DOMESTIC ENEMIES

MATTHEW BRACKEN

Published By:
Steelcutter Publishing
Orange Park, Florida

Sixth Printing 2013

This novel is a work of fiction. The events and characters described herein are products of the author's imagination. Any similarities to actual persons are entirely coincidental.

ISBN 0-9728310-2-9

Library of Congress Control Number 2006905353

Printed in the United States of America

www.EnemiesForeignAndDomestic.com

Acknowledgements

Thank you to Charles Guest of MemorablePlaces.com, who walked with me down this road line by line, always challenging me to make Domestic Enemies: The Reconquista the best novel that it could be.

More thanks to my brother Joseph Bracken, Jefferson Adams, Glenn Bellamy, Kasey Beltz, Joe Brower, Dave Brown, Dave Burch, Charlie Byrd, Michael Dukes, Tom & Donna Eaker, Brandon Estes, Tim Freeman, Cas Gadomski, H.J. Halterman, Rob Henry, Arthur Hines, Wade Jacoby, Larry Lucido, Larry Marshall, Russell McDonald, Kevin O'brien, Frank Parker, Caylen Perry, Greg Price, Oleg Volk of a-human-right.com, Andrew Wharton, Shawn Whisman and my sister Clare Strange who created the cover.

The other novels in the "Enemies" trilogy by author Matthew Bracken:

Enemies Foreign And Domestic
A novel about the true meaning of loyalty and the high cost of freedom in the age of terror.
(2003)

Foreign Enemies And Traitors
The long emergency and the struggle for America, through the Greater Depression and Civil War Two.
(2009)

Over 100 pages of each book may be read at:
www.EnemiesForeignAndDomestic.com

There is no such thing as a hyphenated American who is a good American. The only man who is a good American is the man who is an American and nothing else. We are a nation, not a hodge-podge of foreign nationalities. We are a people, and not a polyglot boarding house.

Theodore Roosevelt

DOMESTIC ENEMIES

Author's note: ***Domestic Enemies: The Reconquista*** contains a major "plot spoiler" for ***Enemies Foreign And Domestic***, the first novel in the Enemies trilogy. This work may be read by itself, but the three books will be best enjoyed in order.

1

Friday June 20

"Yo, Penny! What the hell you doing, girl? Get your scrawny butt back here!"

The woman was new—it was only her second day among the camp's female detainees. She still had the boot camp buzz-cut that marked her as fresh from the "Tombs" in Illinois.

The D-Camp admin staff usually did this with pale-skinned girls: they put them straight out into the fields under the blast-furnace Oklahoma sun. The new prisoner had gamely attempted to keep up with the line of twenty women, weeding her row of knee-high corn with a hoe, but her hands were already cratered with broken blisters.

She walked back down the narrow file to where Big Kendra was waiting. Ranya anticipated what was going to happen next.

"Penny, are all the skinny white girls back in Maine as pitiful as you?"

Ranya kept moving her hoe, while glancing over her shoulder at the drama playing out behind the field crew. The new woman was half the size of Big Kendra, with her broad behind and ample chest straining against her khaki uniform.

"What is this here, woman? What do you see here?" Big Kendra was a "line pusher," an unarmed guard who moved among the prisoners working the fields, telling them exactly what to do. She carried a long rake handle when she was on duty in the fields; now she was using it to point at the ground between the rows of immature corn.

The new detainee was shaking visibly, but Ranya couldn't hear her reply. The woman turned and looked back up the line for the missed weed, leaning over to see where the guard had pointed. The guard moved up close behind, looming over her.

"Are you blind too? That's a big ole' weed—ain't that what you're here for?"

Ranya cringed as the guard booted the new woman down onto her face.

"Now get back on the line, and don't let me catch you slacking off again!"

Big Kendra was one of the most offhandedly brutal guards in D-Camp. The six-foot Philadelphian took special delight in humiliating the new detainees, especially soft suburban housewives from the opposite end of the pigmentation spectrum.

After a few months of interrogation, they arrived at D-Camp in unmarked "moving vans" as pale as Pillsbury doughboys, and were immediately sent out to do field work beneath the unrelenting sun. No hats were provided, and their faces and shorn heads burned an agonizing lobster red. No gloves were supplied, and without calluses, their hands became painfully blistered working the short-handled hoes.

Ranya had seen the black Amazon called Big Kendra put the boot to many new detainees, as part of her own personal "breaking in" procedure.

The new prisoner stumbled back, and took her place among the women working their way up the lines of dusty plants. She was on the next row from Ranya, sobbing quietly. A trickle of blood seeped through the dirt embedded in the abrasion on her left temple.

"It's not my fault, it's a mistake—I shouldn't even be here! It's all a mistake! But nobody will listen. Nobody will listen!"

This was the usual lament of the new Article 14 detainees. It was always a mistake. An old song by an Australian band ran through Ranya's mind. "It's a mistake!" It was always the same heartrending tune. "It's a mistake!"

"My husband disappeared last year, just disappeared! Went to work, and never came home. No word, not one word! Then last March the police came, and found guns in our attic. Assault weapons and sniper rifles, they said! I didn't even know they were there! I swear to God, I had nothing to do with them! But nobody would listen! Now who's taking care of my children? It's all a mistake, but nobody will listen! And now I don't even know where my children are…" Tears slid dirty tracks down her cheeks.

Children. The word stung Ranya like a slap. Who's taking care of your children, lady? Well, who's been taking care of my own baby for five long years? Her thoughts swept her back to the federal prison clinic in Maryland, her wrists and ankles shackled to the cold stainless steel table, and those precious minutes spent with her newborn baby boy. Even then, her wrists were not unchained: a sympathetic nurse held the baby boy to her chest, allowed her to kiss him, to inhale his newborn breath…and that was all of her time with him. Her baby was taken by a grim prison matron, and he disappeared behind a locked door, never to be seen by Ranya again. At least this new prisoner had been able to share a life with her children. Not just a few minutes!

Ranya wanted to say, "Do you think you're the only mother here?" Instead, she answered, "Look, it's not a mistake, your being here. Let me guess: you're here for an Article 14: 'conspiracy to commit acts of terrorism,' right?"

The new prisoner nodded slowly, her face down, broken.

Ranya continued talking, while also looking down at her own work. "Lady, there are no mistakes here. And nobody in admin will listen to you anyway, so just forget it. That life you had is over, that life doesn't exist—not while you're in D-Camp. Hell, Delta Camp, detention camp, whatever you want to call it, it doesn't even exist, haven't you figured that out? Did you get your telephone call yet?" Ranya laughed bitterly. "Listen lady, if you ever want to see your children again, you have to at least make it in here. You have to survive. If you give up on yourself, you give up on any chance of seeing your kids again, ever."

Ranya had tried to stay aloof in the camp, cold inside and hard outside. She avoided close friendships. Nevertheless, she couldn't help but feel sympathy for this innocent woman, thrown defenseless to the wolves, with her husband missing and her children taken away by the state.

"I'm sorry." Ranya reached across, and touched her arm. "What's your name?"

"Stephanie. Stephanie Pennington. I'm from Maine."

"Stephanie, I'm Ranya Bardiwell. I'm from Virginia. Look, you really need to cover your head out here." She paused, scarcely believing what she was about to offer to this stranger. "Here, take my hat." She was giving up a prize possession, the brown ball cap she had found in the drainage ditch by the road, while being marched back to the barracks. A dingy gray rag was attached to the back like a vagabond's version of a French Foreign Legion kepi. "I don't need it so much any more—I'm way past getting sunburns. Don't make a show of it, and the guards will let you wear it in the fields. Hide it in your bunk in camp. You won't get another haircut out here in D-Camp, so in a few weeks you'll have some more protection from the sun. I can't help your hands though…I know how they hurt. I'll try to get some of the weeds on your side, the ones that I can reach. You'll be all right."

The Latina woman working on the other side of Pennington ignored their hushed conversation. They worked their hoes in the red soil with their heads down, their backs to Big Kendra, who was trailing along behind them with her six-foot hardwood pole.

"Thank you, Ranya, thank you." Pennington wiped away her tears with the sleeve of her blue prison shirt, leaving grimy smears across her sun burnt face. "I just think about my children, and I don't know how I can endure it…it's like a nightmare that never ends."

"How old are your kids?"

"Four and seven. Thomas and Michael." The hint of a smile crossed her face and vanished. "Where do you think they are? Nobody will tell me anything!"

Ranya poked through the corn with her hoe: with her experienced eye and strong arms, she was able to weed most of the new woman's line as well as her own. They were a hundred yards from the end, then they would move down twenty lines of corn and work their way back. They would do it until seven pm on this June day, with only a brief water break every two hours. Lunch had been stale peanut butter sandwiches, eaten an hour ago at noon, in the meager shade of a windbreak tree line.

Tree lines were what passed for scenery in this dead-flat part of Oklahoma. Sometimes, in the right light, Ranya would visualize in a distant tree line the fringe of palm trees that often marked a low-lying tropical island on the horizon, as seen from the deck of a sailboat. Sometimes the wind blowing in waves across the wheat fields played the same cruel trick, taking her back to those days of sailing aboard *Guajira* with Phil Carson. He had been her father's friend, before her father had been killed. Then Carson had become her friend, protector and mentor during their months together on the run, hiding out along the coast of Colombia.

That time was now five years in the past, back when she had carried Brad's baby. Brad Fallon, whom she had known so briefly, and loved so intensely, Brad, who had been shot by federal agents. Brad, who had then disappeared into the depths of the Potomac River, leaving Phil and Ranya to flee without him, on the boat he had prepared for his own getaway.

Ranya had returned from Colombia to the USA by herself. By the time she finally decided to come back she was seven months pregnant, and she thought she should not sail across the always windy and rough Caribbean. Instead, she had flown from Colombia to Honduras on her false Canadian passport as Diana Williams, and after a week of switching towns and hotels, she changed her identity back to Ranya Bardiwell for the onward flights to Guadalajara and Phoenix.

She should have risked the sea voyage with Phil Carson and returned to America secretly, off the official radar. Her passport had been flagged even as she reserved her flight to Mexico, and four grim-faced U.S. Marshals pulled her from the Customs line at Phoenix Sky Harbor. Her first day back in America had been her last day in freedom. The immunity deal they thought had been arranged proved to be a dangerous fantasy, nothing but bait to lure them back to the states, and arrest. Ranya had left Guajira and Colombia before Phil Carson, and she still had no idea where he was: abroad or in the states, free or a prisoner, or even if he was alive.

She should never have returned to America. Returning had only meant betrayal and imprisonment, and worst of all, losing her son...and Brad's son. The most bitter irony was that the only reason she had returned to the United States, was to give her son a proper start in life as an American citizen. She did not want to risk ruining his life by beginning it as a baby fugitive, with his mother living under an alias in a foreign country. For attempting to bring her son into the world as an American, she had instead lost him, and lost five years of her life.

From over the eastern horizon a crop duster appeared, a buzzing yellow dot, lining up to fumigate a distant field.

"A-rab! Yo, A-rab! Come here, Bardy-well!"

It was Big Kendra. The black Philadelphian couldn't quite grasp the concept of Christian Arabs, and frequently wondered aloud how an "A-rab" had wound up in D-Camp, instead of in a separate camp for Muslim women. Ranya had never attempted to educate her. Big Kendra was hopelessly stupid; a perfect camp guard, a model employee of the Internal Security Agency. It was a standing joke among the detainees that if government employees were completely illiterate and lacked the people-skills required to work for the DMV, they were still more than qualified for the ISA, the bottom rung of the Department of Homeland Security.

Ranya turned and walked back nonchalantly. She wasn't afraid of the guard, despite Kendra's height and weight advantage. She could easily cleave the guard's skull with the edge of her steel hoe, but after that moment of satisfaction, she'd be shot down by the two trailing riflemen, the so-called "gun guards." Still, Ranya habitually fantasized doing it. She vividly pictured a full steel-edged swing to Kendra's throat, the stark terror on Kendra's open-mouthed and bug-eyed face, the scream that would never make it past the severed windpipe, the spouting arterial blood.

She regularly imagined rushing one stupefied gun guard, and wrestling his rifle away from him before he could unsling it and prepare it to fire. The question was: would the other rifleman fire at them both, rolling on the ground? And even if he didn't open fire immediately, what then? Even if she managed somehow to kill Big Kendra and both gun guards, she couldn't outrun their radios and helicopters. Not out here in the endless open fields of western Oklahoma.

Even so, she wanted to kill a guard, to kill all the guards. She wanted very badly to kill them. She endlessly daydreamed their sudden, painful, violent deaths. She just wasn't quite ready to sacrifice her own life to that end. Not yet. The camp guards were only bottom feeders, they meant nothing in the greater scheme of things. The ones Ranya had a stronger desire to kill were much higher up the food chain. Ranya still valued her life too much to trade it away for the momentary satisfaction of cleaving Big Kendra's empty skull.

After almost five years at D-Camp, Ranya knew all of the guards' weaknesses. One of her infrequent victories had occurred the previous summer, when she had found a king snake in a soybean field. Growing up in rural Virginia, Ranya had no fear of non-poisonous king snakes, which mimicked the deadly coral snake with a similar color pattern. She had carefully pinned the banded red, black and yellow snake with her hoe and grabbed it behind the head, and when Kendra's back was turned, she had flung the snake at her feet.

The guard had broken every Olympic record sprinting from the field, and then she split the back of her too-tight khaki pants climbing on top of the flatbed stake truck. The other guards, male and female, had mocked Big Kendra for weeks after the incident, baiting her with false snake alarms, and leaving rubber snakes in her lunch pail. Ranya's original tossing of the live snake had never been suspected. If any other prisoners had witnessed her defiant act, they had kept their mouths shut.

"A-rab, what you doin' giving that white girl you hat? Why you be doin' that?"

"I don't need it anymore. I'm almost as dark as you now."

"Hah! That'll be the day!" Kendra grinned, her single gold tooth gleaming in the sun. "I don't understand why you is feeling all sorry for a no-good white bitch like that. What she do for you?"

It was pointless to try to explain normal human feelings to a line pusher, one of the bottom guards at D-Camp. Collecting a federal paycheck for following hapless prisoners across fields was about as low a living as Ranya could imagine. Obviously, Big Kendra considered the deeply tanned "A-rab" Ranya Bardiwell to be something other than "white," and therefore she couldn't fathom Ranya's sympathy for the new pale-complexioned prisoner. Politically correct racial solidarity must have been drummed into Kendra's pea-brain in government schools and institutions all of her life, Ranya mused. She ignored the guard's question.

"That ain't why I called you back, Bardy-well. Warden Linssen, she want you back by the tool truck. That little pickup truck over there, that be Warden Linssen. I don't know why, but she just axed for you on my radio. Go drop your hoe in the tool bin, and see what she want."

Without replying, Ranya marched back down the row of corn, between the two male guards with their Mini-14 rifles slung on their shoulders. These gun guards in their khaki uniforms regarded her carefully as she passed between them: they formed the back points of a wide triangle 50 yards behind Big Kendra. The two men tracked Ranya with their eyes hidden behind sunglasses, their faces obscured by wide-brimmed tan desert hats.

No matter what direction a prisoner might try to run, one or both of the gun guards would have an easy shot. Their iron-sighted Mini-14s were crummy rifles, provided to prison guards solely because they were the cheapest of the available alternatives, but she knew that at these distances, even a gun guard with a Mini-14 would not miss.

She carried the hoe across her chest at military "port arms," with her head up and eyes front. She wanted to shoulder the hoe like a rifle of her own, and aim down the "barrel" at them, but that type of rebellious gesture would only earn her another stint in D-Camp's rusty iron "sweat box," where one could neither stand up nor fully lay down.

Besides, she was consumed with curiosity about why Deputy Warden Linssen wanted her, and she would do nothing to jeopardize this meeting.

At the edge of the field was the tool truck, a mud-splashed white full-size GMC pickup. Ranya dropped her hoe into a plastic bin in the back, and the supervisor sitting in the cab made a notation in his ledger book. Beyond the tool truck, on the dirt road leading from the cornfield, was Warden Linssen's black Ford Ranger. The power window on the driver's side rolled down as she approached.

"Ranya? Get in. You're done with the weed line for today. Maybe for forever." The warden was wearing wire-rimmed aviator's sunglasses, and she smiled warmly through the open window.

It was the first time Ranya had opened a vehicle door in five years. She had ridden in the backs of camp trucks on occasion, but never in the cab. The AC hit her with a forgotten alpine blast, pushing out the Oklahoma summer heat. As she settled into the spongy seat, Ranya suddenly remembered riding in another pickup truck that mad September in Virginia, six years before. Brad's pickup truck.

The deputy warden was wearing a crisp Internal Security Agency senior officer's summer working uniform: black pants and a white short-sleeved dress shirt, with the ISA patches on the shoulders. She was an attractive woman about forty, Ranya guessed, with short jet-black hair that was cut flat around the back to keep it the regulation length: just covering her collar, but no more. Like the other senior ISA officers Ranya infrequently saw, she carried no sidearm. She was an administrator, and duty guns were beneath her station and pay grade.

Linssen put her truck into gear and pulled out. "You must be wondering what's going on, right? Why I came for you?" She was grinning, relishing her secret.

"Am I getting out of D-Camp?"

"No, no I'm afraid not." The warden sounded genuinely sympathetic. "But I do have good news for you, some very good news. But let's have lunch first, and get you cleaned up! I think maybe I'm going to take you out of the fields and put you into admin. If you want it—if you have the right attitude for it." She turned and smiled at Ranya again.

The last time she had spoken in private at any length with Deputy Warden Starr Linssen had been in her office in the administration section of D-Camp. Ranya had requested the meeting, after being beaten in her bunk by a group of male and female guards during one of her first nights in camp. Ranya had forcibly resisted their brutal "seduction" attempts, biting and kicking at her attackers.

During that initial meeting, Linssen had appeared sensitive to her plight, and Ranya was able to steer their conversation to the subject of her missing son. The warden had promised to seek out any available information about the child, if she could. Her main concern was that Ranya "fit in," and not invite further abuse by "antagonizing" the guards. As if defending herself against sexual assault constituted antagonizing the guards! Nevertheless, the guards had kept a wary distance after that first unsuccessful attack, and Ranya gave the deputy warden some of the credit for that small mercy.

A series of dirt road turns led to a cracked asphalt track, just inside the ten-foot high razor wire topped perimeter fence. The fence itself presented only a minor obstacle to escape. The real control was exerted by the tiny chips implanted behind her left shoulder, just under her neck: Radio Frequency Identification Devices smaller than a grain of rice. The RFID chips were used inside of the camp to control the movements of the detainees. Every time they passed through a gate or numerous other portals, they were automatically counted to determine that they were where they should be at all times.

Around and beyond the inner camp, sensor wires were buried in the ground, and other wires were strung along the many fences. Any prisoner crossing a buried sensor wire, or approaching within a few feet of a fence, would trigger an alarm at central control. Beyond D-Camp lay unknown miles of rural western Oklahoma: more fields stretching to the horizon, and probably more buried sensor wires.

"Ranya, I hated seeing you turned out as a field worker. Hated it! But after your fight with the guards… Anyway, I know about your background, your education." The warden reached over for Ranya's left wrist. "Let me feel your hand…ugh. All callused, so rough...that's no way to live! But there's no reason D-Camp has to be so bad, not all of it. We have a saying: you scratch my back…and I'll scratch yours, all right?" The warden squeezed her hand.

Ranya said nothing, but withdrew her hand, glancing over at Linssen. The warden had a blue-black tattoo of a grinning quarter-moon visible on her neck, partly above her collar, and a matching sun-face on the opposite side. Her white uniform collar always made them appear to be rising or setting. "Is the good news some word about my son?"

"Ranya, you've been here for almost five years—let's not rush things. Okay?"

Linssen stopped at an open vehicle gate in another fence, which separated different areas of the former Army base containing D-Camp. A few feet opposite an electric eye on a steel post, she held up an ID card against her side window to be scanned. A guard stepped out of his cement blockhouse, gave them both a perfunctory look from a few steps away, and waved them on. In five years, Ranya had never seen this area of the base. It was both unsettling and exhilarating.

They drove past another vehicle gate in the chain link outer perimeter fence. Beyond it to their left lay a two-lane blacktop road, heading south into the distance across endless fields. It was impossible for Ranya to know if the road she saw lay inside or entirely beyond the boundaries of the old military base. The gate itself led into a tractor-trailer-sized double box of chain link fence, all topped with razor wire. Any vehicles leaving the base through it would have to stop inside the steel rectangle for inspection, before the outer gates were opened.

The pickup continued on into an area of trees and white-painted wooden structures, warehouses mainly, parts of what seemed to be an abandoned military supply depot. Warden Linssen made another turn into the interior of the base and in a few minutes, they arrived at what appeared to be a small suburban enclave, complete with sidewalks, lawns and shade trees.

"Home sweet home, Ranya. It was married officers' housing, back in the Army days. Pretty nice, eh? We can have lunch, and talk. I'm sure you'll enjoy some fresh fruit."

Linssen didn't seem concerned about her own personal security, or any escape risk presented by Ranya. She evidently believed the implanted chips made escape impossible. The white clapboard ranch-style house had an old-fashioned key lock in the front door. Linssen opened the door for Ranya and followed her inside, locking it behind them with a dead bolt. She pulled off her sunglasses, revealing startling ice-blue eyes, made more so by the contrast to her raven hair.

"I've prepared a wonderful salad for us, and I can fix you almost any kind of deli sandwich you'd like. But first I think you'd like to clean up, and take a real bath—am I right?" Linssen cocked an eyebrow, almost winking, and smiled knowingly at Ranya. Detainees were permitted only cold showers, twice a week, in the open barracks latrines. Shaving legs and underarms was not possible, and shampoo was a rarely seen luxury. "I've gone to central supply and drawn you some new uniforms. I really don't think you'll be going back to the fields." The warden was now beaming continuously, obviously in anticipation of more than a leisurely luncheon.

Ranya looked around the living room and adjoining kitchen, absorbing the soft homey touches, while noting the absence of evidence of any family. There was a calendar on the wall by the open kitchen door, and she noted that it was Friday, the 20th of June—not that this had much meaning in the camps. She asked, "Why are you doing this for me? I don't understand." But Ranya did understand. She hoped that Linssen would have news of her son, and she guessed what Linssen wanted in return. In spite of her five years in detention at hard labor, Ranya knew that Linssen was attracted to her. The warden had regularly checked up on her, and always used her first name. Ranya was 27, and although the summer sun and bitter winter cold had aged her a bit beyond her years, she still had a face and a figure which made most of the guards, male and female, follow her with their eyes. The meager prison diet kept her slim, and the field work kept her fit.

"Ranya, do you think I like the way detainees are treated in D-Camp? I don't! I try to make the conditions as…tolerable as I can. But I don't set policy! And our budget—oh, our budget! It's still set in dollars, as if that meant anything these days… That's why the farm and cattle operations are so important to us—we could never get by, otherwise. Anyway, I'm hopeful that the Civil Emergency will be lifted soon, maybe after the election, and you'll all be released! Amnesty! But it's a political decision, and I have nothing to do with it. Nothing. You know, I'm just a tiny cog in the machine." Linssen half-smiled wistfully. "In fact, I'm almost as much of a prisoner out here as you are…"

Ranya's reply was cold and matter-of-fact. "We'll never be released. I was sent here for three years 'detention,' that's what the judges said at my first Article 14 hearing. But after my three years were up, they just tacked on another three. No hearing, no nothing. In five years, I've never seen a lawyer. I've never sent or received as much as a phone call or a postcard. How can they ever release us, when they don't even admit they have us in detention? When they don't even admit these camps exist?"

"It's the Civil Emergency, and when it's over, I'm sure there'll be an amnesty."

"I don't think it'll ever be over."

"I don't believe that. I can't believe that! But neither of us can do anything about it—we have to play the cards we've been dealt. In the meantime, I can…I can make life a lot better for you. You went to the University of Virginia; I went to VPI…we have a lot in common, you know! You almost graduated, and someday I'm sure you'll be able to finish your education. But for now, I can move you into the admin section. You'll work inside, in air conditioning! And I can move you to the trusties' barracks…they have some privacy; they even have their own washer and dryer. It's really not so bad there."

"I guess I should be grateful…even though…"

"Yes, I think so too…and we can talk about that, later. But first, why don't you enjoy a nice long bath? I know that's what I'd want, after nothing but cold showers for so long…"

The bathroom was lined in yellow tiles, cracked in places, but the porcelain tub was long and deep, a throwback to another era in government housing. Under the single window, there was a shelf built on top of an old steam radiator. Fresh denim pants and a clean blue work shirt were neatly folded on top. Ranya closed the door behind her, but there was no interior lock. Behind the frosted glass window, Ranya could see stout burglar bars.

She wondered how many young detainees the forty-something deputy warden had brought to her house for a bath and some coerced "afternoon delight." She thought of the detainees she had seen working in admin, they were mostly all young and pretty. Instead of a violent gang attack in the barracks, the warden was using the promise of a hot bath and a transfer to easy duty to achieve the same result. The deputy warden held all the cards; she probably succeeded at seduction every time she tried, given the temptation of the warm tub…

Whatever was going to happen, there was no point in missing the rare opportunity to take a hot bath, and use real shampoo on her dirty shoulder-length hair. Ranya ran the water, pouring in fragrant liquid bubble bath, and then checked herself in the mirror over the sink. There were no mirrors in D-Camp, not even stainless steel ones. She saw the faint lines around her hazel eyes; her skin was tight and drawn. She was grateful that her nose was almost imperceptibly askew, where it had been punched the night of her attack. None of this mattered. Beauty had held little added advantage in D-Camp, unless being leered at by guards and administrators was counted as an advantage. Well, today at least, it seemed to be the key to getting her out of the fields…and into a hot bath.

On top of the blue uniform were neat stacks of underwear, white socks, and a new cotton prison bra. A new pair of blue canvas prison-issue sneakers, with laces, was on the floor beneath the clothes. It figured that Linssen would have access to all of her sizes. Ranya pushed off her dirty prison-issue sneakers, which were held together with a single plastic wire tie in the middle, instead of proper laces. She piled her dirty clothes into a corner and slipped into the bath, and pulled the rubber band from her ponytail, letting her grimy brunette hair spill across her back and into the water.

It was the first time her body had felt the silky envelopment of hot water in longer than she could remember. Then she recalled another warm bath, shared with Brad Fallon in the little cabin by the river a lifetime ago… Ranya slid down until her hair was entirely submerged. She lay still for several minutes, enjoying the exquisite pleasure of the warm bubble bath, guessing what was coming next, not knowing how she would react when it inevitably happened. In D-Camp, a single warm bath with perfumed soap and aromatic shampoo held more seduction value, she thought, than a trip to a luxury resort in Hawaii might hold for girls who were free.

So Ranya wasn't at all surprised by the light knock on the door.

Starr Linssen entered the bathroom wearing a beige terrycloth bathrobe, carrying two goblets of chilled blush wine. She sat on the edge of the tub and handed a glass to Ranya. "I'm so glad to be able to get you out of the fields, you deserve much better than that." She looked directly into Ranya's eyes. Ranya drew her knees up to her chest in the bubbly water, and set her wine glass in the corner of the tub behind her. Linssen put her feet into the bath by the silver spigot and slipped off her robe, then slid smoothly into the bath facing Ranya, smiling warmly.

Besides the sun and moon tattoos on the sides of her neck, she had large stars tattooed on her breasts, centered on her nipples. Ranya caught herself glancing at them, unsure where to look, since she was even more uncomfortable returning Linssen's smile, a smile made more inviting by freshly applied frost-pink lip gloss.

"I know, I know, a mistake from my youth," said the warden, referring to her tattoos. "But what can I do? It seemed like a good idea at the time…" She forced a breezy laugh. "But they're a part of me now. Do you hate them? You don't have any tattoos—that was *so* smart of you."

"I don't mind them—I really don't care one way or the other. Warden Linssen, in your truck…"

"Ranya, please…call me Starr."

"In your truck, Starr…in your truck you said you had news for me, good news."

"I do, but why don't we get to…know each other better first? We have all afternoon. I signed out early for the day, and I put you down for 'special duties.' Oh Ranya, this camp is so harsh, I hate it so much! We need to find our pleasures where we can... We can talk…later. You know, you have such beautiful eyes…like amber sprinkled with tiny emeralds…" Linssen's crossed shins rested against Ranya's feet. She slid her hands underwater and began to caress Ranya's legs, while smiling at her and leaning closer, her lips parted.

Ranya struggled to suppress her distaste, to disguise it. Over the years, many of the female detainees had paired off, finding solace in something closer than mere companionship. But not Ranya Bardiwell. "I'm sorry, I can't relax—my mind is going a mile a minute—I'm trying to guess what your good news is! Tell me the news first, and then I'm sure I'll relax, and then…"

"Oh, I can relax you Ranya; I'm *very, very* good at it…"

"Yes, I can see that you are…but please, tell me what you know! I can't stand not knowing, I'm just dying to know!" Not only had Ranya not made a phone call or received a letter in five years, there were no radios or televisions in D-Camp.

"Well, I suppose..." The assistant warden's fingernails were tracing lines up and down Ranya's calves and brushing her thighs, as she locked her eyes onto Ranya's. "I found out about your son—that's the good news!"

"My son! Oh my God, my son! Tell me; please tell me everything you know about my son!"

"I thought you'd be pleased! Well, he's fine, doing fine, perfectly healthy I suppose...I mean, there's no medical record on him to speak of. He's just great—he's a healthy, happy five year old boy." Linssen smiled at Ranya, and attempted to take her hands into her own, but Ranya jerked them back. The last time she had shared a bath with another person, it had been with Brad, in the lost cabin, on the little river island in Virginia. Poor Brad... Now, sex was being forced on her in another tub, and by a federal officer no less! The contrast between the two encounters battered her sensibilities. Yet as long as there was a chance of finding out about her son...

"But where is he? Who's taking care of him? You have to tell me everything, you can't just tell me he's 'fine' and let it go at that! Don't tease me! Where is he? Please, please tell me!"

"Oh Ranya, what good will it do to know? Let it go... From the records I've found, he's being raised by a terrific family, top notch. Isn't that enough?"

"No, it's not enough!" Ranya pushed all the way back in the tub, her arms wrapped around her upraised knees, her chin down upon them.

Linssen stroked Ranya's wet hair, but Ranya shook off her touch. "Well. Hmmm. Oh, all right, I suppose." The warden sighed, resigned. "Your son is living in Albuquerque, New Mexico. His name is Brian Garabanda. His parents are...federal employees."

"His parents? His *parents*?" Ranya looked up, imploring.

"He was adopted, Ranya. Of course, he was adopted."

"But—but I never gave up my rights! I never agreed to this! How could they?"

"Oh Ranya, be realistic. You wouldn't want him living in foster homes. Trust me, I know... He's in a fine home, and his parents are wonderful people, I'm sure."

"You said they were federal employees. What kind of...federal employees?"

"What difference does it make?"

"I just want to know!"

Linssen exhaled audibly. "Oh, I guess it doesn't matter. Brian's father is an FBI Special Agent. He works out of the Albuquerque Field

Office. Actually, he's a Supervisor. His name is Alexandro Garabanda. A very fine man, I'm sure. The FBI is the top..."

"His…father…is FBI? Oh my God! Is this true? An *FBI agent* is raising my son? An FBI agent…is his father? His father? How can that be true? I suppose I should be grateful, but…"

"Ranya, it's for the best! How could you retain…how could you possibly raise him, in here? There are no children in here, there couldn't be, you're an intelligent adult, you have to understand that! Brian is being raised by federal agents—just think of all of the advantages that will give him, as he grows up! Plus, think about his future, when he's grown. He won't carry the stigma of…a traitor…a domestic enemy. He'll grow up with all of the rights and freedoms of any law-abiding American citizen! I mean…"

"But an FBI agent! My son is being raised by federal agents? That's twisting the knife! You have to be kidding, this is just a joke, this can't be true, can it? It's just not fair, it's not right!"

"But they can give him everything, and what can you offer him, in here? Nothing. Ranya, please be realistic, and think of what's best for your son. The FBI…" Linssen reached again to take Ranya's hands in hers, to calm her, to sooth her.

Ranya looked up and flung her own hands apart, casting off the warden's offered comforting gesture. Her five years of smoldering frustration over not knowing the fate of her son had at last been settled, but the hollow aching pain was instantly replaced by a rolling wave of burning anger. Five years of seething resentment crystallized into blind rage. Her hands, strong and callused from the fields, shot to Linssen's throat. Her long fingers encircled the warden's neck as Ranya exploded forward, propelling the warden backward in shocked surprise.

Linssen's mouth was wide open in amazement as her own hands sought Ranya's wrists beneath her chin, when the back of her head slammed down on the protruding bathtub faucet. Then Ranya was over her, straddling her, still shaking and choking her, Linssen's terrified blue eyes disappearing beneath the fragrant bubbles.

"The FBI! The FBI! You feds, you feds think you own the whole world and everything in it! Steal a baby? Why not! Take five years of my life? Who cares! National Security, right? Right! You own everything, don't you? Well, that's it! That's it! Enough! Too much! No more! No more! And I'm not a traitor! I'm not a traitor, damn you!" Ranya continued strangling Linssen under water, with all of her 130 pounds bearing down on the helpless warden's throat, crushing her larynx.

Whether it was after one minute or much longer, she would never know, but eventually Ranya comprehended that Starr Linssen was not struggling, was not moving at all. No carotid artery pulse surged through her neck against Ranya's pressing thumbs. No desperate fingers clawed at her wrists. When this fatal realization finally struck, Ranya bolted upright and shot out of the tub to escape the warden's limp body. She dropped and sat Indian-style, naked and wet on the throw rug in the center of the bathroom floor, staring at the warden's legs, which were partially exposed above the bubbles. Linssen's slick breasts formed two star-tipped islands surrounded by sudsy foam.

Now she couldn't go back. There was absolutely no going back to D-camp. There was no explaining away the death of Deputy Warden Starr Linssen, in her own house.

But now she also had a new idea tugging at her, at last she had a real reason to try to escape, regardless of the odds. Assuming that Linssen had been telling the truth, Ranya finally knew where her son was! She had a name to search for, and she knew his "father" was an FBI agent in Albuquerque, and that was enough. If she could escape from D-Camp, and make it to New Mexico…if she could do that, she could find her son, and rescue him from his kidnappers!

Ranya knew that Starr Linssen had planned to spend several intimate hours with her, which meant she probably had these hours to make her escape. It was Friday afternoon, and if Linssen had signed out for the day, then perhaps her presence wouldn't even be missed before Monday morning. She had the advantage of time, a few hours at least.

Starr Linssen was roughly her size, it occurred to her… She pushed down the lever under the silver faucet, and the tub began to drain. Gradually Linssen's face came back into view as the bubbles disappeared. Ranya studied the dead woman's slick black hair, just a bit gray at the roots. She opened the medicine cabinet, then looked under the sink, and found an unopened package of black L'oreal hair dye. It could be done, maybe. It was possible! Anyway, what else could she do? What choice did she have? She knew where her son was living, she knew his new name, and she knew who had stolen him from her life!

In less than two hours, Ranya was driving the dead warden's black pickup back toward the double-box of high chain link and razor wire, which surrounded the back gate leading away from the base. On their way to her house, the warden's ISA identification card had gotten them through the inner gate leading out of the D-Camp area into the rest of the old Army base. Ranya could only guess if that same ID card would be sufficient to allow her to pass entirely out of the base, and into the civilian world.

Her hair was dyed black and scissors-cut to resemble the warden's, as closely as Ranya had been able to manage in the bathroom mirror. A sun and moon, approximating the warden's tattoos, were inked in ballpoint on the sides of her neck. She wore the white blouse and black pants of the dead woman. To defeat the RFID implants in the back of her left shoulder, she had stripped the circular magnet from the speaker of a portable radio, and secured it in place with generous strips of duct tape. Another detainee had explained this trick to Ranya, but she had no way of knowing for sure if the big magnet would override the RFID microcircuits or not. Well, she would find out soon enough…

Ranya wore Linssen's gold-framed aviator's sunglasses and a black ball cap with the ISA patch on the front, to obscure her face. She hoped that the gate guards would not study her too closely, but would be basing their judgment on Linssen's familiar black vehicle with its ISA bumper and windshield decals, and her ISA uniform and ID card. If the warden's vehicle had any special RFIDs placed in it, Ranya could only hope that they would indicate that it was authorized to depart the base via this back gate. The vehicle gate was already outside of D-Camp, in another part of the old military base, and she hoped that it had less stringent requirements for permitting outward passage. In any event, Ranya had no way of knowing the overall scheme of the security protocols that were in effect.

In case it didn't work, if the guards became suspicious and stopped her for a close inspection, Ranya had the warden's Glock 19 pistol, loaded with sixteen 9mm hollow points. She had found it in the locked drawer of the warden's bedside night table, hidden in a hollowed-out Bible. Now the ugly black pistol lay on the seat beside her right thigh, concealed beneath a copy of "Homeland Security Today" magazine. No matter what happened next, Ranya was finished with D-Camp. She was finished with around-the-clock interrogations, and with months buried alive in solitary confinement, in an underground "supermax" cell. She was finished with troikas of unseen judges, who handed down sentences of "non-judicial detention" from behind face-blurring translucent screens.

She was not going back. Deputy Warden Starr Linssen lay beneath her own bed, wrapped in her shower curtain, strangled and drowned and dead. The pistol beside Ranya's hip had a round chambered, ready to fire in an instant.

Ranya slowed and made the right turn toward the vehicle gate, her heart hammering inside of her chest. The inner gate rolled back on grating steel rollers with a clank of chains and the whine of an electric motor, and she pulled the little truck inside the inspection zone. One of the two middle-aged guards on duty was sitting on a stool inside of his cement block guardhouse, and he unenthusiastically raised himself up to do his duty. She noted that the service pistol on his belt was hidden beneath the flap of a black nylon holster. It would be no match in speed for her Glock, if they both had to draw in a hurry. Shooting both guards and activating the outer gate from inside their guard house would be a last ditch desperation measure, but she would attempt it if they tried to stop her now.

She held the ISA card up against the side window a yard from another optical scanner on a steel post, the way she had seen Linssen do it, while keeping her eyes forward. It was obvious the truck was empty in the back, and held no passenger other than the authorized driver, the easily recognizable deputy warden of D-Camp. The guard took a step toward the truck, paused just two paces away, stopped for a moment…

And then he waved her forward with a casual flip of his hand.

The outer gate squealed open, and in a moment Ranya was through, bursting forth with immeasurable bounding joy. In seconds, she had the pickup truck going sixty miles an hour on the ruler-straight blacktop, heading south toward Interstate 40.

Ranya Bardiwell was out of D-Camp, but she was still far from free.

2

Alex Garabanda had tried to call Karin several times, but his cell phone had not been able to make a connection. Finally, when he had gotten through to her phone, she didn't pick up and he didn't want to leave a voice mail message. He knew she was using the caller ID to screen her calls, one of her favorite tactics in their ongoing psychological war. As much as he dreaded it, he needed to speak to his ex-wife personally, in real time. Leaving a voice mail would give her too many ways to play him, to blame him if Brian wasn't picked up from day care.

It was so ridiculous. It was beyond absurd, because she was working in the same Federal Building only thirty or so feet beneath him. Karin was three stories below the FBI Field Office, where he was one of the five Supervisory Special Agents. He could take the elevator down to the IRS offices and physically locate her, but he ruled that option out. Any such pursuit could and would be written up as "stalking" or "intimidation." It had been many weeks since he had entered the IRS offices where she worked as an admin assistant.

He left his little office and went out into the bullpen, to use a landline that she wouldn't recognize on her cell phone's caller ID. Finally, she picked up. "Hello?" She sounded pleasant enough, less than an hour from the close of business on Friday afternoon.

"Karin? It's me."

Several seconds went by without a response, dead air. He wondered if the connection had dropped, which happened frequently enough for it to be his first thought. When she did answer, the warmth in her voice had evaporated.

"What is it?"

"Something's come up. I can't pick up Brian from kindergarten." Their five-year-old son was in the day care center, on the first floor of the Albuquerque Federal Building.

"Well, sorry, I already have plans. You have to pick him up."

"Karin…I can't. Really. I have no choice; it's a meeting I can't get out of. Somebody's come down from Washington…"

"From Washington? Should I be impressed? Deal with it, Al!"

"I can get Brian at home after six, maybe seven at the latest."

"Oh, no you won't! If I'm getting him from kindergarten, he has to come with me and…with me. I've already made plans—I actually have a life! And you're certainly not picking him up after his bedtime. If you can't get him from daycare at five, then you'll just have to come by tomorrow morning and get him, at the house."

"Karin, I'm sorry, but…"

"That's right, you are sorry. I'll get Brian at five. You'll just have to get him tomorrow. Okay? Buh-bye, Al."

"Karin…"

She had already disconnected.

Ranya was slumped down in the driver's seat of a rusted-out ambulance, behind a defunct auto repair shop that bordered a truck stop. She was staring across the backs of a row of eighteen-wheelers, toward the truck stop's mini-mart. High up on the red and yellow Love's sign facing the interstate, diesel was advertised for $28.99 a gallon. Below the price were the words "Cash Only."

She finished a plastic container full of fruit salad from the warden's kitchen, while watching the store for the return of a driver. Much of the fruit she recognized from D-Camp's fields and orchards. Linssen's brown backpack was on the seat beside her, ready to grab. After 45 minutes of observation, Ranya had narrowed her attention to a pair of trucks that had entered from the direction of Oklahoma City, and immediately gassed up. The driver who returned from the Love's mini-mart first would be her initial target.

In the meantime, she listened to AM talk radio through the ear plugs on Linssen's jogging radio, dreading a breaking news announcement about a murder and a prison escape. The host was yelling about an upcoming Constitutional Convention scheduled to take place in Philadelphia. It was the first she had heard of it. Any news that had dribbled into D-Camp was at least a couple of months old. The new detainees spent at least that long in interrogation centers before arriving.

An hour earlier, she had watched the dead warden's black pickup roll into a half-acre cattle stock pond. With the hood, doors and tailgate open, the truck had disappeared without leaving more than ripples and a trail of bubbles on the opaque water. The water would hide the pickup from helicopters, even from their infrared scopes, but by abandoning the vehicle so permanently, she had committed herself to finding transportation at the insignificant crossroads town. Ranya had changed out of Linssen's ISA uniform in the concealing shade of a willow tree by the pond. The dead warden's casual clothes were loose on her, but with the belt cinched tightly around her waist, the pair of khaki hiking pants she had selected fit tolerably well. The nylon pants had legs that zipped off above the knees. Ranya decided to remove them and stash them in the warden's backpack. She was grateful that the dead woman seemed to have been an outdoorsy type. Linssen's camping and hiking gear was now being put to good use.

From the cattle pond, it was only a short hike across bare fields to the abandoned junkyard behind the truck stop. She was halfway between

Oklahoma City and the Texas line. Her newly dyed black hair fell just to her neck, cut straight around at the level of her earlobes. She was wearing a pale green scooped-neck sleeveless t-shirt over her khaki pants: effective low-key camouflage. Her neck 'tattoos' had been mostly rubbed off with spit and elbow grease while waiting in the ambulance. She had forgotten to look for makeup remover or cold cream in Linssen's house.

One of the double glass doors of the mini-mart opened with a flash of reflected afternoon sunlight. A man wearing jeans, a white t-shirt and a black cowboy hat walked out, he was one of her chosen westbound drivers. Ranya slipped from the abandoned ambulance, swung on the backpack, and walked through tall weeds behind several other junked cars to the truck parking area. The trucks were all slant-parked at a 45-degree angle, with their cabs toward her. She crouched behind a wrecked mini-van, and she watched. His truck was a dusty red Peterbilt, with a generous sleeping compartment behind the seats.

The Stetson-wearing driver walked from the back of his rig carrying a plastic shopping bag, inspecting his tires as he went. He paused by the passenger side of his cab, unlocking the door with a remote control on his key chain, then stepped up on the platform over his fuel tank. He was a sunburned and clean-shaved Caucasian about forty or so years old, Ranya guessed. Not bad looking, but a bit on the hillbilly side.

She moved out from cover, stepped over the guardrail at the property line, and walked toward him displaying her most fetching smile. She hoped that she came across like an eager-beaver small town truck stop whore. The Glock was in her right hand, hidden behind her hip. They were isolated from casual view in the narrow slot between two trucks.

"Hiya, cowboy! Listen, you wouldn't be heading west, would you?"

The driver was just opening the door, taken completely by surprise and turning toward her. "Huh? Uh…well…I…I can't take hitchhikers. It's…uh, company policy…" He was standing above her, his eyes flicking between her face and her chest.

Ranya wasn't having it. "Oh please, I insist." She raised the Glock and leveled it at his stomach, moving to within a few feet of him, just out of kicking distance. "Get in. I can handle this rig just fine, no problem, but I'd rather have you drive. So please, don't make me put a hole in you. Really, I just want a ride." Her smile was gone, her pistol steady. "Drop the bag inside, climb in and slide across behind the wheel. Keep your hands where I can see them. I'm getting in right behind you. Please believe me: I'll shoot you if you do anything stupid."

The driver stared open-mouthed at the pistol. She waved it toward the cab's open passenger door to get him moving, and he dropped the bag into the foot well area. "Look, the company… Oh shit, forget it. J-just get in, a-and watch that trigger, okay lady? Don't slip or any…"

"I won't slip. I just want a ride, that's all."

"What's the matter?" he croaked, "A boyfriend after you? Or the law?"

"Just get this thing started, and get on the highway, heading west."

"Yes ma'am." He slid behind the wheel and did as he was told, starting the massive engine, releasing the brake, and pulling smoothly out of his spot.

In short order he was going through the gears, merging into the right lane, westbound on I-40.

She kept the pistol aimed at him, resting it across her stomach. "I'm going to Albuquerque. How long until we get there?"

"Albuquerque? I'm not going that way."

"Oh really? Change of plans. This Glock says we are."

"Look, you don't understand. I'm not routed there. If I go off my route, the GPS is going to alert my dispatchers, and they'll check me out. Automatically." He pointed through the roof with his finger, presumably indicating the location of the GPS transceiver, or perhaps the orbiting satellites. "Then they'll call me. And then if I don't check in, they'll call the highway patrol, and they'll come looking for that trailer I'm pulling. I can't turn off the GPS. I'm sorry, but that's how it is."

"Shit. So where *are* you heading, then?"

"Salt Lake City. I'm going to take 287, up into Colorado. We don't hardly ever go into New Mexico, not anymore. Almost never."

"What's the matter with New Mexico?"

"What's the matter with New Mexico? Where have you been, darlin'? First of all, it's Nuevo Mexico now, that's what they call it. I can take you as far west on 40 as Amarillo, but that's where I turn north, and if I don't..."

"I know. Your GPS rats you out." She heaved a sigh in frustration.

"Mind if I smoke?" he asked. "Makes me mighty nervous, you pointing that thing at me."

"Go ahead."

He withdrew a Winston from a pack in his console, and lit it one handed, his left hand on the big wheel. "You in trouble?" He glanced over at Ranya, taking in the incongruent tan lines on her arms, the residual ink marks on her neck, and the choppy haircut. "Look, I've had my own run-ins with the law. I've done some time, in my younger days."

She changed the subject. "So, what's the deal with New Mexico?"

"Shit. That place is messed up bad, even more since last year. That's when they passed the 'Spanish only' laws. *Español Solamente*, they call it. You speak Spanish?"

"I can speak it okay."

"Well, you'll need to speak it good in *Nuevo Mexico*. Most of the highway signs are in Spanish now; almost everything is. They made all the cops take a Spanish test, and fired everybody who didn't pass it. All the gringo cops got the axe. They did it after Idaho passed an English-only law—at least I think Idaho was the first. That's what I heard on talk radio, anyway. Montana and Wyoming did it too—passed English only—and then they started booting out the illegals. You know, illegal alien Mexicans, mostly. Even ones that had the amnesty—they said the federal amnesty didn't count, at least not in Idaho and Montana."

"How could they do that, if the illegals had been given amnesty?"

"Well, it was amnesty, but not exactly citizenship, not yet. It was pretty complicated. Anyway, they said the illegals had gotten faked, I mean forged—no, that's not the word either—no, it was 'fraud,' that's it. Up north, they said the illegals had gotten the amnesty 'by fraudulent means,' so it was no good. They started checking, and thousands of illegals were all supposedly living at the same addresses for years and years, and working at the same labor centers. The records were all the same, just Xerox copies with different names! Can you imagine? So they started taking away the amnesty, and kicking them out."

"Kicking them out to where? Mexico?"

"No, just over their state lines—but they couldn't stay there either. Like in Wyoming and Colorado, the state police met the deportation buses at the state lines, and they escorted them south."

"They deported all of the illegal aliens out of Idaho?"

"Oh no, they didn't have to. Once Idaho and Montana took away the bogus amnesties and went after the employers, the illegals started leaving on their own. No jobs, no more free school, no more free medicine, no food stamps, stuff like that. Washington raised hell, but they stuck at it. They didn't have to use a lot of buses—mostly the illegals left on their own, when the gravy train dried up. I mean, if you're picked up and deported on a bus, that means your car gets left behind, right? Most of the illegals decided they'd rather drive out and keep their cars, than get put on a bus. This was really big news—where were you that you didn't hear about it?"

"If I told you, you wouldn't believe me."

"Well, okay. Anyway, that's part of why it's so crazy in New Mexico now: the ones that got booted out of the other states are really pissed off—they seriously have it in for gringos. It's nothing but hassles, driving through. You'd think you were in friggin' Castro Cuba or some damn communist country! Trucks get impounded and confiscated right and left. And now they've got these new cops, called *Milicias*. They're the 'brown berets,' and they have special checkpoints all over the place. Anyway, I won't go into *Nuevo Mexico*, no ma'am, not if I don't have to.

I'll take 287 straight up into Colorado instead, even though it's longer. This is my truck we're sitting in, and I aim to keep it."

Ranya sighed again in resignation. "Sign we just passed says it's two hundred miles to Amarillo. Three hours, right? Any problems at the Texas state line? Weigh stations, checkpoints, things like that?" She still held the Glock across her lap, now only casually pointed at him.

"There's an inspection station a few miles in. It's not open, or it shouldn't be. And Texas doesn't care about the federal gun laws, if that's what you mean by checkpoints. Nothing like back East. I can find out about it out on the CB." He reached for the radio microphone, mounted in the ceiling.

She waved the pistol at him, bringing his hand quickly back to the wheel. "No radio. We'll take our chances." Traffic was sparse out here in western Oklahoma. An unusual percentage of the vehicles that she did see seemed to be loaded down with luggage, furniture, and jerry cans, somehow reminiscent of a distant generation of Okies fleeing the dustbowl days of the 1930s. "The Grapes of Wrath." She remembered the Steinbeck classic from high school English class. It had seemed like ancient history at the time.

After long minutes of silence between them, he glanced over at Ranya and said, "Look, if you're really set on going to Albuquerque, I know where you want to go first. It's a place in Texas, north of Amarillo. If I wanted to find the best way into New Mexico, with no hassles, it's where I'd go. I mean, I've been in trouble with the law, I know how it..."

"Save it. You don't know anything about me."

"Oh, I think I do know! Look, can you please put the gun away? Point it somewhere else? I don't need a heart attack, okay? If I wreck this thing, it won't do either of us any good. And grab a couple of sodas out of the bag down there. Please? If my mouth was any drier, it'd catch on fire." He turned and looked at her. "Listen lady, I'm trying to help you, okay? I'll drop you off at a place where you'll be clear, and then you can find your own way into New Mexico. It's a campground a little west of 287. Honest, it's your best bet. Deal?"

Ranya kept her hand on the Glock, but she pointed it forward, away from the driver, her finger well clear of the trigger. "Deal." Then she reached into the plastic shopping bag on the floor with her left hand, and twisted out a pair of cold Mountain Dews from a six-pack.

It was after dark when he let Ranya out. He stopped the eighteen-wheeler on the shoulder of the highway before an overpass. She climbed down, thanking him before she slammed the truck's door shut, and watched as his red taillights diminished and disappeared. If he was going to call the police, there was nothing stopping him now.

She hiked an hour west from 287 on the dirt shoulder of the asphalt county road. She stepped away from the road and crouched behind scrub at the first hint of headlights, until the occasional vehicles were past. Finally, she left the road and walked up a dry wash, and found a place to sleep rough. The driver had given her a green wool Army blanket from his truck's sleeping compartment. Before finding a flat grassy spot, she zipped on her pant legs and pulled on a black hooded sweatshirt from her pack.

Each time she put on another article of stolen clothing, she thought about Starr Linssen, wrapped in her seashell pattern shower curtain, concealed beneath her bed. She wondered if the warden had been found yet. Linssen had said that she had signed out for the rest of the workday. She might not be missed until she failed to show up for her next scheduled duty shift, or she failed to answer her phone or pager too many times. It was Friday night, so it was even possible that she wouldn't be missed until Monday.

There was no news of any prison break (or a murdered assistant warden) on any of the AM radio stations Ranya could tune in. Still, she knew that the alert could have been put out only to the police on their own radio and email networks. In the meantime, she was engrossed in catching up on the current news. It was the fourth night of deadly "arson riots" in Los Angeles, despite martial law, curfews and shoot-to-kill orders. The tense standoff was continuing in the besieged Muslim Quarter in Detroit. Marines were engaged in heavy combat in some city called 'Nazeer-Bakaf,' wherever that was. An emergency meeting of the Federal Reserve Board was scheduled for Monday. The first thousand representatives of the "Poor People's Party" had set up their planned tent city encampment on the National Mall in Washington.

Headlights passed less frequently as the night wore on. She slept fitfully, with her head on the warden's pack, and the Glock beneath it. She was wrapped in the blanket on a bed of flattened range grass, with her black sweatshirt hood pulled up, the string tied tightly in a circle. Mosquitoes buzzed around her exposed face, other insects trilled and chirped. It was miserable attempting to sleep this way, but she was hardened to misery. Through a slit in the folds of her blanket, she could see a brilliant swath of stars, and she found Orion standing guard among the constellations.

The real Spiderman wouldn't be afraid. Not one little bit. *But I'm not the real Spiderman, and I am afraid,* thought Brian Garabanda. Spiderman pajamas wouldn't fool real bad guys or monsters. Something was scratching the roof of his house, right over his bed. This happened sometimes when it was windy, or even worse, when there were thunderstorms.

It was the middle of the night. Brian was awake, but lying perfectly still, while something terrible scratched at the tiles on the roof. He carefully opened his eyes, just barely. If anything terrible was in the room, or looking in through his window, he was ready to shut them tightly again in an instant. But there was nothing. The Snoopy nightlight cast its reassuring glow across his room.

Once when he had opened his eyes in the night, he thought he had seen Daddy looking in the window from just a few feet away, but he wasn't sure. Maybe it was a dream. Daddy was very brave, he even had a gun. He worked for the FBI, catching bad guys. Brian hoped that his Daddy was outside somewhere, guarding him from terrible things. Daddy had told him that when it was windy, the tree branches scratched the roof sometimes, and not to worry.

But Daddy didn't live here any more. Now, Daddy only came and got him on Fridays, and took him to his small house, his apartment where he lived now. His Daddy and Mommy used to get so angry all the time, that he had finally left. Brian knew that it was his fault. He was sure that Mommy and Daddy had been happier before he had come along. He had heard his Mommy say this, and he knew it was true.

But even though today was Friday, Daddy did not come to get him. Instead, he had been picked up at day care by Mommy and her friend Gretchen, and they had gone to a boring meeting, which had lasted forever. Grown-ups in a big room, talking forever, blah-blah-blah. He didn't even have a game-boy to play with, so he had to play with boring Legos and coloring books instead.

He wondered why his Daddy didn't pick him up at day care. Mommy said he had other things to do. Brian worried that his Daddy was probably getting tired of picking him up. Probably, Daddy didn't care about him very much any more, since he had moved away. This fear stabbed deeply into Brian's five-year-old heart. *Maybe Daddy will come and get me tomorrow morning...or maybe he will have other things to do again.*

From his bed, he could see out his window and up at a part of the sky above their neighbor's roof. It wasn't cloudy, so there would probably not be any thunderstorms tonight, thank goodness. Thunderstorms at night were the worst, with the booming and crashing and lightning flashing.

Tonight there were stars out. Daddy would get him in the morning, he hoped.

3

Saturday June 21

Ranya awoke before it was fully light, stiff from sleeping on the hard and uneven ground. She unwrapped herself from the blanket, stood and stretched while surveying the desolate landscape. She breakfasted on bottled water and saltine crackers from the pack, and then quickly brushed her newly cut hair and rolled up the blanket. She had slept fully clothed and was ready in a few minutes.

She walked back to the cracked asphalt road and picked a hidden location, sitting Indian-style behind the desiccated carcass of a road-killed steer, where she could observe any cars coming in the distance from either direction. The grim mound was disgusting, but there was not enough other natural cover near the road to screen her from view in broad daylight. The dried animal was literally skin over bones, and long past being a source of interest to either insects or vultures. The steer's skull had become detached from the rest of the remains, and was picked clean and bleached white. Only when she was certain that an approaching vehicle was not a cop, would she stand and step out to hitch a westbound ride. If the police had been alerted to her escape, she knew that a young female hitchhiking on a rural Texas two lane road would draw their immediate attention.

It was eighteen hours since Starr Linssen had drawn her final breath of water and foam. Ranya was guessing that by now the police in all of the states around Oklahoma would be searching for her, even if their hunt was not publicly announced on the radio.

It was over twenty miles to the safe haven the truck driver had suggested. If she had not heard any news accounts of escaped prisoners on her mini radio, then the odds were that neither had any other ordinary civilians who were out driving today, and presumably, it would be safe for her to catch a ride. Otherwise, it would be an all day hike across sage land and cattle country. She unzipped her tan pants legs, took off her black sweatshirt, and stowed them in her pack.

A dark sedan appeared from the east, a possible police cruiser, so Ranya lowered her head, her huddled form blending in with the steer carcass. A black Mercedes flew past at better than 90 miles per hour, the driver unseen behind tinted windows. Other cars passed but she was afraid they might be police, so she stayed hidden. Almost two hours later a camper came into view, a boxy RV with an extension over the cab. Ranya weighed her chances, and stepped to the edge of the blacktop, waving her arms enthusiastically. The camper drove past with a small push of air, and then came to a stop several hundred yards beyond her. The taillights blinked indecision as Ranya slung on her pack and ran after it.

The big camper had a faded green and white body like a bloated cocoon. A sleeping area extended out over what appeared to be the vestigial front of a full-sized van. The camper was made even taller by the addition of antennas and cargo on top. Metal and plastic Jerry cans and a pair of bicycles were strapped in racks along the back.

The front side window was down when Ranya jogged up alongside the weathered RV. The passenger was a plump black woman somewhere past sixty years old, wearing a gold velour tracksuit and a purple crocheted cap. The driver was a thin bald black man at least as old, staring out at her through gold-framed glasses. He was gawking and grinning through ill-fitting dentures, but his wife inspected Ranya more skeptically. She said, "Sorry to make you run so far, but we had to be sure you were alone."

"No problem, I understand." Ranya had already rehearsed what she would say. She assumed the most fresh-faced college girl smile possible under the circumstances, considering that she had slept on the ground in the same clothes she had worn since yesterday. A tiny statue of Jesus glued to their dashboard buoyed her spirit. "You wouldn't be heading to Barlow's Creek by any chance, would you?"

The old driver said, "We sure are, Missy! You're in luck, because that's right where we're going today." He was wearing a white short-sleeved shirt and gray pants. His left hand was on the steering wheel; his right hand was out of sight behind the woman's ample hips. No doubt he was prudently holding a gun, Ranya thought.

The woman looked Ranya up and down and asked, "Lord, what happened to you?"

"My car died last night, back on 287. I walked as far as I could. I have friends at Barlow's campground. If I can make it there, I'll be fine."

The husband was nodding, already convinced. The wife studied Ranya and then said, "Well…I see. It's tight up here in front—there's no room for your pack. So let's throw it in the back, and then you can sit up here with us. How's that sound?"

"Wonderful!" She put her hand out, and shook their hands through the open window. She understood that they wanted her sitting in front with them, to keep an eye on her. It didn't matter, she was just glad for the lift. She would have cheerfully sat on the roof with the other strapped-on cargo.

"Well, okay then," said the woman. "And I can get you some orange juice and something to eat. I don't guess you've had breakfast yet today?"

"No ma'am, just crackers and a little water. Breakfast sounds great."

"I'll bet it does, honey, I'll just bet it does."

In a minute, her pack was in the back of the RV, and she was up front sitting in the middle between them. There was a cloth napkin spread across her lap, she was enjoying canned juice and biscuits with strawberry jelly, as they rolled west at a steady sixty miles per hour.

The woman said, "By the way, my name's Olivia, and that's my husband, Melvin."

Ranya didn't hesitate to give them an assumed name, her last false name from before her arrest. "I'm Diana. Diana Williams." This was the name from her long-gone counterfeit Canadian passport. Now the name held only sentimental value to her, from her last period of living in freedom, down in Colombia on the sailboat with Phil Carson.

"Pleased to meet you, Diana. We're coming from Houston, heading to Utah. We just couldn't stand living around Houston anymore. We just couldn't take it. It got too dangerous, too crazy. No way for civilized folks to live. We lived in New Orleans all our lives until the flood in oh-five, and then we thought we'd finish our days in Houston, but there's no way, no way at all."

"You were in the flood?"

Olivia answered, "No honey, when they said get out, we got out. We were in Baton Rouge in this very camper when Katrina hit, but we lost our house. Thank God, we had some insurance so we could start again in Houston. But then Houston went right straight downhill too, even without a flood."

Melvin said, "We finally figured if we were going to get shot or stabbed anyway, it might as well be on the way to the free states. So we decided to go for broke and make a run for it. We hoarded up all the gas we could, and when we had enough, we loaded up and we left. We bolted. We just walked away from our new house, we just up and left it behind. Gave it back over to the bank, I guess. Or the looters… Now we're heading for a safe place to live out the rest of our lives. We hear Utah's a safe place, a God-fearing place, even if they have a funny religion. That's all we want—a God-fearing place."

"We just want peace," said Olivia. "If we got to spend the rest of our days in this camper, then so be it. And if we don't make it…well…it's better than staying in South Texas, getting robbed every other week, waiting for one of them gangs to kill us for what little we got left in our pantry."

"I don't care if it does get cold up there in the free states," said Melvin. "I just want to live free again, that's all. Free from being afraid all the time."

His wife nodded agreement.

Barlow's Creek was a makeshift RV campground on a private ranch, visible from the state road. It stretched along one bank of a marshy stream that bisected endless miles of scrub prairie and cattle grazing land. Beyond the paved road, a dirt track led to a barbed wire fence, and a cattle guard made from pieces of railroad track.

Next to the break in the fence, a middle-aged guard sat on a lawn chair, beneath an awning made from a gray plastic tarp. A bike leaned against the last fence post. The man stood up from his chair at the approach of the new camper. He had a revolver openly holstered on the belt of his cutoff shorts, and he wore a gray Texas Rangers t-shirt tucked in under it. He carried a notebook and a walkie-talkie as he walked over to greet them.

"You folks ever been here before?" he asked the driver, studying the unusual trio composed of an older black couple and a young white woman.

"Nope, first time," Melvin answered.

"Where you coming from?"

"Down by Houston."

"Houston huh? Any of you all been east of the Mississippi in the last two years? No?" He studied them closely, gave each of them a long hard look, and they each replied that they had not.

"Well then, fine. Here's the camp rules. Read them, and then put your John Hancock here on the next line in my book. We don't have enough copies of the rules left to give you one to keep, so read it and hand it back." The gate guard passed over a well-worn sheet of paper with a dozen numbered sentences printed on it, and then he began to rattle them off from memory.

"You can only stay three weeks. If you like it, you gotta leave for a week, and then come back. This keeps the grass fresh, and we don't wind up with broken-down heaps that can't move. We don't want homesteaders or squatters—this here is a transit camp. Cost is eighty dollars cash a day, for now, subject to change any time the boss feels like it. If you want, we can take barter in ammunition, gold, silver, canned goods—all the usual stuff. We don't take credit cards, debit cards, E-bucks or bank checks, so don't even ask.

"It's an open-carry camp, but if we think you're unsafe with your weapons, you'll be politely asked to leave. You can carry concealed if you prefer, but nobody cares either way. You can drink, and you can shoot at our range, but if you drink and fool around with guns at the same time, you'll be run out of here *pronto*. You can only shoot on the range, during range hours, nowhere else. We got a mobile sewage pump out, the cost is reasonable, and if you dump on the ground…well, don't. We keep quiet hours from ten PM to seven AM, and that means no motorcycles, generators or loud music or even talking that bothers anybody. They're pretty reasonable rules, and you don't look like jerks anyway. I think you'll like it here. You plan on staying a full three weeks?"

"Not sure," replied Melvin. "We're heading to Utah, once we figure out the safest way there. New Mexico's out and we're not too sure about Colorado."

The gate guard offered, "Lots of people are heading that way, so you'll find plenty of company if you want it. Folks 'convoy up' here. Convoys leave all the time. You can even find gas, if you have enough cash or anything worthwhile to trade. I think you'll make out fine. You made it here from Houston, so the worst is behind you. If you can find gas along the way, you'll make it the rest of the way to Utah, no problem."

"Praise be! That's mighty welcome news, mister," replied the driver. Visible relief flowed into all three of the visitors at the prospect of a layover in a safe refuge.

"I'll lead you to your spot now; it's a nice grassy place. Just follow behind me, okay?" He turned and spoke into his two-way radio, then clipped it onto his belt and mounted his bike.

They drove in at the guard's unhurried cycling speed, jouncing down a dirt track with tents, trailers and RVs on both sides. Most sprouted a wide variety of antennas, solar panels and wind generators mounted on top. The wind generators all whirred madly, their sounds merging from one campsite to the next. Everywhere, flags were whipping back on the breeze: Texas Lone Star flags, the Stars and Stripes, several yellow Gadsden "Don't Tread On Me" flags, and other banners in every color and dimension. Specific state flags appeared among clusters of RVs, evidence of regional clannishness, or convoy intentions.

Ranya asked, "Why did he want to know if we'd been east of the Mississippi?"

"Are you putting me on?" asked Olivia, turning to look at her. "Cameroon Fever, what do you think? But ain't none of us got them poxy scars, thank the Lord."

Ranya simply said, "Oh, yeah. Of course," and let it drop. She had heard rumors from new D-Camp prisoners about a lethal epidemic that had swept through Florida and Georgia, but didn't know how far it had spread. Evidently, traveling east of the Mississippi put one into a greater risk category, at least as far as Texans were concerned. The RV continued to follow the gate guard on his bicycle, swaying and bumping along the path.

Kids rode bikes, chased one another on foot, played catch and threw Frisbees. Their camper passed a wide bend in the creek, where a few people waded and splashed in the sluggish water between cattail covered banks. They passed a redheaded woman riding a mountain bike in the other direction; she had an AR-15 carbine slung nonchalantly across her back, its muzzle down. She exchanged waves and hellos with the gate guard on his bicycle. The staccato popping sound of pistol and rifle shots could be heard in the distance.

The woman beside Ranya asked, "Honey, do you see your friends yet? What kind of a rig do they have?"

"Not yet," she lied. "They should be here, somewhere. At least, that's what they told me last week. We haven't seen half the place yet. They're around here somewhere, I'm sure. I'll just ask around, I'm sure I'll find them. So listen, thanks for the ride, but I don't want to impose on your hospitality…"

The woman smiled and said, "Nonsense, honey, it's no trouble. If you need…"

"If I know my friends, they'll be hanging out at the shooting range. If you let me out now, I'll just walk out there."

"Well that's fine, if that's what you want," said the woman. "But listen…first let me finish cutting your hair: it's kind of rough in the back."

"Olivia's right, honey," said her husband, chuckling. "If you're going on the lam, you'll need a better hair-do. If you didn't cut it yourself, I'd say your hair stylist needs to find a new line of work!"

"Is it that obvious?"

"Sure it is honey child, but who cares?" responded the woman, turning more serious. "We're all escaping from something these days, ain't we? Well, join the club. And if you don't find your friends…you're welcome to stay with us for a time. We'll squeeze you in—it'll be tight, but it'll be all right. The good Lord will provide."

The range was a half-mile walk down another dirt road, away from the creek into the scrubland, past scattered trees and immobile rocking-horse oil pumps. Ranya felt more confident with her hair trimmed evenly, and the residual ink on her neck scrubbed off with Olivia's cold cream. She had gratefully accepted the offer to wash up in their camper's tiny bathroom, and felt much better with a fresh face and clean teeth.

As she walked, she reflected upon the fact that all of the clothes she wore belonged to a dead woman, from her tan leather hiking boots, to her green ball cap and even Linssen's gold-rimmed aviator-style sunglasses. This was more than a little bit creepy, but after years of nothing but prison denim, it felt nice to be dressed in casual civilian clothes.

She walked on, enjoying her aloneness, reveling in her anonymity. There were no terrain features to speak of anywhere around Barlow's Creek, it was practically dead flat over vast expanses of land to the horizon. Willows, cottonwoods, and cattails defined the course of the creek to the east and the west. Only trees, oil pumps and occasional houses broke the monotonous uniformity of the land.

The slap-dash outdoor shooting range was like many she had visited in Virginia before the troubles. The firing line consisted of a dozen rough unpainted wooden tables, with a plywood roof extending above all of them to protect the shooters from the mid-day sun. Two hundred yards from the firing line, there was a bulldozed dirt berm for a bullet backstop. This berm was the only "hill" in the vicinity. A few cars, pickup trucks, motorcycles and bicycles were parked on the grass behind the firing line.

A red flag twenty feet up a pole announced that the range was open. Nobody paid her any attention as she dropped her brown pack on an empty table at the left end. There was a small plywood range shack behind them, with a hand-painted sign advertising reloaded ammunition and targets for sale. The firing line was hot. Four men were shooting rifles from sand-bagged positions on the tables at paper and cardboard targets 100 yards away.

Ranya had only the Glock pistol and two full magazines of 9mm bullets, just thirty rounds in all, which she had taken from Linssen's bedroom. She had no plan, no itinerary, just a general desire to get to Albuquerque somehow, and the range had drawn her back to the sights and sounds of her youth. Any shooting range was familiar, friendly territory, a place where she felt that she had the best chance of making the kinds of contacts that she would need to assist her on her way.

A pair of men behind one table fiddled with a Mini-14 rifle, they couldn't get the stuck magazine out. The rifle reminded her of the 'gun guards' in the fields back at D-Camp, she wondered if they knew that she had escaped yet. A full size black AR-15 also lay on the table, along with gun cases and nylon zipper bags. Going back five years to the last she had heard, semi-auto rifles had been outlawed, but here they were, lying out in the open. A tall range safety officer wearing a red ball cap walked over. He tersely admonished the two for inadvertently pointing the muzzle of their rifle sideways down the firing line, while they tugged at the magazine. The lanky RSO appeared to be in his mid-fifties, she thought. The same age her father would have been, if he had not been murdered.

The range master finished with the two men, and walked over to Ranya's end table. "Howdy. You new around here?" He noted her pack, with the rolled-up blanket tied underneath.

"Just got in," she replied.

"What're you shooting today?" She had no visible gun case or range bag.

"Glock 19." She pulled the 9mm pistol from a side pouch on her pack. "I'd trade it for a .45 though, a model 1911. That's more what I'm used to. Anybody around here trade guns?"

The man laughed. "Anybody here trade guns? Who doesn't?" Random rifle blasts split the air just to their side. "Look, you need ear protection. We're not very formal around here, but we do insist on that. I'll cut you a break though—wait just a second." He walked over to the range shack and returned in a moment, and handed her a pair of plastic earmuffs. The man had sandy hair sprinkled with gray; he wore jeans and a faded blue polo shirt with the lightning bolt logo from Thunder Ranch. A .45 caliber pistol, a model 1911, was holstered in leather high on his right hip.

She gestured with her head toward the rifles on the nearby table. "Weren't semi-automatic rifles banned a few years ago?" she asked.

He took a half step back and regarded her carefully. Questions posed by strangers about firearms legality were regarded with suspicion at gun ranges. The realistic fear of ATF entrapment stings ran deep.

"Where are you from?" he asked her, his hands on his hips.

"Virginia."

"Virginia—back east. Well that explains it. Sure, semi-auto rifles were banned, after the Stadium Massacre. And they still are banned, I guess. But this is North Texas, not Virginia, and we sort of do things our own way out here. We're not too worried about the federal gun laws, as you can probably tell. I mean, if the feds tried to come out here on gun raids, they'd have a real time of it! Anyway, I'm thinking they've already got their hands full in Detroit and LA, places like that." The man snickered. "Yeah, they've got plenty enough on their plates as it is, without declaring war on Texas."

"So, there're no feds in Texas?" she asked.

"Oh, no such luck. I'd say we still have our share, but they tend to mind their own business. They don't get out of the office much, you might say. They're not stupid: they want to go home at night, like everybody else. Meaning no disrespect to Virginia, but trying to enforce the old federal gun laws in Texas these days, well, that would be just about purely insane."

She nodded, and then asked, "Say, I noticed those two guys couldn't even get the mag out of their rifle. Are there any instructors around here? I could stand to earn a few bucks."

He chuckled. "Yeah, you might say there're a few instructors here. In fact, you're looking at Numero Uno. But you seem kind of young to be a gun pro—you're a firearms instructor? NRA certified? Or maybe you're just some kind of a natural Annie Oakley?"

She grinned at the mention of one of her childhood nicknames. "Something like that. All of the above, I guess. I grew up around guns. My father was a gunsmith; he owned a gun store with an indoor range. Back in Virginia." She pointed to the logo on his shirt. "He even came out to Texas, to Thunder Ranch a few times, back when..." She cleared her throat, her voice cracking. "So yeah, I can shoot. I'm a little rusty, but I can shoot."

"Say, what's your name?" He put out his hand, and she took it.

"Diana. Diana Williams."

"Diana, I'm Mark Fowler. I run this range, and I know everybody that matters around Barlow's Creek. Hey, you know what? If you can shoot, I mean really shoot, you might be able to make a little money, or maybe win some prizes later on this afternoon. There's not much to do for excitement out here but watch the grass grow and the wind blow, so shooting is pretty much the big sport. Of course, we encourage it: we keep the spent brass, and I get to reload it and sell it all over again. It's how we stay in business, you might say. Hey, you gotta be creative to make a buck these days." He paused, looking her up and down, considering. "You know, if you want to shoot for money, I might even lend you one of my .45s. You don't want to be shooting reloads out of that Glock, not even my reloads."

"No kidding—I don't want to lose any fingers. And I've only got two magazines of factory nine mil."

"Well then, let's see how you do with one of my .45s. If I think you can beat the local talent, I'll sponsor you, and spot you the ammo. How's that sound?"

"That sounds great Mr. Fowler, I appreciate it." She flashed him a toothy smile, forming cheek dimples, and he grinned right back at her.

"Mark. Please call me Mark—I'm not that old! Let me get a competition pistol out of my truck, and we'll see if you can shoot. None of the suckers around here will shoot against me anymore, so it might be fun to enter a ringer in the money matches. We usually have some macho men show up, and their pride just won't let 'em quit when a lady's whoopin' on 'em. Now let's grab my race gun, and see what you can do with it."

It took Ranya only a hundred rounds through Mark Fowler's custom-tuned .45 to get her shooting reflexes back up to speed. More shooters began arriving after lunchtime, mostly on foot or bicycle, or packed into the backs of trucks. It was becoming evident that gasoline was not only expensive, but it was hard to come by. She did as much listening and as little talking as she could, concealed behind her ball cap and aviator's sunglasses.

They started with a contest shooting steel targets for time. A judge with a stopwatch followed behind the competitors. Skillet-sized steel plates were balanced on steel bar frames, at ranges from ten to thirty yards from the firing line. When hit, they made a loud ringing clang and flopped over. Shooters had to run from position to position, firing at specific groups of targets, knocking them all down before moving on, changing magazines as needed.

If nothing else, she figured she would get in plenty of pistol practice, after five years without firing a shot. Practice that she might put to good use later, when it was time to rescue her son from his kidnappers.

4

The toy store was air conditioned, but not so cold that you would notice it. Not unless you had just walked in from the asphalt parking lot in back, where the temperature hovered around 95 degrees Fahrenheit. It was bearable inside, and in Albuquerque in June, that was enough, considering the frequency of citywide power outages. The shop's dusty ceiling was low, the aisles were cramped, the shelves half-filled with last year's toys and overlooked games. In its favor, it had entrances both in front on Central Avenue, and in the back behind the mini shopping center.

Luis Carvahal entered through the rear doors. He was wearing shorts, running shoes and a plain gray t-shirt that was dark with sweat. Carvahal had the physique of a much younger man, but his deeply lined face betrayed his late middle age. He propped his sunglasses up on his curly gray hair, and as his eyes adjusted to the relative darkness, he found his contact seemingly shopping in the middle of a center aisle.

His contact was more than a decade younger than he was, perhaps only in his mid-forties. Carvahal thought the man looked like a typical *Telemundo* or *Unavision* network newscaster. He was the standard clean-shaven and fair-skinned Latino from central casting, with wavy chestnut hair and gentle brown eyes. Both men were exactly the same height, five feet eleven inches, so when they met, they literally saw eye to eye.

His contact was an FBI Supervisory Special Agent named Alexandro Garabanda.

After the brief eye contact, he turned toward the shelves and stage-whispered, agitated. "I don't like meeting in stores. You know I don't like meeting in stores! You're supposed to be a pro at this—didn't they teach you this in spy school? And the Toy Hut? What am I supposed to be doing in a toy store? I'm 58 for God's sake—I look like a pervert trolling for kids in here. I stand out like a sore thumb!"

They didn't shake hands, but pretended to be looking at games on the same shelf. "No Luis, you look like a grandfather. A grandfather, shopping for a special birthday gift for a favorite grandson."

"Well, I don't have a grandson. Or any son, not any more." He sighed, and grew pensive. He pulled off his daypack and removed a small white towel, and used it to wipe his face dry. "You know, after 300 years, I'm the last Carvahal in Albuquerque. The end of the line." He took a clear plastic bottle of water out of a side pouch and drank from it.

"I'm sorry for setting up our meeting here, but this place was the best I could do on short notice. I had to bring my son, and he can play with the toys while we talk. Half of the time when I leave my house or I leave work, I'm getting plain-clothed Milicias tailing me. The Special Surveillance Group. I needed a decent cover, in case I was followed here. Father, son, toy store."

"I forgot: it's Saturday. You've got weekend custody, right?"

"Barely. I'm supposed to, but it hardly ever works out that way. It's not like I work nine to five, and my wife, my ex-wife…"

The toddler was near the end of the aisle, sitting on the ground playing with wind-up racecars, letting them go and chasing after them, smiling and laughing. The child was dressed in denim shorts and a camouflage pattern t-shirt.

"He's Brian, right?"

"Right, Brian. Five years old."

"I'm sorry Alex, I get so damned nervous. I always feel like I'm being followed. There are people in here…"

"Not on this aisle," said the FBI agent. He was wearing jeans and a Navy-blue polo shirt, with a brown vest on the outside. The unzipped vest resembled one that might be worn by an angler or a photographer. It covered his belt, and concealed his .40 caliber Sig-Sauer pistol. Thin layers of ballistic cloth sewn inside the vest would stop bullets from most standard pistols. "Don't worry, I checked the place out. Nobody followed me today, and nobody came in after me, or after you. It's clean. The Toy Hut's not a chain store, so it's not in the National Surveillance Network. It's too old, too small. Its cameras aren't linked to the NSN; they don't go anywhere. I checked."

"Well they better watch out anyway: they've still got 'Toy Hut' on all the big signs outside. Putting up a couple of 'Casita de Juguetes' placards, that won't satisfy the hotheads. The Spanish has to be on the biggest signs, not the English."

"Well, why don't you tell them, then?" Garabanda snapped. "Sorry, I know, it's not your fault. I mean, can you even believe this crap? Any of it? 'Spanish Only'—what the hell is that? Is this America, or not?" He shook his head slowly, resigned. "You know, a year ago when you told me that Agustín Deleon would be elected governor, I said you were nuts. But you called it Luis, you called it."

"Yeah, well, that and twenty bucks will buy me a cup of coffee. Alex, I don't want to complain too much, but at least you drove here. I had to ride my bike, three miles and every inch uphill. I can never get enough gas. I can't afford it, and I can't get enough gas coupons."

"What's the matter, the Mountain Lion can't toss some gas cards your way? I thought you were in tight with El Gobernador?" Garabanda was ribbing him—Deleon's stinginess was infamous. The governor retained the lifelong habits of frugality, which had sustained him during his years of exile, during his hard years in the wilderness.

"I am, but…"

"But no extra gas cards. I thought you were an insider now, Deleon's buddy?"

"Alex—enough joking around. I've got important information. You know the Democrats in the Senate—the U.S. Senate—they're supporting the revolution in Mexico…"

"I look at the computer from time to time," said Garabanda. "Sometimes I even turn on the TV."

"Funny. You know I was up in Santa Fe yesterday, with Deleon? Anyway, he got a call from Senator Kelly while I was with him in his office, after dinner. He was showing off—he let me listen in on another line."

"Why would he do that, Luis?"

"Why? Because I'm ghostwriting his memoirs, why else? The man is 82 years old. He wants me to know everything, see everything from his point of view, right? He trusts me a hundred percent, and he's very, very serious about his memoirs. Believe me, this was a proud moment for the Mountain Lion, taking a call from the senior senator from Massachusetts! I mean, it validates him, he thinks. Everything from the courthouse raid in '70, to prison, to exile, to the election—his entire life! So of course he wanted me to hear it...for his memoirs."

"So what did Kelly tell Deleon, that the FBI should know? You don't actually think I can send up a report on it, do you? On a private conversation between a U.S. senator and a governor?"

"Shit. I didn't consider that. Well, I'll give it to you anyway. Do what you can with it. Kelly's not going to object to the New Mexico land reform laws. He's going to support them in Congress, so they're a done deal. The special tax on ranches over a thousand acres, the Spanish Land Grant Commission—everything. Looks like Washington's not going to oppose any of it, as long as the state stays away from federal land. And you already know the President won't say a word. With Los Angeles burning, she can't afford to alienate the Hispanics…"

"I could've told you that. Our instructions from headquarters have been the same ever since this mess started: New Mexico 'land reform' is not a federal issue. We've already been directed by the DOJ to stay out of it, no matter how ugly it gets. So it really doesn't matter if Senator Kelly confirmed it to El Gobernador."

"Alex, that's all just background. There's more. I haven't gotten to the interesting part. This is why Kelly called: there's going to be a conference next week up north, some kind of mega-meeting of big shots. Politicos and tycoons are coming from all over. Heavy hitters only. Senator Kelly is coming down, and he said Senator Montaine is coming over too! Imagine those two cooperating on anything! Deleon didn't even know about the conference before this call, but it sounded like Kelly didn't know that he didn't know. Kelly must have assumed that El Gobernador was already in the loop about the meeting. Well, you know how cagey Deleon is—he played it like he knew all along—he didn't miss a beat. It's going to take place up at Wayne Parker's ranch next week. You won't believe who's coming: Orozco…"

"Pascual Orozco's not in charge of Mexico yet—there's still a revolution going on! Zorrero is still El Presidente."

"Not for long," replied Carvahal. "Zorrero is going to go on a permanent vacation in Ireland any time now, that's the rumor. He already owns a castle there, or at least his brother does. Zorrero is finished. Orozco will be the next El Supremo, one way or the other, and he's coming to Parker's ranch next week."

"Then this meeting must have been cleared with the White House."

"That's what I think too. It must have gotten the okay from on high; it had to have. And you wouldn't believe the guest list—thank God Senator Kelly is such a namedropper. Actually, he sounded pretty drunk. Besides the Senators, Paul Warburg is coming, and maybe Nicholas Biddle and Norman Montague. Imagine those billionaires, sitting down for dinner with a socialist like Pascual Orozco! Something huge is going to happen up there, something important."

"Like the Davos meetings, it sounds like." Garabanda was referring to the annual meeting of the so-called "World Economic Forum," sometimes held in the Swiss town of that name.

"No, not like Davos. Not hundreds guests, only a dozen or so. And all in private, all in secret. You know, Wayne Parker's ranch has its own jet runway—I mean, the Vedado Ranch is almost a million acres! I'm guessing it has something to do with Orozco taking over in Mexico, or maybe it's about the Constitutional Convention in September. Maybe it's about the 'North American Community.' I'm just guessing—Senator Kelly wasn't specific. But whatever it's about, it's going to be major, judging by who's coming."

"Luis, what am I supposed to do with this kind of information? Send an Intel report to Washington, saying that a couple of U.S. senators are meeting secretly with foreign leaders and billionaires in New Mexico? Just because a well known drunk like Senator Kelly made a private phone call to the governor? I can't send a report like that! You could leak something like that to the media—that might work. Put it out on the internet, the blogs might run with it. But it's political—it's completely out of my area of responsibility, and believe me, it's way, way above my pay grade. I need something else, something tangible. Maybe more information on the foreign fighters you said are coming over the border.

Something hard, with pictures, with names and some solid documentation. Then maybe they'll pay attention at headquarters. Maybe."

Carvahal stage-whispered, "My God, you already know they've practically got a damned Mexican Ho Chi Minh trail running straight across the border and up into Colorado, and that's not enough? What more does Washington need?"

"Calm down Luis, don't make a scene... I don't know what it'll take, I just don't know. I can't even tell who's really running the show back at headquarters. It seems like sellouts and UN carpetbaggers are in most of the key positions. The way I see it, nobody's left back there who gives a damn about a sovereign America any more. New Mexico…face it, we're a backwater, a sideshow. Washington has bigger problems to deal with than tinhorn radicals in 'Nuevo Mexico.' As long as they fly the Stars and Stripes over the capitol in Santa Fe, I don't think Washington gives a damn what else happens here. Not with LA burning and half of Detroit in a state of siege."

"Then what's the point, Alex? What are we doing this for?"

"What are we doing this for?" Garabanda repeated his question softly, taken aback. "Luis, that's a question I ask myself about a hundred times a day." He paused, and said quietly, "I suppose I'm just hanging on until retirement, is one answer. Maybe the only one…"

"Aren't you already over twenty years? I guess you got screwed on that deal."

"You got that right. I was at nineteen when they changed the minimum to twenty-five years. 'Take it or leave it.' Bastards!"

"Listen, you weren't the only one who got screwed. Remember, my entire pension evaporated into thin air when the Herald went belly-up. At least you feds will still get paid, even if they're only going to pay you in blue bucks."

"Luis, by the time I retire, they'll probably be pink or red or purple bucks. Worthless paper—just change the color, and whack off a zero."

"Tell me about it! You know what my IRAs are worth today?"

Garabanda muttered, "Yeah. BOHICA. Bend over, here it comes again."

"So what keeps you going Alex, why are you still working for the feds? I know why I'm here, why I'm doing this. My reporting days are finished, so if I'm anything any more, I'm an historian now. Deleon's confidant and biographer by day…and secret historian by night. At this stage in my life, it's enough for me to be where history is being made, and write it down. And maybe—just maybe—do what I can to keep New Mexico in the United States. But why do you keep at it? You're not even from here, so what do you care?"

"Shit, now you're getting all existential on me? Here in the Toy Hut?" Garabanda laughed quietly for a moment and gestured toward his son, playing on the floor. "Well, I've got Brian there, that's one reason to keep going. And besides the paycheck, as long as I stay in, I can get into the federal stores and shop on the Air Force base. And getting free gas for the bureau cars, that's another nice bennie. I can't imagine how you civilians manage it, without getting into the federal stores and the military bases."

"But is that enough?" replied Carvahal. "Enough to keep you working for the whores in Washington? Alex, that's like being a stoker on the Titanic, and staying in the engine room shoveling coal while the ship goes down! For what?"

Garabanda pulled a shiny black "Magic 8-Ball" from the shelf in front of him, and was slowly turning it over. "It's what I do, Luis. It's all I've ever known. Protect the country; try to warn headquarters…it's all I can do. Finish the career, hope for a pension, and raise Brian as best I can when I've got custody. It's all I've got left. Like your memoirs and your history of New Mexico."

"Speaking of which," said Carvahal, "There's something else: Deleon is seriously paranoid about the Vice-Governor. He's as much as told me he thinks Magón is planning something, maybe some kind of a move against him. Finding out about the Vedado Ranch conference backchannel from Senator Kelly—that really did it. Now Deleon knows for sure that Magón is operating behind his back. He thinks Wayne Parker set up the Vedado Ranch conference with Magón, making a private deal. Probably protecting Parker's million acres from the Land Reform Act."

"And Félix Magón is a total whack job," added Garabanda. "He's another Castro wannabee, if you ask me. He's worse than Hugo Chavez."

"You've got that right. You should see his 'Falcon Battalion.' They make the regular *Milicianos* look like Girl Scouts. Half of them are right out of the MS-13 and the Mexican Mafia—the worst scum from El Salvador to LA. They're not just another unit of the Milicia, they're Magón's enforcers. They'll do anything he says, anything at all. Deleon has no control over them at all. The Falcons only answer to Magón, and I don't think there's an American in the whole bunch. And Washington doesn't want to hear about it?"

The FBI agent stared intently at his informant, absorbing these latest rumors about the neo-communist Félix Magón. He was allegedly born in New Mexico and was therefore a U.S. citizen, but he had spent most of his adult life in Cuba, Bolivia and Colombia, before returning to America and entering politics. He replied, "Exactly right—Washington doesn't want to hear about it. DC is still in the PC lockdown mode. 'See no evil, hear no evil.' If Montana and Wyoming can pass 'English only' laws and start kicking out the illegals, then Nuevo Mexico can pass '*Español Solamente*' and fire all the gringo cops. Washington doesn't see any difference at all. They don't see 'land reform' as confiscating private property—they prefer to think of it as 'helping the little guy.' Like they say: 'no justice, no peace,' right? Meanwhile, they've got a bunch of hard core neo-Marxist narco-gangsters taking over an American state right under their noses."

Carvahal added, "An American state, but for how long? Listen Alex, I'm going with Deleon up to Tierra Andalucia Monday. He's going to inspect the Milicia training camps with Magón. He has to show himself, make sure the *Milicianos* all know he's really in charge, and not just the party figurehead. I'll take some pictures, and try to get you something you can send back to headquarters. Something that might wake them up."

"What the hell Luis, give it a shot. Watch your back though—if Magón's gunning for Deleon, he'll take out anybody near him."

"I'll be careful. I'll be back sometime Tuesday. Let's meet again, maybe midweek, okay? But not in another store. How about the old Mount Calvary cemetery?"

"We've used it before," replied Garabanda, dubious.

"So what? It's huge, and I won't have to pedal five miles to get there. I've got enough gas left to drive there, from home. Say, Alex, about the gas…"

"Don't worry about it. I'll bring the hose; I'll fill you up. Bring some extra Jerry cans in the trunk, and I'll fill them up too."

"Thanks, I appreciate it," said Carvahal. "The blue bucks…they don't go far. Thank God I own my family home free and clear… But trying to find gasoline on the open market, it's tough. Nobody wants to sell gas for blue bucks, not with the price freeze, and the money going down by the hour. All the gasoline is winding up on the black market, and I can barely afford it. At least you feds can get gas, on the federal bases."

"Thank God for that. I know it's tough—I can't even imagine trying to live on the civilian economy. So I'll bring you some gasoline, that's the best I can do for you, my friend."

"No my friend, the best you do for me is listen to my stories. You take the time to listen to an old reporter." Carvahal paused, looking briefly at Garabanda, and then turned back to the toy shelf. "You know, I used to admire a lot about Agustín Deleon. I still do, in some ways. I used to be such a star-struck lefty, in my younger days…such a naïve idealist. Oh, what a fool I was!" Carvahal smiled weakly, and shrugged. "You know, the Mountain Lion and I, we go way, way back together. All the way to Tierra Andalucia, and the courthouse raid. He's actually mellowed in many ways. At least he's not completely crazy! But the people around him today, oh my God! It's like being trapped in a Marxist insane asylum, up in Santa Fe. They think it's Barcelona in 1935, or Havana in '58! You wouldn't believe it, the lunacy of them! They're trapped in a time warp."

"They are?" asked Garabanda. "Or we are? Maybe we are."

"Us? Trapped in a time warp? My God, maybe we are. Maybe we all are! But who's going to stop this merry-go-round? And how the hell do we get off? Where does all this insanity end?"

"That, my friend, I haven't figured out. Not yet." Supervisory Special Agent Garabanda turned over the Magic 8-Ball. "Where does this insanity end?" he mused to himself.

He read the secret message that floated up into view.

It said: "*Better Not Tell You Now.*"

The tin-roofed two-story farmhouse had a screened-in veranda, which extended completely around the first floor. The private RV campground spread along the bottomland almost a mile away to the west. The sun was lost in gunmetal overcast across the creek, near setting. The dozens of trucks and campers were dark blocks silhouetted across the fading horizon.

A ceiling fan circled quietly above the polished pine dinner table, which was located just outside the kitchen on the side of the house facing the campground. Brass hurricane lamps suffused the screened-in porch with a soft golden glow. The dishes had mostly been cleared away after a dinner of steak, salad, and fresh corn. Four diners remained from the original group, including Caylen Barlow. His family had owned all of the land to the horizon for a century and a half.

Barlow sat in his wheelchair and stared intently at Ranya, while sipping bourbon from a heavy glass. He had a full head of snow-white hair, combed straight back, piercing blue eyes, and a face chapped red and deeply lined from a lifetime spent outside in all seasons. It was his house, the house he had grown up in, moved away from, and returned to in his later years. He was seated in his wheelchair at the head of the table opposite Ranya. Mark Fowler, the range master, sat on one side facing the screens and across the fields. Another man sat across the table from him, he was a middle-aged black man with a shaven head, wearing a red Western shirt with blue piping.

After devouring a plate-sized steak and all the trimmings, Ranya had told them her real name and her story, going all the way back to Virginia. To before her escape to Colombia, her return to America, and her betrayal. Before her baby had been born in prison, and was then stolen from her.

Before D-Camp.

Before Brad Fallon.

Back to her father's murder, the week after the Stadium Massacre. Back to the day her world had been turned upside down.

She didn't mention her sniper killing of Eric Sanderson. That secret had gone to the bottom of the Potomac with Brad, five years before. But she told them the rest.

Barlow said, "Come around here; let me see your hands."

Ranya got up, walked around the table behind Fowler, and extended her hands to the old man. He took them into his rough hands like a palm reader making an initial appraisal. He turned them over, stroked them, and fingered her calluses.

"Well," he said, "you certainly didn't just get these today. These are from field work, years of field work. I've never seen a government employee yet with hands like that. In fact, if you hadn't of had these calluses, you'd have torn your hands bloody today. What did you fire up there, 500 rounds?"

"At least," she replied, returning to her seat. "I lost count." She was wearing her khaki-colored nylon hiking pants with the legs zipped on, and a plain black t-shirt, which matched her dyed hair.

"Closer to 800," added Mark Fowler, beaming. "And she did pretty well, I'd say. She won a couple of pistols, a ton of ammo, and over nine thousand bucks. Those boys just had to keep trying again and again; they were regular gluttons for punishment! It purely kills 'em to get beat by a woman."

The black man in the fancy cowboy shirt raised his long neck beer bottle in toast to her and said, "You know what they say: 'your ego is not your amigo!' Those Tennessee boys just didn't know when to quit."

Ranya toasted him back, sipped her own beer and said, "I just sort of slipped into the zone. I was pretty much floating along after the first couple of steel plate matches. Mark kept me fed with fresh mags, and all I had to do was pull the trigger."

"Pull the trigger!" exclaimed the black man, snorting his beer. "Hell, you won everything from bowling pins on the table to long range metallic silhouette!"

"I guess I had a good day, considering I haven't touched a gun in five years. But remember, I was raised in a gun shop with an indoor range. I mean, I was shooting against grown men since I was a little kid! I used to just shoot for free ammo; it was strictly for fun. I never won a pile of cash money like I did today! Not to mention the guns..." She took a pull off her own beer. "Pretty weird to see the new dollar bills though. There was no money at all in the camps. When did they switch over to blue money?"

"Blue bucks," said Mark Fowler. "They're new, just this year. All the old greenbacks had to be turned over in January. Everybody's bank accounts had a zero knocked off, just like that! Ten for one—and the prices are still going through the roof."

Barlow said, "You did well by yourself today, Miss Bardiwell. Very well. We're all impressed with your shooting skills, especially after not touching a gun for five years. I'll admit that had us all wondering about you, but our law enforcement sources confirm most of your story. A female prisoner did escape from a federal facility in Oklahoma yesterday. That's just gone out on the police wires."

The black man winked across the table at the mention of "law enforcement sources," but Mark Fowler kept a poker face.

The old man continued. "The police report says it was from the Federal Transit Center at Oklahoma City, but I suppose we can't expect them to blow the cover on your secret D-Camp. Your story holds up, what we can check of it. I'm real sorry about your father, and Mr. Fallon, and of course about what happened to your baby son."

Fowler said, "It just amazes me that I know Leo Swarovski personally, and that he told me years ago how he was tipped off about the ATF raid. It never made any sense, not until now. He never knew who tipped him off, or why. It's just the damnedest thing, and now it all fits, it fits right into your story. I suppose it's one of those 'six degrees of separation' things: me, Swarovski, your father, and you."

"So here we are now, Miss Bardiwell," said the white-haired Caylen Barlow. "We believe you. It's one hell of a story, but we believe you. We'll have a doctor carve that chip out of your shoulder tomorrow morning. That's no problem. In fact, we know some folks who would love to study it; we'll send it on to them. But I still don't understand what you want to do. Nobody in their right mind would drive straight through to Albuquerque from here! No gringos anyway. Say, how's your Spanish?"

"Pretty good. *Más que bastante*; more than good enough. I had a lot of practice in the camps—I always figured it would come in handy, eventually. Like when we were in Colombia. I can't pass for a native speaker, but I speak 'Spanglish' about as well as millions of American Hispanics can. I'm not afraid to go into New Mexico, if that's what you mean. Mr. Barlow, I intend to find my son, no matter what it takes. I'll walk to Albuquerque, if I have to."

"I'll bet you would, too. Hmm..." Barlow looked at his two friends. "Mark, Sam…you wouldn't mind going inside for another round of beers, would you? I'd like to talk to Miss Bardiwell for a little while, please."

When they had left, he paused, stared up at the ceiling fan, and then quietly spoke. "I can get you a ride in. Not all the way to Albuquerque, but close. Close enough. Close enough to get past most of the checkpoints and roadblocks, at least all of the ones we know about. The permanent ones. We can get you close enough for you to rendezvous with somebody we trust, somebody who can drive you the rest of the way into the city."

"How will I get through the checkpoints? I don't have any ID."

"Not through the checkpoints. Over them. In an airplane, a light airplane. You're game to fly, aren't you? If you can ride motorcycles, a little hop in an airplane shouldn't be a problem, right?"

"Oh no, no problem! No problem at all."

"Okay then, it's settled. You'll take off tomorrow night, at dusk. We'll have until then to get you ready. There's some folks in the camp from near Albuquerque; they got thrown off their land. Got 'land reformed,' you might say. They can fill you in on what to expect in the city. If we're lucky, we'll get an address for your son. We still have some good law enforcement sources in New Mexico, but I don't know about finding an FBI agent's home address…"

"That's all I really need: an address for Special Agent Alexandro Garabanda."

"We'll do our best. And we might be able to find you an ID card. I'm not sure, I'll have to ask around, see what's available on short notice. Nothing that'll stand up for very long, mind you. Not if they scan your thumbprint or your eyes. From what we're hearing, there's not too much of that. Just something to get you past a regular Milicia checkpoint. If you're lucky, if they don't have a print scanner. If they scan your prints into the wireless network, well…after that, you'll be on your own."

"Mr. Barlow, that's all I could ask for. More than I could ask for! I don't know how to thank you…"

"Oh, it's not much. The smile on your face right now is all the thanks I need. The plane is going in anyway; you'll just be a straphanger. Since you're bound and determined to get to Albuquerque one way or the other, I figure it's only fair to give you a head start. After what you've been through for the last five years, I guess you're in line for a break. And I'll admit it: I've always been a sucker for a good-looking gal who can shoot! You remind me of…well, never mind that…" He looked away from her, toward the last fading light, beyond the RV camp.

"Mr. Barlow, if I could, I'd like to do something for you in return, to repay…"

"Repay? No. No need. But…something in return? In return…" He cleared his throat, and took a drink. "Miss Bardiwell, for at least thirty years I've watched the politicians of both of our so-called parties selling our country like a twenty peso whore in a Juarez alley. America's being carved up like a Thanksgiving turkey, and sold out by political prostitutes for their own personal gain. I've watched it happening for most of my life." He slowly shook his head.

"Ranya, I do wish you well in your quest to find your son, and I'll do what I can to help from here." He hesitated, and cleared his throat again. "Now maybe, just maybe there is something you might be able to do for me. You'll hear about this tomorrow, when you talk to my friends from

New Mexico." He took another sip of bourbon. "The University there is a magnet for radicals from all over America and Latin America. UNM has become a center of the radical Hispanic movement. The 'Aztlan' movement. Have you heard of it?"

"Aztlan? Sure. All that *la raza* crap. The new homeland for the Hispanics, after they ethnically cleanse out all the gringos."

"That's it. Well, if you have any chance of blending in, it'll be with that crowd, with what they call the 'Voluntarios.' You look Latina enough, and you can *habla* the *Español*, so if you can spout off Marxist gibberish, you'll be able pass muster."

"I went to UVA for three years—most of my professors were socialists. I can 'spout off Marxist gibberish' all day long. I had to, to get decent grades."

"Good. You'll need to, if you want to pass yourself off as a new Voluntario. And if you're questioned, that'll be your best cover for coming to Albuquerque. So, if you do wind up at the university…well, one of the professors there, you might say he's a personal enemy of mine."

Barlow's eyes and lips narrowed. He finished his whiskey and clapped the glass down on the table. "Robert Johnson. He's a gringo transplant from up north, but he's 'gone native' you might say. He's a complete America hater, what we used to call a crypto-communist in the Cold War days. If you find yourself near the university, you might come across him. I understand he's advising the state government on 'land reform' policy.

"This Robert Johnson—this so-called professor of American history—he's helped to poison the minds of thousands of students over the years. And believe me, that's bad enough, but then he made it personal. *Very* personal. He turned my only granddaughter against America, against her own family, and against me. Robert Johnson was her 'guru' at UNM. Her guru…and even more than that. He pulled her in, and turned her into a real one-worlder, a socialist true-believer. I haven't seen or heard from her in a couple of years. Last I heard, she was down in Mexico with the Army of the Poor. Before that, she was in Venezuela, and before that, Cuba. This Robert Johnson—to me he's the worst kind of traitor. He poisons our children, and turns them against their own country."

Barlow paused, and stared directly at Ranya. "So if, and I only say if…if you happen to come across him…well, let's just say I wouldn't mind hearing that he came to a bad end. Wouldn't mind it at all." Barlow placed his elbows on the dinner table, rested his chin on his knuckles, and looked hard at Ranya. "No, I wouldn't mind it at all."

"Mr. Barlow, I'm just going to New Mexico to find my son. I…"

He spread his hands and said, "It's all right, I understand. Forget I brought it up. It's only a personal family matter; it has nothing to do with you. Now if you're finished, Maria will take you upstairs and show you where you'll be staying tonight. You'll be sleeping in the girls' room. They've all grown up, and moved on."

Barlow made a mirthless chortle without smiling. "You know what's ironic? The last one who lived in that room was my own sweet granddaughter, before she went away to college. My granddaughter Jessica, the communist."

5

Sunday June 22

Bob Bullard knew that nothing impressed the ladies like a visit to his yacht. The Eldorado was docked downtown on San Diego Bay, just a few blocks from the Federal Building and his high-rise penthouse condominium. The Department of Homeland Security's Southwest Regional Director had offices in a half dozen states, and his main office was in Los Angeles, but he spent as much time as possible in San Diego.

Who wouldn't? Los Angeles had become unlivable. It was practically a war zone, almost as bad as Tijuana or Juarez. That was no shock, because LA was virtually a part of Mexico today. Most Angelinos were dual citizens, and no Mexican election season was complete without campaign stops in LA by every serious Mexican candidate. You could drive for miles in any direction in Los Angeles (if you had a death wish) and not see a single word of English on a sign or billboard.

On the other hand, Bob Bullard knew that the federal government had drawn a bright red protective line around San Diego, because of the national security importance of the world's second largest concentration of naval power. The better parts of the city and county would not be allowed to collapse into a state of anarchy and gangsterism, like so much of the rest of urban California.

This was especially true of the narrow coastal strip west of Interstate 5, where most key government personnel and other influential persons lived and worked. Coastal San Diego County remained an oasis, a refuge from the Mad Max reality of California. Coastal San Diego was a hot ticket, the place where people wanted to live…if they could afford it. And an eighty-foot yacht tied up right on San Diego Bay? When it came to impressing the ladies, that combination could not be beat.

Wendy Larmouche and her girlfriend (Sandra somebody-or-other) were TSA airport screeners, babes who stared at x-ray machines and wanded passengers' crotches for a living. Bullard had met them at San Diego International on a public relations visit to the terminal, while showing the media the TSA's latest imaging technology. He had lucky timing in meeting the newly hired women. As a customary habitué of the Gulfstream, Citation and Learjet end of air operations, he rarely ventured over to the public side of any airport. He considered public terminals to be prime places to catch diseases like Cameroon Fever or the Bird Flu, and he avoided them like the plague.

Wendy had caught his eye immediately, and so on his instructions, his PR flacks selected her to serve as a model TSA representative for the media demonstrations. She was from Nashville, just past thirty and single. Best of all, she was natural blond with an impressive rack, which looked oh-so-inviting, straining the buttons apart on her tight white TSA uniform blouse. Everybody had a great laugh when she went through the new skin-revealing body imaging equipment. Bullard knew that he had found a live one when she laughed along with them, and gleefully sashayed through it several times to their obvious enjoyment.

He had 25 years on her, but that didn't matter much. Not when he was the Regional Director of the Department of Homeland Security. Besides, he kept in great shape lifting weights, and he still had most of his hair, even if it was kept black with men's hair dye. Lately, he was even winning the Battle of the Receding Hairline, now that his implants were taking hold and showing steady progress. (It was a mystery to him how a man so covered with thick black body hair could go bald precisely where he needed hair the most, but this problem was steadily being conquered through expensive applications of modern medical technology.)

The airport visit had taken place a month earlier. Through his underlings, Bullard let Wendy Larmouche know that he was personally responsible for her rapid promotion to assistant supervisor. After that, Wendy had needed little coaxing when she was invited out for a Sunday morning boat ride on San Diego Bay with the Regional Director.

If the chauffeured Lincoln Navigator bristling with antennas and radios had impressed the girls when it picked them up at their apartment, the sight of his eighty-foot yacht sent them almost into a swoon. The driver was waved through the security gates onto the government docks at the foot of Broadway, and he drove right out onto the hundred yard long concrete pier and parked by the Eldorado. Bullard met them there, casually leaning against the hood of his black BMW 745, wearing a sky-blue polo shirt, khaki slacks, and Docksiders boat shoes.

He had checked himself carefully in the mirror before leaving his penthouse condominium: his hair was combed straight back and he was closely shaved. Someone had once told him that he looked like "Robert De Niro in his prime," and he clung to this façade. Bullard was slightly self-conscious about his height (or lack thereof) of only five feet nine inches. His self-image as "De Niro in his prime" helped him to overcome that shortcoming, and he did what he could to affect the look and mannerisms of the great actor. Maybe he had a bit more nose than De Niro, but when seen directly from the front, he knew that he was almost a dead ringer.

A mile across the bay beyond his yacht laid the gigantic gray slab of the nuclear aircraft carrier Ronald Reagan, presenting a suitably awesome backdrop for the girls' visit. They stepped down from the Navigator, and looked over at the eighty foot converted power yacht with wide eyes. Wendy twanged, "This is your boat, Bob?" in her Tennessee drawl.

"Yeah, sort of, you might say. I mean, since I'm the regional director, yeah, I guess it is."

Wendy's red-painted mouth hung agape as she made for the aluminum ramp, which led from the cement quay down to the floating dock where the yacht was tied up. Brunette Sandra was right behind her, grinning. Today, instead of their usual white TSA uniform blouses and black slacks, both girls were wearing colorful Polynesian-style wrap-around sarong skirts, skimpy halter-tops and sandals. Wendy had insisted on bringing a girlfriend—as if that would guarantee her pretended chastity. Bullard had to smile at her naiveté. Broads always thought that bringing along a gal-pal would mean safety in numbers, but as a strategy, it rarely worked. Not after the girlfriend met Cesar, his boat captain! Bullard followed them down the metal ramp.

His captain was dressed in a white short-sleeved uniform shirt with black shoulder boards and white pants, affecting the look of a naval officer. He was a trim man, a young forty, with black hair and a thin black mustache. He stepped down from the yacht's stern boarding gate to greet them, and graciously helped them up the steps from the floating dock. "Good morning ladies! I am Captain Escoria, but please, just call me Cesar—we are all friends aboard the Eldorado." He extended his hand to help the women aboard, making direct and prolonged eye contact with each of them in turn.

Bullard boarded last, enjoying the shapely rear view of the two women as they climbed up onto the yacht. He noted that Cesar was already laying his Latin-lover shtick on Sandra. Antonio Banderas himself had nothing on Cesar Escoria, not when it came to romancing the Midwest farmer's daughters! He had perfected his wingman role; he had it down to a science. As usual, Cesar knew in advance that his boss was after the large-chested blond hottie. He would be more than satisfied with bedding her mousy brunette friend, if that was how the day played out.

Wendy couldn't stop smiling. "I still just *cain't believe* this is your boat! Bob, you are just so, so…"

"Well…I'll admit it's one of the nicer fringe benefits of the job."

"It sure is a pretty *thang*—that is sure enough true!" Wendy scampered through the open side bulwark and into the cockpit, gawking in all directions at the varnished teak rails, and the polished stainless steel fittings. Her brunette friend Sandra returned a lingering look at Captain Escoria, as he helped her aboard by her hand.

The sleek yacht had been seized by Customs three years ago while attempting to smuggle five thousand pounds of cocaine into San Diego Bay, concealed in auxiliary fuel tanks. The vessel had subsequently spent two years sealed shut and moldering away at a south bay boatyard, which was used by Customs to impound drug boats. After being appointed the regional DHS director, Bob Bullard had spotted the Eldorado during a routine facilities tour. Today, she was in better-than-new condition, after spending almost a year undergoing a bow to stern conversion to official government duty. On paper, Eldorado was now a DHS "Mobile Emergency Management Platform," an entirely new species of floating government asset that Bullard's sharp young assistants had invented at his "suggestion."

By no means was Eldorado the queen of the San Diego waterfront. At "only" eighty feet, the power yacht was less than one-half the length and a quarter of the tonnage of the serious megayachts, belonging to the international ultra-wealthy jet setters who frequently visited San Diego. On any given day, a helicopter tour of San Diego Bay might reveal fifty yachts larger than this one.

On the other hand, the Eldorado had excellent range for her size, and her twin Caterpillar diesels could take her across more than a thousand miles of open ocean on the three thousand gallons of fuel in her tanks. This was a critical factor, because when the time inevitably came to bug out, this would be sufficient range to carry him non-stop from San Diego to any point between Cabo San Lucas and Acapulco.

And this was why Bullard had selected a moderately sized vessel. While there was no way to hide the hundred-foot-plus megayachts, the eighty-foot Eldorado would easily blend in among the larger Bertram, Hatteras and Ocean sportfishers. Blending in was going to be essential, when the time came to disappear south of the border. Toward that end, her beautiful (but distinctive) original gleaming red hull had been repainted in plain vanilla, matching the deck and superstructure. An all-white powerboat with classic sportfisher lines was the ultimate in yacht harbor camouflage—and he would need all of the camouflage he could get, after he split from California.

Despite his high position, Bob Bullard had no illusions about the long-term viability of the federal government, or its ability to stave off the steadily deepening economic crisis. As a member of the Senior Executive Service within the DHS, he was now an insider, a member of the American *nomenklatura*, and he had access to the most highly classified reports. Even though it was never stated in plain English, for those who could interpret the bureaucrat-ese, it was obvious that total financial collapse was only a matter of months away, or a year at the outside. The conversion to blue dollars, the mandatory "gold repurchase" laws, the limits on bank withdrawals, the restrictions on currency exports and all of the other gimmicks were only Band-Aids, applied over terminal economic cancer.

They were just temporary confidence-boosting measures, stopgaps designed to keep Joe Six-pack calm and buy a little more time.

Meanwhile, elite insiders with sufficient foresight were making their own private arrangements to ride out the gathering storm. All of the intelligent top-level players he was meeting recently were preparing their own parachutes, ratlines and escape tunnels. In fact, this was the number one subject of their private off-the-record conversations. For many, these preparations meant buying homes in exclusive walled and gated communities with plenty of private security, far from the urban megapolises. For others, there were retreats on remote islands, complete with their own generators and fuel supplies.

Some optimists believed that because the port and the naval bases were so important, the federal government would never let San Diego go down the toilet. Many of them had moved into high-rise condos near the key government buildings downtown. Bob Bullard currently lived atop just such a luxury condominium, but he thought of it as a temporary sanctuary at best. It was a standard perk of his office, it was convenient, and it cost him nothing, so why not? He could drive between the Federal Building, his condominium and the yacht in less than five minutes, or walk it in ten. All three were located in a high security zone that was regularly swept clear of homeless bums, junkies and petty street criminals. With a heavy police presence, the downtown office district was safe enough—for now—but a suffocating air of dread permeated the California landscape.

Bullard knew the truth: there was simply no federal operating budget left, and there were no more currency-propping tricks left in the bag. The federal government was out of gas, and running on sheer momentum. The wheels had begun to come off the wagon two years ago after the oil crisis, when the hedge funds and derivatives markets had imploded, a hundred trillion dollar supernova sucked into a black hole. Like most Americans, Bullard had only a hazy grasp of the meaning of the derivatives disaster, but the effect was crystal clear: trillions of dollars had somehow disappeared in less than one week, leading to the failures of several of the largest banks in America. Their doors had only been kept open through a massive intervention from the Federal Reserve's so-called "New Bank," pumping in brand new make-believe money created from thin air.

That had only been the beginning of the ongoing slide into national economic ruin. After a year of widespread corporate bankruptcies, factory closings, layoffs and massive pension defaults, bitterly angry (and often hungry) Americans had taken to the streets by the millions. Local and federal government buildings in every state capital and major city were surrounded by seas of demonstrators banging empty pots and pans, demanding that the government "fix the problem, and fix it now!" Leading politicians and senior bureaucrats were forced to sleep in their offices, or in some cases commute via rooftop helicopters. They were unwilling or literally afraid to run the pan-banging gantlets that had taken over the streets and sidewalks around their offices.

After two weeks of massive around the clock protests, the federal government had been panicked into action by the unending din of clanging pots and pans. For the policy makers, all that remained were the printing presses, both the paper and electronic money producing kinds. Their secret economic "cure" was printing endless truckloads of Federal Reserve Notes to stem the danger of bank runs and head off a deflationary spiral.

Since the Federal Reserve had ceased publishing their "M-3" money figures back in 2006, the exact amount of this new currency creation could be concealed from the American people. The runaway inflation it caused could not. As an insider with well-positioned friends at Treasury, Bullard knew that once the President and the Chairman of the Federal Reserve decided to inflate their way out of default, the money supply had been doubling every three months!

Hundreds of thousands of laid-off workers, as well as retirees suddenly without pension checks, continued to bang their empty pots together as they marched around the U.S. Capitol and White House. The penniless unemployed and the abandoned pensioners banged their pans and demanded their dollars…and lo and behold, they got them! Predictably, hyperinflation of the U.S. dollar had been ignited.

Foreign countries (beginning with China) holding US dollar-denominated assets began a mad rush to unload them for tangible goods, even as their value plummeted. The entire world was soon awash with unwanted and increasingly worthless dollars. The economic dominos continued to tumble, one after another. The Treasury Bond market collapsed next, and the United States was unable to borrow new money, even with interest rates soaring past 20%. There was simply no faith left in the enduring value of the dollar. The trust had been shattered; "full faith and credit" became a bitter joke.

The most recent ploy of converting the old greenbacks to "New Dollars" at ten to one to stem the runaway inflation had only bought a few more months reprieve at best. The switch to the new "blue bucks" was clearly not a one-time-only permanent solution, although that was the official government spin. The national leadership understood that the economy was gasping and choking on life support, even while they preached sermons of hope, courage and patience to the masses. The synthetic "plasma extender" of new thin-air money could not substitute for a solid currency. None of them knew the week or the month that the remaining economy of the USA would grind to a halt, but most of them felt in their bones that the final days of reckoning were fast approaching.

When that final reckoning occurred, Bob Bullard did not plan to be standing at attention on the deck of the American Titanic, singing the national anthem while the ship of state slipped beneath the waves. The regional DHS director was nothing if not a survivor, and he had his own eighty-foot lifeboat fueled up, stocked up and ready to go. He fully intended to run away, to live to fight another day…and not for the first time, either.

His thoughts returned to the notorious attack on his former boss's home, which had launched him onto his current ascending trajectory. Five years ago, Wally Malvone had been the leader of the covert "Special Training Unit" of the Bureau of Alcohol, Tobacco, Firearms and Explosives. They had both been at the STU leader's house on the Potomac River, just south of Washington, when it had been attacked by domestic terrorists. After Malvone's capture by the terrorist snatch team, Bullard had shot and killed his old superior. He had regrettably been forced to seal Malvone's lips forever, before he could be taken away and made to divulge the dark secrets of the Special Training Unit. Secrets that might have pinned numerous murder raps on Bob Bullard…

After shooting Malvone, Bullard had run away, and yet, incredibly, in the aftermath of the attack, he had been called a terrorist-battling hero, and he was promoted! This dramatic reversal of fortunes only confirmed to Bullard that it was his fate to rise inexorably upward, even as his colleagues sank all around him.

He had first felt this strange destiny within him on that ill-fated day in Waco Texas, when most of his ATF assault squad had been wiped out. Yet even that disaster had improbably led to him winning ATF valor awards, and a key early promotion. These two experiences had convinced him that even while America broke apart and sank, he would be able to skip across the burning wreckage, and somehow achieve an even higher station. This was his karma. He accepted it and he welcomed it.

His full-time boat captain Cesar Escoria knew the deal, and was an integral part of Bullard's escape plan. He had brought Cesar over to the DHS from the ATF's Special Training Unit, after that radical endeavor had gone up in flames at Malvone's house on the Potomac. Escoria's fluent Spanish and abundant Latin charm would be critical for enabling Bullard to make the transition to a comfortable life in Mañanaland. Bullard had the high-level police, military and governmental contacts that would make the transfer possible, but his Spanish was less than fully adequate to the task. With Cesar as his *Capitán del Yate*, melding the Eldorado into the luxury marina landscape of the Mexican Riviera was going to be *no problema.*

Just as it was going to be *no problema* coaxing Wendy down below into the Eldorado's luxurious master stateroom, after today's boat ride. When you had money, power and a yacht, broads were never a problem. It already promised to be a great day on the water. The sun was burning through the light morning overcast, and Bob wondered how long it would take Wendy to peel off her wraparound skirt and her halter-top to catch the rays. He gave her ten minutes, max.

Wendy's friend Sandra had scampered around the pilothouse up onto the forward deck, shedding her own halter top and wrap, revealing a skimpy red bikini. Cesar was giving her a personal tour of the yacht. All the way back in the cockpit, Bob could hear Sandra giggling and squealing at Cesar's familiar jokes.

Wendy asked, "Bob? Can I call you Bob?"

"Of course you can, doll face." Bullard had heard De Niro call broads "doll face" in a movie. If De Niro could pull it off, so could Bob Bullard. And why not? He was the regional director of the DHS! He could call broads whatever the hell he wanted to—and Wendy was just a hick airhead anyway.

"Are we going to take this big ole' boat out for a ride today?"

"No, not today. It's a major hassle to get it underway. Instead, we're going to go out on one of my Homeland Security speedboats. It's a real screamer; it'll be a hoot! You'll just love it, I promise. They're going to swing by and pick us up right here in a little while."

"You mean like a race boat? One of those long skinny *thangs*, with the great big motors?"

"That's right, one of those. Just like NASCAR on the water, only better. It's a real Fountain racing boat—it was confiscated from the dope smugglers." Just like the Eldorado was, he thought, but didn't say.

"Oh Bob, you really are something, you are just full of tricks, aren't you?" Wendy unwrapped the gold sarong from around her waist and let if fall to the deck, revealing long tan legs, and a tattoo of a spread pair of wings above her round buttocks.

"I try to be, Wendy. I try to be." Bullard sat on the blue canvas upholstered bench seat which ran across the transom, leaned back and crossed his legs, and appraised her very promising curves. She was wearing only a thong bikini bottom under her wrap, another hopeful sign. When they returned to the Eldorado from their seventy mile-an-hour jaunt out past Point Loma on the Fountain, Bullard knew that the two ladies would be as excited as bitches in heat. They always were—it never failed. There was just something magical about the wind on their faces, the pounding waves, and the roar of the motors.

"Say Bob, what's a girl got to do to get a drink around here anyway?"

He smiled. "Name your poison, sugarplum. Just name your poison."

Ranya awoke from a catnap lying on her back. She had been resting on the wild grass, her brown pack for a pillow. She was wearing dark blue jeans and her black hooded sweater, her booted ankles crossed, her fingers intertwined across her stomach. The two men who were going to be the other passengers on the plane were occasionally talking, while sitting on opposite sides of a picnic table twenty feet away from her.

In the camps, she had become accustomed to making the transition to consciousness in a sly way, in secret. In D-Camp, they had slept in open barracks on bunk beds. Useful information could sometimes be overheard, if one was skilled at pretending sleep. She knew that a giveaway was sudden perfect stillness and quiet on the part of the faker, so she gradually began a light snoring sound, her mouth partly open. After five years internment in the camps, the natural sleeping sounds women made were all very familiar to Ranya Bardiwell.

She had been dropped off at this place by Mark Fowler, in his truck. The two men were already waiting there, clad in desert camouflage uniforms, sorting through their gear on the wooden picnic table. Fowler asked her to wait in the truck while he went over and talked with them, and he returned in a few minutes. "Don't bother trying to make friends with those guys. They've got their game faces on, you might say. They're in the tactical mode now. They'll accommodate you, and that's about it. It's Caylen Barlow's plane and pilot, so they don't have any choice about taking you, but don't expect them to like your showing up. Just listen to the pilot. He's already been briefed, and he knows exactly where to drop you off. You're clear about the link-up in Mountainview?"

"Sure, no problem."

"You've got the New Mexico road map? You'll be forty miles southeast of Albuquerque, when you jump out."

"I've got the map in my pack, and a compass. We're landing on a dry salt lake. After I get out, I walk four miles south, across the salt flats, until I hit State Road 60. Railroad tracks run parallel to 60; I follow the tracks five miles west toward Mountainview. Right at 6AM, I walk into the Ancient Pueblos Restaurant on State Road 60, and order breakfast. I ask the waitress for Don, and then I tell Don that C.B. sent me. He'll keep me in the back room until the bread truck makes its delivery, and that's my ride into Albuquerque. It's a good plan."

"Yeah, it is," replied Fowler. "Now, most of the folks in Mountainview are still on our side, but watch out. Milicias could set up checkpoints or do sweeps while you're there. When they show up, it's always at least fifteen or twenty of them, sometimes a lot more, and they're usually kind of twitchy on the triggers. Especially around gringo cowboys, like in Mountainview."

"I'll be careful."

"Don't put your pistol together until you're in the city. It won't do you any good at a checkpoint anyway; it'll just give you away."

"I won't."

"You've got my knife..."

"Right here." She patted her right side front jeans pocket. "Thanks."

"Well, okay then, good luck. I hope you find your son, I really do. Getting his address, that was a lucky break. If you make it back here, you know you've got a place to stay. Both of you."

"Thanks for everything you've done..."

"No problem, I'm glad to help. Say, how's your shoulder?"

"Sore, but I'm damn glad to be rid of the chip." An adhesive butterfly closed the tiny incision.

"You've got everything you need?"

"Yes, thanks. I'm ready." Barlow and Fowler had seen to her outfitting with the gear and clothes she would need. After much discussion, she had decided to keep Linssen's 9mm Glock pistol. It was broken down into its main parts, and concealed against the metal internal frame of her pack. They were concerned about magnetometers being used in Albuquerque in portals, and metal detecting wands being used at checkpoints. The Glock had plastic ammo magazines and a plastic grip and frame assembly, and hence fewer steel parts to conceal. These parts and the ammunition were hidden inside the modified seams of the pack's heavy-duty nylon fabric, against the metal alloy internal pack frame.

The downside was that the pistol had to be carried in such a way that it would not be readily available in the case of an unexpected emergency. She was simply smuggling it into the city, to have it ready to use at the time of the hoped-for rescue of her son. Fowler did provide her with a wickedly sharp Strider folding knife for self-defense, in situations where the Glock would be disassembled, hidden and unavailable.

While resting on the grass she reviewed her conversations with Barlow and Fowler. She visualized her forthcoming rendezvous and pickup at the restaurant. She imagined various possible rescue scenarios in Albuquerque. Even through closed eyelids, she could tell that the sun was almost gone. Their plane was going to arrive at last light. She continued to feign light snoring, her mouth agape in an unladylike pose, while she listened carefully. Finally, she was rewarded with unguarded conversation by her two reticent companions.

"She's sure a sweet piece of ass, ain't she? Pretty face, nice long legs... Looks real inviting, laying there on her back..."

"Too hard for my taste. I can't abide women that tough. Women should be softer. And she looks like a butch with that short black hair."

"You're just pissed off because she won your HK off of you yesterday."

"Naw, it ain't that."

"The hell it ain't. You're pissed off because you had to buy your own pistol back from her. You should be grateful she let you have it back for only fifteen hundred blue bucks."

"Yeah, she don't have a clue what guns are worth."

"Lucky you didn't bet your rifle, or she would've took that too."

"Like hell she would! Okay, I'll give her she's a crack shot with a pistol, and not half bad running around with a little bitty carbine. But take us out to the thousand-yard range, and I'd eat her lunch! Nobody can touch me at a thousand yards with my .338."

"Shit you say! I can beat you left handed at a thousand! Hell, I made a sixteen hundred yard kill with this here fifty caliber last December. Confirmed it with the laser range finder, in front of two witnesses."

"Where, across the Rio Grande, down by El Paso? Man, that ain't sniping, that's just plain murder."

"So? It's a free-fire zone out on those river islands, ain't it?"

"Yeah, I suppose it is, but it's still nothing to brag on. Nobody's shooting back, to speak of. Nobody serious. Did I ever tell you about when I was in Iraq, when—"

"Only about two dozen times."

"Yeah, well, that was *sniping*. The real deal. Once I spent three straight days in a sniper's hide, right in Ali Baba's back yard. Peeing in a bottle, not moving an inch. You earned your kills over there—they were shooting back!"

"Well, we're going to earn them tomorrow morning, that's for sure. A whole bus load of armed Milicias and only two of us…"

"Don't worry; it'll be a turkey shoot. We used to do it the same way in western Iraq, taking out Syrian infiltrators in SUV convoys. We'd put a round from a suppressed fifty cal through the lead vehicle's engine block, and they wouldn't even know they were being shot at. They'd think they busted a rod or something. Once they'd stop, they'd all climb out to look at the engine, take a leak, stretch their legs..."

"And that's when the fun begins!"

"Yep, you've got that right. I've flown recon over our ambush position. It's in a draw, on a long upgrade. Once the bus comes to a stop, there's nowhere for them to go, no cover or concealment at all. You'll be 400 yards in front with the fifty, so if anybody feels like staying inside the bus, just put rounds straight through it. Then they'll get out! I'll be on the flank, and I'll have the angle to pick off anybody who tries to find cover under the bus, or behind it. We'll both take out the runners, and they'll all be dead in five minutes, max. Then we'll call for the bird. You wait—it'll be even better than Iraq."

"How many, you figure?"

"Intel report says they change the guard at 0800 hours, and usually it's about twenty of them Milicias in a ratty old school bus. Brown berets, M-16s, the whole nine yards. So they'll be getting to the ambush site just after seven. We'll do the job and be in the air before they know what hit them."

"You think they'll have any shooters, anybody who can put out counter fire?"

"Naw, these Brown Berets are all show and no go. They're good for scaring old ladies at checkpoints, that's about it."

"What if the plane doesn't show up for the extraction? We'll be a hundred miles from nowhere if the shit hits the fan."

"It'll be there. Anyway, we won't initiate the ambush unless we're in radio contact with the plane. He'll be sitting on the ground just a few minutes away, like we briefed it. And just in case, we've got a solid escape and evasion plan. Hey, you didn't mark it on your map, did you?"

"What, you really think we could be captured? Man, I do *not* plan on being captured by those Milicias—that is *not* in my plan!"

"I didn't say it was. It's just not professional to mark your map, just in case. The guy's taking a big risk, being our E & E contact. So marking his ranch or anything else on your map…well, it's just not right. It's not professional."

"Look, just because I didn't fight in Iraq, doesn't mean I'm not a professional!"

"No offense, but Albuquerque SWAT isn't exactly the Army Special Forces."

"Now, don't start on—"

"And anyway, why couldn't you pass that Spanish test? You're born and raised in New Mexico, and you couldn't pass the Spanish test? Hell, I learned some Arabic, and I hated those freakin' rag heads! All those pretty little señoritas you got over in New Mexico and you couldn't learn Spanish in 28 years?"

"Look you dumbass Tennessee hillbilly, I do speak Spanish! I mean, I speak it okay for a gringo cop, right? But that test was a son of a bitch! No way could a gringo pass it. It was rigged so only beaners could pass it, I swear to God!"

"Listen…quiet."

Both men were instantly silent. Ranya heard it at the same time, the faint buzzing sound of a distant airplane engine. She opened her eyes, stretched, and stood up, then slung on her pack, her back to the two men in desert camouflage.

It was now last light, and the unlit plane wasn't visible until it was very near. It was flying only a hundred feet above the ground, a high-wing single engine prop plane. The dirt strip was just a designated scrap of flat pasture, identical to any other 500-yard long parcel of dirt and grass. Only the picnic table, some fifty gallon drums of aviation fuel, and a faded windsock on top of a metal pole identified these 500 yards as an airstrip.

The plane turned into the wind, tipping a wing, leveled out and landed gently, rolling past them and coming to a halt only a few hundred feet away. The little aircraft was a tail dragger and it maneuvered awkwardly on the ground, swinging around and taxiing back toward them. It seemed to be painted in shades of tan and beige, but this was difficult to determine in the fading light. It finally came to a stop with its high right wing tip almost over the table. The big three-bladed prop wound to a halt and the field was suddenly quiet again. It was clear to Ranya that whoever was flying was intimately familiar with this crude landing strip.

The pilot opened the cockpit door beneath the left wing and hopped down, while the two other men opened another pair of doors on the right side of the fuselage. These two doors swung to both the front and to the rear, revealing a second bench seat behind the pilot and copilot's seats, and behind that an open cargo area. The two-man sniper team ignored Ranya, and loaded their tan packs and rifle bags into the empty space behind the rear seats.

One of the snipers then took a black hose and clambered up on the angled wing strut, and put the nozzle into the fuel inlet on top of the wing above the cockpit. The pilot walked to the drum by the picnic table and began manually pumping gas, topping off his tanks. They worked without words; it was evident that they were well practiced at loading and fueling the airplane in near darkness. As instructed, she approached him, and he greeted her. He was a lanky forty-something, about her height, with crew cut hair. He was wearing fatigue-style pants and a dark t-shirt. Military, or ex-military, she thought.

"Howdy. You're my mystery passenger?"

"That's me."

"Pleased to meet you, mystery passenger." He continued rotating the pump handle while speaking to her. He might have been smiling, but the light was fading fast and it was hard to tell.

"You're getting out first, so you'll sit in back, on the right side. You just have the one pack? Stow it on the floor, between you. We'll be in the air for an hour and a half on this leg, and when we land, we won't be hanging around. Once we stop, I'll holler go, and out you go. Open the middle door, chuck out your bag, hop out quick and get clear 'cause I'm going straight out. That's it, that's all there is to it. Almost a touch-and-go, and then we'll be gone. Just hike south till you hit the tracks. The half moon's going to rise at 2300 hours—that's eleven PM. It'll be easy going for you."

"I really appreciate this, and I'm sorry if I'm putting you at any extra risk."

"Nah, forget it. It'll look just like a false insertion. We do a couple of false insertions on every run, to make it harder for them. Just in case they're tracking us. So far, we haven't had any problems—I generally fly too low for radar—but it's SOP. Doing false insertions, I mean. Anyway, that part of New Mexico is just one big landing strip for a Maule 7. The dry salt lakes are even easier. It ain't no big thing."

"Well, I appreciate the ride."

"Hey, it's my job. But you're welcome."

The sniper who was leaning over the wing whistled, and the pilot finished pumping the aviation fuel. He retrieved the hose nozzle and the sniper stepped down from the strut. The pilot walked around the plane giving it a final visual check, and then stood well off by himself and lit a cigarette. When he was through with his smoke, he ground out the glowing butt with his boot, and climbed back up into the left seat.

The older sniper from Tennessee, who Ranya recognized from the shooting range, sat in the right front seat next to the pilot. They conferred quietly over a folded air map, using a pencil light. She had been proud to overhear during her recent "nap" that she had won the Heckler & Koch pistol off of a Special Forces combat veteran—a Green Beret. She had been happy to sell it back to him after the matches were over: she needed the cash, and couldn't take any extra firearms into New Mexico. At the time, she had thought fifteen hundred dollars was a great price. Oh well. "Blue bucks"—it took some getting used to. Five years was a long time to be away.

The other sniper—the former Albuquerque SWAT cop—climbed into the back seat from the right side and slid across without a word to her, and pointedly looked out the left side window. So he was one of the cops who had been fired for failing the Spanish test… She already knew from the big-rig truck driver that this was a new form of governmental ethnic cleansing—Nuevo Mexico style.

Ranya climbed up and in after the SWAT sniper, placed her pack vertically on the floor in the middle, found her three-point seat belt mostly by feel, and buckled herself in. Finally she latched the door beside her closed. It was a tight fit in the narrow cabin, and she was uncomfortably close to the sniper beside her. They were almost touching at the hips, with their knees bent around her pack.

It was now fully dark, and the pilot fitted a pair of night vision goggles over his face, adjusted the straps, did final checks and switched on the engine. The moment he let off the brakes, the propeller began to pull the plane forward with a powerful surge. Ranya couldn't see any of the gauges or dials in the front of the cockpit; she supposed that the pilot had no problem seeing them with his night goggles. He taxied to the center of the field, adroitly swerved into the wind, and gave the Maule full throttle. The acceleration pressed Ranya back into her seat and the plane immediately hurtled forward with a roar, bumping down the unseen pasture like a runaway dune buggy. In what seemed like only seconds, they lifted smoothly off the ground, and began to climb into the night sky.

Unnoticed by the three men, she couldn't stop smiling.

Bob Bullard awoke in the darkness and checked the glowing face of his watch. It was still Sunday, almost midnight. He was lying on his back, on the king-sized bed in the master stateroom. Eldorado was gently rolling alongside the dock, probably from the wake of a tugboat churning out of the bay. One of Wendy's long sleek legs was crossed over his. He made no effort to keep from awakening her, while he pulled off their covering sheet and extricated himself.

It was time for Wendy to go. She'd been a great lay, and a hell of a lot of laughs, but when you let chicks sleep over all night, they began to get ideas. Next thing you know, they're in the galley making breakfast, and after that, they're setting aside closet space. No thanks. Been there, done that, paid the alimony. He switched on the brass desk lamp, and pulled on his khaki trousers.

"Wha…what time is it?" she asked, arching and stretching.

"It's almost Monday, that's what time. Look, something's come up—duty calls," he lied. "I've got to go. Cesar will drop you off. Come on doll face, get dressed."

"But ba…by, I'm slee…py…" she yawned.

"Yeah, me too, but I gotta get up, and so do you. You can sleep when you get home. Cesar will take you. Come on, get up." As a rule, he never let broads spend the entire night in any of his beds. And above all, he never let them stay in *this* bed, especially while he was off of the boat.

Not with what he had concealed beneath it. No way in hell.

Ranya lay on her stomach among the weeds, on the gravelly slope where the two-lane State Road 60 bridge rejoined the earth. Behind her was a hundred yards of dry wash, the final pinched remnant of the barren salt flat. Almost an hour earlier the insertion plane had landed and braked to a rapid stop four miles north. The pilot yelled go, she threw her pack well clear of the open door, and jumped down. The plane immediately accelerated away with a roar and a rush of prop blast, pelting her with salty grit. She had been prepared for this, so her hood was up and she had faced away as the unlit Maule 7 took off. When she turned around and looked, the single engine plane had already disappeared from view. She found the North Star to get her initial bearings and began her walk to the south, crunching across the saltpan.

All around her was nothing but salt, faintly glowing bone white in the starlight. At 11:07 PM the half moon edged above the low eastern horizon, above Caylen Barlow's ranch, above D-Camp, above her old life in Virginia. The emergence of the half moon brought a weird sort of dawn. The cool horizontal light left crazy shadows across the flats, pointing to where dead trees and tough plants had tried to survive at the margins of the harsh alkaline environment. The walking was easier in the moonlight, with less chance of stumbling into a gully or hole. In the distance, she could see the occasional flickering headlights of a vehicle driving across State Road 60.

In the sky ahead of her, she noticed an extra bright star, which was both blinking and moving from right to left across the firmament. After a while, she decided it was a passenger jet, perhaps heading from Los Angeles to Dallas. She wondered what other aircraft might be above her, which she could not see.

She remembered a story told by another female prisoner in D-Camp, a woman who had been arrested in the wilderness in Oregon. She had been doing some shooting practice with her husband and a few close friends. Nobody outside of this circle knew about their clandestine weapons training. Just the same, they had been ambushed in thick forest, on the remote Jeep trail leading back to the state road. On a tight switchback, a platoon of screaming camouflage-clad federal ninjas leaped out from cover and surrounded their SUV at submachine gun point. They were forced out and down to the ground, and zip-tied with their wrists behind their backs. The federals' boots had literally been on their necks, as their faces were ground into the dirt.

After being frog-marched and dragged to a nearby clearing, before being loaded onto a Blackhawk helicopter, these unlucky Oregonians had seen a UAV drone making low "victory passes" over them. The federal agents looked up and waved skyward for the remotely operated video camera. Later in D-Camp, Ranya and the woman from Oregon surmised that the UAV had been on a routine patrol, and had possibly homed in on the acoustic signature of their firing, the location of which did not correspond to an "authorized" public shooting range. The distant operator of the UAV could have then zoomed in with powerful video cameras, and seen their semi-auto "assault rifles," which had been banned since the Stadium Massacre. Next, it would have been a simple matter to vector in the platoon of ATF agents, who were themselves carrying everything from MP-5 submachine guns to 50 caliber sniper rifles.

So tonight, Ranya wondered what airborne platforms might be slowly circling above, studying the anomalous heat signature moving southward across the saltpan, after a small airplane had briefly paused on an unauthorized flight…

Well, the feds couldn't be everywhere, she reasoned. They couldn't watch every inch of America, every minute of every day. As long as Caylen Barlow's private air force maintained security, there would be no reason for any governmental agency to be focused in on this saltpan, on this particular night…she hoped. If they were, well, she could easily be surrounded by helicopter-borne troops, or she could simply be blown to smithereens by a missile released from above.

Such things were beyond her ability to affect, so she trudged on.

She passed the carcasses and skeletons of numerous cattle and sheep that had wandered onto the unforgiving salt. She had a sudden fright when an immense black-winged bird dived at her unsuspected from behind. She felt and heard the whoosh from its wings as it glided down and brushed past her, touching her hood, and then skimmed low above the ground until it was out of her sight.

By 11:15, the vast saltpan was narrowing to within clearly visible borders on either side, and by 11:30 it had squeezed into a dry creek bed. She could see ahead where a wide bridge carried the state road safely above the infrequent flash flood torrents. According to her New Mexico highway map, the railroad tracks ran parallel to State Road 60, on the other side. Her plan was to walk under the two-lane road bridge on the dry wash, and climb up the bank at the steel trestle railroad bridge a hundred yards beyond. She would hike the remaining five miles to Mountainview on the tracks.

Cars were crossing the bridge only every fifteen or twenty minutes. She turned away and froze when they passed, a black stump to anyone who might chance to look north across the moonlit salt flats. The closer she walked to the highway the more vigilant she became. The moonlight didn't penetrate to the floor of the dry wash under the bridge. She wondered if any dangerous wildlife lurked troll-like beneath the overpass. The yard-thick concrete pillars that supported the roadway could have hidden a platoon of zombie ghouls, she imagined in her rising fearfulness.

She pulled the big folding knife from her sweatshirt's front pouch, thumbed open the blade, and held it at the ready as she entered the shadows. The Strider knife was worth more than many pistols, and she silently thanked Mark Fowler for the extravagant personal gift. It was no pistol—the Glock was useless, in pieces hidden inside her pack—but it was the next best thing. She began to edge her way into the moon-shadow under the bridge between a pair of concrete supports, the space jammed with a helter-skelter tumble of flood-driven rocks and timbers. She was finding a pathway, watching intently for wild animals or other lurking monsters, when she heard a sudden male voice, loud and clear across the still night air.

"Is that you? Finally! You know, we've only been waiting here for three frikkin' hours!"

Ranya spun around and dropped to a crouch behind a boulder, as a vise of fear clamped around her chest and throat. Who was above, waiting for her? This was not in the plan!

Then a shrill female voice demanded, "God Derek, what took you so long? You've been gone forever! My cell phone doesn't work out here, and we were really, really scared! You got the gas?"

"Yes, I got the gas, any other stupid questions?"

"Was the gas station open in Mountainview? Do they have any food?" asked the female.

"No Destiny, the gas station was not open! First, I had to find a hose, and then I had to steal this gas. I had to! Then a dog heard me and almost woke up the whole fucking town! I thought any minute some redneck was going run out and blast me full of buckshot, while I was stealing the gas right out of his pickup truck! So don't even tell me about how scary it was, waiting in the van for good old Derek to go get the fucking gas!"

Twenty feet below the unseen quarrelers, Ranya's heart gradually dropped back below a hundred beats a minute, and the garrote of sudden terror slowly eased its pressure around her neck. She continued listening, putting the pieces together, and crept in the moon shadow beneath the side of the bridge to the slope at its end, and up the sandy bank to the highway.

"B-b-but Derek, if the gas station is closed, how will we be able to get to Albuquerque tonight?" asked the young female.

"We won't, obviously!"

Ranya could hear the sounds of a vehicle's gas cap being unscrewed and removed.

"But I'm hungry, and I want to sleep in a real bed…"

"And your rich Daddy isn't here to make it all better, is he? What kind of a comrade volunteer are you? They want fighters for the revolution, not crybabies!"

"We're not crybabies Derek," said another female voice, lower. "We just need to take showers and wash our hair! That's not too much to ask, not after four straight days in the van! We thought for sure we'd be in the dorms by now."

The other male voice said, "We would have been, if we hadn't gotten off the interstate back at Santa Rosa. That's why we ran out of gas!"

"Don't you start that shit again, Kalil! You've got NO room to talk! If you hadn't of talked us into going all the way to Kansas City just to score some weed, we would've been in Albuquerque yesterday! And then you got ripped off and lost almost all of our money, and for what? Two friggin' ounces of shitty ditch weed! So don't you even talk to me about…"

"But if we had stayed on the I-40, we…"

"Kalil, you don't know shit about cars! The front end is shot on this piece of crap! Above 50, it's shaking so bad it's going to…"

"Then let me drive it, if you can't handle it! A little shaking isn't the end of the world! It can take it…"

"You don't know shit! If we…"

"Look guys, it doesn't matter!" said the first female, the one who had been called Destiny. "Stop fighting, okay? The blame game, it's so over, like, it's so yesterday! Let's look at tomorrow, okay? We can handle another night in the van, what's one more night, right Lisa? We'll get more gas in the morning, and we'll be at the university by lunchtime. Like, it's okay! Really!"

"If they even have gas in Mountainview," said Kalil. "And if they'll sell it."

"Let's just get the hell out of here," said Derek.

Ranya snaked up the slope between prickly weeds and cactus until she could peer under the steel guardrail at the western end of the bridge. A dark full-sized van was parked on the dirt shoulder, partly obscured by tall spiked shrubs along the side of the road. How had she missed seeing it? She must have been too fixated on getting under the bridge—not a good sign. Literally tunnel vision, she reflected.

A man was tilting a gas jug above the fuel inlet on the left side of the van. Another man stood on the other side, looking out to the north, across the dry salt lake. A smaller person, a female, stepped out of the van and hugged this man from behind, and then pulled him back inside. The one with the fuel can finished, closed the gas cap, and tossed the empty jug into the back. Then he went around to the driver's side, climbed in, and began turning over the engine.

After a few tries the engine caught, the lights went on, and the dark van drove off with a backfire, amidst a cloud of smoke. Ranya watched its tail lights disappear down State Road 60 toward the west, toward Mountainview. 'Comrade volunteers,' heading toward a 'revolution?' Were they for real? She guessed their accents to be from the upper Midwest. Well, whatever they were, wherever they were from, they were apparently heading for the University of New Mexico, in Albuquerque.

Score one for Caylen Barlow. Evidently, he knew what he was talking about.

6

Monday June 23

Ranya slept in the backseat of an abandoned Cadillac, on the outskirts of the crossroads village of Mountainview. Even in June the high plains were chilly at night at 6,000 feet of elevation. Mountainview was in fact entirely flat, but it did enjoy a spectacular view of the Monzano and Sandia mountains erupting to above 10,000 feet just behind it. On the other side of these mountains, forty miles northwest as a crow might fly, lay her destination: Albuquerque.

She washed her face with a baby wipe from her pack, and applied light makeup in the Caddy's rear view mirror. Ranya hated the length of her hair: too short to tie back in a ponytail, but too thick to stay put behind her ears. She wasn't used to loose hair rubbing her face this way, it irritated her. But at least the chopped and dyed-black hair had gotten her out of D-Camp, so she really couldn't complain. She brushed it back, and pulled on her newest ball cap: tan, with a leaping blue marlin on the front. It was one of her untraceable Barlow ranch acquisitions, along with her cheap Timex digital watch, her folding knife, and other items. She wore the same clothes she had hiked and slept in: blue jeans and the dead assistant warden's black hooded sweatshirt.

At six AM she was standing outside the front door of the Ancient Pueblos Restaurant on State Road 60, when it was unlocked from the inside by a plump middle-aged woman. The gray-haired lady smiled and said, "Good morning, honey, c'mon in," and flipped the "Closed" sign inside the glass door over to read "Open." Evidently, the *Español Solamente* laws had yet to take root in Mountainview.

Ranya followed her inside and picked a table near the kitchen. The restaurant was humble, but homey, with just eight tables in the main dining room. The place was neat and clean, the tables were covered with fresh white tablecloths, and mouth-watering aromas were emanating from the kitchen.

The waitress returned to her table with a steaming pot of coffee, and Ranya turned over a porcelain cup already on the table to be filled. "I'll be right back with the cream, all right?" she said. "Will you be having breakfast? We only take cash, hon." She gestured to a hand-painted sign above the kitchen, which read, "In God We Trust, All Others Pay Cash."

Ranya understood that the woman had noted her brown backpack, her lack of a car outside, and the dust on her slept-in clothes. "Cash is fine. Can I see a menu?" Ranya guessed that the regulars at this small town diner probably knew the selections by heart.

"Sure thing—just a sec."

While the server was gone, the front door opened again with the jingle of a bell. Four young people, college age, entered the dining room. Two guys and two girls. Ranya pretended to examine the mural of an ancient Indian mesa dwelling painted on the wall behind them, while observing them in her peripheral vision.

It was 'the comrades' from the bridge. Ranya glanced over at them. They were wearing jeans and khaki shorts, and sweaters and sweatshirts. One very tall guy, at least six foot four, had dirty blond shoulder length hair and wore wire-rimmed eyeglasses. The other was a young black of medium height and build, with a bushy Afro hairstyle. Both had several days' growth of whiskers on their oily faces. One girl was a blond with a long ponytail, attractive except for the rings through her eyebrow and lip. The other was a dumpy brunette with her hair in tight braids, and too many silver earrings to count. Derek, Kalil, Destiny and Lisa...up close, and in the light of day. Derek had large blue oriental character tattoos visible on the back of his neck above his gray University of Michigan sweatshirt, and silver rivets punched through his ear lobes big enough to serve as pencil holders. Ranya turned away, disgusted.

The waitress returned with Ranya's menu and cream, and four more menus for the other table. Derek asked the woman, "What time does the gas station open up around here? We need to get back on the road." The town's independent service station and mini-mart were visible through the front windows across State Road 60.

"Don't worry, by the time you finish breakfast, they'll be open. You're having breakfast, right?"

"Um, sure. Yeah, we're having breakfast," said the tall one.

"We only take cash. Cash or metal. No checks, no credit cards, no e-bucks."

Ranya watched their obvious discomfort out of the corner of her eye.

"Uhh…yeah, no problem. Let's see the menus."

Ranya studied her own plastic laminated folding menu. The prices were marked in black grease pencil over the old printed figures. Pancakes, bacon and two eggs were $64! Suddenly her bankroll of nearly $9,000, mostly in crisp new hundred dollar "blue bucks," didn't make her feel quite as rich as it had yesterday.

The waitress came back to take her order. The glass-plated front door opened again, and a genuine cowboy, about fifty, held it open for his wife. He was wearing a black cowboy hat, cowboy boots, jeans and a jean jacket. Ranya could see at a glance that he was the real thing, not a poser. The man nodded to the waitress, and they both raised eyebrows at the table of unsavory young people.

"Have you decided yet, hon?" she asked Ranya, her pencil poised over her blank pad.

"I'll have the Western omelet, with the home fries, and a side of bacon. And a glass of orange juice."

"Okay, coming up."

"And, ahh…" She lowered her voice. "Is…Don here?"

The waitress looked directly at Ranya, skeptically, sizing her up. "Don? You want to see Don? You know him? You related, or something?"

"Ah, no, not exactly, but somebody told me…" Ranya was flustered and floundering slightly, afraid of being overheard. The meticulously planned linkup was suddenly not going according to the plan.

The waitress just stared blankly at her. "Don's not in yet. He'll be in later, most likely. You want to leave a message?"

"Ahh, no. Wait—actually, well…maybe. After breakfast. If he's not here by then."

"Sure thing." The waitress turned for the kitchen.

Damn, thought Ranya. Now what? Hang around and wait for Don? Leave a note for him, and kill time in this remote village, where a stranger without a car will stick out like an Eskimo in the Sahara? While pondering her options, she overheard the college-aged group talking quietly among themselves.

"I've got four hundred left, but it's got to go for the gas," said the longhaired Derek. His hair was parted in the middle, and hung in dirty strands under his whiskery dimpled chin. "We can eat when we get to the university; they'll have something there."

The pony-tailed blond grumbled, "I can't get my cell phone to work in this crappy little town! Daddy…um, my f-father…well, he could zap me a thousand e-bucks, if I could only get this stupid cell phone to work!"

"Des, didn't you hear her?" whined the chubby brunette Lisa. "They don't even take e-bucks here! Cash only, she said."

"Shit!" exclaimed Destiny, getting a look from the cowboy's wife two tables over. "How much is toast and coffee?"

Ranya looked across at them again, sizing up the situation. She got up and sidled over to their table, drawing their hushed attention, and leaned among them and said softly, "Hey, you guys go to Michigan? I go to Virginia—UVA." She addressed herself primarily to their apparent leader, Derek with the neck tattoos and the rivet-punched ears, smiling while suppressing her revulsion.

The longhaired young man had a greasy face and terrible body odor…or perhaps his entire group did. He replied, "Yeah, I do…I mean, we do…or at least we did."

"You wouldn't be heading to Albuquerque by any chance, would you? If you are, I could chip in for gas, if that would help. I could even pay for a full tank, if you can give me a lift up there."

The four of them broke into smiles, sudden relief flooding their faces at the prospect of both a hearty country breakfast, and an easy non-stop drive to the University of New Mexico, their neo-Marxist Mecca.

It had taken Special Agent Garabanda only five minutes to walk up 5th Street from the Federal Building to the Bernalillo County Courthouse. This was where the latest skirmish in the ongoing custody battle with his former wife Karin was going to be fought. They were the first case on the docket this Monday at nine AM, and the judge was only fifteen minutes late when she appeared from her chambers.

The chubby family court judge had a long brown ponytail, and a pierced nose. Alex Garabanda knew he was in deep trouble going before Judge Galatea Balfour-Obregon. Prior to becoming a judge, she had been a New Mexico left-wing radical activist and public defender for decades. It was not his first time going before her, and so far, it had never turned out well.

His ex-wife Karin was seated at the other table on the far side of her female attorney, and would not even make eye contact with him. Instead, she had stared straight ahead while they all waited for the judge to appear. He had to admit Karin looked terrific, with her long blond hair teased out. She was wearing her beige pants suit, with the ruffled blouse showing at her throat and cuffs.

Alex's former wife had already dropped his name. Now Karin Garabanda-Bergen was once again simply Karin Bergen. She had divorced him, dropped his name, and was now attempting to take Brian away. The fact that the female judge also had a hyphenated last name filled him with additional foreboding.

His attorney whispered, "No matter what, don't let the judge bait you into losing your temper. That's what she wants, an incident—I know how this bitch works. Remember, if it doesn't go our way today, we'll straighten it out on appeal. Just keep your cool." Rudy Contreras was a local Albuquerque lawyer with a good reputation for successfully defending fathers' custodial rights, even if he came across as somewhat sleazy, with his thin mustache and slicked-back hair.

Judge Balfour-Obregon began, while slowly shaking her head in obvious disdain. The proceedings were being conducted entirely in Spanish, in accordance with recently passed state laws. Her Spanish was adequate, but choppy and ungrammatical, with a residual New York accent. "Special Agent Garabanda, I've reviewed the case file. I'm particularly concerned with that absolute disaster two weeks ago at the

Federal Law Enforcement Officers annual Memorial Day picnic. I must say, I find it hard to believe that the federal government entrusts a firearm to an FBI agent who can get drunk and assault a woman, in front of over a hundred witnesses!"

"Your Honor, my client was not under the influence of alcohol, and he did not 'assault a woman!' What happened at that picnic was deeply regrettable, but an initial board of inquiry has determined that it was Ms. Bosch who initiated…"

"That's enough, counselor! Don't even go there! Special Agent Bosch, let us not forget, had to be hospitalized after your client put her in a choke hold!"

"My client was only restraining Ms. Bosch, so that she could not strike him again with an aluminum softball bat—"

"Silence! I've heard enough! More than enough! The irrational homophobic attitude of your client is very well known to this court! He's lucky he wasn't charged with hate crimes after that picnic incident! If Special Agent Garabanda can't deal with the fact that his ex-wife is dating a woman, that does not speak well to his stability nor to his socialization, not to mention his fitness to share in the raising of their son."

"But…"

"Therefore, it is the decision of this court that your client shall lose all custodial rights and privileges. Mr. Garabanda, your joint custody agreement is hereby terminated. And furthermore, I'm granting Plaintiff's motion to make the temporary restraining order against you permanent. Special Agent Garabanda, if you so much as come within two hundred yards of Karin Bergen, Brian Garabanda, or Gretchen Bosch, I'll have you arrested and thrown in jail for contempt!"

Garabanda's lawyer tried again, "Your honor, I—"

"Save it counselor! It's time that homophobes like your client were dragged into the 21st century! The fact that he is an FBI supervisor doesn't mitigate the facts of this case. In fact, I should have expected a far more socially progressive attitude from someone of his ethnic background."

"Your honor, the fact that my client is—"

"I told you I was finished, counselor! We'll re-examine limited visitation rights in, oh, six months. Until then, I would strongly advise your client to stay well clear of his former wife, her fiancée Ms. Bosch, or their son Brian!"

Special Agent Alex Garabanda slowly lowered his forehead to the table. Behind him, he heard Gretchen Bosch snickering in her unmistakable female baritone voice.

The back of the old Dodge van had a thick yellow foam mattress pad covering the cargo deck. That was the extent of the custom furnishings and creature comforts. Derek and Kalil sat up front in the separate "captain's chairs," arguing about road directions, arguing about the exact form of the perfect socialist utopia, and arguing about their best speed to avoid shaking the van to pieces. Because of their limited top speed, there was no benefit to taking State Road 60 all the way west to I-25, which ran north along the Rio Grande, on the other side of the mountains. Instead, they decided to take the narrow two lane State Road 355 north from Mountainview, along the eastern slopes of the Manzano and Sandia mountains. This was shorter in total mileage, and their wobbly front end meant holding their speed below 60 miles per hour anyway.

The green van was a clapped-out windowless commercial model, with exposed steel frames on the insides. Destiny and Lisa wedged themselves into sitting positions in the back, leaning against luggage bags and heaps of mixed-up clothing. Ranya was not surprised to see that the male "comrades" took the two comfortable front seats. She guessed that Derek, the driver, owned the van. He looked to be the oldest, probably a graduate student, and he was clearly the "alpha male" of the motley pack.

The interior of the van stank of unwashed clothes and stale food, but it was a ride, and it was heading to Albuquerque. The twenty gallons of gas Derek had put into the tank at the service station in Mountainview had cost Ranya eight of her crisp blue $100 bills. This was a flat non-negotiable $40 a gallon, well above the posted cost, and even then it required extensive pleading to get the fuel at all. This was a serious chunk of her working capital, but she knew that if she couldn't make it to Albuquerque, the money meant nothing anyway.

The girls were quiet, zoning out with tiny music buds planted in their ears. The guys were talking almost nonstop, providing a running political debate and travelogue from the front seats, almost shouting over the music blasting from their stereo. Ranya didn't recognize the rock group or the songs. It appeared that Derek leaned toward classical Soviet or Cuban-style Marxism, leavened with a dash of Trotsky. Kalil seemed to be a garden-variety America-hating anarchist; primarily out to take part in what he believed was his best opportunity to "strike back at the white corporate power structure."

Ranya sat on an overturned plastic milk crate just behind them, between their two seats. From that makeshift seat, she could see out of the front windows, and enjoy the odor-dampening fresh air. She had peeled off her sweatshirt as the morning warmed up, and was wearing a plain black t-shirt above her long blue jeans. They occasionally plied her with questions as they drove up the cracked asphalt.

"That's right, I came from Virginia."

"You hitched all the way from Virginia to New Mexico?" asked Derek. "That's like, so totally awesome! I'll bet you had some sick adventures along the way, eh?"

"Yeah, you'd win that bet."

"So, did you see any of that Cameroon Fever back east? The Monkey Pox? Man, that was some bad shit down there in Florida and Georgia last year, eh?"

Ranya put this question together with what Olivia and her husband had mentioned in their RV, and groped for enough of a response to satisfy them. "Not in Virginia. I didn't see it in Virginia."

"Those Monkey Pox scars really freak me out," said Derek, shuddering. "I think I'd rather die from the fever than live with those scars."

Ranya was tempted to ask him why, then, he had punched giant rivet holes in his earlobes, and had tattoos on his neck…but she resisted the momentary impulse.

Kalil said, "I know how bad the crackers are back there in Virginia—you'd never catch me in those redneck states! They'd probably lynch my black ass just to keep in practice. You see any of those KKK dudes back there?"

"No, I guess I got lucky. Didn't see any Klan this time," Ranya answered.

"How about the Klan down in North Carolina, burning out the immigrants?" asked Kalil. Ranya thought that he resembled Jimi Hendrix, from the posters she remembered seeing in college. Bushy Afro hairstyles must have made a fashion comeback while she was imprisoned.

"I don't think that's just the Klan," said Derek. "I saw it on TV. There were lots of African-Americans right in there with the rednecks in those riots."

Kalil responded angrily, "Man, that is bullshit! Well, some Uncle Toms maybe, but that's all. Real brothers wouldn't be hangin' out with no crackers, attacking no people of color!"

"Hey man, I saw what I saw—it was on television! Blacks and whites were together, going into those immigrant shanty-towns with clubs and Molotov cocktails!" Derek turned around to their new passenger, one hand on the wheel. "What do you think? You're from back there. How bad are those anti-immigrant riots in the Carolinas? It's ethnic cleansing, right?"

Ranya had to stall and evade, hiding her lack of current knowledge. "It's not so bad in Virginia…but I've been on the road for a few weeks. I haven't been following the news much. What's the latest?"

Derek answered his own question without a pause. "Some kind of new Minuteman militia is trying to terrorize the Hispanics into leaving the

South. They call themselves the 'American Patriot Party' and other bull-shit fascist names like that. American Nazi Party is more like it! They've been firebombing housing developments built by immigrants, you know, the ones who used to be undocumented workers. Before the federal amnesty, I mean. The fascists still call them 'illegal aliens' and say they're not real citizens. Hispanic day workers can't wait outside of home supply stores anymore, or rednecks in pickup trucks will jump them with baseball bats. Or sometimes they get in a truck, they think it's for a job, and that's it—they're never seen again. Gone! The rednecks say all the jobs are going to immigrants—that's what they say."

"Same old racist KKK, if you ask me," said Kalil, disgustedly. "Now it's the Minuteman Klan! I mean, how can a worker be illegal? Man, the whole idea of borders and nations: that is so 20th Century! It don't matter where a worker is from, does it?"

"It might matter if he took your job, don't you think?" ventured Ranya. "I mean, that's what all those rednecks and Uncle Toms probably think."

Kalil appeared confused, forming thoughts and mouthing words that he could not articulate. Clearly, his internationalist orientation was at some level in fundamental conflict with the idea of American blacks losing jobs to newly arriving "undocumented" Hispanic immigrants, whether or not they were granted some kind of guest-worker amnesty along the way. In a nation seemingly in an economic depression, Ranya guessed that losing a job could mean losing a home, or not putting food on the table.

While Kalil shook his head and muttered curses, Derek continued with his lecture. "And this ethnic cleansing, it's not just in the South. The fascists have been terrorizing Hispanic immigrants in New England, Michigan…hell, almost everywhere. I mean, in Idaho, the police have been rounding up immigrants and bussing them right out of the state, 'for their own protection,' they say! The immigrants all got the federal amnesty, but some states say the amnesty is bogus and the immigrants are still illegal. It's bullshit any way you slice it, the way Hispanic immigrants are being treated!"

Kalil added, "And lots of them are heading right here to New Mexico: this is where the oppressed peoples of color are finally making a stand! This is where the revolution is happening, I mean really happening!"

Derek switched the subject to Ranya, and her intentions. "So, umm, you're going to UNM to join the revolution too…right?" He kept pushing his loose hair behind his ears, and it kept sliding forward across his oily and unshaven face. "That's where we're going. Time to put up, or shut up, right?"

"Right, put up or shut up." Ranya fervently hoped they would shut up. She didn't want to sit this close to them, but she felt compelled to look out the front windows, and she needed the fresh air from the open side windows to subdue the pervasive stench of body odor in the back. It stank worse than a D-Camp field latrine.

Derek continued, “Michigan sucks so bad anyway. Other than school, there’s nothing left for us back there. Nothing but reactionary fascists up there anymore! Real Nazis! Except for Detroit and Lansing of course. But what’s the point of just preparing ourselves to join the intellectual class? I mean, how’s that going to help the people? Sitting around Starbucks, bitching and moaning about the fascist plutocracy, while we swill their corporate coffee? What good does that do? Right here is where the front line in the revolution is today! *Viva la revolución*, right?”

“Oh yeah, *viva la revolución*,” she replied. “Say, Derek, speaking of *la revolución*, how’s your Spanish? You know, with the *Español Solamente* laws?”

“Oh, that…that’s no problem. That was just so they could fire all the reactionary white racist pigs. That won’t matter for us, because we’re coming to help—we’re joining the cause. We’re on their side.”

“So…you don’t actually speak Spanish?” Ranya asked.

“Uhh…*yo quiero* Taco Bell?” Derek twisted around and winked at her, and laughed at his own joke. The holes punched in his ears disgusted her more each time he turned in profile. “I’m a quick study. I’ll learn it fast, I mean, how hard can it be?”

Ranya asked, “Do any of you guys actually speak Spanish?” She repeated her question twice, and the blond girl pulled out an earpiece to hear her question.

“I’ve got Spanish One loaded on my music pod,” offered Destiny. “I’ve been listening to it when I can, sometimes. ‘*Yo habla Español mucho bueno*.’ See, I’m picking it up.”

Derek said, “It won’t matter. They have volunteers coming from all over, like an international brigade! Kind of like the Spanish Civil War in the 1930s. You know, last semester we took the most incredible course on the history of the international proletarian struggle. That’s where we all met. That’s how we found out the real truth about New…I mean...*Nuevo* Mexico’s new revolution.”

“Yeah,” added Destiny. “Professor Ruskin, he was just so awesome! He really opened up my eyes, I want to tell you. He was just…the best…ever. Hey, show her his letter, Derek! Show her Rusky’s letter to Professor Johnson.”

“Oh yeah,” he replied, opening the lid on top of the center console between the front seats. He pulled out a folded sheet of personalized stationery. “Check this out…with this letter; we’re like, totally golden! We’ll be so totally in, man!” He held it up for Ranya to see, and then put it back into the console. “Professor Ruskin at Michigan is in tight with

Professor Johnson at the University of New Mexico…there I go again! *Nuevo* Mexico! Hah! I gotta watch that! Anyway, he's vouching for us, in this letter. When we find Professor Johnson, and give him this letter, we'll be all set. Land reform, that's Professor Johnson's gig. We'll probably be able to help him, you know, like researching the old Spanish land grants and deeds and titles, stuff like that. I mean, the Mexicans were so totally ripped off after 1748! Or maybe it was 1848… Well, anyway, it's like, all their land around here, you know?"

Destiny was nodding enthusiastically, gazing up at Derek. "Professor Ruskin was really the one who gave us the idea for all this. Joining the revolution, I mean! At least for the summer. Who knows, maybe for even longer! Maybe we'll be able to transfer into UNM, you know? But it's definitely going to be good for a master's thesis, at least."

Kalil opened the glove box, found a brass cigarette case and extracted a pre-rolled joint. He fired it up with a butane lighter, took a prolonged drag and passed it over to Derek. After holding his breath for an inordinate time, Kalil exhaled most of the smoke through the open passenger side window, and choked out, "Yeah man, the revolution, that's the real thing! No more talk—talk is bullshit!"

State Road 355 headed in long straight lines toward the mountains, and then began to curve and twist as it followed the contours where the high plains met the foothills. The junipers and grasslands gradually turned to pines, as the van rolled down into valleys, and struggled back up again. Small and not-so-small ranches were visible on both sides of the two-lane asphalt road. Some houses were close to the road, some were set far down paved driveways. Some of the ranches had Western-style arched gates created from iron or timber, often decorated with their particular cattle brands. There were some rather shabby trailers and private junkyards, but also many comfortably affluent homesteads and a few of what might almost have been called mansions.

"Look at that, another burned-down house!" announced Derek, slowing the van to gaze to the left at a heap of ashes punctuated by a pair of standing chimneys. "That's the third one in just a couple of miles, what's up with that?"

Destiny was now kneeling behind Derek's seat, to look out the front windows and take a hit off the joint. Her clingy green Sierra Club t-shirt was riding up and Ranya couldn't help but notice the hideous platter-sized sunburst tattoo across the small of her back. Destiny said, "Oh, I heard all about that on NPR. The rich white ranchers who have to leave, you know, to give back the stolen land…well, sometimes they're burning down their own places. Just so that nobody else will be able to live in them! Can you believe that shit? It's so typical of the greedy white man. You know, 'if I can't have it, then nobody can'."

"Yeah," said Kalil, "That's whitey for you all right." Then he turned to her, beaming a glassy-eyed smile. "But hey, you all, you're not like that, at least most times! I mean, for white folks, you is all right. Now pass that joint back up here, Destiny girl."

"You remember what Susan Sontag said about the white race?" asked Derek.

Destiny answered him, nodding. "Sure. That's Diversity Studies 101; everybody knows that quote. 'The white race is the cancer of human history'..."

"...And treason to whiteness is loyalty to humanity," he finished for her.

"Right on!" exclaimed Destiny. "I just wish Professor Ruskin could see us now!"

"Oh, hey, look at that sign!" said Kalil, exhaling another cloud of dope smoke out the right side window. "Check it out: *¡TIERRA O MUERTE!*" What's that mean?" He was pointing to a crude homemade red and white billboard, painted on a dilapidated barn along the right side of road. The former ranch house, which was a few hundred yards away across a pasture, was a pile of ashes, with only some charred timbers and a stone chimney still standing.

"Land or death," replied Ranya. "It means land or death."

"Oh wow!" said Derek excitedly, "We must be getting close to the liberated zone! No more rednecks! No more racists! *Viva la raza*!"

"Looks like the party is over for whitey in Nu-e-vo Mex-i-co!" added Kalil. "Oh yeah, this is gonna be so sweet! Payback time!"

"Derek, stop the van!" said Destiny. "Let's get out and take some pictures! I can send some back to Michigan on my cell phone. We can show everybody that we've actually made it to the revolution. We've made it! I can't believe it, we've actually made it! This is going to be the best summer ever!"

There was no other traffic in sight on the long straight run of ranch land. Derek slowly reversed back down the road and pulled off on the dirt shoulder. The four giddy comrades piled out of the van, with Ranya following the girls out of the sliding side door. Destiny handed Ranya her cell phone and her Nikon digital camera, both already opened up and ready for use. The four "Voluntarios" stood in front of the barn, the white and red *¡TIERRA O MUERTE!* sign behind them against the backdrop of the Manzano Mountains. They were smiling ecstatically, standing side by side with their right fists raised high in the air, as Ranya filmed them for posterity.

7

Bob Bullard spent Monday morning in his corner office in the San Diego Federal Building, prior to taking his helicopter up to Los Angeles. The maroon-colored five-story building spread like a malignancy between the feet of soaring glass and steel office towers in downtown San Diego. Most people hated the grim prison-like appearance of the Federal Building, but Bullard loved it. Its forbidding appearance instilled a healthy dose of fear into those unfortunates commanded to enter it on official business.

In front of the main entrance foyer, in the middle of an enclosed quadrangle, was quite possibly the most hideous piece of public sculpture ever commissioned, anywhere or anytime. This was an angular black steel pinnacle, leaning over precariously, and tapering to a needle sharp point at the end of its fifty-foot length. Bullard liked to imagine screaming tax delinquents being thrown down and impaled on its brutally cruel tip, to slowly perish like insects stabbed by an entomologist's pin. (Of course, he kept these private thoughts *strictly* to himself.)

Today his staff had scheduled a half hour of "community outreach." This could often be turned into a profitable exercise in public relations, with photo opportunities showing the deeply concerned regional homeland security boss lending his ear to a stream of noteworthy whiners and malcontents. Artfully staged, these photo ops could perform the miracle of turning Bob Bullard into a kindhearted uncle, with a twinkle in his eye and a ready pat on the head for the kiddies.

This morning it was the turn of the local Muslim Sheiks, Imams and Muftis to moan and complain. Bullard's secretary buzzed them into his fifth-floor corner office at nine AM. He was amused to see the three of them wearing traditional Middle Eastern garb, including colorful dish towels draped over their heads, held in place with what looked like coiled fan belts. Together the three ran part of the Montclaire section of San Diego (known locally as Little Baghdad) as their personal fiefdom. Montclaire was situated atop a mesa surrounded by cliffs and canyons, a natural redoubt. The enclave, just on the eastern side of I-5, was home to the largest mosque and "Islamic cultural center" in California. Even years before the walls had gone up, Montclaire had proven to be a comfortable haven for a number of the 9-11 hijackers.

Several major San Diego surface streets ran through Montclaire, but except for these public roads, access into the enclave itself was strictly controlled. Licensed armed guards with full beards, wearing green military uniforms and checked Arafat-style kefiyah scarves, were stationed at the few unbarricaded streets leading into the "Muslim Quarter." These menacing guards were the only visible face that Montclaire showed to the outside world. Bullard often wondered why some of the thousands of Marines who called San Diego home didn't shoot them on sight while driving past, simply out of habit. This thought gave him a minor smile, and propelled him up out of his black leather executive chair as they entered his office.

"Good morning gentlemen, good morning. What can the Department of Homeland Security do for you today?" After a prolonged exchange of double-pumping handshakes, flowery greetings and one attempted cheek kissing (Bullard would have bitten off a nose or ear first) the Imams got down to business.

"Director Bullard, we have complained and complained to the mayor about the continuing anti-Muslim harassment, yet our complaints fall on deaf ears. So in desperation, we are coming to you for help."

"All right—fair enough. That's what I'm here for. So what's the problem?" Bullard returned to his executive chair, sat behind his desk and cracked his knuckles.

"The law clearly states that we may play the call to prayer of the Muezzin five times a day from our minarets. Yet we continue to have loud 'rock' music blasted into Montclaire when we do so! Even worse, our Muezzin's loudspeakers are fired upon on a daily basis! This is intolerable! You must see that the local police take their responsibilities seriously!" The other Imam's nodded their heads vigorously.

"I'm sorry about that, I really am. I'll do what I can. However, in all frankness, as long as you play that 'Allah Akbar' tape with the volume turned way up, folks might choose to send their own message back at you. It's still a free country, you know."

The transformation of Montclaire into "the Muslim Quarter" had been startlingly rapid, once the amplified loudspeaker broadcasting of the "call to prayer" had been approved by the city council. Non-Muslims began a mass-exodus from within audible range of the muezzin's cry, and property values plummeted. Newly arriving Muslim immigrants moved in to snap up the vacant homes at fire-sale prices. Other Muslims living scattered across Southern California moved to the enclave to avoid "religious persecution," and the process continued until the Montclaire mesa was virtually 100% Islamic. In ten years, the Muslim population of San Diego County had tripled to an estimated 300,000—most of whom lived in and around Montclaire.

"But what about the shootings?" asked the leader of the Imams. "Our minarets look like Swiss cheese!"

"Maybe if you turned down the volume on the call to prayer, maybe that would help? Or what if you turned the loudspeakers around, facing inside? So you could hear the prayer in Montclaire, but not all over San Diego?"

"Mr. Bullard, sir! We have our rights, under the First Amendment!"

"Yes, you do..."

"It is a hate crime to blast idolatrous satanic rock music into Montclaire during the call to prayer! We insist that the perpetrators be pursued and charged! It is disgraceful, it is anti-Islamic bigotry, it is…"

"I'm sure it is. Now, while we're discussing Montclaire, I'd like to pass along a concern coming up from the mayor's office. He says they've been seeing a steady stream of folks showing up in San Diego emergency rooms without right hands. You wouldn't know anything about that, would you?" Bullard held up his own knobby right hand and wiggled his fingers.

"I don't see how this is any concern of yours! You know very well that we have an agreement with the city to observe Sharia Law within Montclaire. I'd like to point out that within our walls we have the lowest crime rate of any urban area in California."

"Sure, and you also have the highest rate of one-handed vagrants all around you."

"Director Bullard, we didn't come here today to suffer another assault on our faith! We came here to reach some understanding, not to suffer an attack."

"Oh Jesus…keep your turban on. Personally, I don't care how you take care of business inside of your own walls. But outside is another matter. Like when the local girls start getting gang-raped…"

"That is a lie! A slander against all Muslims! I refuse to listen! And those harlots should not dress that way near Montclaire! What are decent Muslim boys to think, when they see those teenage girls half-dressed, like *charmutas*, like whores?"

"Then stop complaining about your minarets getting shot up. It goes both ways. That's all I'm saying."

"Director Bullard, this is outrageous! You sound as if you are condoning these unprovoked attacks on Montclaire! You know what is happening in Detroit, and I'm certain that you would not want to see a similar situation here in San Diego!"

Bullard rose to his full height and leaned forward across his desk, staring hard at the sheik. "Now listen here Abdul, you're not in Detroit, and I'm not a liberal pussy like the Mayor and Governor back there. You throw up barricades and block traffic on the through-streets like they did in Detroit, and I'll bulldoze right through them! And while we're at it, we'll bulldoze all of your unapproved dead ends and cul-de-sacs, every last one of them! I'll run bulldozers through your walls, and leave Montclaire wide open! I'll have all of your security guards' gun permits revoked, and let the gangs back in! Trust me: you don't want that! You have a cozy little situation going on in Montclaire—but you're not fooling anybody. We haven't come down hard on you, but believe me, we can. So turn down the volume on your Allah Akbar, and stop chopping off hands, all right? And tell your boys to leave the infidel girls alone outside of your walls!"

Bullard paused, looking at each of them in turn, and quieted his tone before continuing. "That is, if you three want to keep on playing Grand Pooh-bahs with your own little harems… Oh yeah, I know all about your harems, and how young some of those girls are. Girls and boys, I should say… Now if you'll excuse me gentlemen, I've got other appointments."

That should hold them for a while, he thought as they spun in their robes and departed his office, sputtering and muttering and fuming in impotent rage.

After they were gone, Bullard's young chief of staff entered the office and sat on the black leather couch across from his mahogany desk. "That went well, boss. I think they know you mean business."

"Damn right I do," said the Homeland Security honcho. "We won't be having any of that Detroit bullshit in the Southwest Region! I'll burn Montclaire to the ground and bulldoze the ashes into the Pacific first."

"Sounds like they realize it now, if they didn't before."

"You know what they say about Arabs," said Bullard. "They're either at your throat, or at your feet."

"Yeah. Say, listen boss, you know that special list of yours, the, umm…folks who are presently incarcerated?"

"Sure, the scumbags I helped put away. What about it?"

"Well, you wanted me to inform you when any of them were released."

"Okay, so who was released?"

"Actually, nobody was released, exactly."

"Then what are you telling me this for?"

"One of them escaped."

"Escaped? Who? From where?"

"Umm…it would be a certain Ranya Bardiwell. A female prisoner."

"Bardiwell…Bardiwell…I remember that name. Go ahead, refresh my memory. Who is she, and why do I care about her?"

"She's from Virginia. She was involved in the Malvone affair…"

Bullard leaned back in his leather chair, his fingers laced behind his thinning hair. "Oh yeah…Ranya Bardiwell. Now I remember. Hot little number. Brunette. We tried to pin the Virginia Attorney General's assassination on her boyfriend, but they both disappeared. When we finally grabbed her, she got put away under Article 14."

"Right. Conspiracy to commit acts of terrorism. There was no solid evidence, so she just got three years of non-judicial preventive detention. When that stretch of NJPD was up, it was rolled over for another three."

"So, where'd she escape from?"

"Officially, she bolted from the Federal Prison Transit Center in Oklahoma City. You know, 'Air Con.' But actually, she escaped from an NJPD camp in western Oklahoma. All women, mostly Article 14s. And she killed an assistant warden on her way out."

"Hmm. Okay. All right. Shouldn't be a problem, but you never know. Keep an eye out for her, tickle your search engines, and check the traffic going into the Field Offices. If she surfaces, if you hear anything at all, let me know right away."

"Okay boss, will do. Now, your next appointment is with the California Director of the Border Patrol. He wants to know why you're ordering his men back off the line in the Campo sector again."

"Christ, whatever happened to just emailing? All right, send him in."

"Whoa...there's another one of those red X's," said Kalil. The giant X was painted on State Road 355 directly in front of an antler-decorated gateway arch, at the beginning of a long private driveway. The terrain was more forested and hilly now, and the ranch house, if any, was invisible from the road. "What do you think it means?"

"Probably means the land was stolen from the Mexicans," answered Derek. "Probably marks a 'land reform' area. Spanish land grant territory."

"That's some serious shit, then," said Kalil. "X marks the spot... must be some kind of a warning."

"What did you think *'Tierra o Muerte'* meant?" asked Ranya.

Derek said, "Man, that Governor Deleon, he's not messing around! Hey look, there's another sign! At least this one's in English."

This sign was also written in red paint, on a white sheet of plywood, attached to a pair of timber posts just off the shoulder of the road next to a barbed wire fence. Derek stopped in front of it and they all read it together, the girls crouched behind the front seats. While they paused, a black crew-cab pickup truck blasted past them from behind, crossing over to the oncoming lane, going at least one hundred miles an hour and quickly disappearing from sight.

The sloppily hand-lettered sign read: "Warning Gringo! You are trespassing on Land Grant Territory! This is stolen land! Do not attempt to buy any property on this Territory, it is stolen and your deed will be invalid! If you are occupying stolen Land Grant Territory, leave now! You have been warned!"

They were all quiet, reading the sign. Derek whistled softly and said, "Man, I'm glad I don't live on any stolen land around here. Sounds like the day of reckoning has come at last for the white cattle barons."

"Yeah," added Kalil, "And payback's a bitch. Come on, let's go."

"What's the next town?" asked Destiny. "Maybe they'll have cell phone coverage. I can't send these pictures; I can't get a signal at all! I don't understand why they don't have cell phone coverage out here. I mean, this is America, right?"

"Chulada. The next town is Chulada," replied Derek. "About two miles ahead." He had his road map, folded to the right section, lying on top of the center console between the front seats. "Doesn't look like much on the map."

State Road 355 ran through wildly beautiful country now, at times alongside flowing creeks choked with willows, oaks and cottonwoods, at times winding up and through the foothills of the Sandia Mountains, with its peaks on their left side. The van crested a rise where the roadway had been blasted out of live rock, leaving jagged granite walls fifty feet high on either side of them. After the top, the road dropped and turned suddenly to the west, and all at once they saw the roadblock, but too late.

Derek slammed on the brakes, coming to a sudden stop just in front of a row of 55-gallon drums. The steel barrels were painted red, and extended across the asphalt from the right shoulder to the yellow centerline. Another row of drums ran across the oncoming lane, but twenty feet further down. Any traffic in either direction would have to come to a complete stop, and weave slowly between the two barricades to continue on their way. The barrels might have been empty, filled with water, or filled with dirt or cement. There was no way to tell by their outward appearance.

Ranya was impressed by the setup. Empty barrels were a bluff, but highly mobile. Water-filled barrels would be too heavy to ram at full speed, yet could still be drained and easily moved around, as long as a water supply was available to refill them on site. Dirt or sand-filled barrels would mean a semi-permanent checkpoint. Vehicles that were parked on either shoulder prevented anyone from driving around the obstacles.

"What in the hell is this?" asked Derek. As if in answer, from behind both of the barricades of steel drums, more than a dozen men suddenly stood up in one movement. Armed men, weapons shouldered, aiming black rifles directly at the van's windshield from a range of twenty feet. Armed men wearing brown berets, and brown t-shirts.

One of them screamed, *"¡Salga! ¡Salga del carro! ¡Ahora mismo!"*

Ranya looked between Derek, the armed men, and Kalil. "They're saying to get out, right now!" Sudden fear rose from her guts, nearly paralyzing her.

"Don't worry, it's just the New Mexico Milicia, it'll be cool. Remember, they're on our side," replied Derek. "I'll do the talking. Just chill, all right?" He kept his hands on the steering wheel as two pairs of the men moved around the sides of the nearest wall of barrels, their weapons still shouldered and pointed at the van's windows. The pairs advanced toward each side of the van, remaining a bit in front to avoid a crossfire while aiming at the driver and passenger. The rest of the *Milicianos* behind the barricade kept their rifles trained on the windshield.

"¿Estás loco, gringo? ¡Ya te dijé salga! ¡Ahora—rápido!" The Milicia man shouting the demands kept his rifle aimed directly at Derek, through the open driver's side window, emphasizing his words by thrusting the muzzle forward. Ranya noticed his finger wrapped around the trigger, and she slowly shrank down and back in the van. She recognized the rifles, old M-16A1's, the original Viet Nam era Armalites with the smooth black plastic forward stocks. Each rifle was loaded with a long curved thirty round magazine.

"*Es* okay, *amigos...*" said Derek, calmly. "We're on your side. Really, we're coming to help. Umm…*E-stamos…con…u-sted-es*."

Kalil was frozen in his seat, but still whispered, "Derek, man, I think we better…"

"¡Silencio! ¡Callate! ¡Ciera tú boca, y salga—no voy a decirle otra vez!" This *Miliciano* continued to advance toward the driver, weapon shouldered, until his rifle's quivering muzzle was only a yard from Derek's face.

Derek spoke, slowly and quietly. "Listen, *mi amigo*…calm down, okay? Calm…down. *Tranquilo*. I've got a letter of introduction for Professor Robert Johnson, at the university—it explains everything." He slowly moved his right hand toward the center console, brushing aside the folded map, and began to open the hinged compartment on top.

Ranya was almost in the middle of the back of the van, kneeling, her hands on the foam mattress, when a burst of rifle fire exploded just a few feet from her. She saw most of Derek's head disappear in a red eruption and she fell prone, just as Lisa jumped to her feet screaming, "Don't shoot!" There was another burst of fire, and glass fragments rained down on Ranya's back. There were the sounds of the muzzle blasts, and the sounds of bullets pinging through van's sheet metal skin. There were men yelling and orders shouted, and after a few endless seconds, the full-automatic firing abruptly stopped.

The side door of the van was slam-rolled back and Ranya went limp, as many strong hands dragged her out and flung her on the ground. She buried her nose into the dirt, and felt a hot muzzle tip against the back of her neck, and another against her spine.

She was instantly filled with sorrow that she would never see her son, after coming so far. She saw Brad's face, and somehow she felt him beckoning her forward. She saw her father and mother, and a little girl with pigtails running through a sunny field to meet them with her arms held out.

But the expected flashing plunge into eternity didn't come. She still tasted the dirt of this good earth against her lips.

Gradually the ringing in her ears subsided, she heard the moaning and wailing of another girl, and then Ranya began to return to the present. Two college girls. Destiny and Lisa. She slowly turned her head to the side and saw them lying not far from her, a spreading lake of blood under their bodies.

"¡Hijo de la chingada, qué maldita porquería! ¡Qué desastre! What a damned disaster!" spat out a voice in guttural foreign-sounding Spanish. *"Who the hell told you to fire?"*

"The big gringo was reaching for a gun in that box, Jefe! I had to shoot!"

"So, where's the gun, you idiot? Go ahead, check the box!"

Ranya's mind was now spinning at incalculable speed, sifting through the probabilities that added up to life or to death. Without consciously considering the risk or the alternatives, she said, *"No hay fusil, Jefe. There is no gun. There is only a letter."*

"What? Who speaks? One of the gringas speaks Spanish?"

"Sí, Jefe, I can speak it. The tall one was only reaching for a letter in the box. A letter explaining that we are revolucionarios, Voluntarios, coming to join in the people's struggle."

"Is this true? Shit! Then why didn't the fool simply get out of the truck when he was told?"

"He didn't speak our idiom, Jefe. He was a fool."

"Get up. Get up. Help her up, you clowns!"

"Gracias Jefe. Gracias."

The "Jefe" was examining the Ruskin-Johnson letter, while they were being driven up State Road 355 to Interstate 40 on the way from Chulada to Albuquerque. They were sitting in the comfortable rear seat of the black crew-cab Ford pickup, which had sped past the doomed van an hour before. Ranya was handcuffed, but the cuffs were in front, and not too tight. At least she was still alive…

Three *Milicianos* were in the front seat, and four more sat in the cargo bed behind her, their loaded rifles carried in various casual positions, sometimes pointed at one another. All of them wore brown berets and brown t-shirts. The t-shirts were decorated on the front with the state logo, the red "Zia" tribal design from the New Mexico flag, the circle with four lines extending out to the top and bottom and left and right. In the center of the circle was a red star, apparently a new addition to the state symbol.

Some of them wore olive drab or camouflage utility pants, and some wore blue jeans. Some had boots on their feet, and others wore sneakers. Several of their faces hinted at Central and South American Indian origins. Their hair was worn in every length from shaven to shoulder-length. Some of the shaven-headed *Milicianos* had gang tattoos covering their arms and necks, and even their cheeks and foreheads. These seven troops all carried identical M-16A1 rifles, but the rest of their gear was a hodge-podge of various military cast-offs and civilian daypacks and belt pouches.

When Ranya had been pulled up from the ground, some of the men had lip-smacked lewd sounds at her while suggestively grabbing their groins, and she feared being gang-raped. After being patted down and searched, she had been shoved into the back seat of the pickup truck without any more than a few rough gropes through her jeans and her black t-shirt. Her knife, her compass, and her nylon wallet holding part of her cash as well as her recently acquired Texas driver's license had disappeared.

She wondered if Destiny was alive, and if she was, what was happening to her. The blond had been left crying on the ground at the scene of the attack. Derek and Kalil she knew were dead, and she was all but sure that Lisa was also dead by now, judging by the amount of blood she had seen pooling on the ground beneath her unmoving body. Ranya, although sprayed with blood, had not been injured beyond scrapes and bruises.

The Jefe was sitting across the seat from her, behind the driver. He was the oldest of the *Milicianos*, at least forty-five or fifty, with a short black Vandyke beard going gray on the sides, beginning at the creases of his mouth. Instead of a brown t-shirt for a uniform, he wore an old style woodland pattern camouflage utility blouse and trousers. Like his men, he wore the brown beret of the Milicia. Unlike his men, he wore a holstered pistol on a green web belt, and carried no rifle. He wore no other visible insignia of rank, but clearly he was an officer or leader, or as they called him, *el Jefe*—the Chief.

He slipped on reading glasses, and studied Derek's infamous bloodstained letter. "Tell me again what this word means. My English is not very good." He spoke to Ranya in deliberate Spanish, understanding that she was not completely fluent in his tongue.

"It means trusted, trustworthy," she answered in her more than adequate *Español*. "The famous socialist Professor Ruskin from the University of Michigan, he tells Professor Johnson that these four of his students are all trustworthy and valiant, that they believe in the armed revolution and the people's struggle. Professor Johnson should trust them, and use them in any way he can."

"Huh," he grunted. "But you're not on this list of four. Why not?"

"I met them only this morning. I was traveling by my thumb, hitchhiking. I met them in the gringo town of Mountainview, at breakfast. They offered to bring me to Albuquerque, to join the struggle."

"Well, we're going to see about that."

As they neared Interstate 40 at the town of Tijeras, the Jefe pulled a cell phone from his camouflage blouse pocket and punched several numbers. After a few attempts, he gave up in disgust. "The cowboys, they shoot the cellular telephone towers, and not only for sport, I think. *¡Pendejos!* The mobiles work better closer to *Búrque,* most of the time."

"*¿Búrque?*"

"Albuquerque. Same thing." The Jefe removed a walkie-talkie clipped to his web belt, and called ahead to the Milicia checkpoint before Tijeras, to make them aware of their imminent arrival. Finally, he tapped his driver on his shoulder, and the driver took a bright red rag and tossed it onto the dashboard against the windshield. A checkpoint recognition signal, Ranya guessed. A crude form of self-identification, to avoid accidental friendly fire shootings.

"Jefe, the other girl, the blond, was she hit by bullets? Did she live?"

"Stop asking too many questions—some things you don't want to know. Believe me, you don't want to know. But I will tell you that you have much luck that your name is not on this letter! Very much luck. Because these four on this letter, understand me very well, they were never seen, they never came here at all. They have disappeared, and you must forget them completely. That is the ugly reality of dirty war—sometimes accidents happen. Mistakes. Yes, pretty one, you have much luck that your name is not on this letter, or even now you would be with those four in hell."

"But why did your soldiers fire? Why were they so quick to fire? The students were not armed; they were only coming to join the revolution."

"Why did they fire? I'll tell you why! Because gringo cowboys killed almost twenty of our *Milicianos*, only three hours ago! Slaughtered them on a school bus, and some of them were practically only children! Gringo snipers shot them, just fifty miles northeast from here! Shot children, running for their lives! Then your green van-truck was seen, with a license from a distant Northern state, driven by two gringos—that is why they were very fast to shoot!" He folded the fatal letter, slipped it into his breast pocket and sat pensively, looking out his window, away from her.

After a while, he spoke softly, still staring up at the mountains to his left. "You know, I have been in many wars, pretty one. Many wars…for most of my life. And in war…you either kill, or you are killed. There is no other way." He sighed loudly, and then he said, "Until now, I have not been killed."

A few minutes later she said, "Jefe…"

"No! I'm not your Jefe. You may call me…Carlos."

"Carlos… You're not from around here, are you? Your accent…"

He turned to face her, piercing her with the intensity of his obsidian eyes. "Do you mean I was not born as a *Norte Americano*, with the silver spoon of the gringo in my mouth? Or that I am not one of the insufferable 'Spanish' New Mexicans, who trace their blood back to the white-skinned *Conquistadores*? Well, that may be true, but I am an American now and forever more, believe me! I have a driver's license—in fact, I have three! I even voted three times for *el Gobernador* Deleon! So don't tell me I am not an American! I am three times an American, and what the hell are you? Nothing more than my prisoner!"

They were waved through the Milicia checkpoint at Tijeras without stopping, and merged onto I-40 for the fast fifteen mile run west to Albuquerque.

Ranya was petrified when she saw the black hood. The Jefe asked for the *cubierta* when they approached the outskirts of Albuquerque, and the trooper in the right front seat pulled the cloth bag from the glove box and passed it back to him. The Jefe simply told her to put it on, and crouch low on the floor of the truck. She almost fainted when she slipped the dark sack over her head with her cuffed hands, thinking initially that it meant they were going to kill her. Her pulse raced as she began to breathe fast and shallow against the suffocating fabric. It soon occurred to her that if death was to be her fate, they had no reason to keep her from seeing the world around her until her final moment of life. No, she reasoned, hoods were to prevent prisoners from seeing their surroundings, prisoners who might possibly be released.

Unless the Jefe simply wanted to depersonalize her, to dehumanize her, prior to ordering her execution. She tried to banish this possibility from her mind, but could not.

She lay doubled up on the floor of the truck and tried to guess their speed, the turns they made, the traffic and city sounds but it made no sense. She had never been to Albuquerque and had no frame of reference. After ten or twenty minutes—she had no way to tell, exactly—the truck came to a final stop, and she was pulled from it. She could feel warm sunshine on her bare arms and hard pavement under her boots. She was led by a hand on her shoulder for a hundred or so steps and several turns, thrust forward, and heard a door close behind her.

A new voice said in harsh Spanish: "You may remove the *cubierta*. When you hear the key in the lock, you must put it back on. If you try to escape, you will be killed. Do you understand what I'm telling you, *gringa*?"

"Sí, lo entiendo."

She removed the hood and found herself in a cinderblock cell, a narrow room only six feet deep and just a bit wider than the door. Some light seeped in from a mesh-covered air space over the door. There was no bed, cot, or blanket. There was a white plastic five-gallon bucket for a toilet, and a one-liter clear plastic bottle half-filled with water. There was nothing else in her cell. It was 2:25 PM according to her black plastic digital watch. They had not taken it when quickly searching her at the ambush site—evidently, it was too cheap in appearance for even a Miliciano to bother to steal.

The white bucket was clean and empty, so she turned it upside down by the door, and stood on it to look out of the ventilation hole. The opening was the size of one missing cinder block. It was covered on the outside with dusty wire mesh too fine to put her fingers through. Stretching on tiptoes, she had a limited view of the outside. She was looking out onto a narrow white-painted hallway, with a bare fluorescent light tube at the limit of her vision a few yards to her right. Across the hallway was another door, and next to it were more doors to the right and left as far as the rectangular vent permitted her to see, eight doors in all. Each door had a heavy steel hasp. Three were locked with padlocks and five were not. There was no sound or sign of any other prisoners on the hallway.

It was not a real jail, but she knew what it was. She had been in such places under other circumstances. She was a prisoner in a commercial mini-storage. The Milicias were using a private mini-storage business as a covert prison. It made sense. It was probably an easy matter for the new state government to close down a business on any number of pretexts, in order to commandeer it for their own purposes. Most of the mini-storages Ranya had visited were surrounded by their own high security fences or walls. Many were in fact built completely inside of a high surrounding wall, virtual fortresses, with power-operated high security gates. All types of closed panel trucks—bringing prisoners—could come and go without attracting outside attention. Interior alleys would wind between garage-sized units with metal roll-up vehicle doors. The smaller units were usually inside of a structure within the walled complex. There was no doubt in her mind: she was locked up in a mini-storage, a ready-made clandestine prison.

The entrance was not an actual prison cell door; it was crudely made of wood covered with a sheet of steel bolted on the inside. But how could she escape? Even if she could somehow remove the handcuffs and break through the door, an armed guard could be waiting just out of her sight. And she had been warned: if you try to escape, you will be killed. After what she had seen at the Chulada checkpoint ambush, she had no doubt about the sincerity of the threat.

Ranya stepped down from the bucket to consider her situation. It was doubtful the cell was meant for long-term occupancy. There was no bed, no cot, no blanket, nothing. After her secret arrest five years before, she had survived months of solitary confinement in the underground supermax "Tombs" in Illinois. Ranya knew about living in a small cell, although her five by eight foot cell in the Tombs had been a palace by comparison, with its cement bed, mattress, toilet and sink.

She tried pacing, but the room was too small. One, two, about face, turn. One, two, about face, turn. She remembered Brad's story of being crammed inside a small steel locker for hours at a time, a narrow box where he could neither stand up, nor sit down. The "hell box," he had called it… Well, if Brad could survive the hell box, she could survive being locked in a mini-storage unit, even one this small and stifling hot.

Poor Brad, dead and gone these five years… Now, only their unseen and unknown child still linked Brad to her in this world of the living. Their five year old son, now named Brian Garabanda, was somewhere in this city—perhaps only a few miles away. Did he even now feel her nearby presence? Could he somehow sense the physical closeness of his real mother? She had memorized his address; she could find and rescue him, but only if she was free.

But there was no way to get out, not yet. She would have to wait for events to unfold, events that were beyond her control. She sat on the upturned bucket, and sipped some water from the plastic bottle, weighing and considering the story she would have to tell, when the time came.

She didn't have long to wait, only an hour by the glowing face of her digital watch. She heard footsteps stopping outside her door, and she hurried to put on her black hood while the door was unlocked. She stood by the door, it opened, and she was hauled by both shoulders to the right and down the hallway, through a series of turns, out into sunlight, and into another shadowy room.

"*Sientate.* Sit down." The hood was pulled from her head. The two Milicianos who had led Ranya from her cell pushed her down onto a stool. She was in a bare room about twenty by twenty feet, in the middle of the space. She was facing a long table, the kind used in cafeterias, with folding legs at each end. On the wall behind the table was a sheet-sized red cloth banner, showing a black fist inside of an outlining black star. Above the fist was written *¡Socialismo O Muerte!* Socialism or death.

Seated across the table were a woman and two men. The woman sat in the center. She was about fifty, with gray-streaked black hair drawn back in a bun, and narrow reading glasses perched on the end of her nose. She was wearing an austere dark green pants suit, with no frills or adornments. The man on the right was in his thirties, skinny with a receding hairline and a beak-like nose over a thin mustache. He was wearing a white and black checked short-sleeved shirt, open at the collar, and had a notebook in front of him. The man on the left was "Carlos," the *Jefe* from the black pickup truck, still wearing his camouflage uniform, with his brown beret on the table in front of him. He was puffing on a cigar, ignoring the woman's apparent discomfort.

The stern-faced woman began, with no exchange of pleasantries. "So. You say you were coming to join us, that you are a *revolucionaria*. Well, I don't believe you. I think that you are a spy. We shoot spies. Why shouldn't we shoot you?"

Ranya answered her without hesitation, operating on both instinct and anger. "I don't know if you shoot spies. Today I only saw your soldiers shoot unarmed students. Students who believed with all their hearts in the people's struggle!"

"How dare you! How dare you!" shrieked the woman, half standing, leaning on the table. "Enrique, don't write that down."

The *Jefe* turned to her and said, "But it is true, *Camarada* Inez. She tells only the truth. Our Milicianos did kill the gringo students today."

"But you were there, Carlos! You were there! Why was it not your own fault?"

"The Milicianos at the road block were not my own. It was only an accident of fate that I was there. This prisoner is alive before you now only because I took control. If it was up to your half-trained Milicianos, she would be just as dead as the others."

"Carlos—now is not the time! I insist that you stop this line of critique."

"Fine with me. But she is correct." The *Jefe* sat back and puffed on his cigar.

Ranya inwardly breathed a sigh of relief. By going on the counter-offensive, she had successfully derailed the comrade commissar's accusatory and threatening line of questioning.

"Let's start this again," said the woman, taking a deep breath and making an effort to appear calm and in control. "Who are you, where do you come from, and why did you come here?"

"My name is Ranya Bardiwell. I escaped from a United States federal camp for political prisoners last Friday. In Oklahoma. I came to New Mexico because I thought I would be safe here from the United States *federales*. I killed one of them in my escape, and they will kill me if they find me. That is why I am here."

The three stared at her, amazed at this frank revelation.

After a long pause, the man with the notebook asked, "How do you spell your name?"

"R-a-n-y-a, B-a-r-d-i-w-e-l-l." She pronounced the letters in the Spanish way. She was trying her best to use well-accented and grammatical Spanish throughout the questioning, attempting to bond with them at least on that linguistic level.

The woman in the middle asked, "Bardiwell—what kind of name is that? What national ethnic origin?"

"Arab."

"Arab?"

"Yes, Arab. Lebanese-Palestinian Arab," Ranya lied, embellishing her biographical legend to best suit what she guessed to be her audience's prejudices—and outside of their ability to fact-check. Both of her parents were dead, and she had no known relatives in America. They would have to go to Lebanon to discover the truth.

The woman looked at Ranya in a new way. "Palestinian? Are you Muslim?"

"No, my family was Christian."

"And you?"

"I…I have no religion."

"I see." The woman seemed pleased at this. "So this identification card here…" The woman held up a shiny driver's license, the one Ranya had been provided by Caylen Barlow at his ranch house.

"I stole it. When I was hitch-hiking across Texas."

After answering a few more questions, she was hooded again and returned to her mini-storage cell, but this time, her handcuffs were removed at the cell door.

8

Tuesday June 24

The amount of light in the cell never varied. There was no way for Ranya to know the time of day or night except by checking her digital watch. When she heard the footsteps on the cement floor outside, she quickly checked the time: just after nine AM, on Tuesday. When she heard the key in her lock, she stood and slipped on her black hood. Rough hands on each shoulder once again guided her by the same path as the day before. Once again the hood was snatched off, and she was made to sit on the stool in front of the tribunal.

This time, the three judges from yesterday were joined by a fourth, sitting at the left end of the table next to the *Jefe*. He was the youngest of them, she guessed in his mid to late thirties. He was clean-shaven, and had wavy brown hair extending over his ears and the collar of his camouflage utility shirt. Unlike the *Jefe,* he wore his brown beret while seated at the table. It had a coin-sized silver medallion depicting a stylized bird of prey pinned to the front. He was a handsome man, with high cheekbones, and a straight nose and square chin. He was already staring at her when the hood was removed. He had bright hazel eyes similar to her own, and she returned his gaze.

After a few moments, she broke their eye contact and examined the items that had been arranged on the table. She saw her folding knife, and Destiny's Nikon camera. She saw her 9mm Glock, still disassembled. The parts were all in a clear plastic bag.

The woman spoke first. "Come here, Ranya Bardiwell."

She stood and did as she was told.

"Show me your hands." Ranya leaned across the narrow table. Once again, her callused palms were given a careful examination. "Well, you do have the hands of a field worker. That is undeniable. Now, do you recognize this pistol? We found it in your pack, very carefully concealed. Where did you get it?"

Ranya didn't hesitate in answering. "From the house of the assistant warden of the camp for political prisoners. Before I escaped."

"Before you killed her, you mean. Before you killed the woman in her house."

"Yes."

The four judges on the tribunal looked at one another. The man in civilian clothes scribbled in his notebook.

The *Jefe* spoke. "Please assemble the pistol for us."

Again, she did as she was told, efficiently mating the slide and barrel and plastic pistol grip receiver, as they scrutinized her level of expertise. Then after laying the Glock down on the table, she stepped back, and stood at a relaxed version of the position of attention, with her hands at her sides. She stared at the black and red banner on the wall above the tribunal. *¡Socialismo o Muerte!* It almost seemed as if they were offering her a choice. Perhaps they were.

The woman picked up the pistol and then said, "Ranya Bardiwell, we have checked your story through our police channels. We believe that you did escape from the gringo *federales*. We know that this pistol belonged to Starr Linssen, a federal officer, whom you killed. We know that the *federales* killed your father, who was a gun dealer, and that later you were arrested on suspicion of domestic terrorism. All of that doesn't concern us.

"What concerns us is what we must do with you now. We have many, many volunteers already. We don't need you, and believe me…we will not simply release you. We could return you to the gringo *federales* for the sake of diplomacy with Washington. Or we could have you shot here and now, simply to close the book on yesterday's fiasco once and for all. So why should we keep you? What can you do for us?" She stared up at Ranya over her half-glasses.

In her cell, Ranya had thought long and hard about the comments the Jefe had made on their ride to Albuquerque. "Gringo cowboy snipers" had massacred a busload of Milicianos only yesterday. (And she knew who the snipers were, a fact she was not about to share.) She had heard that "gringo cowboys" were shooting cell phone tower transmitters to hinder Milicia communications. The Jefe himself traveled in an unmarked civilian truck, and only dared to put the identifying red cloth on the dashboard when close to his own checkpoint. It was evident to her that these leaders were concerned about the Milicia's deficiency in weapons training, and were fearful of the "gringo cowboys" who still out-gunned them. Knowing all of this, she had prepared several lines of argument.

Ranya began, "Your rifles are in terrible condition, and your Milicianos don't know anything more than how to pull the trigger. I doubt they could hit a house at one hundred meters. They are clowns with rifles—*payasos*. I can make them real marksmen."

She had their full attention.

"Look at that soldier by the door, how he holds his rifle like a loaf of bread under his arm. Look at him, he is aiming at all of us, and his finger is on the trigger! Even so we may be safe, because his rifle is probably so dirty inside that it will not fire. I can show you."

The Jefe was flushed with embarrassment, but the younger officer wearing the brown beret with the silver pin was laughing. He said, "Soldier, step forward and give her your rifle. Unloaded, please."

The Miliciano who had been standing by the door had been holding it casually in the crook of his right arm, leveled horizontally. The stocky Mayan-faced soldier straightened the rifle up while extracting the magazine, which he placed in a pouch on his web belt. He marched across the room and thrust it violently at Ranya, while giving her a vicious look. She was ready, and grabbed the rifle as he pushed it at her. She then turned her back on him dismissively, and faced the tribunal.

She remembered some AR-15 tricks she had learned many years before, growing up at Freedom Arms in Virginia. Back in those days, semi-automatic versions of the military M-16 had been legal to own. How long could that type of ingrained "muscle memory" last, she wondered?

Ranya held the black M-16 rifle vertically in front of her, and then pulled the charging handle rearward; checking that there was no chambered round. (She noted the weapon's empty chamber with keen interest. If it was Milicia SOP to carry their rifles with empty chambers, she might gain critical seconds when the time came to escape.) Then she swung the rifle behind her back and held it horizontally in both hands, the barrel pointing to her left. Next came the tricky part, which she had mastered years before as a teenager in her father's gun shop.

By feel, she found the rear cross pin, slid it out with her fingernails, and dropped the lower half of the rifle down to the vertical, hinged on the still-inserted front cross pin. She pulled back the charging handle and removed the ten-inch long bolt carrier assembly with her right hand, brought it around to her front, and snapped it toward them.

"Look at it, it's filthy. The bolt should pop out of the bolt carrier when I do that, but it's so caked with carbon that it can't move. This rifle will jam after one or two magazines, if it fires at all. Somebody needs to teach your Milicianos to keep their rifles clean, so that they will always fire. And somebody needs to teach them to shoot accurately, or the gringo cowboys will continue to kill them with ease, like yesterday on the bus. That is what I can do for you." She brought the L-shaped half-disassembled rifle back in front of her, and reassembled it in a few seconds, snapping it back into line while keeping eye contact with the young officer.

Once again she held the rifle vertically, and then she surprised even herself by doing a quick drill team routine with loud stock slaps and spins, moving the M-16 smartly from shoulder to shoulder. She remembered the Viet Nam veterans who had taught her these fancy rifle tricks back in Virginia at Freedom Arms, and she silently thanked them. It had amused the old soldiers to see the teen swing and spin the familiar rifle like a drill instructor on a parade ground, and she had basked in their approval. She had never dreamed that their drill team routines were still waiting dormant inside her, until this M-16 had been in her hands, in front of the tribunal.

The four Milicia leaders stared at her. The young one with the longish hair and the beret was smiling broadly.

Camarada Inez said to the guard, "Take her back to her cell." Ranya tossed him his rifle with both hands when he was a few feet away, and he almost dropped it. He was still red-faced as he reloaded his magazine. Another Miliciano handed her the black hood, and Ranya accepted it casually. She made and held eye contact with the young Milicia officer as she slipped the cloth over her face. Then she was marched from the room, but this time without the indignity of handcuffs.

The four Revolutionary Council advisors argued her fate. There were a total of seven appointed members of the clandestine *Consejo Revolucionario*, all of whom were picked by *Vicegobernador* Félix Magón for their ideological pedigree and personal loyalty. Today's tribunal was composed of the members who were locally available. The woman called Inez said, "Well, strictly from an ethno-geopolitical standpoint, she's acceptable. She's a Palestinian Arab…I mean, she's not Indo-Hispanic, but…she is from another oppressed racial group. At least she's not an Anglo, so that's in her favor, even if her credentials as a sincere Marxist are in doubt."

The mustachioed note-keeper with the receding hairline said, "I think at least we should ask *el Gobernador's* office if they want to send her back to the gringo *federales* in Oklahoma. We could turn her in at the Federal Building, here in Albuquerque. Deleon's state government would gain favor with Washington, and this in turn would reflect well on the professionalism of the *Milicia de Nuevo Mexico*. As you mentioned Comrade Inez, this would be the diplomatic thing to do."

The woman said, "But then the story of what happened yesterday at Chulada will be known to the gringos, and many questions will be asked about the missing students. I think Bardiwell should simply be disappeared, with the other four. Or…perhaps used as a rifle instructor, if that benefits us."

"These M-16's are too delicate anyway," said the Jefe. "They are a ladies' rifle! We only need to ask our Chinese friends, and they would begin to send thousands of Kalashnikovs next week. Now that's a rifle that doesn't need to be cleaned! That's a real man's rifle!"

The female comrade cleared her throat at these sexist remarks. "You miss the point, Carlos. We must use weapons obtained locally, gringo weapons, if we are to maintain our appearance as 'indigenous' New Mexico Milicia fighters. The minute our troops were seen carrying foreign weapons, our honeymoon with Washington would be over. They would no longer turn a blind eye to us, if we were to openly carry foreign weapons.

And then they might even begin to question where 'advisors' such as you come from."

"Well, most of the troops won't accept shooting lessons from a woman," el Jefe stated flatly. "They are very macho, and it would insult their manhood to have to learn from a female how to shoot their own rifles. This attitude may be primitive and reactionary, but it is reality. Frankly, many of them are little more than *criminales, pistoleros* who have joined the Milicia for the promise of citizenship and free land. They won't like it at all, to have a *gringa* as their rifle instructor. It will cause unnecessary friction."

The younger officer said, "Well, I can use her right away. So far, we have been given 2,000 rifles from the National Guard armory, but most of them are *mierde*, worn out crap with crooked barrels. I need to find one hundred good rifles from that mountain of junk, and I need to find them as soon as possible! The Falcon Battalion is providing security next week at the Vedado Ranch, and we have damn few riflemen who can shoot as well as they should. I think this Bardiwell can find the best rifles quickly, and make them ready in time. My Falcons will listen to her, if I tell them to. So I can certainly use her, if none of you want her."

"Ah yes, the dashing '*Che*' Ramos can *use* the pretty young lady," said the bearded Jefe, mocking him. "Yes, I'm very certain that you can *use* her very well."

The young officer ignored the intended meaning of the Jefe's remark and replied, "My Falcons are not too proud to learn from an expert: man or woman. And after your Milicianos did so well in battle yesterday, I'm sure they need no lessons! How many were killed on the bus, eighteen, twenty? And how many gringo snipers did your troops catch after that epic battle? None! Only four gringo students from Michigan. Bravo, *Comandante 'El Condor,'* bravo!" The young officer slowly clapped his hands several times.

The bearded Jefe stabbed out his cigar in an ashtray, then pointed a gnarled finger at the one he had called 'Che.' "First of all, they weren't my Milicianos—they were not under my operational command. Now, if I was given actual command of the 5th Battalion, that would be another matter! And second, let me tell you that a real battalion has many more than one hundred men, despite that pretty silver chicken on your beret—"

"All right, enough!" The older woman in the middle stopped their growing argument with a two-handed slap on the table. "Comandante Ramos can take this Ranya Bardiwell to find the best rifles, and instruct the *Batallón Halcón* in marksmanship. I have decided, and it is finished."

But the Jefe was not quite finished. "No, *Camarada* Inez, that is *not* enough! I demand at least a loyalty test! A *prueba*, a proof. It is my right to demand this, before a stranger is brought into our group! It is my right!

We have all been tested in one way or another, and I demand it of this Ranya Bardiwell!"

The woman turned and looked at the Jefe, and then she asked, "What kind of a test?"

The helicopter pilot said, "Watch out for laser lights, gentlemen. And if we get any ground fire, I'm taking evasive action—so be ready."

Through the cabin windows of the sleek blue Eurocopter, Bob Bullard and his young chief of staff were surveying the sheets of flame and smoke still burning across South Central Los Angeles, after a week of what the media was calling "arson riots." This was Bullard's own executive helicopter, or more properly, the helicopter serving the Southwest Regional Director of the Department of Homeland Security. They had lifted off from the roof of the Los Angeles Federal Building in Westwood for a quick aerial survey of the firestorms raging through and across South Central, on their way back to San Diego.

Director Bullard, as a rule, never put his feet on the ground in LA County outside of federal property, and even then only when surrounded by a phalanx of heavily armed security men. The rest of Los Angeles was controlled by criminal organizations of such size and reach that it was impossible to determine where the gangs ended, and the city government began. The telegenic young mayor of Los Angeles was the nephew of one of the leaders of the Mexican Mafia. The police chief was a cousin of the gang's second in command, and so on and on.

After the Great Riots, after the last Anglos had fled, Los Angeles had been recreated socially and politically in the image of Juarez, Nuevo Laredo and Tijuana combined. The sprawling city was virtually a foreign enclave within the USA. For federal agents, it was essentially a hostile "denied area." If they were identified on undercover assignments, they would be kidnapped and tortured to death, just as if they had been captured south of the old border. Federal agents who thrived and produced good results working in LA were assumed to be on the take.

In the new Los Angeles, it was easy to tell who the honest cops, politicians and reporters were: they were regularly found covered in blood, slumped over the steering wheels of bullet-ridden cars, machine-gunned to death by assassins who were never arrested. It was the chronic answer to the age-old Mexican question: *"¿plata, o plomo?"* The foolhardy brave ones who refused the dirty silver of corruption received hot lead instead.

For Bob Bullard, a "working visit to Los Angeles" in reality meant a stopover at the massive Federal Building, within the barricaded and fortified "Green Zone" on Wilshire Boulevard in Westwood, with his helicopter landing him safely on the rooftop helipad. He pitied the poor suckers who actually had to live down there in the city with the animals…as he streaked two thousand feet above them, at 120 miles an hour.

His CSO asked, "The mayor wants to know how soon we're going to bring in the air tankers." James Holcomb was a nervous type, who was going prematurely bald at only 33 years old. This was probably from the stress of keeping up with the crushing workload the DHS regional director piled on him. Bullard considered Holcomb smart, efficient, power-hungry and a convincing enough liar to suit his purposes.

"Keep stalling him," said Bullard.

"What? Excuse me?"

"You heard me, Jim. Keep stalling him. He's not going to get any federal air assets."

"But…then the fire's going to burn all the way to—"

"All the way to where? Where's it going to go? They've got it contained inside of the 710 freeway on the west, and it won't get past the Los Angeles River on the east. So what's the problem?"

"What's the problem? The problem is hundreds of thousands of people live down there! You're talking about most of Compton, Watts, Huntington Park…"

"Exactly! Like I said, what's the problem?"

"Bob…we can't…we have to…I mean…"

"Look Jim, you've got to see the big picture. Not just Los Angeles…the entire country. Long Beach and the Port of Los Angeles are national lifelines. When they talk about 'critical infrastructure,' they're it. Together, they're the third biggest port in the world, for God's sake! The biggest port in America! And over half of the gas and oil in California comes out of those refineries down there—think of it, over half of this state's gas and oil! The federal government can't keep paying those damn gang bosses to keep the Alameda Corridor open, if they can't deliver. It's just not working. I mean, it would be another matter if they could actually keep the corridor safe and secure. Hell, the rails have been basically closed for most of the last month. Ships are backed up clear to Shanghai, and more factories are closing over there! We can't let it continue, Jim, and that comes from the top. I mean, the very top."

"You're talking about letting it burn?"

"Look, we didn't start these arson riots, they did! Those animals shoot at fire trucks, they shoot at police, they shoot at ambulances, so what do they expect? Then we're supposed to bring in air tankers from Colorado, to put out the fires they keep starting on each other's turf? Well, they've got their own fires in Colorado! So fuck 'em! Let it all burn! The best outcome is if it burns from the 110 to the 710 and the LA River. Let it all burn—then at least we can patrol the tracks and the pipelines, and keep the trains rolling and the oil flowing."

"But that's...that's five miles, from the 110 to the 710!"

"Right! Five miles of hostile territory. Five miles of a no-go zone! Five miles where cops haven't been able to step foot in years, outside of armored vehicles! Five miles of animals who would cut your throat and rape your kids just for a laugh!"

"But the mayor, he's never going to agree to—"

"Jim...Jim, that's not our problem, it's his. So what? What can he do? They didn't vote for the President last time anyway, so who cares? Hey, they love Mexico so much down there, then let them ask the Mexican government to send air tankers!"

"But I don't think Mexico has any air tankers..."

"Exactly."

"Bob, seriously, they're still waiting for the air tankers, they're expecting to get them today or tomorrow."

"There's still forest fires burning in Colorado and Montana, right? And isn't that foam toxic to people? Just find a reason we can't drop foam on urban areas, all right? Hell, those animals would just shoot at the air tankers anyway, when they're down low making their runs. So screw 'em, let it burn, let it all burn, clear it way back—just keep those tracks and pipelines open. I want to see a free-fire-zone for at least a mile on both sides of the Alameda Corridor! I don't want to see one single shack still standing within rifle range of those railroad tracks! If this fire's going to do it for us, then fine. Let it burn. And maybe it'll teach the rest of those animals down there how to act like civilized freakin' human beings for a change!"

Ranya was led from the cell once again, but in a different direction. This time she was not made to wear a hood, but instead was handcuffed behind her back. Four Milicianos carrying M-16 rifles marched in two pairs in front and behind her. They escorted her from the building containing the smallest units, out onto the asphalt pavement beneath a brilliant blue sky. She blinked up at the sun, seeing it for the first time in 24 hours. On all sides she saw rollup storage garages; some open, some closed. They marched her around a corner and down a long alley toward a dead end, where closed garages on both sides of the lane terminated against a high cement wall. The top of a mountain was visible above the wall, and she guessed it was Sandia Peak, off to the east.

A man was already standing against the sunlit wall. He was blindfolded with a thin black rag. As they marched nearer, Ranya saw that he was not merely standing, but that he was bound somehow to the wall with his hands behind his back. A yard from his waist on either side there were thick steel rings bolted to the wall. She had a sinking feeling in the pit of her stomach as the horrifying realization flooded in. She had failed to convince them. Instead of trying to promote herself as a mercenary rifle expert, she should have "spouted off Marxist gibberish," as Caylen Barlow had suggested back at his North Texas ranch. It had been a terrible blunder; it was her greatest and last mistake!

The unpainted cement wall around the man was riddled with chips and dings, pocked with bullet marks, and splotched with dark stains…

She recognized the man by his Afro haircut and chocolate skin tone. It was none other than Kalil, with blood-soaked battle dressings taped across his bare upper chest. His lips were split and his once-handsome nose was flattened. She had assumed that Kalil was as dead as Derek, but evidently, she was wrong. Now it seemed that she was off by only one day.

At the sound of their approach he began to curse and mutter in English. "Yeah, motherfuckers, real brave, ain't you? Beatin' up on a niggah, just like you was back in Alabama! That's all you jive Aztlan mothers is—nothin' but brown-skinned Ku Klux Klan! Call yo'self *la raza*, now I know what you really mean: you just a bunch of jive-ass *la raza* racist motherfuckers! Yeah, you real brave ain't you, with me chained to this damn wall!"

One of Ranya's escorts belted him across his face with the muzzle of his rifle, then butt-stroked him in the gut, and Kalil slumped forward and groaned, spitting out blood.

Two of the troops turned her around by the shoulders, and using a second pair of handcuffs, attached her wrists to the ringbolt on Kalil's left side. She saw a dozen more brown-bereted Milicianos appear, marching toward the dead end in single file, their M-16 rifles held haphazardly.

Another of her escorts pulled a black sash from the front cargo pocket of his utility trousers, and quickly tied it around Ranya's eyes, knotting it in the back. He had obviously done it before, she noted grimly.

There was no time for anything now but to prepare to meet God…if God did exist. She wished that she could think of something witty and cutting to shout at her firing squad, but instead random thoughts and faces flashed through her consciousness like a runaway slide show.

"Ready!" a voice shouted in Spanish. She heard a dozen M-16 bolts being charged and released, a chorus of rasping metallic clacks.

"Aim!" She tried to picture Brad's face. Her knees began to go rubbery, her gut turned to water, and she took in one last breath and held it, bracing herself for the blow, her ears already ringing.

"¡Fuego!" There was a mass detonation of rifle blasts. She felt no pain and wondered if she was already dead. Then she heard another chorus, of laughter and loud jeering. After a moment someone pulled off her mask, while another unlocked her handcuffs, both sets, freeing her

hands. She clasped her arms around her chest, shaking, wobbling, and nearly collapsing. Her escorts pulled her away from the wall.

"Ah, well, I guess you're happy to be alive!"

"Ha! Look, she didn't even piss herself! Good for you, *chica*!"

"The *pelotón de ejecución* must be very bad shots—the entire execution platoon missed!"

The Jefe appeared among the brown-shirted troops in his camouflage uniform.

Kalil yelled out in English, "Hey! Hey! Very damn funny! I'm laughing out loud here! Ha ha ha! Now turn me loose, motherfuckers! Turn me loose, you…!"

Then the Jefe did something totally unexpected. He took a rifle at random from one of the Milicianos, and said to Ranya, "Now *chica*, let's see if it's so dirty that it won't fire!" He yanked back the charging handle, ejecting a chambered live cartridge onto the asphalt, and let the handle fly forward, chambering another round from the magazine, holding the rifle so that she could be certain that it was loaded with live ammunition and fully functional.

They were standing thirty feet from the wall and Kalil, who continued in English to alternately shout abuse and plead for his life. The fifteen Milicianos slowly formed a wide half-circle around Ranya, away from the wall, their rifles nonchalantly trained toward her from their hips. The Jefe thrust the loaded rifle at her, and hissed, "Shoot that damned noisy ape! Shut him up! Kill him right now! Do it or we will chain you back beside him, and this time, I will not tell them to aim at the mountain! Do it now!"

She held the loaded rifle at port arms, across her chest at an angle, her right fingers wrapped tightly around the pistol grip, her left hand on the smooth black plastic fore stock. Ranya looked at the Jefe; he was staring intently at her with his coal-black eyes as he backed away from her. With her right thumb, she could feel that the safety was already pointing up, ready to fire single shots. She glanced at the semi-circle of Milicianos fanned out behind her. She looked at the blindfolded Kalil, still chained to the wall and loudly protesting. A dozen M-16 rifles were pointing in her direction. The Jefe had his pistol out, in his hand, twitching by his leg. His eyes burned her with their intensity.

She ruled out trying to reason with him—the Jefe was in deadly earnest, and the brown-shirted troops would obey him no matter what. Ranya quickly weighed her options as they all stared at her, in the dead-end alley thirty feet from Kalil on the wall. She could thumb the safety back to full auto, spin and shoot the Jefe, and maybe a few of the other Milicianos besides, before she was riddled with their bullets and killed.

The Jefe made a slight nod, and the fifteen rifle barrels slowly began to rise.

Talk was out. Running away was out. Shooting the Jefe and then being killed was out. Crying, begging or showing any form of feminine frailty was out.

Time was out.

She threw the black rifle to her shoulder, flicked back the safety while taking aim through the rear peep sight, and emptied the magazine in a single ripping three second burst. She saw her M-16's bullets shred Kalil from his belly to his throat as the front sight climbed his body on full auto, giving him at least a swift death.

Well, the radical anarchist had come to New Mexico to find a revolution.

And he had found it.

They were silent and still when her rifle went empty, and after a moment she lowered its barrel toward the ground. As the echoes of her shots died, she turned to the Jefe and said,

"In war, you either kill, or you are killed. And I am still alive!"

9

In her best Spanish she asked him, "Are these all of the rifles?" Ranya was holding a small plastic bottle of spring water, handed to her by the young officer from the tribunal. He was just a few inches taller than she was, perhaps six feet. He was wearing a camouflage uniform and black boots, with a green web belt and a pistol in a black nylon holster, and of course his brown beret. She was still in the same jeans and black t-shirt she had been wearing since Texas.

"Most of them are in here," he answered *en Español.* "A few hundred are already out with the regular Milicia patrols, and some others are at the academy."

"What is 'the academy'?" she asked.

"Another place we use. A private high school. Or it was. Now my group uses it—the Falcon Battalion."

They were looking into an open garage, in another part of the mini-storage complex from the dead end alley where she had shot Kalil. The young officer with the long dark hair had taken custody of her from the Jefe immediately after the forced execution. He had arrived with four of his personal bodyguards, and flatly said, "The test is over, and now she is mine." The Jefe had nodded acquiescence, staring above the killing wall.

Ranya shook her head at the sight in the garage: a jumbled mountain of black plastic and gray metal. "It's a shame to see rifles treated this way, even if they're old. If they are stored properly, they should last forever."

"I wasn't here when they were unloaded."

The twenty by twenty foot garage was filled with a heap of black rifles, chest-high in the center. If the unloading had begun in an orderly fashion, it had obviously ended with rifles being thrown into the garage.

"How many are in here?"

"About a thousand five hundred, I have been told."

"About a thousand five hundred," thought Ranya. She wondered if there was any accounting for the exact number of rifles, much less their serial numbers. As always, when it came to firearms, there was one set of rules for the common folks, and quite another set of rules for the government—even in this lunatic state of Nuevo Mexico. A lifetime ago back in Virginia, her father would have been jailed for misplacing even one "class 3" full-auto rifle due to sloppy paperwork. In the end, the Special Training Unit of the ATF had simply killed him. Here, fifteen hundred fully automatic M-16s were treated as casually as swap meet junk.

She said, "Well, I can't do anything with them in a pile like this. Have some men bring them out and stand them against the walls, this way." She picked up the first rifle she could extricate from the jumble, and leaned its muzzle against the wall outside of the rolled-up garage door. "It doesn't matter how much space it takes, get them all lined up. Then I can begin to grade and sort them."

"How long will it take?"

"To get them stacked along the walls?"

"No, I mean to sort them, to grade them, after they are lined up for inspection?"

"Hmm…if I can show some of your men what to look for, maybe a few minutes each. So at least a day, maybe two, if I have some help."

"All right, we'll do it that way." He looked her square in the face. He was standing just a few feet away, and she did not avoid his gaze. "Ranya, I want to tell you directly, that I had nothing to do with that disgraceful episode with the firing squad. That was completely El Condor's idea."

"El Condor?"

"Correct. The Peruvian, Carlos Guzman. I think you may have heard him called El Jefe. He has many other names as well."

She sipped from her water bottle, while returning his eye contact. "It hasn't exactly been my best day. But I will do my duty, for the cause." She was gaunt and hollow-eyed after spending the night in the cement cubicle, her hair and face unwashed for two days.

"Well, I'm sorry that it happened. Very sorry. Say, are you hungry? You must be dying of hunger. I'll have some of the men line up the rifles. Let's go get something to eat." The young officer told one of his trailing bodyguards to get a detail of regular Milicianos moving on organizing the rifles for inspection. Then he said to Ranya, "Come on, let's get out of this dump."

Near the front office of the complex was a small parking lot. A black Chevy Suburban with opaquely tinted windows was parked by the gate, its engine already rumbling. He opened the door behind the driver, and motioned for her to get in. She studied the modified door as she climbed inside—the window glass was at least two inches thick. It was a customized, armored luxury SUV, the type preferred by Latin American executives and government officials with reasons to fear kidnapping or assassination.

His bodyguards followed, and took the other places. Two besides the driver climbed into the front, and three more climbed in through the rear doors. The rear bench seat had been turned around to face backwards, allowing the three men to climb in and out without interfering with the passengers in the middle. Ranya noted that this also allowed them to keep their weapons trained to the rear, to fight off any attackers in that direction, as well as to leap out at a moment's notice to go on the attack in a counter-ambush. There was a custom "moon roof" over the rear seat—she guessed this opening was to allow the men in the back to stand and fire in any direction, while the vehicle was on the move. All of the windows were closed, and the air conditioner was running.

Instead of the standard full-length rifles, his bodyguards carried newer carbine versions of the M-16, with short barrels and collapsing stocks. The bodyguards all wore khaki-colored combat vests over their brown t-shirts, with pouches and compartments for extra M-16 magazines. Each of them had a black drop-leg tactical holster strapped to his right thigh for a pistol. They wore the brown beret with the same silver falcon as their leader, woodland camouflage utility pants and a variety of boots. They had the self-assured, almost cocky demeanor of serious operators.

These bodyguards seemed fitter and more alert than the Milicianos she had seen at the Chulada roadblock, or in today's firing squad. Elite troops. The Falcon Battalion, he had called them. Ranya thought that if this personal detachment accompanied their leader everywhere, it would be extremely difficult to escape from them. Two of them had intricate blue prison tattoos on their bare arms and up their necks, but unlike some of the ordinary Milicianos, not on their faces. Several of the tattoos depicted machetes dripping with blood. From the accompanying tattooed Germanic calligraphy, this machete logo seemed to be one of the signatures of the MS-13 *pandilla*, or gang faction.

The chain link gate rolled open, and the SUV pulled out of the complex and onto a wide street. It looked like an area zoned for light industrial and commercial use. She could see the Sandia Mountains on their right side, to the east. A second black Suburban was waiting outside, and fell into line behind them.

"Whew! I'm glad to be out of that shit hole," said the young officer. "Pardon me…that dump. That place makes me nervous—it's too much like a prison, with that cement wall around it."

"It was a prison, for me," said Ranya.

"Well, yes, and I'm glad we got that straightened out. Anyway, let us begin again. I'm called Basilio Antauro Ramos. Or if you prefer, you may simply call me Basilio, and I'll call you Ranya…if that is all right with you." He extended his hand, and she accepted it politely. His grip was firm and smooth, his fingernails were well manicured, and he was wearing a gold Rolex watch.

"It's fine with me…Basilio." She knew instinctively that escaping would depend on befriending this Basilio Ramos, and gaining his trust. She was glad to be traveling with him rather than with Carlos, the bearded Jefe. Ramos was more refined, he seemed better educated, and of a higher class. And of course he was younger, in his mid or late thirties she guessed, and much, much better looking.

"Excellent. Now, first, you must be starving. We'll stop somewhere right away and get you something to eat, and then I was thinking that perhaps you would not mind too much a change of clothing? And a chance to wash up?"

"As you wish…Basilio. Yes, that would be very generous of you."

"And this afternoon, we can begin to inspect the rifles."

"As you wish."

"Oh, we have your pack," said Ramos. Without being specifically asked, one of his bodyguards in the back passed over the brown backpack, which had begun its odyssey in Starr Linssen's house in Oklahoma. "*Camarada* Inez, she kept the Glock pistol. But everything else of yours is in here."

Ranya accepted the bag casually and placed it on the seat between them. After her night in the cement cell, unfed and sleepless, she was exhausted. Then after the firing squad experience, her nerves were badly shaken, but she was pleased to be moving again. Any place had to be better than that secret prison in the mini-storage facility.

The Suburban had a color GPS display in the center of the instrument panel, and from the middle seat, Ranya could see that they were northbound. She saw from street signs above intersections that they were on Tramway Boulevard. From her map study back in Caylen Barlow's ranch house in Texas, Ranya had the general layout of Albuquerque memorized. The city roughly resembled a square, with the lazy Rio Grande forming the outward-curving left side. The famous Route 66 was the bottom of the square, with downtown in the lower left corner. The University of New Mexico was east of downtown along Route 66, which was called Central Avenue in the city. The right side of the square was defined by Tramway Boulevard, which ran due north for ten miles along the base of the Sandia Mountains, and then turned westward to form the top of the box defining Albuquerque. Interstate 40 crossed the city from east to west, just above Route 66, and Interstate 25 bisected the city from north to south. Seeing the GPS map display, and matching it to her memory and to her current observations, encouraged her with a welcome sense of orientation.

Tramway Boulevard was also State Road 556, a number that echoed the caliber of the bullets she had fired at Kalil: 5.56mm. Before arriving in Albuquerque, this number had already been planted in her mind, from her map reading at Barlow's ranch. This was because Tramway Boulevard—556—was the primary route leading to her son. Alexandro Garabanda, his wife, and their "adopted" son lived in the Glenwood Hills subdivision, on the east side of Tramway, above the east-west running Montgomery Boulevard. She studied the neighborhoods as they drove north. There was a dry streambed and a bike path along the right side of Tramway. Beyond this path were comfortable suburban neighborhoods, in the predominant Southwestern architectural styles, mostly stucco boxes and faux-adobes in beiges, tans and corals, topped with red Spanish tiles. The streets rose uphill on the east side of Tramway, and after only a few blocks, the rocky high-desert foothills of the Sandia Mountains loomed above them all.

Ranya had never been to Albuquerque before, never been to New Mexico at all, yet it seemed to be a town in serious decline. Many of the stores in the strip shopping centers were closed, out of business, boarded up or even burned out. The potholes they were driving across were the worst she had ever seen in any American city. Many of the traffic signals at intersections were only flashing red, or they were entirely unlit. It was obvious that the local economy was suffering. The gas stations they passed had signs that all read the same price for a single grade of gasoline: $26.95 per gallon. This was cheaper than she had seen in Texas, but there was a difference. Here, the gas stations also had crude hand-written signs that read, “No Gas.” Unoccupied cars were parked in long lines leading to the pumps, waiting for the next gasoline delivery, she presumed. She decided to hazard an ‘innocent question.’

“Why are they out of gasoline? Is there no gasoline in this city?”

Ramos appeared pained. “*Ay...la gasolina.* It’s very complicated, I’m afraid. Not so much comes in from Texas, anymore. *La economía...es terrible.* There is a problem with credit, with payment for gasoline to be delivered. Anyway, don’t worry. We get enough for the Milicia.”

After ten minutes of traveling north, she saw the sign above the intersection with Montgomery, but as the Suburban rolled through on the flashing red light, she could not see beyond the first residential streets. She could not see 4875 Camino Del Cielo NE, where even now her son might be innocently running and playing in the yard. Or would “Brian Garabanda” be in day care on a Tuesday morning? She didn’t know if his bogus mother worked or stayed home.

Ranya’s heart pounded faster and faster as she possibly came within scant blocks of him, but the trucks continued driving steadily north. At least she had seen the actual approaches to his neighborhood with her own eyes. Finally, she knew the reality, instead of the merely imagined. She was so very close, she had taken the lay of the land and she would return, as soon as she possibly could.

A few minutes later, the black Suburban turned left at the light on Academy Road. “Something to eat” was a foot-long tuna sub, devoured in record time and washed down with a tall lemonade. A “change of clothing” turned out to be a whirlwind shopping spree in a medium-sized mall. Basilio Ramos and his entourage of heavily armed bodyguards swept into ladies' garment boutiques, athletic stores, and outdoor outfitters, and they simply took what she wanted.

They bypassed the cash registers without a backward glance, or a single challenging look from the cowering store personnel. The mall rent-a-cops actually came to sloppy positions of attention as the group passed by. Basilio Ramos's bodyguards not only wore the brown beret with the silver pin of the elite Falcon Battalion, they had the tattoos of the toughest of the hard core of criminal gangs: the MS-13 and the Mexican Mafia. This deadly combination of official Milicia sanction and evidence of a partnership with the gangs instilled paralyzing fear in all who saw them.

For Ranya, a "chance to wash up" involved their group sweeping into a women's health salon in the same mall. The uniformed female staff was idle; she was their only customer. The bodyguards checked out the sauna area, and stationed themselves outside of each exit while Ranya showered. After finishing, a spa staff member handed her a white terry-cloth robe to wear, while the Spanish-speaking hair stylists went to work. They began by showing her various pictures in fashion magazines, and discussed how they could best "save" her hair. Ranya decided on a tapered and layered pageboy cut, which would keep the hair out of her eyes and for the most part off her face. She also decided to return her hair tint to its natural brunette shade, so that it would not change colors from the current black as it grew out.

While the hair color was setting, she received a manicure and a pedicure, reclining in the padded leather salon chair with her eyes closed. The ambient room temperature was ideal, and soft music was playing to make the experience even more pleasurable. After five years of twice-weekly group showers, it was heavenly, and she was in no hurry to leave.

Finally she was finished and she changed into a new outfit, which she thought was suitable for the task of sorting through over a thousand rifles. She wore green slacks and a loose khaki short-sleeve shirt from an outdoor store, both of which had extra pockets patterned after those on military fatigues. For footwear, she had picked ankle-height brown and black cross trainers. If she saw an opportunity to escape, she wanted to be able to run far and fast. Importantly, the shoes had none of the usual reflectors sewn in, reflectors which would betray her at night.

She had selected a brown leather fanny pack for her "purse." She wanted the bodyguards to grow used to seeing her wear it, so that if she was able to obtain a pistol, she might carry it without their knowledge. If she was presented with a fleeting chance at escape, the element of surprise might mean the difference between success and failure, when she unexpectedly drew a gun and fired.

On the way out of the women's spa, she heard Basilio Ramos advise one of the Latina staff to be sure that they changed all of their signs completely to *Español*, by Saturday at the very latest. Ramos helped to carry her shopping bags, while the bodyguards maintained their loose square around them, with their eyes searching, and their weapons held ready. When they walked out of the mall's side exit, the black Suburbans were waiting at the curb with their engines running.

"Oh—hey Alex, I'm glad I caught you. Got a minute?" The female Assistant Special Agent in Charge of the FBI's Albuquerque Field Office was standing in the doorway of her office. The diminutive woman was talking to a male agent when Supervisory Special Agent Garabanda passed by, on the way back to his office with a stack of file folders. She looked like a librarian rather than a federal officer, in her unfashionable black pants suit, with her dark hair pulled back in a tight bun.

"Sure, what's up?" Garabanda was wearing a light blue dress shirt and navy slacks. His pistol was visible on his right hip.

"Harry, get back to me on that after lunch," said the ASAC, curtly dismissing the agent with whom she had been talking. "Come on inside, Alex." She shut the glass door behind them, twisting the louvered blinds closed. "Have a seat, please."

Frederica Chupatintas was five years younger and almost a head shorter than Alex Garabanda, but she was still his superior in the federal law enforcement hierarchy. This was par for the course in the FBI, where the vast majority of Special Agents remained at the grade of GS-13 for most of their careers, while a select few—the anointed—shot rapidly up the ladder of success. It was widely believed that Ms. Chupatintas had been deep-selected for early promotion during her days at the Academy in Quantico. She was of the "under represented" gender, and a member of a preferred ethnic group, as well as a native speaker of Spanish. Like most of the women in the FBI's management track, she was single, 'married to the Bureau,' with no husband or children to distract her from her duty. It was not hard to understand why she had remained unmarried: behind her back her nickname was "toothpick."

She slid behind her desk and Garabanda sat in one of the gray government chairs against her 'me wall,' with its obligatory plaques and pictures of herself in the company of the high and the mighty. Her position behind her desk normally gave her a view through a glass wall and door out onto the bullpen—cubicle city—but for this meeting all of her blinds were closed. Garabanda, on the other hand, could look past her, out of her Federal Building window and across Central Avenue toward the Central Plaza and the County Courthouse, the scene of his latest marital defeat.

"Any new information on the radio towers?" she asked.

"We're working it, but it's not easy. As you know, there were over a million scoped hunting rifles in New Mexico before the sniper rifle ban went into effect, and it's safe to assume most of them are still out there. We've done a time and distance analysis, and we know that there are a minimum of ten active tower shooters across the state, but there could be more. Maybe a lot more—ten is the minimum. We have some leads, but nothing that's actionable yet. So far they're just generic tips like, 'my brother-in-law still has some rifles with scopes on them.' If we followed up on all of those leads, we'd have to investigate about half of the state, as I'm sure you can understand."

"Well, sabotaging interstate communications makes those sniper rifles a serious federal matter. I have to tell you Alex, we're looking weak, awfully weak. Can't you set up a sting or something? Put some cell towers under observation?"

"Frederica, there are thousands of exposed communications towers in this state. Thousands, and I only have nine agents in my squad."

"We're all understaffed Alex—we have to do the best we can with the resources that are available. Face it, New Mexico isn't exactly Headquarters's top priority."

"Well, I don't think it would be a good use of our manpower. Why don't you call Santa Fe and ask the State Police and Milicia to look into it?"

"Oh my God, don't bring them up. After what happened to that bus yesterday morning…Jesus, what a disaster for the Milicia! At least it's not a federal crime—thank God—and so far, Santa Fe hasn't asked us for assistance. It's a big body count, but it's not federal. Interstate communications, now that's another matter. That's us."

"Well," said Garabanda, "It's Santa Fe's fault if the cell towers are getting shot up, after they fired half of the law enforcement officers in New Mexico. What did they expect would happen, nothing?"

She paused, and looked at him quizzically. "Alex, do you actually believe former law officers could be doing some of the sabotage? Are you talking about the 'FLA'?"

"I'm not even convinced that the 'FLA' really exists," he answered. "Graffiti and a few internet messages don't necessarily mean there's an actual 'Former Lawman's Association.' So far it sounds more like some people are playing head games with us."

"Well, somebody's sure taking out the radio towers—and that's not a head game, that's damned serious! It's affecting business, with all the dropped calls and the erratic internet service, and I don't need to tell you how it's degrading law enforcement operations."

Garabanda responded, "Did they really think that they could just fire all of the Anglo cops, and not get blowback? That just because Idaho and Wyoming passed 'English only,' they'd be able to tell every Anglo from Carlsbad to Four Corners to change their signs to Spanish? What the hell were they thinking, up there in Santa Fe?"

"That's not for us to judge, one way or the other. The Governor…"

"Don't you mean '*el Gobernador*'?"

"Don't be a wise-ass, Garabanda," she snapped back at his attempt at humor. "The *Asamblea Legislativa* was duly elected by the people, and their state language laws are their business."

"Just like the Land Reform Act?"

"You've got to lose the bad attitude, Alex. You need to respect New Mexico law."

"Or what? Headquarters will banish me to Albuquerque?"

"Very funny. You know perfectly well that transfers are a part of every FBI career. You're just bitter about being transferred from Washington, and out of Foreign Counterintelligence."

"Me? Bitter?" he replied. "But speaking of Foreign Counterelligence, while you've got me in here, I thought I'd mention that we've been seeing some interesting faces around town. And some of them are even in Milicia uniforms…like this man." Garabanda opened a folder and slid a large color photograph across her desk.

"So who is this bearded gentleman?" she asked, slipping on reading glasses.

"In past lives he's gone by too many aliases to list. We're reasonably certain his real name is Carlos Baza Guzman. Fifty-two years old. He's Peruvian, we're pretty sure. He sometimes goes by the nom'd'guerre of *El Condor*. Cut his teeth with the *Sendero Luminoso* in Peru, and when that played out, he moved in with the FARC in Colombia. He's basically a guerrilla advisor for hire, but he's ideologically motivated. Trained in Cuba and the former Soviet Union as a young man. Graduated from Patrice Lumumba University in Moscow. He's left a back-trail through Peru, Bolivia, Ecuador, Colombia, Venezuela, Mexico—anywhere the neo-communists are fighting for power. Now he's right here in Albuquerque, wearing a Milicia brown beret."

"Alex…oh, please! So now we're supposed to be afraid of *communists*?" Frederica Chupatintas tittered, suppressing her laughter. "So, which investigation is this 'communist' a part of?"

"Actually, we've sort of been doing it on our own, as a sideline. Looking at interesting foreigners, especially in the Milicia."

Chupatintas recoiled in her executive chair, her eyes wide. "On your own? Alex, we are professionals in this Field Office—we do not conduct investigations 'on our own!' Do I need to remind you again that you are NOT part of FBI Foreign Counterintelligence anymore? Your squad may be stepping on other deep-penetration operations by other agencies that you know nothing about! You could compromise ongoing intelligence operations! I insist, I demand, that you cease free-lancing this way, immediately!"

Garabanda was not impressed by her shocked outburst. "What other 'deep penetration operations?' You know that's a crock! Frederica, doesn't it bother you that half of the Milicia is made up of illegal aliens, and the rest of them are Mexican Mafia gangsters?"

"That's your perception, Alex, that's only your perception. Moreover, we do *not* refer to undocumented immigrants as 'illegal aliens' in this Field Office."

"For crying out loud, they have gang tattoos! They're felons!"

"They're felons? You can determine that they're felons, simply by looking at them?"

"When they have gang tattoos, yes, I think I can!"

"Alex, tattoos are a cultural and ethnic manifestation. Are you suggesting that we racially profile members of the New Mexico Milicia? Because of some tattoos? Are you serious? You really need to back off—the Milicia is entirely a matter of New Mexico state law. There is no federal interest in the Milicia—none."

"Then you might try telling the Milicia that they have no interest in the FBI. Send them a memorandum! They've been tailing my squad on a regular basis—how about you, Frederica?"

"Well, did you ever stop and think that maybe it's only counter-surveillance, if your squad has been stalking Milicia leaders? That's all the more reason to back off on them! The FBI has no reason—no interest in the Milicia de Nuevo Mexico!"

"No interest? Oh really? Then where did they get hundreds of fully automatic M-16 rifles? At gun shows? Oh, I forgot," he responded sarcastically, "There aren't any more gun shows. But for pity's sake, they have hundreds of U.S. government-made M-16s, and that's not under federal jurisdiction?"

"Alex, you need to remember your position, and your area of responsibility in this Field Office. I want your squad to find out who is shooting at the communication relays and stop it from happening. That's it! The Milicia is a New Mexico state matter—and none of our business! They were duly authorized by the *Asamblea*, and that's the end of it. Anyway, that's not why I asked you to come in here."

"Can't we at least stage a friendly pretext to check some of the rifles' serial numbers, and find out where they came from?"

"No, we cannot. Let's move on." Chupatintas sighed deeply, calming down, ritually smoothing papers on her desk, taking off and folding her reading glasses. "I heard about the custody hearing. You may not believe me Alex, but I'm highly sympathetic to your situation. Losing your partial custody…it must be tough on you. Very tough. And I want to help you, I really do. So I've arranged for you to fill an open slot in Santa Fe next week, at the bi-annual Southwest Regional Diversity Workshop. Park

Luecking can handle your squad while you're gone—he's up to speed on the radio tower investigation."

"But, I…"

"No buts. I already cleared it; it's a done-deal. Alex, you could even qualify as a Federal Diversity Instructor—now that would be a terrific bullet point on your next proficiency evaluation! High marks from the workshop will go a long way to getting you a new hearing from Judge Obregon. A long way."

She paused, and adopted a quieter, almost conspiratorial tone. "As it so happens, I know Galatea Obregon. Socially, you might say. We work out at the same gym, and sometimes we golf together. Anyway, I've tried to convince her that you're not a complete Neanderthal. It was simply inexcusable that you were attacked with a baseball bat at the picnic. And I said so at the Board of Inquiry, I put it on the official record."

"Thanks, Frederica."

"No problem, I was glad to. But obviously I have no control over the IRS, so if they're not going to discipline Gretchen Bosch, then it's out of my hands. Now, back to your custody problem. If you get high scores at the diversity workshop, if you qualify as a diversity instructor, that would be a big help. Maybe you can pick up a letter of commendation, something concrete showing a decisive attitude correction concerning your homophobia. A little extra credit, if you catch my drift. If you did, then Galatea—I mean, Judge Obregon—she *might* be open to holding new custody hearings in only three months, instead of six. This is all informal, mind you, very back-channel…"

"Three months before I see my son again? He's only five years old!"

"Well it's better than six months! You should be grateful. At least the judge is leaving the door opened a crack."

"Depending on my 'attitude correction'?"

"That's right. It all depends on you, Alex. On your attitude. You've been your own worst enemy—you need to get in step with the times."

"You saved us at least a day getting the rifles ready," Ramos told her.

"It was simple," she shrugged. "The new rifles still had their delivery tags on them."

"Well, you're the one who noticed them. The rifles were delivered at night, and I never saw them until they were already thrown into that heap. Anyway, I want you to know how much I appreciate it, saving us this time. I'd like to take you out for a nice dinner, if you wouldn't mind." The rifles were now sorted into three categories, neatly stacked in separate adjoining garages. It was almost 7 PM, and they were pulling down the overhead doors at the mini-storage.

“That would be nice, thank you for the offer, Basilio.” What else could she say? In spite of his courtesy, she was his prisoner.

“All of these rifles came from the National Guard Armory,” he said. “They were so old, that it never occurred to us that many of them had never been fired.”

Growing up in a gun store, the M-16’s evolution was well known to Ranya Bardiwell. “The military switched to the M-16A2s in the 1980s, the ones with the round hand guards and the heavier barrels. I guess the New Mexico National Guard received one of the last shipments of the old style rifles, and never issued them.”

Ramos said, “So they’ve just been collecting dust for thirty years.”

“I suppose so. But why didn’t the Milicia choose the newer rifles, the A2’s? Why did they give you these old A1’s?”

“You’ll have to ask somebody else—that was a political decision,” he replied. “The Milicia has official status, that is, we have the full support of *el Gobernador*. The *Asamblea Legislativa* created the *Milicia de Nuevo Mexico* by law, but they couldn’t create much of a budget. Even after firing the gringo cops and saving all of that money, the budget is still a shambles. The new money is a joke! Our troops are barely paid, they receive just a pittance in blue dollars. What really motivates them is the promise of free land, and citizenship for those without papers. There was no money in the budget for fancy new weapons. We have to take what we can find, or what is given to us. What else could the *Asamblea Legislativa* do? They had to create the Milicia, even without a proper budget.”

“What about the National Guard?” asked Ranya. “Why didn’t Gobernador Deleon just activate the New Mexico National Guard, after the gringo police were fired?”

“Most of the guard is still in the Middle East, and they’re under federal control, so that was never an option. Somebody had to maintain order and enforce the Land Reform Act, and that’s why the Milicia was commissioned. It’s not a new idea; it’s been very successful in South America. We created similar ‘popular forces’ in Venezuela and Brazil, after they passed their own land reform laws. Otherwise, the rich land-owners would never give up an inch! But I’m not sure how Santa Fe decided which weapons we would receive. I’d like to get some M-203s, the M-16 rifles with the 40mm grenade launchers, but I’m told we can’t have them. At least not yet! It’s something to do with our official status as a ‘paramilitary police auxiliary’.” He laughed. “We’re paramilitary, but we must not appear too military, not for the time being.”

“Can’t you get into the armory?” she asked. “Couldn’t you just take what you need?”

“It doesn’t work that way, I’m afraid. We have certain… arrangements with the federal agencies. Cooperative arrangements, you might say. So these rifles were carried out of an armory without, shall we say, all of the correct paperwork. That may be the reason why we were given the oldest rifles. They arrived one night in a rented truck, and that was that. I'm not sure who approved the transfer. I don't know how high up the decision was made, on either side. We just received the rifles, magazines, and ammunition, that's all I know. But your discovering that 280 of them were brand new, and unfired…well, that saved us at least a day of preparation. We know that at least these 280 rifles won't jam, and that they'll shoot straight."

She pretended a smile. "No problem, anything for the people's cause." After her firing squad experience, Ranya had decided to wholeheartedly "spout Marxist gibberish" at opportune moments.

"Please, call me Basilio."

He was at least a very good-looking man, she thought. She hoped she wasn't overdoing the eye contact, or coming off as excessively flirtatious. She worried that her acting was too transparent. "Okay…Basilio. I know the gringo snipers have been causing problems, from what the Jefe said. He told me about what happened to the bus, yesterday. Your own men are carrying the short M-16 carbines, and they're okay for very close fighting, but they'll be useless if you get attacked from longer range. You'll want your Falcons to carry these rifles, these unfired M-16A1's. With their longer barrels, they'll have much greater velocity and range than your carbines."

Ranya wanted to give him enough information to appear to be genuine in her desire to improve the Falcon's combat effectiveness, but she was conflicted on how far to take this. In reality, the M-16s, with their tiny 5.56mm bullets, would never be a match for the 7.62mm and larger bullets the "gringo snipers" would be firing at them. Their enemies, with scoped high-powered hunting rifles and other semi-auto military style rifles in 7.62mm, would continue to slaughter the Milicianos from well beyond the effective range of their 5.56mm M-16's. She knew this and much more, but she had no desire to impart this information unbidden. As soon as possible, she planned to escape from Basilio Ramos and his men. The less she taught them about marksmanship, the better.

They walked from the garages toward the parking area by the mini-storage offices. Ramos's four personal bodyguards, with their carbines hanging at the ready from slings, shadowed them in a box formation.

10

"Let's take another car tonight," he told her, walking toward a forest green Jaguar sedan. He held the passenger door open for her, and then went around and climbed into the driver's seat. He thought the "Jag" would impress her, and judging by her wide eyes and her body language, it did. Inside, the plush leather front seats embraced one's body in exquisite comfort, and the burnished walnut interior was a treat for the eyes. He tossed his beret onto the dashboard, and ran his fingers back through his hair.

They left the mini-storage with one Suburban in front and another behind, and headed north on Tramway Boulevard. The sun was low in the western sky across the city, casting deep shadows on the furrows and folds of the Sandia Mountains looming above them to their right. The little convoy put on their flashing caution lights, and moved swiftly around the sparse traffic and through the red lights with only a pause.

Ramos said, "Perhaps it's not my position to say so, but you look very nice with your new hairstyle. I like it."

"Thank you. I was afraid that I might look like a boy with it this short."

"A boy? Not a chance of that!"

"I'm glad to hear it, Basilio."

"The ladies at the salon did a fantastic job."

"And I want to thank you for that. I felt like I was reborn."

"Oh, you're very welcome. It was my pleasure." He turned and smiled at her, and she smiled back. "So, how do you like the car?"

"I love it, is it yours?"

He laughed. "Not exactly. The former owner had tax problems with the state government. Now, the people let me use it."

"The people have good taste. A Jaguar for a Falcon. It suits you perfectly."

"Thank you, I agree. I hope that I will always be able to serve the people in this leadership position." He chuckled softly to himself, and switched on the FM stereo. An old song by Shakira was playing: *Dónde Estás Corazón*. When it was over, Ramos pushed the button to listen to the AM stations, and quickly tuned in to the sound of an Anglo voice speaking English with a cowboy's drawl.

"Rick Haywood!" he snapped, "Oh, I hate this gringo bastard! He makes me so furious; he makes my blood boil! Every day he incites the Anglos to resist the land reform, every day he makes insulting jokes about the *Español Solamente* law. He calls our Gobernador 'Fidel-Deleon', as if comparing him to the great Castro was an insult! Haywood is the king of right wing 'hate radio' in Albuquerque, but believe me—we're going to deal with him very soon." Then Ramos unexpectedly switched from his Spanish to speaking in lightly accented English. "Listen Ranya, I hate this guy Haywood, but I like to listen to him sometimes. I like to hear what the Anglo resistors are planning. It's very useful for keeping up with their next moves. Oh yes, I speak English! I was raised in Los Angeles; are you surprised?"

"Not at all, you're obviously very well-educated," she answered, switching languages in step with him.

"Thank you. Your Spanish is also quite good."

"You are being generous, Basilio."

"When we are in private like this, I want to speak with you only in English, okay? I want to be able to speak English as perfectly as I can, and I don't get enough practice these days."

"That's fine with me. We'll speak English together."

"You know Ranya, I was born in Buenos Aires, but I was raised since a small child in California. My mother was Larissa Ramos; she was a news broadcaster. She was on Channel 43 in Los Angeles every night, and she was on Telemundo on the weekends, on an international show. She was very famous in California, on Latino television. You know, she came to America when she was only 18, when she was a fashion model. She was on many magazine covers; she was very popular. Maybe you heard of her, of Larissa Ramos?"

"No, I'm sorry, I never did. I was raised in Virginia, and for the past five years…"

"I know…the prison camp. In Oklahoma."

"Yes."

"Well, when she was a fashion model my mother was living back and forth between Argentina, Brazil, Mexico and California. I had the 'luck' to be born in Argentina. This was just before she moved to Los Angeles, and got her first television jobs. No big deal, right? That's what you might think, when you are very young, and your life is like one long party. My mother was very famous, almost like a movie star. Very beautiful, very intelligent. We had a wonderful life, in Los Angeles. Private schools, tennis and horse riding lessons, our own swimming pool…"

"What happened to her? Is she…?"

"Yes, she's…she passed away, I'm afraid."

"I'm so sorry to hear it, Basilio. Both of my parents are also dead."

"Do you know what happened, Ranya? Do you know what happened to her? The Jews. The damned fascist neo-con Jews run that city—they own LA! My mother was very progressive in her views. She was a supporter of the people's struggle in Latin America, and in the Middle

East. Especially in the Middle East. So even though she was on Spanish television, the damned Jews found her, and they had her fired, to silence the truth of her ideas. The Jews!" After a minute of silent seething anger, Ramos composed himself, and said, "Only two years after they had her fired, she died from taking too many pills, and too much alcohol. It was so sad, so sad... She was only 37 when she died... Anyway, when I discovered that you were an Arab, I knew that in you, I would find an ally."

"I'm so sorry, Basilio."

"I was fifteen, when she died." Ramos took a deep breath, and looked across at Ranya, then up toward the mountains. He wanted to tell her about his father, the Brazilian-Mexican fashion photographer, who had left them when he was only a small child. He wanted to tell her about the sudden and unexpected end to the private schools, their Colorado skiing vacations, and the private plane flights after she lost her television job. About living with a series of distant relatives in South LA after she died, and discovering how the poorest of these undocumented immigrants lived in wretched hovels, hidden among California's wealth. How the long-forgotten accident of his Argentine birth made him a fugitive from *La Migra*, Immigration, despite his growing up in California as a son of privilege.

He wanted to tell Ranya about being beaten bloody by black, white, brown and yellow thugs on the pitiless streets, about learning to fight, and learning to love to fight. Then about discovering the richness of his true Latino identity in the Los Angeles public high schools. About dedicating himself to the Chicano people's struggle against Anglo domination and imperialism, while he was a student at UC San Diego and a member of *FEChA* and *Nuestra Raza,* "Our Race." About his years of fighting for the people in Venezuela, Colombia, Ecuador and Mexico, first as a spy, and then as a guerrilla. And about the Jews, always the Jews, who were the true capitalist puppet masters, and who had always been the enemy of his people...

However, he was hesitant to share his inner feelings, his deepest fears, and his darkest hatreds. Even though she was an Arab, and thus a victim of the same Jewish and Anglo oppressors, he had just met her. She was untamed and beautiful, and he felt she was a kindred spirit, but it was too soon for that. After a while, after being lost in his thoughts, he just shrugged, and sighed. "You're really going to enjoy dinner, where we're going."

Ranya could easily believe that his mother had been a fashion model, based on the looks and charm that she had bequeathed to her son. Basilio Ramos could certainly pass for a television or movie actor. Despite his being way out beyond the left field wall politically, she was grateful for the opportunity to ingratiate herself with him, instead of any of the other three members of the tribunal. Perhaps it was a case of like being drawn to like. They were both outcasts and orphans, rejects and renegades, who had found one another despite the wildly different paths that had led them both to New Mexico. She even had the thought that the two of them could pass as brother and sister, with their similar dark brown hair and hazel-green eyes, and both of them tall and lean… Basilio Ramos, the son of an Argentinian fashion model and television personality, was undeniably a handsome man, and Ranya had certainly heard over the years that she was not exactly unattractive herself…

Once again they drove north past Montgomery Boulevard, and she tried to look up each street, hoping to catch a glimpse of a five year old boy named Brian.

In ten more minutes, the three-vehicle convoy was at the northeast corner of Albuquerque, where Tramway Boulevard suddenly turned and veered to the west. Here she found the reason for the name of the boulevard that wraps itself around the city on two sides. Here at the leftward bend in Tramway Boulevard, the two-lane Tramway Road jutted off to the right, and wound its way up into the stony foothills.

A small sign by the road read "Sandia Peak Tramway Straight Ahead."

"I was wondering what the tramway was. Is this where we're going to have dinner?" asked Ranya.

"No, not down here. Up top."

"Up top?"

"Right. Ten thousand feet up, at the top of the mountain. You're not afraid of heights, are you?"

"No, not at all."

"Well, that's a good thing then. We're taking the tram to the top."

After a mile on a winding road, they arrived at the lower station of the tramway, a stone and timber building the size of a football field, with an enormous chalet-style roof over one side. Instead of stopping on the almost empty visitor's lot, the three vehicles drove around the building past the employees parking area to the mountainside. They pulled alongside the building in the fire lane, almost under the tram wires that led up toward the distant peak, and parked. A dozen bodyguards spilled from the two black Suburbans and spread out, some going up the employees' steps and into the building. One of the guards returned to the upper doorway and signaled to Ramos to come ahead, and Ranya followed him up the stairs and inside. This employee entrance bypassed the ticket booths and nearly deserted waiting areas, and brought them directly to the boarding platforms beneath the high angled metal roof, over the tram docking area.

A blue tramcar was waiting in one of the docking ports; next to it was another U-shaped docking port that was empty. The car was a rectangular glass and metal box, twenty feet long and ten feet wide, with sliding doors shut on either side. It fit snugly into the docking port with boarding platforms flush against it on both sides. A massive twenty-foot tall aluminum A-frame was attached to the roof of the tram. This lifting frame was topped with multiple sets of substantial pulley wheels, which in turn rested on a parallel pair of two-inch thick steel cables. Other cables led from above the empty tram dock, running up toward the mountain, where they converged and vanished in the distance.

Ramos left two men to guard the vehicles, and the rest of his ten-man entourage accompanied them into the loading area, fanning out, their carbines at the ready. The tramway staff seemed nervous, uncertain of what was expected of them. None of the employees asked to see their tickets, and no tickets were offered.

In Spanish, Ramos said to one of his men, "Genizaro, stay down here with your squad, and make sure everything is secure at the bottom." Six of them spread out and took positions to dominate the area around the tram docks and the waiting areas. Then he spoke in English to the young attendant operating the controls, and moved toward the waiting tram. "We're ready to go. Open it."

"But sir, it's only 7:20. We'll be leaving at 7:30."

"Well, not tonight. Tonight we're leaving at 7:20. Now. Let's go."

"I'll have to ask my boss…" The young man looked imploringly toward a door stenciled "tramway staff only." There was a large one-way observation mirror inset into the wall by the office door. A middle-aged man peeked out of the door and nodded yes, then ducked back inside.

The attendant said, "We still have to call the top—both cars leave at the same time. When one goes up, the other comes down. That's how it works."

"I know how it works," huffed the Comandante. "Don't you recognize me?"

"No sir, I'm new here. We have to tell them to get ready, up on the mountain. They need time to board their passengers."

"Well, do it then!" snapped Ramos, annoyed. Then he, Ranya and four of his bodyguards stepped into the empty tramcar after its doors slid open. Three tourists who had been milling about with their tickets in hand moved to board with them. One of the Comandante's men stood in the open door, blocking their entrance, holding his carbine across his chest.

"What the hell is this?" asked one of the visitors, a slim man about fifty years old. He was wearing a black cowboy hat, a black Harley Davidson t-shirt, jeans and boots.

The tattooed bodyguard in the tram's opening stared impassively at him, then glanced over his shoulder at Ramos.

The impatient man said, "We've got tickets. We paid, and we waited. We want to go up, or we'll miss the sunset. What's going on here?"

"What's going on is you wait for the next ride, cowboy," said Ramos, in perfect English. "You don't run this state anymore."

"Whoa-whoa-whoa there fellah! That ain't how it works in America! This is still America, right? We paid for our tickets, and we're getting on!"

A middle-aged blond woman accompanying the man said, "Chuck, it's not worth it. Let's just go home. We can use the tickets some other time." She was tugging at his shirt, trying to pull him back.

"But Rhonda, I'm leaving tomorrow! Anyway, that's not the point. The point is we paid for these tickets, and now these Brown Berets are throwing us off! What the hell is up with that?"

"You don't have to live here Chuck, you're going back to Texas tomorrow, please don't…"

"I'm sorry little sister, but that's just not…"

"Chuck…please…please don't make trouble for us." The woman was trembling, her voice quaking. "We live here, and you don't. You don't understand…"

The man in the cowboy hat was getting angrier. "Yeah, well, I think I do understand! New Mexico's going to hell in a basket, when they've got brown shirts carrying machine guns, throwing people off of rides they already paid for! Hey, you, *Jefe*, where's your damn ticket? Or do only gringos have to pay in Nu-evo Mexico?" The man addressed the questions to Basilio Ramos, who was obviously the leader of the armed group.

"Okay, that's enough you asshole," responded Ramos, drawing his pistol and half raising it. "Show me your ID!"

The irate Texan stood his ground. "No, you show me your ID first! Who the hell are you to ask for my ID anyway? You're not even real police! So you show me *your* ID! Hah! If you even have one, I'll bet it was printed in Mexico! And how about your little goon squad, are they even Americans at all? Hey you," he said, addressing the Miliciano blocking the tram door, "Who's Babe Ruth? Who's Neil Armstrong? You don't even speak English, do you?" He shook his head in disgust, his hands on his hips.

The Texas man's sister and brother-in-law were shrinking back in horror at their belligerent relative's outburst. Ramos's men had raised the barrels of their rifles, waiting for a sign from their leader on what to do next. They were visibly angry, but staying in control. The other six bodyguards moved behind the small group of tourists.

Only yesterday, Ranya had been on the receiving end of an unintended volley of rifle fire. Now she feared that this situation was again on the verge of spinning out of control. The guards' fingers were literally on their triggers, the same as they had been at Chulada. She tugged at Ramos's arm, and whispered to him, "Don't let this happen Basilio…put your pistol away. Think—the parking lot here is already almost empty as it is. This will only ruin their business, and then the tramway will probably close down. Don't let this happen, it's not worth it. There's plenty of room here for all of us. Please Basilio, don't let this happen."

Comandante Ramos drew a deep breath, glaring daggers at the Texan, who was glaring right back at him with ice-blue lasers from beneath the brim of his hat. The cowboy was completely ignoring the closest guard's rifle, aimed at his chest from only a foot away. In Spanish, Ramos told his men, "It's okay boys—let them pass. We don't want to deprive the restaurant of customers." He holstered his pistol, and then he did an about-face to turn his back on the Texan, while clenching and unclenching his fists.

The bodyguards backed up, lowering their weapons, standing in a line across the middle of the tramcar. The tourists looked behind themselves, looked at each other, and hesitantly stepped aboard, following the Texan. The doors were slid shut on both sides by attendants, and the tram lurched, and then with a rumble of machine clatter it rose swiftly into the air.

Basilio Ramos had been up the tramway many times, and had no fear of the experience. He was also a qualified small plane pilot, and the sensation was not entirely different from being a passenger in an ungainly transport aircraft, albeit one without seats, or wings.

He knew that the experience was especially exhilarating for people making their first ascent to the top of Sandia Crest. He had taken many pretty university students and bright-eyed young "*Voluntarias*" on this ride, and invariably the reaction was the same: raw physical excitement. The tram took 15 minutes to rise 4,000 vertical feet, up to the mountaintop at 10,400 feet, over a horizontal distance of 2.7 miles. It was said to be the longest tramway in the world, and he believed it.

Ramos had taken position in the front of the car, facing through the windows up at the mountain, pointedly ignoring the troublesome gringo tourists. His guards were behind him, watching them for him. As the tram swayed in the wind, dangling from the suspended wires, he found himself shoulder to shoulder with Ranya, and then felt her lean against him for support. The tram was more than a thousand feet above the granite cliffs where the Sandia Mountains soared up in pinnacles and spires, and in a few minutes they approached the midpoint, a hundred foot tall steel frame tower perched on a protruding shoulder of mountainside cliff.

The tram rumbled as its trolley wheels passed over the tower's arm, and he slid his arm around Ranya's waist to steady her. Then the tram wire actually dipped down as it shot out across the final mile-wide canyon, and the passengers all felt the momentary stomach flutter of weightlessness. A few hundred yards out into the dizzying space they passed the other tramcar coming down on the other wires fifty feet away, then it was quickly out of sight, beyond the mid-point tower and running almost straight down toward the lower station.

Quietly he said to her, "Thank you for what you did down there. You were right, of course."

"I just didn't want to see our dinner ruined."

"No, of course not. And you have a point, tourism is already suffering badly. We don't want to see the tramway go out of business." Especially, he thought, because he enjoyed bringing his new girlfriends up the mountain for their first romantic dinner together.

Soon the tram had crossed the halfway point of Baca Canyon, and the cable wire began its final steep ascent to the upper tram station. The sides of the mountains that were not sheer granite were now covered in pines; they had risen from a high desert climate to an alpine zone in only minutes. Looking upward through the front windows, the mountain top station looked industrial and ugly, like a giant mining operation. The tram slowed as it approached its dock, and smoothly nested between two boarding platforms, finally coming to a stop with the platform deck level with the floor of the tramcar. The doors opened, and Ranya and Basilio were the first two off.

"Oh my God, I had no idea, it's so beautiful!" she said, looking out over the canyon, the city and the Rio Grande Valley.

"It's almost sunset, the best time up here."

"It's just…stunning."

Ramos said, "On a clear day, they say you can see for a thousand miles from up here. All the way to California. I'm not certain that it's true, but I like to think it is."

"This is where we're going to have dinner?"

"Right there, at the Altavista. It's one of my favorite restaurants in Albuquerque."

"Oh my, but the view!" She hugged her arms around herself; it was suddenly cold at over 10,000 feet of altitude, with the wind whipping over the mountain crest. Ramos put a friendly arm around her shoulder, to provide her some warmth and protection from the chill. The last pinks and reds were disappearing from the sky, as far to the west a parade of thunderheads were transformed to gunmetal gray. Flashes of summer lightning lit up curtains of rain low on the distant horizon, and yet the sun found a sliver of clear blue before disappearing over the edge of the world.

They lingered in silence by the railing, and watched a solitary hawk soaring through airy space hundreds of feet below.

Finally he said, "Let's get inside and order dinner—I'm hungry, and I'm sure that you are too." He thought she seemed genuinely thrilled to be on the mountaintop with him. The thin alpine air, the cold clear wind, the incredible views in all directions never failed to excite first time visitors to the top of Sandia Peak. In the case of beautiful young women, the excitement frequently lasted for an entire night.

And just to ensure that it did, he had brought two capsules of strong medicine, a potent new prescription pharmaceutical one could purchase easily in Mexico, to stir as a powder into her drink. One capsule of *Libidinol* was the normal dosage for the treatment of "diminished sexual desire." He knew from prior experience that two capsules were enough to turn even a novitiate nun into an insatiable nymphomaniac, for several mutually pleasurable hours.

Basilio Ramos was a strong believer in the adage that all was fair in love and war. He genuinely enjoyed the company of this wild Arab girl, Ranya Bardiwell, and he hoped their relationship would flower…for a while. The *Libidinol* would merely guarantee that his physical desire for her would be abundantly reciprocated, on this first of what he planned to be their nights together.

The Altavista Restaurant was only a few dozen steps from the tramway boarding platform. Just behind the platform was the ticket office and souvenir shop, where a handful of tourists were waiting to board the tram for the next trip back to the bottom. There was a red-painted wooden deck with a high timber railing extending around the office and over to the restaurant. The restaurant was built in an octagonal shape, with a low bungalow-style roof, and plate glass windows all the way around. The *maître d'* greeted them at the door, said, "Right this way, *Comandante*," and led them to a table with a spectacular view of Albuquerque and the Rio Grande Valley. Ranya noted that the restaurant had seating for at least a hundred guests, yet there were only a handful of diners scattered about. Two of Ramos's personal bodyguards stayed outside, and two came in with them. These two took up discreet positions in the raised area in the center of the restaurant, on either side of the bar.

The view was beyond spectacular, Ranya thought. No doubt about it, Ramos was a smooth operator. The *maître d'* had not blanched at the sight of the uniformed Milicia officer with his armed bodyguards—an unusual non-reaction, unless one was well accustomed to such visits. She guessed that many other women had warmed the same seat she was occupying across from him, and who could blame them for enjoying the experience? Ramos was quite striking in appearance, a clean-shaven combination of

Antonio Banderas and Che Guevara. In the political world of Nuevo Mexico, he was a powerful man with much to offer a young woman.

"This is my favorite part," he said, "Watching all of the lights coming on across the city. I just love it up here."

"It looks like somebody spilled diamonds across a velvet sheet…it's just mesmerizing." This time her reply was a genuine reaction, it needed no dramatic exaggeration.

"And look," he said, "You can still see the Rio Grande, see the line there? Watch how it shines like quicksilver, but in a minute it will turn to gold."

A uniformed waiter appeared, and handed them both menus. He asked them in Spanish, "Will you be having something to drink?"

"I'll have a margarita," said Ramos. "They're excellent here."

"Do you have strawberry margaritas?" she asked the waiter.

"Of course, señorita. *Por supuesto.* Two large margaritas: one regular, and one strawberry for the lady."

The waiter disappeared, and Ramos said in English, "After being in prison, the food here may be too rich to suit you."

"I don't think so! Honestly, I think I could eat everything on the menu. Twice! What do you recommend?"

"Well, their steaks are fantastic, especially the filet mignon. Or, you could try the seafood. The mahi-mahi is usually very nice. Perhaps we should begin with an appetizer; would you like to try the shrimp quesadilla?"

"Oh yes, please, that sounds wonderful," she replied, sliding back her chair. "But first, I've got to go and wash up—I'll be back in a moment." The bodyguards eyed her carefully but didn't impede her path. Why should they? There was no way down the mountain in the darkness, except for the tramcar. Besides, she was enjoying the cozy ambiance and spectacular views from the Altavista. It was absolutely hypnotic, after five years of seeing nothing but desolate Oklahoma prairie. Moreover, after five years of prison rations, she badly wanted to enjoy the delicious dinner to come, beginning with the strawberry margarita she had ordered.

She could think about escaping later.

The tramcar seemed to go faster and faster on the way down, as the lights of the city drew closer. Ranya had drunk too much, two of the large margaritas. Basilio supported her as they stood together in the swaying tram. The descent was dizzying, she was bordering on vertigo, but it was not at all unpleasant. She felt like she was floating and gliding, freefalling weightlessly as she stared out through the front windows at the approaching city lights.

Upon leaving the tramcar, Basilio guided her down the back steps from the platform, and she slid into his Jaguar. She would have gladly stayed in his Jag forever. She was quite certain that it was the finest automobile ever conceived by the mind of man, a masterpiece of human engineering. Its seat drew her in like a gentle embrace; the soft jazz pouring from the stereo speakers seemed to pluck at strings and keys within her very heart.

After leaving, they drove a short distance down Tramway Road, and then Basilio smoothly made a right turn into a residential area. Once again, there was the reassuring presence of the black Suburbans in front and behind the Jaguar, protecting them from any possible harm. The Suburban in the lead stopped by a little guard house under an intensely bright light. Soldiers wearing berets and carrying rifles allowed it to pass. Basilio merely nodded to the soldiers as they waved him through, and he took another right turn, and began to climb up into the foothills again.

Ranya periodically glanced across at him. She was quite certain that she had never been so close to any man as strikingly attractive as Basilio Ramos, this dashing leader of the elite Falcon Battalion. In the soft instrument panel glow within the Jaguar, his profile shone like a god. When he turned and smiled back at her, she almost melted into the soft leather seat, overcome to breathlessness by his movie star handsomeness. Now she understood why he wore a gleaming gold Rolex watch: any other wrist adornment would have been beneath him.

They passed fabulous luxury homes on multi-acre lots, and finally they reached another gate at the very top of the road. At this gate they were greeted by more troops wearing berets and carrying M-16s. This property was surrounded by a high ironwork fence; the top of each bar was crowned with a small black arrowhead. On either side of the driveway there was a tall column made of stone masonry. An arched iron double gate swung apart in the middle to allow them to enter.

The private driveway curved upward for another hundred yards, and then she saw the house. It was more of a mansion than a mere house, she observed.

"Basilio, whose place is this? Who lives here?"

"Actually, the people own this property now. The former owner decided he didn't want to pay his taxes, and he gave it to the state. Now it's designated as the official headquarters for the leader of the *Batallón Halcón*."

"And that would be…you?" she tittered. It seemed like the most incredible good fortune that she had met Basilio Ramos. The house was a palace, a fairy tale castle, and certainly no less than this prince of men deserved.

"Yes, at the present time, that is my privilege, to serve the people in that capacity."

She giggled again. Besides everything else, Basilio was so incredibly witty!

The three-story pueblo-style mansion was built into a steep slope. Wide curving stairs on the left side led up to a veranda and the front doors. Ramos pushed a console button, and the middle of three garage doors on the right side of the house rolled open. He pulled the Jaguar into the garage, and turned off the motor as the door slid down behind them. There were two other cars already in the garage: a silver Mercedes to the right, and a black Jeep with a hard top to the left.

He opened Ranya's car door, and took her hand to help her up from the Jaguar's cushiony embrace. She thought it was the most incredibly gallant gesture she had ever experienced. He led her by the hand through the garage, and into a tastefully decorated recreation room centered around a billiard table, and up two sets of stairs. Then he guided her down a short hallway lined with elegant artwork, and into and across an enormous bedroom to a pair of French doors, which he opened before her. The summer breeze was a sweet caress, carrying the scent of jasmine.

They were standing side-by-side at the edge of a room-sized balcony, against its ornamental-iron railing. He said, "We're not as high as we were on the top of the mountain, but it's still a nice view, don't you think?" The lights of the city spread below them toward the horizon.

"It's just as beautiful, Basilio, just as beautiful. I never knew Albuquerque was so lovely. I don't know what I expected, but I never imagined it would be like…this."

Then Ranya turned to him, pressed her hungry body against his, ran her fingers through his gorgeous hair and slid her arms around his neck, finally lifting her parted lips to his, unable to deny herself for another moment. Basilio Ramos was the most astonishingly handsome and charming man she had ever met, and she was going to show him her affection tonight, in every possible way that she could imagine. It must have been the margaritas, or perhaps it was the altitude, but she felt an entirely new kind of sensual urge spreading warmth through her body…and her needs would not be denied.

After their first prolonged embrace and deep kiss on the balcony, she whispered to him, "Please Basilio…please…take me to your bed."

11

Wednesday June 25

The San Diego police cordoned off a hundred yard stretch of the cement boardwalk, and all of the beach behind it, for the on-location film shoot. It was the first full light of Wednesday morning, and only a few walkers and joggers paused from their daily exercise to observe the modest production. The director was fussing over the spokesman, making final adjustments prior to shooting the public service announcement.

"I'm sorry Bob, but the hair is just not working," said the gaunt director, who was dressed from head to foot in skin-tight black leather. From behind, he could pass for a teenager, but his boyish body was betrayed by his deeply lined face. "The light is perfect, but your, um…*new hair*…how can I put this delicately…it looks like it was planted in little rows. It's…thin. When we come in for the close-up, it won't look *natural.* It just does not convey *charisma.* Bob, are you really, *really* sure we can't try one of the toupees?"

"We've been over this: no wig! What do you think I am—a friggin' fairy?" Bob Bullard chortled when he said this, and the diminutive director was not sure if it was meant as a good-natured jibe or…something else. Earlier, during makeup, Bullard had threatened to rip his arms off and use them for shark bait. He had exactly the same strange smile on his face when he had made those other jokes…if they were jokes.

The fat unshaven cameraman was wearing a stained gray sweat suit. He was standing behind his tripod-mounted Sony, a lit cigarette in one hand, and a cup of 7-11 coffee in the other, waiting. In a raspy voice he said, "Listen Bjorn, we're losing the light. We've got maybe ten minutes to get this shot before the sun is all over us. Put the Homeland Security hat on him. It'll be fine."

"The baseball hat? Oh, that is *so* cliché! Are you certain?" implored the director. A female assistant appeared with the cap, and placed it on Bullard's head.

The gruff cameraman said, "Look, it'll work, and we haven't got all day. It's more Bob's image anyway. That's it Lindsey, a little higher—right there!" The ball cap was navy blue, with the letters DHS across the front in white. "Now, Lindsey honey, just bring the reflector in tighter, with more of an up-angle. Yeah, that'll do the trick—perfect. Come on people! Is everybody ready?"

Bob Bullard was wearing a light blue windbreaker and khaki slacks, casually standing on the boardwalk in the Pacific Beach section of San Diego. The film location was overlooking the ocean, with a long fishing pier and a distant point of land jutting toward the horizon in the background. He had his hands in his jacket pockets, an avuncular smile on his face and a sparkle in his blue eyes. On the boardwalk off to either side, extras were waiting to move on cue. An animal trainer had seagulls penned in a dozen wire cages, ready to release one at a time.

The skinny leather-clad director gave one more look around and called, "On my mark: three—two—one…ACTION!" The plastic timing slate snapped shut in front of the camera lens.

After a beat, the center of all of this attention began his rehearsed script. "Hi, I'm Bob Bullard, your regional director for the Department of Homeland Security." As he spoke, he walked a few steps across the board-walk toward the camera, and then he stopped on his mark. A circular logo patch on the left breast of his windbreaker read "U.S. Department of Homeland Security" around a tiny blue eagle.

Off camera, the director pointed a finger, and an attractive twenty-something girl in a red one-piece swimsuit walked behind Bullard from the left. She was carrying a small surfboard under her arm, her golden hair lifting on the breeze created by an unseen fan.

Bullard continued with his memorized lines of text. "As we all know, this has been a year of difficult problems and unique challenges. But with challenges, also come opportunities."

A seagull wheeled off into the sky and out over the sea behind him.

"Once again, the Southwest Region has led the nation in security awareness and preparedness. We should all be proud of that record, but we can always do better. I don't need to remind you that improving homeland security means improving the economy, and increasing everyone's prosperity and well-being."

From the right, a middle-aged Hispanic couple pedaled behind him on a pair of bicycles, grins plastered across their health-exuding faces. In the distance beyond the white sand, a pair of surfers paddled out through the smallish waves.

"So let's all pitch in, and help your Department of Homeland Security to help you! Let's do everything we can to win the war on terror and economic sabotage. Report suspicious behavior, and please give your full cooperation to law enforcement at safety checkpoints. And don't forget: you can earn cash rewards for reporting illegal firearms, or stockpiles of hoarded gold. Call 855-GUN-STOP, or 855-USA-GOLD, and you can help to support your family, while you help to defend your homeland."

The camera closed in on Bullard's smiling face, while a sailboat glided across the shimmering water in the distance.

"Okay, CUT!" screeched the director. "Let's try it again, people! Surfer girl—Shauna—next time, walk like this: show a little hip action, all right? We're selling the American dream here sweetie, so don't hobble by like you're walking on broken glass, okay?"

"Can I just wear my sandals, then?" she whined, clutching her arms around herself against the morning chill, her board was lying on the cement.

"No, you cannot wear sandals. Barefoot! See, it's right here in the script: 'barefoot surfer girl walks by.' And think warm everybody, think warm! Okay now, places...get ready…and…on my mark, three—two—one—ACTION!"

"…Hi, I'm Bob Bullard, your Southwest Regional Director for the Department of Homeland Security..."

The convoy rolled out of the city on I-40, westbound across the chaparral scrubland under a cloudless sky. There were more than a dozen pickups and SUVs, each carrying a squad of riflemen from the Falcon Battalion. The trucks bristled with black M-16s. The troops carried over one hundred of the "new" rifles Ranya had found among the mini-storage garage full of surplus rifles.

They were taking them to what had previously been a public shooting range to sight them in, that is, to ensure that the spot where their adjustable sights were aimed would precisely coincide with the spot where the bullets would actually strike. This was no trivial matter. As delivered from the factory, the sights could be a foot or more off from the point of bullet impact at 100 yards, making the rifles useless beyond close range. Once properly sighted-in, the rifles would be capable of hitting a man-sized target at 400 yards or more.

Ramos had said that the full unit movement would also serve as a show of force, to show the obstinate gringos exactly who was the new boss. Eventually, they had to accept the fact that they were no longer in charge in Nuevo Mexico. If they didn't like it, he had said, there were plenty of other Anglo states where they could choose to live.

His black armored Suburban was in the center of the column. Once again he sat behind the driver, next to Ranya, but this time another soldier was seated to her right. She felt trapped. At no time since her capture at Chulada did she have an opportunity to escape. To make her predicament even more difficult, she had to pretend to enjoy the company of Basilio Ramos, and echo the Falcon Battalion's enthusiasm for overturning the old order in New Mexico. She stared straight ahead, her hands folded across her lap, recalling her bizarre and disturbing morning.

Basilio was already gone when Ranya had finally awakened, with a crushing headache and a mouth like sun-dried pond scum. It had taken her several minutes to orient herself in the strange bedroom, and determine that she was alone. Naked and alone, in a strange bed, in an unfamiliar city. She untangled herself from the silk sheets, slowly raised herself up to a sitting position, and the room tilted and whirled. She fell back, staring up at a stationary ceiling fan, bracketed between mahogany bedposts.

When she was able, she loosely wrapped the pink top sheet around herself, staggered across the room and checked the bedroom door, which was made of dark wood against the surrounding white plaster walls. The brass handle turned at her touch, but she didn't open it, afraid that there might be a guard waiting outside. Instead, she quietly locked it from the inside by pushing in its gold button. Her brown backpack and yesterday's shopping bags were lined up against the wall near the door.

Her eyes were only partly opened as she stumbled to the bathroom, looking for a glass of water and a bottle of aspirin or Tylenol in the medicine cabinet. She averted her gaze from the mirror until the cabinet door was open, unwilling to see herself in her present condition. Straining to focus, peering at the rows of prescription and non-prescription medicines while leaning against the sink and quenching her thirst, she had her sudden revelation, and the memories came flooding back. Oh, the things she had done with that man…

Ranya leaned against the pink marble counter top, her eyes closed and her temples throbbing.

She found some Tylenol and washed down two caplets, then began reading the other prescription labels, printed in both English and Spanish. She returned to the bedroom and found a pencil and a scrap of paper, and then with weak fingers she laboriously copied down the names of a dozen unrecognized pills and capsules, careful not to disturb their positions on the shelves.

With the list safely hidden, she showered quickly, afraid that Basilio might return unexpectedly at any time. She was grateful that her short hair took only a minute to shampoo and rinse. After drying, she wrapped a bath towel around herself, and cleaned her teeth with a new brush, studying them carefully in the mirror, appreciating her slow transformation back to something approximating a human. Then she opened the small makeup kit she had picked up yesterday at the salon, and applied just a little blush and clear lip-gloss. She enjoyed these routine feminine rituals again, after her five years of Spartan life in the camps. Wanting to blend inconspicuously with the Milicianos, she dressed in her green fatigue-style pants and a matching green shirt from the mall's outdoor outfitting store, and laced on her black and brown ankle-high cross-trainers.

The glass-paned doors to the bedroom balcony were not locked, and from outside she could see far down the driveway toward the wrought iron double gate, and its guardhouse. A high fence of iron bars with arrowhead tips delineated the property line, leading to the gate. A half dozen

Suburbans and pickups were parked along the drive, and there were armed guards on duty at the gate. The backs of other luxury homes were visible on the dusty slopes descending toward the city. A pair of iridescent black and purple butterflies distracted her for a moment, twirling over the balcony railing and above the house, spiraling high in the sunlight. Then she went back inside.

The bedroom had an office alcove with a desk and a computer, facing a window with a panoramic view of the city. She sat down to search the internet for the names of the unknown drugs on her hand-written list, but the screen informed her that it was "unable to establish a connection, try again later." On the screen there was an icon of a stack of books, she clicked on it and found the computer's own internal encyclopedia. The "Omnipedia's" home page informed her that it had been automatically updated only yesterday.

One at a time she carefully typed the scientific names of each unknown drug into the search box, and on her third try she found a "morning-after pill" which had been approved by the FDA. She pondered only a moment and decided she would take it. The possibility of having another baby, this time fathered by Basilio Ramos, horrified her. God might not forgive her, but she would not risk bringing another innocent child into the world inside a prison, while shackled to a steel table. If there was a new life even now growing within her…well, God could add yet another to her growing list of sins.

But Ranya had not made a list of the drugs in Basilio's medicine cabinet in order to find a morning-after pill. On her fifth search, she found the information she was seeking. After carefully typing in *dioxyselbrin-phenthalozine*, the computer informed her that this concoction was commercially known as *Libidinol.* The blue and yellow 100-milligram capsule was prescribed for the treatment of "diminished sexual desire" in both men and women. According to the Omnipedia, it was a controlled pharmaceutical in the United States, subject to certain unspecified abuses, but it was commonly bootlegged and sold in South and Central America. Having found her answer, she quickly logged off the computer.

So that was it. *Libidinol—the bastard drugged me!* Probably slipped it into the margaritas, she thought. She supposed she'd been date-raped…whatever that actually meant, when under the influence of Libidinol. She had certainly not been unconscious. Last night, she had been a willing partner. Wide awake, and more than merely willing. *She had reveled in it.* Could she blame all of her behavior on the Libidinol? Would she have slept with Ramos, even without the drug? Basilio was surely a handsome man, trim and muscular, but then, he was only her second lover, after Brad...

Brad Fallon had not needed Libidinol to coax her into bed that first time, in the midnight cabin by the nameless river. Basilio Ramos had drugged her, had taken away her choice, and that made all of the difference.

And now Basilio might return at any moment, anticipating, even expecting, a replay of last night. The thought repulsed her on one level, and yet... She drove those unexpected thoughts away, and refocused on escape, and her mission to reclaim her son.

Brad Fallon's son.

Their son.

To escape, to be able to find little Brian and take him away, she would need freedom of movement. Escaping from this house destitute, unarmed and without a vehicle would be almost pointless. She would need valid identification papers, plenty of cash for food and gasoline, weapons of course, and gear for surviving on the run with a small child.

To acquire these things, she would need to win the complete trust of Basilio Ramos. She would have to bend him to her will. In order to escape, she would need to continue and even amplify her pretense at being a dedicated Marxist, goose-stepping beside him toward a bright socialist future. That would be the easy part: many of her leftist university professors had unwittingly prepared her to play the role of revolutionary.

The difficulty would be in maintaining and even increasing Basilio's personal affection toward her. But how could she accomplish that seduction, while at the same time refusing to submit to him physically? She found no simple answer to that quandary. She would just have to cross that particular bridge later, when there was no other way around it.

She checked in her brown backpack—her folding Strider knife was there, as well as Destiny's Nikon camera from the van and other items. Ranya wondered if anybody had checked the pictures on the digital camera. Once she had been grilled by the tribunal, and had passed the various tests and been accepted into their fold, they might have lost interest in what they considered to be her personal effects. It took Ranya only a minute to figure out how to check the pictures contained within the camera on its LCD screen.

The first photograph in the queue showed the four students from Michigan, their right fists held high, in front of the red and white *Tierra O Muerte* sign painted on the roadside barn. The picture was only 48 hours old, which seemed astonishing. So much had happened since she had taken that photograph! Now the four grinning student radicals were dead—one of them killed by Ranya's own hand.

Above all, she didn't want to be in the bedroom when Basilio returned, so she slipped the folding knife into her right front pants pocket, and left to explore the house. She wanted to see what limits—if any—

would be put on her movement. There were no guards or anyone else in sight on the third floor.

The rest of the house outside of the bedroom was tastefully decorated in a Mediterranean style, with oil paintings on the walls. The floor was inlaid in parquet hardwood tiles. She passed an open door to a small library office with another computer and a huge flat screen monitor. The other doors were closed and she did not try them.

At the end of the hallway double glass doors led to another balcony, the doors were unlocked and she went out. The left side of the balcony offered her a view of the back of the beige stucco mansion; it was only two stories high on the up-sloping side toward the mountain. Beneath the balcony, only a few yards across a patio from the house, was an oval-shaped swimming pool with a connecting Jacuzzi. Ranya strolled nonchalantly around the wide balcony; it was large enough for several outdoor chaise lounges and tables. She looked carefully up the rocky hillside toward the mountain, and saw a uniformed soldier with an M-16 rifle standing a little higher than the house, but about 150 yards away. In between them was a broken landscape of sand, rocks, boulders, cactus and a few raggedy juniper trees.

The iron fence wrapped around the side of the property beyond the swimming pool, terminating against a cliff-like part of the slope. The steep uphill side of the property was not fenced, but it was guarded by at least the one rifleman that she could see. The same fence ran downhill and in front of the house; she had seen it from the bedroom balcony. She carefully noted the overall physical layout of the grounds, and the sentry's location.

The present reality, however, was that she was trapped inside of a fenced compound within an exclusive gated neighborhood, which was swarming with armed Milicianos. If she was caught while trying to run away during a poorly conceived and executed escape attempt, she knew that she would not be given a second opportunity to flee.

When Ramos had finally returned to the house after a training run with his troops, he informed her that they were going to a rifle range to sight in their new M-16s. He had seemed pleased to find that she was already showered and dressed appropriately.

An hour later Ranya was leaving the city, but she was still a prisoner in every sense. She was in the exact middle seat of the Suburban that was in the center of the armed convoy. On this trip, Ramos was accompanied in his command vehicle by other leaders of the Falcon Battalion. She saw no overt signs of rank, but she could tell by their ages, lack of visible gang tattoos, and complete uniforms that Ramos was with his officers and noncoms. Only the driver and one Eurasian man in the back, whom she recognized from yesterday, were from Ramos's personal bodyguard detail.

Ranya was still angry and disgusted, keeping a measured distance from Ramos, avoiding eye contact, doing her best to disguise her feelings as cool professional detachment. Discussion of the procedures they would use to quickly and efficiently sight-in the 100 rifles competed for the attention of her mind, which otherwise drifted between thoughts of escape, and last night's activities. Despite the discomfort caused by her present company and circumstances, she was interested in seeing what the "new" forty-year-old M-16A1 rifles could do in the hands of the Falcons.

Ranya sat between Ramos and a short but powerfully built man about fifty, who had the look of a career professional noncommissioned officer, right down to his bristly gray crew cut. His woodland pattern camouflage uniform was sharp and crisp; his black jump boots gleamed with a high polish. They spoke in Spanish.

Ramos asked her, "How long do you think we'll need, to finish all of the rifles?"

"What kind of range is it? How many shooting positions are there?"

"It was a public shooting range before, but now the public has no need for weapons. Today it's the property of state security. It has, I think, more than fifty firing positions on a two hundred meter target line."

"Then we can do it in two relays. Even if we go slowly, I think it will take less than one hour for each relay. How much ammunition do we have?" Ranya's use of "we" was deliberate and calculated.

"Don't worry; we have a mountain of ammunition. A truckload."

"Well, okay then, first you'll want to fire a few magazines through each rifle. Aimed or unaimed, it doesn't matter. That's just to smooth off any burrs or defects in the barrels, since they are new and have never been shot. Then let them cool down, and fire groups of five shots at a very small target, only fifteen meters from the shooters."

"Fifteen meters?" asked Ramos, skeptically. "That sounds too close."

"She is correct, Comandante," said the sergeant on Ranya's right side. "This is the best way, for the M-16. If you try to shoot at a more distant target without first sighting in this way, you may never even hit the paper around the target, and you won't know which way to adjust the sights. With an M-16, at fifteen meters the bullet strikes exactly where it will also strike at 200 meters. In the first case, the bullet is still going up, and at the longer range, it's coming down. But at both fifteen and at 200 meters, the sights are aimed at the same point where the bullet will hit. Once we have the rifles sighted in at fifteen meters, it will be easy to hit the targets at 200 meters, and then adjust them more precisely. Then when the rifles are perfectly sighted at 200 meters, you simply flip the rear sight over to shoot at 400 meters. The *señorita* knows her rifles—that's just how we did it in the army. That would be the Mexican Army, señorita. In the *Fuerzas Especiales*."

Ramos asked him, "You've done this before, *Primer Sargento* Ramirez? Sighted in so many rifles in one day?"

"Sí Comandante! Many times! But never with forty-year-old 'virgin' rifles. And these M-16A1's are excellent rifles, believe me. They weigh a full kilo less than the newer model A2 rifles, and these old rifles are true *ametralldoras*, machine guns. They can shoot either single shots, or fully automatically. The newer A2s fire only single shots or three rounds at a time. I never understood why the gringos changed the rifles. They were better before."

Ranya said, "It was to make them more accurate at longer range, out to about 500 meters. They have a heavier barrel, with a faster twist to the rifling grooves inside. And with heavier bullets, the newer rifles are slightly more accurate—but it's only a small difference. There is nothing wrong with these old rifles. Nothing at all, as long you have the right ammunition for them, and they are kept very clean."

The middle-aged senior sergeant laughed. "I heard about the trick you did in front of the *junta*, with that stupid Miliciano's dirty rifle! You became famous that day señorita, yes you did! Now the men call you *la ejecutora*, the executioner. But don't worry—you won't find a dirty rifle in the *Batallón Halcón*. These men are all chosen, they are not common trash like they accept in the regular Milicia. Most of the *Batallón* have served in elite units in their old countries—paratroopers, *fuerzas especiales*…

"And yes," the sergeant continued, "Some of them may have the tattoos of the *pandilla*s, the criminal gangs, but don't let that deceive you. They're excellent troops, or they would not be Falcons—we pick only the best of the best. Every Falcon is a double volunteer, first for the Milicia, and then for the Battalion. They are all making a clean start in Nuevo Mexico, even the worst *pistoleros* and *criminales*. They are tired of always running, of always being hunted like animals. You could say that the Battalion is their French Foreign Legion: it's a chance for a new life! They are extremely motivated. Believe me, they keep their rifles very clean, and they obey orders without question."

"And if they don't," added the Comandante, "*Primer Sargento* Ramirez puts his big paratrooper boot right up their ass. And if they would dare to disobey a direct order, they would be shot."

"That is the only way, señorita," said Ramirez, smoothing the brown beret resting on his lap. "It is harsh, but it is the only way. Not like in the gringo army, where they permit *maricón* soldiers to sleep with one another, and curse at their officers to their faces."

Ramos said to her, "This morning while you slept, we ran ten kilometers of the La Luz trail, half way up the mountain above our battalion headquarters. Not one man fell behind on the run—they don't want to lose their Falcon insignias!" Then Ramos addressed one of his personal bodyguards, seated behind them facing to the rear. "*Camarada* Chino, what does that Falcon badge mean to you?"

"*¡Tierra y libertad*, Comandante*!* Land and liberty!"

"Yes, yes man, I know all of the slogans. But what does that insignia mean to you, personally? What is that badge going to bring you? Speak freely, *camarada*."

"As you said, a new life, Comandante! A new name and papers to stay in *Nuevo Mexico* forever, and someday even a house of my own, so that I can have a wife and raise a family. Yes, it means a new life, a good life, with respect, *con safos*, and nobody can mess with that!"

"And what will you do to keep that silver falcon on your beret, Chino?"

"Anything, *mi Comandante*! Anything at all!"

12

Alex Garabanda arrived for the meeting first, in his unmarked Crown Victoria. He had the only automobile in the northern part of the Mount Calvary Catholic Cemetery, and no other visitors were in sight on this Wednesday before lunchtime. He parked the burgundy four-door sedan in the shade of a row of leafy maples, on the left side of the narrow asphalt road. The car was facing out of the graveyard, in case he needed to make a quick exit. The driver's side, the gasoline cap side, was toward the trees.

Garabanda kept his windows up and the air conditioner running, even though it wasn't oppressively hot outside, only in the low eighties. His tinted windows were closed to make it more difficult to see him, in case anyone was watching. He had detected no sign of surveillance as he meandered the two miles from the Field Office to the meeting site. When the new state government's security teams followed him, they were usually clumsy and obvious, following him openly to send a message of intimidation. Today he had detected no tail while conducting his SDR, his surveillance detection run.

The hundred-acre *camposanto* was a refuge for the living as well as the dead, a cool green oasis in a dry and dusty city. The old cemetery was nestled in the southwest corner of Albuquerque's "Big I," the intersection of north-south running Interstate 25, and the east-west Interstate 40. Soaring ribbons of concrete weaved and curled atop colossal pillars only a few hundred yards away on the other side of the trees. The sound of traffic made a steady rumbling background hum. Surface streets and highway access roads ran beneath the "Big I" in all directions, permitting myriad opportunities for ingress and egress from the neighborhoods around the graveyard, for one versed in their intricacies. The FBI often stashed witnesses at several of the nearby chain motels on the other side of I-25, and Alex Garabanda knew the area well.

At 11:15 AM, Luis Carvahal's battered Toyota Celica arrived and slowly passed Garabanda's FBI "bureau car" going in the opposite direction. The men nodded subtle greetings through their windshields. The white Celica drove on a short distance, traveled around a loop in the memorial park's road, then returned and pulled over. Its front bumper was almost touching the back of the Crown Vic.

The two men climbed out of their cars. Garabanda slipped on a black Arizona Diamondbacks ball cap and dark sunglasses; he left his jacket and tie in the Ford. They didn't shake hands, but stood by their respective vehicles.

Carvahal said, "I'm on fumes, I barely made it here. I don't know what I would have done if you hadn't of been here—there's no way I could have made it home. I really appreciate this. Gasoline is liquid gold these days." He was wearing jeans and a navy polo shirt, his curly gray hair was uncovered by any hat.

"No problem," replied Garabanda. "I can fill up on the Air Force base anytime. That way I can keep my accounts square with the office, and not attract any attention from the bean counters. Did you bring the extra jerry cans?"

"I couldn't. I've got a neighbor lady across the street who watches me like a hawk, and she was home today. Hell, she's practically always home. I have a tenant living in my garage now, so I have to park out on the street. Then just when I was getting ready to leave, the old witch came over to ask me about the March for Social Justice. I couldn't load the gas cans in front of her, so I left them behind. I guess maybe I'm getting paranoid in my old age."

"What, is she your 'block captain'?"

"Something like that. Fat little commie bitch! When they get around to organizing 'committees for the defense of the revolution,' she'll be *numero uno* in line. She was the first one in our neighborhood to fly the flag with the star." Flying the modified New Mexico flag with the red star inside of the circle at the center of the Zia design, was a sign of support for the Deleon government and its socialist ideals. The new Zia with the red star was also showing up on bumper stickers, car magnets and ball caps, and of course, it was on the front of the Milicia's brown t-shirts.

"You take what, eleven or twelve gallons?" asked Garabanda.

"Eleven, max."

"Okay, I've got the hose ready, let's do it quick." Garabanda had created his own transfer system from three-quarter-inch clear vinyl hose, and a 12-volt fuel pump, which was wired to a cigarette lighter plug. In a price-controlled economy where there was little of value to purchase with the rapidly inflating Federal Reserve "blue bucks," it was useful to reward informants such as Luis Carvahal with precious gasoline. He ran the hose from his own gas tank and passed the other end to Carvahal, who stuck it into the Toyota's. A long twisted wire led from the small black pump to the 12-volt plug.

When Garabanda stuck the plug into his cigarette lighter the pump began to whine, and orange liquid filled the clear hose. Racing air bubbles showed the direction and speed of the fuel's passage. The hose and small electric pump lay on the asphalt against their tires, shielded from casual view. Even if someone drove past, they would not be able to see the operation in progress. Anyway, in this era of chronic gasoline shortages, "private deals" were common and for the most part accepted as a part of normal life. That is, unless one's staunchly socialist neighbor took a personal interest in your private business.

Garabanda asked, "So, how is El Gobernador? How was Tierra Andalucia? At least both of you made it back."

Tierra Andalucia was a town north of Santa Fe, thirty miles from the Colorado line. For generations the surrounding area had been a flashpoint of anger and confrontation over the lost "Spanish Land Grants." As a part of the 1848 Treaty of Guadalupe Hidalgo ending the Mexican American War, these *mercedes*, or land grants, had been promised in perpetuity to the heirs of the families with grazing and hunting rights on them. During the decades after the signing of the treaty, most of the land grant territory had been lost in swindles, stolen, or was simply absorbed by the U.S. federal government as National Park and National Forest land. The heirs of many of these original New Mexico land grant families had nursed their family resentments across the generations. Now, the more radicalized among them were strongly backing the Deleon "Land Reform Act" in hopes of seeing their land rights restored.

"What can I say about Tierra Andalucia?" said Carvahal. "They're crazy up there, they always have been. Sure, we made it back, but the training camp visits were a disaster for el Gobernador. Magón ran the entire show—it was bad. He made Deleon look so damn old… He didn't disrespect him outright, not in front of the troops, but he made it clear who was the real boss. And it sure wasn't Gobernador Deleon."

"Well shoot, the Mountain Lion *is* old."

"Yeah, and now it's showing. Magón kept the inspecting teams moving fast, and Deleon just couldn't keep up—he was staggering along behind like a Methuselah. Magón's people kept pulling petty stunts like that. It was really a set up—Deleon was suckered. I actually felt sorry for him. Magón was getting the recruits all fired up, strutting around, waving his pistol like Hugo Chavez, giving his 'República Del Norte' speech. You know, 'Aztlan, we have returned!' and all of that crap."

"He must be practicing for Saturday, for the rally," said Garabanda. Although Agustín Deleon and Félix Magón were still nominally members of the Democratic Party, they were also leaders of *Nuestra Raza,* the *Movimiento A Socialismo* and the international *Partido del Ejercito de los Pobres*. This group was the "Party of the Army of the Poor," more commonly referred to as *Los Pepes*. A mass rally was scheduled for Saturday on the Civic Plaza in downtown Albuquerque, and Deleon and Magón were the keynote speakers.

There were rumors that Deleon was going to announce the formation of a new Chicano political party, separate from the Democrats. This new party would run its own slate of candidates for office, candidates dedicated to turning the Southwest into an autonomous region from the Gulf of

Mexico to the Pacific. Their long-standing goal was to see the states of the Southwest form an independent "República Del Norte," which would be closely aligned with other socialist-leaning nations from Mexico to Argentina.

Carvahal said, "I was thinking the same thing: Magón's getting warmed up for the big rally. Rehearsing. And I've got to admit, he's good in front of a crowd. Damn good. When he pulls out his pistol or he starts waving his machete, the troops go wild! Deleon looked so old and tired beside him, it was kind of sad. I rode with Deleon in his Cadillac, but Magón set the agenda, and we just followed him around like puppy dogs. It was the vicegobernador's show all the way."

"Luis, keep an eye on the gas. There's no automatic shutoff."

"I know. I'll be able to hear it when it's almost full."

Garabanda leaned through the open window into his Ford, his hand on the cigarette lighter plug. "Tell me when."

"Just a minute…a little more. Here it comes…a little more…okay—that's it!" Garabanda yanked out the 12-volt plug, but some gasoline still back splashed from the Toyota's gasoline fill, down the side of the car, and onto the ground.

While Garabanda drained the hose, rolled it up and put it away in his trunk, Carvahal said, "Listen, Alex, let's not talk here. There's something I want to show you."

"That's fine. We shouldn't keep our cars together anyway."

"Leave yours here and follow me, okay?" Carvahal climbed back into his Toyota, backed up, and pulled around the Crown Victoria. Garabanda waited until the Toyota was almost out of sight among the shrubs, and followed on foot. The burial ground was almost a mile by a half mile of grass, headstones, monuments, hedges and trees.

They met up again in a more open part of the cemetery, near the old Santa Barbara section on the west side. Carvahal was waiting by a rough-edged granite tombstone. It was pleasantly cool there, in the shade beneath a cottonwood tree.

"Here's my grandmother."

Garabanda read the inscription aloud. "*Davita Ester Flores de Carvahal y Nuñez, 1891-1963.*"

"She was a great woman. The family was never the same after she died."

"Davita Ester…not exactly your typical Spanish Catholic names." Garabanda crouched low by the tombstone, running his fingers over the Spanish inscriptions below the dates. A cascade of flowers was carved under the words.

"No, not exactly Catholic," agreed Luis Carvahal.

"These flowers, in the middle, they remind me of something. I've read about it, but I've never seen it." Garabanda looked up at his friend, then back at the stone monument. "These are Hebrew letters, aren't they? Here in the petals?"

Carvahal hesitated, and said, "Yes, that's what they are. I don't read Hebrew, but I know that one is the letter 'Shesh.' It was a code for the holiest Jewish prayer, the Shema. I guess you've figured it out by now, G-man."

"Your family were crypto-Jews?"

"Yeah, it seems that way. The Carvahals were 'conversos,' Jews who were forced to convert. All the way back in 1492, the same year that the last Moors were pushed out of Spain, and Columbus sailed the ocean blue."

"Only they didn't convert?"

"Only they didn't convert. Well, they did here, outside." Carvahal made a sign of the cross, blessing himself in the Catholic way, and then he pointed to his heart, and tapped his chest with his finger. "But not in here. They kept their Judaism alive, in secret, right down the centuries. The crypto-Jews ran to the furthest ends of the Spanish empire, always trying to stay one step ahead of the Inquisition."

"And this was about as far as they could go."

"That's right. New Mexico was the far frontier, the ragged edge of the empire." Carvahal snorted a small laugh. "Just about like it is today, for America. I guess the more things change…"

Garabanda finished the saying. "…The more they stay the same. But the Inquisition ended hundreds of years ago. Why did they keep it a secret?"

"I don't know. Habit, maybe? The family tradition was to practice the faith in secret, so even when they didn't have to, they still kept the secret. Secrecy became part of the tradition, I guess. And for all that time, our family observed the Sabbath, in the back rooms of our houses with the curtains closed. For five centuries! And we weren't the only ones…we only thought we were. There were probably dozens of crypto-Jewish families in New Mexico, but it's been only in the last years that we've broken out of the secrecy. I was just a little boy when my granny died, but I remember those days. Putting a coded signal on a tombstone was about the limit in those days."

"In a Catholic cemetery," added Garabanda.

"Yes, in a Catholic cemetery. I mean, we were Catholics too, in our way. It was strange growing up—we had a Christmas tree in the front parlor, and a Menorah in the back. We went to Mass, and we kept the Sabbath. But in the end, after she died, I didn't believe in either faith. I lost them both."

"It's a fascinating family history, Luis, but why are you telling me all this? Why now?"

Carvahal exhaled slowly, hands in his blue jean pockets, looking up into the top of a lone Ponderosa pine. "Deleon's trusted me since the old days. You know what a radical fool I was back then!"

"I've seen your COINTELPRO files."

"Todo Por Nuestra Raza—everything by, for and through our race. I bought all that 'brown power' crap, hook line and sinker."

"But you were just a kid, what, in your twenties?"

"Right. Just a kid, fresh out of college. Ready to save the world, to right all the wrongs, with my journalism degree and my brand new Smith-Corona. Anyway, Deleon liked what I wrote about him. I got the only interviews from him when he was a fugitive in the mountains, and later when he was in exile in Mexico. He always trusted me, and I always liked him, as a man. Crazy as a bed bug, I know that now, but he was a real man! And such charisma, such a natural leader you never saw! Then, after my politics changed, after I grew up you might say, he still came to me. As a reporter for the Herald, I was always fair to him, even when he was in jail. And now, all these years later, he came to me to be his scribe, to ghostwrite his memoirs, even though I'm not the same radical jerk he befriended 35 years ago. Far from it."

"But that old personal connection is still enough to get you access inside of the new government."

"Sometimes. Like on this trip to Tierra Andalucia. I just stay in the background, I don't participate, but they speak freely around me. I'm trusted. And you wouldn't believe what they say, you just wouldn't believe it! That's why I contacted you in the first place, and that's why I brought you here today, to show you this grave marker. Understand Alex, I'm not an observant Jew. I haven't been, really, not since my grand mother died back when I was a little kid. I couldn't juggle two religions, and my own father and mother didn't care much either way. So I just dropped them both. But inside, I guess I always understood that I was a Jew. I even had the genetic test done."

"I've got it, your family was Jewish. Is this leading to something?"

"Yes! Be patient Alex, this isn't easy for me. It's my life, and I have nobody else to confide in, nobody! Anyway, the new government …they're unbelievably anti-Semitic. It just oozes out of them. I can't explain it, other than they're 'red fascists.' It's the old *Nuestra Raza* gang, and the 'Sword of Aztlan' maniacs. It's all about race to them: race and ideology. They're really into something they call *etnogeopoliticos*—ethnogeopolitics. They're not just harmless old Santa Fe hippies, like they think up in Washington. They're not just 'New Agers' doing the peace and love thing, with a little socialism-lite on the side. They're hard core!"

Carvahal was agitated, the words spilling out in the presence of the one man he trusted. "The state government is full of committed Marxists, I mean real live communists, and you know how the commies were always in sync with the Middle Eastern terrorists. Now they call the Southwest their 'Palestine', they call it 'occupied territory.' When they say they plan to reconquer Aztlan by any means necessary, they're comparing it to Palestine and Israel. They're talking about using terrorism to get what they want, if that's what it takes. And man, they sure brought over that old-time Jew hatred. There's even a training camp just for Muslims, north of the town of Española. Dar al Harb, it's called—the House of War. That was the one camp we didn't visit, but the word is that the graduates from Dar al Harb aren't staying in New Mexico—they're heading north."

"You didn't get any pictures, did you?"

"No, that's just what I heard them talking about when we drove past the place. I couldn't have pulled a camera out, and anyway, a picture would have just shown trees."

Garabanda sighed. "And now these Aztlan lunatics are running New Mexico."

"It's amazing. Even they can't believe it. They can't believe they're in power. And I'm not even talking about the 'Old New Mexicans' either, far from it. The 'Old New Mexicans' are some of the most loyal Americans in the state—it's not them, it's all the illegals! Probably a half million of them are illegals—or they were. But now they all have ID's, they all have New Mexico driver's licenses, and they damned sure all vote straight Democrat."

"What a bunch of suckers we were, for so long…"

"You know Alex, I guess we should have seen it coming. I mean, looking back, it was all so predictable! The New Mexico Democrats thought it was all up-side political gain for their party, letting the illegals vote. Hell, that's what 'motor voter' was all about, right? No photo ID's being needed to register to vote, all of that. Even at the Herald, illegal alien voter fraud was always off limits. Every 'undocumented worker' crossing the border was going to be another good little Democratic Party voter, so why rock the boat? Legal, illegal, what's the difference? Anybody with a pulse could vote in New Mexico, and half of the dead in these graveyards voted too! And that's how it worked, for years and years.

"But then it started to change. The illegals became a voting bloc, and then they became THE voting bloc. They took over the state party. The tail grew stronger than the dog! Almost every year there was another amnesty. The federal government just couldn't resist, so every year there were more amnesties, and more 'citizens' were made out of illegals. And that's when the flood gates really opened up, and the momentum became unstoppable."

Garabanda said, "I remember. They were holding those mass swearing-in ceremonies every week in sports arenas like The Pit at the university. Five thousand at a time, all in Spanish. Raise your right hands, and become instant citizens. Sign your voter registration card on the way out."

"Yeah. I guess the Democratic Party thought they could have a steady flow of new voters coming across the border, just enough to keep control of state politics. But sometimes trickles become floods, and floods don't always stop where you want them to, do they? They develop their own dynamic—and sometimes they just wash away the old riverbed. They carve their own new channel, like the Mississippi. And that's what happened in New Mexico, once the flood of illegals became unstoppable."

"Completely unstoppable," agreed Alex Garabanda. "And then came Ortiz."

"Yeah, Ortiz sealed the deal. Whammo! Sixteen million brand new illegal alien voters."

"With five anchor babies each."

"At least," agreed Carvahal.

"Who could argue against 'no taxation without representation'?"

"Not the Supreme Court, that's for sure."

Fernando Ortiz was an undocumented "landscape engineer" who had demanded the right to vote, on the basis that he had been paying state and federal taxes for ten years, while living and working on Long Island. Actually, he had been stopped from casting a ballot by an alert poll watcher who had suspected his citizenship status, and (illegally, as it turned out) demanded proof of his identity and legal qualification to vote. Ortiz won a multi-million dollar settlement against the Republican Party of New York in the subsequent "racial profiling and ethnic intimidation" civil suit, but he did not stop there.

Instead, with massive support from various Hispanic "immigrants' rights" groups and other left-leaning foundations, he had pressed his demand to vote all the way to the Supreme Court…and he had won. The Supreme Court, in its famous 5-4 decision, ruled that negligence in securing America's borders against illegal immigration on the part of the federal government, could not be held against "undocumented workers who played by the rules and paid their taxes," once they were established in America—legally or not. The State of New York had sleepwalked through an aimless and desultory case for denying the vote—and citizenship—to "undocumented workers."

Following Ortiz v. New York, a stunned America woke up to discover that there were not only an amazing forty million illegal aliens hiding in plain sight across the land, but that sixteen million of them immediately qualified to vote. In a nation split 50-50 down party and ideological lines, these sixteen million brand-new voters were recognized to be the certain majority-makers in future elections. Both parties immediately set record lows for cravenness in pandering to their perceived "needs." Chief among their "needs" were liberal new family reunification laws, and these instant citizens—illegal aliens only the year before—began bringing the remainders of their families to the USA.

Over night, wavering Democrat states became locks, and swing states with large Hispanic populations went solidly "blue." The result was the recent election, which had swept Gobernador Deleon to power in Nuevo Mexico, and had also brought radical Democrats to power in the White House and both houses of Congress.

Thus came the political tsunami that swept all before it, a tidal wave triggered by a mere pebble, an undocumented lawn maintenance worker named Fernando Ortiz.

Carvahal continued with his history of political upheaval in New Mexico. It was a subject that consumed him, yet he rarely had an opportunity to share his passion. The former newspaper reporter burned for a receptive audience for his stories, and today, Alex Garabanda was it. "Meanwhile, at the same time, more and more Anglos began to feel unwelcome down here, threatened even, and they began to leave the state in droves. They were voting with their feet, until that became another flood—leaving! And the Anglos took a lot of the tax base with them when they went, which sure didn't help. Our demographic tilt kept gaining momentum from both sides, and as it did, the politics became more and more openly socialist. Just look at where the new voters were coming from—socialism was all they knew! Now we're practically a little Venezuela, on our way to becoming the next Cuba."

Garabanda said, "Believe me, I'm familiar with how ethnic politics works. I've been living it too, in a way. FBI Headquarters thought that just because I have a Hispanic name, I'd be perfect for 'Nuevo Mexico.' It's the federal version of '*etnogeopoliticos*,' only they call it 'multi-culturalism.' I mean, I speak terrible Spanish, and anyway, my father was Cuban, and my mother is Italian. As if Cuba and New Mexico have one damn thing in common, other than Spanish names on the maps! But to FBI headquarters, an Hispanic is an Hispanic, whether he's a blue-eyed Basque from Northern Spain, a *mestizo* Indian from Peru, or a black Dominican. To the FBI, Hispanic is Hispanic is Hispanic! It's just crazy!

"Hell, my own father was first-generation Cuban, but he sent me to military boarding schools in Virginia when I was a kid, just so I'd grow up thinking and speaking in English, 'like a real American' he said! He just wanted to make me a regular 'un-hyphenated American,' which is what I am. But then the FBI flipped it all back around on me. The FBI considers me just another Hispanic on their ethnic diversity chart, all because of my last name! 'Oh, Garabanda, why don't you go on down to New Mexico? They're *your people*, you'll fit right in.' My people? Hello? Uh…no offense, Luis."

"None taken. I know what you're saying."

"And now the same FBI Headquarters is telling us to look the other way, while the Milicia is terrorizing the state with M-16 rifles! It just makes no sense; it's making me completely crazy! Those Marxist Aztlan lunatics have hundreds of fully automatic M-16 rifles from God knows where, and my bosses could care less!"

"Not hundreds, Al. Thousands."

"What? Thousands? How do you know that?"

Carvahal answered, "I heard Vicegobernador Magón's staff talking about the rifles, when we were up in the training camps. They're from Belen."

"There's a big national guard armory at Belen."

"Yeah. That's where the rifles are from. I'm not sure who approved it, but the rifles are coming right out of the armory there. They're not stolen, or bought on the black market or coming from south of the border. They're surplus government property, being turned over to the Milicia."

"Damn… You know… Aw, crap. I should have figured as much," said Garabanda, disgustedly shaking his head while looking at the ground. "So the federal government, my government, our government…is arming the Milicia. Shit. Oh, shit…" He sighed deeply, one hand on top of the gravestone, leaning against it for support. "You know, ordinarily, we'd investigate something like this as a major theft of government property. I mean, the Bureau and the ATF, man oh man! We'd be all over a redneck militia in Alabama that had even a couple of fully automatic weapons. Or semi-autos, for that matter. It'd be SWAT City, Waco time! But I've already been told to back off, and stay away from the Milicia de Nuevo Mexico. Period—end of story."

"So the federal government is either totally brain dead and unaware of what's going on down here…"

"Oh, they're aware of it," Garabanda interjected. "They're not only letting it happen, they're obviously facilitating it, if they're passing out rifles. So they know what's going on."

Carvahal was equally disgusted. "They're basically neo-communists up in Santa Fe, and Washington is helping them get a foothold in the United States. Helping them! No wonder Wayne Parker feels so at home here," he said bitterly.

"Wayne Parker always was a commie-loving son of a bitch," said Garabanda. "He made his first billions trading with the Soviets, and now he's into Chinese factories up to his eyeballs."

"That's nothing new," added Carvahal. "It's just like Armand Hammer, cutting deals with Lenin and Stalin. Or like Peter Kosimos today. He comes to America, becomes a citizen, makes billions of dollars speculating on currencies—and then he gets into bed with the Red Chinese. One thing I'll never understand is how billionaires like Wayne Parker and Peter Kosimos can turn around and shaft their own country."

Garabanda replied, "Wayne Parker owns almost a million acres up in Torcido County, and I'm sure he doesn't want it taken away under the Land Reform Act. You just know he's cutting deals with the state to hang onto his ranch."

"No Alex, it's beyond that, it's not just simple greed. He's a one-worlder, just like Kosimos. A true believer—it might as well be his religion. He's donated billions of dollars of his own money to the U.N., for God's sake! Governor Deleon says that Parker is going to 'donate' most of the Vedado Ranch to the World Conservancy Group. Of course, he'll get to stay on, as the 'manager'."

"Of course," agreed the FBI man. "So his ranch is the perfect place to hold this little meeting next week. The one you told me about in the Toy Hut."

"Oh, the Vedado Ranch is totally perfect for secret meetings," said Carvahal. "It has its own jet runway, and miles and miles of privacy. The next President of Mexico will be there, and so will U.S. Senators from both parties."

"Has the governor mentioned what the meeting's agenda is going to be yet, or any more of the guests who are coming?"

"No, he's still out of the loop—Magón is still running the show behind his back. Deleon just knows what Senator Kelly told him on the phone."

"Thank God that Ed Kelly is such a drunken idiot," said Garabanda. "So what do you think the meeting's going to be about?"

Luis Carvahal, paused, gathering his thoughts. "Well, I'm guessing it's about a new federal status for New Mexico, and maybe for the whole Southwest. They wouldn't be hosting the conference in New Mexico, if there wasn't something in it for Santa Fe. Wide open borders, for sure. I mean, that's already a given. Probably the right for New Mexico to control its own 'immigration policy,' without any interference from the feds. Maybe some kind of 'autonomous region' set up, so they can loot the state and not have to worry about any federal investigations. Maybe they'll get to stop paying federal taxes, like Puerto Rico. And they'll probably send you feds packing, any way you look at it."

"Then say goodbye to America, and hello to Aztlan," Garabanda replied sarcastically. "But hey, what's the big deal about America keeping all fifty states, if we're just going to be a region of the North American Community anyway? You just know the new Constitution is going to sell us down the river. Luis, I've been thinking about this a lot, ever since the Toy Hut. I think the Vedado Ranch meeting is going to be about more than just the Southwest. I think it's going to be the 'private convention' before the public Constitutional Convention—but it'll be the one that really counts. Kind of like the secret Jekyll Island meeting in 1913, before Congress passed the Federal Reserve Act. You know about that scam, right?"

"Jekyll Island?" answered Carvahal. "Oh sure, I know about it. Hey, I'm an historian now, not just a reporter. 'The Creature from Jekyll Island' is probably the most important economic history of the 20th century ever written, even if almost nobody ever heard of it. That was when J. P. Morgan had all of the big New York bankers and some crooked Senators sneak down to his place in Georgia to set up the Federal Reserve. Then they had their paid-for Congressmen rubberstamp it in Washington."

"Right, that's exactly what happened," agreed Garabanda, pleased that his informant was familiar with this little-known episode in American history. "Only this meeting won't just be about letting the bankers print all the funny money they want. I mean, Jekyll Island was bad enough, look where that got us in the end—a ruined economy, and worthless blue bucks! No, this is going to be even worse, a lot worse. I think this Vedado Ranch meeting is about the big prize—the new Constitution."

13

The Falcons' pickups and SUVs parked along the dirt road behind the rifle range. The troops took their M-16s, magazines and ammunition and set them on the shooting tables, two rifles to a table, their barrels pointing down range.

Comandante Ramos told Ranya that he'd be back in a few minutes, and she should wait in the Suburban. With the windows of the Suburban down to let the morning breeze pass through, she watched the hundred men gather by the tables. There was nobody guarding her, nobody near her at all. Nonetheless, she knew that there was zero chance of successfully escaping now, even if the driver had left the keys in the Suburban's ignition, which he had not. How could she outrun a hundred men armed with rifles, pursuing her in a dozen other vehicles?

Ranya briefly entertained the fantasy of finding the keys in another unwatched truck, then sabotaging all of the other vehicles and driving off in a cloud of dust…but she quickly discarded the idea. She was ten miles west of Albuquerque, in a God-forsaken land where you could spot rolling tumbleweeds a mile away. There was nowhere for her to run that they could not easily catch her, so Ranya had to accept that her best opportunity this morning lay in establishing her trustworthiness. She could be left unguarded in a vehicle, and she would not run off. If her guards learned this lesson today, it would be enough. The next time that they left her alone, she might be able to suddenly escape and disappear.

So she waited and she watched. Assembled behind the line of shooting tables were one hundred lean troops in brown t-shirts and camouflage pants. One hundred brown berets, one hundred pins flashing silver in the New Mexico morning sunlight. One hundred ardent faces turned to their leader.

"Falcons! *Primer Sargento* Ramirez will be in charge today while you adjust the sights of your rifles. He has done this many times in the Mexican Army, in the *Grupo Aeromóvil de Fuerzas Especiales*. Listen to him, and this job will be done quickly and efficiently. Do your very best, because the ten riflemen with the highest qualifying scores will then compete in a separate championship. I will be here for the contest, to award the prizes. All ten finalists will win a telescopic sight that fits onto their rifle's carrying handle. These optical sights provide four power magnification, and they have an illuminated crosshair for shooting at night. The ten best marksmen will also be given special consideration for promotion, and for a position in the Zeta Squad."

Ramos paused for dramatic effect, and then he said, "In addition, as a special reward, the three shooters with the highest scores will also win Canadian Maple Leaf coins. They each weigh 31 grams, or one solid ounce of gold!" Ramos held a gleaming golden disc aloft, where it caught the sun. "Three of the golden coins will go to the winner. Two will be given for second place, and one for third. They were 'liberated' from rich Anglos, and there are many more where they came from, if you will fight with me for *La Liberación*!"

At this offering of rewards, the hundred Falcons began to shout and cheer, and many cried out that the golden coins would soon be theirs!

However, Ramos did not finish with the mention of the prizes. "And the bottom ten shooters will run the La Luz trail tomorrow morning, to pay for their sins! All the way to the top of the Sandia Mountain! If they cannot shoot straight, by God at least they will be able to run fast!"

His men burst out in raucous guffaws and laughter, and many picked up a chant of "Che! Che! Che!"

Ramos allowed them to cheer and call his nickname and whistle for a few moments, and then held up his palms to them, quieting them back down. "Now, some of you may be concerned that these rifles are not powerful enough, because they fire only the small 5.56mm bullet. Some of you say that the M-16 will only make a wound like an ice pick, and that you must shoot your enemy many times to kill him. Well, stop worrying. Chino, get the dog."

Chino, taller than average and with the narrower eyes of the half-Asian, was one of Ramos's personal bodyguards from the *Escuadra Zeta*. They were distinguishable by their tan combat vests, while the rest of the Falcons were wearing green web belts and H-harnesses over their brown Milicia t-shirts. Each web belt held four green pouches on the front, enough for twelve magazines. Some of the men had short military-length haircuts, but others, particularly the Zetas, had longer hair showing beneath their berets, in emulation of the Falcon leader whom they admiringly called Che.

Ranya observed the group, looking for their officers and noncoms. She could not see any distinguishing stripes or chevrons, but she did notice that some of the older and taller troops wore camouflage blouses that matched their trousers, instead of brown t-shirts. Several of this group had made the trip to the range with her in Ramos's Suburban. These men did not have on H-harnesses, but only web belts with holstered pistols. They must be the leaders, she mused. Good socialists, they were eschewing overt symbols of rank. Nevertheless, all Indians need chiefs…and for an officer, the pistol is the ultimate symbol of authority. Not to fire at the enemy in battle, so much as to potentially use against one's own disobedient or cowardly subordinates.

Ramos's bodyguard led a limping mongrel pit bull from the back of a pickup truck onto the range, and tied its leash to a wooden target frame 15 yards from the shooting tables. It was obvious that the brown and white bulldog had placed second in a recent fight. The troops all turned to watch the animal on the other side of the range tables.

The stout dog panted in the sun, oblivious to its fate. Chino returned to the closest shooting table and picked up an M-16, inserted a magazine, charged it, shouldered it and aimed at the doomed creature. A hundred pairs of eyes flickered between the shooter and his living target.

A single shot was fired, and the dog collapsed onto its side, without making so much as a twitch or a growl. A shower of blood and tissue was visible on the bare dirt beyond its body, while a dark pool spread beneath the dead canine and soaked into the ground. The bodyguard placed the rifle down on the table and trotted back out, grabbed the dog by two legs and rolled it over to expose the gaping wound. A ragged exit channel the size of a fist had been blasted from the dog's right side. The hundred Falcons crowded around the shooting tables, studying the terminal effects of the bullet, murmuring approval to one another with keen professional interest.

Ramos continued with his pep talk, and his troops turned around to face him again. "Men, in all of Nuevo Mexico, only the *Batallón Halcón* has this new ammunition. It's specially made for the gringo anti-terrorist units—it's the best stuff around. The bullets are very light, and very fast. They'll go straight through armored glass and soft body armor, but when they hit a person, watch out! The bullets aren't solid. They're made of compressed powdered metals inside of a copper jacket, and when they strike flesh, they explode, as you have just seen. So don't worry that you'll have to shoot these big fat gringo ranchers three or four times with your M-16s to kill them! With this new ammunition, our motto will be: one *cartucho*—one cowboy!"

The men burst into peals of laughter once again.

"Make no mistake: we are going to drive the *Yanqui* oppressors from this sacred land! And after we set the example and push them out of Nuevo Mexico, then our brothers will push them out of Alta California, out of Arizona and Texas, and out of all of the Indo-Hispano territory of Aztlan! We will drive the dough-faced *gabacho* settlers from all of the rightful lands of our fathers! No longer will our undocumented brothers and sisters from the south be forced to cut the gringos' lawns and clean their toilets, smiling and groveling, while burning inside with humiliation!"

Ramos gestured broadly with his hands and arms, shaking his head. "No, instead we will burn the shameful treaty of Guadalupe Hidalgo, which was signed by sold-out Mexican *vendidos* at gunpoint! We will end the illegal *Yanqui* occupation of our land, and create a new *República del*

Norte, based on socialist principles of equality for all! We will begin new lives as free men, free from *Yanqui* imperialist domination forever! In time, this rich new Indo-Hispano nation will extend from the *Golfo de Mexico* to the *Mar Pacífico*, and the world will not be able to ignore us! We will take our rightful place at the world's table at last! So my Falcons, I ask you, what do we fight for? We fight to throw off the heavy yoke of *Yanqui* oppression! We fight for our own place under the sun, we fight for respect, and we fight for a free land in America! Men, we fight for... *Tierra y Libertad!*"

"*¡Tierra y Libertad!*" the troops roared the slogan in unison.

"Men, I can't hear you! What do we fight for?"

"*¡TIERRA Y LIBERTAD!*" was screamed from a hundred throats like a clap of thunder.

"Men, the *Batallón Halcón* will be growing rapidly in the coming months. Each squad will become the basis of a new platoon, until we are at full battalion strength. But I know that you all understand that we must not sacrifice quality for quantity, so this process will take some time. In the meantime, however, we have several critically important missions before us. First, none of us has forgotten the bloody *matanza* on the bus. We will never forget nor forgive this massacre of our brother Milicianos! Friday, we will begin to exact our just revenge for this unprovoked atrocity!"

The Falcons erupted again in screams and whistles.

"Then on Saturday, we will provide security and carry out special missions during the March for Social Justice. And next week, we will be providing security for an important meeting that concerns the future of Nuevo Mexico, and all of the stolen lands of Aztlan. This meeting will include foreign leaders, as well as important gringos who are secretly on our side in the struggle. The success of this conference will be vital to the future of a free and independent Nuevo Mexico, so we must continue to train hard, and operate at the very highest level. That's why we must make sure that our new rifles are as accurate as possible. We are the vanguard of the *revolución* in Nuevo Mexico, and if we fail, all of the hopes of our people might be crushed. So today, let every man shoot with the sharp eyes and the unerring aim of a Falcon!

"*Primer Sargento* Ramirez will direct the sighting-in of your new rifles. Remember: the ten best sharpshooters will win valuable prizes and the ten worst will run the Sandia Mountain trail tomorrow, to the very top! Now, *Primer Sargento* Ramirez, carry out your orders!"

Ramos stepped back away from the group, turned smartly and strode to his left. Ramirez stepped toward the troops and bellowed out, "*¡Pe-le-tones!*" Five of the leaders Ranya had identified stepped forward from the mob at even intervals. Platoons of about twenty men immediately formed into neatly ordered groups behind each of the leaders. The troops stood at rigid attention, their backs to the shooting tables and the range. A smaller group, all wearing the tan combat vests of Ramos's personal bodyguard detail, were formed up on the left of the platoons. Ramos walked past his Zeta Squad and said, "Chino and Genizaro—let's go. We have a different job today."

While First Sergeant Ramirez barked out his instructions, Ramos and his two picked men walked back to the black Suburban.

They drove a short distance away from the rifle range, the two bodyguards in front, Ranya and Basilio Ramos in the middle seat. The land here was less than perfectly flat, and they stopped with a low rise between themselves and the rest of the *Batallón Halcón*, well off to the side of the rifle range. The Suburban was parked by a pair of picnic tables in the shade between two oak trees. Forty miles to the west, the peak of the 11,000-foot tall Mount Taylor was visible above the dry plain.

The two Zetas carried seven hard and soft rifle cases from the back of the SUV, and then began opening them and carefully laying the rifles on the table parallel to one another. Five of the rifles had gleaming hardwood stocks; two were stocked with black synthetic material. All seven had long black telescopic sights mounted on top of their receivers.

Ranya and the Comandante stood by the table, studying the weapons.

"You know what happened to the bus, Monday morning?" he asked.

"I heard about it. Fascist snipers ambushed a bus carrying Milicianos, somewhere east of Albuquerque, on the other side of the mountains. The enemy snipers killed many of them."

"Yes, that's right. Twenty-two Milicianos were killed, and eight more were wounded. The *Yanquis* stopped the bus with a bullet through the engine, probably from a fifty-caliber rifle. The Milicianos were unable to return effective fire, so they could not stop the gringos from killing them, one at a time. They were as helpless as babies to defend themselves from the long-range snipers, so they died. And that's not the only time that fascist snipers have hurt us—the bus massacre was only their most recent atrocity. That's why it's so important for the regular Milicianos to receive proper rifle training, and of course, that is why it's even more important for our Falcon Battalion. We have a very important mission next week, and we need to be ready, all of us."

Chino carried what looked like gym bags from the truck, and placed them on the table. From the nylon zipper-top bags, he removed small cardboard and plastic boxes of cartridges, and set them by each rifle, corresponding with their calibers. Though half Asian he was tall, six feet or so, with a shaved head beneath his beret. The other bodyguard, Genizaro, was shorter but more powerfully built. He had the straight black hair and profile of an Indian, but the light skin color and gray-blue eyes of a northern European. Acne pits and several knife-fighting scars had ravaged his face. Both men had blue tattoos on their arms: indecipherable calligraphy, symbols and numerals. Chino had additional tattoos on his neck, and tear drops beneath the corners of his eyes.

An old term jumped into Ranya's mind: halfbreed. Both Chino and Genizaro were half-and-halfs, but they could not have been more different in appearance. In contrast, Basilio Ramos appeared to be 100% European. Yet here were all three of them, fighting for a common Hispanic homeland. And here am I, she thought—ethnically Arab, born in America, and raised Catholic. A Christian Arab—another misfit.

Ramos continued, while Ranya looked over the weapons. "But I've also considered what you said about the Zeta Squad's short carbines, about how they are no good at long range. I want some of my men always to be ready to shoot back at the gringo snipers. Even our new M-16 rifles won't be enough, not when the gringos are shooting their big guns."

"You're asking me to train the Falcon Battalion's counter-snipers?"

"Yes, counter-snipers for my *Escuadra Zeta*. To begin with, I want you to teach these two *Camaradas* to be my personal counter-snipers, in case we are attacked from long range. I want you to sight-in all of these rifles, and then I want you to pick the very best of them. After that, I want you to show Chino and Genizaro how to shoot them."

"Well, I'm sorry, but it's not as simple as that! Being a sniper is more than just a matter of aiming a rifle and pulling the trigger. Firing the rifle is only one part of sniping. It takes many weeks just to learn the basic skills a sniper needs, and I'm hardly qualified to teach that course of instruction."

"Yes, I'm sure you're right, but for now I only need these two men to be able to shoot very well, with the best of these rifles."

"Whose rifles are they?" she asked innocently.

"They are mine—I mean—they belong to the state now, to the people. They were confiscated from gringos, on their ranches and at road blocks."

"What crimes did they commit?" she asked with an earnest expression.

"What crimes? What crimes did they commit? Why, they had sniper rifles! Just look at them: every single one of these rifles has a telescopic sight on top. All sniper rifles have been illegal for years now, if you hadn't heard while you were away. So, which ones are the best?"

"The best for what? For out here on the flatlands, in the mountains, in the city?"

"Well, for all of that. For shooting enemy snipers, before they can shoot at the leaders of our government." The two bodyguards snickered at this remark. "Can you find the best ones, and sight them in today? Right now? Say at…200 meters?"

"Sure, that's no problem. You'll want to get bipods, and mount them under the front of the rifle stocks. Most of the time, your snipers will be shooting from…" Ranya searched for the words in Spanish. "From the prone position, laying down on the ground. Bipods will make the rifles steadier, and much more accurate."

"Yes, of course. We can get bipods."

"But Comandante, why at that distance? Why at 200 meters? That's too close, I think. These are rifles for hunting big game animals. Elk, moose, brown bears…" She checked the calibers of the weapons, stamped on their receivers. "You only want to keep the ones that are very high velocity, the ones that will shoot with a flat trajectory. Forget these two—they're too slow. They'll shoot like a rainbow at long range. Now these are better: you have a 300 Winchester Magnum, a .338 Lapua here, this one's a 7mm Remington Magnum…keep them. This .308's not bad either, and match grade ammunition is easier to find for a .308. You know that .308 caliber is basically the same as 7.62 NATO, right?"

"Yes, of course I knew that," replied the Comandante, sounding less than certain.

"Well then, okay, these four are a good start. These are all serious rifles, and so are their scopes. My father used to build custom rifles like these. Today we'll find out which are the most accurate among the four, with the ammunition that we have."

Ranya picked up and shouldered each rifle in turn, hefting them, looking through their scopes, working their bolts with her right hand. "These are all fine for what you want. I think that these can hit a man at a thousand meters if you have match-grade ammunition, but we'll need to shoot them to know for sure. But we should sight them in at 400 meters, or even 500. That way, your counter-snipers will only have to make a smaller elevation correction, if they need to shoot at very long range. If somebody is shooting at you from 800 or 1,000 meters, your rifles need to be set up to get right on them fast. In my opinion, 200 meters is too close to zero-in these rifles."

"No, I think 200 meters is better for now," said Ramos. "I don't think it's likely that our counter-snipers will have to shoot past 500 yards, so let's zero them in at 200 meters. It's more realistic for my men. Maybe later you can train them to be better marksmen, at longer ranges."

"Well, it's not usually how this is done. That's all I'm saying." She caught herself: why was she actively helping these men to become better snipers? To ingratiate herself with Basilio Ramos, and to gain his trust, of course. Even then, there had to be limits to her assistance. She just didn't know where the limits were.

"But you can do it, can't you? Sight them in so that they'll hit precisely where the crosshairs are aimed, 200 yards away?"

"Yes, of course I can do it, if that's what you think is best, Comandante."

There was the sound of a shrill whistle blast from over the rise, which was immediately swallowed by the much louder sound of a solid fusillade of rifle fire. The unbroken volley from one hundred M-16's tapered off after a few seconds, then regained its full volume, tapered off and rose again, and then died off, the final bursts finishing suddenly with another whistle blast. The three men and Ranya grinned at one another.

The Falcon Battalion had just test-fired and broken-in their "new" thirty-year-old rifles, with three magazines each, just as she had suggested. These nine thousand rounds had also been fired as a morale-boosting "mad minute" for the Falcons, demonstrating to them the fearsomeness of their combined firepower.

It also boosted Ranya's confidence, to know that Ramos and his battalion were accepting her advice. She smiled back across the table at them and she said, "Well, those old M-16s aren't virgins anymore," and they laughed with her, nodding approval at their Arab rifle expert Ranya Bardiwell, *la ejecutora*, the executioner.

"Now," she said, "Let's forget those M-16s, those little dog shooters. Let's see what some real rifles can do."

As a security precaution, the battalion left the range by an alternate route, returning to the city from the northwest. The convoy was preceded by a scout vehicle driving a mile ahead: a small gray pickup truck with four troops keeping a low profile in the back. In keeping with Ramos's personal preference from previous conflicts in other countries, it had a radio call sign named for a dangerous creature, in this case "Scorpion."

After five miles, the two-lane blacktop made a right turn to the east and ran ruler-straight back towards Albuquerque. The convoy only rarely passed a private sedan or work truck on these barren high desert outskirts of the city. Ramos's black Suburban was once again embedded in the middle of the column.

For the return trip, Ranya arranged to be sitting against the passenger side door of the middle seat, staring out through the armored glass while the others spoke in rapid Spanish, discussing the day's training evolutions. Often it was too fast for her to follow.

"*Primer Sargento*, I think it went well," said Ramos. "I was pleasantly surprised to see that most of the men qualified at the expert level. You've done a fine job of training them."

"Thank you sir. All they needed were good rifles."

"Well, they seem to be satisfied with them."

"Yes sir, especially with the new ammunition. The rifles shoot very well, that's true, and we want the men to be confident with them. But even so Comandante, out here in this kind of open country, the M-16's are marginal at best. Even with the special ammunition, we'll be outranged. The fact is, past a few hundred meters, the 5.56mm is just too light to do much damage, and the desert winds will push the bullet off target. We really need to get some serious battle rifles—7.62mm rifles. If there is any way we could obtain M-14s from the same armories which supplied the M-16s, well, that would be very beneficial."

"M-14's? With the wooden stocks? They're even older than our M-16s."

"That's true, but it doesn't matter. They can hit targets much farther away than our rifles, and with a much heavier bullet. Old or not, they'd be better for us in the plains and the mountains. This is not like the jungle fighting you were accustomed to in South America."

"Hmm… I see your point, *Primer Sargento*. I'll pass your request up the chain, but I don't know if we'll be able to get them, or not. I don't even know if such rifles as these M-14's are available."

"And some real machine guns, belt-fed machine guns, to protect our vehicles. I don't have to tell you how vulnerable we are, with the troops in unarmored vehicles."

"Belt-fed machine guns will have to wait. For now, M-16s are all we will be allowed to use. It's a delicate balance…a matter of appearances. It's a political matter."

"*¡Malditos políticos!* It's always the politics over the soldiers! When I hear that, I want to line those politicians up against a wall!"

Ramos laughed, as did the other men in the vehicle. "I understand how you feel, *Primer Sargento*. I feel the same way, at least ten times a day. I'll keep pushing for heavier weapons, but you know how the politicians are. *Pendejos políticos*, all of them."

"Well even if we can't get better weapons, we should look into armoring more of our vehicles. It's simple enough to put steel plates inside the backs of the trucks. The extra weight will slow them somewhat, but on balance, armor is…"

The ceiling-mounted radio above Ramos crackled with sudden urgency, and he grabbed the microphone from its clip.

"Falcon leader, this is Scorpion, we're taking fire…"

Immediately another voice came over the radio: "What the hell? Falcon Leader, this is Falcon 1, we've been hit! We've been hit!" Falcon 1 was a Dodge crew cab pickup, the first vehicle in the actual column, not counting the scout far out ahead.

Ramos grabbed his radio and spoke into it. "Scorpion, Scorpion, report, over?"

"Falcon leader, this is Falcon 1—Scorpion is off the road, it's rolled over, it's on its back, on its back, over!"

"Falcon 1, this is Falcon Leader, do you have casualties, over?"

"Negative, no casualties."

All of the men and Ranya slid down in their seats as they passed the area where the first vehicle in the column had taken fire moments before. They were already nearing the location of the overturned advance scout. "Falcon 1—keep going, keep pushing, let's get up there!" Next Ramos contacted their on-call Piper Supercub, call sign *Avispa*, or wasp. "*Avispa*, *Avispa*, do you read me? Get airborne, we have contact on Paradise Road, one mile east of the turn, over."

"Falcon Leader, this is *Avispa*. We're rolling now; we will be over your location in five minutes."

"Roger *Avispa*—Break—Scorpion, do you read me?"

There was no reply from the scout vehicle. The front of the column was drawing even with the wreckage.

"Falcon 1, cover Scorpion from the front and take care of his casualties—we're going ahead. All forward vehicles, stay out of the left lane, we're going past you." In the black Suburban, Ramos said, "Get down everybody; we're going to swing into the front."

They passed the overturned gray Toyota pickup that had been their scout vehicle at 60 miles per hour, traveling in the oncoming lane. Falcon 1, the point vehicle of the column, had stopped in front of the scout, which was lying wheels-up in the ditch on the right side of the road.

They briefly noted bodies on the road and the shoulder as they blasted by, the rest of the convoy following close behind them, swerving and barely missing colliding with the vehicles that had stopped to render aid to the scouts. They all hunkered down low, fully expecting to hear and feel bullets tearing into the Suburban, wondering if its three-inch-thick Lexan front windshield would stop rifle slugs. Even the driver was down so low, that he was peeking out from the level of his steering wheel.

Ramos spoke into his radio and to the passengers in his own truck at the same time. "Okay, get ready, get ready to stop, we're pulling off to the right, keep control everybody, drivers, both sides, contact front, okay now, STOP!"

The black Suburban braked and hit the shoulder at a slight angle, tearing through the dirt and creosote bushes and bouncing off the rocks, negotiating the transition from asphalt to scrubland and sliding to a halt in a thick cloud of dust at a 45 degree angle away from the road. As soon as the Suburban was halted, the passengers leaped out of the right side and rear doors with their weapons. Ranya went to the open back doors of the Suburban and pulled out a rifle case, they were still loaded from the range for this type of contingency. She grabbed a tan range bag and crouched behind the SUV's back wheels near the shoulder of the road, where she could see straight up the pavement. In a moment the .300 Winchester Magnum was uncased, its gleaming black barrel lying across the range bag for support, and then she was prone on the dirt behind the rifle and seeking the enemy sniper through her own scope.

On both sides of the road, the other vehicles had disgorged their troops. They were kneeling or sitting with their rifles across their knees for support where the grass and weeds were taller, or lying prone where there was less cover. The riflemen with their M-16s began laying down suppressing fire, peppering likely enemy hiding places ahead of them. Some of the Falcons on the forward perimeter were in Ranya's likely line of fire, but she saw no enemy targets and thus had no reason to shoot.

Comandante Ramos was standing hunched over behind the Suburban with First Sergeant Ramirez; both men were scanning ahead through binoculars. Ramos said, "There he goes, look at his dust trail. Ahh, he's already gone. Have the men cease fire." A rough dirt road angled away to the right, a half mile ahead. The road ran in a straight line, but over rolling terrain and through cuts where the rocky ground was broken with small escarpments. Occasionally at the front of the dust trail, the helmet and shoulders of a man could just be seen—he was on a motorcycle and already well out of range. Through magnified optics, he could be seen riding southeast toward the Albuquerque suburbs on the western bank of the Rio Grande, traveling through the uninhabited volcanic badlands of the Petroglyph National Monument.

The stocky middle-aged First Sergeant blew his silver whistle and bellowed "Cease Fire! Cease Fire!" and the shooting abruptly stopped.

Ramos said, "He's gone. Shit! He'll disappear before the plane gets here. How many casualties do we have?"

Another Sergeant, in his full camouflage BDU uniform and pistol belt, reported. "Two dead, three injured Comandante. One of them needs to be evacuated immediately. He may die—not from bullet wounds, but from the crash. Our *medicos* cannot do anything more for him here."

"Yes, yes. Let's get the helicopter—call the state police, have them contact the air ambulance and get it here. Do it!"

"Yes Comandante!"

Ramos's Lieutenants and Sergeants gathered around him to hear his orders. Ranya was still on the ground behind her rifle, almost at their feet. Ramos said, "If he left on a *moto*, then he arrived on a *moto*. If he carried his rifle on a *moto*, then he must live nearby. We can find this bastard, if we move quickly. Chino!"

"At your orders, Comandante!"

"Take the Zetas up to the dirt road cutoff, look for his firing position. Check for booby traps, see what you can find."

"Yes sir." Chino left at a trot and jumped into the front of a brown Toyota 4X4 pickup, which immediately peeled out with a hail of dirt and gravel, and then tore up the paved road. The rest of the troops fanned out in a circular perimeter around the vehicles, their rifles pointing outward.

Ramos pulled out his cellular phone, and checked it. "*Teniente* Almeria, we have cellular coverage, thank God. Find out about any calls handled by nearby cell towers in the last two hours. The shooter was probably informed about our presence on the rifle range, and then he put himself into position in case we returned to the city this way. These calls may lead to the conspirators. Find out, get the records."

"Yes sir." Lieutenant Almeria was sitting in the back of a gray Toyota Land Cruiser that was bristling with antennas. The Land Cruiser had traveled behind Ramos's Suburban in the convoy, and had pulled up close behind it when they stopped.

"Also, there may have been other ambushes placed on the roads we used to come to the range. If there were, then those shooters might be leaving their positions now. Contact Milicia headquarters, have them put flying roadblocks on all of the Interstate 40 interchanges, looking for weapons. They might get lucky."

"Yes sir. Right away." Almeria, the Falcons' young communications officer, was round-faced, and wore gold-rimmed eyeglasses with dark sun lenses clipped over them. Besides Almeria and the driver, two other Falcons also were busy on radios and computers in the Land Cruiser.

The walkie-talkie on Ramos's belt crackled, and he pulled it off. The handheld radios were digitally encrypted, so he spoke freely.

"All secure up here, Comandante. We located the position, and we found fresh shell casings, over."

"Excellent. What kind of ammunition, over?"

"It's Russian sir. 7.62 by 54, rimmed. Ten shells, over."

"What does that tell you, Chino?" Ramos already knew the answer; he was testing his subordinate's knowledge.

"Dragunov, sir. I'd say a Russian Dragunov."

"I agree. Good work. Get back here now—we're not finished today."

The Russian Dragunov was a semi-automatic sniper rifle issued to Soviet and Eastern European troops during the cold war. The cartridge it fired was the same fired by many Russian belt-fed machine guns, and was slightly more powerful than the .308 or 7.62mm NATO round. Different versions of the long, sleek and deadly rifle had been legal to purchase in the USA, before the ban on semi-automatic rifles had gone into effect six years earlier.

"*Teniente* Almeria, do we still have a network connection? Can you get into the police sites?" Fortunately for the Milicia, they were still able to access the same law enforcement-only internet sites used by the other New Mexico police agencies. This was one of the residual benefits of flying the United States flag over the Capitol in Santa Fe…for the time being at least.

"Yes, we're in the net." Lieutenant Almeria had a keyboard on his lap, and a screen in front of him on a flexible bracket mount.

"See if you get any hits on people who owned Dragunovs, or who have purchased 7.62 by 54 ammunition. Give priority to the western Albuquerque zip codes."

"I'm already working on it. This should only take a minute—if we keep the connection."

Although there had never been a formal law passed creating a national firearms registration database, that minor legalistic hurdle had been bypassed years before. The same search engine technologies that powered Google and other data mining systems had been converted to law enforcement use long ago. Although firearms purchase information was not supposed to be held by the federal government, those privacy laws had been superseded by a secret Presidential Decision Directive buried within the third Patriot Act. Terrorists, it was reasoned, should not get a free pass, merely to ensure the confidentiality of right wing gun nuts. The complete record of all firearms purchase information was collected and maintained on classified Department of Homeland Security databases.

"No luck, Comandante, it's not showing any Dragunovs. Now, wait a moment, here's another list of Dragunov clones and imitations... There's a Romanian PSL, it shoots the same ammunition, and uses a similar ten round magazine. No, I don't see any Dragunovs or PSLs still on the list in Albuquerque. They were all collected and destroyed five years ago, all the ones that were listed in the national data base."

Lieutenant Almeria cracked his knuckles, stretched, and lit a cigarette. "So let's look at ammunition next. I'm bringing up credit card sales of shooting supplies. Okay, now here's a list of ammunition purchases by zip codes…I'm narrowing the field to only 7.62 by 54 Russian. Got it, here it is. Now let me overlay this on the map…

"All right, I've got twelve ammunition buyers west of the river. Well…look at this. This fellow also bought four magazines for a Dragunov—the fool ordered them on his VISA card! Hah! Now, let me go into the DMV for a moment…and…here's our man!" Almeria jabbed the "enter" key with a flourish, and a New Mexico driver's license and vehicle registration information popped up in a full screen view. "Guess who owns a Kawasaki KLR 650 motorcycle, and spare ammunition magazines for a Dragunov, and who bought five hundred rounds of 7.62 by 54 Russian 'sniper grade' ammunition six years ago?" Almeria turned the computer screen toward the side window.

"Jan Pieter De Vries?" asked Ramos. "What kind of a name is that?"

"Dutch, or maybe South African," replied his commo officer. "He's also a member of the NRA and Gun Owners of America, and *ay, chihuahua*! Look at all of these gun magazines he subscribed to!"

"Well, why don't we go pay this Mr. De Vries a visit, right now?"

First Sergeant Ramirez, at Ramos's side, said, "It might be a trap, Comandante. Bait, to lure us into another ambush."

"No, it's too clumsy for that. His attack was on impulse. I think someone telephoned him a tip, and he acted on it. He identified the scout truck and shot it eight times, and then he fired two shots at our lead vehicle to stop our column, and then he fled. One magazine of ten bullets, and gone. Good fire discipline—fairly professional. But now he's hiding, and his heart is beating like a rabbit's. So let's go see if the rabbit ran home! *Teniente* Almeria, find his house on your electronic maps. We'll brief the mission right now. Maybe we'll get lucky, and catch this Jan Pieter De Vries before he can make any escape plans."

"¡Maldita sea!" swore Lieutenant Almeria. "I just lost the internet connection!"

"It doesn't matter now," stated Ramos, "We have enough information."

"Here it is," said Almeria, zooming in on his computer's map. "7518 Cuttner Court is right here at the end of the Warner Ranch development, in this cul-de-sac." He swiveled the screen toward the open window for Ramos and his gathered lieutenants to see.

Ramos studied the color map for a minute, and made his plan. "Okay…first stage: we'll send Gamma Platoon as a blocking force out here almost behind his house, in case he runs out the back. Then the Zetas will go in the front as the assault team, with Alpha as backup. Beta and Delta will cordon the neighborhood. We've done this many times, the only thing different is it's daylight, and we've never done it so quickly. Chino, are your Zetas ready for this mission? Do you have your assault bags?"

"Yes, Comandante. We are ready for these contingencies. Always."

"Sir, the helicopter is inbound," reported one of the other troops in the commo truck. "It's two minutes away."

"All right. Are the casualties ready to be transported?"

"Yes sir," answered First Sergeant Ramirez.

"Good. Now, let's get back to the plan. *Sargento* Ramirez…"

The radio crackled again. "Falcon Leader, this is *Avispa*, over." It was the pilot of the Milicia's Piper Supercub, just arriving overhead.

"*Avispa*, this is Falcon Leader, can you downlink your video to us, over?"

"Roger, I'm streaming it now."

Lieutenant Almeria said, "We've got it."

"*Avispa*, take a look at 7-5-1-8 Cuttner Court Northwest. Let's see who is home."

Cuttner Court was like many streets in the new Warner Ranch subdivision: nice upper middle class pueblo-style homes on half-acre lots. Seen from above, each house in Warner Ranch was a red tile roof. Like many similar neighborhoods, it was dotted with houses that were frozen in a partial state of construction, dreams which had not been completed when the currency had failed. Many other finished homes in the area were vacant, "walk-aways" abandoned to the banks by newly destitute owners, and by Anglos who had simply given up on living in New Mexico under the new regime. The abandoned homes were easily distinguishable from above by their dusty yellow lawns, the rapid result once the daily watering stopped.

The back of Cuttner Court opened onto the broken rocky expanse of Petroglyph National Monument, thousands of acres of ancient volcanic rubble, where prehistoric Indians had left their graffiti on hundreds of stone monoliths. The twenty Falcons of *Pelotón Gamma* now lay in wait behind Cuttner Court, a hundred yards from the north side of the subject's back yard, well hidden behind black volcanic boulders. If De Vries bolted in that direction, even on his motorcycle, Gamma Platoon would take him down.

The little Piper, orbiting soundlessly high above, provided a sharp video picture of 7518 Cuttner Court. By now, Ramos and his men knew that Mrs. De Vries was still at work, and their two grown daughters had moved out of state. The presumed Mr. De Vries himself could be seen from above, puttering in his backyard, apparently gardening, or working on his underground sprinkler system.

His personal information, retrieved by the computer, indicated that he had a lot of time for gardening—he had been laid off from his position as a facilities manager for the University of New Mexico. Mr. Jan De Vries's master's degree in mechanical engineering from the University of Johannesburg had not helped him to pass the state's mandatory Spanish proficiency test with a sufficiently high grade. He was evidently shown the door, after seven years of keeping the university's infrastructure humming.

Three blocks from the De Vries residence, Ramos, Ranya and First Sergeant Ramirez sat in the middle seat of their air-conditioned Suburban, watching a laptop's color video screen. The perspective on the house constantly shifted as the Piper circled, but the stabilized zoom image was more than adequate to follow the action.

The man they assumed was Mr. De Vries could be seen digging along the rear fence of his back yard, while four Zetas crept around each side of his house. For this suburban mission, the Zetas were disguised as a police tactical unit, wearing black Kevlar helmets, black uniforms, and black body armor. They were carrying their short M-16 carbines, with sound suppressors attached to their muzzles.

There was a chain link fence with a hedge growing along it on the back of De Vries's property line; beyond it began the vast Petroglyph National Monument. His back yard was an emerald-green rectangle when seen from above. Along with a few sparkling blue swimming pools, it was one of a handful of colorful gems scattered at the edge of the desolate brown "high desert." On the video, a black dog was briefly seen running to the north side of the backyard, and then it went down, shot by one of the Zetas sneaking in from that direction. Mr. De Vries jumped to his feet, turning and looking at that side of his house as he drew a pistol from his waist. Then the Piper's orbital position put Mr. De Vries into the image shadow of a leafy sapling tree for a few seconds, and when he reappeared, he was lying motionless on the ground on his back, with several Zetas standing over him, their M-16 carbines pointing at his head and chest.

Chino's voice hissed over the radio. "Falcon Leader—Zeta 1. Subject is down, area is secure, over."

"Roger Zeta 1, we're on our way."

When Ramos's Suburban arrived, Chino walked down the driveway to greet them, carrying the captured Dragunov rifle as a prize. The weapon was sleek, with a long slender black barrel extending well out beyond the almost yellowish wood of the fore stock. The black steel receiver showed a strong family resemblance to the Russian AK-47, except for the long telescopic sight mounted above it, and the square cartridge magazine protruding from the bottom. The exotic-looking hollow shoulder stock was laminated from layers of yellow and brown wood, with a pistol grip forward and a hollow skeletal frame behind. The Dragunov was one of the few weapons ever commonly referred to as sexy or beautiful. There was no mistaking the classic Russian sniper rifle for any other, except perhaps for its Romanian and Chinese cousins.

Chino was sweating profusely in his armor as he met his leader, but he was cheerful, his narrow eyes reduced to slits beneath his black helmet as he smiled. He passed the rifle to his Comandante, who cradled it appreciatively. Ramos then shouldered it and peered through the sight, scanning the rifle toward the distant mountains, before lowering it and returning his attention to the Zeta squad leader. A green off-road motorcycle could be seen in the De Vries's now-open garage. It had been hidden behind a folded ping-pong table and covered with a blue plastic tarpaulin, which was now cast aside.

"Where was the rifle?"

"He was trying to bury it. He already had a place prepared under his back fence, but we were too fast for him."

"Good work, Chino. Very good work."

"Thank you, Comandante."

"Do you know why he was going to bury this rifle under a fence?"

"I would say…to defeat metal detectors. It's a steel fence."

"Very good, Chino, very good. Say, do you like this neighborhood?

"Yes Comandante, it's fine."

"Well, you know what? Maybe we'll keep it."

14

"Mommy, why can't I see Daddy? When is Daddy coming home?" asked five and a half year old Brian Garabanda. The barefoot child walked across the kitchen and looked directly into his mother's face from a yard away. Karin Bergen was sitting Indian-style on the speckled terrazzo floor in her gray tracksuit, wrapping china plates in packing paper, after removing them from a cabinet under the counter. The dinner set had been a wedding gift, a decade ago. "It's complicated, Bri-bri. It's a grown-up problem."

Little Brian pondered this new concept for a minute while she continued packing, and then he said, "Well, I think it's a kid problem too. I want to see Daddy! I miss my Daddy!"

"Oh, sweetie, right now you can't see Daddy." She didn't return his gaze, but continued wrapping dishes. Both of them had sky-blue eyes and medium blond hair—an accident of fate, not genetics.

"Why not, mommy? Why not?"

"Because…"

"Because why?"

"Because a judge said so."

"A judge? What's a judge? Judges are stupid!" Brian quickly reached over and snatched up a bone china teacup and then threw it down hard, shattering it on the kitchen floor. A dozen large and small shards skittered across the room.

Karin turned and grabbed the straps of his denim overalls, and shook him, his head snapping. "What's the matter with you? That was part of a set! Damn it! You're going to clean that up, mister!"

Brian burst into tears, and buried his red face in his little hands. Karin softened, and hugged him against her shoulder, rubbing his back.

"I'm so sorry sweetie, I am so, *so* sorry."

Between wracking sobs, he wailed, "I don't wanna go to Sandy Eggo! I don't wanna see a killer whale named Shampoo! I wanna see my Daddy! I hate Mommy Gretchen! I hate her! I already have a Mommy! Why can't I see my Daddy? Why?"

If the battalion felt any great degree of sorrow or regret for the loss of their three comrades in the sniper ambush, they managed to hide their lamentations more than adequately, while chasing a soccer ball around the field with raucous abandon. It was Beta Platoon versus Gamma, shirts versus skins, with both teams wearing their camouflage BDU pants and boots. They had returned to the *Batallón Halcón's* base an hour after the ambush, and the subsequent immediate-action raid on Mr. Jan De Vries's house. Perhaps the swift revenge taken against the Anglo sniper had erased some of the sting of losing their comrades.

In any event, the Scorpion casualties had come from Alpha Platoon, the remaining members of which were currently licking their wounds and commiserating in their dormitory barracks. Their dead and injured had already been airlifted to the UNM hospital.

Ranya marveled at their base, the former New Mexico Academy, previously an ultra-elite college prep boarding school. It was located in northeast Albuquerque, only two miles from Basilio Ramos's mansion in the Sandia Heights. The academy was a lush 200-acre oasis enclosed by high walls, and surrounded by calm tree-lined suburban neighborhoods. Now, instead of preparing the children of New Mexico's wealthiest families for college, the academy was home to the Falcon Battalion.

The officers sat on wrought-iron patio chairs drinking cold beers from an ice chest, in the shade of a long row of maple trees. Their brown berets and cigarette packs lay on the glass-topped tables. The sleek and deadly Russian Dragunov rifle, which had been captured on the raid, was passed from one leader to another to be examined and admired.

Across the sports fields, five miles away to the east, the Sandia Mountains presented a suitably dramatic backdrop. The small group of Falcon leaders was gathered behind the former headmaster's brick residence, where his back lawn merged with the complex of sporting fields. They watched their troops playing soccer and discussed the day's events, from the rifle range, to the one-man ambush and the ensuing raid, which resulted in the gringo sniper's death.

Ranya had not been specifically invited to join them, neither had she been given any other instructions, so she sat near Basilio Ramos, on his right side. She didn't partake in their discussions, which were conducted in Spanish too rapid and colloquial for her to follow in detail. Wearing dark wraparound Oakley-style sunglasses, she was able to discreetly study the men around her, or tune them out, as she chose.

She was confused by Basilio's on-and-off, hot and cold reaction to her. Ranya marked it down to his shifting priorities—when he was with his mini-battalion, she was an unneeded accessory. When he needed a rifle expert, he would call upon her. Now, amidst his subordinate officers, her function seemed to be purely ornamental. She was el Che's current *amiga*, a living, breathing symbol of his alpha-male macho supremacy.

Today at least, she was able to pop open her own can of Tecate beer, and not worry about something being slipped into it. After her experience with the strawberry margaritas, she had decided that she would not drink anything which did not come directly out of a tap, or which she had not opened personally.

A wooden gazebo on the former headmaster's back lawn had been enclosed with wire mesh and converted into an aviary. Inside, a raptor was perched on a T-shaped stand, tearing with its cruelly-hooked beak at the remains of a small furry creature pinned in its talons. The reddish-brown bird was probably a Harris hawk and not a falcon at all, Ranya decided. No doubt a battalion mascot—and another decorative prisoner like herself. Was the bird ever allowed out for hunting, she wondered? If the hawk was allowed to fly free, would it return to a master's gauntleted hand? Or would it disappear forever, back into the wild?

Four of the Zetas, including Chino and Genizaro, sat at a separate table thirty feet behind the Falcon leaders. Ranya noted that they were sipping non-alcoholic soft drinks. They were once again wearing their tan combat vests, with their carbines resting close at hand. Even within the walls of the academy, Basilio's security detail was plainly taking their duty seriously.

The conversation among the leaders alternated between animated commentary on the soccer game, and an informal after-action debrief of the day's activities. It was decided that in the future major battalion convoy movements should be accompanied by the Piper or another aircraft overhead, equipped with video and infra-red cameras. The consensus was that the isolated sniper and his motorcycle would have been ferreted out by an aircraft on patrol, or even by a UAV drone if one was available. An aircraft waiting on the ground even five minutes away was too slow in its reaction time to be of any use in warding off danger.

Ramos and his subordinate leaders spent several more minutes discussing the need for more airplanes and helicopters to be tasked in support of the battalion. The fuel for the extra flying hours this would demand would have to be found, somehow. Ramos assured his lieutenants that he was going to personally take the matter to his superiors, and demand they be provided the airplanes and helicopters they needed in order to conduct their missions properly. Their Spanish was fast, diversely accented and full of colloquialisms Ranya couldn't catch, but the gist of their discussion was perfectly clear.

They also discussed the merits of confiscating the houses on the cul-de-sac in Warner Ranch, where the sniper Jan De Vries had been killed. Most of the houses were already vacant or still unfinished, and the cul-de-sac had potential as a battalion stronghold in far western Albuquerque. It would benefit battalion morale to begin providing selected troops with concrete, tangible rewards for their efforts toward the liberation of Nuevo Mexico.

Ranya sipped her cold *cerveza* in silence, hiding her thoughts behind her dark sunglasses, brooding. She was getting nowhere. Her son was only a few miles away, and she was stuck, trapped, a virtual prisoner.

When the attention of the group turned to the soccer field, after a bold take-away and a fast race toward the distant goal, she leaned in towards Basilio Ramos, and said, "I need to speak to you."

"What? Go ahead."

"In *private*," she replied, so that only he could hear.

"Eh? Oh, yes. Come on, let's go for a walk. I'll show you around our new Falcon Academy." He picked up his brown beret from the table, put it on and carefully adjusted it, and they left the informal officer's assembly. The four Zetas rose at the same time, slinging their carbines to hang in front at the ready. They spread into a wide box, the four corners a hundred feet from their Comandante.

Once they were alone (except for his ever-present shadows), Ramos switched to English. "You know, most of the people who live in this city have never seen the inside of this place—it was for only the rich. For *la gente*, the ordinary people, the New Mexico Academy was known only by its outer walls—if they even knew it existed."

They strolled side-by-side on a paved walkway, which meandered between brick faculty homes and a half-dozen enclosed tennis courts. His hands were joined behind his back, hers were at her side.

"If they were so wealthy, then why did they give up their academy?" she asked.

"Well, the richest families began leaving New Mexico when Deleon was elected, and the school lost many of its students. Then there was a new tax put on properties over 100 acres inside of the city. Frankly, the law was passed to allow us to confiscate this place, and a few others that we needed. But even without that law, we can basically take any property we need."

"What about the Constitution?"

"What Constitution? The gringo Constitution?" Ramos smiled, and laughed. "Who bothers about that any more? Don't worry—the gringos are too busy putting out fires in their big cities to worry about what we do here. This academy was an important symbol of Anglo power in New Mexico. It was important to take it away, as a lesson to the oligarchs. Look around you: the rich *gabachos* enjoyed baseball, tennis, handball, racquetball…there's even an indoor swimming pool! Nothing was too good for those rich boys! I'll tell you something, my troops have never lived so well. For my men who come from dusty little villages and crowded barrios, this Falcon Academy is a paradise. Now, what did you want to discuss?"

What indeed! Was last night's ardor already forgotten by him? She had planned her words on the return drive, and while half-listening to his officers discussing the day's events. Now that she could address him alone, her words came haltingly. "Basilio, I have to know what I am, who

I am. To you, and to the battalion. Outside of New Mexico, Ranya Bardiwell is hunted by the gringo *federales*. Here, I have no name, no identity. I can't live like this, I just can't! Who am I? What am I? I have killed for the Milicia, and I have taken up arms for the battalion, but still I am nobody. How long can I exist as your shadow, as only the Comandante's *amiga*?"

He turned in front of her, his hands on his hips, cocked his head and smiled. "It's not so bad to be my lover, is it?"

She looked briefly into his eyes, hazel like her own, and then away. "I don't know. Basilio, that wasn't me, last night. I must have been very drunk. No—I'm sorry—I didn't mean it that way. I mean, I don't regret it, what happened, but still… That's not how I am. Not who I am. You must think I'm very cheap, after last night." She folded her arms across her chest, turned and stared at the captive hawk caged in its gazebo aviary.

"No, of course not…"

"You have to lead your battalion—I understand that. I respect that. There are many important missions coming for the Falcons, I know that. But I want to join the effort too, and to do that, I need a name of my own, so that I can win my own place in the people's struggle."

"I understand. We can give you a new identity, that's not a problem. Most of my men have new identities."

"I don't belong with your men, with the Falcons. There must be other units where I could fit better. Perhaps as a translator? Or with the student Voluntarios? Or even as an ordinary Miliciano."

"Hmmm… Well, you can't simply join the Milicia, just like that. First, you need to go through their training course to qualify, and that means six weeks in the north, in the mountains. It's very rugged, even brutal. I'm sure you can handle it; there are some female Milicianos, but…frankly, not all of the regular Milicianos are the best troops. And forget about the student Voluntarios: most of them are trash, completely useless. We tolerate them only for the propaganda value their presence brings to the *revolución*. Very soon we'll be sending most of them home."

"Then I would prefer to join the regular Milicia, to earn my own brown beret." Ranya had thought long and hard about her best escape options, and was making this offer as a gambit, to transform the current status quo. She hoped that by volunteering for the Milicia, she would clearly demonstrate her dedication to the 'people's struggle.' By volunteering, she would prove her ideological reliability, and increase the chances that she would be allowed to slip from her gilded cage. It was certain that as long as she was merely "el Che's woman," she would not be able to escape the encircling grasp of his bodyguards, wherever they went.

"Yes, of course, you could do that. A new Milicia training class begins Monday. If that's what you really want…"

“Yes, it is. It’s what I want, very much.”

“Well then, we’ll need to get you a new name and identity papers. Fortunately, this is standard procedure. We control the entire process now, from birth certificates, to driver’s licenses, to registering to vote. Everything. In the meantime, you are welcome to stay at my house.”

“Thank you Basilio…but I have to tell you, that after last night…I’m…I don’t know how to put this. After five years in the camps, without a man, and then last night… I’m afraid I’m really rather…”

“I understand.”

“I couldn’t…”

“Don’t worry. I really do understand.” He turned, and they resumed their walk together. “Ranya, would you like to go out to dinner again? If you’re going to go up to the camps for Milicia training, I can assure you, you will not enjoy the meals. You may even wish you were back in your old camp in Oklahoma.”

She laughed. “Oh, no, there’s no chance of that! Thank you Basilio. Yes, I would very much enjoy going to dinner with you.”

“Well, I’m finished here anyway. Let’s go back to my house, and you can do whatever you need to get ready for going out.”

They returned to the patio area near the soccer field, walking side by side but making no public display of affection. Ramos was in uniform, and he had his appearance as Comandante to maintain. His junior officers and NCOs respectfully stood up as he approached.

“*Caballeros*,” Ramos began in rather formal Spanish, “I have an announcement to make. Our Arab friend ‘Señorita X’ has enjoyed her time with us so much, that she is joining the Milicia. She will begin her training next week!”

His officers and NCOs broke into grins and actually applauded. “Oh, she’ll make a fine troop! She’s already a dead shot! She should be an instructor, not a student!”

Ramos excused himself from the group. He quietly told Ranya, “Come on, let’s go,” and they headed for their vehicles with his four bodyguards in tow. When they reached the parking area by the gym, he said, “We’ll take a Suburban, but this time I’ll drive. I like to be unpredictable. It’s better for my health.”

His four Zeta bodyguards, in an identical black SUV, preceded him through the main gate and out of the Academy. This security vehicle circled through the quiet residential neighborhood outside of the wall, and then looped back and gave the ‘all-clear’ on a walkie-talkie. Only then did Comandante Ramos pull out to follow them. Ranya was sitting across from him in the front passenger seat.

Ramos noted the time on the console's digital clock, it was five PM. Alone with her again, he spoke in English. "Don't get the wrong idea, but I like to check the gringo radio stations. I want to know if they've heard what happened today."

He switched the radio to the AM band, and then he tuned in an English-speaking talk radio station. They caught the national news headlines first. The Compton fire in Los Angeles was still inexplicably raging out of control after a week, destroying several square miles of the city. This was tentatively blamed on an incipient three-way civil war between Hispanic, African-American and Asian gangs. Lawlessness and anarchy were spreading across greater Los Angeles, with a flood of desperate refugees fleeing the zone of total destruction in Compton. Martial law had been declared, and Marines from Camp Pendleton were being sent in to restore order. Fortunately for the national economy, the vital railroad tracks and fuel pipelines leading out of the ports of Long Beach and Los Angeles had not been seriously damaged by the fires.

The standoff and siege of the Muslim Quarter was ongoing in Detroit. The Imams were asking for the International Red Cross and Red Crescent to be allowed in, to witness that children and the elderly were dying of hunger. Police marksmen were picking off armed Muslim gunmen inside of the barricaded enclave, and in return police cars were the targets of snipers and improvised explosive devices. So far, the President was resisting enormous pressure to send in regular infantry troops, and terminate the insurgency by force of arms. The grim specter of an impending "American Fallujah" lay over the nation.

The private ownership of more than five ounces of non-jewelry and non-numismatic gold had been outlawed. The new amnesty period for redeeming gold coins and bullion (at the fixed exchange rate of $1,000 per ounce in "New Dollars") would not be extended beyond the end of June. The collection of the now-illegal gold was expected to run smoothly, since privately owned gold had already been registered under the previous "gold amnesty program," which was no longer in effect. The President was glowingly compared to FDR, for having the resolute courage to take these stern but necessary measures, intended to shore up the faltering dollar and stabilize the national economy. A recent public opinion survey showed that large majorities supported confiscating the illegal bullion from "ultra-rich speculators and gold hoarders."

Meanwhile, "currency regularization" with Canada and Mexico was back on the fast track in Congress, as part of the President's "North American Community" initiative. The new "Amero" was expected to replace dollars and pesos within one year.

At six minutes after the hour, local afternoon talk host Rick Haywood began an angry monologue. "We have an update on the story the KNMR radio news team broke this morning. That was about last night's fatal one-car accident, where three people died when their car ran off of Tramway Road. Here's what we know so far: a reliable source says that only hours before the fatal accident, the three victims were in a verbal altercation with some of our 'brown-bereted guest soldiers' at the Sandia Tramway lift station. The argument was so heated that the 'brown-bereted guest soldiers' felt the need to point machine guns at the three Americans—who 'coincidentally' were later found dead. That's the story as we reported it earlier today."

Ranya stared straight ahead, trying not to tremble, picturing the three Americans alive at the tramway last evening. She remembered Chuck, the mouthy Texan wearing the cowboy hat, and his two timid local relatives. Murdered, she was quite certain, for embarrassing Basilio Ramos in public. Murdered, no doubt on his orders, on the very night that she had been so charmed by him.

"And this next part is brand new—it's another tip from one of our many loyal and patriotic friends still working in law enforcement. The victim's car was a white Nissan Ultima, but when it was towed out of the ravine this morning, our police source reports that it had black streaks along its driver's side. Just a wild guess, but if you can find enough gas to be out driving today, you might want to look out for a black SUV or pickup with fresh white paint on its passenger side. Just a suggestion, just a thought, not that it will matter in the long run—except maybe to a few of us stubborn gringos they can't run out of New Mexico."

Haywood paused and took a deep breath, muttered to himself, and continued his monologue. "In other news, or perhaps, just perhaps, it's related news, there seems to have been a serious traffic accident out on west Paseo del Norte earlier this afternoon. It seems that a truckload of 'brown-bereted guest soldiers' flipped over for no apparent reason. No reason at all. This accident may or may not be related to the brown-bereted guest soldiers making an armed house call in Warner Ranch shortly after the accident. During the armed house call, one lone holdout gringo seems to have succumbed to acute lead poisoning, along with his dog.

"As I said, it's impossible to know for certain if the 'accident' on Paseo del Norte is related to the 'lead poisoning incident' in Warner Ranch. Some folks have even suggested that the driver of the brown-bereted guest soldiers' truck might have suffered from a severe case of lead poisoning himself, right before his truck flipped over. But of course, there's no way to really know for sure. And since none of this will be in your local Quisling newspaper or on traitor television, I suppose it's possible it never really happened anyway. But hey, what do I know? I'm just your humble radio host, passing along what comes in, broadcasting as always from a secure, undisclosed location…"

Ramos stabbed the radio on-off button, silencing the talk show host. "Shit! That filthy gringo bastard! Now even the police are calling him with tips—even after we fired all of the gringo cops! Oh, that *pendejo*! Of all of the right-wing reactionary fascists on the radio, he's the worst!"

Inwardly Ranya was applauding this feisty Rick Haywood—he sure had plenty of guts to talk the way he did about the Milicia. She had to suppress her laughter at each mention of "brown-bereted guest soldiers," so only with difficulty, she mirrored Ramos's stern visage. She knew that she needed to continue wearing her Marxist mask, to convince him of her dedication to *la causa,* the cause.

And anyway, what was it to her if the gringos or the Hispanic radicals won the battle to control New Mexico? Why should she care if New Mexico went socialist, or even communist, and broke away from the United States? What had the U.S. federal government done for her, other than murder her father, kill Brad Fallon, imprison her and steal her baby? She was here to find her son, not to take sides in this budding civil war. All she cared about was finding her son, and to do that she needed to escape.

"Basilio, why don't you have that fascist arrested, for sedition? Or for conspiracy—it sounds like the terrorists are using him to pass along information. Why isn't he arrested?"

Ramos looked across at her, then back at the road ahead. "Well…that's a complicated question. Believe me—I'd like nothing better than to see Haywood chained to a wall in front of a firing squad. He's been a thorn in our side ever since I arrived. But he's also been a valuable source of intelligence. Our Special Surveillance Group traces every call, every email that he gets. It all fits together quite well, and so far it's been useful to let him spew his hate. But don't worry: his usefulness is almost at an end. We'll grab Haywood when the time is right, and make an example out of him. It's all a question of timing. Just wait until Saturday—Saturday will change everything."

15

Thursday June 26

Basilio Ramos wasn't accustomed to waiting in public. Sitting on a park bench for ten minutes, even obscured beneath the hanging branches of a willow tree, made him feel like he had a bulls-eye target taped onto his oxford shirt. On the other hand, he knew that there were few places in New Mexico as safe for him as the university, especially with his four primary bodyguards surrounding him at a discreet distance.

On short notice, Comrade Inez from the clandestine Revolutionary Council had asked to meet him at nine o'clock Thursday morning, and she was late. She was only now walking around the duck pond in the center of the campus, in the green space between the imposing Fidel Castro Library and the university administration building where she worked. For the meeting, Ramos had discarded his usual camouflage uniform and brown beret, in favor of wearing jeans and a pale blue button-down shirt, open at the collar. He could easily pass for a young professor, he thought.

With school finished for the academic year, there were not so many students strolling around the shady paths on the perimeter of the small lake, which had always seemed to him to be the lively heart of the university campus. The duck pond's fountains were not working, and a froth of yellow scum was beginning to build up on the water's edges. For some unknown reason, the overall maintenance of the university's physical infrastructure seemed to be in serious decline. Probably due to various parts shortages, he reflected. Another symptom of the faltering economy.

Most of the young *Voluntarios* who had come to Albuquerque were staying on the other side of the campus, in and around the dormitories and sporting complexes. Apparently, these idealistic volunteers had little interest in the library, and why should they? They had come to Nuevo Mexico to make history, not to read about it on dry and dusty pages.

Inez arrived alone, wearing a navy blue pants suit, her black and gray hair pulled back in a ponytail. Ramos didn't rise to greet her, or make any overt display of even knowing her. She gave a last look around, and then sat on the open end of the bench, in the obscuring shade of an overhanging willow tree.

"So, Basilio, how is the girl working out? The Arab?"

"Bardiwell? She's been fine. Just fine."

"You have your rifles sorted out? She was of assistance to you?"

"Oh, very much so. She found hundreds of perfectly new rifles in that garage. More than thirty years old, and never fired."

"Excellent. So, you're ready for the March for Justice? Your men will not be in their uniforms, correct?"

"Some of them will be, and some will not." She had no need to know the details of the operational planning.

"Saturday is going to be a very important day, a very exciting day for our movement!"

"Yes, of course." He mused that Comrade Inez had no idea just how exciting.

"And you are moving ahead with the punishment mission? For the bus massacre?"

"It's on for tomorrow, if nothing causes the plan to change."

"Good. Attacks like that *matanza* must be answered in blood. It's a simple calculation: if we don't return blood for blood, we lose face, we lose respect, and *la revolución* loses momentum. Our enemies must fear us: they must understand that when they strike at us, we will exact blood revenge! How did you select the target? The closest ranch to the bus attack?"

"Not entirely, it's a few miles from where the bus was ambushed. We found part of a topographical map near the bus massacre; we think it was dropped by one of the snipers. The ranch has a dirt air strip—it was marked with an X on the map."

"You don't think it was left intentionally, as bait for a trap?"

"We considered that, and we'll be ready for anything, but no, we don't think it was deliberate. Not at all. This ranch has been a problem for a long time; the owners are 'Old New Mexicans.' The idiots must think that because they have some Spanish blood, they're immune to land reform! So anyway, they're being obstinate and holding out. It's 14,000 acres, and it's the last big ranch in Monterey County that's not under state control. They've been ignoring the land reform laws, and they've been setting a bad example for the other ranchers. Now we're going to make an example of them."

"Good," she said. "Resistance is contagious. It has to be smashed."

Ramos continued, agitated. "They were offered a hundred acres and some of their buildings if they complied, but they wouldn't listen to reason. Even after the Land Reform Commission settled two hundred landless *pobladores* on part of their ranch, these stinking *pocho* bastards still didn't get the message."

"That was under the Idle Lands Act?"

"Right, we used that to put the settlers on their ranch, but they're still holding out and refusing to give up one damned acre! Then after the bus *matanza*, we found the map with the X…and we're not giving them any more chances. We're going in hard, and we'll be prepared for anything. This land reform mission is a top priority for Vice-gobernador Magón, and we have everything we need. We've even have two state guard helicopters for the air assault, and a transport plane…"

"A transport plane? Really? I didn't realize we had them."

"It's a Canadian twin-engine plane; it used to fly sport parachutists out of Coronado Field. It's called an Otter, and it's amazing—it can even take off from a soccer field! I had a frank discussion about aviation support with the *vicegobernador*, and now the plane is ours, whenever we need it. It's perfect for us—in a state this big, it gives us the kind of speed and range we need."

"You're dropping paratroops on the ranch?"

"No, not this time, there is no need. Maybe in the future we will. This ranch has its own runway. The plane will land right after the helicopters, and bring in twenty more troops. The rest of the battalion will arrive in trucks after that. On a ranch that big, there are a lot of areas to secure, all at once."

"Don't be soft with them—if they show any hint of resistance…"

"I understand the mission, Inez—I was briefed by *Vicegobernador* Magón himself. But that's not why I'm here: you said you had something to show me?"

"I do. Something very important, I think." She handed him a manila mailing envelope. "Take a look, there's a surveillance report and some photographs."

Ramos slid out the papers, scanned the printed sheets of text, and turned to the large color photos. "Do I know these men? Should I know them? Where is this, a *camposanto*?"

"Mount Calvary Cemetery, yesterday. Beneath where the interstate highways cross. The one wearing the baseball hat is an FBI agent named Alexandro Garabanda."

"FBI?"

"Actually, he's a supervisor, the leader of a squad of agents. The gray-haired one is Luis Carvahal—he used to be a reporter for the Herald. That was an old Albuquerque newspaper; it closed a few years ago. Did you ever hear of him?"

"No."

"Well, now he's Deleon's biographer. They were friends from the old days, Deleon and Carvahal. They go all the way back to the Tierra Andalucia courthouse raid—did you ever hear of that?"

"Yes, of course. I have a degree in Raza Studies."

"Anyway, this Carvahal has been spending a lot of time with el gobernador, helping him to write his memoirs."

Ramos sighed, flipping through the photos. "And reporting everything Deleon says, right to the FBI."

"Yes, apparently. However, we can't touch the FBI agent, that's part of our, um, *understanding* with Washington. We can't punish this race-traitor Garabanda, at least not yet. We can follow him, intimidate him to a certain extent…but that's all. Next year maybe, but not now. And we certainly can't push his car down into a canyon, like some…"

"Inez, I…!"

"Don't worry about it Basilio, those gringos from the tramway meant nothing." She grinned and cut her eyes at him like a schoolgirl, seemingly pleased with herself to have caught him out in an unsanctioned peccadillo. "But my section has been monitoring their talk radio—you should exercise more discipline, control your temper."

Ramos ignored her mild rebuke, and didn't mention that he too had heard the same radio report by Rick Haywood. There was no need to mention that he was practicing his English with Ranya Bardiwell, or listening to gringo talk radio. It might give Inez an idea that he was 'unreliable,' which of course he was not. Inez might put such questionable items into his personal dossier, and who knows what kind of trouble that could cause later?

Instead, he said, "What about exposing this Garabanda as a Yanqui spy? We could cause a lot of embarrassment for the FBI in Nuevo Mexico with these photographs. The federal government running a spy operation against a United States Governor—now that's a juicy story! The Yanqui news media will go crazy if they hear about it! The scandal will force the FBI to back off of us."

"Well, that's worth considering. I'll suggest it. We still have certain ongoing arrangements with Washington—there may be no point in antagonizing them for no good reason. Not yet. If we have indeed caught the FBI spying on Gobernador Deleon through this *gusano*, this traitorous worm Carvahal, well, something like your idea may be worth exploring. We don't have recordings of what they said, but clearly, Carvahal is a spy and a traitor. Look at this picture—do you see the line on the ground here?"

"What is that, a hose? He's getting gasoline from the FBI man's car?"

"That's right. He's a *vendido* traitor, sold out for free gasoline. And there is more: look at the picture of this gravestone. They were standing near it when they were talking later, away from their cars. It was taken by our Special Surveillance Group team after the spies left the cemetery."

Ramos studied the large photograph carefully. "Davita Ester Carvahal? Strange name."

"Not so strange, if you look at the carved flowers. Look at the center of the bouquet: what do those petals remind you of?"

Ramos squinted and stared at the photo, then shook his head. "This is just a guess, but they almost look like Hebrew letters. But that doesn't make any sense."

"Basilio, you were raised in California. Did you ever hear of the crypto-Jews of New Mexico?"

Inez had his full attention now. "Crypto-Jews? No, never. Who are they?"

Alex Garabanda's phone vibrated in his shirt pocket. This was the first call to his cell phone all morning, indicating that the service had been restored. The service outages were a constant reminder of the failure of his squad to find and stop the tower shooters, a fact which was not overlooked by his peers at the Field Office. When phone service was suddenly cut in mid-call, or during a computer download, it was common to hear "Dammit Garabanda! Your snipers just got another one!" shouted across the office. On the other hand, he received no words of appreciation when service was restored.

He flipped open the phone, glanced at the caller-ID display and raised it to his ear. The caller's number was unknown, and Garabanda said a tentative hello.

"It's me," he heard through the phone.

He recognized the voice of Luis Carvahal. "Hi. What's up?"

"Is this a good time to talk?"

Supervisory Special Agent Garabanda was alone in his small office. "Ahh…sure, go ahead." There was always the chance the call was being monitored and recorded, but if Luis was careful with what he said, it was probably worth that risk to listen to him. At least he hadn't called from home, or from his own cell phone.

"Oh, umm… You know about the big party on Saturday? We've discussed it."

"Sure. Downtown."

"Right. I've got some more on that," said Carvahal. "And, ahh, if you were thinking about attending the party, well—don't. I don't think it'll be safe. Things could get…out of hand. That's what I'm hearing. I'll be right there, front and center, but you probably don't want to be anywhere around that place on Saturday. And none of your associates, either."

"I got it, thanks. Is that it?"

"That's it. I'll call if I hear anything else."

"Okay then, bye now." Garabanda pushed end, concluding the brief conversation, wondering if anyone else would ever hear it or read a transcript. The meaning of the call, the reference to the March for Social

Justice, was transparent. Working with amateurs, even a friend like Luis, was enough to give him an ulcer.

The oblong pool was about thirty feet across at the its widest. There were steps at each end, so it was impossible to do speed-turns on the very short laps. Ranya wore the same stretchy black jogging top and black nylon running shorts she had worn on the La Luz Trail, going up the mountain with the battalion's poorest marksmen.

When she woke up after seven, Basilio was already gone. She was more comfortable in his house now, and she slipped on a plush bathrobe and wandered downstairs to find something to eat. She knew that she had been accepted into the household on some level, when the plump cook rose from her kitchen chair and asked politely if "the lady" would like breakfast. The middle-aged cook was very dark, pure Mayan, and less than five feet tall. Clearly, certain cultural and class aspects of "la revolución" had yet to affect the Comandante's house staff.

The eggs for her omelet were being cracked when, from the dining room window, she had seen a group of Falcons down the driveway below the house. The men were dressed alike in black shorts and brown t-shirts, stretching and evidently preparing for a run. She remembered the marksmanship contest at the rifle range, and Ramos threatening punishment for the ten shooters with the lowest scores. She quickly decided to try to join them, both to test the limits which would be placed on her freedom of movement in Ramos's absence, and because she simply wanted to run.

She reasoned that going for a run in the company of ten Falcons could not possibly be construed as an escape attempt. Running would simply be taken as sensible preparation for her forthcoming Milicia basic training. She abandoned her breakfast plans and quickly went upstairs to change into appropriate clothes: her new cross-trainers, black nylon shorts, and a loose gray t-shirt over her jogging bra.

The ten Falcons had been pleased, even excited, by the unexpected appearance of "el Comandante's woman." One coyly asked her if the rumor was true that she had been a *prisionera,* and she joked that she had merely been on "an extended vacation" paid by the government. The tattooed Falcons were obviously a rough bunch, who would consider prison to be a standard rite of passage. Her vague non-answer was greeted with knowing smiles and nods. She told them that she had not run for a long time, and she would not make it all the way to the top with them.

They laughingly called themselves *los diez ciegos*, the ten blind men, for their lack of shooting prowess, but they proved to be mountain goats on the run. She ran two rock-strewn miles up the trail, losing ground steadily to the ten, and then she stopped and rested on a flat boulder overlooking Albuquerque and the Rio Grand Valley. The morning sun was still on the other side of the mountains, so the trail was thankfully all in shadow. After a few minutes to catch her breath, she descended by herself, while the ten Falcons continued steadily toward the summit.

The topographical contrast between flatland Oklahoma and the rugged Sandia Mountains of New Mexico could not have been greater. Her lungs had burned while running at the 7,000 foot elevation, but she was used to heat and discomfort from her forced labor in Oklahoma. The dramatic vistas of jagged cliffs and soaring pines around every twist of the stony trail pulled her upward, but she knew that she had to be cautious, and not risk an injury that could jeopardize her upcoming escape attempt.

On her return down the trail, she waved to the riflemen standing watch above the house. They did not have the silver Falcons on their berets; they were ordinary Milicia, wearing the standard brown t-shirt and camouflage pants and boots. They each carried an M-16 with a thirty round magazine inserted, and an extra magazine pouch and a canteen on a web belt. At the driveway gate, the same two guards who had waved to her on her way out with the ten Falcons were unconcerned by her solitary reappearance. They opened the wrought-iron double gate for her from their little guardhouse, both sides swinging outward with an electric whine.

The run had been a worthwhile exercise on several levels, beyond conditioning herself for high altitude endurance. She had seen the trails above the house, and learned that she could not possibly hope to outrun the Falcons as part of any escape attempt. The men were uniformly tough, lean and physically fit, even if at five feet nine, she was as tall or taller than most of them.

But most importantly she had established that she could be trusted to leave the compound, and return on her own accord. Once the guards became accustomed to seeing her leave the estate on her own, her escape would be straightforward, and could be initiated at the time of her choosing. She had waited for five years, she would wait a few more days and do it right.

The strenuous trail run had made her subsequent plunge into the swimming pool behind the house an experience that was blissful beyond compare. The pleasure of the moment made her feel a twinge of guilt for accepting and enjoying the hospitality of Basilio Ramos. Yes, he was handsome and charming, but he was a heartless bastard at the same time. Ranya had not forgotten the fate of the three unlucky gringos, who had the misfortune of crossing his path at the Tramway lift station. She had certainly not forgotten that he had drugged her with Libidinol, or the night of unbridled lust that had followed.

Since then, he was getting his own bit of payback in return for that sleazy trick. So far, he had bought her explanation that after their night of endless passion, she was far too sore, too abraded and tender for any more lovemaking. So far, he was accepting this feminine stratagem—which anyway, was half-true.

And in the meantime, why not enjoy the fancy restaurants and expensive dinners with Comandante Basilio Ramos, "el Che?" Why not enjoy his magnificent house, and the benefits his power could bring to her? Why not enjoy a trail run with his Falcons, followed by a dip in his pool? Why not enjoy a little slice of this New Mexican *vida loca* that she had been thrust into, while she could? Why not turn the tables, and *use him* for all he was worth?

Why the hell not? Hadn't she already done enough penance in her life? In fact, every enjoyable moment this week: the shopping, the beauty salons, the expensive dinners…they were all completely justified. They were all a deliberate part of her campaign to win his trust, so that she could escape at the most opportune moment, fully outfitted and equipped.

She dolphin-kicked under water, her legs together and her arms at her sides, using only her body movement to propel herself from one blue-tiled wall to the other. The cool water slid around her skin. She could float and spin, or hover a foot above the bottom, weightless, the sun rays from above flickering around her. With eyes closed, she could disappear into an internal space within her mind, emptiness without pain. If not for the need to occasionally surface to breathe, she would gladly stay underwater forever.

When Basilio Ramos returned home, his chief housekeeper nervously mentioned that *la señorita* was in the swimming pool. Consuelo looked down at the tiled floor when she stammered that *la señorita* had gone running up the mountain with a group of his Falcons, and had later returned alone. It was obvious that while middle-aged Consuelo disapproved of him bringing home girlfriends, she considered it completely without shame—*sin verguenza*—that a half-dressed girl would consort with his troops on the mountain. Ramos merely thanked her, and swept through the house and out to the back patio, eager to see Ranya again.

She was gliding underwater, twisting and rolling. She surfaced like a dolphin for a quick breath, facing away from him, and then dived again, her shapely *culo* emerging for a moment, followed by her long legs, which ascended to vertical before slipping back underwater with her toes pointed. He sat on one of his wood and canvas deck chairs to enjoy the sight of her, memories of his first night with her flooding his mind, causing him to swell in anticipation of future lovemaking.

Unfortunately, he had been such a stallion during their one night together, and she had been without a man for so long, that he had done some unintended injury to her feminine parts. It was most regrettable that she was unable to repeat her ardor for the time being, but he knew that like all women, she would heal quickly, and like any woman he desired, she would want much more of what Basilio Ramos had to offer!

He had been attracted to her from the start, even when she was dirty and smelling like a common *vagabundo.* Even as a prisoner with a dust-streaked face, her features had struck him as remarkable, with her full lush lips, high cheekbones and wide-set hazel eyes, upturned and almond-shaped like her Arab ancestors. She had captured him at the first sight, locking onto his eyes with her intense gaze, even as the black hood was pulled down over her head before the Revolutionary Council.

Certainly, none of the succession of naive young gringas taken to his bed could compare with this wild Arab girl! Ranya Bardiwell had not only made love with burning passion and wild abandon, she had a hard and even bitter side, which also resonated with him. She could shoot rifles like a man, and had indeed taken up arms alongside his Falcons when they were ambushed by the gringo sniper. She even had the natural courage to go for a mountain trail run, unasked and uninvited, with ten of the roughest *maleantes* in New Mexico! So even if he had not given her permission to leave the grounds, how could he scold her for doing so? And after all, she had returned.

While she was choking on dust in the endless fields of Oklahoma, Ranya had constantly fantasized about swimming, but it was an impossible dream. The wind was another pitiless tormenter, rippling waves across the grain fields and reminding her of past ocean horizons…but wheat and corn were waterless seas which brooked no swimming. Twice-weekly cold showers (in open view of prisoners and guards alike) were only another spiteful reminder. Thankfully, that cruel five-year chapter of her life was over, if not forgotten.

She had grown up swimming in Tidewater Virginia, which had led to summer time employment as an ocean lifeguard. During her three years at the University of Virginia, she swam endless laps at least three times every week. Best of all she swam with Brad Fallon, and later she swam and skin-dived alone in the warm Caribbean, while a fugitive on poor Brad's sailboat. She imagined Guajira's black underwater profile, with its slim fin keel and spade rudder suspended above her in the clear Caribbean water. She remembered that first race with Brad down the chain to touch its anchor…and her first time, ever, with Brad afterwards aboard his magical boat. Now, drifting underwater with her eyes closed, all of her best aquatic memories merged into the same tranquil reverie.

Ranya pushed off the side with her feet, gliding through the water like a human torpedo until she touched the other side with her fingertips. She slowly arced upward for a breath, opened her eyes…and Basilio was only a few yards away, watching her. He was sitting on one of the deck chairs, wearing a pale blue oxford shirt and long blue jeans. She was pleasantly surprised to see him out of his usual camouflage; he looked young, lean and sexy. He smiled at her, and Ranya smiled back.

She rested her chin on her crossed forearms, on the edge of the pool. "How long have you been there, you sneak?" she asked in English.

"Long enough to see how lovely you are, when you're wet."

She swept her arm back and splashed him, laughing.

He didn't flinch, his eyes remained fixed on hers, ignoring the water on his shirt. "But I already knew that. Ranya, you seem very comfortable in the water, were you ever a competitive swimmer?"

"On a team, you mean? No. But I was an ocean lifeguard, a long time ago. And I used to swim laps in a pool when I was in college. I love to swim, and it's been so long…"

"And you love to run as well, that's what I hear."

She grinned broadly. "Word travels fast! Sure, I enjoy running, but I'm so out of condition I could only make a couple of miles. I have an excuse though: five years in detention. Running was…not encouraged."

"I'd say that's a good enough excuse. And I'm glad to see you're preparing for Milicia training." Ramos leaned forward. "Listen, do you want to swim in a real pool? Fifty meters. I have to go to the academy—we're getting the battalion ready for an operation tomorrow. You can swim as many laps as you want."

"Really? Oh, I'd love to! You have no idea how much I'd love to!"

"Well then, let's go. We'll pick up a Speedo suit for you on the way."

She cut her eyes at him. "Basilio, you're spoiling me."

"Yes, I know. Are you really sure you want to join the Milicia?"

"I'm sure."

"You don't have to, you know. You could stay here, with me."

She brushed aside his offer. "Be a gentleman—help me up, please?" She coyly tilted her head, threw him a wink, and stretched her arms out toward him, rolling her hands over with a graceful flourish.

He stood above her, blocking the sun, his chestnut hair a glowing corona around his face. "You won't pull me in, will you?" he asked.

"I haven't decided. Do you trust me, Basilio?"

"I don't trust anybody—not even myself."

"Well, you should trust me."

They locked hands, and he pulled her smoothly from the pool, dripping shiny slickness in the sunlight. Ranya fell against him as she pretended to lose her balance; he ignored her wetness staining his shirt and jeans. He slid his hands around her narrow waist and down to rest on her bottom, as she slipped her arms around his neck. He gave her a light kiss, which landed chastely on her cheek as she turned her face.

"You see Basilio, you can trust me," she whispered in his ear. Over his shoulder, Ranya observed the closest up-slope guard with his M-16 rifle. He was standing on a ledge 150 yards away, half-concealed in a patch of shade among the junipers and piñon pines. The guard was observing them both intently, just as she had seen him watching her during her swim. She knew that the word would be passed from him to the rest of the estate's security force: this *señorita* with the short dark hair is el Comandante's special woman. She comes and goes on her own. That information, shared by the guard force around the compound, was going to buy her ticket to freedom.

But not today. Not today.

Ranya had disappeared into his bathroom ten minutes before, carrying her fresh change of clothes. Through the locked door he asked, "Why are you dressing in there? It's not as if I haven't seen every inch of your body."

"Don't be a pig, Basilio. I'm a woman—I can't dress like I'm in a locker room, with strange men walking around."

"I'm not a 'strange man', and this is not a locker room."

"I had five years of living in an open barracks, now let me enjoy my privacy. It takes time to be pretty, you know. Especially with no hair! Do you know what it's like to be seen with 'El Che,' when he has longer hair than I do?"

He laughed as he stood by the door, wearing only his camouflage pants, cinched around his narrow waist. "Can you at least pass out my toothbrush then? And your hair is just fine the way it is: with a face like yours, too much hair just gets in the way."

In a moment, the door opened a crack, and his toothbrush was thrust out.

Ramos accepted it, smiling broadly. She was a delicious enigma to him. "Listen, on the way to the Falcon Academy, while we're picking up some swimsuits, let's get you a dress, all right? You do wear dresses, don't you?"

"I've been known to, but not lately. Dresses weren't issued for field work."

"You know about Saturday, about the March for Social Justice, don't you?"

"I heard something about a march. You mentioned it to your troops."

"From the university, to downtown. Anyway, all of the important people from Santa Fe will be in town: the governor, the vice governor, their staffs, lots of dignitaries and guests. I'm having a reception here at the house afterwards. A dinner party, actually. It's going to be a catered affair—live music, everything. I thought you might like to pick out some dresses…" He sat on the edge of his bed, lacing his black jump boots.

"I won't need dresses for Milicia training." He strained to hear her voice over the running water.

"You don't start training until Monday. I want you to be with me Saturday night at the reception, and I'd like you to look, well…sexy. Pretty. Just because we're socialists, it doesn't mean you have to dress like a soldier all the time! Okay, we're *revolucionarios*, but we're also Latinos. Women are allowed to flaunt their feminine beauty—in fact, it's encouraged!" While talking, he stood and finished buttoning up his camouflage BDU blouse, and then he pulled his web belt with its holstered pistol from where it hung on the back of a chair, and buckled it around his waist.

"A dress or two would be very nice, Basilio. I'd be honored to accompany you at your reception."

"With your legs and your figure, I think you'd look fantastic in a black mini-dress, but you can choose any style that you'd like."

"A little black dress sounds fine. And heels to go along with it, and the right accessories, of course."

"Of course—whatever you need."

"Basilio, what I really need is a name I can use! Yesterday, you said I could get a new identification. I can't go around using my real name. Not after Oklahoma. I mean, if you're going to be introducing me to people, I need a new name. And please, something more believable than '*Señorita X*.' My God, I almost broke out laughing when you said that yesterday!"

"I understand. That's no problem at all. How many IDs would you like? Two, three? After all, a proper *nom d'guerre* is almost mandatory during a *revolución*. We'll stop by the DMV and get them made—it will take only a few minutes. You might say that I have front of the line honors in all government offices."

"Hmm…I'm sure that you do, *Señor Comandante*."

"As the gringos say, 'rank has its privileges.' Just choose the names that you'd like, and I'll have your drivers licenses custom made to order."

They left the house through the garage. Ranya was wearing her green fatigue-style slacks and a tan short-sleeved shirt. Basilio was in his usual camouflage uniform and brown beret.

"What are we driving today?" she asked him.

"Why don't you choose?"

"The Jeep? It looks like fun."

"Why not? It's a good idea to be unpredictable."

He pushed a button by the inside door to the garage, and the panel to their right rolled up into the ceiling, allowing brilliant daylight to pour onto the black hardtop Jeep. Under the buttons for the different garage doors was a row of brass hooks, from which dangled car keys for the Mercedes, the Jaguar and the Jeep. Along the wall by the Jeep was a machine that gave Ranya pause: the green Kawasaki KLR 650 taken from the ill-fated Mr. De Vries. It had been five years since she had twisted the throttle on a bike, but that fact didn't discourage her in the least. Her pulse quickened involuntarily.

The vague outline of a plan began to form in her mind. She was no longer worried about escaping from Basilio's house and compound, not after going on her mountain run. If she was able to escape in one of his vehicles, or even on the Kawasaki, and if she was able to find and then snatch her son, they would have a good chance of making it out of Albuquerque together. If they could somehow make their way across two hundred miles of New Mexico and get back to Caylen Barlow's ranch in North Texas, they would be safe. If she was able to accomplish all of that, she might actually be able to carve out some kind of a future, for herself, and for her son. If…

There were so many ifs! But at least, there was now a fighting chance. The Jeep's passenger door was already unlocked, and she climbed inside. She stole another glance at the green Kawasaki.

16

Friday June 27

Basilio Ramos stood in the open field between the pair of Blackhawk helicopters. His troops were sitting on the ground in two squads of a dozen men each. The long sleek helicopters were painted a flat dark green, almost black. The doors on both sides were rolled all the way open, revealing their Spartan gray metal troop seats. It was Friday morning, and the Falcon Battalion was poised to attack, waiting on barren sun-beaten pastureland forty miles east of Albuquerque. The rugged Santa Fe Mountains loomed on the northern horizon. Even before nine in the morning a breeze was already coursing through the tall grass. He resisted an urge to bite his fingernails, while waiting for the radio clipped to the left side of his web belt to send a specific message to his earpiece.

The two squads of *Pelotón Beta*—Beta Platoon—were smoking and talking quietly to one another to pass the time. Today they were all wearing their complete camouflage uniforms, including Kevlar body armor and helmets, and load bearing gear with pouches for extra magazines. Comandante Ramos was similarly uniformed and equipped, but he carried no rifle, only his holstered .45 caliber pistol, the symbol of his officer's rank.

The body armor, including hard ceramic SAPI plates in the front pouches, had been taken from the National Guard armory after Wednesday's sniper attack on their convoy. The rectangular armor plates covered most of the vital organs, and would stop a rifle bullet fired point blank. Each troop held a black M-16, their rifle butts resting on the earth, their long dark barrels aimed skyward above their helmets like the spines of a cactus. Each troop was made even fiercer looking with diagonal stripes of black, brown and green camouflage grease paint across his face.

The Falcons were waiting for the radio message that would signal them to begin their air assault on the Hacienda Lomalinda, twelve miles away to the east. It was nine o'clock in the morning, and the 200 civilian *pobladores,* the ranch squatters, would be moving out now. They were unaware that their movement would commence the attack plan. These settlers would be leaving their encampment by the state road, marching toward the main house of the Hacienda Lomalinda. Two of Ramos's Zeta Squad, Chino and Genizaro, had already infiltrated the ranch on foot in the dark of night. The hidden snipers waited only for the column of squatters to move to within sight of the main ranch house to initiate the action.

A hundred yards away, twenty more Falcons sat in the shade, under the wing of a white twin-engine transport plane. "Coronado Air Sports" had been covered with white paint on the boxy fuselage, but the old name was still somewhat legible. Just behind and below the high wing on the left side of the fuselage was a gaping square opening, the cargo door his troops would use. Ramos thought the huge tail at the back of the plane seemed to be mismatched, taken by mistake from a much larger aircraft.

The Canadian-built DeHavilland Twin Otter had carried countless thousands of sport parachutists up into these same clear blue skies in happier years, up to twenty-five jumpers at a time sitting on its bare aluminum cargo deck. Today it would land on the targeted ranch's grass airstrip at the same moment the helicopters touched down by the main house. The platoon embarked on the big plane would dash out to secure significant out buildings, and the homes of key ranch employees. Still other Falcons waited in trucks, concealed at various points outside of the ranch, ready to race to critical targets on the 14,000-acre property.

Lomalinda wasn't the largest ranch in New Mexico, in fact it was only a splinter compared to the major ranches. But Lomalinda was almost entirely prime land, amply watered by a tributary of the Pecos River, which ran through its 22 square miles of rolling hills, forests and pastures. Comandante Ramos had made several reconnaissance flights over the property in the battalion's Supercub, and he knew the *Hacienda Lomalinda* was a jewel, a long emerald oasis following the stream's watercourse.

The operation would have been easier if they could have planned to simply burn the main house, as they had done on many of the other ranches the Falcons had liberated. However, Vicegobernador Magón had given Ramos specific orders to preserve the *casa solariega*, the ancestral house. This meant that if the owners (and possibly some of their more loyal ranch workers) decided to fight to the end from within the heavily built three story stone and timber manor house, the Falcons would have to go in and root them out in close quarter combat, at far greater risk.

Nevertheless, the Vicegobernador had given explicit orders: preserve the hacienda's main house at all costs. Félix Magón had seen pictures of the beautiful Lomalinda residence, when Ramos briefed him on the pending reprisal mission. It was almost a rustic mansion, really. It didn't surprise Ramos when he heard through Santa Fe back channels, that Magón had decided to present Lomalinda to his daughter and future son-in-law as a wedding gift. (The Comandante of the Falcon Battalion knew that he was in no position to object, considering the manner in which he had obtained his own luxury villa.)

Comandante Ramos knew his assault teams would be quietly questioning the rationale for storming the strongly built mansion with its stone first floor walls, instead of simply launching pyrotechnics into it through the windows, as was their standard operating procedure. They would not challenge his orders verbally, but he detected an air of doubt.

He considered giving the troops one last pep talk, before he received the radio signal from the sniper team already in place on Lomalinda. He would remind them that among the dead at Monday's bus massacre were young *Voluntarios*, teenagers who had been shot in the back while running away. He would tell them again that the ranch was part of a Spanish Land Grant, but that it had been stolen by the gringos, even though the infamous Treaty of Guadalupe Hidalgo had promised to respect the communal land grants forever.

But really, he reflected, the Falcons didn't need much extra motivation. They already believed that they were going to have the opportunity to shoot some rich gringo cowboys with their new M-16 rifles with the devastating bullets, and that was more than enough reason for them to get their blood up. (They had not been informed that the occupiers of the ranch were in fact of Spanish ancestry. There was nothing to gain by relating the convoluted history of the ranch's ownership to the Falcons.)

Ramos sighed, remembering other mornings like this one. He had led more than a dozen land reform actions in Venezuela, Brazil, Ecuador and other countries over the past decade. The only difference today was that Nuevo Mexico was still technically part of the United States. But if the Yanqui bosses in Washington would not stand up and fight for their Southwestern territory, then they deserved to lose it, and they would lose it.

He remained silent and still, his arms folded across his chest, standing between the two helicopters, watched by his troops. While waiting for the word to come over his radio, he stared out at the dry grass blowing in waves across the high plains, so much like the Pampas of his first *patria*, Argentina.

Dolores Parada was standing behind a tripod-mounted telescope, which was aimed down the mile-long road that was the Lomalinda Ranch driveway. She was a sprightly woman in her early seventies, with long gray hair falling in a single thick braid to the small of her back. She wore a floor length wrap-around skirt, banded in green and yellow horizontal stripes, and a white cotton blouse.

Lomalinda, the "beautiful hill," was crowned by the Parada's century-old family home, built of local stone on the first floor, then solid timber on the second, crowned with a smaller central third floor that had been added in the 1920s. The third floor was now her own personal apartment containing her bedroom, closets, reading room, and private bathroom. It was her refuge.

The third floor also served as Dolores Parada's observatory, with telescopes behind four dormer windows pointing to the cardinal points of the compass. The four telescopes gave the 72-year-old matriarch of the hacienda eagle eyes. The lenses were each adjusted for her vision, and the tripods for her height, just an inch over five feet tall. Two telescopes were in her sitting room, and two in her bedroom. In normal times, they were useful for tracking wildfires or spotting cattle herds or lost horses, and checking that work groups were moving to their assigned tasks. These were not normal times, and the south-facing telescope in her sitting room was fixed upon the squatter camp, which spread along the state road all around the main gate.

Five weeks ago in early May, the first contingent of squatters had arrived. They were dropped off from Albuquerque school buses, and were protected by the new "Milicia" in their rag-tag uniforms and brown berets. Amazingly, the Monterey County Sheriff's Department had bluntly informed the Paradas that they would take no action against these trespassers, while "the case" wound its way through the courts. According to both the Sheriff's Department and the Parada's own family lawyer, the squatters had the law on their side, in occupying several hundred acres of the Lomalinda Ranch under the so-called "Idle Lands Act." According to this cockamamie new "law," any privately owned ranch land not under cultivation or being grazed could be "settled" by landless *pobladores*, squatters, if the property had ever been part of a Spanish Land Grant!

The new sheriff even warned the Paradas that if they took any actions to expel the squatters and defend their property rights, *they* would be arrested! Not the squatters, but the Paradas, the rightful property owners!

Property rights sure didn't mean what they used to anymore, Dolores reflected bitterly. The United States Supreme Court had seen to that… stretching and twisting the definitions of public use and eminent domain like silly putty. Now just about any government body—local, state or federal—could seize any land they coveted. They could keep it for any kind of so-called public use, or even sell it to cronies in blatantly corrupt private deals. Legalized theft is what it was.

Dolores often wondered if old Sheriff Brickwood would have responded in the same cavalier manner to the blatantly unconstitutional property laws passed by the new *Asamblea Legislativa* in Santa Fe. The question had been mooted last year when Dan Brickwood had been fired, after refusing to take the Spanish language test required of all government employees in "Nuevo Mexico." Now Dan Brickwood wasn't around anymore. He'd taken his family and moved out of New Mexico lock, stock and barrel, moved up to what he called "the free state of Wyoming."

So for several weeks the family had patiently waited out the squatters, hoping that they were just making some kind of political statement, and would give up once the temperatures climbed into the nineties and hundreds with the approach of high summer. Through her eighty-power telescope, it was clear that the squatters were city folks, mainly students and hippies she thought, judging by their grubby and disheveled looks. She hoped that they would soon grow weary of "roughing it," and head back to Albuquerque and Santa Fe, or whereve they came from. But instead of leaving, almost every day there were more colorful tents to be seen through the telescope. Worse, sham "survey stakes" with red rags blowing from their tops began to sprout on the bottomland below the state road.

Next, the squatters had run their own hoses to ranch irrigation pipes, diverting water to their encampment. The Paradas were having none of this, and cut off the water, leaving some of their own bean fields to whither and die as a result. The squatters retaliated by bringing out their own gasoline-powered drilling rig, trying to put in their own water wells. Plywood shacks began to sprout among the tents. The camp was beginning to take on an air of permanence.

Then, two weeks ago, trucks had brought out large diesel generators, the tent city began to be lit at night and the nonstop music and threats had begun. This was harassment and psychological warfare pure and simple, but again the Sheriff's Department refused to intervene. "Free speech," they called it!

Driving directly from the house to the state road meant running a gantlet of jeers and obscene gestures, and lately, rocks launched from slingshots. The Paradas and their employees quit using their driveway after screaming gangs of tattooed and face-pierced thugs had broken their car windows. They had been forced to use remote unpaved secondary routes to reach the state road, to avoid the increasingly hostile army of squatters. At least the mob was staying in that one area along the state road, an insignificant percentage of the 14,000-acre Lomalinda Ranch. Insignificant, except that the occupied land choked off both sides of their only paved access to the state road.

Then early on Monday morning, a bus carrying Milicia troops and squatters had been ambushed only a few miles east of the encampment, and the daily confrontations became uglier and more threatening. New loudspeakers, bigger and more powerful, were brought into the squatter camp. They began issuing curses and threats for the Paradas—whom the agitators called "traitors" and "*gusanos*," or worms! They were abused as *pochos* and *tio tacos*, "brown Anglos," sold-out *vendidos* who did not love their own *raza* or race. They were warned repeatedly to leave immediately, "for their own safety." The Lomalinda Ranch belonged to "all of the people of *Aztlan*," the speakers claimed. It was like living in some communist nightmare. Things like this happened in Venezuela or Brazil or Zimbabwe, not in the United States of America!

But it was not just a bad dream. Each day more of the bed-sheet signs were visible from the house. Through her telescope, Dolores could clearly read them. "Land for the Landless," they said in Spanish. "Land or

Death," others threatened ominously. "A Place to Live is a Human Right!" What had that socialist clap-trap to do with the Parada's family ranch?

The sign that angered her the most said, "Return What Was Stolen!" As if the Paradas had stolen Lomalinda! It was true that at one time the ranch had been part of a so-called Spanish Land Grant, dating back to before the Treaty of Guadalupe Hidalgo in 1848. And without a doubt, thousands of Old New Mexicans had been swindled and deprived of the use of their ancestral lands after the treaty. Entire National Forests were expropriated by the federal government from the land grants, and millions of more acres had been "legally stolen" by the Santa Fe Ring and other shady conspirators.

However, the land grants affecting Lomalinda were only *Ejidos*, which merely granted communal grazing rights to the inhabitants of distant pueblos, pueblos that no longer even existed. The *Ejido* land grants were nothing like proper land deeds: the land belonged to the king of Spain. Anyway, the property had been bought and sold several times before it was purchased by Emiliano Parada in 1879. This had been settled once and for all in 1892 by the Court of Private Land Claims, giving the Paradas clear title to Lomalinda forever.

In any case, the Paradas had put down six generations of deep family roots on Lomalinda since then. Paradas had built every house and barn and shed, strung every mile of fence, drilled every well. Six generation of Paradas had bled, sweat, laughed, and cried on every acre, through fires and floods, droughts and blizzards.

And now foreigners, illegal alien Mexicans mostly, were trying to use those ancient so-called Spanish Land Grants to seize the Lomalinda Ranch! They might as well offer to pay for the land with Confederate money, she thought. The Confederate flag had once briefly flown over New Mexico, and as far as Dolores Parada was concerned, the Confederates had just as much of a right to claim it as these newcomer Mexicans. Exactly none!

The Paradas had not for one minute ever considered themselves to be Mexicans. They were proud United States citizens, New Mexicans, and before that, they were Spanish, but never, ever were they Mexicans! The first Paradas had come to Santa Fe in 1693 with Don Diego de Vargas, thirteen years after the bloody Pueblo Indian Revolt had driven the Spanish out of northern New Mexico. They had come "with a cross in one hand and a sword in the other," in the name of the King of Spain, when there was not even a country called Mexico, but only a colony called New Spain.

Now they were being threatened, warned daily to pack up and leave, by a gang of red communists and upstart Mexican illegal aliens! The world had indeed turned upside down.

But today, this Friday morning, something else was happening, something new. Just after dawn, two more school buses had turned off the state road into the squatter camp, followed by several pickup trucks that seemed to be carrying extra Milicia troops. Her son Max had stayed by the house, instead of going out on his rounds, after noting their early arrival. Perhaps most worrying, many of the Lomalinda ranch workers were absent this morning, or had quietly scattered to distant sections.

After their breakfast of *huevos con chorizo*, Dolores had walked up the thirty eight winding hardwood steps up to the third floor, to keep an eye on the encampment. Now, at nine AM, there was a flurry of fresh activity in the squatter camp. The flags and signs made from painted bed linens, which had been attached to wooden poles and planted in the ground for weeks, were being uprooted. It seemed like hundreds of the squatters were forming up on the Lomalinda driveway road in a deep line, flags and signs in front, as if in preparation for a march on the house.

A simple code word in Basilio Ramos's earpiece informed him that the settlers were moving. The New Mexico Air National Guard pilots were already in their cockpit seats, wearing their standard issue green flight suits and helmets, watching him. He nodded and gave them a sign, twirling his right index finger in a circle. The turbines wound up with a shrill whine, the jet engines blowing out waves of kerosene exhaust. Their four black rotor blades began to turn.

A tiny stalk microphone extended from his left side earpiece, leading by a wire to the radio on his web belt. He pushed the button on his radio, and twice he spoke the code word *flecha*, or arrow. After a pause, he said *hazlo*. Do it.

In his earpiece he heard his distant sniper click the transmit button two times, confirming the order. Ramos had complete faith that Chino and Genizaro would do their duty, according to that far more secret part of the attack plan, about which the rest of the *Batallón* had no need to know.

The Falcons were pleased to rise from the ground and stretch, their white teeth grinning from behind camouflage face paint, cheerfully joshing one another as they strapped on their helmets. They climbed aboard the helicopters and sat packed tightly together on the aluminum pipe frame seats, and buckled in. The rotors picked up speed and whipped the air above them, a blur. Ramos sat on the gunner's seat on the right side, across from the crew chief and behind the pilot's seat. The crew chief passed him a gray aviator's helmet; it was wired into the Blackhawk's intercom system. He slipped it on and adjusted the microphone. The machines shook furiously, the pilots pulled pitch and the blades bit, the Blackhawks dipped their noses, rolled forward and they were off.

There was something uniquely stirring, glorious even, about lifting away from the brown earth in a rush of wind and jet turbine noise for an air assault, preparing to drop like hell's hammers onto an unsuspecting enemy.

Basilio Ramos hated the Yanquis with a burning passion, but oh, how he loved their Blackhawk helicopters!

"They're moving Max, they're coming now, over." Dolores spoke these simple words into her new walkie-talkie. Max said that the radio was "digitally encrypted," so the squatters and the Milicia wouldn't be able to hear what they were saying. Max knew all about these things, and Dolores took his word that this was true.

"Okay Mom, we're locking the new gate. I've been trying to call the sheriff again, but I'm still just getting the run-around."

"I don't see any sheriffs down by the encampment Max, just squatters and Milicia. No deputies, no state police, nothing. Be careful, over."

Her son Maximilio had installed a new galvanized steel gate across the driveway, over the last open cattle guard 200 yards down from the front of the house. The shiny silver gate and the barbed-wire cattle fence around the house had been specially topped with a roll of "razor wire." If the squatters wanted to seize their home, they'd have to cut through or climb over that last chest-high barbed-wire cattle fence. In that case, Max had said, the squatters would have crossed the Rubicon, crossed the line in the sand. Trespassing and camping on so-called "idle lands" was one thing. Climbing the final locked gate to invade a family's home…that was an entirely different matter.

Max had strapped on a heavy revolver after breakfast this morning, and had taken his Winchester saddle rifle. He had also loaded another 30-30 Winchester for her, "just in case," but they seriously doubted whether the squatters would dare to cross that last fence. The rifle now lay on the sitting room reading table, just a few steps behind her. Dolores Parada had handled firearms for most of her life, but had not done any shooting for at least two decades. It didn't matter: some things you never forgot.

She didn't need a telescope to see her son riding his chestnut gelding down by the new gate, with her daughter-in-law Carly on her palomino mare beside him. Max was almost fifty, but despite his age he cut a fine figure astride a horse, a modern day cowboy, and still the handsomest man in Monterey County. Carly was just as tough as Max, in her own way. Dolores had never questioned Max's decision to marry the pretty blue-eyed blond Carly Drake. They had met at the University of New Mexico, but she was not even a New Mexican. Worse, she was a city girl, from Denver! At least she was a Catholic, *gracias a Dios.* Carly had made them all proud, she truly became a Parada, and she bore Max four wonderful children, all grown up and moved away…

The horses stood quietly now, on either side of the ring of whitewashed stones around the base of the flagpole, half way down to the new galvanized gate. The pole was over seventy years old, hand-hewn and arrow-straight, cut from a single pine by Dolores's own father. An American flag flew just below the level of her third floor window, rolling and tossing on the breeze as it did every morning. The wind blew much harder in the afternoons, and the frayed flags with their tattered stripes had to be replaced almost every other month. The Paradas bought their American flags by the case.

The squatters were all on the driveway now, less than a mile away, signs and banners in front. Many of them were carrying those bastardized New Mexico flags, with the red star inside of the Zia's circle. Others carried red communist flags of one sort or another, as well as the rainbow flags preferred by the homosexuals, the black flags of the anarchists, and the baby-blue U.N. flags of the one-worlders. After five weeks of eighty power telescopic observation, she knew all of their subtypes, could almost read their tattoos. A sound truck was behind them, mounting loudspeakers that could be heard clearly from a mile away. She had heard them for weeks and she knew what they were saying. They were saying leave now. Flee. Run. Give up the "stolen land." Hand it over to "the people of Aztlan," whoever they were, and whatever "Aztlan" was...

Never. These thieving socialists, these Mexican illegal alien squatters, they were never going to put their dirty communist feet on the hundred year old pinewood floors of Lomalinda, they would never sit on the leather-covered oak chairs her father had built with his own hands, they would never eat a meal from Dolores Parada's kitchen!

Never!

Then shots rang out, slow fire from booming center-fire rifles Dolores guessed, and she put her eye back to the telescope. Max frequently sighted-in his own elk rifles behind the house, and she knew the sound well. Pandemonium engulfed the column of marchers, who were at that moment scattering off of the driveway and diving onto the ground!

The two Blackhawks flared out and made rapid landings only a hundred yards from the side of the house, inside a small line of trees, sending twirling eddies of dust in all directions. As they came in Basilio Ramos saw two cowboys mounted on horses, just like in an old movie, wheeling and rearing as the helicopters roared overhead. Through the open gunner's port of the helicopter, Ramos clearly glimpsed one of the cowboys on a dark horse raising a rifle.

The first dozen troops hopped down from both sides of his helicopter even before its wheels hit the ground, the other chopper had landed fifty yards away to the side. The squads immediately formed up in a line abreast for the assault. Both mounted cowboys were immediately taken under fire, but not before one of his Falcons fell to the ground beside him, his face a crimson ruin beneath his helmet. There was a flagpole just downhill from the front of the house, where the two horses staggered and fell. Both cowboys were riddled with volleys of well-aimed bullets from the Falcons' M-16s, dead even before their mounts ceased twitching.

Another bullet snapped past his head and thudded into the helicopter behind him. Someone was firing from the ranch house, even as the assault platoon dashed for the stone front steps and the wide covered porch.

Dolores Parada heard the helicopters before she saw them, and then they were landing right over there on the side of the house, just inside of their apple trees, blowing them around like a tornado! Max and Carly were firing at the helicopters even before they landed, so Dolores picked up her own Winchester from the table and did the same, the heavy rifle's blast deafening her the first time she squeezed the trigger. And then Max and Carly were somehow both on the ground, their horses too, rolling and crawling, but then they were so very still, and all in the blink of an eye, even as camouflaged soldiers in full battle dress dashed for the house!

She had already decided what she must do in the event of this ultimate calamity, but the shock of seeing her son and daughter-in-law shot down before her very eyes kept her at the open window, working the lever and blasting away through angry tears while the soldiers swarmed toward the house. When at last she dropped the rifle's hammer on an empty chamber, with a start she remembered her final responsibility. Earlier she had brought a one gallon metal can of lamp oil and a box of kitchen matches to the sitting room, "just in case."

If the invaders and thieves and communists were going to come up the varnished pinewood steps to the third floor, to drag her away from her beloved ranch house, they were going to have to run through fire.

Dolores Parada wasn't leaving Lomalinda.

By Friday, Ranya had lost her fear of doing exactly as she wished in Basilio Ramos's house. The Falcons were off on an operation, and once again she had been left to her own devices. She dressed in one of her new outfits: a green silk blouse, black designer jeans and Gucci sandals.

There was a full-length mirror on one bedroom closet door, in which she briefly checked her appearance. Curious, she opened the closet, which turned out to be a large walk-in. A Spartan wardrobe of men's suits and starched camouflage uniforms lined each side. In the back of this small room was a black Liberty gun safe the size of a double refrigerator, with an electronic combination number pad in the center. She was familiar with these heavy steel vaults from her youth as a gunsmith's daughter, and she wondered what types of firearms Ramos had stashed inside this one. She guessed that the safe had been the property of the mansion's previous owner, and it probably contained hunting rifles, and perhaps some expensive pistols. If she could open it, she thought she would be able to obtain a carbine or other weapons to help her during her escape.

While considering various stratagems for cracking the safe, she walked downstairs to the spacious and ultra-modern kitchen. The cook, a small dark Mayan woman of fifty or more years, sat at a side table reading a colorful tabloid. Ranya matter-of-factly asked for a breakfast of coffee, juice, fruit and cereal. Then she turned and let herself out, and waited imperiously at the patio table by the swimming pool, nonchalantly observing the up-slope guards with their M-16s, as they observed her. In five minutes, the meal was brought out to her on a silver tray.

It certainly wasn't the case that Ranya Bardiwell was used to dominating servants in this way. It was simply her calculated take on what was expected of her as the new "lady of the house." She decided that slinking around like a kept-woman would not win her any respect in the eyes of the house staff or guards. Only by dressing well and demanding service could she do that. If they were going to consider her their exalted Comandante's lady, she would have to live up to that high status.

After breakfast by the pool, she spent some time in the master bedroom at Basilio's computer, cautiously surfing the internet. Not only was she interested in news from outside of New Mexico, more importantly she wanted to try to reestablish contact with Phil Carson, her old friend from their time together as fugitives on Brad's sailboat. She had not heard from him or about him since she had stepped off Guajira in Santa Marta Colombia, seven months pregnant with Brad's child. A week after leaving the boat, she had been arrested by the U.S. Marshals after landing at Phoenix Sky Harbor.

Now, sitting at Basilio's computer, she considered risking a search for Phil Carson. She worried that any direct internet search for his name would immediately ring alarm bells deep within some federal alphabet agency, and this would in turn lead them straight to her again.

Before leaving Colombia, they had agreed upon a system to reestablish communications via new and unused free email addresses. Messages could be posted to these free internet accounts, with only the two of them knowing the exact email addresses and account login passwords. She checked Yahoo and Hotmail to see if the email accounts had already been created by Phil Carson, but she only received generic notices indicating that no such accounts existed. Further messages told her that due to unspecified reasons pertaining to national security, creating a new email account would require going through an extensive process of proving her identity. A small section of frequently asked questions told her that due to various unstated abuses, free email accounts could no longer be created anonymously, outside of official supervision.

National security. There it was. Once again, she had been tripped up by changes occurring during her five years in captivity. She wondered what the latest rendition of the Patriot Act was called. She could well imagine the articles she would read, if she wanted to risk searching for such security-related material. Free anonymous email accounts were too helpful to criminals and even to terrorists, to let them skulk in secret on the information superhighway. Big Brother had to know who was texting away on the internet, and to whom. So much for reestablishing contact with Phil Carson the easy way, via email, she thought.

Ranya gave up on the computer, and switched on the enormous flat screen television, which dominated a wall on the other side of the four-poster bed. Clicking around with the remote, she discovered that the same cable news channels were still in business, along with a few new ones.

After recognizing some familiar talking heads, she paused to hear a panel discussion. The subject on the table was the impending Constitutional Convention, scheduled for September in Philadelphia. The bow-tied conservative was whining that the entire process was a fraud and a sham, and that any resulting Constitutional Amendments would have no legitimacy. He said that four of the states that had originally voted for the "con-con" (as they were calling it) had rescinded their votes, after the original purpose of the convention had been "hijacked" by Congress.

The fat and pasty-faced liberal was shouting back that the four "insurgent" states in question could not withdraw their decisions to call the convention. Their state convention delegates were already in Philadelphia, and the convention would proceed as scheduled. The necessary total of 34 state legislatures had voted to call the con-con, and by God, that was that! There was no stopping the train: it had already left the station!

Mr. Bow Tie retorted that the renegade convention delegates would have to stay here on the East Coast forever, because if they returned to their Western states, there might be ropes awaiting them, tied to trees! He said that these so-called state convention delegates were simply Congressional patsies and paid front-men, without any valid authority to vote in the names of their states. Indeed, Bow Tie said, these fraudulent delegates were now too afraid to even step foot back in their nominal states of origin!

The fat liberal snarled back that the conservatives were obviously afraid of the "Economic Democracy Amendment," which Ranya mentally translated to mean the forced socialist redistribution of wealth.

The heated debate broke for a commercial, the angry demeanors of the panelists immediately changed to amicable bonhomie, and she switched channels. It was coming up on twelve noon. Basilio had advised her not to miss the local Spanish language television news, because the Falcon Battalion promised to be featured in it.

She sat barefoot and Indian-style on the bed, and skipped between Albuquerque channels. She stopped when she saw the male and female co-anchors of a Spanish language station touting the "liberation" of a large ranch, the *Hacienda Lomalinda* in Monterey County, east of Albuquerque. The hacienda, the pretty female reporter said, was on a Spanish Land Grant territory, and was therefore subject to the Land Reform Act. The female anchor breathlessly described how the current occupiers of the ranch had rejected every offer by the new state government to negotiate a settlement.

Despite the lack of cooperation from the occupiers of the disputed territory, the state government had given permission for several hundred landless *pobladores* to settle on unused portions of the 14,000-acre ranch, under the terms and conditions of the Idle Lands Act. These valiant settlers had been harassed and harried by the ranchers, but had stood fast at every turn. File television footage showed a colorful tent city spread beneath a line of trees, with a rocky escarpment in the background.

The male news anchor said that the settlers had run their own water hoses from the ranch's irrigation system to the tent city, but the ranchers had retaliated by cutting off the pipes they had tapped, leaving them without a source of water in the hundred-degree heat.

Finally, today, the settlers had reached the limit of their patience, and had marched in a body toward the main ranch house to demand that the water flow be restored. Television cameramen must have been just in front of the procession. The in-studio reporters were silent as they played the video. The view cut back and forth between the colorful line of singing, drumming and flag-waving marchers, and the distant ranch house atop a prominent hill. Without warning, there was a series of cracks, and the marchers scrambled in confusion and then fell to the ground, as the camera swung wildly amidst shouting and screaming. There were chaotic camera shots of people wailing and crying over a pair of bodies lying on the road, face down and still, blood flowing from them in dark rivulets.

In the footage aired by the television station, the next scene showed a pair of helicopters swooping down beside the ranch house. The male anchor reported that after the unprovoked shooting into the column of unarmed settlers, Milicia forces had been flown in aboard state guard helicopters to regain control of the situation, and arrest the snipers who had apparently fired on the peaceful marchers. The news anchor mentioned that last Monday's notorious bus *matanza* had happened only a few miles from the Hacienda Lomalinda, allowing viewers to draw their own conclusions about the identity of today's shooters. The reporters didn't question the amazing coincidence of the Milicia helicopters being only minutes away when the marchers were shot, supposedly by the obstinate ranchers.

The Milicia troops were seen only at extreme range, and there was no way to tell from the blurry television images if they were the Falcon

Battalion. Ranya had no doubt that they were, just as she had no doubt who had actually fired on the squatters to trigger the swift helicopter assault. Her experience in Virginia six years earlier had taught her to question the publicly announced version of any event involving the use of violence by the government. She assumed that the Lomalinda ranch attack was in reality nothing like it had been portrayed on the news show. She had no doubt that a massive injustice had just been perpetrated and innocent blood shed on both sides, in the name of "Land Reform."

Well, Chairman Mao—who certainly knew about these things—had said that to make an omelet, one needed to break some eggs. He also said that power grows out of the barrel of a gun. Unquestionably the same held true today, even in New Mexico's simmering slow motion revolution.

Nevertheless, it just wasn't her problem. As long as she was able to rescue her child and escape from this *casa de locos* called Nuevo Mexico, it was not her business how they redistributed the land. Not when the land was taken from the Indians by the Spanish conquistadors, nor when it went to the carpetbagger Anglos after 1848, and certainly not when it went to well-connected Comandantes like Basilio Ramos today. As she saw it, this was no more and no less than the rusty iron wheel of history, breaking loose and turning once again—lifting some, and crushing others.

From a long distance, shaky video footage showed the ranch house sky-lined on a hill, engulfed in flames. Black smoke was streaming away on a stiff breeze. The newscaster solemnly announced that the owners had burned their mansion, rather than hand it over to "the people." In front of the blazing house, an American flag could be seen falling away from a pole. The television camera's lens zoomed in on this movement, suddenly blurry at its extreme magnification. A few seconds later, the red-on-yellow flag of Nuevo Mexico ascended in a series of quick tugs. There was a single red star filling the circle in the center of the Zia design, as the new flag whipped straight out on the wind, framed in fire.

17

Saturday June 28

Early Saturday morning, the Falcons mustered in a local restaurant across Central Avenue from the university. The restaurant, a popular student and faculty hangout, had wisely changed its name from the Country Kitchen to *La Cocina del Campo* in compliance with the *Español Solamente* law. After their arrival, the Falcons proceeded to commandeer the establishment by not permitting any new guests to enter. By nine AM they were the only customers—and non-paying customers at that.

The management of *La Cocina* made no outward objection to the unexpected presence of the elite Milicia unit, and retreated to their office. The predominantly Hispanic kitchen staff was delighted, apparently regarding the undercover *pistoleros* as some kind of folk heroes. This morning's breakfast was on the house, no questions asked.

Most of the Falcons were wearing jeans or solid-color BDU fatigue-style pants, and a wide assortment of civilian shirts. The shirts were left untucked, to cover the pistols jammed into concealment holsters inside their belts. Some of them wore brown Milicia t-shirts, with the modified New Mexico Zia design on the front. Their brown berets went into personal daypacks, or were rolled up and tucked away in pants cargo pockets.

Sergeants passed out special items for today's march and rally. The men were handed plain white baseball caps, *gorras blancas*, without logos or markings. The hats would allow the Falcons to recognize one another among the crowds, and enable them to help one another in the event of trouble. Along with their own sunglasses (which they had been instructed to bring) the ball cap visors would help to conceal their faces in the bright sunshine's glare.

From large cardboard boxes, each Falcon was handed a new t-shirt. Most received bright red shirts featuring an upraised black fist design on the front. *Partido Internacional del Ejército de los Pobres* was printed in a circle around the fist. This was the logo of the International Party of the Army of the Poor, more commonly referred to as the Army of the Poor, or simply as *Los Pepes*. Other Falcons were given green shirts from the Armed Ecological Group, or the black shirts of the Popular Revolutionary Insurgent Army. These were just three of the largest of the radical groups participating in the March for Social Justice, along with the Nation of Aztlan, FEChA, Nuestra Raza, and other more mainstream Hispanic rights organizations.

Black bandanas were also distributed to each man, to hide their faces if that became necessary, and to serve as a secondary recognition sign. Some of the men quickly tied on their new bandanas just below their eyes, laughing and aiming their fingers at one another like *bandidos*, before removing them and shoving them into their pockets.

Ranya was handed her own issue of gear along with the rest of them—an honorary Falcon for the day. She was given a red Army of the Poor t-shirt to wear over her own black one. The other special items included a cardboard "get out of jail free" card. It was made of stiff gray paper covered in a swirl pattern, and was the size of a pair of business cards creased lengthwise down the middle. The printing was intricate and faint, deliberately difficult to read, to make the card next to impossible to photocopy. It read in formal Spanish:

The bearer of this pass is acting under the orders of state security. Do not stop, detain, hinder, question or interfere with him. This person is authorized to carry non-standard firearms and other weapons, in or out of uniform.

A single phone number was lightly penciled-in for verification purposes. Ranya slipped the folded card into the back pocket of her jeans.

In sharp contrast to his men, Falcon leader Basilio Ramos was wearing his usual camouflage uniform, complete with his brown beret and pistol belt. Today he would not be marching with his unit, but instead he was driving directly to the Civic Plaza by a roundabout route. The sleeves of his BDU blouse were carefully folded above his elbows, his trousers were sharply creased and his black jump boots were gleaming. Around him, his men were busy pulling on their new t-shirts, or adjusting their caps and bandanas. Ranya looked about the restaurant for familiar faces. She saw the men who had made the run up the mountain with her on Thursday morning; they smiled and gave her the thumbs-up sign. She did not see Genizaro or Chino, the Zetas who had been with her when she sighted in the hunting rifles at the range.

When they were finished, Comandante Ramos gave them a final briefing. For the most part it was the same information they had heard several times before at the Academy. He stood on a bench built along a wall so they could all see him. The Falcons fell silent and listened intently.

"Men, yesterday we fought together as combat soldiers, wearing helmets and carrying battle rifles to liberate stolen land. Today you are *soldados clandestinos*, but your mission is just as important, and it could be just as dangerous—so be on your guard." Ramos scanned the room, making eye contact with each of his troops.

"As you know, the final deadline for changing all business signs to Spanish has already passed. The Anglos have been warned many times that if they ignored the law, severe consequences would result. They have had more than sufficient time to comply with the new law. Now, the time of warning is over. Anglos who have decided to ignore the law have chosen their path, the path of defiance, and today they will be taught a *hard lesson*." He made a fist, and waved it slowly in front of him, glaring.

"Now the important thing, and the reason we are here today, is to initiate the direct actions. Even in a revolutionary movement, most people are like sheep. They are naturally afraid, and like sheep, they have to be led. Fortunately, it takes only a few leaders in a crowd to break the ice, by smashing the first windows. That is your primary task during the march. The others will find their courage when they see that the police won't interfere with them. I have seen this many times, in many countries.

"Now, about the police. The police have been ordered to stay away from Central Avenue, but anything could happen, and that is why you have your pistols. Let me be clear: any police who interfere with the march are traitors. They are enemies of the state who are disobeying their orders, and they should be dealt with accordingly!" Ramos patted his own service pistol, within its black nylon holster on his web belt, to emphasize the point.

"After you march under the railroad bridge into downtown, link up in your squads and platoons, then move out and undertake your assigned missions. Depending on your next missions, you will get rid of these new shirts, obviously. There may be some city police around the plaza, but they also have orders not to interfere. If the police won't let you through, show them the special pass cards you have just been issued. Don't take any crap from the police, but don't start anything with them either, not if you can avoid it. Are there any questions?"

There were none.

A Falcon posted outside opened one of the glass doors to *La Cocina*, and indicated that the march had gotten underway by giving a thumbs-up sign. Ramos said, "Okay, here come *Los Pepes*—let's go." All morning thousands of marchers had been assembling on the complex of intramural sports fields a few block north on the University. Now the din of drums, whistles, horns and loudspeakers could be heard growing in volume as the crowd approached. The "Army of the Poor" was on the move.

In only a few years, this international socialist organization had become a powerful political force from Argentina to Guatemala, and now it was growing rapidly inside Mexico. The so-called Army of the Poor was paradoxically one of the best-funded of the major international radical leftist groups, with its leaders and cadres traveling from country to country with all of their expenses paid by unknown benefactors.

The first group coming down *Avenida Central* appeared as a crimson wave, with almost all of them wearing red shirts identical to the ones just handed out inside of the *Cocina Del Campo*. If the march and rally went completely out of control, any blame would fall on the groups the Falcons were infiltrating as *agents-provocateurs*. The Falcons could melt away simply by removing their new shirts and white ball caps.

A line of giant puppets led the Army of the Poor. There were huge caricatures of Uncle Sam, bankers wearing top hats, and fat-cat capitalists. All of them had shark teeth, dripping red-paint blood. Behind the puppets, enormous banners spanned the Avenue. Even at a distance of several blocks, the larger signs could easily be read, held aloft between poles:

¡Devuelva Lo Qué Fue Robada!—Return What Was Stolen!
¡Nuevo Mexico Para Los Mexicanos!—New Mexico for the Mexicans!
¡Gringos Vayan de Nuevo al Carajo!—Gringos Go Back to Hell!

And the most common messages:
¡Sí Se Puede! and ***¡Tierra O Muerte!***

The west side of the Civic Plaza was bordered by government office buildings, the east side by the Albuquerque Convention Center. Marquette Street ran along the north side, just beyond the stage. Across Marquette from the plaza were public parking lots, and the Albuquerque Police Department Headquarters. The twenty-five stories tall Regent Hotel dominated the south end of the plaza opposite the stage, looming above it.

Concealed in a vacant office, Alex Garabanda could see the entire plaza. He was spending his Saturday morning on the fifth floor of the twelve story Bernalillo County government building, in the empty office of a neighbor who worked for the county water district. This casual acquaintance was impressed enough by the fact that Garabanda was an FBI Supervisory Special Agent, that he had not raised the slightest objection to the request for weekend access to the office. The building was located near the stage, at the north end of the Civic Plaza.

Garabanda brought along a Sony digital video camera and tripod, FBI property. This was no problem—the cameras were one of his squad's basic tools of the trade. He knew he could have more easily stayed home and simply recorded the rally from any of several local television stations, but he did not trust them to provide uncut footage. Besides, much of what he was interested in filming was going to take place backstage, or in areas of no interest to the local news stations. Finally, he just wanted to watch the rally in person. He wanted to see it with his own eyes.

In fact, Alex Garabanda shouldn't have been there at all, not even alone and on his own time. He had been instructed repeatedly by his superiors and in no uncertain terms to stay out of the politics of Nuevo Mexico, but he had been drawn to the Civic Plaza rally like a moth to a flame. Memos had been circulated in the Field Office stating explicitly that the March for Social Justice was entirely a local matter, and that there would be no federal involvement unless it was specifically requested by local authorities. His Saturday surveillance was unauthorized, strictly unofficial, solely a matter of personal curiosity.

If the tinted windows of his office lookout post could have been opened, Garabanda would have been able to toss paper airplanes down onto the stage area, less than fifty yards away and five stories below him. The permanent concrete stage was raised six feet higher than the rest of the Civic Plaza. Continuous steps ran around both sides and across the front of the stage, lending it the appearance of a miniature Mayan temple.

Just beyond each corner of the stage was a thirty-foot tall cement pillar. An enormous sunshade made of welded tubular steel was supported above the entire stage by the four pillars. Hundreds of pieces of sky-blue canvas, angled to deflect the sun's rays, were laced into the three dimensional pipe structure. Garabanda had selected the fifth floor office for his observation post, because it was just low enough to permit him to see all of the stage, beneath the immense sunshade.

Giant poster images of revolutionary icons were attached all around the perimeter of this overhead structure. He recognized Castro and Che, Mandela and Malcolm X, Arafat and Farrakhan, Cesar Chavez and Hugo Chavez. Many other faces were unknown to him. Garabanda studied the posters while he waited, looking for but not finding Marx, Lenin, Stalin or Mao. Not this year, he mused. The local socialists were still keeping their craziest uncles locked out of sight in the ideological attic…at least for now.

A band was already set up on the far side of the raised stage, blasting amplified *baladas* and *corridos* to the nearly empty Civic Plaza. The sound of guitars, violins, accordions and trumpets echoed off the surrounding buildings. Some reporters, concessionaires and others who had skipped the march had already staked out prime locations around the plaza. There was no sign yet of the marchers, or the guests of honor who would be making the speeches. He noted that the plaza's unique fountain was back in operation after several dry months, the water cascading in all directions over the rectangular blocks, once again a cubist's fantasy waterfall.

Ranya stood near the Falcon leader by the front of *La Cocina*, wearing her own white ball cap and dark wrap-around sports sunglasses. Like most of the others, she wore a red Army of the Poor t-shirt, and jeans. The Falcons (who already knew her as "the executioner") had seemed to increase their respect for her after learning that she was about to begin

Milicia training. She detected no overt sign of resentment at her inclusion among them today.

When Ramos finished his talk and stepped down from the bench, he turned to her and said, continuing in Spanish, "You don't have to do this, you know. You can ride downtown with me in the Suburban."

She pretended to be disappointed at his offer. Also in Spanish she replied, "What? And miss being a part of New Mexican history?"

"That's the spirit! Then after all of the speeches, we'll go home and get ready for the reception." The Comandante appeared distracted, frequently checking his watch and his cell phone for messages. She noted that his gold Rolex had been left at home today, replaced by a more proletarian black plastic digital sports watch.

Ranya looked through the restaurant's plate glass windows at *Los Pepes*, who were just beginning to march past, and asked him, "Why are they all carrying weapons? They look like they're ready to attack a castle." There were seemingly thousands of them coming, mostly young Hispanic men dressed in red t-shirts. Many of them were waving machetes, axes, sledgehammers and rock-picks above their heads as they streamed past.

Ramos smirked. "*Los Pepes* are simply bringing their tools, like all good workers. Their tools will be used as weapons only if any stupid gringos or *gusanos* try to stand in their way."

"*Gusanos*? Worms?"

"That's right, worms. Traitors. Latinos who are traitors to their own people, who support the Yanquis. Believe me; we hate these race-traitors even worse than we hate the gringos! And we know there are still some *gusanos* hidden among the police, so we have to be very careful today."

The undercover Falcons left the restaurant in pairs, mingling with the Army of the Poor as they came streaming down Central Avenue. Ranya said a quick goodbye, and went out with two of the troops from yesterday's mountain trail run who had volunteered to accompany her. Basilio Ramos had permitted her to take part in the march, proving that she had nearly won his complete trust. She understood the trust was not complete, because she had not been offered a pistol like those carried by his undercover Falcons.

In any event, she had already decided that she would not attempt to escape during the march, in spite of the fact that she was carrying a brand new driver's license in her wallet. The best time to escape—fully equipped and with a vehicle—would come later tonight. Her behavior during the march and the rally would further cement Ramos's confidence in her ideological reliability, and in her personal commitment to him.

As they had been previously briefed, a dump truck had tipped off a load of broken bricks to be used as missiles. The brick fragments lay in heaps along the curb on the north side of Central Avenue, the University side. As they passed the piles of brick fragments, most of the marchers picked up a selection for later use. Ranya left the rocks on the ground.

A short distance beyond the bricks was a jumbled pile of random lengths of half-inch thick steel rebar, thoughtfully provided for any "workers" who had not brought a sledgehammer or an ax along on the March for Social Justice. She selected a two-foot piece of rebar, feeling that it might come in handy for self-defense if things went crazy during the march, or later at the rally. As usual, she also had her folding knife in the front right pocket of her jeans.

Alex Garabanda scanned the roads leading into the Civic Plaza, but there was still no sign of the main column of marchers. There were already a few hundred people on the plaza, between the government buildings and the Civic Center across from his position. There were no uniformed police visible, even though the squat three stories tall Albuquerque Police Department building was located only a block away to his left, north of the plaza across Marquette Avenue. Numerous small groups of rifle-carrying Milicianos stopped and searched street vendors and other pedestrians who were walking onto the plaza early to take up the best spots.

The raised stage area itself was surrounded on all four sides by temporary chest-high festival railings. The galvanized steel sections were linked together to form a physical barrier between the speakers and other VIPs on the stage, and the expected crowds on the plaza. Garabanda noted that the Milicianos were now checking the IDs of those already within the stage area, comparing their names to lists on clipboards. Security was tightening up, prior to the rally. Non-official traffic was blocked off on Marquette Avenue north of the plaza, and on Third Street, which ran along the east side in front of the Convention Center.

More Milicianos carrying M-16s arrived on two yellow school buses, and were stationed at close intervals all the way around the temporary fencing that surrounded the stage. These troops wore the standard Milicia brown berets and brown t-shirts. Garabanda observed that they had all been issued camouflage pants and combat boots—gone were the old Milicia trademark hodge-podge of jeans and sneakers. Each man was wearing a load-bearing harness, with GI magazine pouches and canteens on their web belts.

He looked for their leaders, and found them standing in a small cluster on Marquette Avenue by the front of the buses. There were four men in complete camouflage uniforms, including matching BDU blouses, and pistols on web belts. One he recognized immediately from previous surveillance, by his black and gray Vandyke beard: Carlos Guzman, the Peruvian communist military trainer-for-hire. He zoomed the video camera in on these leaders' faces, for later close examination and possible lip-reading.

A lone bicyclist pedaled around the traffic barricades on Marquette, and up onto the sidewalk behind the stage. He dismounted and walked his bike onto the grassy area between the stage and Garabanda's position in the Bernalillo County government building. The man removed his helmet and leaned his bike against a small tree. It was little more than a sapling, one of a dozen or so planted in the grassy areas on both sides of the stage. As he locked his bike to the tree, he looked up and nodded a subtle greeting. Luis Carvahal had arrived, alone. Despite the heat, Luis was wearing dark slacks today, and a cream-colored long-sleeved shirt. He walked a dozen yards to a gap in the temporary fencing, showed some sort of credentials to a pair of Milicianos, and was allowed into the stage area. Luis Carvahal, Garabanda's informant and formerly a local reporter, was once again covering the New Mexico political beat.

The Milicianos gave him no trouble about entering the speakers' area, not when he showed them his New Mexico press credential and the hand-written note on El Gobernador's official letterhead, signed by Agustín Deleon himself. After granting him entrance, the young Milicianos paid no attention whatsoever to the skinny old man with the curly gray hair. Luis Carvahal didn't even warrant a quick frisking when entering the stage area, which suited him just fine.

Metal folding chairs were set up in four rows parallel to the front of the stage, but only a few were occupied. The front row of chairs was reserved. Toward the back of the fifty-foot-wide stage there was a long table with several yellow igloo coolers on it. Luis Carvahal poured himself a paper cup full of ice water, selected a second-row chair on the right side with a nice view of the podium, and settled in to wait.

Fortunately, the day was partly overcast, and not as hot as it might have been, because he was wearing long pants and a long-sleeved shirt, an old guayabera that had turned off-white after years spent languishing on the hanger. The four-pocket shirt, with fancy embroidered piping down the front, had been worn to a traditional wedding years before and then forgotten. Deleon had told him that the leaders were all going to wear guayaberas today, as a demonstration of Hispanic solidarity meant to symbolize some sort of cultural changing of the guard.

Deleon, Magón and the rest would arrive in vehicles from behind the stage, from Marquette Avenue, thus avoiding the crush and danger of actually participating in the March for Social Justice. It was understood that the march would in all likelihood turn violent, especially on the east side of the railroad tracks away from downtown, up Central Avenue toward the university. By arriving separately from the marchers, the state leaders would not be tainted by direct responsibility for any unpleasantness that might occur during the march itself.

Carvahal looked around him for information that might be of value to his FBI contact, Alex Garabanda. He sought out undercover security operatives, or hidden counter-snipers, but did not see any. He thought that the Milicianos around the stage area seemed to be ordinary troops. They carried black M-16s, and wore brown berets and brown t-shirts. Their t-shirts were printed on the front with the modified version of the New Mexican Zia, containing the red star inside of the circle.

The sun came out from behind a patch of clouds, so he moved over one chair to a shadier spot, and leaned back and enjoyed the music. The band was set up on the convention center side of the stage, toward the back. Each member of the band was dressed entirely in black, from their sequined sombreros to their cowboy boots. They were playing "The Ballad of Tierra Andalucia," an old tune celebrating the radical exploits of a much younger Agustín Deleon.

Carvahal allowed the ringing guitar chords and plaintive trumpets to carry him back to his glory days, when as a young man he was the reporter with the closest access to the reclusive "Mountain Lion," Agustín Deleon. What an incredible life the man had led! Deleon had come a million miles from his days as a fugitive hiding in the northern mountains, when he had been called "the most dangerous man in New Mexico."

The clandestine Falcons walked behind the first ranks of the Army of the Poor, tramping their way down Central Avenue. This would enable them to lob their bricks, without being seen instigating the violence. A low concrete median divided the avenue, but the marchers swarmed in a mass across both sides of Central from sidewalk to sidewalk.

The leading edge of the mob passed a run-down motel, built around a central parking lot and swimming pool. The motel's name on top of a thick steel pillar had been removed, and the marquee sign's black plastic letters announced *¡Bienvenidos a la Marcha de Justicia!* in ungrammatical Spanish. In place of the old name sign atop the steel tower, a flagpole had been erected, flying a large Nuevo Mexico flag with a hand-painted red star in the center. Other modified flags were hanging over the windows by the reception office. Clearly, this business owner had gotten the word and heeded its message, and as a result, his windows were spared.

Some foolish people had left their cars parked in front of stores along Central, and they were among the first targets. Automobiles sporting American flag stickers were pointed out, kicked, spat upon, and scratched down their sides with steel tools. The cars singled out for the worst treatment had red white and blue *"Kent Braswell for Governor"* bumper stickers, left over from the previous gubernatorial election. Eventually a passerby in a red t-shirt, often a fit young man wearing a white ball cap, would take a length of steel rebar or a chunk of a brick and shatter the windshields of these cars.

These first unpunished acts of vandalism emboldened the ranks of marchers swarming down Central Avenue. Once damaged, vehicles became targets for further abuse. All of the other windows were soon shattered into glass pebbles, car bodies were scraped and dented with iron rebar and hammers and tires were cut. In some cases, rags were stuffed into gas tanks and cars were set afire, blazing furiously. Ominous pillars of noxious black smoke from the burning vehicles soared aloft, clearly signaling the advance of the march to the far corners of Albuquerque. Still, there were no police officers to be seen as the drumming, whistling, horn-blowing mob stomped and thundered its way down Central Avenue. A spirit of animalistic joy pervaded them, as they smashed, slashed and burned without any fear of reprisal or reprimand.

The power of mob psychology spread like an infectious intoxicant. Thousands of voices screamed in unison: *¡La Raza, Unida, Jamás Será Vencida!*—The Race, United, Will Never be Defeated!—until it echoed and reverberated from block to block. Their "workers' tools" rose and fell in rhythm with the chanted slogan *¡Sí Se Puede!* Many of the marchers were carrying two pieces of rebar, or a piece of rebar and a tool, and were clanging them together. The cumulative sound they made was like a non-stop car wreck, an iron avalanche. Others were beating on the tops of improvised drums, made from upturned five-gallon industrial buckets. Some group had obviously passed out hundreds of whistles, which were all being blown in cadence. The crashing of glass and the smashing of car roofs and hoods added another percussion section to the anarchical orchestration of the "March for Social Justice." The acoustic din created by the mob rolled away in all directions, an unambiguous warning of approaching violence.

There were no police along the route of the march, and no foolhardy shop owners standing guard in their doorways against the human flood tide. If anyone witnessed their cars being vandalized, they did so from hiding. To confront this mob at any point would be to confront a psychotic human tsunami brandishing hammers, axes and iron bars.

A few minutes later, the leading ranks of the horde came upon the first row of stores still displaying signs written in English, and their fury found new targets. Apparent "Army of the Poor" hotheads (many of them wearing plain white ball caps) instigated the initial acts of vandalism against the offending businesses. Pulled along in the crowd, Ranya found herself with her two escorts in front of a store in a small strip shopping center. She had not picked up any bricks and she had no desire to take part in this mayhem, but nevertheless she was absorbing the frenzy all around her, almost like a contagious fever.

On one roof, yard-high metal letters rimmed in neon tubing announced to the world that the shop below was the Toy Hut. Taped inside its four plate-glass windows were poster-sized hand-painted paper signs now calling it the *Casita de Juguetes*. The temporary paper signs written in Spanish were not sufficient to placate the marchers' rage at the offending six letters of outlawed English.

A brick sailed over the edge of the crowd, digging a chunk out of a window, leaving a milky star pattern. A "worker" in blue jeans and a red shirt stood in front of the window with a sledgehammer, tapped the window twice, reared back and took a full-armed swing. The window dropped, a glass Niagara cascaded onto the sidewalk as the crowd around the hammer-wielder roared approval. The other shop windows quickly followed as the tool-swinging mob joined in the frenzy. Emboldened "marchers for social justice" ran into the suddenly wide-open store, its alarm bells ringing unheeded, and still there was not a policeman in sight.

Every business along Central with signs in English fell to the bricks and sledgehammers. A car dealership prominently displaying American flags lost all of its ground-to-ceiling plate glass windows, and had every car trashed. A restaurant still called the New York Deli was plundered, a bakery was "liberated" of its bread and pastries and was then wrecked, and so it went, block by block. Each business with smashed windows quickly became a target for looting by following groups, as the Army of the Poor marched through broken glass, heralded by alarms and sirens and rising towers of black smoke, down Central Avenue toward the Civic Plaza.

Ranya's little team of three stayed near the leading edge of the crowd. Most of the crowd around her seemed to be made up of young Hispanic men, but she thought perhaps a quarter of them were Anglos, of university age or a little older, including some other females. She guessed they were mainly *Voluntarios* like the four doomed students from Michigan, coming to Nuevo Mexico for an exciting summer vacation of riot, revelry, and *revolución.*

With the lights out in the small office and the bright sunshine on the plaza, Alex Garabanda was confident that he was invisible behind the tinted glass. Still, it was an unsettling feeling to stand by a window only a hundred yards from so many enemies, enemies who would cheerfully skin him alive merely for being an FBI Special Agent. For a time he scanned the Civic Plaza with his binoculars, and left the video camera running on its tripod to film the stage area. A special wafer microphone was taped to the window glass, with a long black wire leading to the camera to ensure decent sound recording.

He was especially interested in the guests who had been given access to the stage, in advance of the expected arrival of the official parties. Some were seated on folding metal chairs and some were standing by a refreshments table, chatting in small groups. Luis Carvahal sat by himself on the near side of the stage in the second row of chairs, writing in a notepad.

Garabanda was almost certain that he was seeing some old faces he remembered from his days in Foreign Counterintelligence. Was that short man with the droopy mustache a Cuban DGI operative he had known in New York, who had been working under UN diplomatic cover? He was talking by the beverage table with a well-groomed gentleman in a gray suit. Garabanda thought that he was a so-called Venezuelan oil minister named Rogelio Lechuga, who was considered to be one of Hugo Chavez' leading itinerant bagmen. Chavez' oily fingerprints were all over the destabilization of New Mexico. He had been exporting arms, explosives and cash from petroleum-rich Venezuela to subversive groups all over Latin America for years, but the United States was by far his most hated enemy.

And who were the other paramilitary officers with Carlos Guzman, inspecting the Milicianos around the stage? Were they Americans, or were they other foreign "advisors?" The FBI supervisor continued to film and photograph interesting persons on and around the stage—he could load their images into the Facial Recognition System databases later.

But would anyone in Washington actually care if there were hostile spies and agents operating openly on American soil, with the goal of subverting the government of a border state? Was anyone back East concerned that there was a foreign hand guiding the supposedly homegrown *revolución* in Nuevo Mexico? Did the State Department have any position on the matter? Might the President even support the foreign interference, perhaps because she privately shared their goal of advancing the cause of international socialism?

Would FBI Headquarters even give a damn about what happened in New Mexico, given the enormity of the crises it was dealing with in Detroit and Los Angeles and elsewhere? Would anyone ever analyze this videotape and his digital photographs, other than himself? To whom in Washington could he even send this tape, who would not simply toss it in the circular file? Why was he even bothering with this exercise in futility?

I suppose, he mused, it's because I still believe in the United States—all fifty of them, together. And maybe, because I still believe in my sworn oath to defend the Constitution—even if I'm the only one left who does. Even if I'm only shoveling coal into the furnace of the Titanic, I'll continue to do my duty.

Ranya and her two comrades linked up with the other Falcons after they walked beneath the railroad underpass, and emerged on the downtown side of Central Avenue. Still hidden among the throngs of marchers, they removed and discarded their red, black and green temporary t-shirts. Some of the Falcons had been wearing ordinary brown Milicia shirts underneath, these men now slipped on brown berets, but without their silver Falcon emblems. Their M-16's and web belts would be given to them behind the stage.

Other Falcons now showed a variety of civilian clothes, depending on their next assignment. Some of them tied their black bandanas around their left upper arms, as recognition signs. Ranya was now in her own plain black t-shirt and jeans, still anonymous. The human river turned right and flowed up Third Street in front of the Convention Center, to the top of the Civic Plaza. A few of the bigger Falcons set themselves at the point of a wedge formation, and the group shoved its way through the crowds.

Seen from the plaza, the back of the main stage was a high brown wall. Behind this backdrop, the ground-level backstage area was the rally point for the Falcons with operations around the plaza. Other platoons and squads broke off and headed for their own missions elsewhere. The Falcons who were now wearing brown Milicia t-shirts and berets (including Ranya's two escorts) were allowed through the temporary steel railings into the backstage area.

She was briefly stopped here, until she produced her special pass card. Her two comrades told the ordinary Milicianos guarding the fence, "she's with us," and she was allowed inside with the others. A sergeant was handing M-16 rifles to the Falcons who were now dressed as ordinary Milicianos (except for their distinguishing black armbands). After seeing her briefly detained at the fence, the Falcon non-com in charge of issuing the rifles found Ranya a spare brown beret. He just told her, "Wear this, and nobody will bother you." And so she did.

While adjusting her beret, she saw the Jefe from the van's ambush at Chulada. She recognized him by his distinctive beard and mustache. He was wearing a complete camouflage uniform, and seemed to be in charge of the Milicianos providing security around the stage area, outside of the steel railings. Seeing him here, and seeing the black M-16's, brought the memory of the firing squad flooding back into her mind. What was it he had he said? "In war, you either kill, or you are killed." Both of them were wearing dark sunglasses, and neither of them gave the other any hint of acknowledgment, but the Jefe had seen her, she had no doubt.

18

Luis Carvahal watched the plaza fill with thousands of marchers, many carrying signs and banners. There was a twelve-foot-tall mockup of Uncle Sam, with long white fangs dripping red blood. On one side of Uncle Sam was a scar-faced puppet general, clutching rockets in each hand. The general's nametag identified him as Jack D. Ripper. On his chest were medals labeled Genocide, Rape and Torture.

On the other side of Uncle Sam was a gigantic hook-nosed (and stereotypically Jewish-looking) banker in a black top hat, clutching dollars in both fists. Lest the point be missed, there were dollar signs, Stars of David, and Nazi Swastikas tattooed on the sneering banker's face. With these radical Aztlan socialists, it always came back to the Jews. Carvahal didn't consider himself Jewish, not really, but still he shrank into his seat, glad that his secret roots were unknown.

Hundreds of flags waved back and forth above the cheering throngs. They included the flags of Nuevo Mexico, Cuba, Mexico, Venezuela, Bolivia, Peru, Brazil, Palestine, the United Nations, the red hammer and sickle flag of communism, and the black anarchists' flag. He scanned the plaza, and finally he did see one American flag: it was flown upside-down, with the blue field of stars on the bottom. A black Swastika was spray-painted across the red and white stripes.

Swastikas and Stars of David. Luis Carvahal did not miss the irony of those two symbols being linked, even if the irony was lost on the gathered protestors. The irony of course was that the Swastika was the symbol of Germany's National Socialist Party, the Nazis, who were the authors of the Jewish Holocaust. Carvahal sighed in resignation, having long since given up on today's youth and their utter historical illiteracy, a product of their deliberate educational brainwashing.

The band on the other side of the stage now belted out a fast *corrida*, competing with the chanting crowds for maximum decibel supremacy. Finally, coming toward the plaza from across Marquette and heralded by blasting air horns, was a convoy of trucks. These were open stake-side flatbed farm trucks, which Carvahal knew were symbolically delivering the downtrodden Hispanics to the positions of ultimate power in New Mexico. The fronts, cabs and sides of the trucks were festooned with more banners, ribbons, and posters. The truck convoy came to a stop on Marquette, along the north side of the Civic Plaza behind the stage. The first truck was loaded with brown-bereted Milicianos, holding black M-16 rifles. The second and third trucks brought the VIPs, and more soldiers.

The crowd cheered madly as Gobernador Deleon, Vicegobernador Magón, and the other state leaders climbed down, and made their way through a lane formed by outward-facing parallel lines of Milicianos. They walked through an opening in the railings to the side of the stage, and up the wide rows of steps. The new state leaders were all wearing guayabera shirts in various hues, symbolically throwing off the Yanquis' detested suits and ties for uniquely Hispanic formal attire. The crowd roared approval at their appearance. The ovation continued for several long minutes, as the Gobernador and Vicegobernador and their staff's stood shoulder to shoulder across the front of the stage, pumping their fists toward the sky, beaming with the full expression of total victory.

When the dignitaries arrived, Ranya was standing with the other Falcons just inside of the railings, by the side of the stage. These state officials filed in between rows of Milicianos and ascended the steps to the stage, to the roar of the crowd. Comandante Ramos was about the fifteenth person back in the line, and when he passed by he greeted her with a broad smile and pulled her along with him, nodding in approval at her brown beret. He led her to a front row seat on the right side of the stage.

Higher ranking state officials and other VIPs were seated in the center directly behind the podium. The Jefe from the roadblock attack on the van came up on the stage with the other leaders, but sat on the far side of the stage, away from Ramos. Ranya also recognized the stern-faced female comrade from the drumhead tribunal at the mini-storage detention facility, the one who had taken her Glock pistol. The governor and the other leaders lined up across the stage, their hands raised high, basking in the crowd's adulation.

Alex Garabanda adjusted his video camera on its tripod, bracketing the center of the stage area around the podium. Once the state leaders had settled into their seats, an Albuquerque Spanish-language TV news anchor served as Master of Ceremonies. Taking his cue from the state political leaders, who were all wearing Latin-style guayabera shirts, Francisco Chavero had taken off his jacket and tie and left them on the back of his chair. He had his own portable microphone, and moved around the stage like the professional he was. "*¡Bienvenidos!* Welcome, people of Nuevo Mexico, to our Rally for Social Justice! Can you believe it? Just look at us today! ¡Sí se puede, Albuquerque!" This "impartial newsman" gushed on in typical crowd-pumping emcee fashion for a minute before finally introducing the first speaker. His muffled voice was understandable through the tinted double-pane window, even with the inevitable echoes bouncing off the buildings surrounding the Civic Plaza.

"Now, let's begin the Rally with a special benediction by Albuquerque's own 'first padre,' Father…Antonio…José…Mar—tínez!"

A plump middle-aged man with slicked-back hair bounded up from a front row chair and strode to the podium. The only hints that this obviously well fed man was (or had ever been) a priest were his black short-sleeve button-down shirt and matching black slacks. There was no Roman collar under the shirt, which was open at the neck. The TV emcee Francisco Chavero stepped back and took his seat, when Martínez approached the array of microphones atop the podium.

"Thank you Francisco, thank you esteemed guests, thank you people of Nuevo Mexico, and especially, thank you Gobernador Deleon!" Martínez paused, while the crowd erupted again. After a minute of basking in the reflected adoration, he used his hands to settle the spectators down, so that his amplified voice could again be heard.

"It's hard to believe that it was thirty years ago, that I was attending the trial of a so-called 'Chicano radical' named Agustín Deleon in that courthouse, right over there!" Martínez pointed to the Bernalillo County Courthouse to his right front, and the crowd roared. "And wasn't he a prisoner in the jail a few blocks behind us for a time as well?" Martínez quipped, "In fact, was there a prison in Nuevo Mexico that did not count Agustín Deleon among its guests, at one time or another?" and the crowd roared again.

"But seriously, like Jesus and the apostles, Agustín Deleon has spent his entire life struggling to reclaim the lost dignity and the stolen rights of the poor and oppressed of our state. All his life, the governor has fought to bring dignity and honor to all of God's children in Nuevo Mexico, by fighting the rapacious forces of Yanqui imperialism and neo-colonial exploitation, which have been imposed from outside upon our native peoples for over a century and a half.

"But instead of simply mouthing worn-out platitudes, Agustín Deleon has spent his entire life actually living the gospels, in a way few humans ever find the courage to do. In the Gospel of Matthew, Jesus warned that eternal condemnation awaits those who do not feed the hungry, clothe the naked, and visit the prisoners. Well, who can deny that Agustín Deleon has lived according to these commands of Jesus himself?"

"Father Tony" went on for several more minutes, but Alex Garabanda tuned him out. He had no time for the defrocked ex-priest's liberation theology, which wrapped the traditional terminology of Christianity around Marxist dogma, in order to resell it to a gullible population long steeped in Catholicism.

Luis Carvahal endured the convoluted preaching of the excommunicated priest, Tony Martinez. He smelled the same old socialist snake oil, and he wondered how many in the audience would buy it with the new Jesus Christ label slapped on the bottle. Martinez had been officially defrocked years before, but this had not stopped him from serving as the new state government's semi-official "chaplain." His off-brand of "base community" Catholicism might not have been popular with the Pope in Rome, but he seemed to retain currency with New Mexican leftists who fancied themselves as religious—when it suited them.

Carvahal, bored by the stale liberation theology rhetoric, looked around him. He knew many of the others now filling all of the rows of folding metal chairs on the stage behind the podium. He saw Basilio Ramos, the smooth-shaven Hollywood version of Che Guevara, looking quite dashing with his brown beret sporting a silver falcon. Ramos, sitting in the first row and several chairs to Carvahal's left, was accompanied by an attractive young woman who was wearing a brown beret, but not a Milicia t-shirt. Ramos, perhaps feeling Carvahal's gaze upon him, turned and held direct eye contact with him, causing a shudder to pass through the old reporter. Carvahal didn't notice the end of the benediction, or when Father Tony took his seat.

Ranya half-listened while the priest without a collar gave a brief sermon: it was Karl Marx, wrapped in swaddling clothes and lying in a manger. When the so-called priest finished, he introduced Vicegobernador Félix Magón, who stood and walked briskly to the podium. His black pompadour was combed back; he was wearing black pants and a white guayabera. She was close enough to see his acne–pitted face in fetid detail. Ranya noticed from her position behind him that Magón was standing on a small wooden crate for a step. This step was hidden from the crowd's view behind the podium. Magón launched into a fiery speech, full of rage and invective against Yanqui imperialist domination, neo-colonial exploitation, wars of genocide and oppression, and numerous other Anglo-Zionist sins.

Magón whipped the crowd into a frenzy, and at the crescendo of his oratory, he pulled out what amounted to a theatrical prop from within the open-backed podium: a machete which had been chromed to a brilliant silver. He waved it around above his head like a pirate's cutlass, declaring that the era of the Yanqui oppressor was over at last! Today the Anglo exploiters had been given their first "Spanish lesson," and more hard lessons were coming! The workers and peasants of Nuevo Mexico were going to cut the chains of domination, which unjustly bound them to Washington! The Vicegobernador didn't come out explicitly for formal secession; he left just enough room not to force the federal government's hand. Even so, his intentions were clear to the massed crowd in front of and around the stage, and they went wild with excitement as his amplified voice boomed and echoed off the surrounding buildings, and his machete flashed in the sun.

After several more violent machete thrusts at the sky, Magón replaced the blade in the open back of the podium. He calmed himself with visible effort while holding both sides of the podium, and in a reverential tone he introduced the next speaker, the old Mountain Lion himself, the founding father of the new state of Nuevo Mexico, his most excellent and esteemed Gobernador…Agustín Deleon!

The governor rose from his chair to thunderous applause, and was greeted by his vice governor at the podium with a hearty and prolonged *abrazo* or embrace, complete with mutual back thumping. The assembled thousands again thundered out their approval, as a sea of flags and banners waved with renewed fury. Félix Magón then returned to his front row seat, several yards to the left of the speaker's platform.

Gobernador Deleon held onto the sides of the podium, and launched into his speech. It seemed as if El Gobernador was beginning by reading a slightly revised version of *El Plan Espiritual de Aztlan*, the credo of the radical *reconquista* crowd. Well, thought Alex Garabanda, why not? El Plan de Aztlan had been written in 1969 during Deleon's heyday as a Chicano leader. If he was not the actual father of El Plan, he had been there when it had been born.

Like Hitler's Mein Kampf, "El Plan" was quite explicit in its goals. Like Mein Kampf, the plan was ridiculed as a bad joke for years. Also like Mein Kampf, it had been brutally honest in its aims, and most importantly, it had never been forgotten, renounced or abandoned by the true believers.

Every year, another generation of Hispanic university students, members of FEChA, Nuestra Raza and the Nation of Aztlan, rededicated themselves to putting El Plan into action. By the turn of the century, scores of these former student radicals had become judges, mayors, governors and congressmen. Today, El Plan de Aztlan suddenly seemed to be within the reach of reality, and it was a natural point of connection between Deleon and the younger people, mostly students, in the crowds. It occurred to Alex Garabanda that the reading of El Plan at the rally today sounded almost like the recitation of the Apostles' Creed in a Catholic Mass.

"In the spirit of the new people, that is conscious not only of its proud historical heritage, but also of the brutal gringo invasion of our territories, we, the Chicano inhabitants and civilizers of the northern land of Aztlan from whence came our forefathers, reclaiming the land of their birth and consecrating the determination of our people of the sun, declare that the

call for our blood is our power, our responsibility, and our inevitable destiny.

"We are free and sovereign to determine those tasks which are justly called for us by our house, our land, the sweat of our brows, and by our hearts. Aztlan belongs to those who plant the seeds, water the fields, and gather the crops and not to the foreign Europeans. We do not recognize capricious frontiers on the bronze continent!

"Brotherhood unites us, and love for our brothers makes us a people whose time has come and who struggle against the foreigner gabachos who exploit our riches and destroy our culture. With our heart in our hands and our hands in the soil, we declare the independence of our Mestizo nation! We are a bronze people with a bronze culture. Before the world, before all of Nuevo Mexico, before all of our brothers in the bronze continent, we are a nation, we are a union of free pueblos; we are Aztlan!

¡Por La Raza, Todo! ¡Fuera de La Raza, Nada!

For The Race, Everything! Outside of the Race, Nothing!

Deleon began his speech by reading, word for word, the prelude to the Plan de Aztlan. Luis Carvahal had not been invited to help him to write it, Deleon had prepared it on his own, as he had written all of his own speeches over the last three decades. Still, it surprised him to hear Deleon begin by reading El Plan. Many of the people in the crowd were obviously familiar with the words, and a hush fell over the Civic Plaza, broken only by the amplified voice of the governor, echoing off the walls of the buildings surrounding the plaza. When he arrived at the concluding phrases, the crowd erupted in cheers, and recited along with him:

¡Por La Raza, Todo!
¡Por La Raza, Todo!
¡Por La Raza, Todo!

They picked up the chant and made it their own, repeating it over and over until their thousands of voices joined, swelled, and reverberated around the plaza. Finally, Gobernador Deleon was forced to put up his hands and implore them to quiet down, so that he could continue, now with his own words.

"When the Anglos came to Nuevo Mexico, they found a new culture already in place, a culture born of a new race created in the land of the sun, the Mestizo race, the bronze race of the Indohispano people. Neither European nor exclusively Indian, this new race was born of the soil more than three hundred years before the Yanqui robbers and thieves invaded our homeland!

Carvahal considered Deleon's peddling of the Indo-Hispano fairytale to be almost comedic—the delusional pretense that the Native Americans had greeted the Spanish conquistadors as some kind of long-lost soul brothers! In fact, the first time the Spanish met the Indians living in what was to become New Mexico had been during Coronado's gold-seeking expedition in 1540. Some horses were stolen, perhaps the first horses ever introduced to the American west. In retaliation, Coronado ordered over 200 of the closest Indians his soldiers could find to be burned alive in their dwellings. That was the bitter reality of the brutal Spanish conquest of New Mexico, not Deleon's "Indo-Hispano bronze race" fable!

"Since 1948, the Yanqui imperialists have championed the cause of the Jews to illegally occupy what they call their land, 2,000 years after they abandoned it. Yet the same Yanquis have been deaf to the cries of the Indohispano peoples, to reclaim their rightful lands only a century after it was stolen from them! Only the long-suffering Indohispano peoples, who have never left their land, who have never renounced their legitimate claims to their land, only they are ignored! Why do the Yanqui bosses in Washington and New York always hear the cries of the Jews in far off Palestine, but they never hear the cries of the Indohispano people of Nuevo Mexico?

"Why? Because for hundreds of years, the Anglos have always been thieves and pirates and despoilers, ever since the first Pilgrims stole the land from the native peoples of so-called New England. Even at America's birth, God Almighty Himself put the mark on that wicked country, by cracking its so-called Liberty Bell the first time it was rung. Yes, the broken liberty bell, which rang for African slavery, and the genocide of the Indians, and the theft of Aztlan from the Indohispano people! What other nation goes to war just for corporate profit? What other nation has dropped atomic bombs on defenseless civilian cities? Only America, the wicked, America, the destroyer, America, the Satan of the world!"

Comandante Ramos was seated in the first row of folding chairs, but well to the side of the podium, with Ranya seated next to him in turn. Deleon had been speaking for approximately five minutes. What was taking Genizaro so long? Genizaro had been briefed to execute his mission soon after Deleon began, just in case the governor might give an uncharacteristically short speech and leave. His speech was another collection of clichés and half-truths about Aztlan, but it seemed to work on the crowd, silencing them. Even many of the flags and banner were still, just rolling softly in the breeze.

What was Genizaro waiting for? Had he gotten cold feet? Had he been compromised and deserted his mission, or possibly even been detained or arrested, somehow? Ramos checked his watch again, and then searched the Regent Hotel with his eyes, looking across the Civic Plaza for any sign that Genizaro's seventh floor location had been discovered. Deleon droned on—at least he showed no sign of quitting any time soon.

"But now, our long period of humiliation has ended! Finally, the Treaty of Shame, the Treaty of Guadalupe Hidalgo, which was broken by the Anglos from the very first days, will at last be thrown into the trash heap of history where it had always belonged! The Anglos have never honored their part of the treaty, and now it is only justice that we, the rightful inhabitants of Aztlan, will put it aside. As promised in the Treaty of Shame, the Spanish Land Grant territories will be returned to the rightful communal ownership of the entire people of Nuevo Mexico. This time, our sacred land will not be carved up as so-called private property, to be raped and plundered for corporate profit. This time, the land will be held communally, for all the legitimate, rightful members of La Raza, the new bronze race, the Indohispano peoples born of..."

Ranya, Basilio Ramos, Luis Carvahal, Vicegobernador Magón, Alex Garabanda and every other person on the stage was watching Deleon when, without the slightest hint or warning, a red fountain sprayed out of the back of his yellow guayabera shirt. He immediately crumpled and fell backward, his heart turned to pulp and his spinal column severed. The muzzle blast of the assassin's rifle, muffled inside of the sniper's lair two hundred yards away, was no louder than a truck's backfire. The sonic crack of the single bullet passed unnoticed, lost among the echoes of the governor's last amplified words.

After a few seconds for the reality of what they had just witnessed to be absorbed, most of the people on the stage sought cover from any following shots by simultaneously attempting to duck behind one another. Under most conditions, this hopeless exercise would have been comical, but there was nothing funny about their visceral fear during those first moments after the shooting.

Vicegobernador Magón, unlike the others who were cowering in huddles and fleeing off the stage, rose from his seat and advanced directly to the side of his fallen superior. He sat on the stage by Deleon's body and cradled his lifeless head and chest against himself. After a quick check to determine the governor's absolute, unambiguous, and irrevocable state of death, Vicegobernador Magón bravely stood in the open, with Deleon's blood visibly staining his own white guayabera with dark red splotches.

In complete disregard for the hidden assassin's possible next shots, Magón once again took to the podium to calm the crowd. This time, he forsook his usual overheated rhetoric, and his trademark theatrics with the silver machete. With his voice low and solemn, he informed the assembled masses that the governor, their hero, had been shot and tragically, it appeared that he had been killed. The thousands of clamoring protestors let out a collective gasp and wail of No-o-o! Magón let them moan for a little while, and then he used the microphone to address the people, urging them to disperse peacefully, in memory of the late Gobernador Deleon. They should go home, and await further events…

Basilio Ramos, the Comandante of the elite Falcon Battalion, also bravely stood beside Magón with his pistol drawn, as if to personally defend him from the unseen assassin. After a few moments, a squad of Milicianos armed with M-16s surrounded the vice-governor, pulled him off the stage and led him away to safety. Later, observers would remark on Magón's incredible composure and state of calm in the seconds and minutes after the assassination. It was almost as if he sensed, somehow, that no second bullet would touch him on that fateful day.

After half an hour, the Milicianos cleared a path through the crowds. An ambulance with its lights flashing backed in toward the stage area from Marquette Avenue. Most of the demonstrators had gradually dispersed from the Civic Plaza, leaving a carpet of abandoned signs and banners and trash in their wake. The diehards converged on the vicinity around the stage, not willing to leave while Agustín Deleon's blanket-covered corpse still lay where he had fallen. The back stage area all around the ambulance was a tightly packed mass of anger, grief, confusion and despair, with people crying, screaming, clinging to one another and swearing blood oaths of revenge.

Luis Carvahal followed Deleon's body as it was carried from the stage on a gurney, traveling the last yards with him. Félix Magón and the other VIPs had already departed in swarms of SUVs. Milicianos in brown t-shirts and berets tried to clear a path in front of the ambulance out to Marquette Street, firing shots into the air from their M-16s. This rifle fire sent the panicked crowds diving to the ground for cover, and again stranded the ambulance in a sea of bodies. With kicks and curses and shouts, and help from someone's amplified voice over the PA system imploring the crowd to make an opening for the ambulance, the vehicle was at last freed to move forward. Once out of the grip of the mob it quickly disappeared across Marquette Avenue, up Third Street past the police headquarters.

There was nothing left for the old reporter to do now but to go home, to reflect, and to write the final pages of the biography of Agustín Deleon.

The last groups of protestors who had spent an hour jammed tightly into the Civic Plaza began to leave. Only the area near the stage was still crowded with the most ardent true believers, clinging to the fresh history they had just witnessed, unwilling to let it go. Some still appeared shocked, but many more were furious, swearing to kill the gringo bastards who had assassinated Gobernador Deleon!

He wound his way through the milling crowd to where his old mountain bike was chained to a small tree, and unlocked it by twisting the three wheels of his combination to the correct numbers. The tree was in the grassy area between the side of the stage and the county government building. As he was pulling his cable lock free, he heard someone call his name, from behind him.

"Carvahal!"

He began to turn, and half way around he was knocked senseless by a blow across his face from an iron bar. His eyes exploded with white light, he felt the skin over his left cheek split. He staggered, and would have collapsed if two men had not seized him by his arms and supported him. The world tilted and dropped from under his feet, as his field of vision began to shrink into a hazy circle surrounded by blackness. The two men who held him up by the arms kicked his bicycle away and roughly shoved him back against the tree. He had the momentary idiotic thought that they were going to extreme measures to steal his bike!

Another man, who was wearing a black bandana across his face, took the cable bicycle lock and swiftly wrapped it several times around both his neck and the slender tree and snapped the ends together. The plastic-covered steel cable was tight against his throat, forcing him to choke and gasp, still stunned, and still reeling from the blow across his cheek.

The men on his shoulders released their grasp and stepped away. Carvahal, his knees rubbery, sagged against the steel ring binding his neck. He pulled at it with his fingers under his chin, as he struggled to stand up on his weak legs, trying to relieve the suffocating pressure on his throat. Then another black-masked stranger loomed in front of him, improbably holding a huge white bucket.

The man snarled, "You want some free gasoline, you Jew bastard? The price of your soul is a few gallons of gasoline? Well then, here it is! Have all the gas you want, traitor!"

With that, he dumped several gallons of a reeking liquid over Luis Carvahal's head and body, and one more incredible shock piled upon the others which had hammered him since the bullet had struck Agustín Deleon less than an hour before.

Five stories above, Alex Garabanda watched the doors of the ambulance close after the rolling gurney was slid into the back. Deleon's body was strapped down, zipped into a white body bag or perhaps wrapped in a sheet, he couldn't tell. He briefly caught sight of Luis Carvahal, recognizing him by his curly gray hair; he was standing near the back of the ambulance. Garabanda lost him in the swirl of the agitated mob, as the ambulance tried to inch forward. Then the crowd all around the stage hit the ground, as Milicia troops fired rifle shots into the air to clear an open path ahead of the ambulance.

At last, the ambulance moved forward, driving across Marquette. He continued scanning the crowd, and in a minute he found Carvahal again, but this time he was surrounded by masked men, who were pushing him back against a sapling tree. The tree, an Aspen perhaps, was topped by a crown of green leaves almost resembling a large bush, but its foliage was high enough above the ground not to impede Alex Garabanda's view.

A group of masked men seemed to be working Luis over, mugging him. Then the gang stepped back away from him, and Luis appeared to be tied or attached to the tree, facing obliquely toward Alex Garabanda's observation post. The front of his pale shirt was covered in blood, and Luis seemed to be clutching at his throat with both hands. It was hard to see what was happening in the mob, but then a larger space suddenly cleared around Luis, the crowd melted further back seemingly almost in concert, and somebody else wearing a black mask inexplicably threw a container of liquid on him. What the hell was going on? None of it made any sense!

Ranya was behind the stage when the ambulance left, trying to make her way toward Basilio in the crowd. She had seen him with the Jefe, standing with other Milicia officers near a line of dark SUVs on the avenue behind the stage, but then she lost sight of him, pushed along by colliding eddies of moving humanity. When she saw him again, he was on the side of the stage near a little tree, where there seemed to be some fresh commotion brewing.

She forced her way against a current of people until she was also at the edge of the mob, where she could cut through some small open spaces and get over to Basilio. She needed to link up with him—he was her ride back to his villa. She had not seen her two comrades from the march since before the speeches and then the assassination, when everything went crazy. She could have easily disappeared into the crowd and escaped amidst the confusion, but she decided to stick to her plan, and escape from his house later, fully equipped and prepared.

As she pushed between more men and reached another open space, she noticed there was a circle of protestors standing around the small tree, which was topped with shimmering green leaves. A gray-haired fellow in a bloody shirt was tied by his neck to the tree, writhing and groaning.

Suddenly a man with a five-gallon plastic bucket appeared, and doused the man with liquid. The man with the bucket was wearing a black mask like a cowboy movie bandit. The scene was so bizarre that it struck Ranya as surreal, almost Dali-esque, until she made the connection between the black mask and the bandanas given to the Falcons, including the one that she herself had shoved into her fanny pack…

Someone spat out, "You like gasoline, Jew? Here, take your gasoline!" A moment later, a lit cigarette or a match was tossed and there was an audible *whoomp* sound. Instantly the man on the tree was alight. In seconds he was on fire from his legs to his hair, yet he was fully conscious, his face clearly visible behind the orange corona of flame. He screamed and shrieked, swinging his arms and kicking his legs to no effect, his mouth and eyes impossibly wide open, his face a mask of sheer horror.

Instead of burning out as the gasoline was consumed, the fire only intensified, but the new fuel was the flesh of the man himself. Before Ranya's eyes, he became a human torch: bubbling, screaming, and turning brown. It was obvious that the man was still all-too aware of his mortal predicament, and feeling the blazing heat with every nerve ending.

The leaves of the tree above him browned and then suddenly ignited in a flash, creating an instant updraft and intensifying the fire, which was literally consuming the burning man. The smell of cooking flesh was unexpectedly horrible, beyond sickening. The smell was in its way as terrible as his agonized shrieking, and the sound of his crackling skin.

After several minutes, the man's screaming died down to a keening wail from somewhere deep within him. His lips had burned off revealing teeth frozen in a scream, as his blackened limbs curled and twisted, his entire body still alight, and still held by his neck to the burning tree. His bicycle had been kicked to the ground beside him, and it had also been splashed with gasoline. Its tires had ignited along with the man and the tree, adding the smell of burnt rubber to the nauseating potpourri of death.

Ranya wept openly, involuntarily, remembering another Saturday morning almost six years before, when she had seen her own father, newly dead. When she had found him, his body had been burned…and now she had witnessed the entire horrifying process first hand, and at close range. The sight and the smell sent her back to that Saturday morning in Virginia...when her entire life had been turned upside down and ripped apart, never to right itself again.

Basilio Ramos would have enjoyed an even closer view of Carvahal's well-deserved immolation. In fact, he would have enjoyed throwing the first lit match himself, but he was in uniform and was all too aware of the ability of a random camera lens to make unwanted and indelible linkages. As planned, Carvahal was locked to the tree that had secured his pathetic bicycle, and then he was doused with gasoline and set afire. It was quite satisfying to see the traitorous Jew bastard suffer, but by the end even Ramos's feelings were just a little bit touched, imagining Carvahal's inconceivable pain and agonizing death.

Nevertheless, it was important to remain strong, and maintain a coldly impassionate heart, like that of his revolutionary guide and spiritual mentor, Che Guevara. *El Che* had not flinched from his duty, not even when sending the Cuban people's class enemies to their deaths before the firing squads. *El Che* had understood what needed to be done, and he always did it, without pity, without remorse.

Today in New Mexico, as before in Cuba, it was critically important that the enemies of the revolution be ruthlessly crushed. They needed to serve as clear illustrations, in order to dissuade the ideologically weak from betraying the cause of social justice during its fragile and vulnerable infancy. The New Mexican revolution was now entering the consolidation phase, when cruel examples became most necessary. Traitors and potential traitors had to be rooted out and mercilessly executed, before they could even think of organizing a counter-revolution. In their deaths, the traitors could at least serve as examples to the living.

Che had shown the way in Cuba, back in '59 and '60, sending thousands of possible enemies of the revolution to the firing squads. It was Che's firm conviction that it was necessary to execute class enemies en masse, in order to terrorize the rest into rapid submission. This was a necessary step to guarantee the permanence of the revolution, when half measures would only put the revolution at risk. It was Che's dictum that it was better to execute one hundred innocent men, than to allow one clever traitor to live to challenge the revolution. In the furtherance of the glorious cause of promoting social justice, the ends always justified the means.

A generation later in South Africa, Winnie Mandela had updated the method of execution for greater public impact. At her orders, her followers had introduced the gasoline-filled automobile tire "necklace" to the world, punishing suspected collaborators with the most agonizing death imaginable. However, it was Basilio Ramos's own proud contribution to reintroduce the old Spanish tradition of burning heretics and traitors at the stake. Unlike those who died in the burning embrace of the gasoline-soaked tire, Carvahal had not collapsed to the ground in an unrecognizable blackened heap, out of sight. He had remained upright and visible to the very end, chained by his neck to the little Aspen tree.

The way Comandante Ramos understood things, this was much more than simply a matter of revolutionary justice for one traitor. Today this traitor Carvahal had received his punishment within full view of the Albuquerque Police Department headquarters building across *Avenida Marquette*. Any *gusanos* hiding themselves within the police department would now understand the stakes they were playing for, if they continued to support the counter-revolutionary elements. The message conveyed by the public execution would be very clear to the police: do not interfere in Milicia or other state security operations.

Comandante Ramos was certain that the APD would not so much as open a notepad to investigate Carvahal's immolation, any more than they would investigate the hundreds of smashed windows and scores of wrecked and burned cars up and down Central Avenue. During the economic chaos that often accompanied a social revolution, public civil servants were among that lucky segment of the population with a guaranteed paycheck. This always meant that the police, eager to keep their jobs, could be depended on to look the other way, while revolutionary forces conducted necessary (but often extra-legal) operations.

While reflecting on these matters, he spotted Ranya in the circle of spectators around the scorched tree. She was still wearing her borrowed beret, but she was weeping with her hands covering her face. He pushed his way through to her, reaching for her shoulders from behind, turning her around and embracing her. He wanted to shield her from this disgusting spectacle, as the smoldering Jew was reduced to a twisted, blackened cinder.

Women were generally too sensitive to appreciate all of the brutal necessities involved with making a successful revolution. Trying to show some semblance of human caring, he pulled his own black bandana from a pocket and dried her tears, and then quietly suggested, "Come on, let's go home." His own security detail cleared a path for them to *Avenida Marquette*, where three black Suburbans were parked in a line.

Alex Garabanda stood transfixed at the window, not caring if he could be seen through the tinted glass, standing right up against it. His informant, his friend...*had been burned at the stake!* It seemed impossible, a nightmare beyond comprehension. The governor had been assassinated, and Luis Carvahal had been burned alive, tied to a tree! This had happened across the street from the city police headquarters, yet not one single police officer, nor for that matter firefighter, had responded!

His cell phone buzzed on his belt. After a while the sound penetrated his mind, and he pulled it out and flipped it open.

A lightly accented male voice said in English, "Did you see it, Garabanda? Did you see your Jew spy baptized in the name of your Uncle Sam? I'll bet you did, didn't you? Well, since your friend likes so much to receive the free *gasolina*, we thought we would also give him a little gift, but this time we would give it to him right out in public, and not hidden in a *cemetario*."

Garabanda struggled to form words, his mouth gone dry. "Who is this?"

"It doesn't matter who I am. What matters is we know who you are: the federal agent who sent the traitor to spy on Deleon. Now, remember this: anytime we want, we can give you the same baptism we gave to that Zionist spy. Anytime at all, *gusano*. Think about it."

Garabanda was staring at his cell phone, when he saw a new text message come in. The CIRG, the Critical Incident Response Group, was being recalled to the Field Office. Garabanda text messaged a coded response, stating that he had received the instruction, and was on his way in. It would only take him five minutes to walk to the Federal Building, if he didn't run into any hassles with the mobs of demonstrators who were streaming out of downtown.

19

Ranya was seated next to Ramos in the middle of the Suburban, as they drove out of downtown on unfamiliar surface streets. Long suppressed memories of her father were flooding her mind, brought to the surface after seeing the man burned alive. She remembered receiving the fateful call while she was at school in Charlottesville, her wild high-speed motorcycle ride home, and then finding her dad sprawled on the ground, dead and burnt. Was he already dead from his bullet wounds, before he had been doused with gasoline and set afire? After what she had just seen, she sincerely hoped so.

Watching the man burned alive back by the stage, tied to the tree by his neck, had been beyond horrible. Her mind was spinning with a kaleidoscope of images from recent and past traumatic events. She could have escaped during the march, when she had passed up numerous opportunities to slip away, and she would have avoided poisoning her mind with those searing images. She could have run away in the mass confusion, after Deleon's assassination. However, she had not. Now she continually flashed back to her father, charred on the ground, between the smoking ashes of their house and the burnt shell of their store.

But even in shock, numb with new and old pain, priorities rose in her mind, allowing her to control or at least to mute her outward display of emotions. She knew that no matter what, she had to keep up her act and stick to her role as a determined revolutionary, in order to make good her escape. She could not fall apart now, she could not betray her feelings, or she would destroy her best chance to rescue her son and escape from the insanity of Nuevo Mexico.

Sitting next to her, Ramos pulled out his cell phone and made a call. According to the half of the conversation that she could hear, he was referring to the man who had been burned alive as a "Jewish spy." He said he could do the same thing to the person he called, anytime that he wanted to. This was the kind of man Basilio Ramos was. She retained her outward composure only with great effort.

Then he made another call, arranging a rendezvous, and in a few minutes the three Suburbans pulled onto the shoulder of a deserted road, within a sprawling gravel or cement manufacturing complex. A dusty gray sedan pulled over in front of their convoy, and four men in civilian clothes emerged, dragging out a fifth man who had his head and shoulders covered with a dark pillowcase. The man's wrists were zip-tied in front of him, his hands were a livid purple. While she watched, a length of rope was secured to his wrists. Ramos stepped down from the Suburban to greet the four undercover men, who Ranya recognized as members of the Zeta Squad. He left the side door open.

One of the Zetas snatched the sack off their prisoner's head, as they pulled him back toward the Comandante's SUV. The man was wearing khaki shorts, and a blue t-shirt. He was a slender man, an Anglo with light brown hair, possibly in his forties. His age was hard to guess, because one of his eyes was partially swollen closed, and the rest of his face showed signs of a recent severe beating.

"Well, well, well. Rick Haywood, we meet at last," said Comandante Ramos. "I guess you might say that I'm a long time listener, but not exactly a fan."

Ranya heard the name, and in a moment made the connection. Haywood was the radio talk host who had poked fun at the Milicianos, calling them "brown-bereted guest soldiers." She knew that Ramos hated him.

Haywood stared back at Ramos through his one fully open eye, but said nothing.

Ramos walked up to the prisoner, their faces inches apart, and addressed him in English. "What is the gringo expression, 'the cat has your tongue?' You always have so much to say on the radio, but today you are suddenly very quiet. Now, why is that?"

Haywood worked his jaw, glaring back at Ramos with his good eye. Finally, he muttered, "It doesn't matter. You're going to do what you're going to do."

"That's all you can say, that's the best you can come up with? 'You're going to do what you're going to do?' That's it? You, a professional radio talker? That's all you can think of to say? Man, if I was in your place, I'd be doing some very fancy talking! Aren't you at least going to beg a little?"

"Go fuck yourself." The talk show host stared evenly at Ramos, making a display of his courage, but at the same time, his skinny body was visibly shaking.

"I'm really disappointed, Haywood. I thought you'd have some unforgettable words for the occasion, something worth remembering. So let me tell you something instead. You always told your audience of one hundred gringo drunks and whores, that we'd never run you out of New Mexico. Oh yes, you used to say that a lot, the little man with the big mouth, hiding in a studio behind a big microphone. We would never run you out of New Mexico, that's what you always said. Well let me tell you something now, Haywood, let me give you a news flash: today is the day we are going to run your gringo ass out of New Mexico! Today is the day!"

With that, as if by prearrangement, Ramos nodded to the plain-clothed Zeta man holding Haywood's rope leash. The Zeta tied the free end of the rope to the trailer hitch of the black Suburban parked in front, directly in Ranya's view. Ramos climbed back in next to her, and closed the door hard.

"Now, just watch this. This should be good."

Ramos was smiling, she noted with disgust. She forced her own tight smile in return, trying hard to stay in revolutionary character.

The Suburban in front slowly pulled away, doing no more than five miles per hour. Rick Haywood was yanked forward by his wrists, and broke into a jog to keep up. They drove along the deserted road like this for a few minutes, circling around the abandoned cement and gravel operation, with Haywood running in the space between the two black SUVs. Finally, Ramos pulled out his cell phone, and spoke two simple words: "*Más rápido*."

The Suburban in front gradually picked up its speed until both SUVs were going ten miles an hour according to the speedometer. Haywood now had to run full out to stay on his feet. The other Suburban was about fifty feet ahead, gradually pulling away. Ranya watched in horrified fascination as Haywood lost one of his shoes, a leather moccasin of some kind, and still he managed to hop and run at top speed for another minute before he seemed to trip—and that was it.

He went over.

Pulled by his wrists, dragged along the hot asphalt and gravel, twisting and rolling, Haywood's body was quickly reduced to raw meat, bloody red, his clothes and his skin peeling off in strips, his flesh scraped away down to the bone. She watched him struggle to keep his head up off the pavement, he managed to roll onto his side, and then his back, struggling for his life, hoping, she could only imagine, that his tormenters would show some human mercy and stop before the damage was irreversible. Ranya looked down, unable to watch, hating herself for her cowardice in permitting this sadism to occur without protest.

But Haywood's tormenters had no pity within them, and they showed no sign of human mercy for their enemy. In another minute when she glanced up, Haywood had ceased struggling. There was no sign of life, his head was turned to the side and bouncing along the pavement, there was no face left, he was almost unrecognizable as human.

Ramos spoke into his cell phone again. "Drag him into the gravel pit, and make him disappear." The Suburban in front, pulling its limp cargo of bloody meat and broken bones turned off of the road trailing a plume of dust. Ramos's Suburban continued northward, reentered a public highway, and quickly picked up speed.

He turned toward Ranya and cheerfully said, "Well, I told you that Saturday would change everything. For one thing, there won't be any more problems with Anglo talk radio. Haywood's radio station just had a serious fire, and believe it or not, their transmitting tower fell over at almost exactly the same time. Talk about 'bad luck!' The other stations are going to get the message, loud and clear." Ramos tapped the Zeta in the front passenger seat on the shoulder. "Mario, turn on the radio, on the AM band, and push the middle button."

Mario did so, but only the crackling sound of static came from the speakers.

"You see," Ramos joked, "Our new media campaign is already bearing fruit. I think that in the future, we can expect more responsible reporting on the other stations." His men laughed, Ranya tried to smile with them.

"Listen *cariño mio*," he said softly, calling her his sweetheart, "We have some Falcon business at the Academy, maybe an hour. Do you want to swim some laps in the pool while we're there? Or would you rather go shopping?"

She turned to him, only able to glance at his face, struggling to appear unaffected. "I'd like to swim, thanks. Swimming would be nice."

It took Alex ten minutes to reach the FBI conference room in the Federal Building. The extra time was spent evading angry mobs of demonstrators who were not yet ready to disperse and go home. He exited the Bernalillo County Government Center on the side opposite the Civic Plaza, and walked down 5th Street with a ball cap pulled low over his face. He wore his brown utility vest to cover his Sig-Sauer pistol, and hold his spare ammo mags. His camera equipment, video camera, binoculars and other gear were in a gray daypack, to keep his hands free.

Up close, the roving bands of marchers looked dangerously feral. Black and red shirts predominated, and he was reminded of the colors of the Nazi swastika. He could have spent a productive couple of hours photographing tattoo-faced gangsters and metal pierced anarchists and seditionists, but he was not about to pull out a camera. Most of the gangs of men (and some women) he passed would have killed him on the spot if they knew who he was.

He even wondered if the bullets contained in his pistol and those in his two spare magazines would be enough, if he was cornered by one of these mobs in an alley. He knew that he was not the only person on 5th Street packing a pistol today, and that if he drew his weapon, he could not rely on merely flashing it to make an escape. If he drew his pistol, the odds were high that he would be involved in an immediate gunfight, alone and far outnumbered. It was not a good feeling.

He had to walk several blocks out of his way to approach the Federal Building from the south, because another impromptu protest was taking place in front. The fact that the sidewalks around the Federal Building had been cordoned off with heavy-duty chain link fences did not deter the radicals. The demonstrators, drawn from the Rally for Social Justice, were blocking several lanes of Gold Avenue, screaming and throwing rocks over the security fence, but the missiles merely bounced off the ballistic plastic the building used in place of glass.

This type of demonstration was actually a common occurrence in front of the Federal Building, and the unstated rules were well understood by both sides. As long as they hurled only rocks and profanity at the unbreakable plastic windows, their antics would be tolerated. If they tried to climb the fences, or brandished Molotov Cocktails or other deadly weapons, they would be doused with pepper spray fired from high-pressure hoses and hit with plastic bullets, beanbags and pepper balls.

Garabanda was glad to flash his ID, scan his thumbprint, and get through the gate in the back of the building. With the energy cutbacks, the air-conditioning inside was set at only eighty degrees. Still, it was a relief to get in from the street, fully scan-in at the security desk, and take the elevator up to the Field Office. It was Saturday, so his jeans and brown polo shirt raised no eyebrows in the conference room. He dropped his daypack onto the floor behind the chair he picked to sit in, the camera equipment hidden inside. He did not intend to volunteer the information that he had just come from his own freelance surveillance operation, and had seen the assassination of the governor with his own eyes.

In the absence of the SAC, who was at Headquarters in Washington, Frederica Chupatintas was the acting Special Agent in Charge. While they waited for the other Supervisory Special Agents and the rest of the Critical Incident Response Group to assemble, they watched local television coverage of the rally and the assassination, flipping between English and Spanish stations. The actual shooting of Deleon had been filmed from a half dozen angles, as had the emergence of the vice-governor to calm the crowd.

Garabanda watched with special interest for any film showing the subsequent immolation death of Luis Carvahal, but there was none. Either the camera crews had left before his burning, or the program managers had simply decided not to report it. He supposed that they already had more than their quota of breaking news in the assassination of Gobernador Deleon. Perhaps they didn't want to confuse their viewers with a discordant report on the other political murder that had happened on the Civic Plaza today—how would they explain it? The studio news anchors were all practically on the verge of tears describing the "martyr's death" of the "heroic" governor. Alex Garabanda could think only of how swift and merciful a bullet from the blue was, compared to the prolonged and agonizing death his friend had suffered, burning alive while chained by his neck to a tree, fully conscious even as his flesh was consumed.

Chupatintas took several phone calls while they watched the television reports, as the other SSA's and CIRG members straggled in. Finally, she asked for the television to be muted, and made an announcement. She looked slightly confused and a bit flustered. "Umm, here's the deal. They don't want our help. The city and the state have both informed us that they don't want us to be involved in the investigation. I'm still waiting for instructions from Headquarters on what our next steps should be." She paused, looking at the dozen men and four women assembled around the conference table in their Saturday casual attire.

"They don't want us. They don't want any federal help." She fumbled with her cell phone, as if hoping a new message might be found there.

20

Ranya was wearing a new strapless black mini-dress, the stretchy fabric fitting tightly against her body. The built-in bra was under-wired and moderately padded, giving her breasts a rounded profile, and pushing them up and together to maximize her visible cleavage.

She was choosing the lipstick she would wear for Basilio's party, while sitting at the desk in his bedroom. She had set up a portable vanity mirror with a vertical row of lights on either side. He was putting on his uniform behind her, after finishing his shower. The dress, vanity, perfume and makeup had been picked up on another shopping trip, after she had swum 500 meters in the academy's indoor pool. This was a short distance, but she had resolved to save her energy for tonight. The swim had left her very relaxed, acting as a partial antidote to the dreadful events she had witnessed earlier.

The swim had also left her feeling sleek, toned and sexy, which had put her in the mood to select this rather extreme black mini-dress. She knew that if she had to spend much time sitting in it, it would be a constant battle to keep it pulled down over her hips. This inconvenience would be worth the effort: the dress was a perfect fit both for her body and for her plan. Watching Basilio in the mirror, she decided to playfully taunt him, in order to lead him on and then frustrate him yet again.

"You're going to wear your uniform tonight? Don't you ever get tired of it? You have so many nice suits in your closet." As usual, when in private they spoke English.

"Of course I'm wearing my uniform. This is a meeting tonight, not just a reception. Especially now that Deleon has been killed, and we have a new governor. There will be more than enough politicians in their pretty suits. Or do you think I should wear a flashy guayabera like they all wore today, maybe with a pocketful of Cuban cigars to pass around?"

"I think you just don't want them to forget who the Comandante of the *Batallón Halcón* is." She pointed to his beret, lying on top of a nearby bureau, the silver falcon insignia prominent.

"Well…maybe. Is that so wrong?"

"No, not at all. But why camouflage again? Even pressed and starched, it's just…boring. Don't you have any dress uniforms? This might not be a party, but…I mean, you're not exactly liberating a ranch tonight."

"Very funny. You are aware that my First Sergeant was shot and killed on that Lomalinda operation, standing two meters from me? Don't ever take our missions lightly—I don't! Anyway, the Milicia doesn't believe in dress uniforms. At least not yet—not while we're still in the revolutionary phase. Perhaps they will be added later."

"I think you'd look quite dashing in a fancy dress uniform. With red stripes on the pants, and fancy shoulder boards, and a sword, perhaps? Of course, you'd need to get a proper haircut."

He flicked his damp hair back with a toss of his head, picked up the green web belt with its holstered pistol from the back of her chair, and cinched it around his waist. "I think you're deliberately teasing me."

"Always!" she said, flashing him her sexiest smile.

He stood behind her and ran his fingertips across her bare shoulders, and up to her neck. "You know, it's only seven thirty. We still have time to…"

"To what? After all the effort I've just put in to become beautiful for you, so that you can show me off like a prize mare?" Ranya twisted in her chair and pouted her freshly painted red lips at him.

"Hmmm…" He leaned down to kiss her, but she quickly turned back to the mirror, and he managed only a peck on the top of her head. He asked her, "You are…all better now, aren't you?"

"Oh yes, I'm not a bit sore. But Basilio…there will be much more time after the party. I don't want your fastest effort now—I want your best effort later!" She grinned, and poked him in the stomach with her finger. "And by the way, how late do your important guests usually stay at these 'meetings'?"

"Well, it's not up to me. It all depends on Vicegobernador Magón."

"You mean Gobernador Magón."

"Yes. Gobernador Magón. As long as he wants to stay, the reception…that is…the meeting will continue. But after his entourage leaves, I'll throw the rest of them out and chase you back upstairs!"

She tilted her head coquettishly. "Promise me?"

"Of course!"

Gobernador Magón had been preceded by his own six-man advance security team, their suit jackets bulging with concealed firearms. They all wore discrete earpieces, and spoke quietly into throat mikes concealed under their collars as they swept through the house and surrounding property. Their team leader gave Basilio Ramos regular updates on the expected arrival time of the new governor. When the governor's motorcade swept up the driveway, Ramos was waiting just inside the massive oaken double doors at the top of the wide flagstone steps. Ranya stood beside him; she was an inch taller than Ramos was while wearing her black stiletto heels.

Six more security men surrounded Magón as he exited his black Lincoln Navigator SUV and ascended the steps. He was wearing a dark, almost funereal suit, far different from the cheerfully casual guayabera he had worn at the rally. In mourning for Deleon? Ramos thought Magón looked much like Manual Noriega, the former Presidente of Panama, who had mockingly been called "the pineapple" for his round and pockmarked face. He noted with satisfaction that Magón was staring up at Ranya's long sexy legs as he mounted the steps, probably trying to peek up her miniskirt. Basilio Ramos accepted that he was not the highest ranking of the state's new leaders, but they all knew who attracted the most beautiful women!

The new Gobernador and the Comandante of the elite Falcon Battalion met on the villa's threshold and shook hands. Magón's rough, stumpy fingers disgusted the well-manicured Ramos. The security men backed away, to allow them to converse privately.

Magón said, "Terrible what happened today, but life must go on." He held a tight grip, while peering directly into Ramos's eyes. "As usual, the Falcons came through, and did their duty."

The Comandante made a slight bow. "Always at your orders, my Governor." Ramos understood the nonverbal subtext, they both did. The facts surrounding the assassination were not a mystery to either man. "We are all very sorry for the tragic loss of Gobernador Deleon."

"Indeed. His death was a great blow to us all, but I will do my utmost to carry on his sacred mission in his place." Magón released his handshake.

"I'm certain that you will," Ramos agreed.

"Comandante, what happened afterward? I heard some…disturbing reports. The fire, I mean. By the stage. The man…on the tree?"

Ramos lowered his voice. "We eliminated the Zionist spy."

"Yes, I fully understand eliminating spies. But were the public…theatrics necessary?"

"Theatrics? I would not call it that. I would call it necessary revolutionary justice, just as publicly necklacing traitors and spies was important for the ANC's victory in South Africa. Harsh, but necessary, in order to frighten the enemies of the revolution into submission."

"Yes, perhaps, but Comandante, it's not your place to make that decision!" Magón pushed a blunt forefinger into Ramos's chest. "In the future, you will not take any more such unilateral actions, understood?"

"Yes, Governor. Understood." Ramos pulled himself to a position of attention, his face flushed at being dressed down by the new maximum leader of Nuevo Mexico.

"I really don't think that you appreciate the delicate situation we're in with Washington. Your theatrics could put us into a very bad position. Thank God it was not shown on television—at least our media campaign is getting results! That reminds me, I understand that we won't be having any more trouble with Anglo talk radio, is that correct?"

"That is correct, Governor."

"You know, Comandante, I was also disappointed that yesterday's ranch liberation did not go as well as it might have."

"Yes sir, First Sergeant Ramirez was a fine soldier. His death beside me in battle was a great loss to the *Batallón Halcón*. But fortunately, the pilot of the helicopter is expected to recover from his wound."

"Eh? Who? A pilot? Sergeant Ramirez?" Magón seemed confused. "No, not that—I meant the house. *La hacienda*. It's really a shame that you failed to save it. I was looking forward…that is...it's a pity that it burned. An unfortunate waste. Even as we move ahead with land reform, we should try to retain as many of the finer artifacts of the old regime as possible. It was a beautiful house, a true classic of the type." Magón looked around him, at Ramos's villa. "It was almost as beautiful as this place. You know, you're really quite fortunate to be able to keep your 'headquarters' here, as the Comandante of the Falcon Battalion."

"Yes, quite fortunate, Governor. I assure you, in the future the Falcon Battalion will take better care to preserve the classic homes of the old regime."

"Yes, see that you do. It's just a matter of attention to detail, discipline and training. We don't want any more treasures like Lomalinda to burn."

"Yes sir, I understand, completely."

Magón shifted his gaze to Ranya, and reached for her graceful hand with his thick fingers. Even with lifting heels in his shoes, he was only five and half feet tall. His gaze darted between her face and her cleavage.

While ravishing her with his eyes, he said, "So, Basilio, I see that you've been busy off of the field of battle, as well as on it. Who is your lovely lady friend?"

"This is…Angela Carrasco, Governor." Ramos used the name on Ranya's new state driver's license. "And she is more than just a lovely lady. In fact, she will be attending Milicia training, beginning on Monday."

"Really! Well Angela, I wish you luck! I must say that I haven't met any other *Milicianas* as pretty as you…"

"Thank you sir. I'm honored to be able to contribute to the cause of bringing social justice to Nuevo Mexico."

"Yes, yes. So, Basilio, who else is here tonight? Is there anyone of interest?"

"The Revolutionary Council, of course. But in their overt, official capacities."

"I know that. I said anyone of interest." Magón laughed at his own joke, his mouth splitting in a simian smile.

"Well sir, there are several notable academics who have been helpful to the cause. There is Professor Robert Johnson; he helped to formulate our new land reform policy, so that it would be acceptable to Washington..."

"That boring windbag? You know, I can never trust a man who betrays his own people."

"The gringo movie actor Blake Bradford is here…"

Magón made a sour face. "That old goat hasn't made a film worth watching in twenty years. Still, I suppose he's influential enough. Who else?"

"Well, there are several famous Yanqui news reporters who are sympathetic to our struggle. Ricardo Mentiroso from CBA News is here—he's collecting background for a Timeline special report on 'The New New Mexico'."

"CBA News eh? Excellent!" Magón clapped his short hands together, grinning. "They've always been…*more* than fair in their coverage."

"And Wayne Parker might drop in."

"Wayne Parker? Did you know that his Vedado Ranch is bigger than the entire Yanqui state of Rhode Island? Well, let's get inside—what have you got to eat?"

Alex Garabanda lay on the sofa in the cramped living room of his apartment, his TV on mute across the room. His Sig pistol was on the end table within easy reach, next to a half-finished bottle of bourbon whisky. He was staring up at the circling ceiling fan, thinking about the quick death of the governor, and the agonizing death of his friend Luis Carvahal, burned alive while tied to a tree. He had come home after the Critical Incident Response Group was stood down, their federal assistance unwanted by the state. He had nowhere else to go, and was not the type to publicly drown his sorrows in a bar.

He had been watching television news all afternoon, and into the evening. On the national news channels, the assassination of the governor of New Mexico did not even rate top billing, pushed aside by a critical refinery complex ablaze near Los Angeles, and a fresh outbreak of Cameroon Fever burning through eastern Tennessee.

On the local channels, the assassination received wall-to-wall coverage, as was to be expected. On the other hand, the horrific immolation murder of Luis Carvahal did not merit a single mention on the news. There was not even one picture of his friend's horrible death, either before, during, or after. Garabanda even checked the most reliable Anglo talk radio station, but he inexplicably found it off the air, producing nothing but a steady hiss of static on its assigned frequency. None of the remaining English language radio stations mentioned Carvahal's murder. They were kept busy covering the governor's assassination, which had happened only minutes and yards away.

His cell phone chirped. Guessing it was FBI business, he pondered for a moment whether to answer it or let his voice mail catch it. Finally, he decided he might as well, and reached over and grabbed it. The number on the screen said that it was Karin, calling from her cell phone. He wondered if she was at home—at his old home.

"Yeah? What's up Karin?"

"Al? Have you been drinking?"

"My, how…*perceptive* of you."

"Whew. Al, you never fail to disappoint. I thought you'd be out on the case, what with the governor being assassinated right under your noses."

"Well, as a matter of fact, no. We're not on the case. The state wants us nowhere near the case. Karin, is this why you called, to talk shop and lend moral support? For old times sake?"

"No, it's not. It's not. It's Brian. He wants to see you."

"Is that so? Well, put him on, I'll talk to the tiger right now."

"I can't, he's…asleep. Tomorrow. Come by tomorrow."

"To the house? What about your restraining order? Is this a setup? Karin, I might have had a couple, but I'm not drunk."

"No Al, it's not a setup. Come to the playground by the house, at eight o'clock. We've got things to do tomorrow, so if you want to see Brian, be at the playground at eight, okay?"

"Karin, you have got to be bullshitting me. If you think…"

"Eight o'clock sharp."

Click.

There was something new on the television. Some type of a news conference was about to begin. The text crawl beneath the local news anchors said, "Assassin's rifle found in Regent Hotel." Alex Garabanda picked up the remote control from the carpet by the sofa and turned up the sound. The news scene switched to a hotel hallway, swimming in bright television lights. Set in an alcove was a stainless steel ice-making machine. A uniformed police officer was pointing to the area behind the machine, describing where the rifle had been discovered. The scene switched again, this time to an ad hoc press conference, with police and civilians in suits crowding around a podium. Garabanda recognized the place as one of the Regent's meeting rooms. Microphones were still being added even as reporters began to fire questions at the Chief of Police.

"You're sure that the sniper rifle has been recovered?"

"No, we're saying we found a rifle. It's been taken to the crime lab for forensic testing."

"Why would an assassin leave it where it could be found so quickly?"

"You'll have to ask him, when an arrest is made. Maybe he panicked. Maybe he was in a hurry to leave the hotel, and he didn't want to be seen carrying a rifle. We're checking all of the hotel's security tapes."

"Have you found the room the sniper fired from?"

"Yes. Next question."

"Have you connected the rifle to a suspect yet?"

"We may have an announcement on that very soon."

"When?"

"Soon."

As the evening wore on, the reception gravitated to the patio area behind the mansion, around the swimming pool and the jacuzzi. The blackness of the mountain loomed up close behind them, providing a sense of safety, an immense rock-solid wall. Out of respect for the death of Gobernador Deleon, the entertainment had been canceled and the Mariachi band sent home. Heartfelt toasts were made to the ascending spirit of the old Mountain Lion, who had battled for the rights of his people until his very last breath. The catered buffet line and bar were still open. A string of yellow party lanterns hanging between the house and the pool provided soft light. Mesquite wood crackled in a *chimenea* fireplace on the far side of the hot tub.

Félix Magón, cigar in hand, was the center of attention. He was seated on one of the upholstered patio chairs, in a small circle with billionaire tycoon Wayne Parker, aging leftist movie star Blake Bradford, CBA news star reporter Rich Mentiroso, and a member of his production staff, a stunning blond in her late twenties. Basilio Ramos, puffing on his own cigar, was standing just behind the governor's right elbow. He was laughing at Magón's jokes, paying rapt attention to his well-worn anecdotes. Ranya leaned against the uniformed Comandante; his arm was snaked around her narrow waist.

Mentiroso's pretty assistant, who had an audio plug in her ear, put up one hand and then made an announcement that a sniper rifle had just been discovered in the Regent Hotel. This revelation prompted a brief flurry of speculation concerning the probable identity of the shooter. It was agreed that the assassin must have been a gringo with a grudge against Gobernador Deleon, driven to commit murder by the course of events in Nuevo Mexico. Ranya thought that Magón and Ramos seemed rather unimpressed by the news, and the conversation soon drifted back to state politics.

She thought the talk might have been fascinating to anyone who was interested in the future of New Mexico, which she was not. She knew that history was being made here tonight, but it was not her history. Her stay in New Mexico was drawing rapidly to an end…she hoped. Her time in the compound under the control of Basilio Ramos was now down to hours and minutes.

She was bored with their political chat, so she studied the subtle maneuverings going on around her. There were other seated groups scattered around the pool area, but most of the 'A' list guests clustered around the stars, mingling oh-so-casually, while trying to penetrate to the inner sanctum. Wait staff in white uniforms moved discreetly among them, bringing drinks and trays of savory *tapas*, and surrounding them all were phalanxes of bodyguards.

When the new governor arrived at the house, Ranya had learned that Professor Robert Johnson was attending the party. She remembered his name from Caylen Barlow's ranch in north Texas, and from the fateful letter of introduction in the Michigan students' van, before the Chulada ambush. When she overheard two party guests introducing themselves, she learned that one of them was Johnson.

Professor Johnson was a paunchy man in his fifties, shorter than Ranya in her black high heels by several inches. He had shoulder-length brown hair in the back and was bald in the front, with a thin beard trimmed close to the bottom of his jaw line like a feeble imitation of Abe Lincoln. He was wearing a red guayabera shirt, obviously trying to assimilate with the state power structure, after seeing their new style of dress at the Civic Plaza rally. Ironically, the governor and most of the power elite were wearing dark suits tonight, leaving the sycophants clearly identifiable by their newfound sense of Latin chic.

Ranya watched and eavesdropped as Johnson tried to put the moves on an attractive young Hispanic couple, assistants to one of the state cabinet members. The two were *Voluntarios*, university graduate students. Curiously, the professor had seemed more intently focused on the handsome young man than on his girlfriend. Johnson wasn't too blatant about his attraction, but Ranya's 'gaydar' was twitching, triggered by the invisible sparks shooting between the two men.

Now, while Ranya was standing by Comandante Ramos, she observed as the professor completed his methodical advance toward the center, until he found himself standing in the gap between Rich Mentiroso and Blake Bradford. During a pause, when the chuckles were dying down after another stale joke told by Gobernador Magón, Johnson asked, "So, Governor, now that we have rejected the treaty of shame, will you push for Nuevo Mexico to leave the United States and rejoin Mexico?" His Spanish was fluent but painfully accented, revealing his New England origins.

Magón half-choked on his martini, sitting upright in his padded chair, his eyes wide in his pockmarked face. "Rejoin Mexico? Why in the hell would we want to join with Mexico? Who are you?"

"Uh, I'm Professor Robert Johnson, from the university. I helped to write the Land Reform Act." Johnson smiled, showing crooked teeth, thrilled to be sharing in Magón's spotlight if even for a moment.

"Oh yes, I remember you. No, we will not be rejoining Mexico. Clearly, that is not in our interest. Anybody who supports reunification with Mexico is an idiot."

Having been rudely dismissed, Johnson was mortified into silence and slunk back away from the inner circle.

CBA reporter Rich Mentiroso followed up. "But what about the United States? Is Nuevo Mexico going to remain in the Union?" Mentiroso was also wearing a fancy guayabera shirt tonight, a blue one with the original creases from the store packing still visible.

Magón waved his cigar hand airily. "It's not certain. In the long term, I don't think Nuevo Mexico will simply remain as one of the fifty states. Eventually, what the gringos call their Southwest will have to achieve some level of political autonomy. Perhaps we'll see some changes in the federal system after the gringo Constitutional Convention. *¿Quien sabe?* Who knows?"

Mentiroso pursued the subject. "Nuevo Mexico has always been a large net receiver of federal dollars. If we…I mean…if Nuevo Mexico left the Union…"

"That may have been true in the past, but not any longer. Except for the money going to the air force bases and the national labs, the state isn't getting much at all from the federal government, especially not with the dollar falling by the week. What good are the new blue dollars anyway, at one dollar for ten? The Yanqui federal budget just doesn't carry over from one year to the next. We can't depend on it."

"So, you'll let the federal government keep the military bases?"

Magón paused, and then replied, "For now, yes."

"And the National Forests?"

"They are ours! This will be announced very soon. The stolen lands will be returned to the people—that is, the stolen federal lands. The President has already indicated that she will not stand in the way of justice. The private ranches, they will be dealt with on a case-by-case basis, under the Land Reform Act."

Wayne Parker hadn't participated in the discussion yet, but he perked up at the mention of private ranches. Ranya knew that the left-wing billionaire "philanthropist" was at least seventy years old, and she could see that he had not mellowed with age. His wild shock of white hair appeared not to have been combed in some time. Alone among the guests, he was wearing a loud Hawaiian shirt, white pants, and boat shoes. Tonight he appeared to be quite drunk, using a slurred mixture of English and Spanish. "Félix, what about our goddamn *República Del Norte*?"

Magón turned to him, and said, "What?"

"La República Del Norte! La goddamn República Del Norte. You know what the hell I'm talking about—our own damn country! Don't play coy Félix, we've already been through this."

Magón had no difficulty in understanding Parker's drunken Spanglish, but he answered in deliberate English for the benefit of the tycoon. None of the guests seemed to have any problem following the thread of the conversation, as it shifted between idioms. Even Ranya paid close attention. "Well…of course, some kind of federation with California, Arizona and Texas is always a possibility. That is, when they are liberated, which, of course, we all hope will be soon. Colorado, Utah and Nevada …they are not so simple. Denver and Las Vegas are ours, of course, but where will the final line be drawn? Who knows? I'm sure that the idea of La República will come up at some point in the future."

Wayne Parker lurched forward, spilling some of his drink on his pants. "You can bet your sweet New Mexican ass it'll come up! Even if La República is just one damn state. You can bet the ranch on that one—we got a deal!" He fell back against his chair, mumbling incoherently, winded from his exertion.

Professor Johnson had been edged out of the discussion, shunted aside. Ranya saw an opening, and a new plan began to form in her mind. She detached herself from Ramos, and sidled over to him. Johnson looked miserable, like a pampered house cat that had been hurled into the alley by a new owner.

It was usually quite easy for her to open a conversation with a man, or at least with a heterosexual man. Normally, all she had to do was smile and make eye contact. Ranya wondered how he would react, considering his dubious sexual orientation. "Hi! You're Professor Johnson?" she asked in English.

"Yes, but please, call me Robert." He was obviously flattered by her attention. "Do I know you? Are you in one of my classes?"

"No, I'm sorry to say. But I did read some of your work on the Spanish Land Grants. You might even say that *you're* part of the reason I came to Nuevo Mexico."

He smiled back at her, his recent sense of rejection easing. "Then…do I understand that you're a volunteer?"

"Yes, I am…or I was, anyway. I'm joining the Milicia—in fact, my basic training starts Monday."

"Well! That's quite impressive! You must really be dedicated to the cause, to be willing to make such a sacrifice! Obviously, you're not just a 'summertime comrade' like so many of the other student volunteers." Johnson glanced back over to the inner circle, still clustered around the governor. "I see that you're with Comandante Ramos?"

"Yes, you might say that he's been my mentor, ever since I arrived in the city."

"Then you're very lucky. Very! You know, some of my students say that Basilio Ramos is our revolution's 'Che.' Personally, I can't think of a higher honor than to be compared to the great Che Guevara."

Ranya suppressed her loathing for the professor, while nodding in feigned agreement, thinking of the thousands of Cubans who had been executed on Guevara's orders. "Yes, the Comandante is a wonderful man, just wonderful. Actually, I've been very fortunate to get to know him personally. And you know Robert, Basilio is actually quite a fan of yours."

"R-really? Seriously?" Johnson stammered, flustered by this welcome surprise.

"Yes, seriously! He often says that land reform is the very cornerstone of our revolution, and he frequently quotes your work."

"Oh…my! Well…I'm just so *honored* that the Comandante has even heard of me!"

"He's very familiar with your body of work—he's quite a serious student of land reform."

"Yes, but the Comandante does much more than just write papers! We have all been so proud, watching his Falcons liberate the stolen lands from the gringo invaders!"

Ranya almost choked at these words, coming from a pale-faced Anglo, who by his accent had spent most of his life in New England. "Yes, Basilio is truly a man of action."

"A...man of action." Even in the dim torchlight, Johnson appeared flushed.

"And you know, Robert…" She paused, as if carefully considering her words. "Really, I shouldn't say this at all…" Ranya dropped her voice to just a whisper, stepping back, leading him further away from the main body of guests.

"Shouldn't say what?" Johnson slurped his drink, staring hard at her.

"Basilio would absolutely *kill* me if he knew I was going to mention this…"

"Kill you? What?" Johnson's eyes opened wide, as he leaned toward Ranya, his gaze flickering between her face and her well-exposed bust line.

"Robert, as I'm sure you know, Basilio is *quite* a ladies' man."

"Uh, yes, so I have heard," Johnson nodded eagerly.

"Well…umm…he's also, well…quite a *man's man*—if you follow my meaning." She gave him a sly wink, and squeezed his arm. Johnson appeared to be choking, and Ranya wondered if he would soon need CPR, or perhaps the Heimlich maneuver.

"A…*man's*…man?" Johnson replied weakly.

"You know, sometimes…Basilio…he's really quite…*adventurous*."

"I'm sure that he is…"

"And sometimes he enjoys a bit of…*variety*…but only with someone he knows he can trust intimately, of course…"

"Of course…"

"Someone that he sees eye-to-eye with."

"Yes, yes, eye-to-eye…"

"So…Robert…after the governor's group leaves, after Wayne Parker and Rich Mentiroso and the rest have gone…well, perhaps you can stick around? I'll come and find you…and we'll go upstairs. Then you can meet Basilio…on a *personal* level."

"Yes… I—we—uh…" Johnson's voice was cracking.

"A very…*personal*…level."

Johnson slurped another sip of his drink, while staring at her face. "Oh, I'll wait. I'll be here!"

"Good man, Professor." Ranya dragged a fingernail under his chin while pursing her lips as if to blow him a kiss, then turned to go back inside the house, trying hard to suppress her laughter. She left him standing frozen, his mouth hanging agape like a fish.

21

Ranya and Basilio Ramos walked the new governor and his entourage down the steps of his villa to the driveway, to his waiting motorcade of SUVs and luxury cars. She was pretending to be tipsy from drink and unsteady in her black pumps, so that she could fall against the Comandante, pressing her breasts against his side. While she was leaning against him, she brushed his ear with her lips and whispered, "Basilio, I'm so horny—I just can't wait any longer! Please *cariño*, get rid of these clowns, and hurry upstairs!"

Then she spun away from him, and strode back toward the house, exaggerating the swing of her hips, fully aware of how tight her mini-dress was. She saw the guests and bodyguards turn to follow her progress back up the curving stone steps to the front landing. She instinctively knew that they were all watching her; she felt all of their hungry eyes. Then she disappeared inside, the doors held open for her by one of Ramos's own Zeta Squad, still on duty, wearing a tan combat vest, a carbine slung over his shoulder. She knew that all of these men from the governor to the guards were thinking the same thing: *Dios mio*, that Comandante Ramos sure is one lucky bastard! *Ay caramba*, he is going to nail that *chica guapa* tonight—and wouldn't I like to be him!

How wrong they all were, she thought, savoring the delicious moment. Now she had to move quickly—there was much to do in a short period of time.

Ten minutes later, Basilio Ramos eagerly entered his bedroom where he knew Ranya was awaiting him. He had hurried his farewells to the new governor, anxious to get inside the house and upstairs to her. As he rushed through his foyer, he had seen Wayne Parker and the gringo professor in his downstairs library. They were standing over maps and atlases laid across a table, marking them up with pens like common vandals. He paused only a moment, and then continued. He didn't have time to bother with them now. They could let themselves out when they finished with their felt-tip marker fantasies of *La República Del Norte*. No doubt Wayne Parker already saw himself as the new power behind the throne, with Félix Magón serving as his brown-skinned puppet. How could a man so monumentally stupid have amassed so many billions of dollars?

Ramos took the steps two at a time, almost broke into a run on his upstairs hallway, and threw open the door to his master bedroom. The room was dark, except for the flickering light of a dozen red and yellow candles. Soft music was playing on his stereo system. Ranya was sitting on a chair in the darkness across the room, the open doors to the balcony behind her. The bottom of her black mini-dress was pulled up around her waist. Her long slender legs were crossed, showing the flesh of her thigh all the way to her curvaceous *culo*. He could see the tops of her black stockings; she was still wearing her black stiletto high heels.

"Wait, stop right there!" she commanded in English. Her unexpectedly authoritative tone brought him up short in the doorway. "Comandante Ramos, I think that you are far too accustomed to giving orders. Tonight, I am going to give the orders. I am going to command you, and I demand that you will obey me! Will you give me this gift of your obedience, Basilio? If you will indulge my fantasy, I promise you, I will exceed your wildest desires tonight. I want tonight to be a night like no other, a night that you will never, *ever* forget. Tonight will be my gift of thanks for all that you have done for me."

Ramos stood transfixed, unused to any woman ever demanding to take charge of him in this manner. Well, he had certainly never had any woman like this wild Arab girl before! Why not, he thought? What can be the harm in fulfilling Ranya's fantasy of role reversal? What can she possibly deal out that I cannot handle?

He answered with his own question. "I guess it depends on what you want to do, doesn't it?"

"I only want to please you Basilio, in a way that you have never been pleased before. I want to give you more pleasure than you have ever known. But I have to be completely in charge, at first. Will you agree to this, *cariño mio*?"

He breathed deeply. In the flickering candlelight, he could see that her nipples were just exposed above the top of her dress...and he suppressed a groan. This Arab girl was hot, burning hot, she was eager, and she wanted to begin their lovemaking by acting out some deep personal fantasy. The time they had spent together without having sex must have finally driven her to an excess of pent-up lustful desire. Well, why not satisfy her cravings, in the way that she demanded? At least, at the beginning. As soon as she lost her self-control he would take over and forcefully dominate her, the way that he knew she really wanted him to, despite this artful charade.

So after a moment's consideration he said, "I agree. Yes, I'll play my part, as you wish. And then afterwards, I'll give you even more pleasure in return."

"Excellent—that's what I wanted to hear you say. Thank you. Now, close the door and undress, right there. I want to watch you."

When Basilio agreed to obey her instructions, Ranya took a deep breath, relieved. This was the most unpredictable—and dangerous—part of her plan. She needed to give an Academy Award performance to pull it off, and so far, it had worked. After dropping his gun belt he slowly undressed, one button at a time, while staring at her. When he was naked she said, "Now, you just lay down like a good boy, and I'll do the rest." He did as he was told, his head propped up on thick pillows to watch her, his hands behind his head, his manhood growing across his flat stomach.

She stood and walked the few steps to the bed, and leaned over him, allowing him to savor the sight of her exposed breasts, which were jutting over the low-cut top of her dress. On her last shopping trip, she had picked up a dozen pairs of black nylon stockings, with this final night in mind. Where the sight of ropes or cords might panic him, she hoped that soft and feminine hosiery would instead be a tease and a turn-on. She had placed several sets of the new nylons under the bed, hidden beneath its matching mattress skirt. Each nylon already had a slipknot tied in one end.

Now she took one soft nylon and looped the slipknot around his left ankle, and then tied the other end to the mahogany bedpost. She left enough slack for it to feel safe and unthreatening, only a play-act of mild bondage. A second set of nylons was under the other bed corner, and in another minute both of his feet were securely tied to the posts. They smiled at one another, and he willingly offered her his right hand to be tied. His eyes on fire, he said, "Oh baby, I knew you were a wild one, but I had no idea how wild!"

"Basilio, you still don't know! Trust me, *cariño*: you will never, ever forget this night." In another minute he was tied hand and foot to the four bedposts, the soft and stretchy nylons seemingly only make-believe restraints for playful fantasy games.

She said, "One more, lover, one more." Ranya sat on the bed and leaned over him, and wrapped a last nylon stocking around his eyes, and pulled the slipknot tight behind his head. As an extra touch, she placed his brown beret on his head, the silver falcon medallion prominently displayed in front. He groaned, tried to lift his head up and forward to reach her but she was already gone. After a moment, she returned and sat on the right side of the bed again, and placed one hand gently on his shoulder, causing a shiver to run through him. He really did have a nice body, she thought...trim, narrow hips, broad shoulders, not too hairy…

Too bad he was such a psychopathic monster. She held a tumbler in her right hand, it was filled with a dark liquid. She slid her left hand behind his head and helped to lift it, and said, "Drink this, *cariño*," while holding the glass to his lips.

"W-what is it?"

"Oh, just a little something I know you'll like. A very special drink I made, just for you. I think it's your favorite, in fact. Now…drink."

He continued to play his role and obeyed her command, and swallowed the contents in a few gulps, spilling only a little on his chin. When he finished he was still smiling, no doubt in anticipation of the unimaginable sexual pleasure about to commence.

The cocktail consisted of only a half of a can of ice cold Pepsi, and the dissolved contents of four capsules of Libidinol. The Physician's Desk Reference on his computer had said that the normal dose for "diminished sexual desire" was one capsule, and warned strongly against taking more within a 24-hour period. When emptying the capsules into the glass, she had wondered if four would kill him, knock him out, render him impotent, or turn him into a raging sex machine. Well, she would soon find out.

"Now, lover boy, just wait for a little while. I need to freshen up and get ready, and then you're going to have the most unforgettable sex you've ever had in your life. That, I promise you."

He could feel her sitting on the edge of the bed, but then she had left. At first, he had been uneasy at the idea of Ranya binding him with the nylon stockings, but a few minutes after drinking her potion, he had seen the magnificence, even the genius of her idea. She was by far the most gorgeous, sensuous and seductive woman he had ever known, and she was presenting him with the gift of herself, but not too quickly or easily. Ranya was going to make him *earn* her love tonight! She was truly brilliant, besides being by far the most breathtakingly beautiful woman he had ever known! Compared to Ranya Bardiwell, Salma Hayek and Catherine Zeta Jones were ugly ducklings!

Willingly blindfolded, lying on his back on the softest bed he had ever felt, he remembered how she had smiled at him, and his heart melted again. Her eyes had shone like amber jewels, her lips were like ripe tulip petals, and her pink, erect nipples, peaking above the top of her dress, well, he had never seen anything half as erotic in his life!

Ranya spoke to him, her voice a melody, a symphony, and his heart turned somersaults. (Did she really have to join the Milicia? Was she really going to leave him? Panic struck him at the thought!) Then she spoke again (Oh, that voice!) and his momentary fears blinked away to insignificant nothingness.

"Basilio, do you know that tall black safe in the back of your closet? I'll bet it's just full of wonderful, beautiful things."

"Oh, yes it is! Many beautiful things! I think you would love the jewelry." He was proud, even excited, that she shared his deep appreciation for the Liberty gun safe, which was already in the closet when he had moved in. Ramos smiled, visualizing all of the treasures that it contained.

"You know, I would really enjoy seeing your beautiful things. Please darling, tell me the numbers to push to open it, so that we can enjoy your wonderful, beautiful things together. I'd like to wear some jewelry, to be as beautiful as I can for you, before I take off your blindfold."

He was astounded by the perfection of her idea—the perfectly lovely Ranya Bardiwell, wearing the perfectly lovely jewelry he had collected. His Falcons were true champions, dutifully bringing to their Comandante the valuables that they discovered on land reform operations, to be donated to the People's Cause. Now, Ranya wanted to please him, by wearing some of these gems. Why hadn't he thought of this before? Naturally, she should wear the jewelry, any that she liked!

"The combination is 8-2-4-7-5. The best jewelry is inside the drawer on the top shelf." Her happiness was more priceless to him than all of the gold and all of the jewels in the world. He only hoped his little collection would please her.

"Thank you Basilio—I'll be right back." Ranya laughed, the Libidinol was definitely working its black magic. It was not only making him super horny, but it was leaving him determined to please her in every conceivable way. She remembered what a bliss ninny she had become after drinking his spiked Margaritas up on the mountain, and she felt no pity for him in his present condition. She left him tied up on his bed, and went to the closet, where she quickly punched in the combination on the electronic number pad. When the light blinked green, she turned the three stainless steel bars protruding from the center of the safe, and pulled the heavy door open. After a quick glimpse within, she left his bedroom for the next phase of her plan.

Ranya had specifically picked the stretchy black mini-dress with the built-in bra, because while wearing it she could switch from a half-naked dominatrix to sufficiently modest, simply by making the proper adjustments at the top and bottom. Now she pulled the top of the shelf bra out, fitting her breasts back into their proper positions, and then she tugged the hem down over her hips to the tops of her thighs. She was once again presentable enough to walk through his house at just after midnight.

Three minutes later, she led a dazed Professor Johnson into the bedroom by his hand. He had been waiting in the downstairs library, seated in a wing chair, reading a history book. The billionaire tycoon Wayne Parker was lying on a leather sofa on his back, snoring to rattle the windows, while watched over by a trio of unsmiling thick-necked bodyguards in business suits.

On the way upstairs, she gave the dumbstruck professor his instructions, and on the stairway landing she presented him with his own waiting glass of cola, pre-spiked with Libidinol. He drank the concoction eagerly and without any questions, unfazed. She guessed that the horn-dog professor was accustomed to plying his students—male and female alike—with strong drinks and mood-enhancing party drugs.

There was no need to wait for the Libidinol to kick in; the professor was already eager and ready. In the hallway she said to him, "You know Robert, Basilio is still in a bit of denial about his bisexuality. He likes to begin with a blindfold on. You'll know what to do when you get there, but don't say anything. Just let me do the talking, while we begin the fun and games."

After quickly undressing (and revealing a disgustingly pale and flabby body), Professor Johnson had indeed known what to do. Ranya was not personally interested in the sight of the professor performing on the Comandante of the Falcon Battalion. She had a different purpose in mind, while she took picture after picture with poor dead Destiny's digital Nikon. She moved around the bed, carefully framing each shot to include Basilio's face in unmistakable paroxysms of pleasure. After several minutes of receiving oral attention, Ramos seemed to go almost berserk, and even with his arms and legs loosely bound by the hosiery, he clamped the professor's head between his thighs.

Ranya had underestimated the stretchiness of the nylons. They were hardly an impediment as Basilio was able to pull the more-than-cooperative professor up into a bear hug, and then roll him over onto his stomach. The nylons were like rubber bands, elongating as Ramos wrestled the professor to a position underneath him. At first, he received enthusiastic assistance from the professor,who willingly raised his chubby posterior high up from the bed to meet the frenzied thrusts of his hero, the leader of the Falcon Battalion, the Che Guevara of New Mexico.

The Comandante's blindfold had come off during all of the twisting and rolling, but still he seemed to take no notice of the sexual gender of the recipient of his desire, or of Ranya behind him with the flashing camera. During this violent homosexual act, Ramos threw one arm around the professor's neck, effectively putting him in a chokehold while continuing to batter him from behind. Basilio's face was red from exertion, a mask of both lust and anger, as he alternately kissed and bit the professor's back, ears and neck. The bites were hard enough to draw blood, which, almost unbelievably, Ramos then eagerly licked, while Ranya snapped more flash photographs. The quadruple dose of Libidinol had done the job and more.

After several minutes without oxygen, Johnson's face went from blue to purple, his eyes and tongue were bulging out, and still there was no letup in Ramos's maniacal tempo. The Comandante actually sped up for a final minute, grunting and groaning in time with his pounding as he arched up high over the professor's back. Ramos was pulling Johnson's head back, the professor's neck still trapped in the crook of his elbow between his forearm and bicep.

Ranya heard bones cracking, but she thought that Johnson was already deceased by the time that Basilio Ramos achieved his climax, jerking and spasming above his partner, and then finally collapsing on top of him, his chest and back heaving like a lathered stallion. Gradually his breathing diminished to a steady droning snore. Ramos was out cold, his entire body limp, his head nestled serenely over Johnson's shoulder, next to the professor's purple-black face, with its swollen tongue and bug eyes. Ranya took a few more pictures, from wide shots to close-ups of both of their faces, one above the other, one possibly sleeping, and one clearly dead. Then she put down the camera, turned away, closed her eyes, and held herself to stop from shaking.

Alex Garabanda sat up on his sofa now, wide-awake, clicking with the remote between the local late news programs. Details surrounding the governor's assassination were pouring in. The assassin's rifle had already been found, in a hallway of the Regent Hotel overlooking the Civic Plaza. He had apparently (the theory went) been spooked on his way out after committing the murder, and had ditched his rifle behind an ice machine as he fled. The sniper had fired from well back in a room on the seventh floor. News crews had been permitted to film the jury-rigged shooting table, which was the writing desk pushed into the center of the room. An upturned waste-paper basket, with a pillow draped over the top, had been placed on the table. Apparently, it had been used as a support, to prop the rifle at just the correct downward angle.

The curtains and the twin sliding glass doors to the balcony were left exactly as they had been found, opened with a gap in the middle only a few inches wide. TV news cameras had already captured the "money shot," the sniper's view of the Civic Plaza stage. Even in the darkness of the night, the illuminated speaker's podium was clearly visible in the slot between the curtains. The sniper had fired between the metal railings of the narrow balcony outside of the sliding doors. Zoomed in to mimic the sniper's telescopic sight, television viewers could see that it was an easy shot. The podium, some 200 yards away, seemed close enough to hit with a slingshot.

The 7mm magnum bolt-action rifle had already been linked by its serial number to the son of an Anglo rancher. The rancher and his son had not been seen for more than a month, ever since their family's property had been confiscated under the Land Reform Act. Pictures of the thirty-two year old suspect were flashed on the television, as were pictures of the scoped bolt-action rifle. They showed his New Mexico driver's license blown up to full-screen size. His name was Daniel Thomas Milbank, and he had the shaggy blond hair and wide blue eyes of a California surfer. Milbank was an Iraq War veteran, and simple revenge was speculated as his motive. All the way around, Garabanda thought, it was extremely fast work by the state and local police. No wonder they had not needed help from the FBI—they already had the case sewn up! All they needed to do now was make an arrest…

Garabanda wondered if the Anglo rancher and his son were already in custody, or already dead.

Surprisingly, the *muy macho* Comandante Ramos had turned out not to be a firearms enthusiast. For pistols, Ranya could find only the .45 he kept holstered on his web belt. This turned out to be a pleasant surprise—it was a Jardine's Custom, handmade by that master pistolsmith. Well, why should the quality of Ramos's sidearm be a shock? Basilio had consistently demonstrated excellent taste in stolen property. Was there any doubt how he had acquired his Jaguar, this villa, or his gold Rolex watch? She dropped the magazine, and pulled back the slide. It rolled back as smoothly as buttered ball bearings, and she remembered another custom .45 her own father had once created for her.

Jardines had on rare occasions passed through her father's gun shop. They were strictly top of the line, selling for over $2,000 "old dollars" back in those days, and only to those customers who were willing to wait for months. What the name meant to her now was not worrying about a failure to feed and fire—ever. With its precision sights, she would be able to hit human targets at extreme pistol range, out to about a hundred yards. The sights had tritium inserts that would glow at night for shooting accurately in darkness. There were eight hollow point bullets filling the magazine, but she could find no other .45 caliber ammo or extra pistol magazines in the room, not even in his open gun safe.

The one long arm in the safe was a souvenir she was already familiar with—Mr. De Vries's Dragunov, the semi-automatic Russian sniper rifle. She was hoping to find a submachine gun or a compact M-4 carbine like those carried by the Zetas—some concealable firepower—but this was not to be. The Russian rifle was four feet long, which would be quite a liability during her exfiltration. She decided she might need it later, so she would take it.

When she searched the safe, she found Canadian Maple Leafs, South African Krugerrands, American Eagles, Chinese Pandas and other types of gold coins stacked on several interior shelves. Most of the gleaming coins were kept in specially made plastic tubes, in stacks of ten or twenty. Many others were in coin-sized clear vinyl envelopes, and some were simply piled loose in cloth or leather bags and small boxes.

How much was gold going for today? She vaguely recollected that an ounce of gold had been worth seven or eight hundred of the old greenback dollars, before she had been arrested five years ago. She couldn't begin to guess what they were worth today in blue bucks, after factoring in the recent conversion from greenbacks at ten to one. Probably enough to start a new life with her son—after she rescued him.

On a top shelf of the gun safe, she found two extra magazines for the long rifle, and five small cardboard boxes with Russian Cyrillic writing on them, all packed together in a large zip-lock bag. The boxes were a bit larger than cigarette packs: ammunition. She opened a glued flap with a fingernail, and pulled out one of the twenty golden cartridges. It was a thirty-caliber bullet, about the overall size of a round of .308 or 7.62mm NATO, but it had a protruding rim around the base, confirming that it was the correct ammunition for the Russian rifle.

Ranya held the single gold-colored brass rifle cartridge in one hand, and selected a loose one-ounce gold coin with the other. They weighed about the same. If each of the gold coins was worth $800 or more, how much were the 100 cartridges in the five boxes worth? Should she take all of these five or six pounds of bullets?

She thought, what good would extra gold do for her, if she ran out of rifle ammo, and was killed or captured? But how likely was she to get into a fight where she would need all 100 rounds of the high-powered ammunition? Anyway, what good would the extra ammunition do for her, if she was forced into a prolonged shootout against the Milicia? What good had the extra ammunition done for Jan De Vries?

Not much good, she reflected—especially considering that he had been shot while trying to bury his rifle.

Burying the Dragunov was something Ranya Bardiwell had no plan to do.

She decided to take all of the ammo, one hundred rounds. The Dragunov rifle was dead weight without bullets, so she loaded the three rifle magazines on the spot, with their maximum of ten rounds each. There was now too much to fit into her brown backpack, along with her clothes, so she found another bag on a closet shelf. This was a heavy-duty green canvas zipper bag with strong carrying straps. She hoped it might contain some useful tactical gear, but it was only half-full of sweaters, which she dumped out on the closet floor. She continued packing. Besides her clothes and most of the gold, she also shoved into her pack several thick stacks of crisp new $500 and $1,000 "blue bucks," bound with rubber bands. Her backpack and the gear bag were quickly getting heavy. Her pack alone now weighed at least fifty pounds and the kit bag another thirty. The gold was the main culprit—it was amazingly heavy for its size.

She now mentally ruled out trying to escape on the Kawasaki off-road motorcycle she had seen down in the garage. She couldn't handle the bike with all of this extra weight, along with a five-year-old son who might struggle and fight with the "strange woman" who had grabbed him. Realistically, she'd need to take one of the cars.

Ranya didn't know how many (if any) guards might be roaming around downstairs. There hadn't been guards inside of the house during the rest of the week, but then, the rest of the week, the governor hadn't come for a visit. If any of the Zetas or even the regular Milicia estate guards saw their Comandante's girlfriend slipping out of his house at half-past midnight, laden down with heavy bags and a rifle… No.

She went out onto the balcony, and looked down over the driveway. There were only a few other cars left inside of the fenced compound. While she watched, she saw someone being carried bodily down the front steps to a waiting black limousine. It was Wayne Parker, being hauled out by his three bodyguards like a side of beef. They seemed well-practiced at the drill, with one man on each leg, and a huge fellow supporting him under his shoulders while his arms flopped down.

Ranya studied the remaining cars, and had a new idea. If she took one of Ramos's vehicles from the garage, the gate guards might balk at seeing it driven away without him. Certainly, they would all go on alert the moment one of his automatic garage doors noisily rolled open.

On the other hand… She went back into the bedroom, found the professsor's pants and checked the pockets, and found his key chain. One key was to a "Solaris," whatever that was. She went out onto the balcony again. A mini station wagon was parked on the uphill side of the drive, across from the garages. The light was bad, but there appeared to be solar panels covering the hood and the roof. Solaris?

What if she took the professor's car? There was no reason for the guards not to let a guest's car leave the compound. Could they have kept track of which guest went with which car? Not likely. Their security was focused outward, not inward. Parker's limo and an escort SUV were leaving now, with no hassles. Why not the professor's Solaris?

And the professor, well, the creep had been single—no huge surprise there. He probably wouldn't be missed by anyone at all until his first class on Monday morning, if he were even teaching any summer session classes. What would his little Leninist lemmings do then? Probably leave after the mandatory ten minutes, without so much as looking into the cause of his unexplained absence. The school might not get serious about searching for their wayward professor for another day or two. And if he wasn't teaching this summer, his absence might not be noted for weeks.

This left the question of the unconscious Basilio Ramos to deal with. She could kill him now, easily (and God knows he deserved it). A knife or a nylon stocking garrote, and it would be done. In fact, after what she had seen today, she considered it an injustice to allow him to live at all. If anything, he deserved to burn, like the man at the rally—after being dragged behind a car as a warm up. Would God take care of his punishment, if she didn't? She paced his bedroom, glancing at the two naked men, one alive and one dead. In the end, she made the hard, cold calculation to allow him to live.

Alive, he would have every motive to cover up his crime. When he woke up, his first order of business would be to get rid of the professor's corpse. She would actually be helping him with the cover-up, if she removed Johnson's car from the compound. No body, no car—no crime.

If she killed Ramos now and then she escaped, the entire episode would blow wide open in the morning at the latest, when he was missed and both of their bodies were inevitably found. After that gruesome discovery, the Comandante's last girlfriend would be everybody's number one suspect—and Ranya did not want that type of attention, to say the least.

A floodlight mounted on the outer right corner of the balcony shone down upon the front landing of the house, from the doors and the flagstone stairs, toward the driveway and the gate. Immediately beneath the balcony on the ground floor was a window room, protruding six feet out from the house. On the other side of the balcony, the up-slope side of the house toward the three garage doors, there was no spotlight. Better, there was a row of shrubs along the front of the house on that side, between the window room and the garages. It was only fifteen vertical feet straight down the stone corner between the balcony and the house, into the darkness…

Peering over the right side of the balcony she could see the guard leaning back against the door, illuminated in the beam of the floodlight. His head was tipped forward…was he even fully awake? If he looked up toward her on the balcony, he would be blinded by the spotlight. Presumably, any late straggling guests might come through the house, but perhaps not. Was he now relying on the door being opened up from within to give him a nudge to wake him up, if any straggling guests were coming out? If she descended down the other side of the balcony, could she make it to the professor's car in the near darkness, without attracting this sleepy guard's attention?

She considered the guard's probable reaction if she went downstairs through the house, and opened a noisy garage door. Could the Comandante's girlfriend get away with driving off in one of his well-known vehicles, without being challenged? That was a dicey proposition, at best.

Instead, she decided to lower the bags and the Dragunov rifle down into the hedge, directly beneath the left side of the balcony, and go for the professor's Solaris.

Back in his bedroom, she went on a search for rope to lower down the bags. She hoped to find a coil of rappelling line, a roll of 550-pound test parachute cord, anything at all capable of holding the two bags and the rifle, but she found nothing like this. In his room, he had one pistol, one rifle, and no rope or paracord.

Quietly laughing to herself, Ranya was beginning to wonder just what kind of "commando" Basilio Ramos really was. Clearly, the kind who was more interested in collecting gold than guns. The only useful gear she found in his room was a set of compact Steiner binoculars, and a small tactical flashlight. She packed both into a side pocket of her pack, and continued looking for rope.

Finally, as a last resort, she settled on his rack of civilian neckties. Each tie was silk, five feet long, and with a series of quick square knots, she created two uniquely colorful ropes, each twenty feet long. Another pair of neckties became a sling, so that she could carry the rifle as unobtrusively as possible across the driveway. Slung across her back, barrel down, the Dragunov would blend with her dark form as she crossed the open ground.

If she was challenged and had to fight, she would only have the eight .45 caliber pistol bullets, and the ten rounds in each of the three rifle magazines. There would be no way to shoot her way past the gate, and certainly no way to ram the gate with the tiny Solaris wagon. The bars of the fence around the front of the house were ten feet high, and each was tipped with a wrought-iron arrowhead. If she was seen, compromised and challenged, if she had to battle her way out, she would have to go all the way around the house and up the mountain trail. She harbored no illusions about her chances of outrunning the swift-footed Falcons, but regardless, she would not surrender. One way or the other, she would get out of the compound tonight.

Now, faced with the difficulty of an escape that had seemed so simple in the abstract, she questioned why she hadn't simply bolted today during the march or the rally, when she had had every opportunity. Before, it had seemed like such an easy thing to slip out of the compound. Looking over the balcony at the reality, it didn't seem simple or easy at all. It looked like long odds, very long odds.

Back inside the room, she had only a few more tasks to take care of with the camera, and then she changed into her long blue jeans, her black hooded sweatshirt, and her cross trainers. She adjusted Ramos's web belt so that it fit snugly around her waist. The .45 was a comfort to her in its black nylon holster. It was cocked and locked, with a round chambered, the safety engaged and the hammer back. She looked around the room again, at Basilio passed out on top of the dead professor. With her folding knife, she sliced through the four nylons that still held him to the bed, lest he wind up strangling himself tonight if he tossed and twisted around.

Then it was time to go. She took the bags and the rifle outside and quietly closed the two glass doors behind her. She crouched on the left side of the balcony and lifted the backpack over the low stone wall. A rope made of neckties was already tied to the grab handle on top of the pack. She leaned over on her stomach and lowered it down hand over hand. It slid behind the bushes with just a rustle and nudged the ground, and she let go of the necktie rope, dropping it down as well. She was fully committed now: there was no turning back. Next over the stone parapet went the green canvas zipper bag and the rifle, tied together. She was careful not to let the weapon bang or scrape against the walls on the way down.

One more glance over the right side of the balcony: the guard was still leaning back against the front doors. Nothing left to do now but slide out over the ledge, hanging down by her fingers, and find the first foot holds where the rocky walls joined in a corner between the balcony and the house. The uneven stones made easy hand and toe holds. It was no problem pushing against the two rock walls, spread ninety degrees apart, and inching her way down.

After a few rock-climbing moves, feeling with her fingers and probing with the tips of her shoes, she settled the outside edge of her right foot against the top of a protruding stone. She moved her hands to new positions, shifted her weight to the new foothold—and the tiny ledge crumbled and snapped. She pushed away as she fell so that she wouldn't scrape her way down the rocky corner, and landed on her back with a loud crash, in the middle of the dry bush.

The wind was knocked out of her; she lay still and clumsily drew the pistol from its holster even while she gasped for air. The dozing front door guard was only yards away on the other side of the window room, and she expected to hear a cry of alarm. After a few moments to recover her breath, she extricated herself from the hedge, rolled and lay prone on her stomach in the space next to the house. She allowed a minute to pass, waiting in the hidden spot for her heart to stop racing, and then she raised herself to a crouch, and continued with her escape.

She bunched up the necktie ropes, and stuffed them into side pockets on both bags. There was just adequate space to move along the wall concealed by the hedge, so she slipped the rifle over her back with its necktie sling, barrel down, and picked up a bag with each hand, and slowly, hunched over and turned sideways, she carried them a yard at a time toward the garages, twenty feet away.

After a few careful, silent minutes, she was at the end of the shrubbery near the first garage. Basilio's black Jeep was behind this door, but it might as well not have existed. The professor's little Solaris wagon was only thirty feet away now, across the asphalt driveway. It wasn't parked in complete darkness, but neither was it bathed in the spotlight shining from the other side of the balcony above the window room.

Take a deep breath, shoulders back. Muscles primed. One heavy bag in each hand. She told herself that there was no way to be perfectly, invisibly stealthy now, even wearing dark clothes, with a black hood pulled up over her head. Just do it! She slipped away from the shrubbery by the first garage door, and covered the thirty feet to Professor Johnson's Solaris in a few seconds, stopping on the far side, away from the front door of the house and the driveway gate. The driver's side door was unlocked, thank God. There was no need to fumble with the key.

She pushed her heavy backpack over into the passenger side foot well. The rifle and the other bag went into the back, and she slipped in behind the wheel. She closed the door, firmly but quietly. No alarms, no guards, no notice at all…so far. She unfastened the web belt, and took the pistol out of its holster, sliding it into the gap between her right thigh and the center console. If she had to, if they stopped her at the closed gate, she'd shoot the guards and try to open it herself. But with only eight bullets in the .45…the odds were very long.

She found the keyhole on the side of the steering wheel and turned on the car. There was no motor noise, but the digital dashboard display instantly lit up. Softly glowing red numbers and letters informed her that the battery bank was at 27% charge. After a few fumbling moments, she found the anemic headlights and turned them on, sending their light away from the house. She pushed the centerline shifter into reverse, and gently depressed the accelerator pedal. The car eased back as she turned the wheel to head out the driveway. She could handle it. Electric or not, a car was a car.

The guards, having recently opened the gate for Wayne Parker's entourage, were ready when they saw another vehicle approaching. On the way out, the guard shack was on the right side of the driveway, away from her. Two bereted Milicianos with slung M-16 rifles were standing together by it, smoking and having a conversation. They had been opening the gate for departing guests for several hours, and they didn't hesitate for one more. The automatic twin gates pivoted outward and she was through, heading out of the Sandia Heights neighborhood toward Tramway Road, the miniature electric car easily getting up to 50 miles an hour rolling down hill.

Once on level ground, southbound on Tramway, the display informed her that she was at 22% charge, and the car could travel thirty more miles at the current power output. Well, Brian lived only five miles away, so this would be plenty. After taking down his "parents," Ranya's evolving plan now called for her to escape with Brian in one of their gasoline-powered vehicles. She could ditch the professor's crummy electric car somewhere near Brian's house.

With luck, if all of them were home, she could break in and catch his two "parents" together in bed. Alexandro Garabanda was an FBI agent, so without a doubt he would have some type of a security system in place, and of course, he would have a weapon close at hand. It wouldn't be easy, it would take some study, take some care. Perhaps she could lure him outside with some type of ruse. She would have to see his house, and study its layout. Until then, all she could do was think up hypothetical situations, and plan to use the element of surprise to the maximum.

22

Sunday June 29

Professor Johnson's electric car was painfully slow and it was running out of battery power, but it did have one superb quality: it was virtually silent. No one, no matter how alert, could hear it as it prowled around the Glenwood Hills subdivision in the early Sunday morning hours. Only a few of the local streetlights were functioning, which was another plus during Ranya's stealthy reconnaissance. The little wagon might have been detected if someone was already outside, but there was no one. Camino Del Cielo was abandoned, it was hers alone. She had no difficulty finding the Garabanda's house—a single dim porch light illuminated the number 4875 near the front door.

Many of the houses in the neighborhood appeared to be unoccupied. There was an obviously vacant home diagonally across the street from 4875 Camino Del Cielo. The front yard was knee high with dry weeds, and there was not even a hint of light from inside. No cars were parked at the curb out front, or in the driveway. The place was worth a look on foot. The garage door was rolled open and the space within was empty. She checked it with a little penlight she had taken from the top of Basilio's dresser. She found a broken ladder, canvas drop-cloths, empty paint cans and other trash littering the interior. After clearing away sufficient open space, she backed the Solaris into the garage, parking it just far enough inside to be able to observe the Garabanda residence from the driver's seat.

By the collection of junk and debris in the garage around her, it appeared that home renovations had been aborted mid-stream. Was the owner tying to sell the house when it had been foreclosed, or was it another "walk away," a product of the broken economy? She remembered the older black couple in the RV, who had given her a lift in Texas. They said they had given up on trying to live in Houston and walked out on their mortgage, giving their house back to the bank.

A white plastic bucket in the front corner of the garage was identical to the one used to throw gasoline on the man after the rally. She stared at the empty five-gallon pail, so white that it appeared to be glowing in the darkness. She remembered the bucket being raised above the man chained to the tree; she saw the gasoline poured over him and the match arcing through the air. Ranya shuddered at the memory of him bursting into flames, and again she heard his screams. She had stared at his burning face, it seemed that he had looked into her eyes, but there was no way to know what the man had seen through his veil of flames.

What a day of excruciating memories it had been, beginning with the jolting shock of Deleon's assassination twenty feet from her, followed by the man being burned against the tree, and then the radio man's dragging death, flayed alive while tied to the back of a Suburban. In the quiet and dark of the night, the misery brought by these painful memories filled her with deep regret at having left Basilio Ramos alive.

After the loss of her mother to cancer, the loss of her father to the federal assassins, the loss of Brad Fallon in the river, the loss of her son only minutes after his birth, and the loss of five years of her life in the camps, Ranya had thought that she had lost the ability to experience normal human feelings. Nevertheless, today had been too much even for her armor-plated soul. Today's new store of pain penetrated to the remaining core of her humanity, and found a tender spot to stab with a burning poker, and she wept with her face in her hands for a long time.

Eventually she returned to the present, staring at glowing red and amber LED lights. The soft dashboard display lights told her that the Solaris now had only 12% battery power remaining. The car was a two-seater, configured like a micro station wagon. She guessed that all of the space in the back beneath the small cargo area was given over to batteries. The car was not going to recharge from sunlight any time soon, that was a given. At best, even a small urban commuter like this one was going to get only a supplemental boost from the black solar panels contoured into the hood and the roof. She assumed the car had a cable for recharging from household power, and she found an orange cord rolled up on a spool, inside of where a gas cap might have been. When she put the plug into the garage's outlet, she only confirmed that the house power was off.

After failing to find an outlet with power, she examined the garage by penlight, especially where it joined the rest of the house. There was an interior door leading from the garage into the house, and it had only a doorknob lock. The houses in Glenwood all appeared to be variations on the same layout, so she guessed the Garabanda's house would also have a similar interior garage door.

The house where her son was living lay at an angle to her left across the street. After traveling hundreds of miles to find him, Brian was now sleeping only a hundred feet away. The thought crossed Ranya's mind to just walk across the street and ring the doorbell, gun in hand. There was no car in front of the Garabanda residence, but their garage door was rolled down, so their car might have been inside.

After watching for an hour from the empty garage, she slipped out to do a walking recon around the Garabanda's house. The .45 went under her belt, hidden beneath her black sweatshirt. Instead of a grass lawn, their small front yard was covered in pebbles, interspersed with small desert plants and bushes. After gingerly stepping from the sidewalk into the dark space between the Garabanda house and that of his neighbor on the right, a floodlight on the roof snapped on, and she had to hop back and quickly walk up the street and out of sight. She knew that these motion-activated lights often gave false alarms, but still she wondered if it had alerted Special Agent Garabanda.

A gunfight on his front sidewalk was not what she had in mind. After returning to her hiding place in the garage, she decided to wait for dawn and signs of activity. If the Garabanda family went to church, she thought she might boldly cross the street and ambush them at gunpoint when they backed their car out of their garage. She could take them unaware, carjack them and climb into the backseat with the barrel of her .45 leveled at their heads. If they didn't go to church…well, she would have to think of another ruse to gain entrance to their house.

Once she managed to overcome and subdue them, she would escape in the Garabanda's own gasoline-powered vehicle. She tried to guess what type of a car an FBI agent might have in his garage. Perhaps a big sedan, or an SUV? She wondered why no second car was parked on their driveway, or on the street in front of their house. The homes on this street had only single-car garages, but surely, the Garabanda's had two cars? Or had the difficult economy forced them to economize?

In the abstract, her mission had seemed so uncomplicated. Find this address, grab her child and leave. Now, back in the Solaris and looking across the street at his house, it seemed anything but simple. She wondered if Brian would scream and struggle, and how she would deal with him if he did. It wouldn't be easy to subdue the two adults, while gaining control of her five-year-old son.

At four in the morning she switched on the car radio, figuring the extra electrical output would be minimal. The AM band was preset to a Spanish language station, which dramatically announced itself as *¡Radio Regeneración, La Voz de la Revolución!* Two men were discussing the assassination of the governor, and the Anglo fugitive who was the main suspect. The alleged sniper's name meant nothing to her, but she sat straight up when they mentioned the rifle that had been found in the Regent Hotel behind an ice machine: a Remington, in 7mm magnum caliber!

On Wednesday at the rifle range west of the city, she had sighted-in three scoped bolt-action hunting rifles, and she could recall each of them in detail. One of them was a Remington 700, in 7mm magnum. Ramos had insisted the rifles be zeroed in at only 200 yards, and she mentally estimated the distance from the stage, across the Civic Plaza, to the Regent Hotel. She would never forget the sight of the blood and tissue jetting out of Governor Deleon's back. Now she had little doubt that she had personally fired the killing rifle, that she had zeroed it in and readied it for that single fatal shot.

It was time to get out of New Mexico, way past time.

The porch light illuminating the number 4875 gradually faded, as the dawn spread over Albuquerque. Morning twilight was a long and gradual process, with the rising sun still hidden behind the Sandia Mountains. The Garabanda's house had an angled roof topped with red Spanish tiles. Like all of the homes in the neighborhood, its stucco surfaces were painted in shades of tan and beige. About half of the homes on the street had grass front lawns, and half seemed to be using pebbles instead, like 4875. She'd never seen pebble "lawns" before, and guessed that the cost of watering real grass might be exorbitant, given the dry local climate. Some of the homes on Camino Del Cielo were two story or split-levels, but most, including the Garabanda's, were one story high. If she had to go in and take over the house at gunpoint, its single-story layout would make the task much easier.

There was a one-car garage on the left side of the Garabanda's house, and Ranya presumed that one of their cars was inside it. Again she wondered where their other car was, assuming that they had a second car. Perhaps it was in the shop, or perhaps, she thought hopefully, Garabanda was away on FBI business. It would greatly simplify grabbing Brian, if she had to deal with only his phony mother. If their primary vehicle was now parked inside of their garage, as she assumed, then she could get Brian into the car and under control before taking off with him. The most difficult part of the snatch could be done out of sight, avoiding any ugly scenes on the street in view of the neighbors. She could leave Brian's bogus mom tied up inside the house, or take her along and dump her off in some remote place on the way out of New Mexico.

Ranya went over her primary immediate action plan. If the garage door opened and their car backed outside, and it looked like they were heading to church, she would wait until they returned. When they did, she would quickly walk across the street and follow the car inside the garage while the door was still rolled open, and jump them at gunpoint. If they didn't go to church but she saw them inside, she considered various ruses for getting into the house. She could ring their doorbell with a clipboard, like a polltaker or petition signature gatherer. Did people still do things like that in Albuquerque, she wondered? Would they be too suspicious to open their door to a stranger, even a woman on Sunday morning?

She imagined that they would open their door for a young woman on their doorstep on a Sunday morning. Why wouldn't they? Once the door was opened, she could use her .45 to force her way inside and subdue them. She ran through various scenarios and permutations of scenarios.

What if the wife opened the door, but the husband was in another room? What if she screamed and alerted him? She went over possible variations until she couldn't think anymore. Finally, she decided that she would just have to rely on her instincts when the opportunity came.

"Mommy, I gotta go to the bathroom." The five-year-old boy was buckled into a child's car seat, diagonally behind the driver on the passenger side. Boxes, bins and bundles were packed into almost every other cubic foot of the vehicle.

"Brian, we just left, and I asked you if you had to go." His mother was driving her mid-sized SUV. She was wearing faded jeans, a gray jersey and running shoes, ready for a long road trip.

"But I didn't have to go then!"

"That was only five minutes ago."

"But I can't help it—I've gotta go!"

"You know, we're going to be in the car all day. You're going to have to learn how to hold it. We won't be able to stop for you every five minutes."

"But I have to go!"

Karin Bergen sighed loudly in exasperation. "Okay Bri-bri, let's see what we can do." She picked up a slim walkie-talkie from the center console of her Toyota 4-Runner. She was following behind a black Chevy Avalanche pickup, which was pulling a trailer. "Gretch, it's me, over."

"What's up?" Gretchen Bosch's gravelly voice came back through the radio.

"Brian's gotta go to the john. I'm going to swing by my old house."

"Okay girlfriend. We're early—we'll still be at the playground by eight."

"Roger."

Brian asked, "Mommy, is Daddy at our house?"

"No sweetie, we're going to see him at your old playground."

"Mommy, is Daddy coming with us?"

"No sweetie, Daddy has to stay here."

"But why?"

"You know why."

He said nothing for half a minute, thinking about this. "Mommy, how far is Sandy Eggo from Albakirky?"

"Very far, Bri-bri, almost a thousand miles. It'll take us all day. All day today, and some of tomorrow. We're stopping half way tonight, so we'll be there tomorrow."

Ranya was scrunched down low in the driver's seat of the Solaris, when a big black crew-cab pickup truck pulling a trailer rolled up Camino del

Cielo and passed in front of her. The truck was followed by a silver-gray SUV, which slowed, and made a left into the driveway of 4875! The truck continued and made a round U-turn at the next four-way stop sign intersection a half block up the street. Then the truck slowly came back down the street, and pulled to the curb directly in front of 4875. What the heck? Had the Garabanda family been away over night? Were they returning from a vacation? Why two vehicles? Was it FBI-related business? That might make sense. The truck was jammed with cargo in the back, covered by a gray plastic tarp. The silver SUV in the driveway had a black luggage carrier attached to its roof rack.

The driver's door of the silver SUV opened, and a woman with a thick mane of blond hair stepped out. She walked around to the other side, opened the rear passenger door and leaned inside. In a moment, a toddler climbed down. Ranya's heart raced, she grabbed for Basilio's small binoculars. Was she seeing her own son, who was now named Brian Garabanda?

The blond woman was wearing jeans and a gray sweater. Ranya thought the child was about the right size to be a five year old, but he was wearing pink overalls. Was this child a girl? Then the driver's door of the black pickup parked on the street opened, and a man stepped out, wearing denim farmer's overalls, showing muscular tattooed arms. His light brown hair was cut very short on the sides, and brushed straight up in a crew cut on top. Was this Special Agent Alexandro Garabanda? If so, he was undoubtedly armed at this very moment. FBI agents always were armed, she thought, on duty or off.

He was standing directly in the path Ranya would take to approach the woman and child in the driveway. She briefly considered attempting a one hundred foot pistol shot with her untested .45, but ruled it out as unrealistic. Despite it being an excellent pistol, she had never fired it. She could not know with certainty where its bullets would hit, when fired at a target a hundred feet away.

At best, taking the shot would result in a suburban street battle with an uncertain outcome, especially if the agent was wearing concealed body armor. To make matters worse, his black pickup was blocking the driveway, trapping the silver SUV. Even if she nailed the man in the coveralls, she would have to somehow race across the street and seize Brian from his false mother, and then what, escape in the pickup truck, towing the trailer? Or move the truck, and escape in the SUV?

The Dragunov rifle was behind her in the back of the mini-wagon, covered by a blanket. Could she get the four foot long rifle unlimbered and into position, sticking out of her driver's side window, without attracting the attention of the man waiting in the street? No, she decided, and besides, the angles were all wrong for shooting from her driver's seat position. She'd have to climb out of the car to make the shot. He was certain to notice all of that preparatory movement.

And even if she managed to shoot both adults, could she make a clean escape from New Mexico with Brian, after waking up the entire subdivision with gunfire, and leaving two corpses lying on the street? How would Brian be likely to react to seeing his "parents" shot down? How would he react to a strange woman grabbing him, after witnessing that kind of violence?

The blond woman and the child walked up the short path to the front door. She put a key into the lock and both of them disappeared inside. The blond had her own house key, so she must be Garabanda's wife.

The man standing by the pickup turned and stretched his arms out, and bounced on his toes, apparently limbering up. For a moment, he seemed to look straight at Ranya. She was already hiding far down in the seat, with just her eyes above the dashboard. She froze like a deer, hoping the interior of the garage was in deep shadow from the man's point of view. Then Ranya noticed something unusual about the shape of the man, very unusual, and it suddenly became clear—all too clear—he was a she! The big guy with the brush cut and the muscular tattooed arms was a woman! A very big woman, but still a woman, with breasts and all!

Ranya was stunned, trying to make sense of the situation. The tattooed woman in the overalls didn't go into the house, but instead she walked around the bed of the black truck, tugging at the lashings that secured the gray tarp over the load. Ranya's head was spinning, trying to come up with a new plan. This might be her only chance to get Brian! She could now see that the big woman by the truck was carrying a pistol. Its butt was visible, sticking out at the waist of the overalls on the side. Could she get out of the Solaris and take down the tattooed woman with her own .45, while her back was turned? Rush her and subdue her without a gunfight or a loud struggle, while her son (if it was her son!) was in the house? But then what? Then what?

The front door of the house opened again, and the woman and the child returned to their silver SUV. The burly female driver slid back into her truck, and all of their doors closed. The truck pulled down Camino Del Cielo, followed by the SUV. In a minute, they would be back on Tramway Road, headed for God knows where!

Would they be returning to this house later today? Not likely, the way both vehicles were loaded down. And was that child Brian anyway? Ranya had to admit, she had seen no sign of anybody else in the house during the hours that she had been watching it.

Where was Alexandro Garabanda, and who was that tattooed woman in the overalls?

The two vehicles were already a block down the street when Ranya decided to follow them. But with the little electric car at only 12% charge, just how far could she follow them? If she ran out of power, what then? She'd be stranded and on foot until the car could recharge in the sun, and how long would that take?

Perhaps they were going only to another house nearby, or perhaps they would stop for gas. But was the child even Brian? What if it was some other child? What should she do? If she followed them, at least she could see which way they were heading, and at least that would be something…but what good would that information do if she couldn't keep up with them?

Why had she decided to take Professor Johnson's pathetic electric car in the first place? She had stupidly assumed that the Garabandas would all be waiting for her at home, fat dumb and happy, ready to politely cooperate with a straight-up home invasion, and (from their point of view) the abduction of their son. But reality, dammit, was not working out as neatly as she had visualized!

Ranya pulled out of the garage. The trucks were two blocks ahead, almost back down to Tramway Road, where they would accelerate to a speed the Solaris could not hope to match. Then the black truck slowed for a stop sign, and both vehicles made a left turn, staying within the subdivision. Ranya followed, a sliver of hope creeping back in. Perhaps they really were going to another house, where she might get a second chance to grab Brian.

The black truck pulled to a stop along the side of the new road, next to a waist-high chain link fence. On the other side of the fence was a small playground: there was a swing set, seesaws, a jungle gym made of pipes, and a colorful multi-level playhouse structure. She couldn't park the Solaris on the same stretch of the road with the vehicles she was following. Instead, she stopped just before the corner, where she could observe the two trucks by the playground. The power was down to 11% when she switched off the ignition—the electric car's nearly depleted battery banks lost power by the block!

She watched the drivers' doors of the pickup and the SUV open. She scanned the playground. A man was already there, sitting on a bench by the swing sets. He was clean-shaven, wearing jeans and a tan vest over a t-shirt. He had no children with him that she could see. Perhaps he was a smoker, who was not allowed to enjoy his habit in his own home. But he wasn't smoking, or feeding birds, or walking a dog or anything else.

The man was waiting for someone.

Alex Garabanda stood up from the bench when he saw Gretchen Bosch's black pickup approaching the playground. It was five minutes after eight

AM, and he'd been on the playground for twenty minutes. Her truck was loaded down in the back, and it was hauling a cargo trailer. Karin's 4-Runner pulled up behind the truck and they both parked. It figured that Gretchen would come—they both knew how her presence would piss him off. He'd have to be extremely careful, and control his temper. Karin had surreptitiously taped their conversations in the past, and he knew she was probably carrying a recorder today. If he said anything which could be construed in any way as threatening, she'd run straight to Judge Galatea Obregon with the tape.

Gretchen Bosch got out first, looking around in all directions. Garabanda could see that she was wearing her blue denim farmer's overalls. She liked to show off her steroid-enhanced weightlifter's shoulders and arms, with their encircling rings of blue-black Polynesian tattoos. While he watched her from about fifty yards away, he saw her lift her right hand, almost as if to wave to him, but instead she was hoisting a small camcorder into position. He'd have to keep his distance from Karin, or Gretchen's "videotaped evidence" would be used to show him making "threatening movements or gestures." He knew how it would go down: Karin would flatly deny inviting him here to see Brian. Instead, she would allege that he was stalking them in violation of his restraining order. She was setting him up like a bowling pin.

It took an effort of will not to give Gretchen Bosch two middle fingers to record for her video. He idly wondered if he could draw, fire his Sig and hit her before she could duck behind her truck. He hated the Beast even more than he hated Karin, if that was possible. The overalls, bare shoulders, tattooed arms and crew cut summed up her thuggish personality. At least today, she wasn't carrying an aluminum baseball bat. He often thought that her personality was perfectly suited for her position, leading one of the Internal Revenue Service's new Contraband Asset Recovery Teams. "Contraband assets" my ass, Garabanda thought. "Contraband assets" was federal Newspeak for gold, unregistered cash, foreign currency accounts and other prohibited forms of private wealth, which were now outlawed in the name of stopping "money laundering" by "terrorist and criminal organizations."

No longer satisfied with merely plundering taxpayers' diminishing paychecks, the IRS was now also in the business of legally looting the "contraband assets" of American citizens. Since the creation of the CART teams, the IRS's Criminal Investigations Division was enjoying a boom within federal law enforcement. Under the CID's "Recovery Incentives Program," agents received a percentage of the value of the "contraband assets" that they "recovered" from Americans. Their standard mission involved kicking down doors and stealing people's property and life savings, while dressed in black uniforms and body armor. Then, the

CART teams would literally "cart off" the citizens' formerly legal "contraband assets," supposedly for delivery to the U.S. Treasury. What the IRS teams couldn't haul away went under the gavel at public auction, and the IRS agents received a percentage of the take.

Karin climbed out of her SUV next, and went around and unbuckled Brian from his child seat. She led him by his hand as they walked together down the sidewalk, toward the opening in the playground fence. That's when he noticed Brian was wearing pink coveralls. Pink! She is definitely trying to provoke me, he thought. He looked back to Gretchen Bosch; she was holding the camcorder up in front of her face.

As soon as they entered the playground, Brian began to pull and twist, trying to break loose from his mother's tight grip on his wrist. "Let me go Mommy—let me go! There's Daddy!"

Finally, Karin relented. "Okay Bri-bri, go ahead. Give your father a hug, and say goodbye."

He leaned forward and dashed the fifty feet across the rubberized playground surface, and leaped from a yard away into Alex Garabanda's open arms. His father pulled him up the rest of the way into his embrace, while spinning into a turn so that Brian's legs flew outward in a circle. He hugged his son tightly, kissing his face and neck.

"I missed you tiger, I really, really missed you."

"I missed you too Daddy. So much!"

They said nothing for a minute, and then Alex Garabanda let his son slide down, and knelt on the rubberized surface to get to Brian's eye level. Karin stood twenty feet away, watching silently with her arms folded. Gretchen Bosch stayed back by her truck, also watching.

"Daddy, are you coming to Sandy Eggo too? *Please* Daddy…"

"San Diego?" He stood and faced Karin. "What's this about San Diego? What the hell are you trying to pull?" Brian scampered off and climbed up the play tower, and started to rock and swing on a little chain suspension bridge.

"We have permission from the court." She snapped a white business-size envelope against her leg. "It's right here. There's nothing you can do to stop us."

"Oh no—no way!"

"Oh yes, yes way," she said, mimicking him. "And if you interfere in any way, you'll be breaking your restraining order, and the judge will put out an arrest warrant. They'd just love that down at the Field Office, wouldn't they Al?"

"Karin, this isn't right! The TRO didn't give you permission to take Brian out of the state!"

"It does now. It's all right here." She tossed the envelope onto the ground between them.

"Karin, this is not right, and it's not fair to Brian."

"We're leaving, Al. You can keep the house. We're out. Everything that's left in the house, you can have it. It's all yours: keep it, give it away, burn it, I don't care. But we've got to go now—we're leaving from the annex at nine. We're traveling in a federal convoy and they won't wait, so we have to get going."

"Karin, why are you doing this? Why? You've even got him dressed in pink for God's sake. Pink! What are you trying to prove?"

"That's not pink, that's *orchid.* Anyway, what's it matter to you?"

"Orchid, pink, what's the difference? He's a boy, damn it! Why are you twisting the knife like this? Does this give you pleasure?"

"Pleasure? This has nothing to do with pleasure! We just think you've already done enough damage to Brian's psyche, that's all. You've tried your best to turn him into a little macho man, always playing with toy guns and wearing camouflage. Well, we're breaking your chain of patriarchy. We're not going to inflict another heterosexist creep like you on the world!"

"Karin, this isn't right. It's not right, you can't do this—I'll get an injunction!"

"You're too late," she hissed. "It's all perfectly legal, and we're doing it. But you know, I hope you do try something stupid—a little time in jail might just do you some good. And after you get out, you'll be done with Brian forever—*finito*. So go ahead, try to stop us!"

"Karin…please…"

She turned and walked over to the play tower and pulled Brian down, keeping a strong grip on his wrist. "Come on Bri-bri. We have to go now. We have a long drive ahead of us. Say goodbye to Daddy."

Ranya studied the scene through her compact seven power Steiners. She could almost lip-read what the man was saying. The little boy—Brian?—had run to him when they arrived at the playground. What was going on? Slowly, she guessed at some theories that might explain the meeting. A custody turnover? Maybe. On Sunday morning? Possibly. Are the Garabanda's separated, or even divorced? The boy ran to him, and his father swung him up into a tight hug. Their mutual affection was genuine and obvious.

The man and the blond woman had some words together, standing fifteen or twenty feet apart. The woman waved some papers at the man, and dropped them on the ground. Then she walked over to the playhouse, pulled the child down, and dragged him back toward the street by his arm.

The man followed them, the woman turned around and they had some more words, and he stopped.

After the two women and the child got back into their vehicles, they quickly pulled out, made a right turn and drove the last block down to Tramway Boulevard. The Solaris had only a small residual battery charge remaining, so pursuit at this point would be meaningless. Even if she could catch up to the two vehicles, how could she overcome them with her little electric car? Shoot out the black truck's tires, and then go after the silver SUV? It was all too far-fetched. Her son was gone, at least for now. She had to face reality. She was back to square one.

The man—Brian's so-called father—dropped back onto the cement park bench and sat motionless, staring. Brian was gone, beyond the possibility of pursuit for now…but his "father" was still a connection to his "son." If this man were in fact Special Agent Alexandro Garabanda, he would at least know, presumably, where Brian was being taken.

She screwed me and she screwed me good, Garabanda thought, staring at the rubbery textured playground surface between his feet. She did it on a Sunday morning, when finding a judge to issue a fast injunction would be virtually impossible. Now she was already on her way out of the state, in an armed federal security convoy. By the time they stopped for gas, they'd be far into Arizona. There wasn't one damned thing he could do about it. Gretchen Bosch had videotaped the brief encounter, and if he'd so much as touched Karin or kept Brian from her, he'd only have wound up under arrest…and the arrest would stick, in Judge Galatea Obregon's politically correct kangaroo court. Those radical witches were tight; they were like a little coven the way they worked together.

And now they're going to take Brian to California, the land of fruits and nuts, and raise him to be a sissy. Karin and Gretchen are going to get 'married' and raise poor Brian to be a *maricón*, God help him! Even now, they were dressing him in pink! Oh, that woman, she screwed me but good—a bullet would hurt less than this!

After five minutes of sitting on the bench, Garabanda left the playground. He walked slowly down the sidewalk away from Ranya, to a wine-red Crown Victoria. If it's government issue, he probably gets his gas free, she mused. That was a car that could easily catch the mid-sized SUV her son had just been taken away in. She wondered if the FBI souped up its sedans to high-performance standards. Each one of its eight cylinders probably put out more horsepower than the Solaris's electric motor on its best day.

If she could get the Ford, and if she found out where Brian was being taken, she could overtake the truck pulling the trailer and catch the silver

SUV. She could shoot out a tire on the trailer to stop the black pickup, and force them to pull over while they were in a remote area. It could work.

The Crown Vic pulled past the playground and made the left, heading back uphill in the direction of the Garabanda house. She would have to go after him. There was no better alternative that Ranya could see. He would presumably know where Brian was going—if the man in the Crown Vic was indeed Alexandro Garabanda.

The truck pulling the trailer had been loaded down with more than just gear for a weekend camping trip. They were taking two vehicles, so they were moving, and not just making a vacation road trip. If she could just find out where they were going…she could pursue them.

Ranya had to suppress her urge to follow the FBI man's car immediately. If she did, he would probably spot the boxy little wagon with the solar panel hood and roof trailing behind him. She couldn't afford to spook him. In any event, if Garabanda didn't go straight to 4875 Cielo, she couldn't follow him anywhere else, not with the Solaris almost out of juice. Even fully charged, the electric car would be hard pressed to follow the powerful V-8 Ford.

She silently cursed Professor Johnson again, this time for being a tree-hugging eco-pansy. Why couldn't he at least have driven a car with some power, instead of this glorified golf cart? She guessed that he drove the electric car because he had found a power outlet where he could mooch free electricity, probably at the university. No doubt his students thought he was a hero for his choice of vehicles, even though most of the electricity to charge it probably came from coal-burning power plants.

There was no alternative except to return to the house on Camino Del Cielo, and hope to spot the FBI man there. She was running out of options. Basilio Ramos might be waking up at any time, if he had not already. It was not lost on her that she was only five short miles from his villa, driving the very distinctive car belonging to the dead man left in his bed. She decided to leave the car where it was, around the corner from the playground, where it could at least begin to recharge its batteries once the sun climbed over the mountain.

Garabanda's house was only three blocks away. She could walk there in few minutes, for a daytime sidewalk recon. If he wasn't at home, she could return later after dark and hide the Solaris in the same empty garage across the street. Then she could break into the empty house through the interior garage door, and set up a long-term surveillance. Garabanda was her last link to Brian. If he didn't go back to his house at all, well then, she was just out of luck.

First, however, she needed something to eat and drink. She had eaten nothing since enjoying the catered buffet line behind Comandante Ramos's villa. In hastily packing her escape gear, she hadn't even considered food or water, a huge oversight! In the back of the wagon were two bags containing what was probably a fortune in gold coins, plus an exotic four-foot long Russian sniper rifle, but not as much as a water bottle or a sandwich.

There was a convenience store on the corner of Montgomery and Tramway. She could walk there, buy what she needed, then walk back uphill to 4875 Camino del Cielo. She found a black and red UNM "Lobos" ball cap in the back of the Professor's car. With her short hair and her shapeless black hooded sweatshirt, she thought she could almost pass for a man, once she pulled on the ball cap and her sunglasses. The wolf on the front of the hat even matched her mood. The .45 caliber pistol went inside of her jeans on the front left side, its grip to the right, "Mexican carry" style. It was invisible under her loose sweatshirt. Eight rounds weren't much, but they were all she had. She certainly couldn't take the Dragunov. The Russian rifle was as long as a canoe paddle, and a lot heavier.

23

He was deep inside a forest. It was a world of dark shadows and radiant sunbeams. The sun's rays were painfully bright when they struck him in the face. He tried to move, but his feet were stuck. He looked down, and saw only rough brown bark, the skin of a tree growing twenty or more feet straight into the ground. He tried to look at his watch to check the time, but he could not move his arm, which was a rigid tree branch, extending straight out from his side.

With no warning, he simultaneously heard and felt a bang, then another bang, and another! Suddenly he realized that his mortal enemy, the woodcutter, had discovered him. His enemy was down behind him where he could not turn to see, chopping into his lower back with a heavy axe! Bang! Another deep cut was hacked into his defenseless wooden body. Bang! Another deep chop. How many more, until he went over? Bang! Then he both heard and felt the fatal cracking and splitting, the world tilted away under him, and he was going down, down, down!

Basilio Ramos tried to open his eyes, but they were sticky with some kind of crusty gunk. With effort he managed to partially open one eye, but the other was jammed hard against whatever he was lying on. Gradually his waking consciousness came sifting back into his mind, and the tree once again became the man. He was lying face down on a bed, his left arm thrust out stiff, asleep, paralyzed.

That God-awful banging continued. Banging on his bedroom door. A familiar voice yelled, "Comandante! Comandante! Are you there? Are you inside?"

Christ! What time was it? For that matter, what day was it? What country was it? "Yes, I'm here," he croaked.

"Comandante, do you wish to reschedule the staff meeting?"

Oh, goddamn it all to hell! He'd slept through his own staff meeting! What time was it? His Rolex watch was on his right wrist, he had to force his head to turn all the way over, but without his temporarily useless left arm to help raise himself. His face turned through the sheets toward the right, and—oh my God in heaven! What in the name of all damnation?

He was not alone in bed. Next to him was a man, a bald and bearded man with a blue-black face! Ramos recoiled away, but he was hindered by his still useless left arm, extended straight out, anchoring him in place.

That voice again! "Comandante, are you all right?"

He coughed, cleared his throat, and struggled to speak. "Yes, yes, I'm fine! Now, go away!"

"But what about the staff meeting?"

The staff meeting! *¡Maldito hijo de puta!* "Ahh, the staff meeting is cancelled today. No—make it later. I'll be at the Academy at…noon." He tried to think, but his mind refused to function. Noon? What time was it now? Was midday too soon? Think! Later…best to make it later… "No! At one. One in the afternoon, is that clear?"

"Sí, Comandante, very clear! One in the afternoon!"

With his weak but still functional right arm, he pushed himself away from the corpse. The dead man's face was turned toward his own, a yard away on his king-size bed. His eyes were open and bulging out, dull and dead. With his swollen black tongue protruding between crooked yellow teeth, he resembled an enormous rodent caught in a human-sized rattrap.

Oh, and that smell! His room smelled like shit, worse than shit! Ramos managed to push himself to the edge of his bed, and swing his legs down one at a time. He tried to stand but only his right arm worked, the left hung uselessly, then the room shifted under him and whirled and everything went black again. He was dropping through a deep well, a spinning vortex leading to the center of the earth, straight down to the fiery pit of hell! Gradually the spinning stopped, and he was able to open his eyes again. He was sitting on the floor, leaning against his bed. There was indeed a body on his bed, a dead man, there was shit and blood and God-knows-what all over his sheets, and all over the man…

What kind of nightmare was this? Last night…he remembered seeing Félix Magón, the new governor. He remembered the girl, the Arab girl Ranya, dressed like a million peso *puta* in a black mini-dress. But after that…what? What? Where was Ranya, and who was this dead man, who seemed vaguely familiar? Ramos slowly pushed himself to his feet, using the side of his bed for support. The dead man was lying on his stomach with his pimply white *gabacho* ass in the air. Blood and shit was all over everywhere! The man's face was purple, his head was twisted more than ninety degrees to the left, his eyes protruding like those of a doomed rat, already halfway down a snake's throat.

What in the name of hell was going on?

Standing unsteadily, naked, he looked down at himself and was greeted by another shock, and he thought, I have to take a shower, right now! Right now! He looked again at his shriveled manhood, at the dried shit and blood encrusted together all over himself, the revolting patina matching the backside of the corpse…

What in the name of Satan had happened here last night?

He staggered and lurched toward his bathroom, and leaned against his computer desk for momentary support. He looked down and saw a sheet of printer paper in front of his keyboard. It said, *"READ THIS"* in large block print. A sinking feeling overcame him, a feeling of dread. He pulled out his desk chair and dropped into it, his shower temporarily delayed.

It was a typed, printed note, evidently created on his own computer. He had to rub his eyes hard and blink several times to focus on the words.

"By the time you read this, I will be far away. In case you cannot remember last night, I left a slide show on your computer.

"If you pursue me, I will send copies of this slide show to every member of the Falcon Battalion, and to all of the leaders of the state government. If anything happens to me, the pictures will be automatically sent out in a way that will ensure that your entire battalion will see them.

"Goodbye Basilio, I won't be seeing you again, or any Falcons or Zetas or anyone else you might send. I won't, because if I do see you or them, the entire world will see all of these pictures."

After a moment of trepidation, he reluctantly pushed the computer mouse, and a full screen image came up. It was unmistakably him, Comandante Basilio Ramos, *"El Che,"* wearing his brown beret with its silver Falcon medallion. The bald gringo, the dead man was …oh… my… God! The image changed, he was on his knees, and that dead man, oh my dear God… The picture switched again, he was now behind the man, taking him in the dog position like a woman! His forearm was wrapped around the man's neck and he was grinning like an idiot, staring directly at the camera!

The photos continued to switch every few seconds, but he could not watch anymore, or he was going to be sick. He lowered his forehead onto the desk. He had to think! But with his head already splitting open, each forced thought was another red hot steel wedge being hammered through his skull. There was one thing that he did know: he knew that no matter what, he could not allow any hint of this…situation…to get out.

Alex Garabanda hadn't been by his house in several weeks. Outside, it didn't look any different. With pebbles instead of grass for a front yard, watering and mowing were irrelevancies. It was an ideal low-maintenance yard for an FBI Supervisory Special Agent, who was often on the road for weeks at a time working cases.

Some "gift" Karin had handed over to him. More like a poison pill. They had bought the place when he had been assigned to Albuquerque, right at the top of what turned out to be the worst real estate bubble in memory. They had taken a loan for $320,000 in old greenbacks to buy the 1,800 square foot place, certain that its price could only go up. Instead, within months, all of the homes in the area began to slide in value. In no time, they owed more than the falling worth of the house. Even worse, interest rates began climbing into double digits, and the monthly payment required by their adjustable rate mortgage nearly doubled.

After the real estate market collapsed, deflation began to hammer the economy down. With their two federal salaries, the Garabandas had hardly noticed the deflation, except for the growing number of for-sale signs, foreclosure and eviction notices, and neighbors packing up and leaving one after the other. Karin and Gretchen were just two of the latest to take off, leaving him without Brian, but instead with this albatross of a house.

Well, at least he would be able to stop paying rent for his apartment. He couldn't sell the house, he realized that was impossible. If he tried to sell it in this economy, he would be lucky to get an offer. It was now worth less than half of what he owed on it. As a federal law enforcement officer, defaulting and walking away from his debts was not an option. After Congress passed the "Fair Real Estate and Mortgage Act," defaulting on a loan with a greater balance outstanding than the value of the underlying property had become a crime.

Because of FREMA, homeowners across the USA were perpetually on the hook for the difference between the money they still owed to the bank, and the money the bank would receive at a foreclosure auction. This hadn't stopped millions of Americans from becoming "bolters," but as a federal officer, if he walked away, he'd lose his job and his pension. If he ever wanted to see his federal pension, he'd have to make the monthly house payments, no matter what. Still, he wondered if it was even worth it.

After the real estate bust and the deflation, hyperinflation had swept in like a fast rising tide, with prices doubling every other month. The Garabandas had to scrape every penny of both paychecks together just to put food on the table. These were hungry times for civilians, many of whom were unemployed. Thank God he'd been able to shop in the military commissaries! Finally, their federal salaries were indexed to the inflation rate, and for a while they were living on easy street, because their monthly mortgage payment (unadjusted for inflation) suddenly seemed like small change.

Those easy days lasted only until the old greenbacks had been swapped for New Dollars, at ten to one. This momentous change occurred after a two-week "bank holiday" to allow the government to "restructure" the financial system to "ensure fairness and stability." (Somehow, "fairness and stability" meant that the banks came first, and ordinary people last.) Congress also passed "FREMA Two" during the bank holiday, and loans were adjusted and repegged to the new currency, in order to keep the banks solvent. Once again, their mortgage payments took most of their paychecks.

There seemed to be no way out of the ongoing financial mess. From month to month, it was impossible for average citizens to make sane financial plans. While you were looking for another sucker punch, your legs would be cut out from under you. When you ducked the roundhouse punch of deflation, hyperinflation hit you with an uppercut. If you had been responsible and saved up a little money, you woke up one fine day and found out that it was now worth one-tenth of the old amount, in crisp new blue dollar bills.

There was no escape. He would just have to suck it up, and continue to hand over most of his paycheck to the bank. But what about when he retired, and his pay was cut in half? Job opportunities for a former federal agent would be slim in New Mexico, but he couldn't move out of state—not while he was caught in the mortgage trap. If he defaulted and bolted, he'd lose his federal pension.

Catch-22.

Like millions of Americans, Alex Garabanda was now effectively a slave to the banks because of his debt. He might not be able to see the steel collar around his neck when he looked in the mirror, but he could feel it every waking minute.

Driving up Camino Del Cielo for the first time in two weeks, he noticed another empty house. Had the owners sold it, or just taken off? Despite the risk of prosecution under FREMA, he knew that people were still walking out on their bank loans. So many civilians had lost their corporate salaries and pensions, that the banks had little or no recourse against them when they took off. Bolters usually had no other assets to go after besides the house, which the bank already owned. Millions of Americans were voting with their feet, and walking away from their homes. And no group more than the Anglos fleeing "Nuevo Mexico," he thought.

Where could they go to begin their lives again, he wondered? He knew there was talk about the Rocky Mountain States and the Deep South being havens for mortgage bolters. He had heard that retiring federal agents were heading to the so-called "free states" in great numbers. Some compared the "mortgage migration" to a new internal exodus, debt slaves running away for what they hoped was a new Promised Land.

Millions of formerly solid middle class families were now living in their cars, or in low rent "campgrounds" in tents. The lucky ones were in recreational vehicles. It was hard to watch Americans, so recently on top of the world, existing in such grinding third-world poverty. Who could blame them for taking off, for bolting out of state to escape their debts?

And to think that it had all happened in the space of just two years!

Alex pulled into his driveway, wondering if his remote control still functioned, if Karin hadn't changed the code. He pushed the button, and the garage door rumbled, rattled, and rolled up like it always had before.

He had to straighten out the garage before he could pull his car inside. It was strewn with empty and full boxes, discarded clothes and the rest of the stuff Karin evidently didn't want or couldn't take. He unlocked the inside garage door into the house and wandered from room to room, taking stock of the furniture and household goods which she had left behind. The bed and some of their older, cheaper furniture was still in their former bedroom. She'd left a television there as well, an old 19-inch model sitting on the carpet. He carried it out to the living room and placed it on a battered end table, and plugged it in to catch the local news. What a day, what a weekend.

What a life.

He twisted the thin plastic handle to open the living room Venetian blinds, and as soon as he did, he noticed the car across the street. It was an old Chevy Caprice, dark blue. The four windows were down, and two men were sitting in the front. He could see that the driver was reading a newspaper. Alex Garabanda knew what was going on—he'd seen them plenty of times before. Not these men or this car, but their kind.

They were from the state's own *Grupo Especial de la Vigilancia*, the Special Surveillance Group. When they wanted to, they could be halfway professsional, and stay out of sight while conducting their business. Obviously, they had followed him here, and he had not seen them. Well, he hadn't been looking...he had other problems on his mind. Now they were not making any effort at all to hide their presence. Their intention was only to intimidate him, and serve as a reminder of the state's power over him.

You'll have to take a number and get in line, thought the FBI man. Everybody has power over me...

He felt a sudden urge to just walk across the street, pull out his Sig, and blow them both away. It would be pleasant, amusing really, and it wouldn't matter much if they drew on him as well. Who cares? He'd lost his friend and informant yesterday, and his son today. So what the hell? Why not? The Sig was still in its holster on the right side, unconcealed now that he had taken his vest off inside the house. He could simply open the front door, walk a dozen paces toward the street, and start shooting.

Why the hell not?

The front door was only a few steps away, but he made no move toward it. Maybe because he was just too tired to care. What possible difference would it make? Why bother? Why shoot those two nobodies? They meant nothing.

He shut the blind, and stood by the window.

Maybe later he'd go back to his apartment, clean it out, and get his things. He could clear out his furnished one bedroom rental unit in a single trip, if he loaded the Crown Victoria up, if he really packed it in tight. Consolidate. Get all of his things under one roof.

Maybe later...if he had the energy.

He wandered into the kitchen, and flipped through a tall stack of mail with no real interest. There was half of a jug of orange juice in the fridge. Karin was addicted to the stuff, and she spent a fortune on it, when she could find it. He was surprised she'd left it behind, a rare oversight. But then, she'd probably been staying with the Beast, Gretchen Bosch. In the back of an upper cabinet, he found an open bottle of Smirnoff, half-full. He poured the entire contents of the vodka bottle straight into the plastic container of OJ.

Alex Garabanda was home. For what it was worth.

Ranya was the only customer in the combination convenience store and gas station on Tramway Boulevard. The establishment had no name. There had once been a sign atop a steel pillar, but now the plastic face was missing, revealing only a row of fluorescent bulbs. Another business with an Anglo name, bowing to the new reality. A line of parked cars snaked from the gasoline pumps outside and down the side street, evidently awaiting the next fuel delivery. Professor Johnson's anemic solar car suddenly seemed less pathetic to her. At least it was still capable of moving under its own power.

The shop was dirty inside, there was no air conditioning, and the dusty shelves were only half-stocked. The solitary clerk on duty hardly glanced up to take her money and make change. She didn't want to make possibly memorable eye contact with anyone, and so she left her sunglasses and hat on inside the store.

The cashier didn't blink when she slid over a crisp blue $500 bill, taken from Basilio's safe. Not when a box of donuts cost $39, and a one-gallon plastic bottle of *agua purificada* went for $19. The total with tax was $73, which Ranya now understood would have been $730 in the old pre-conversion green money. What the hell had happened to the dollar, in the five years since she had been arrested? No wonder they had to grow their own food at D-Camp! She glanced at the bill before it disappeared into the cash register, and saw the smiling face of Franklin D. Roosevelt. Didn't he say that prosperity was just around the corner, or was that Herbert Hoover?

At the end of the transaction, she still didn't know if the cashier spoke English or Spanish. After the recent events, she realized that both sides of the divide had good reason to be guarded about their linguistic leanings. Speaking the wrong language to the wrong person could spark a confrontation, or worse.

Ranya walked back across Tramway against the flashing red light. It seemed like there was very little traffic, even for a Sunday morning. The extent and depth of the potholes in the asphalt were beyond anything she had ever seen before. The road was more a collection of interconnected potholes than pavement. After drinking some water and checking the area around the playground for any signs of surveillance, she put her shopping bag in the back of the Solaris. If Basilio Ramos were sending anyone out to search for her, they would be homing in on the professor's solar-powered wagon. It was hard to imagine that he would be pursuing her so soon, not with the surprises that she had left for him. Still, the possibility could not be ruled out, so she took appropriate precautions.

The sun was now above the mountain, and the car was in direct sunlight. She wondered how long it would take to charge up. How many hours of sitting in the sun would put how many miles of driving into the batteries? She locked up the little car, and left it to do a walk-by of the Garabanda house.

In five minutes, she was striding up the sidewalk on the right side of Camino Del Cielo, the opposite side of the street from the Garabanda residence. The garage at 4875 was now rolled up, and as she drew near, she saw with relief that the dark Ford from the playground was parked inside. Well, hallelujah, something was going right for a change! Alexandro Garabanda was home.

Then she noticed a new car parked at curbside directly across from the Garabanda house. It was an ugly blue American-made four door, facing away from her. She had been so intent on studying the Garabanda house that she was almost next to the car's rear bumper before she saw that its windows were rolled down, and two men were sitting in the front seat.

Her mood went from elation to near panic as the realization hit her that another group was watching the Garabanda house! Shit! How could that be, unless the Milicia somehow knew about the connection between herself and the Garabandas? Could Basilio Ramos have already recovered from the Libidinol overdose, and sent a posse out after her? But how could he know about her link to the Garabandas? It seemed impossible, but what else could explain the two Hispanic men sitting in a car, directly across from his house? Were they just waiting for her to show up?

Ranya continued up the sidewalk at the same steady pace, her head turned slightly away from the street. She was dreading to hear the sound of a car engine, or doors opening, or a voice calling to her from behind. She dared not look back, imagining the two men studying her, comparing her to their search profile. But there was no sound, no shout, no footsteps, and no engine noise as she put distance between herself and the blue sedan. Damn! Now there was no way that she could approach the Garabanda house, not while there was a team staked out across the street, watching it!

The jug of orange juice and vodka was getting lighter each time that he lifted it from the floor to refill his plastic tumbler. Orange juice seemed to go with Sunday morning, somehow. The vodka…well…it was as good a painkiller as any.

Karin had left his favorite living room armchair. She'd hated it and had wanted him to throw it out for years. He was mildly surprised she hadn't put it out on the curb to be taken away, just for spite. It was just covered in cheap plaid fabric, but it fit him like a glove from his head to his knees. When he sank into its padded contours, he was finally, truly all the way home. The chair had flat hardwood armrests on either side. They were wide and level, perfect for holding remote controls, paperback books, magazines, snack bowls…or a large glass full of orange juice and vodka.

His pistol always dug into his side in this chair, so he unholstered it and laid in on the right side armrest. That used to drive Karin mad. She couldn't stand to see his pistol out in the open, afraid that Brian would pick it up. Well, today that was a moot point. No Brian. Now he could leave his gun right where it was until the next ice age, and not be nagged about it.

He used the remote to flip between the Sunday morning talking-head shows, while sipping his vodka screwdriver. The latest Secretary of the Treasury, a weasel-like man with a whiney nasal voice, was explaining the new bank account withdrawal regulations to a skeptical host. The Treasury Secretary seemed to think that Americans should be grateful that the withdrawal limits were being doubled from their current $4,000 a month maximum. The catch was that in order to withdraw more than that amount, depositors would have to "invest" an equal matching amount of their New Dollars in "USA Patriot Bonds," with a minimum ten-year maturity. This was "a vital element of the NEP, the New Economic Plan," he said. "All *real* Americans should welcome the chance to support this vital national recovery effort…"

Alex Garabanda couldn't stand watching the man, or hearing about the administration's New Economic Plan. He clicked the remote control's "up" button. TOP News was showing a rubble-strewn crater in the middle of a city street, with burning cars and blasted windows radiating for a block all around it. A suicide car bomb had gone off on the street outside of the Dearborn Michigan police headquarters. An audiotaped threat had been issued, and was being played. A foreign-sounding voice demanded that the police siege of the Muslim Quarter of Detroit be lifted immediately, or more car bombs would follow. In response, the President had issued her own written statement. "The United States Government will never cave in to threats by terrorists. Furthermore, the misguided bombers were not acting in the name of true Islam, but only a small, twisted fragment of that great religion of peace. We must not…"

Click. Hundreds of tents and tarps were being erected on the National Mall in Washington. The vanguard of the Poor People's Party was vowing to camp there until two weeks before the Constitutional Convention, while growing in numbers every day. Their stated goal was to lead a 150-mile march up Interstate 95 through Baltimore to Philadelphia, where millions of poor people would surround the convention with "people power" and demand that...

Click. The FBI agent continued going through the national news channels, looking for any mention of the assassination of the governor of New Mexico. Maybe it had been covered, and he had just missed it. Or maybe events in *Nuevo Mexico* just didn't rate as national news any more. Maybe the state had slid beyond the national interest horizon.

Well, Alex Garabanda remembered what had happened yesterday. He even had his own personal video recording of the Rally for Social Justice. He wondered if he was ready to watch it again...if he ever wanted to watch it again. He drained his vodka and orange juice, pushed himself up from his easy chair, and dragged his gray daypack over toward the television. He took out his camcorder, fumblingly set up the connection to the TV, and then lurched backward and fell into his chair again.

Ranya kept walking up the sidewalk without looking back, made a right at the top of the block, and then another right, heading back down toward the playground. She was wondering if the two men in the blue sedan were waiting for her to show up, or if they were watching the house for other reasons. Alexandro Garabanda was an FBI agent, so perhaps New Mexico politics were involved. Or maybe they were just waiting for someone else there, a third party. Or maybe they were just innocently killing time. Maybe it was merely a coincidence, where the two men were parked...

No, she couldn't accept that. Now she had a new problem. Garabanda might leave his house at any time, and she wouldn't be able to follow him very far in the Solaris. Neither could she approach his house while the two men were watching it.

What could she do to get them to leave? What kind of diversion could she create, while keeping a low profile? She could take out a neighborhood transformer with the Dragunov, and create an instant power failure. She could burn an empty house. She could torch one of the empty cars parked in the line in front of the gas station on Tramway.

Ranya sat for a while in the playground, on the same cement bench Garabanda had used, watching all around the area for any signs of surveillance on the Solaris. When she was satisfied it was clean, she walked toward the car and then continued past it, again searching for new watchers, her paranoia spiking to astronomical levels. Finally she returned to the car and quickly climbed inside. It was already stifling hot and she had to open the side windows. The indicated power level was up to 19%, a slight improvement. She pulled off her sweatshirt, squirming in the car's tight confines. She was wearing a black t-shirt underneath.

She saw a middle-aged Hispanic woman come out of a house on the other side of the street, walking a Chihuahua on a leash. While waiting for her dog to do its business, the woman seemed to be staring at her in the solar car. Ranya turned the ignition switch and pulled out. Her new intention was to find a spot where she could observe the two watchers across from the Garabanda house. Camino Del Cielo curved slightly to the left as it went uphill. She pulled over to the curb 200 feet behind the blue sedan, obscured behind a long roll-off construction dumpster. The green steel dumpster was sitting at curbside in front of a house undergoing renovation. From her driver's seat, she could just see the back of the blue car, and the Garabanda house across from the two watchers. His garage door was still rolled open. There was finally time for some water, and a few stale donuts.

The open-topped dumpster in front of her appeared to have been in that location for a very long time, long enough to be overflowing with trash. Dirt and crud was piled up around it on the asphalt. She looked more closely at the house by the dumpster. It was empty, with a half-finished room addition on one side. The project had obviously stopped in mid-construction. The bare plywood of the addition was gray and warped from long exposure to the elements. Lumber cutoffs and building debris littered the unkempt yard of dirt and weeds.

Ranya wondered what all of the abandoned houses on Camino Del Cielo were doing to the property values on the rest of the street. It had clearly once been a thriving middle class neighborhood, but now it had fallen to seedy ruin and disrepair. Its rundown condition reminded her of the neighborhood around Mr. De Vries's house, west of Albuquerque.

She briefly thought about the man she'd never met in life, whose Dragunov rifle now lay behind her in the back of the wagon, covered with a dirty blanket. Jan Pieter De Vries, she guessed by his name, was probably a South African Boer. She wondered if he was a recent immigrant to the USA, driven out of that country by a hunger for freedom. Well, at least he'd gone down fighting, which was more than she could say for most Americans.

Ranya had no way of knowing the remarkable journey the Dragunov had already taken, since its creation in the drab central Russian industrial city of Izhevsk in 1979. She would not have guessed that the rifle had been lifted from a dead Cuban "advisor" in 1987, when Lieutenant De Vries had gone into Angola with the South African Special Forces, to battle the communist SWAPO guerrillas. The Dragunov had thereafter stayed continuously in his possession, craftily hidden and eventually smuggled into the USA, when he emigrated from the RSA.

If Ranya Bardiwell had known this particular rifle's unique history, she might have understood why he fired those ten bullets, killing three members of the Falcon Battalion. Jan Pieter De Vries was not the type to avoid a scrap with a Marxist paramilitary unit. Leaving his first homeland had been hard enough. He was no longer a young man, and he was done with running from communists. It was now his turn to fight a guerrilla campaign of resistance—and he had taken his best shots.

These were the stories the Dragunov held, but it lay mute behind her, keeping its secrets. The only time the long rifle spoke out loud, was when someone put eye to scope, and finger to trigger.

Alex Garabanda was sitting in his old easy chair getting quietly sloshed. The digital video recording from the "Rally for Social Justice" was clear enough on the small television, even with some office window glare and contrast problems. The recorded audio quality of the band playing on stage was terrible, and the Spanish lyrics were barely understandable. For the second time he saw the busloads of extra Milicianos arrive, taking up their security positions around the stage area. He saw Carlos Guzman, "El Condor," conferring with a small group that he supposed were junior officers, all of them wearing old-style woodland pattern camouflage uniforms and pistol belts. Each zoom and pan of the camera's lens had been his decision, and watching the video took him straight back to yesterday's events.

He saw Luis Carvahal arrive, and chain his bicycle to the fateful tree. He saw Luis look up toward him, and give a little nod of recognition in his direction.

Two hours, a long hot shower and many aspirins and glasses of water later, Basilio Ramos was ready to deal with the problem of the dead man in his bed, who he now realized was Professor Robert Johnson from the university. By now he remembered that Johnson had been a guest at his post-rally reception last night. The dead man was single, and had come to his villa alone. Johnson's keys were gone, and there were no extra cars inside of the fence. Ramos deduced that Ranya Bardiwell, that Arab bitch from hell, had used it to flee his property.

Basilio Ramos burned with rage, thinking of how she had not only betrayed him, but how she had drugged him and then photographed him in ways that could not ever be explained. To add greater insult to his injury, she had somehow gotten inside of his safe, and had robbed him of his most valuable possessions in the world: his painstakingly collected hoard of gold coins and gemstones. Most of his lovely Krugerrands, Maple Leafs and American Eagles, the fruit of dozens of ranch "liberations," were gone. How had she learned the safe's combination?

Bardiwell had even stolen his custom-made .45 caliber pistol, which he had personally lifted from the cold dead hand of a wealthy Anglo rancher. The bitch even took his web belt and holster! How would he be able to explain the loss, when he had a staff meeting to attend? One of his loyal Zetas would have to provide a substitute, something to put into a replacement holster. He could not attend the afternoon staff meeting without his customary accouterments of leadership. It was unthinkable!

Ramos wrapped the dead professor in the filthy sheet, dragged him across the bedroom floor and into his bathroom, and finally heaved him up into the bathtub. The man was stiff with rigor mortis, and Ramos had to put his foot onto the corpse's chest to shove him down into the tub. The man's dead eyes were still bulging from his purple face, still staring at nothing.

Professor Robert Johnson, the stupid gringo, had to disappear from the planet earth. But first he had to disappear from this bedroom and this property, and for that, Basilio Ramos had a razor-sharp hunting knife. Several inches of the blade near the hilt were serrated into triangular saw teeth. It was going to be a disgusting but necessary job to reduce the corpse to smaller, manageable segments that could be discreetly carried out in plastic bags, one piece at a time.

Ramos knelt by the side of the tub and carefully studied the body, considering which extremity to remove first. The professor was a disgusting specimen, a piece of human shit. He was a traitor to his own people, and a homosexual pervert. Cutting him into pieces was no more than a distasteful job to do. Unpleasant, but necessary. No different than butchering a deer or a pig, he told himself.

On the other hand, he thought (while working the knife's blade through the tendons of the professor's right knee joint) that under the right circumstances this could actually be extremely pleasurable. Oh, yes, indeed it could. That is, if it was Ranya Bardiwell under his blade, and if she was securely tied up and very much awake and alive, while he was doing the cutting.

He remembered with satisfaction how the Jewish traitor and spy named Luis Carvahal had screamed and struggled while burning to death, tied to that tree by his neck. The gringo radio man Rick Haywood had also met a fitting end, skinned alive while being dragged to death, deserving every bit of his pain for the trouble and embarrassment he had caused with his big fat gringo mouth.

As Ramos severed the last gristly knee sinew and the professor's lower leg dropped free and thumped into the bottom of the tub, he wondered how much more gratifying it would be, when it was that Arab bitch Ranya Bardiwell struggling and screaming under his knife blade!

But those pictures! Those pictures could not ever—ever—get out, to be seen by his men! He had to face the ugly truth: as long as she had copies of the pictures, she not only had his gold and his guns—she also had him by his *cojones*.

24

She gazed up the street for a half an hour, munching donuts and sipping water, wondering if Garabanda was going to leave his house before the two men in the blue four-door sedan. She considered more means of creating a diversion that might cause them to leave their position. In the end, she decided to just wait and see what happened.

Finally, at quarter till twelve, the blue sedan pulled away. It headed up the hill and made the right turn at the stop sign, retracing her recent walking route. She gave them ten more minutes, in case they were just circling the block, or they were going to be replaced by another surveillance team. Departing around noon made some sense, if they were on a schedule and acting under orders. She optimistically hoped that their shift was now over for the day, and they were not going to be replaced.

Garabanda's garage door was still open. She knew that there might never be a better opportunity. Another Milicia surveillance team could be on the way. What was she waiting for, an invitation? She decided to go for it. She put the black and red Lobos ball cap back on, mentally slipping back into wolf mode. She smiled at the thought. She was already wearing her wraparound sport sunglasses. The .45 pistol went under her belt, Mexican carry, covered by her untucked black t-shirt. There were no reloads. Eight bullets would have to do whatever needed to be done.

It was time to move. She slipped out and quietly closed the Solaris's locked door, and crossed the street to walk up the sidewalk toward 4875. She passed a nicely dressed family getting out of a mini-van, who were obviously returning from church. The husband stole an appraising look at her, while the wife quickly shepherded their small children into their house. The absence of people out and about, of kids playing or parents gardening seemed strange to her on such a beautiful day. In half a minute she was approaching the Garabanda's short driveway, which led at a right angle from the sidewalk to the open garage. Until this moment she was a lawful pedestrian like any other—until she made that turn toward their house.

The key to success was not breaking stride, was not looking around or acting unsure or furtive in any way. She smoothly turned ninety degrees to the left and walked directly into the open garage, and disappeared into its cool darkness.

She'd done it. Step one, a huge step, was accomplished. She had penetrated the perimeter. There was no reaction from the street, no neighbor coming around to check. Now she could just wait right here, until Garabanda eventually came out through the interior door to get into his Crown Vic. When he came to get into his car, she'd be ready to ambush him. He wouldn't have a chance to defend himself—which was just the way it should be.

Ranya quietly moved between his car and the wall, sliding up to the interior door leading into the house. Her senses were amped up to a state of hyper-awareness. She could hear some sound coming from within the house, perhaps talking, or perhaps a TV or a radio. She put her right hand on the grip of her pistol, and extended her left toward the doorknob, driven forward by curiosity to know if it was even locked. Her fingers encircled the gray metal knob, applied light pressure, and rotated. Her heart was pounding, her pulse whooshing in her ears. She was expecting the doorknob to come to a firm stop after turning only a few degrees.

But the knob didn't stop, it continued turning clockwise a full ninety degrees against the internal spring pressure. A single thought now flowed into her mind: *why wait?* She drew her pistol, and gently snicked down the safety with her thumb. Then she slowly, slowly pushed open the door, the way a soft but persistent breeze might blow it open if it had been left ajar.

No reaction came from within. The odds were slim that the FBI man would be in the room directly on the other side, to notice the door opening. When it was opened wide enough, she stepped back against the wall of the garage. Still there was no reaction. The same noise continued in the house, but at a slightly higher volume with the door open.

Again the same thought returned: *why wait?* She inhaled deeply, took a two-handed grip on the pistol, and slid inside, into a small laundry room with a washer and dryer. There was no door to the next room, just a door-sized opening. She could hear the television now, the program sounded somehow familiar to her. News? It was the rally on the Civic Plaza, yesterday. She remembered the speech. She stepped through the opening into the kitchen. A tall pile of mail was heaped on one counter. A quick look at the address on the top envelope was her first positive confirmation that this was the Garabanda residence. An empty liquor bottle stood near the mail.

Ten more feet into the kitchen, and there was an open portal on the left side, leading into a carpeted room. She could hear the television clearly now, coming from the next room, the living room or den. Still there was no reaction from inside, as the sound drew her forward.

Pistol held slightly down and in front in both hands, she peeked around the corner, and ducked back. The man from the playground, Special Agent Garabanda, was sitting in a big chair watching television, facing obliquely away from her. His back and right side was presented to her, he was completely unaware of her existence. She shrank back against the wall, her heart hammering. He wasn't reacting to her, he wasn't looking her way, he had no idea she was in his house! She had taken only a half-second glimpse, the picture of him frozen like a snapshot in her mind.

Again the same inner voice asked, *why wait?* There was no remembered training, no tactical consideration of cover or movement when she stepped into the portal opening, both arms extended, holding out the .45 caliber pistol with her finger on the trigger. Garabanda was facing away from her, his gaze directed at the television to her right, which for a moment also captured her attention. It was the Civic Plaza rally, seen from above, from the side. The view was centered on the podium, while Governor Deleon was still speaking. She was amazed that she could actually see herself in the picture, sitting on the near side of the stage next to Basilio Ramos. Both of them were identifiable by their brown berets among the civilian guests, politicos and VIPs. She stared transfixed at the images, and heard Deleon's lunatic speech for the second time.

"Why? Because for hundreds of years, the Anglos have always been thieves and pirates and despoilers, ever since the first Pilgrims stole the land from the native peoples of so-called New England. Even at America's birth, God Almighty Himself put the mark of Cain on that wicked country, by cracking its so-called Liberty Bell the first time it was rung!

The video had run almost to the point where Deleon was going to be shot. The jug of OJ and vodka lay empty on the floor, as empty as the plastic tumbler on the left armrest. He was drunk enough, that was for sure. Random thoughts and memories were sliding around his mind. He could easily fall asleep right here in his favorite old easy chair, as he had done so many times before in a happier life. Or he could stumble to the kitchen to make something else to drink, and forget the images on the television entirely. He felt he could not watch much more of the video. Certainly not the part after the rally, after Deleon's body was taken away, when Luis…

Alex Garabanda didn't need to watch the television to see the fiery end of Luis Carvahal. For the past 24 hours he had seen it over and over, with his eyes open, and with his eyes closed.

With his head resting against the soft back of the seat, staring at the wall above the television, his fingertips could trace the contours of the pistol lying on the armrest. It would be so easy. He could pick up the Sig-Sauer, and finish off the wreckage of his life.

Tally it up. FBI career—banished from New York to New Mexico. Karin—left him for a woman. Brian—taken away by Karin and the Beast. Luis Carvahal—burned alive. He could not possibly stand to watch that terrible scene at the tree again. What in the world had he been thinking, to watch this video today? It was beyond mere masochism. A form of penance? Punishment?

Or was he giving himself an intentional nudge, a little push to finally do it, to take the next irrevocable step? For the twentieth time in the last hour, his right hand fell gently across the Sig-Sauer pistol on the chair's right armrest.

"But now, our long period of humiliation has ended! Finally, the Treaty of Shame, the Treaty of Guadalupe Hidalgo, which was broken by the Anglos from the very first days, will at last be thrown onto the trash heap of history where it had always belonged!

It was preposterous, it was purely insane, but standing in the open portal to the living room, ten feet from her quarry, Ranya could not take her eyes off the television. She was unconsciously counting down the words until Agustín Deleon would spout a gusher of blood from his back, and fall.

The Anglos have never honored their part of the treaty, and now it is only justice that we, the rightful inhabitants of Aztlan, will put it aside. As promised in the Treaty of Shame, the Spanish Land Grant territories will be returned to the rightful communal ownership of the entire people of Nuevo Mexico.

For the twentieth time he pondered the mechanics of finality. The means—a pound of cold blue steel—was once again in his right hand. Mouth, head or heart, those were his three choices. The mouth was most certain, he knew that from unwelcome professional observation, but the very idea was distasteful, somehow unmanly.

The well-delivered head shot would be quick, but it left a God-awful mess for whoever had to come behind to clean up. Worse, he knew that a muzzle against the temple could slip at the ultimate moment, a final hesitation flinch deflecting the shot. When this happened, the shooter was sometimes left to writhe and thrash in agony on the floor. Usually they died, but occasionally they lived. He had seen the bloody aftermaths, personally and in photographs. Could he do a better job of it, and make a steady-handed shot straight through his temple, in his current drunken state? Returning to brain-damaged semi-consciousness in a state hospital, a failure even at suicide… No.

That left the heart. Cleaner by far, and very, very final…but less than instantaneous in effect. On the plus side, the easy chair would make an excellent blood sponge, simplifying the cleanup for the unlucky soul left with that miserable duty. Just turn the gun around 180 degrees for a contact shot, as he had already practiced a half-dozen times. On the last dry run, he had put several pounds of pressure on the trigger with his right thumb. His fingers had been laced around the back of the grip, pushing the muzzle against his sternum bone. He had put enough pressure on the trigger with his thumb to watch the hammer begin to ease back from the slide, but he had not been quite ready. Part of him still wanted to see the final moments of Agustín Deleon and Luis Carvahal on his videotape, before he joined them. Another part of him said, *why wait?*

Alex's entire life added up to a catalog of failure. Unable to produce a child with Karin, they had finally been able to adopt an infant son, who became a truly wonderful boy. Then he had lost his wife, and not even to another man, but to *another woman.* Now he would not see his son grow up, he would not play any part in little Brian's life, while his two lesbian mommies set out to turn him into a gay *maricón.* But what could he do about it? Nothing. The entire power of the government was on their side, and it was hopeless and useless to attempt to fight that infinite force. "Resistance is futile," the saying went... He could do nothing, absolutely nothing. He was boxed in from every conceivable angle, buried alive, even while he was technically still above ground and breathing the air.

His video recording played on, and he decided that he could not stand to watch Luis burn again. That was beyond the limit of his ability to bear pain. Would he meet Luis on the other side? What would his friend say to the newly arriving former FBI Special Agent, who had as much as led him by the hand straight to his fiery death? He imagined meeting Luis on the other side, and seeing him burnt, charred and twisted. Bile rose in his throat at the image.

But was there even "another side" waiting for him, after he pulled the trigger? Or was there just a black unknowing nothingness beyond this life? He hoped for black nothingness, because he knew that if another reality lay waiting beyond this world, his well-deserved perpetual punishment would be severe.

It always came back to the eternal question: *what comes next?*

There was only one way to find out.

Was he ready now, finally?

He pushed the Sig's muzzle tip against the center of his chest, holding the gun with the fingers of both hands wrapped around the back of the grip. His right thumb was across the trigger, while watching the final moments of the life of Governor Agustín Deleon play out on the stage. A few pounds of pressure on the trigger, and…

But this time, our sacred land will not be carved up as so-called private property, to be raped and plundered for corporate profit. This time, the land will be held communally, for all the legitimate, rightful members of La Raza, the new bronze race, the Indohispano peoples born of..."

Ranya was waiting for Deleon's final recorded words and the fatal rifle shot, when Garabanda's sudden hand movement caught her eye. She swung her pistol back toward him, but by the time her mind fully snapped into the present, the situation had completely changed—the FBI man was holding a pistol! How had she missed the pistol? She saw him holding it now, but he was holding it all wrong.

It made no sense! He was not turning it toward her, but toward himself, backward toward his own chest. Nothing in this house made sense, nothing! Deleon continued to speak, but she no longer heard the television, as her entire universe funneled down to that hand holding that black pistol.

Without thinking she shouted, "Stop it! Stop it! Don't move!"

Alex heard a female voice, and turned his head toward the kitchen. He found himself looking into the muzzle of a pistol, aimed directly at his face. There was a period of mental turmoil while he oriented himself, and then he burst out laughing. It was the damnedest sight: a woman wearing a baseball cap was staring at him over the top of a pistol, which she held in a two-handed grip. He leaned forward in his chair, still holding his own pistol against his heart, his head rolling from side to side and he laughed.

An odd memory popped into his head, and in Spanish he asked, *"Who the hell gave you a candle in this funeral?"* His parents had often used this Cuban saying, meant as a put-down to unbidden interlopers. It had somehow leapt into his mind and from his lips without conscious thought.

Then he said, "You have a fine sense of timing. Are you from the Special Surveillance Group?" He wondered if the blue stakeout car was still parked across the street. "Where's the rest of your team? Please, don't tell me that I'm only worth sending one single Miliciana?" He laughed bitterly. "No, I guess that's about right. One should be plenty to take care of such a meaningless task. But you know what? You're too late."

The woman spoke again after a moment. "I'm not from the Milicia or from any surveillance group—I don't even know what you're talking about. Now put down your gun—put it down!"

He chuckled again. "Oh really? Or what? You'll shoot me? That's pretty funny: you'll shoot me." Then he turned serious: "Well, go ahead. What's stopping you?"

The woman shook her head, still aiming her pistol at him. Her voice lost its commanding tone. "No, no, that's not why I'm here! So put down the gun…please?"

He gradually rotated the pistol around in his hands, until he had a conventional one-handed grip on it. "You know, I can make you do it."

He slowly extended his right arm and the pistol straight out in front of him, toward the forgotten television. His face was turned toward her over his right shoulder; he was staring at her now with tired eyes.

"No, no, please, please don't do this—at least, listen to me! We need to talk, so please stop!" She seemed to be growing frantic, but she kept her pistol's sights on him.

"Just a little more…should do it," he said, the gun held out on a wavering arm, which was slowly swinging toward her.

Finally, the woman sprang back out of the kitchen opening, sidestepping to get cover behind the wall. "Stop it, stop it! We need to talk—I need to know something important!"

Alex Garabanda continued to bring his arm—and his pistol—slowly around toward her. He knew that she would have to either fire or retreat in a matter of seconds. He wondered if she understood that the interior wall would barely slow down his bullets…if he fired at her. He didn't know what he would do if his pistol made it all the way, before she stopped him.

"Please, don't do this. Stop! Listen to me! It's about Brian. Brian!"

He paused. It finally occurred to him that she had been speaking English all along, unaccented American English. His pistol ceased its traverse while aimed halfway between the television and the kitchen, where the woman was now crouching behind the wall.

He switched to English without thinking. "Brian? What about Brian?" His Sig-Sauer pistol was weaving around in little circles, not quite directed toward her. "Hey, you're not from the Milicia, are you? So who are you then?"

"I'm Brian's mother."

This stranger's armed intrusion during the final moments of his life had seemed like one last cosmic joke, but those three words struck him like a hammer blow. He choked out his reply, trying to claw his way back to sober, rational thought.

"His…mother? No, no, that's not possible." He spoke slowly and deliberately, fighting against the alcohol, trying to find the right words, trying to speak without slurring. "No, you see, I have just this very morning said farewell to Mommy Dearest, and to young Brian as well…"

"No, I'm his *real* mother, you moron! His *real* mother, damn you!"

The pistol slipped from his suddenly feeble hand, and dropped onto the carpet with a thunk. "You're…Brian's…*birth mother?*"

Ranya stepped through the doorway, and moved a yard closer to him. On the television, Governor Deleon collapsed backward onto the stage, unwatched. "Yes, I'm Brian's *real* mother—even if I didn't have the privilege of naming him! Even if I only had five minutes with him in his whole life, well—they were the first five minutes! Five minutes, before he was stolen from me and given to a pair of jackbooted thugs to raise!"

Garabanda had turned ashen and slumped back against the easy chair. "But that's…impossible," he whispered. "That's…not what happened! Brian's birth mother is dead, she was killed in—"

She cut him off. "Do I look dead, you idiot?" Ranya advanced another step toward him, shaking her pistol at his face. "Do I look dead?"

He turned his head back toward her. "No..." was all he could manage to say.

"Do you think I came all the way out here to Albuquerque New Mexico, just to play some kind of a sick practical joke?"

"Um…no. I don't suppose so."

"No, you don't suppose so! So tell me something, was that his mother—I mean—you know what I mean!" She struggled, unable to mouth the alien words. "Was that woman at the playground, was she Brian's…oh, dammit, his 'mother,' I mean…"

"Yes."

"So, you're Alexandro Garabanda?"

"Yes…"

"And the lady who took Brian from the playground?"

"She—that was my ex-wife. Karin Bergen. Formerly Karin Garabanda."

"So who was the other woman, the tattooed lady with the biceps?"

Garabanda shook his head slowly. "That…was Karin's new 'wife.' Or maybe husband? Fiancée? I'm not quite up on their current legal status. If there was a wedding, I didn't get an invitation."

"What? She's…?"

"Karin's…gay. At least, she is now. When we got married? Who knows what she was then. That tattooed freak…"

"Enough—I got the picture. So, where are they going?"

He looked directly at her. "Where are they going?"

"You don't understand the question?"

"California. They're going to San Diego. Gretchen Bosch—Karin's girlfriend, she got promoted and she was transferred."

"Transferred? What's that mean?"

"She works for the IRS. Internal Revenue, Criminal Investigations Division. She's an IRS Special Agent."

"IRS, huh?" Ranya thought about this for a moment, still covering him with her .45. She kicked the empty jug of orange juice with her toe. "So what the hell were you doing here? Drowning your sorrows, and getting up the nerve to shoot yourself? What kind of a man would let all that happen to his son, and then shoot himself?"

Garabanda turned his head away. "No kind of a man," he said miserably, "No kind of a man at all."

"You let your son…MY son…!"

"Yes! And that's not even the worst of it! You want to know the worst of it?" He rubbed his eyes with the back of his hand. "Pull up a chair, watch the movie—we just missed seeing the governor catch a bullet. But the best part is coming, just wait. After you see it, believe me, you'll want to do me a favor and shoot me. Yes, you will. A big favor."

Ranya stooped and snatched his pistol from the carpet, then stepped away, shoving it into her jeans left-handed. That danger out of the way, she glanced toward the TV, and noted the video camera resting on the table beside it. "This isn't a news program, is it?" She pointed at the television with her .45.

"No, it's not."

"You made this movie?"

"…I did."

"FBI work?"

He snorted. "No, not FBI work. On my own. Sort of a hobby."

She was confused by this cryptic disclosure, but let it pass. "I was there too, you know. Right on the stage."

"You're…joking?"

"No, I'm serious. See the guy standing there, in the cammie uniform? This is right after Deleon got shot." Despite the low quality video, they could clearly see the governor's body prone on the cement stage. Vice-gobernador Magón was crouching over Deleon's corpse, in the spreading pool of dark blood. The Comandante was standing behind Magón, while most of the remaining men and women on the stage were scrambling for non-existent cover.

Alex Garabanda focused on the television screen. "I know him. That's Basilio Ramos, the leader of the Falcon Battalion."

"Well, that's me right behind him, wearing a beret. See the pistol he's holding? Here it is." She tipped her .45's barrel up, and briefly held it sideways for him to see.

"Oh…shit." Garabanda glanced between the television and Ranya. The truth of it was obvious. She was wearing jeans and a black t-shirt both on the video and here in his living room. Only her headwear had changed. "Tell me the truth," he asked her, "Have I gone insane? Are you for real, or am I hallucinating this? I'm drunk, but this is too…"

"Yes, I'm for real, and yes, I'm Brian's real mother. That's all the truth."

"You were with Comandante Ramos, at the rally? But you said you weren't Milicia."

"I'm not."

He looked from her back to the television. "But—she—you're wearing a brown beret there, on the stage!"

"I know I was, I already told you that. Listen, it's a long story about how it all happened, but take my word for it: I'm not Milicia. Far from it."

"Then you're undercover, you're on an assignment?"

"No, I'm Brian's mother, that's all."

Garabanda's head fell against the back of the armchair. "New Mexico…and I thought it couldn't get any crazier..."

"Crazier? You should talk—you were the one pointing a gun at himself."

He cracked a wan smile at this observation. "Touché. Good point."

"So—are you still going to try to kill yourself? Suicidal people make me kind of nervous."

"Listen—I wasn't planning to kill myself."

"Oh, really? You always point guns at yourself when you're drinking?"

"Okay, well—maybe. Maybe yes, maybe no. I mean, I didn't plan it or anything. But that's over. That's finished."

"Why? Sudden change of heart?"

He stared straight ahead, his jaw working soundlessly. Finally he said, "Because things are…different now. Everything is different. I want to hear your story, about Brian…about everything. But first, I want to turn off the television. I've seen enough. You know what happens next?" Garabanda used his remote control, and the television screen went black.

"I wish I didn't. I was right there…right by the tree. The burning tree. The man with the bike—who was he?"

"He was my last friend. And I sent him there, to the rally. You see, he was my friend, but he was also my informant. He was close to the governor. Very close. His name was Luis Carvahal."

Ranya made a soft whistling sound. "You know, you really suck at being an FBI agent, don't you?"

He sighed. "Don't worry…I wasn't going to suck at it for much longer."

"But you just said…"

"Oh, forget it," Garabanda said despondently.

"Forget it? That's fine for you, but what about Brian?"

He looked at her, and they held eye contact. "What about Brian?"

"You were just going to shoot yourself, and let Karin and that circus freak have him?"

"There was nothing else I could do. Nothing…"

"Just like that—you were going to give up?"

"Nothing is 'just like that.' I had no alternative, none! The court…"

"Okay, I get it. You gave up, you quit. Well that's your problem—that's on you. But at least tell me where they live in San Diego, before you do yourself in."

"I'm not going to 'do myself in'."

"So you said. But just in case you change your mind again, why don't you tell me where they live?"

"I can't."

"Why not?"

"Because I don't know, at least not yet. They're moving out there now, and I just found out about it today."

"Well, they just left a few hours ago! You've got a fast car, what were you sitting around here for? Why didn't you go after them?"

"It's not like that! It's not that easy! They're traveling in a federal convoy, for security. Ten or fifteen vehicles, and everybody's armed. The convoys usually have armored gun trucks at each end, as escorts. They won't stop for anybody or anything until Flagstaff or Phoenix, and then they'll stay overnight on federal property, or on a military base. They'll drive the rest of the way to California tomorrow. So there's no chance of just grabbing Brian from out of that convoy. None."

She thought about this, evaluating his truthfulness, and weighing the chances. The concept of federal agents traveling between states in armed security convoys was entirely new to her. "Okay, maybe I buy that. Maybe. But you can find out where they're going to live in San Diego, can't you? Even a really bad FBI agent should be able to do that, right?"

"Oh yeah, sure, even the worst FBI agent in the world could do that. But the address won't be enough."

"Get me the address, and I'll take my chances. I got this far, didn't I?"

He looked at her again. "What did you say your name was?"

"I didn't." She thought for a moment about the pros and cons of disclosure. "My name is Ranya Bardiwell."

"I just saw that name. Was that Oklahoma? There was an escape from the federal transit center last week. A female. You?"

"Oklahoma, yes. But not the transit center. From a detention camp for politicals."

"For terrorists, you mean."

"Whatever."

"A federal officer was killed."

"Yeah, well, they weren't going to just let me walk out of there."

"But, you killed a federal—"

"Don't get all choked up, G-man. She was a warden. She made her play, and I made mine. I did what I had to do. Now I'm on a mission, and I'll do whatever it takes."

"To find Brian?"

"Not just to 'find' him. I've come to get him."

"You know…he's my son, too."

Ranya angrily thrust her pistol back out at his face. "Like hell he is! And besides, weren't you just about to shoot yourself? That sort of terminates your parental rights, don't you think?"

"But I'm the only father he's ever known, from the time he was an infant..."

"*You*, his father? You have no idea about his father! You don't even know where Brian is going. His father!"

"Listen, I'm sorry for what happened, but you didn't raise him. He was taken from you—stolen I guess, and I know that's terrible, but you were in detention, and—"

"You don't know anything! Anything!"

"I know you're not going to be able to just go to California and 'get' him."

"I got this far. I'll get to California too."

"But this screwed up place is New Mexico! Nobody's in charge here, they don't know which way is up in this state. The Three Stooges could do a better job of running this state! California is different. You'd be busted on your first day out there, and then you'd go right back to prison. One day, max."

"Thanks for painting the rosy picture," she said icily. "Coming from the world's worst FBI agent, that means a lot, believe me. I think I'll take my chances."

"And how will you get there? Drive?"

"Yes, actually I was planning on taking an FBI agent's Crown Victoria. He doesn't need it anymore."

"Just like that? Traveling alone, one car? You have a plan for getting through all the checkpoints? You have a plan for getting across the California state border? Where are you going to buy gas out there, when there's almost no gas anywhere, unless you can get onto a federal base? Lady, you are so naïve, it's a miracle you ever made it to New Mexico. You'll never make it to California—much less ever see Brian again."

She said nothing as they glared at one another. Finally she broke the impasse. "Okay then, tell me how to do it."

"You? You can't. It's impossible."

"It's possible. Tell me how."

He took a deep breath and said, "Well…there's really only one way."

"Okay, that's enough, that's all I need. How?"

Alex paused again before quietly answering. "I can take you there."

She stared at him, thinking, considering the lack of available alternatives. "Does that mean you're not going to shoot yourself, after all?"

"No. No, I won't. Not now. That's over, that's finished."

"So tell me, why would I want to take the world's worst FBI agent?"

He managed one more partial smile. "Because I'm all you've got. You can't get there without me. You get a better offer, tell me about it."

Alex Garabanda had nothing more to say to her. She would accept his offer, or not. If she didn't, he would not be any worse off than before.

After a minute of silence between them, she asked, "Do you have any pictures of my son around here? Albums, something?"

There were no framed photographs hanging on the walls, only nail marks. Karin had stripped away their memories.

"Pictures? I don't know what my ex-wife left. You'd have to look around in the closets, I guess. She probably took everything. No, wait—my laptop. I've got pictures of Brian on my laptop." His brain was functioning only at three-quarters speed. Now that he was attempting to sound half-intelligent, his tongue felt like a beanbag.

"So where's your laptop?"

"In my car. In the trunk."

"Do I need a password? To see the pictures I mean."

"No, not for the family albums. Just click the camera icon on the desktop."

"Okay, good. I want to see pictures of him, it would mean a lot to me." She walked behind him and over to the window, peering between the horizontal blinds, glancing across the street.

He asked her, "Are they gone?"

"You saw them too?"

"Of course I saw them."

"They're gone," she replied, "Otherwise, I wouldn't have come in. I waited until they left. At first, I thought they were after *me*. I thought that somehow, they knew I'd be coming here. I thought they were already looking for me, and it freaked me out pretty bad. Who were they?"

"I'm not positive, but I think they're from the Special Surveillance Group. They're part of New Mexico's own CIA, since the last elections. I think they're just leaning on me, letting me know they're on my case. Yesterday after the rally, they called me up on my cell phone, and they told me that they were the ones who burned Luis Carvahal. They told me I might be next. They're trying to run me out of the state, I guess."

Ranya leaned against the bare wall next to the living room window and lowered her pistol, still staring at him. "Run you out of the state, huh? You know what? I heard that phone call, from the other end. Basilio Ramos made it. We were in some kind of a gravel mine north of the city, in one of his Suburbans. You ever hear of a radio talk show guy named Rick Haywood?"

"Sure, he's 'the king of Albuquerque talk radio.' He comes on in the afternoon."

"Well, not anymore. Right after Ramos called you, they tied him up behind a Suburban, and made him run for his life. Then he fell, and they dragged him. Dragged him to death. I saw it, right in front of me. It was terrible…almost as bad as your friend being burned alive. Almost…" Ranya was staring out the window between two slats, holding her pistol down against her leg.

"They killed Rick Haywood?"

"The Zetas. They're the Comandante's private goon squad. They blew up his radio station too, that's what they said. Ramos said they're done with Anglo talk radio giving them a hard time. Haywood was the example. After they killed him, they were going to bury him in a gravel pit. At least, that's what Ramos told his men to do."

Garabanda said, "They 'disappeared' him. Deleon was assassinated, Carvahal was burned and now Haywood's been 'disappeared.' That means they're moving to the next level, the next stage. They're going beyond politics now, way beyond 'land reform.' They're settling scores, and making examples. It's a classic progression. Classic. 'Marxist Power Consolidation, 101: State Terror.' There's probably old communist text-books somewhere. Did you notice how fast they found the sniper's rifle in the Regent, and how they already had an Anglo pinned for the shooting?"

"Yeah, I noticed. Ramos told me that Saturday was going to change everything."

"He told you that? When?"

"When? A few days ago. I was…um…staying with him."

"You were staying with Comandante Ramos? Where, in Sandia Heights, or at the Albuquerque Academy?" Alex Garabanda knew about both places.

"At his house."

Garabanda paused, digesting this information. This woman had been staying at Comandante Ramos's house, living under his roof. That could mean many different things. "How did…how did you…"

"How did I wind up staying with Comandante Ramos? It's a long story, are you sure you want to hear it?"

"Why not? I've got nothing but time now."

She was leaning with her back against the wall by the window, and she slid down it until she was sitting Indian style, her pistol held across her lap, but no longer aimed at him. "Well, after I escaped from the detention camp—that was Friday, a week ago…"

Ranya proceeded to tell the FBI agent of her trip across Oklahoma and North Texas, of her night flight in the small plane to the saltpan near

Mountainview, of her ride in the van with the wayward student radicals. She described the accidental ambush at Chulada, which had ended with her under the control of the Milicia, and eventually under the roof of Comandante Basilio Ramos. The story took a long time, and he frequently interjected with his own questions. He paid close attention when she described how she had been shackled to the wall and subjected to a mock firing squad. She left out the next part, how she had been forced to shoot Kalil as a loyalty test.

While she was describing her subsequent mall shopping spree and trip to the beauty salon, accompanied by Ramos and his Zeta squad, she noticed that his eyes had closed. She sat and watched him for several minutes, until she was sure his sleep was genuine.

Ranya could only guess how much alcohol he had consumed, or how long he would be out, but she wanted him secured. There was a long clothesline in the backyard, running from the house to the cement block wall that separated his property from the house behind them. She cut the line down, and brought it inside. She sliced it into four equal lengths, and gently slid them under his wrists and around his ankles, listening and watching him carefully, while slowly and meticulously binding him to the armchair. The cords weren't tight, she just wanted to be able to turn her back on him or leave the room without worrying about being jumped. Despite his promises to the contrary, she had no trust in his declarations. A man who was ready to shoot himself was ready to do anything, rational or not.

Next, she went back into the garage. His car was not locked. She popped the trunk, and found his laptop inside of a black soft-sided valise. The trunk was jammed full of bags and boxes. She brought the computer back into the living room, and then she gave the rest of the house a quick search. It seemed that about half of the furniture had been left behind by his ex-wife.

Papers, boxes and forgotten toys were scattered about. She lingered in Brian's old room, guessing what posters had been on the wall between the tape marks and thumbtacks. There was a tiny red plastic action figure left on his windowsill, facing outward against the glass as if standing guard. She picked it up and stared at the three-inch tall Spiderman, trying to imagine Brian's little hand grasping it. She pocketed the toy and moved on.

With Garabanda tied up and the rest of the house checked out, she could finally sit down on the living room floor with his black laptop computer. She flipped it open and pushed on the power button, and when the screen came up she clicked the camera icon, and was presented with a selection of picture files. She randomly clicked on albums, and studied the photos documenting the life of her stolen son, photos taken during her own five stolen years.

There was another house, brick, and a backyard with a grass lawn and a small swing set. Alex Garabanda must have been the primary family photographer; he was in only a few of the pictures. Karin Garabanda looked happy in some pictures, but Ranya paid little attention to her. Brian was a jolly little fellow, given to wearing overalls and bouncy high-top sneakers. In some earlier pictures, he was wearing only a diaper, splashing in an inflatable wading pool. Album by album, picture by picture, Ranya reached back into the five stolen years of the life of her son.

There was Brian at about two years old on a plastic pony, grinning up at the camera with wide blue eyes. Grinning up at his father. At his father? No, not at his father! At Alexandro Garabanda, the FBI agent who had stolen him—not at his father!

The unfairness of it all was crushing. Five minutes she had spent with Brian, only five minutes, and these federal agents had gotten five years! This child, her child, was a complete stranger to her. This child who looked up with loving eyes at his abductors, never knowing the father and mother who had conceived him in love and brought him into the world. It was so unfair, so unfair, so unfair! When would she get a break? When? She closed her eyes and she wept.

After a few minutes, she went back to clicking through pictures, staring through tears at the stranger who was her son, bitter at the unfairness.

Nevertheless, in so many pictures Brian was smiling, almost always smiling, even if it was not at his real father. He was not smiling up at Brad Fallon, no, not at poor Brad, gone down into the cold Potomac River these six long and lonely years. No, little Brian was constantly smiling up at this other man, at this federal agent. At this willing cog in the machinery of repression, which not only crushed people's lives between unfeeling gear teeth, but also stole the small children of its victims. Stole them, to be handed out like random door prizes to jackbooted thugs.

Even so, her son *was smiling*. Brian was constantly beaming with obvious joy at this man taking the pictures, this man who was the only father he had ever known. Brad Fallon had died before he was born. Didn't Brian at least deserve to have a substitute father?

Alexandro Garabanda didn't kill Brad Fallon. Taking him at his word, Garabanda had believed that the boy was an orphan. Should she hate him, just because he worked for the same federal government that had spawned Brad's killers? The same government that had taken away five years of her life, and stolen her son?

25

Wendy Larmouche was game to go out on the Customs boat again the following Sunday. Bob Bullard appreciated that this was a hit or miss proposition. Most women (and men too for that matter) couldn't handle more than a few minutes of the rolling and slamming involved with taking high performance boats out on the ocean. It was a particular taste, like the enjoyment of roller coasters. Wendy's friend Sandra enjoyed sunbathing and fooling around at dockside aboard the eighty-foot Eldorado, but she could not tolerate the occasionally violent motion of the Fountain racing boat. Bob was not disappointed that Wendy returned the following Sunday by herself. As before, they were picked up alongside the Eldorado, downtown on San Diego Bay.

The Customs boat was forty feet long, with four 200 horsepower black Mercury outboards mounted across the transom. The boat was nicely trimmed out in black, gray and blue paint, with HOMELAND SECURITY written along its hull sides. Wendy and Bob both wore black uniforms for their excursion today, with HOMELAND SECURITY printed on the back in white letters. Bullard had a holstered pistol on his combination inflatable lifejacket and utility vest, which was also black, also with HOMELAND SECURITY on the back.

There were three U-shaped bolster seats in the front of the cockpit, and three more behind them. Bob took the wheel on the right side, the leader of the three-man Customs crew took the center position to navigate and handle the radios, and Wendy took the left side. The other two crew members occupied the second row of padded bolsters behind them. Once the boat was out on the open ocean and leaping across waves, there could be no question of sitting. You could only stand, wedged back against the bolsters, with your knees flexed to take the shock as the hull repeatedly slammed down against the waves. Today it promised to be calmer on the outside, but still they stood, just in case. Even crossing a large wake at high speed could send the Fountain airborne.

The three Customs agents voiced no objection to Bob Bullard taking the wheel, as they headed out the shipping channel between the North Island Naval Air Station and the Point Loma submarine base. He was the boss of all of their bosses, so how could they possibly object? With just one phone call, he could have them promoted, or have them transferred to Alaska. If he liked to go for boat rides on the weekends, well, that was his prerogative. They loved their work, and were proud that the regional director took a personal interest in it, and shared their enthusiasm for high-performance boating.

Running out the ship channel at a leisurely thirty knots, they overtook the usual bright-orange harbor tugs, and passed down the side of a cruise ship coming in. Bob Bullard wouldn't push the throttles wide open until they had cleared the sea buoy beyond Point Loma. He ran up the sterns of several sailboats and then crossed their bows, leaving them wallowing in his wake. Most were typical Sunday morning day sailors, about thirty to forty feet long. Their sails were already raised, as they tacked their way back and forth against the light mid-morning sea breeze. It seemed like a hell of a slow way to go boating, but Bullard understood that at least they didn't need to pay for expensive fuel.

Burning fuel was never a factor for the Customs boats. Uncle Sam kept their tanks full of high-octane gasoline at all times. Even in times of fuel scarcity, the Department of Homeland Security went to the front of every line.

Next, the Fountain overtook a larger sailboat, which was motoring straight out the channel just beyond the tip of Point Loma, the land's-end of San Diego. It was a white-hulled boat about fifty feet long, with its cockpit in the middle between two masts. A woman was standing behind the wheel in the cockpit and hand steering, while a man stood by the larger mast in front, evidently preparing to hoist the main sail. Bullard didn't know too much about sailboats, but he was a quick study, and something alerted him to an opportunity.

He throttled back and turned to the leader of the Customs crew standing next to him, and asked, "What's that contraption on their stern, those pipes and ropes? It looks like an extra rudder, why isn't it down in the water?" Both of them were wearing wrap-around sports sunglasses, and Bullard could see his own double reflection. They had to yell to be heard over the four engines.

"I think it's what they call a self-steering wind vane. Sort of like an autopilot for sailboats, but it runs off the wind, instead of electric power or hydraulics."

"So they can make that boat steer itself, even when it's sailing?"

"Sure."

"And they can cross oceans on boats like that, right?"

"No problem. They do it all the time."

Bullard noted a gray inflatable dingy turned upside down on the foredeck of the boat, and a dozen plastic Jerry cans in assorted colors lashed to the safety lines along the amidships on both sides. "It doesn't look like he's just going day-sailing today, does it?"

"I don't know. Maybe not."

Bullard further eased back the throttles until the Fountain was almost at a dead idle, falling into line behind the sailboat. He read the name from the transom.

"The *Mystic Lady*, from Boston. That boat's already come a long way—let's go have a chat." He goosed the throttles slightly ahead, coming alongside the sailboat with only a few yards separating their hulls. The man and woman on board the sailboat had been studiously trying to pretend that the Homeland Security boat trailing them did not exist. With the boat so close alongside they were beyond pretenses, and the couple forced weak smiles and gave little hand waves of greeting.

"You take the wheel," Bullard told the Customs man beside him, stepping out from his bolster. "Bring her right alongside, I'm going over."

The truth was that despite his present high rank within the Department of Homeland Security, Bob Bullard was at his core a hands-on kind of a guy who missed kicking down doors and busting scumbags. Wendy would appreciate watching him in action. She'd see that Bob was still a stud who could get physical, that he could hang with the young agents and match them step for step.

He gestured to the two Customs agents in the aft bolsters to follow him across. The Fountain edged over until its deck-edge rub rail was pressed alongside the white hull of the sailboat, matching its speed of five knots. He stood on the gunwale of the race boat, grabbed the sailboat's lifelines and climbed over. The two men climbing over behind him carried MP-5 sub machineguns slung on chest slings.

All three of them wore black ball caps with DHS written across the front as their introduction. There was no asking permission to come aboard, no mention of probable cause or warrants. In the eyes of the law, the sailboat was not a home, and was not afforded the protections of even an automobile on an American highway. The vessel was a conveyance potentially used in international travel, and it could be boarded at their discretion, anywhere and anytime, with no questions asked. For all anyone knew, it could be involved in smuggling dope, guns, illegal aliens or enemy terrorists.

The well-tanned husband looked to be about in his late forties, with a shaggy mop of windblown brown hair salted with gray. He was barefoot, wearing cutoff shorts and a t-shirt advertising a bar somewhere in Mexico. His wife was about the same age, but not too bad looking. She was wearing white sneakers, white shorts and a man's white oxford shirt, and a floppy white canvas sailor's hat to protect her face from the midday sun.

The man stepped down from the sailboat's coach roof as Bullard and the Customs team scrambled aboard. He was clearly terrified, which was how Bullard preferred them. The sailor nervously asked, "W-what can I do for you gentlemen today?"

Bullard never answered questions from civilians—he only asked them. "Anybody else aboard this vessel?"

"Uh, no sir. We're alone. Nobody else aboard."

"This is your vessel?"

"Yes sir, it's ours."

"What're your names?"

"I'm Harvey Sumner, and that's my wife Roxanne." He forced a tepid smile and put out his hand, but it was ignored and he slowly withdrew it.

"Where are you heading today, Mr. Sumner?"

There was a short pause, as the man looked between the agents, and over at the Customs boat. "Up to San Francisco."

"San Francisco? Nice town. Nice. You have the papers for this vessel, some ID?"

"Uh…yes sir. Down below."

"Good. Well, why don't we go down below and have a look, shall we? Roxanne can just keep on steering, right?"

"Sure—sure she can."

"My men can keep her company in the cockpit. Why don't you and me go below? After you, Mr. Sumner." The old juices were flowing. There was nothing quite like invading somebody's most personal space with the full force of the government behind you. The companionway hatch was already open at the front of the cockpit, and Mr. Sumner climbed down the short ladder first, followed by Bob Bullard in his black uniform and utility vest.

"Nice, very nice." Bullard pulled off his sunglasses as he entered the main saloon. "Is this all natural teakwood? Fine workmanship. Where was it made?"

"Taiwan."

"Well, those Chinamen, they do mighty good work, that's for sure. Nice table, is this where you eat dinner? I'll just sit here, while you gather your documents." Bullard enjoyed making himself at home, uninvited. He was teasing the man, who had obviously been expecting several Customs agents to come below and search his boat. The documents were in a plastic valise on a shelf across from the dinette table. Harvey Sumner quickly had them spread on the table in front of Bob Bullard, and then he sat down across from him.

"U.S. documented vessel, that's good. Stamps are all up to date. From Boston, huh? What, you came through the canal?"

"Right, the Panama Canal. Last year." Mr. Sumner was about the same overall size and height as Bullard, but with longer and much thicker brown hair. In his silly t-shirt and shorts, he was no match for the muscular homeland security honcho, who was beefed up even further by his black uniform and utility vest. Bullard was clearly the top dog today, no question. The boat owner virtually rolled over on his back, and figuratively offered his throat to the dominant alpha male by asking, "Can I get you something to drink, or maybe a snack?"

"No thanks, Mr. Sumner. Say, do you two live aboard this boat?"

"Uh, yeah. Yes. Yes sir."

"That's nice, very nice. Free as birds, eh? Just go wherever the wind blows, is that right?"

"Sometimes…"

"But the wind's not blowing towards San Francisco, is it Harvey? Must be tough to sail north, against the wind. Have you seen the five day forecast? A low's moving in from the Northwest—it's going to get nasty. I'm thinking it'd be a lot easier to sail south, or west. You know, with the wind." Mr. Harvey Sumner was tongue-tied, off balance. *I've got you*, thought Bullard, enjoying the old cat and mouse game of interrogation, before going in for the kill.

"Uh, um, sometimes it can be. It depends."

Bullard waited, looking at Sumner as if he could read his mind, and already knew that he was prevaricating. "So, where are you going in San Francisco, Mr. Sumner? Which marina?"

"Um, we usually don't stay at marinas. Usually, we anchor out, to save money."

"Is that so? So tell me, where are you going to anchor out, when you get to San Francisco? Maybe you can show me, on a chart? I'm sure you already have it marked, don't you? And I'm sure you've already got the waypoints entered on your GPS, right? Waypoints, all the way up to San Francisco. Don't you, Mr. Sumner?"

The man hesitated, uncertainty written all over his face. He looked down and to the left, unable to meet Bullard's gaze. "I was g-going to put them in today, once we're s-sailing north. The w-waypoints depend on the w-wind direction, and how we have to tack."

Bullard leaned back and snickered, as if he'd just heard a mildly amusing joke. Once they started stuttering, it was close to the end. He'd been trained in facial cues and body language lie detection, and he could list a dozen subtle clues to determine when a subject was lying, but this man was an open book. "Nice try Harvey, nice try. Now, tell me something that's not a 'sea story.' Tell me the truth. You're not going to San Francisco. You're heading west, aren't you? West across the mighty Pacific. That's why you have all those extra Jerry cans of fuel tied on deck, isn't it? That's why you have that self-steering vane on the back? For crossing oceans."

Sumner's face drained, his jaw hung slack.

"Look Harvey, personally, I don't care. There's no law against it, at least not yet, right? You're still free to go wherever you want—I just don't like being lied to. That's all. So tell me the truth: you're not going up to San Francisco, are you, Harvey?"

Mr. Sumner looked down at the varnished table, at his folded hands. Bullard knew that liars arranged their hands that way to keep them from visibly shaking. He could write a book on how liars behaved under interrogation stress. Harvey Sumner could provide an entire chapter.

"Harvey, I don't want to be here, giving you a hard time. Actually, I admire you, I really do. Most men only dream about crossing oceans, and you've done it! I respect that, I honestly do! So please, just to satisfy my curiosity: where are you going? Tell me the truth, and we'll all be on our way."

Mr. Sumner's jaw twitched. He glanced up, could not bear the pressure of Bob Bullard's piercing ice-blue eyes, and looked down again. "Well…um…" He gave a low cough, clearing his throat, stalling. "Actually…um…P-Polynesia." He spoke almost inaudibly, his voice cracking. "The Marquesas, and then the T-Tuamotus. Down that way."

"Nice! The ultimate tropical cruise, that's really terrific. But you know, I'll bet there's one big hassle. Those new currency export laws, they must really be a pain in the ass. I mean, only being able to take $10,000 New Dollars out of the country—that has to be a showstopper. Tell me, how do you manage it?"

"We—we're thrifty. We m-make do. We get by."

Bullard grinned again. "Oh, come on now Mr. Sumner—I wasn't born yesterday. It takes a lot of dough to run a boat like this." Bullard had a hunch, and he was winging it. "I've never met a sailor yet that didn't have a little something hidden away, you know what I'm saying? I mean, New Dollars aren't exactly the flavor of the month overseas anymore, are they? What's a hamburger cost in Tahiti, two hundred blue bucks? Now I'm thinking, an intelligent man like you Harvey, he'd have a few coins set aside for a rainy day, don't you think? You know the kind I mean. Maybe a Maple Leaf or two? Maybe an Eagle or a Krugerrand? Gold coins, Mr. Sumner. I'm sure an intelligent man like you must have seen the wisdom of putting aside some gold."

Sumner looked to be on the verge of tears, the facial tic was really firing now, as he continued to look straight down at his hands to avoid eye contact.

"Mr. Sumner, I'm going to be straight with you. I could have my men take this boat back into port under suspicion of unlawful export. We could handcuff you and your pretty wife Roxanne, and take the Mystic Lady right back to the Customs dock. Then we'd tear this boat apart, down to the last screw. We'd cut open every mattress and cushion; we'd pull up every floorboard and rip out every ceiling panel. We'd take it down to the bare hull, if that's what it took, and then we'd rip the hull apart.

"And we'd find something, I guaran-damn-tee it. We always do. If you have one penny over $10,000 New Dollars on board, we'd get you for felony currency export, and that's five years federal time right there. Federal time Harvey—that means you do every single day—there's no early release. Plus, we'd do an asset forfeiture on your boat, so when you and Roxanne got out, you'd be homeless. And if we found more than five gold Krugerrands or Maple Leafs or Liberty Eagles, well, that's ten more years right there. You know, gold hoarding is economic sabotage, and taking it out of the country, well, tack on some more unlawful export charges. You could be looking at ten to twenty, easy.

"And Mr. Sumner, we haven't even gotten around to the firearms yet. Now, I know that if I was sailing around the world, well I damn sure wouldn't go without at least a couple of guns! No freakin' way! Now, you're an intelligent man, I'm sure you agree with me. No way would I go out there unarmed, what with all the pirates and cutthroats lurking around every third world hellhole, making eyes at Roxanne! So I'm right there with you on the guns. But unfortunately, you have to know, if we did take the Mystic Lady back to the Customs dock, we'd find every last bullet. There's no way on earth you could hide a gun on this boat so that we wouldn't find it, not even a .22 derringer. I don't care if you buried it in the keel or hid it up the mast, we'd find it.

"So what do you say, Mr. Sumner? Should we turn this boat around, and have my men take it back to the Customs dock? Take a minute to decide, get a glass of water if you want. But let me know if you want the Mystic Lady to be heading out across the Pacific today, or back to the Customs dock. It's your decision."

Sumner's eyes were welling, he was on the verge of tears, and he swallowed several times before softly answering. "No…I don't w-want to g-go back."

"That's good. I don't want to either, because once we turn around, everything gets real official. Everything is recorded, inventoried. Paperwork out the old wazoo. Right now, we're still just two men having a friendly, unofficial conversation. So help me out Harvey, give me a reason to get off your boat. Give me a reason to send you on your way across the Pacific, with Uncle Sam's blessing."

"W-what…do you w-want from us?"

"Just the truth, Harvey. No more bullshit. Show me the gold, and show me the cash. No—forget about the cash, you can keep it. Just show me the gold."

Sumner breathed deeply, and stood up from the dinette. He knelt down and pulled up a heavy teak floor panel in the center of the main saloon passageway, and set it aside. Then he reached far down into the bilge, his arm fully extended, and after a few moments of tugging, he pulled out a short section of galvanized steel pipe, dripping with oily seawater. The sailor had struggled to lift it up one-handed; it was obviously extremely heavy for its size.

Bullard felt a momentary chill when he saw the foot-long pipe, with an end-cap on each side. It looked like almost every pipe bomb he'd ever seen—and he'd seen a lot. Sumner wiped it dry with paper towels from the galley, and then unscrewed one steel end-cap and placed it on the dinette table. He tipped the open pipe at an angle, and four white plastic tubes slid out onto the table. Inside of each translucent cylinder was a short stack of what appeared to be one-ounce gold coins.

"I thought so," said Bullard, grinning, a friendly uncle once again. "How many are in there?"

"Eighty."

"What kind?"

"American Eagles," the despondent sailor admitted.

"Call me patriotic, but that's my favorite brand!" exclaimed Bullard. "Now, I'm going to tell you how we can resolve your problem. How we can avoid going back to the Customs dock, and tearing your boat to pieces. I'm a reasonable man, Harvey, very reasonable. And I really do admire you, that's the truth. I'm not the kind of man who would leave you broke, right at the start of your voyage across the Pacific. Tell you what. Let's go fifty-fifty, half-and-half. Forty for you, and forty for Uncle Sam—and then you'll be on your way in five minutes. Or, we can go back to the Customs dock, and you'll spend ten years in prison, minimum. You and Roxanne both. We find any illegal guns or ammunition, and that's another ten. You'll be old by the time you get out Harvey, and you can't get those years back, trust me on that. So, do we have a deal?"

Harvey Sumner finally found the nerve to stare straight back at Bob Bullard. "I don't have any ch-choice. Take them." He reluctantly pushed two of the plastic tubes across the table.

Bullard unzipped a horizontal compartment on the bottom of his black vest, dropped the two rolls of gold coins inside, and zipped it shut again. Then he stood up from the dinette table. "You made a wise decision, Harvey, you'll never be sorry. I hope you have good luck on your voyage, I really do. Fair winds, and all that. Now stay down below for five minutes, and then go give Roxanne a big hug. Tell her how you kept both of you out of prison, and saved your boat. She'll understand—there was nothing else you could do."

He knew that he could have taken the entire stash of eighty gold coins, but half was safer. He wanted Harvey Sumner to keep sailing west today, far away, out of range. If he took all of his gold and left the man dead broke, Sumner might decide to cancel the voyage, and turn around. Then, bitter and out for revenge, he might find the ear of some rabble-rousing reporter, who might raise a stink. No, half was better. Half meant that Sumner was not coming back.

Besides, the sailor probably had another pipe with another load of gold coins hidden somewhere else on the boat. He would do all right.

Bullard ascended the ladder and stood in the cockpit, blinking in the bright sunlight while slipping his shades back on. The high cliffs of Point Loma were receding astern, as the two boats had continued heading offshore while he was down below. Roxanne Sumner was still standing behind the wheel, staring straight ahead, looking right through him. The two Customs agents who had boarded with Bullard were standing near the stern, holding onto the twin backstay wires. Their faces were unreadable beneath their DHS ball caps, and behind their reflective sunglasses.

The Fountain was keeping pace with the Mystic Lady a dozen yards off the sailboat's port side, and Bullard waved it over. When it was pressed alongside the sailboat's hull, he lightly hopped down and across, followed by the other two Customs agents. The leader of the Customs detail slid across to the center bolster, giving him the controls again. Bullard said, "He was clean as a whistle. Fine man, a real gentleman. Everything was in order, we had a nice conversation." He winked over at Wendy, and she smiled back.

Then he turned the wheel to the left and shoved the throttles ahead. The Fountain's four black Mercury engines screamed and the boat shot up onto a plane, leaving the sailboat far behind them as swiftly as if it was at anchor.

Bullard did the rough math in his head. Forty ounces of gold, at roughly $7,000 an ounce, was what? $280,000 New Dollars? Not that he would ever change the gold for paper blue bucks—God forbid! These forty ounces would go aboard the El Dorado to join the rest of his gold stash. And sure, they represented a good day's work. They felt solid and heavy on the left side of his utility vest. But really, the forty ounces were just a drop in the bucket compared to what he already had, or even to what he collected as part of his other routine operations. The Indian casinos alone paid 25 ounces a week for protection. Only keeping the Border Patrol away from carefully selected portions of the Mexican border paid more than that.

26

Ranya spent an hour studying the life of Brian Garabanda, as seen through the digital camera lens of Alexandro Garabanda. There was Brian taking his first steps, Brian coming down a sliding board, Brian riding a Big Wheel, Brian blowing out four candles—and almost always grinning at the camera. Brad would have been rightfully proud of how adorable his son was. Brian had his father's blue eyes, and unruly light brown hair. His dimples and the little freckles on his nose were Brian's alone.

After looking at hundreds of pictures, Ranya found that she could not hate the man tied to the chair, the man who made her son's face shine with happiness in photograph after photograph.

Garabanda certainly didn't look like an evil man, slumped back and snoring softly in his old easy chair. He had wavy brown hair, which needed to be combed. He had a Hispanic surname, but he didn't look Mexican. His ancestors could have been from any number of European nations. Asleep and with his face in repose, she guessed by the tiny lines around the corners of his eyes and the creases of his mouth that he was in his mid-forties or maybe a bit older. His eyes were now closed, but she remembered from their previous stare-downs that they were cinnamon brown, and that they had fire in them when he had shown a spark of anger.

The laptop computer had no electrical cord or AC adapter, and after several warnings, it shut itself off due to a low battery. In the kitchen, she found part of a loaf of wheat bread and half-filled jars of peanut butter and jelly. She made sandwiches and washed them down with tap water, while flipping through Alexandro Garabanda's stack of mail, which consisted mostly of bills and junk mail advertisements. Once she finished her lunch, she took a kitchen chair into the living room, and turned the television back on. After spending five years in detention, Ranya watched even the commercials with interest. They were in both English and Spanish, depending on the station, and whether they were national or local in origin.

The new cars seemed very small, and touted their high gas mileage above all other factors. The local ads were tilted toward security-related businesses: locks, alarms, burglar bars, guard dogs and chain link fences. Then a new commercial came on, with a picturesque seacoast in the background. A kindly looking man stood in front, his hands in the pockets of his sky-blue windbreaker. She guessed he was selling insurance or a medical plan. He was wearing a blue cap with DHS written across the front.

The friendly pitchman said, "Hi, I'm Bob Bullard, your regional director for the Department of Homeland Security." The name jolted her, but it took a few seconds for her to place it. "As we all know, this has been a year of difficult problems and unique challenges. But with challenges, also come opportunities. Once again, the Southwest Region has led the nation in security awareness and preparedness. We should all be proud of that record, but we can always do better. I don't need to remind you that improving homeland security means improving the economy, and increasing everyone's prosperity and well-being."

A man and a woman on bicycles pedaled by, just behind him. There was an ocean pier visible in the background as he continued with his earnest and folksy message. "So let's all pitch in, and help your Department of Homeland Security to help you! Let's do everything we can to win the war on terror and economic sabotage. Report suspicious behavior, and please give your full cooperation to law enforcement at safety checkpoints. And don't forget—you can earn cash rewards for reporting illegal firearms, or illegal stockpiles of hoarded gold. Call 855-GUN-STOP, or 855-USA-GOLD, and you can help to support your family, while you help to defend your homeland."

The camera focused on Bullard's smiling face, with the two phone numbers superimposed on the screen across his chest.

Alex Garabanda was handcuffed to a bicycle, pushing it along while trailed by a screaming mob. If he could just spread his hands far enough apart, he might be able to grasp the handlebars and ride away from them to safety. The handcuffs were passed under the bike's frame, and he could not get a grip on both handlebars at the same time no matter how he tried. It occurred to him that this was a puzzle, and if he could figure out the solution, he might free his arms and escape.

Then someone hoisted a white bucket above him and without warning he was drenched in a foul liquid, the stink of gasoline pungent in his nose. While he watched, a beautiful woman wearing a brown beret was trying to strike match after match, but the flames kept flaring, sputtering and going out. In desperation, he tried to balance on the saddle with both hands together clasping the front fork, but the bicycle fell over on its side while the crowd around him jeered. From the ground, he looked up at the blue sky and saw Fidel Castro, wearing a green utility uniform and cap, lighting a long cigar with a silver Zippo. Then the old Cuban dictator snapped his lighter shut, and casually offered it to the woman wearing the beret. She smiled warmly at Fidel, and promptly dropped her useless book of paper matches to accept his gift.

Lying on the ground in mortal terror, still shackled to the fallen bicycle, Alex Garabanda knew that the silver Zippo lighter would not fail.

The sound of the television brought him back, awareness flowing into his mind like the spreading dawn as his eyes flickered open. He groaned aloud when he felt the cords tying his wrists to the wooden armrests. The female home invader was still here. She was not part of a bad dream. The woman—and these new bindings—were very real. She was sitting a few feet away to his right side, on one of the kitchen chairs that Karin had left behind, watching a commercial on television.

She noticed he had awakened and immediately asked, "Who's that jackass?" while pointing at the TV. The female home invader had taken her baseball cap off. She was an attractive woman with very short brunette hair, something like a pageboy or pixie cut. Judging by her trim figure and muscular shoulders and arms, she was evidently very fit. She could have easily been a new Special Agent, fresh from Quantico. He guessed her age to be mid-twenties, so she must have been about twenty years old when she had delivered Brian…if she was telling the truth.

The woman repeated her question, insistently. "Did you catch that commercial? Who was that guy who was just on?"

"Who?" He was not following her, lost in his own thoughts, and still reacting sluggishly under the residual effects of the vodka.

"The guy who was just on the TV! Who was he?"

For some reason, she was quite agitated about the homeland security public service announcement that she had just seen on television. He had seen it a few times, and had considered it a joke until now. His mouth was dry, his head hurt, and it was an effort to speak. "The guy standing by the ocean? He's my boss, way up the chain of command. Robert K. Bullard. He's the director of homeland security for the Southwest. I think he came up from the ATF. That's all I know about him."

This was not quite true. Alex Garabanda knew a bit more about Bullard's rocket-like rise to the top echelons of Homeland Security, and his peculiar knack for leveraging positive recognition out of disaster. He was a poster boy for the Peter Principle, repeatedly failing his way upward to ever-greater success. Bullard had won awards for valor both after the disaster at Waco, and later after the ATF's Special Training Unit fiasco back east. In each case, he had managed to convert his growing fame within the federal law enforcement community into significant promotions.

She was still going on about the public service announcement.

"Was that California? Where they filmed that commercial?"

"Huh? What? California? Looked like it. Yeah, I guess so."

"Where in California?"

"Where? I don't know where."

"Is that what San Diego looks like?"

"I don't know. I guess so. I've been to San Diego, but it was a few years ago. I didn't see that part, if that's where it was."

"It looked beautiful, in the ad."

"Yeah, well, that's what everybody says. Listen…what's your name? I'm sorry, if you told me before, I…"

"Ranya Bardiwell."

"Well Ranya Bardiwell, honest to God, I've got to use the bathroom. Would you mind untying me? I'm not going to run away. You didn't have to tie me up."

She looked doubtful, but at least she was not waving her .45 around any more. She asked, "You're not going to do anything crazy?"

"I swear, I've just got to use the bathroom. No, I'm not going to do anything crazy."

"How do I know that? Why should I trust you?"

"Listen, Ranya, at some point you've got to. You can't keep me tied up, and you can't keep a gun on me all the way out to San Diego. That's just not going to work. You have to let me go. You have to trust me."

"You say that now, but how do I know you won't jump me the second my back is turned?"

He could understand her worry, it was completely reasonable, given the circumstances. "I don't know how to answer that. I guess it's just that I care about Brian too. You should be able to understand that."

"Were you really about to shoot yourself, when I came in?"

"I…I don't know. I was watching my video, and drinking, drinking a lot. I hadn't planned it ahead of time or anything." Those minutes spent with the muzzle of his Sig pressed against his heart had been the absolute nadir of his life. They were the rock bottom of his well of sorrow. And at the end of those final moments…in walks this woman, saying that she's Brian's real mother. This was not mere happenstance. Not a coincidence. Even in his residually boozy state, he recognized that Higher Powers were somehow at work. They had to be—there could be no other explanation for her astonishing appearance. However, in his present muddled condition, he could not even begin to explain himself, his feelings, or his near self-destruction.

She wasn't satisfied, she wouldn't let go of the suicide question. "But you're okay now, you're not even thinking about it? For sure?"

"For sure." This was true. In fact, Alex Garabanda felt that he *had* died, in a way. The barrel tip pressed against his sternum had been a fulcrum, around which his entire life had pivoted: before, and after. Wasting the gift of this fresh new life was now the last thing on his mind.

She stood up from the kitchen chair and pulled a vicious-looking folding knife out of her right front jeans pocket. She flicked it open one-handed with a steely snap, and approached him, looking him in the face all the while. Her eyes were a uniquely luminescent shade, between hazel and green. The silver blade was leveled a yard from his throat, but he felt perfectly calm. His new life was literally in the hands of his deliverer. He recognized this as the exact moment of surrender to trust, for both of them.

She brought the knife down and skimmed the blade along the wooden armrest, under his up-stretched right palm, slicing through the restraints. Then she stepped back and said, "You do the rest." Her pistol—a .45 caliber model 1911 he could now plainly see—was jammed into her jeans under a wide leather belt. The hammer was back, cocked and locked, in "condition one." It was evident that she knew her way around guns. His own Sig-Sauer was nowhere in sight.

Alex tugged at the knotted cord tying down his left hand, and then leaned forward and loosened the bindings around his ankles. He recognized his backyard clothesline but felt it unworthy of comment.

She said, "I must be an idiot to just let you go like this. If you're lying, if you turn around and try to pull something, I swear I'll kill you."

He raised himself unsteadily, pushing off from both armrests. She backed away from him, keeping a safe distance, while he lurched across the living room and down the hall to the bathroom, pushing against the walls for balance. He noticed his framed family pictures were gone. He said aloud, "Listen, what you saw today when you walked in…that wasn't really me. That's not how I am. I'm not a quitter, no matter what you think. It's just…the things that have happened, the pressure…"

"Pressure? Oh, please, don't you dare talk to me about pressure!"

He turned around in the hallway to face her, holding onto the bathroom door frame. "Okay, fair enough. But I'm not a quitter. And I don't believe it's just an accident, you showing up when you did. Think about it! How can that just be an accident? Think about everything that happened to bring you here, to bring me here—how can that just be a coincidence? So what I want to say, to tell you, is…well…I'll help you. I'll help you to get Brian away from them. I'll go all the way, no matter what it takes."

He stepped into the bathroom and closed the door behind him.

She called after him, "Okay, all right. But don't get any ideas! Just remember, he's *my* son, not yours!"

Ranya found an open jar of instant iced tea in a kitchen cabinet, and stirred up a pitcher with water from the sink and ice cubes from plastic trays left in the freezer. The house was more than half-empty, but some essentials had been left behind, including some kitchenware. She wondered if this was due to a sense of fairness on his ex-wife's part, or because she had been unable to move it all. She concluded that Karin just didn't want the stuff, that it wasn't worth packing.

When Garabanda returned a few minutes later, he brought a child's portable radio with him. He switched it to a rock station and set it on the counter by the stove. “It was Brian’s,” he explained. “I gave it to him for Christmas. I don’t think he listened to it.” Then he shot Ranya a conspiratorial wink and pointed to his ear, and she nodded her understanding. If anyone was listening to them, there was no reason to make their job easy. Next he walked back into the living room and switched the TV on to a news channel, doubling the crosscurrents of background noise.

“I made iced tea. It’s in the fridge if you want some.”

“Thanks.” He poured himself a glass and sat down at the kitchen table across from her. They both sipped their drinks while coolly regarding one another.

She asked him, “So if you’re coming with me to California, what about your job? Can you just take off? Won’t you be AWOL? Can you take emergency leave or something?”

“I don’t need to,” he answered. “I already have next week off. I’m supposed to be attending a diversity workshop in Santa Fe. The PC Nazis want me to get over my ‘homophobia.’ I’m supposed to fix my attitude and get my head right…but I think it’s probably too late for that.” He smiled bemusedly. “You remember that circus freak with the tattoos?”

“The IRS agent. Karin’s…ah…”

“Karin’s ‘special friend,’ Gretchen Bosch. Here’s what happened: we were at the Memorial Day picnic, the annual federal law enforcement picnic. I’d had a couple of beers, and I wanted to talk to Karin. She came to the picnic with Gretchen, but I approached her when she was alone. Gretchen was off playing softball with the coed IRS team, so I thought I could speak to Karin privately. I’d been out of the house a couple of months by then.” He sipped his iced tea, and continued.

“I guess Gretchen didn’t appreciate my sneaking around her girlfriend. I mean, I’m only the ex-husband, right? So she nailed me with an aluminum bat. Gave it to me in the back, from behind—I never saw it coming. More of a hard jab than a full swing, or so I’m told. Otherwise… Well, anyway, after I got up, I guess I kind of forgot I was dealing with a ‘lady,’ and I ended up taking her down and choking her out…which wasn’t easy, let me tell you. Gretchen’s a steroid queen.” He shook his head at the memory. “It was an ugly scene, two federal officers brawling at the annual picnic. Not exactly what you’d call ‘career enhancing.’ I ended up losing weekend custody of Brian for assaulting a federal agent.”

“But she hit you first!”

“Yeah, that’s what you might think. But once the dust settles, it always comes back to ‘angry white man beats defenseless woman.’ Throw in the ‘homophobic hate crime’ angle and you’re doubly screwed. That fight at the picnic, and then losing weekend custody…well that was the low point of my entire life. At least until today, when Karin told me she was taking off for San Diego with Brian. I never thought there’d be any good coming out of that picnic fight, but I suppose every dark cloud hides a little silver, right? And here it is: I already have next week off for diversity training, so I won't be missed at the Field Office."

"But what about after that? What if it takes longer than a week?"

"Well, what if it does?" he said, brightening. "Ranya, I don't care anymore. Don't you see? After where I was a couple of hours ago, after that—the FBI just doesn't seem very important. I can do anything now! If finding Brian takes longer than a week, I don't care. I'll take my chances."

"But what about your job, your paycheck? Don't you have a pension coming?"

"Ah, what the hell… I'll have to send most of it to the bank anyway, just so I can stay in this empty house. And by the time I can retire, they'll probably switch the money again. They'll probably pay us with ration coupons or raffle tickets or something, so who cares?"

"Really?"

"Yes, really." Alex Garabanda knew that he wouldn't be the first career Special Agent to bolt from the FBI and give up his pension, not by a long shot. Luis Carvahal had been right: he had been shoveling coal in the Titanic's engine room. And for what?

"Okay, fine. So tell me how we're going to get to San Diego."

"How? Well, the best way is to fly there."

"Flying? Are you crazy? I can't walk into an airport—I'd be spotted in a minute! I'm a fugitive from everybody—the feds, the Milicia, the Falcons, everybody!"

"Not that kind of flying, not the commercial jets. I'm talking about small planes, like when you flew into New Mexico. Small planes are the best way to go. 'General aviation.' I know people—I can swing it."

"What, are you a pilot?"

"Me? No. Not officially, I'm not licensed or anything. I've spent a lot of hours up in light planes, but I'm not a pilot. It's been a part of my job for years. I've got plenty of stick time, unofficially—but it doesn't matter. I'm not going to fly. I'll get somebody else to do that. It won't be cheap though, and aviation gas…well, if you think gasoline is scarce, just try to find aviation gas!"

"But it can be done?"

"Sure, it can be done, but money's going to be a problem. I can only take $4,000 cash a month out of the bank. $4,000 more if I 'invest' another $4,000 in government bonds. That's the law. Even $8,000 won't be enough to get a plane and a pilot, not even if I call in some favors, and get a friend to help us out. Otherwise, we'll have to drive through, and just take our chances at the checkpoints. At least I can buy gas on the military bases. If you're just a civilian going by yourself, then it's a hell of a gamble to try to drive through. It's easy to get stranded in the desert if you can't find gas, and then what? A woman alone…"

"What would it cost for somebody to fly us straight to San Diego?"

"Straight through? It'd cost a lot, that's for sure—but it's still the best way. No checkpoints, no roadblocks."

"How much?"

"How much? Well…I'm just guessing…probably a least a hundred thousand. Maybe a lot more."

"Blue bucks?"

"Yeah, blue bucks. 'New Dollars.' That's all there is now. For the plane, the fuel, the pilot…everything. That is, if I can even find somebody that'll do it for blue bucks. You can't just walk into a bank with a stack of cash anymore, if you can't prove where you got it. You know the deal, the war on drugs, the war on terror…the banks have all kinds of reporting requirements. And on the other side of the coin, nobody wants to be left with a pile of Monopoly money, if they pull another switcheroo. That's what happened when they went from greenbacks to blue bucks. People who had lots of cash lying around couldn't convert it. Mafia, dope dealers, crooks—they lost out big time. Honest people too, people who just didn't trust the banks, and kept their dough under the mattress. They wound up with green Monopoly money. Wiped out."

"So how can anybody come up with a hundred thousand blue bucks, if you can only take out $8,000 a month?"

"Well, you've just put your finger on the problem: it's damn hard to operate outside of the system. And now Uncle Sam wants everybody to use digital money. You know, electronic transfers, credit cards…"

"So that Big Brother can see what you're doing."

"You've got it. But I have a friend who used to fly for the Border Patrol. He might take us as a favor, at least part way…" Alex poured himself another glass of iced tea from the pitcher, and took a long drink. "And he needs the money."

Ranya asked, "What about gold. Would gold work any better?"

"Gold? You mean, like gold coins?"

"Right. Krugerrands, Maple Leafs—that kind of gold."

His eyes lit up. "Oh, hell yeah! You can buy a whole damn airplane with enough Krugerrands. You've got some?"

She hesitated, scanning his face. "Well…yes. As a matter of fact I do. You fell asleep before I got to that part of my story. I took the Comandante's gold when I split from his house last night. I stole his stolen gold from him, when I escaped from his compound. He had it in his safe."

"You're a safecracker too?"

"No…he sort of left it open," she lied.

"He left his safe open?"

"It's kind of a long story."

"I'll bet. So how much gold did you take?"

"I haven't counted it yet. A lot." She paused again, considering what to tell him, and decided to lowball her answer. "Maybe fifteen pounds."

"Fifteen pounds of gold? Seriously?"

"Right."

"Where is it? Here in the house?"

"No..." She wondered if she was being stupid, admitting this to him. But if getting to California meant paying her way, it was time to pony up.

"Where is it then?"

"Take it easy, it's safe."

"How can you be sure it's safe, if you left it outside somewhere?"

"I know it's all right, because it's in my car. Well, it's not exactly 'my' car. But don't worry—the guy I stole it from won't be looking for it. He's dead."

"What?" he choked.

"Believe me, he had it coming—but I didn't kill him. Basilio Ramos did."

Alex Garabanda was trying to maintain a neutral appearance as these revelations came one after another, but she could read his suppressed astonishment. His expressions amused her, as he tried to retain the tough-guy FBI agent façade. She told him, "The dead guy I stole the car from was just a dirtbag communist professor at the university. Trust me—the world is a better place without him. Hey, that reminds me, I took pictures of the whole thing."

"You took *pictures*? Of a *murder*?" He shot her a look of incredulity that clearly indicated that he doubted her sanity.

Well, she thought, so what of it? What good had sanity ever done for her? Sanity, she was beginning to think, was highly overrated. She replied, "Not just a murder—it was *much* better than that. It was a *sex* murder. But don't get the wrong idea—I didn't participate. I just took the pictures. Well, actually, maybe I did help a little bit...hey, don't look at me like that! Listen, I took the pictures for a very good reason: blackmail. I don't want Basilio Ramos coming after me. Say, that reminds me: I need to make copies. Can I burn a few discs on your computer? And by the way, your battery's dead—have you got a charging cable somewhere? What? What's the matter? Blackmail pictures won't work unless you have lots of copies, right?"

This young woman is clearly a lunatic, Alex Garabanda thought. But to be fair, just who was it who had been aiming a pistol at his heart a couple of hours ago, getting ready to blast himself into the Great Beyond? So who am I to judge anyone's sanity? He knew that Ranya's unexpected arrival was the reason he was still among the living. He was still alive, wasn't he? So many aspects of this conversation were beyond the bounds of the reality he thought he understood. Of course, after the past year, almost any new reality would have to be an improvement. One thing he knew: the chains binding him to his previous life were broken, *and he was free*. Just as free as he chose to be. So she wanted to use his laptop computer to make copies of blackmail pictures, pictures of the leader of the Falcon Battalion murdering a communist professor? Well, why not? "Sure, go ahead and make copies. I've got a charging cable in my trunk somewhere."

"My camera's still in my car. I need to go get it."

"Where's your car?"

"Down the street, on the other side. Behind that dumpster."

"Oh Jesus, you left your car parked right out on the street? It might have been stolen already. You have to be careful—you can't just leave cars parked outside. Not anymore. You'd better get it off the street before it's gone, along with your gold." He thought for a moment about the best way to hide her car, and get her in and out of his house unobserved. "Okay, here's what you do: the house behind this one is empty. I'll go over the back wall and open the garage door. Pull the car in there."

The front of the classroom was draped with poster-sized topographical maps and overhead imagery, as well as equipment lists and personnel rosters. Fifteen Falcon Battalion officers and noncommissioned officers occupied the front two rows of chairs, notebooks open on their laps.

Even though it was Sunday, the leaders were wearing their usual camouflage uniforms for the staff meeting. Ramos had drawn a 9mm pistol from the unit armory at the Academy, claiming that he wanted a firearm that held more that the eight rounds of his .45. The Glock was in another black nylon military holster, attached to a new green web belt. None of his men knew that his .45 had been stolen, but the new pistol hanging from his belt was a constant reminder of his betrayal by Ranya Bardiwell. She had taken his lovely custom-made .45, and now he was reduced to carrying a standard-grade plastic and steel Glock.

The object of their attention this afternoon was Torcido County, in the far north of Nuevo Mexico. More specifically, the top half of the county, which constituted Wayne Parker's Vedado Ranch. This enormous property was to be the site of the upcoming "conference of great importance," about which Basilio Ramos and his troops theoretically knew nothing. For a change, they were not planning how to seize a property from its gringo occupiers. This time their mission was to secure the ranch against any conceivable attack, while its primary buildings were the meeting place for a group of "very important persons." Ramos believed that sooner or later, the million acre Vedado Ranch would be confiscated under the Land Reform laws, but for now Wayne Parker was an ally of Gobernador Magón, and useful to the revolution. For the time being, his false property rights would be respected and even protected.

Comandante Ramos sat front and center among his officers and sergeants, trying to feign some level of interest as Teniente Velasquez droned on about tomorrow's battalion movement up to Torcido County, and the berthing arrangements for the men. The Falcons were expropriating a group of off-season ski lodges for their temporary quarters. They would be fed by the resort's kitchen staff, and so on. These were routine arrangements for battalion deployments, and Ramos had a difficult time keeping his mind on the details as they were presented. He felt slightly self-conscious because his mind was still drifting and given to unexpected detours into surreal imaginings. He avoided talking as much as possible, afraid that his tongue might betray his altered mental state.

He tried to focus on the proceedings. The Falcon Battalion was moving early Monday morning, tomorrow. The conference was scheduled to take place on Wednesday, at the mansion and conference center of the Vedado Ranch. After the officers finalized the plan, the rest of the troops would be briefed at three PM today, giving them ample time to prepare their uniforms, gear, weapons and vehicles for the unit movement.

The million-acre ranch occupied most of the top half of Torcido County, right against the Colorado border. A key attribute of the ranch was its two-kilometer jet-capable runway, which would allow the guests to arrive and depart without fuss or formality, and of course, with no attention from the media. The identities of the guests and the purpose of the meeting were secret, and supposedly outside of his "need to know."

Regardless of that, he had some ideas, some of which he had gleaned just last night during the exchange between Gobernador Magón and Wayne Parker. Certainly, one topic on the table would be a new federal status for Nuevo Mexico, perhaps as an autonomous region with less direct control by Washington. In reality, this would merely be formalizing the evolving facts on the ground. Washington was eventually going to cede control of Nuevo Mexico, because it had no effective means of control.

Because of the high importance of the Vedado conference and its attendees, the Falcon Battalion was going to serve as the primary Quick Reaction Force. This was only to be expected, considering that they were, by any objective standard, the most elite unit of the Milicia de Nuevo Mexico. Four state guard Blackhawk helicopters were being provided for the Falcons, supporting them in their capacity as the mobile QRF. This heavy commitment of fuel-guzzling military helicopters was the best proof of the tremendous significance of the conference.

The areas around the mansion, the conference center and the jet runway were shown in overhead photographs, blown up in tremendous detail and marked with colored tape. The four Blackhawks would be staged on a runway apron, their aircrews and his best troops equipped and waiting only a few meters away, ready to lift into the sky on a moment's notice. Besides the helicopters, the Falcons would also have their own trucks and SUVs to transport them, if they were needed closer to the meeting facilities around the mansion and conference center. The interior security was going to be provided by a private contract firm, brought in to supplement Wayne Parker's usual bodyguard force.

The outer security perimeter around the ranch would be manned by Comandante Guzman's newly formed and hastily trained 5th Battalion. These three hundred troops were only marginally better than typical slovenly Milicianos, having gone through just one extra month of "advanced" infantry training under the tutelage of Comandante Guzman, "El Condor." These troops would be transported solely on trucks and buses, positioned to control key road intersections on and around the sprawling Vedado Ranch. In reality, the Peruvian's 5th Battalion troops would be able to serve only as an early warning trip-wire force. In the extremely unlikely event that a serious attack was mounted against the conference, Ramos knew that his Falcons would do the real fighting.

Teniente Velasquez completed the transportation and logistics portion of the staff briefing. There were a smattering of questions and suggestions, and then he returned to his seat. Next, Teniente Almeria would brief the communications plan. The staff meeting was painfully dull. Ramos had hoped that it would divert his thoughts from the disgusting events of his past night and morning, but it could not. Unwanted hyper-vivid memory flashes continually burst into his mind, and the bald gringo professor was, to say the least, not a sexual partner he wanted to remember!

Ramos compulsively wrung his hands together, still feeling the sticky blood of the dead gringo staining them. In his bathtub, he had hacked and sawn the dead man's corpse into manageable parts, and then placed each grotesque piece into a heavy-duty black plastic garbage bag. He put the bags inside of luggage, and in three trips carried them down to his Jeep, for a solo ride back to the same gravel pit where his men had disposed of Rick Haywood a day earlier. Finally, Professor Johnson's plastic-wrapped body parts were dumped into an empty steel drum, doused with gasoline, and burned. The stink was excruciating, and he could still smell it on his skin hours after his last shower.

The majestic pine-covered mountains of the Vedado Ranch would provide a welcome relief. Hopefully, he would be able to get his mind off the dead gringo professor and Ranya Bardiwell, and try to forget what that Arab whore-bitch from hell had done to him!

While Teniente Almeria went over radio frequencies and call signs, Basilio Ramos daydreamed about the most excruciatingly painful tortures he could imagine for Ranya Bardiwell. He imagined her naked and screaming on a steel mortuary table, with wire binding her wrists and ankles to its four corners. Around the room, within her sight, he would assemble every imaginable tool of torture: the razor sharp, the red hot, and the high voltage. But while he tried to concentrate on her look of sheer animal terror, each pleasant fantasy image he conjured was soon replaced in his mind by one of the filthy and repulsive images she had left for him to see on his computer. He could not erase those disgusting scenes of his coupling with the gringo professor from his memory!

Someday he would figure out a way to destroy her nauseating photographs, or at least to keep them from dissemination. But try as he might, he couldn't think of a plausible way to be certain that all of the digital photographs were permanently wiped out and deleted. They could already have been copied onto a dozen discs, or stored on a hundred websites.

Ramos stared straight ahead at Teniente Almeria, without hearing a word he was saying. He ground his teeth, and dug his fingernails into the palms of his clenched fists, which were pressed hard against his knees. He was torn between his overwhelming desire for painful revenge against Ranya Bardiwell, and his even greater fear of her explicit homosexual blackmail pictures ever being seen by his troops.

Pictures that would also raise the sticky question: *where was Professor Johnson?* Why had the well-known socialist professor suddenly disappeared from the face of the earth, *and who had he been with last?*

27

There was a seven-foot cinderblock wall between the Garabanda's back yard and the yard of the empty house behind his. The walls between the houses were too high for any other neighbors to observe the activity between these two properties. After hiding her car in the vacant garage, Ranya stood on a discarded white plastic chair to peer over the top. Alex Garabanda was waiting on the other side, and she quickly lifted up her heavy backpack and kit bag and passed them to him. Then she carefully handed over the long Dragunov rifle, wrapped loosely in the blanket from the professor's car.

Her .45 was still tucked in front, so she pulled it out and shoved it into her jeans in the small of her back for scaling the wall. She put her hands on top, and smoothly pushed herself up onto her belly, swung up a leg, and slid over. Alex Garabanda carried both bags back into his house. She followed him inside with the rifle and closed the door behind her. The two heavy bags were left on the floor by the back door.

At every transition point, she was expecting betrayal: when pulling into the empty garage, climbing over the wall, and coming back into his house. The FBI man had been given ample opportunity during her absence to drop a dime, cover his ass, and have her picked up. The constant gnawing fear diminished just a bit each time she walked through a door, and was not met by an arrest team.

She unwrapped the rifle from the blanket and laid it across the kitchen table.

"Nice," he commented, picking it up. "Is that a real Dragunov, or a knockoff?" He shouldered the rifle and pressed his eye against the rubber cup at the back of the scope. She sat at the table while he stood and scanned through his kitchen window toward the trees outside. Her makeshift rifle sling, made from two of Basilio's neckties, hung slack beneath the weapon.

"It's Russian, it's the real thing." She said. "Scope's authentic too. Pretty cool rangefinder setup."

"Yeah, it is." He placed the butt of the rifle on the table, holding the barrel up, and ran a hand down the two silk neckties, examining them. One was solid blue, the other a multi-colored paisley. "What's the story on the, uh, 'custom sling'?" he asked. The two ties were knotted together in the middle, and tied to the bottom of the stock and to the gas tube just above the barrel, in front of the fore stock.

"The Dragunov was one of the Comandante's newest souvenirs. Last night I climbed off a second story balcony at his house, and I had to lower everything down first. I made a rope from neckties, it was the only 'rope' I could find. Then I had to carry both bags and the rifle, and it needed a sling, so…"

"Well, it's certainly original," he laughed.

"I like it. Classy, don't you think? They're real silk."

"It looks terrific, but how's it shoot?"

"Good enough. It shot up a truckload of Falcons last Wednesday."

"I heard about that! You were there?" He laid the long semi-auto sniper rifle back down on the table and sat opposite her, casually eyeing it while they continued their conversation.

She understood his interest: there was no other rifle quite like the Dragunov, with its skeletal laminated wood stock, long sleek barrel, and menacing black scope. Not the most accurate rifle in its class, with good ammunition it could still shoot inside of an inch and a half circle at 100 yards. This meant that it could easily hit a man at well beyond 600 yards: certainly nothing to sneeze at.

"We were coming back from the range, in a convoy. The Falcons had a scout truck out in front, and it was ambushed by one guy with this rifle. Ten quick shots, and then he took off on a motorcycle. The Falcons tracked him down. They killed him at his house. Ramos kept his rifle as a souvenir, and now it's mine. I took it, just like I took his .45 and his gold. I wish he'd had something a little shorter in his safe, but this was the only rifle. Anyway, I know it works! I saw what it did to a pickup truck full of Falcons. Straight through the windshield, from long range. It wasn't pretty."

"The bullet it fires, it's about like a .308, right?" he asked her.

"Hmm…maybe a shade more powerful than that. More like a thirty-ought-six, depending on the load. But the magazines only hold ten rounds. Drop the mag, check it out. The cartridges have a funky rim—you'll never mistake them for .308."

"How do you know so much about guns?" He fumbled with the magazine release until the black steel box came free.

"My father was a gunsmith, back in Virginia."

"Really? Is he still there?"

"He's dead."

"Oh—I'm sorry."

"So am I." She wanted to say, *he was killed by another federal agent, like you*, but she didn't. There was nothing to gain by opening up that painful subject with this FBI agent. She changed the subject to break the uncomfortable silence. "Listen, when can you get in touch with your pilot? How soon can we fly to California?"

"I already did, while you were moving your car."

"You called him from here? Was that smart?" She thought: have I hooked up with a moron, somebody who's going to bring her enemies down on their heads with his carelessness?

He countered, "Come on, I'm not stupid, I know how to do this sort of thing."

"You're sure nobody could hear your call?" She felt like mentioning what had happened to his informant after his cover was blown, but she held her tongue. What good would it do? She didn't need him becoming depressed and possibly even suicidal again.

"I just set up a meeting for tonight, that's all. I invited him over. He's a friend, so there's nothing strange about it. I used a good cover story, about Karin and Brian leaving, and my moving back into the house. I'll ask him about flying us once he's here. But Ranya, there's one other thing..."

"What 'one other thing'?"

"We're not going straight to California. I have something I need to do first."

"What are you talking about? For how long? I don't want to wait around, and you only have one week before you'll be missed, right? We need to get going on this thing, right away. I'm done with Albuquerque—I've got too many targets pinned to my shirt already."

"I'm sorry, but I can't just go. I can't leave New Mexico, not yet."

"Why not?" she asked impatiently. "What can be more important than getting your son?"

"Not more important. There's just something I have to do first."

"Like what? How much time are you talking about?"

"A few days."

"A few days? No way—forget it. As soon as we can, I want to be on the way to San Diego."

He replied with his own challenge. "You think airplanes are just sitting around, waiting to go on unauthorized flights? You think it's that easy?"

She tried to read his face, wondering if he was scamming her, or if she was being set up. Would 'his friend the pilot' turn out to be the point man of an FBI arrest team, or the U.S. Marshals? The fear of betrayal never left her mind. If Garabanda was playing her for a fool, he was going to die—no ifs, ands, or buts. If he was setting her up for arrest, she was going to shoot him right in his ruggedly handsome face, first thing. "I'm listening," she finally said, in a noncommittal way. She realized that she had no choice but to hear him out.

"Good. You remember my friend, who was…burned yesterday?"

His mention of that horrific event was completely unexpected. "I'll never forget it. Never."

"Well…that's why I have to stay for a few days. I have to do something for him. I can't leave New Mexico before I do it. Otherwise his life, his death…it would have been wasted. He would have died for nothing. All that suffering, all that pain…and for nothing."

"What are you talking about?"

Garabanda had turned morose again. He had removed the top two cartridges from the Dragunov's magazine and was rolling them in his fingers like worry beads. His mood seemed to be swinging back toward the state of melancholy she had discovered him in just a few hours ago.

"Luis Carvahal was my informant. I was running him, but without the FBI's blessing or knowledge. It was kind of on my own."

"What's the point of doing it then? I don't understand how…"

"Politics, it was all politics. Ranya, I can get into that later, we'll have plenty of time. The point is, he was ghostwriting Agustín Deleon's memoirs. Those two went way back together, more than thirty years. Deleon trusted him completely, and he told Luis everything about what was really going on in New Mexican politics, everything he knew. For his memoirs. So last week, Luis found out about a meeting that's going to happen on Wednesday, this Wednesday. Up north on a private ranch. Wayne Parker's ranch."

"Wayne Parker? Holy crap, you know what? He was at Ramos's house last night! He was a jerk, he was a loudmouthed drunk. What an obnoxious creep."

"Parker was at Ramos's house? You actually saw him there?"

"Of course I did, I was with Comandante Ramos. He had a reception after the rally—you wouldn't believe his house. It's a mansion, actually."

"I've seen it," Garabanda said. "But I was never invited inside, that's for sure. It's at the top of Sandia Heights. It's stone, with a serious iron fence around it."

"That's the place. Félix Magón was there, plus some Hollywood types, and a CBA news crew. Ricardo Mentiroso, among others."

Garabanda seemed amazed by this latest information. "Did Wayne Parker and Félix Magón speak to each other? Did you hear what they said?"

"Yes, and yes. They had some words together. Parker was drunk, he was hard to understand, but he mentioned '*La República del Norte*' a couple of times. It sounded like he had some kind of a deal going with Magón."

"Yeah, I'm sure he does—how else is he going to keep his million acres off the land reform list? And now he's using his ranch to host a secret meeting this Wednesday. There's got to be something in it for Félix Magón."

"I'm still not seeing the point of all this."

Garabanda paused, quietly drawing a breath, looking directly at her. "Ranya, do you know about the Constitutional Convention?"

"I heard something about it on TV. It's going to be in Philadelphia this fall."

"Right. Only it's just going to be a rubber stamp. The real deal is going to go down at Parker's ranch this Wednesday—at least, that's what I think is going to happen."

"You 'think'? What's that mean?"

"Ranya, it's complicated, it'll take a little while to explain. Magón and Parker were organizing the Vedado conference behind Governor Deleon's back, but Deleon found out about it."

"And now Deleon is dead, and Magón is the new governor. Good timing."

"Exactly. You're picking this up fast." He continued. "A couple of U.S. Senators and some VIP billionaires are flying in for this meeting. Luis Carvahal heard all of this straight from Governor Deleon. Vice-governor Magón was organizing it behind his back, and Deleon was left completely out of the loop. But then Senator Kelly called him from Boston, that's how he found out about it. That old drunkard must have assumed that Governor Deleon already knew about the conference, but he didn't. Kelly told him everything. After that, Deleon's days were numbered, I can see that now. He was just standing in Magón's way, more of a risk than a benefit. A thug like Félix Magón could never have been elected—for one thing, he's lived his entire life outside of New Mexico, mostly in Mexico. He just used Deleon. Magón rode his coattails into Santa Fe, and then he had him shot. Had him shot, and blamed it on an Anglo rancher—everybody's favorite whipping boy."

"So Magón killed two birds with one stone—he got rid of Deleon, and he whipped up the anti-Anglo hatred." Ranya considered mentioning the 7mm rifle she had sighted-in for the Falcons, but she held her tongue, unable to think of a reason why Garabanda would need that information. The FBI man was on a roll, and it was better to let him carry on talking and gain as much information as possible from him, while giving up as little as possible in return.

Garabanda said, "This meeting at Parker's ranch is where the new Constitution is going to be ginned up, I'm convinced of it. That's what Carvahal found out from Deleon…"

"And now they're both dead."

"That's right—and now they're both dead. Luis Carvahal was killed for that information. He was burned to death for it! Now you and I are the only ones alive who know about the meeting, and that's why I can't just leave the state, not right now. If I do, then my friend was burned to death for nothing—nothing at all."

It took a minute for Ranya to digest all of this new information, and determine that Alex Garabanda was dead serious. "So why does any of that matter to me? I'm sorry about your friend, I really am. That was a horrible way to die…just terrible. But aren't you just guessing what the meeting's going to be about?"

"I'm not just guessing, Senator Kelly said…"

"Senator Kelly's a drunk!" she snapped. "This meeting could be about land reform, or 'La República Del Norte,' or anything else."

"Not with those two Senators coming. They're not from New Mexico. They've got nothing to do with New Mexico, and neither do the billionaires."

"Well, even if it is about the new Constitution, it's not my problem. Am I supposed to care if there's a plan to write a new Constitution before the convention in Philadelphia? I mean, they've ignored most of the old one for years and years, so who cares if they write a new one? Old or new, what's the difference?"

"Don't you see? A new Constitution will mean the end of the United States! It'll turn America into a socialist country, that's—"

"Oh please," she scoffed, "like it's not already!"

"But not like it's going to be after they pass the 'Economic Democracy Amendment!' The convention delegates are all handpicked stooges, it's a complete joke. The whole thing is a sham—most of the delegates aren't even recognized by their own states! It's all a setup—anybody can see what's going to happen! Have you read any of the proposed amendments? The Bill of Rights is going to be chopped back to nothing—there'll be no Second Amendment, for one thing. Instead, we're going to get the 'Freedom From Gun Violence' amendment, it's already been written!

"And just forget about American national sovereignty—that'll be a thing of the past. Both of the Senators who are coming are big open-borders globalists like Wayne Parker, and there's one from each party so it'll be a bipartisan sellout. They both want to fast-track the 'North American Community,' and just erase the borders. As bad as America's gotten, at least we still have a country, at least we still have fifty states and national borders! I mean, it can be fixed, if the economy recovers. But after the convention, who knows what we'll end up with? I'm sure Félix Magón is getting something out of the deal for holding the meeting here in New Mexico. What did Wayne Parker call it, '*La República del Norte*?' So kiss the Southwest goodbye for starters."

"If you care about the United States so much, then how can you quit the FBI?"

"It doesn't matter if I'm in the FBI or not. In or out, I'm an American first."

"Look, Alex, I'm sorry, but I still don't care. I haven't cared about that patriotic crap for five years. The last time I cared that much about America, somebody I loved got killed."

"Brian's biological father?"

"Brian's *real* father."

Garabanda reacted as if he'd been slapped, and the sting showed on his face as he dropped his eyes to the table.

Ranya kept on, unmoved by his hurt feelings. "Listen, I don't care who writes the new Constitution, or what it says. It has nothing to do with me. It's just words, words on a piece of paper. The government will use half of it to screw people, and ignore the other half—just like they do now."

"Well Ranya," he said softly, "I'm sorry you feel that way, but it still matters to me. This might sound like nothing but a joke to you, but I took an oath to defend the Constitution. I put my right hand up in the air, and I swore to God that I'd defend it. And that doesn't mean just standing around and watching, not while a couple of billionaires and crooked Senators gin up a new one, and get it rubberstamped in a phony convention."

"Your patriotism moves me," she replied coldly, "But come on, even if that's all true—and I'm not saying it is—what could you possibly do about it anyway? Wayne Parker is one of the richest men in the world. Can you imagine the security he's got up there? Besides his own private guards, the entire Falcon Battalion is going up to cover the conference—I heard that from Comandante Ramos himself. What are you going to do, charge in like Rambo and shoot them all? Arrest the Senators and make them confess to treason? You won't be able to get within ten miles of Wayne Parker's ranch! Seriously, what can you do that'll make any difference?"

"Oh, I have some ideas. The meeting's on Wednesday, in the afternoon and evening, so I have three days to plan and get ready. It's completely secret. I've been checking, and I haven't seen a single hint of it. Not in the media, or in FBI message traffic. Secrecy is obviously their top concern—they can't be caught in the act of rigging the new Constitution. So if I can just find out who came, prove who was there…it'll be something. I'm not saying it'll derail this bullshit Constitutional Convention…but it'll be something. I think it's important that people find out that the new Constitution is a con job, that it was pre-cooked at Wayne Parker's ranch by a bunch of billionaire globalists."

"Do you honestly think that Americans will care?" she responded. "As long as they can watch the ball game and find a beer to pour down their throats, they could give a crap less about the Constitution—old or new. They care about finding gas to put in their cars and food to put in the fridge, not what happens in Philadelphia."

"Well, maybe you're right, but it doesn't matter. I still have to do it."

There was no denying his stubbornness, his dogged determination to press on. She said, "I know, I know…you swore an oath to defend the Constitution."

"That's right, I did! Against *all* enemies, foreign *and domestic.* And you know what? I meant it then…and I still mean it now."

"I can hear that you mean it. I believe you. But I heard that same speech once, and afterwards, some good men died—and not one thing changed. The country just got worse."

"Well, I'm sorry, but I still believe it. Go ahead and mock me if you want to, but I still believe it. I took an oath, *and I meant it.* I'm not going to just hang around doing nothing, not while the Constitution is ripped to shreds and put back together in a lab like Frankenstein! Anyway, this is going to be safe, there won't be any shooting. This'll just be an intelligence-gathering mission. Photographic surveillance. If I can find out exactly who attended the conference, that'll be enough. After that, we'll fly straight to San Diego and find Brian."

"But I'm paying for the airplane ride with my gold, and I'm not interested in making a side trip to northern New Mexico! You can tilt at windmills on your own time."

"Okay, fine, if that's the way you want it! Then maybe I won't help you get to California at all! Hey lady, maybe you can just walk there, or drive your little solar car! And what happens when you get there, *if* you get there? I don't exactly think Brian is going to run to the arms of the strange woman who just shot his mother. You'll need me out there if you want to get Brian."

She knew that he had a point, and she wasn't sure if he was bluffing. And at least he was showing some backbone, some spine—*some life.* He seemed to have climbed out of the pit of misery she had found him in when she had first entered his house. He was angry and determined, qualities they'd need in San Diego. "All right, I'll think about it. What did you have in mind?"

"Just aerial surveillance. Some kind of quick aerial surveillance. I'll know more after I talk to my friend. He used to be a Border Patrol pilot, he just retired."

"Who is he? You can trust him?"

"Oh yeah, totally. Plus, he really needs the money—well, the gold. I think he'll fly us anywhere we pay him to go."

Just after dark, the pilot pulled into the driveway and rang the doorbell like any other visitor. Ranya remained in the kitchen while Garabanda went to the front door to let him in. She slid into a pantry corner, her hand on the grip of the .45 against the small of her back, in case this was the moment of betrayal. If it was, she decided that she would make the best possible use of the eight bullets in her pistol. She would not meekly surrender. She would not be thrown to the ground on her face and handcuffed.

She harbored no illusions. She knew that after drowning Warden Linssen and escaping from the federal detention camp, she would rate gold star prisoner status as both a cop killer and an escape risk. The best that she could hope for after arrest would be a silent and solitary life spent in a windowless underground supermax cell. She would never leave the cell unshackled, ever. She would get only an hour of "exercise" in another solitary pen, virtually a dog run, once a week. She'd been there. She knew. She wasn't going back.

The only alternative to this living death would be a one-way trip to death row itself, to await execution. Neither choice was an option. If Alex Garabanda was going to be her Judas, she would try to take him out first. If he was even now letting in an assault team, they would be in full body armor and helmets, and she would aim directly at the first face she saw. She turned out the kitchen light and hid herself in shadow behind the half-open pantry door. She wondered if she should have already run out the back door, instead of waiting here in his kitchen like a cornered animal, but she figured that if an arrest team was coming, they'd already have the back yard covered.

But after a few minutes alone with her dark thoughts, there was still no FBI SWAT Team, no squad of Federal Marshals. There was just Alex Garabanda and a paunchy middle-aged man with dark black hair combed straight back, chatting casually while they strolled into the kitchen. She stepped out from her concealment. Garabanda flipped the kitchen light back on, and gave her a look of mild puzzlement. She shrugged at him in return, while shoving her pistol inside of her pants in the small of her back.

The pilot was no taller that Ranya, no more than five feet nine. He was clean-shaven, with a weak chin and down-turned eyes that gave him a mournful hound-dog look. He was wearing jeans and a royal blue alligator shirt, Joe Average, nobody you'd look at twice. The FBI man looked like a television star next to him. Garabanda introduced him simply as his friend Logan, who used to fly for Customs and the Border Patrol. No other name or personal background information was offered, and Ranya didn't ask. His appearance didn't inspire much confidence.

She introduced herself in return as Robin, her previous nom d'guerre from another undeclared dirty war. If the pilot wondered whether she was another Special Agent or Garabanda's girlfriend or something else, he didn't indicate any overt curiosity. Whatever Garabanda had told him to explain her presence in his house must have satisfied him. Best of all, Logan brought a twelve pack of beer, and a paper sack full of takeout burritos with him. He put them on the kitchen counter and invited them both to dig in, while pulling the first bottle of cold beer from the colorful cardboard box.

Ranya extracted her own brew and twisted it open, then unwrapped the foil from a beef burrito and bit into it, closing her eyes with pleasure. Alex Garabanda turned the radio back up, to block their conversation from possible eavesdropping. The curtains were already closed. The three sat down around the Formica-topped kitchen table to eat, drink, and see where their conversation might lead them. The Dragunov rifle had already been put away, stashed in the pantry. In its place a road map of New Mexico was spread across the center of the table, with beer bottles and plates of burritos on top of the map.

The pilot spoke with a folksy Texas twang. "Al, I'm real sorry to hear that Karin bolted on you. Well, I mean, I'm not so sorry about her…I guess I'm just sorry that she took Brian. It must be tough for you, losin' the little guy."

"Yeah Logan, it's tough, it's damn tough."

"At least you're back in your own house, that's something anyway."

"I suppose." Garabanda shrugged as he looked around the nearly bare kitchen. "So, how's retired life treating you?"

"I'm bored, I'm not flying nearly enough. The flight instructor gig sure ain't working out. Nobody can afford to pay for lessons, especially not with fuel the way it is. Things are tight, there's never enough money…you know how they cut the pensions when they changed the money. Thank God our house is paid off is all I can say—otherwise we'd be living in a tent."

Alex Garabanda knew that this was no mere figure of speech. Thousands of retirees and the unemployed were indeed living in tents and RVs on new "campgrounds," which seemed to be springing up like mushrooms. He adopted a more somber tone and asked his friend, "How's Trudy doing?"

The pilot slowly shook his head while letting out a sigh. "She's holding on. She's a real trooper. She just needs more treatments than what she can get here."

"Can't she get what she needs on the outside? Private care, I mean."

"She could if I was made of money. I just can't play the insurance game any harder than what I already am. You know how government health care sucks for retirees—we're at the bottom of every priority list. She just can't get any more treatments here. Twice a week isn't enough, and the dialysis machines they use are just crap. They're friggin' antiques, and they reuse the filters! You wouldn't believe it, you'd think you were in Cuba or Mexico or something. It's damned depressing. You know how New Mexico is, so just imagine how it is on a pension when you need extra medical treatment." He took a long pull from his bottle of beer. "I swear to God Al, they just want us to shut up and die, without costing them any money."

"So what's the word on the organ donor list?" he asked.

"What list? We're off the list—Trudy doesn't make the cut. It's the triple whammy: she's over fifty, no dependent kids and not working. Three strikes and you're out. The only waiting list she's on is the hurry-up-and-die list."

Garabanda let those words sink in, before responding gently. "Logan, I think we can help each other out. We don't need much, we just need somebody to do a little flying—off the books. We can pay you for it. We can pay you real well."

The pilot slowly shook his head, resignation written on his downcast face. "You must not know what dialysis treatments cost out on the private side."

"I think I've got an idea how much. Anyway, I'm pretty sure we can help you out with it."

"Al, I don't know what you've been up to lately, or where you'd come up with that kind of money—and I don't want to know. But I can't pay for Trudy's dialysis with wads of cash. They won't accept it unless I have about ten kinds of disclosure forms filled out and approved. I have to pay with credit cards or bank drafts. Its all gotta be 100% kosher, legit, traceable electronic money. That's the system, that's how it works."

"I know all about the system—I'm an expert. But I'm not talking about paying you cash."

The pilot appeared puzzled. "I don't understand. What then?"

"First, let me tell you what we need. We want to fly up to Torcido County on Wednesday, stay for a few hours, and then fly to San Diego. That's it."

The pilot quietly whistled. "Interstate. That's a pretty tall order, that's over a thousand miles one way, ballpark estimate. So what's going on up in Torcido? Picking somebody up, or what?"

"Well, I'm afraid it's a little bit more involved than that. You're familiar with Wayne Parker's place up there? The Vedado Ranch?"

"Sure. It's got one of the only private jet-capable runways around, at least that I ever heard of. How much land does he have up there, a half-million acres?"

"More like a million. It's roughly about forty miles on a side. Covers most of Torcido County."

"That used to be Spanish Land Grant territory," offered the pilot, "So how come Wayne Parker hasn't been 'land reformed'?"

"I'm not sure," replied Garabanda. "I think it's got something to do with the United Nations. He's donating most of Vedado for a World

Conservancy Site. It's some kind of a UN deal. You know Wayne Parker—he's a big one-worlder, so the commies up in Santa Fe tolerate him—at least for now. Plus, he practically bankrolled Deleon into office single-handed. I guess if you fork over enough dough, you get to keep your land."

The pilot twisted open his second bottle of beer. "Al, for some reason I'm not getting the impression that Wayne Parker's inviting you up for a party. What's going on?"

"Well, it's kind of complicated. He's having some VIPs fly in for a conference on Wednesday, and I want to know who they are."

"What's the matter with the FBI, can't you get your own airplanes? What are you asking me for?"

Garabanda paused, looking directly across at his friend. "The FBI isn't behind this, Logan. This one is on my own. Well, on our own." He nodded to Ranya, who was devouring her second beef and bean burrito. She had been a silent observer at the table during the exchange, and shot him back a challenging look at that comment.

The pilot replied, "What the hell are you talking about? Al, are you going freelance? What is this, an FLA operation? Or the Federal Underground? Man, I can't afford to get messed up in that kind of shit—I need to keep my federal pension. If I lose the pension, we're eating out of garbage dumps like all the trash pickers! I'll lose all of my benefits, and that includes medical, and then Trudy won't be eligible for any treatments at all! I mean, I'm sympathetic to the cause, but Al, I just can't get mixed up with that underground cop business."

"Logan, I swear that it's got nothing to do with the Former Lawmen or the F.U. This is strictly on my own. I just want to know who's coming to Wayne Parker's conference. That's it."

"You just want to know who's coming?" he asked sarcastically, "Then why don't you just call up there and ask?"

Garabanda ignored his friend's tone. "It's not that kind of meeting. It's very hush-hush, top secret. It'll be enough just to find out who's attending."

"And how do you propose to do that?" The pilot pushed back from the table, his arms crossed.

"Well, I had a couple of ideas. First, I thought maybe we'd shoot a runway approach. Line it up and call it in like we're expected, and then do a touch-and-go while they're figuring out who the hell we are. Touch-and-go, and then haul ass. Film out of both sides of the plane, and record the tail numbers of the jets parked on the runway. Trace them back that way."

"Oh, just like that huh? One shot on a touch-and-go fly-by, with video cameras rolling. You actually think that'll work?"

"You tell me. Would it work? You're the expert."

"Maybe, it might—it depends on a lot of factors. It's iffy though. So who do you think is coming? What's the meeting about? What's so important about it, that you want to go to all this trouble?"

Garabanda explained his belief that the Vedado Ranch meeting was going to be the covert precursor to the upcoming Constitutional Convention. This account took enough time for both of them to drink another beer, with the FBI man talking, and the pilot asking occasional questions and making a few comments. Alex finally concluded, saying, "So that's it, that's what I think is going to happen next Wednesday."

"Well I can believe it," agreed the former Border Patrol pilot. "Folks like Wayne Parker aren't going to be satisfied to just let Philadelphia play itself out. They're not going to just let the chips fall where they may, and actually leave the new amendments up to the delegates. Not even these phony delegates. You can bet they want it all set up first, pre-fabricated, a done-deal. They'll just pay off the delegates. They're billionaires, right? They can buy these delegates for pocket change. And anything Senator Kelly and Montaine are in on together, well, you just automatically know it stinks to hell, and that it's some kind of a sellout. They're both for the North American Community, those Quisling traitor bastards! That's why they always kept a real border fence from being built. Why build a border fence, if you're planning to get rid of the border?"

Alex Garabanda formed a slight smile, seeing that his friend seemed receptive to his ideas. "So, now that you know why I want to do it, what do you think? Can you do it? Will you do it?"

"Well, I'll tell you the truth, I'm not too hot on the idea of flying straight down a hostile runway, just to try to shoot some video. Too iffy. What kind of security will they have up there?"

"You've heard of the Falcon Battalion?"

"Hmmm…elite Milicia. I heard of 'em. Land reform experts. They specialize in evictions."

"Yeah, that's them," said Alex. "And based on their usual M.O., they'll probably have some Blackhawks, and maybe some fixed wing planes too. They've used Blackhawks on their 'land reform' operations pretty often. They like to do air mobile ops, and come in hot."

"Blackhawks? Now that's a fast helicopter. That means we can't use a 172—they're not fast enough. Blackhawks will eat a 172 for breakfast. No way can a 172 get away from a Blackhawk."

"You mean a Cessna 172?"

"Right. I'd have to get something faster. Maybe a 210T, from Tucson or El Paso. That's a Cessna Centurion turbo—top of the line for single engine props. Plus, a 210 has the range to make it all the way to San Diego nonstop. But I'd have to spread some serious money around, this wouldn't be easy to arrange…"

"How much money are you talking about?" asked Alex.

"A lot. A real chunk. I can't borrow the airplane without making it worth some people's while not to notice a few irregularities."

"How much, Logan?"

The retired pilot sipped his beer, looking across at the FBI man. "To do it right? Oh, ballpark figure, about three hundred grand. Two hundred for my part, and another hundred that I'll need to spread around here and there. This is all hypothetical now, of course."

Garabanda turned to Ranya. "Robin, can we handle that?" He had noticed her use of a cover name, and used it to refer to her in Logan's presence.

"I think we can. Let me see." She left her chair and went to her backpack on the floor by the back door, unzipped the flap and returned with a pair of white plastic tubes in her fists. Each compact tube was about three inches long and a bit more than an inch in diameter. She set one in the center of the table between the men. "25 ML" was written on the top in black magic marker. It was clear that the unusual plastic tube was purpose-made to hold something unique, something of value. She pulled an end-cap off the other tube and tipped it over, spilling a neat row of golden coins across the map like a fan of fallen dominos.

All of their eyes grew wide at the sight of the dazzling golden line, and broad smiles formed on their faces as if by magic. Alex Garabanda and his friend Logan each picked up a coin for closer examination. They were all Canadian Maple Leafs, stamped "9999 FINE GOLD, 1 OZ." On one side was the distinctive maple leaf logo of Canada, and on the other, the profile of an English queen.

Alex Garabanda spoke first, while hefting the coin in the palm of his hand. He asked, "What's an ounce worth these days? Seven thousand?" He quickly did the mental math, and came up with an estimate. The fifty gold coins on the table were the equivalent of $350,000 hyperinflated New Dollars. Ranya hadn't hesitated to bring these two tubes full of gold coins to the table. Garabanda remembered what she had told him about stealing ten or fifteen pounds of gold from Basilio Ramos. One thing he knew for sure: he had carried her two bags into the house, and they had weighed well over that amount, by at least double or triple—each. He picked up the other plastic tube still containing twenty-five coins. Despite its compact size, it weighed about as much as an all-steel pistol. $175,000 blue bucks, in his hand.

"Seven thousand an ounce?" the pilot repeated, "That sounds right, but I'm not sure. Probably closer to $7,500. And besides that, you know what else these coins are worth? Ten years in Leavenworth. You know what they say: 'only terrorists and the mafia need gold. America's gold belongs in Fort Knox'."

The FBI man grinned at his friend. "Yeah, well, what the hell. In for a penny, in for a pound, right?"

"Damn right!" the pilot agreed.

Ranya jumped in and insisted, "Twenty-five now, and the rest when we land in California. Okay?" She took the full tube of coins back from Alex Garabanda's open hand.

"Sounds fair to me," Logan answered, still smiling.

Alex said, "You might even find a way to get Trudy back on the donor list with some of these, don't you think?"

The pilot scooped up the twenty-five bright golden coins from the table, jingling them in his two hands. "Yes, oh hell yes, for sure, right to the top of the organ list! These will do just fine—I already know who's going to get them. This is money you don't need to deposit in a bank, with a government permission slip! This is *real money.* You just put it in the doctor's hand. So, when do you want to fly?"

"Wednesday morning," the FBI man answered.

"Up north to Wayne Parker's ranch, then to San Diego?" confirmed their newly hired private pilot.

"That's it. That's the plan," he agreed.

"San Diego is where Karin and Brian are, right?" asked the pilot.

"You never heard that from me."

"Alexandro mi amigo," he responded with a wink, "I never heard any of this."

"Good, let's keep it that way."

The pilot nodded, his enthusiasm visibly growing. "I can do the whole trip in under 24 hours, from picking up the plane in El Paso to returning it. Sure, it's doable. Oh yeah, I can do it! But forget your idea about the runway touch-and-go. There's a better way. Much better."

"What's that?" asked Garabanda.

"Mini-UAVs. Drones. They've got a bunch of them sitting in the Border Patrol hangars in El Paso collecting dust. The brass just hauls them out to show reporters a demo flight once in a while, and then they go back in their crates until the next dog-and-pony show. We can carry a tactical UAV in the back of the plane, and launch it from the ground once we're in range. That way we can stay out of the danger zone, and film the ever-loving crap out of everybody at that Wayne Parker shin-dig, in living color."

"Won't they be able to hear the drone?" asked Ranya, who had finished two burritos and two beers, wiped her mouth with a napkin, burped several times, and was leaning back in her chair with her thumbs hooked into her belt loops. The full container of gold coins was on the edge of the table in front of her, a white plastic tower.

"Naw, we'll just take a Pelican 3. It's too small to see when it's at altitude, and its motor's as quiet as a hummingbird. Sweet little Wankel rotary, runs on regular gas. Smooth as silk. It's invisible and inaudible when it's on the job. You'll see. Then we can just sit on the ground about ten or fifteen miles away, and download the video. Once we've got what you need, we'll recover the Pelican, and then off we're off to San Diego."

"We'll fly under radar?" asked Ranya.

"Where, to San Diego? No way, we'll be on a declared flight plan for that leg. I'll have it all squared away, no problem. Now up north, on the way into Vedado, sure, we'll do a below radar approach for that leg. But don't worry, I made a living chasing coyotes in planes for twelve years—I know all the tricks. I know how not to be seen."

The FBI man told Ranya, "And Logan used to play the smuggler for pursuit training, and let the Customs boys try to chase him down. Hell, he practically wrote the manual on aerial pursuit! Isn't that right?"

"Yeah, that's true enough. But once we're on the leg to San Diego, it'll be a declared flight plan all the way. Well, almost all the way."

Alex asked him, "Are you sure a 210's going to be available on Wednesday?"

"You bet I'm sure. I know who maintains 'em, who schedules 'em and who flies 'em. I know *everybody* down there, and I'm still on the cleared list for check flights, as a private contractor. Al, a few of these gold coins in the right hands, and we could start a regular air taxi service, I kid you not! I mean, it's not as if they're actually *using* those planes or anything. They barely get any operational flying time along the border. It's the same old song and dance: they don't want us actually *catching* illegals; they just want to put on a good show for the media. So sure, it'll be no problem taking one for 24 hours, no problem at all. They go off for maintenance, they do special VIP trips, they haul agents to conferences—you name it. No, it won't be missed for one day. Not when I put some of these Maple Leafs in the right hands."

"So you're cool with doing this job? You know you'll be risking your pension…"

"Al, the gold on this table is probably worth more than all of the pension money I'll ever see in the rest of my life, especially after they switch the currency a couple more times. But that's not as important as just getting this much all at one time. With this much, there's a chance for Trudy to get the operation, and that's a chance worth taking." He looked back and forth between the two of them. "But you know what, that's not even the only reason I'll do it. The truth is, even without the gold, I'd be glad to fly this mission."

He chuckled. "For once, I'll be doing something really worthwhile in a government airplane! Not like back in the Border Patrol, when I was usually grounded while thousands of illegals crossed our sector, night after night. I can't tell you how many times we were pulled back by the brass: 'just stay on your X!' That means don't interdict them, just let 'em through. You want to know what real frustration is? Being told by the whores and sellouts from Washington not to do your damn job, to just shut your mouth and 'stay on your X.'

"So hell yes, let's go on up to Torcido County and stick it to those treasonous rat bastards! Let's film the whole damn party and nail their traitorous asses to the shithouse wall! Name 'em and shame 'em, in living color! You know Al, I always hated traitors like Montaine and Kelly the worst, I hated their stinking guts. It used to make me sick, how they'd come down to the border to hold a press conference, and talk about how they were finally going to get control of it. But you know, after all these years, they still never even built more than a few token miles of the damn fence!

"And now that the socialists are running New Mexico, it's worse than ever. There's no border, no border at all—it's just wide open. They won't even let the Border Patrol get anywhere near the line anymore, can you imagine? It's 'too dangerous,' they say. Too dangerous! Yeah, just let the Mexican Army and the Milicia take care of the border, they do a *fine* job. And after the Constitutional Convention, well, just forget it. There just won't even be a border any more, not even a make-believe border. The new border will probably be the Colorado state line—if we can keep Colorado."

Alex steered him back onto the subject at hand. "Okay, let's talk about how we're going to do this. We'll need to be picked up Wednesday. I have to drive up to Santa Fe early tomorrow morning to register for my workshop, and after that, I'll be free. We'll need the right air maps; we'll have to check out the landing strips…"

"Oh, I can do all of that," offered the pilot. "Wednesday is good. Wednesday gives me plenty of time to get everything squared away for the flight. It'll be a piece of cake—*no problema*."

28

Wednesday June 2

In the bone-dry badlands halfway between Albuquerque and Santa Fe, a small combination mini-mart and diner served the nearby Indian reservation. The humble establishment was located only a few miles west of I-25, but there was no sign of the highway here. In this region of bluffs, buttes, ravines and rock formations, the low building could easily be overlooked as just one more random outcropping. The place might have begun as a doublewide trailer, or maybe it was just a ramshackle structure built one sheet of plywood at a time. It was impossible to tell which part was original, and what had been added incrementally over the decades. The entire exterior was painted the same faded gray, blending to dun brown where the dust crept up the sides.

Besides its small kitchen and restaurant seating area, the mini-mart side of the establishment sold lottery tickets, hunting ammunition, ice, beer, liquor and other necessities of life. Horses were kept in a corral on one side of the diner, and off to the other side was a combined garage and junkyard. A mobile home stood under cottonwood trees at the back of the corral. Chickens pecked in the dirt, unmolested by dogs resting in the shade. The land around the place was relatively flat for this part of the country, and offered views of distant mountains in several directions.

An hour after finishing their huevos rancheros and *posole* grits, Ranya Bardiwell and Alex Garabanda were nursing coffees, waiting by the single large window in front of the dining area. It was Wednesday morning, and they were the only customers. They were dressed for the outdoors. She was wearing her green fatigue-style pants and khaki short sleeve camping shirt. Her loose shirt was left untucked, covering the .45 stuck under her belt. He was wearing gray BDU pants, a green t-shirt and his brown operator's vest.

Alex's burgundy Crown Victoria "bureau car" was parked out of the way on the repair shop side of the diner. It was nine o'clock, an hour later than the planned meeting, but delays were the norm when waiting for an informant to show up. Allowances for time slippage had been built into their plan.

Two days earlier, on Monday morning, Alex Garabanda had made the forty-mile drive up to Santa Fe. The only Milicia check point was on the highway off-ramp leading into the capital, but he was not hassled beyond a cursory glance at his FBI credentials. As he had expected, the state was not ready to provoke a direct clash with the federal government. For this first drive, he brought only his Sig pistol in case his car was searched.

He registered early at the Santa Fe Regent's conference center, and attended a full day of politically correct multiculturalism, diversity and tolerance indoctrination. He made sure that he was seen by the lecturers and group moderators, but without leaving a strong impression. This dry-run process had been repeated without incident on Tuesday. The room was paid for through the rest of the week. He left his FBI-issued cell phone hidden under the mattress, plugged into its charger, the wire concealed behind the headboard. The phone was set to forward calls to his voice mail. The do-not-disturb sign was left on the door.

On both days, Ranya Bardiwell stayed behind and out of sight, at his house on Camino Del Cielo.

Wednesday morning before first light, they both left Albuquerque in the Ford. This time the car was fully loaded with baggage, weapons, communications and other technical surveillance gear, and of course, Ranya's stolen gold in her two bags. Alex Garabanda took one last look at the house in his rear-view mirror, and wondered if he would ever see it again. Probably not, he thought without any real regret. Though it had been the place he and Karin had raised their son, the negative memories of the last few months had taken away any luster from what had once been their happy home.

As planned, Alex and Ranya had arrived at the nameless diner, had breakfast, and waited. They didn't talk much. They were both lost in their own thoughts, and were still uncomfortable with and mistrustful of one another. At 9:15, a rusty brown full-sized pickup truck pulled up in front of the diner. It had a tradesman's lumber rack extending above it from bumper to bumper, so he recognized it as their ride. The welded steel rack was empty except for an aluminum ladder tied down on top. Two men were in the cab of the truck. One got out and walked over to the diner's front door, which opened with a bell's jingle.

A short Indian man, who was some years beyond sixty, shambled over to their table. He was wearing jeans, a plaid flannel shirt and a green NAPA ball cap pulled down low. Wispy hairs grew from several moles on his chin.

"You're Alex?"

"Where's Joseph?" This old Indian was the wrong man, and he was using the wrong protocol for the meeting…but one had to make allowances in New Mexico. The truck with the pipe rack was the key detail.

"Joseph couldn't make it, something came up. I'm his grandpa. He told me you needed a ride. He told me all about it."

This sounded reasonable, and Alex adapted. He had no alternative. "Then you know where we're going?"

"Yeah, I know."

"And I need somebody to take care of my car for a little while, until I get back."

The old Indian gestured with his head toward his truck outside, where the other man waited in the passenger seat. "My brother can drive it. No problem. Let's go."

"We need to get our stuff. Pull your truck behind my car. The Ford over there."

"I know which one."

The Indian turned and walked back outside to his truck. His brother climbed out and followed them over to the Crown Victoria, and waited, standing by the driver's door. Alex and Ranya hauled their backpacks and kitbags from the Ford's trunk when the pickup pulled up behind. When Alex hoisted a gear bag over the side, a mixed-breed German shepherd lunged snarling from the truck's bed. The older Indian whistled and the dog circled low, watching them, and laid down again.

The two drivers didn't bat an eye when Ranya's long Dragunov, wrapped in a gray army blanket and bound with cord, was placed into the bed of the truck. By its very shape it was obviously a rifle, but this was northern New Mexico, and where they were going, rifles were a commonplace sight. Gun laws passed in far-off Washington had never held any sway in this part of the country.

Garabanda told the younger of the two men, "I'll be back in a week or so for my car, just keep it out of sight. Under some trees would be nice, or throw a tarp over it."

The man just nodded, and got into the Ford after he was handed a single car key.

Alex leaned over the open door. "Hey, no joyriding, okay? Just hide it. You don't want to be stopped in this car..."

"No shit." The driver slammed the door.

The other three climbed into the rusty brown pickup truck, with Ranya in the middle. A red and black horse blanket covered the bench seat. A statue of the Virgin Mary was glued to the center of the peeling dashboard, beneath the cracked windshield. They drove northwest on a two lane road, twisting across a sun-baked moonscape fissured with canyons, escarpments and dry-wash riverbeds.

"No checkpoints?" asked Alex.

The old man came close to smiling. "No, not around here. Not on the res. The Milicia, they don't mess with us—they know better than that."

"How's Joseph doing? He sounded happy on the phone." The two men talked around Ranya, while she stared straight ahead.

"Oh, you know Joseph, he's okay," said the Indian. "He's been clean for two years—he's done with his wild life. It's good to have him home. Moving back here was what he needed."

"I'm glad I could help him out. You know, with all that trouble he was in."

"Yeah. He's a lot better now. He's back home with Sarah, and they have a new baby boy. He gets some work. It's not so bad. He's not drinking or using. We make sure of that."

Joseph Mequon was one of Alex's informants. He had decided to help the feds, instead of taking a rap for distribution of marijuana. He'd traded his knowledge of meth labs around Las Cruces for his freedom, and it had worked out well for him. He had already spent two years in the state pen for manslaughter, and that had been enough for him to last one lifetime. Now he had left the fast life around Las Cruces and El Paso and returned to the reservation, where he would be safe from those he had helped to convict.

As often happened, the process of cultivating Joseph's trust had resulted in something approaching friendship. Both parties understood that the relationship might be renewed again at some time in the future, if a favor was needed. Now, Joseph was in a position to help Alex Garabanda. The informant was glad to do the FBI agent a small favor, to be redeemed later when he might need help. Even though Joseph Mequon couldn't make it in person today, he'd seen to it that the job was done by his grandfather.

The truck turned left off the state road, heading west on a single narrow lane of pavement. There was no traffic in either direction to observe their exit. If they were being followed, it could only be from the air. As far as he knew, the Special Surveillance Group was not yet conducting routine aerial surveillance.

Alex Garabanda took a small handheld GPS receiver from a pocket on his vest, and studied their position on its tiny screen map. "About five miles ahead, that's where it's coming in."

"I know where." The Indian smiled, the first expression of emotion that Garabanda had noticed. "It won't be the first airplane to land there. It's a nice straight piece of road."

After they arrived at the GPS location, the pickup truck waited in the dirt well off to the side of the road. This was in case the plane didn't show, and they needed a ride back. The road was indeed as straight as a ruler for a half mile in front of them. The land rose sharply in all directions around them, so that a plane landing here would literally have disappeared from radar. There was a barbed wire fence on one side, but it was too low to cause a problem for a high-wing airplane like a Cessna. There were no telephone or electric power poles near the road.

They erected the ladder in the back of the truck, lashing it upright against the pipe rack. A plastic grocery store shopping bag made a fine windsock, a full white billowing balloon. Alex tied more shopping bags on the barbed wire fence at hundred foot intervals; they blew toward the road at an angle. The white bags were Logan's idea, indicating the exact location of the airstrip, and the wind strength and direction along its entire length. The steady breeze was significant, about ten to fifteen from the northwest making a slight diagonal crosswind. Then they waited, sipping water from plastic bottles, which they had refilled at home from the tap.

Bob Bullard didn't have much of a view from his fifth floor office in the Federal Building. From the outside, the brown concrete structure looked like a massive bunker. If anything, it was uglier than most of the prisons he'd ever visited. From his window he couldn't even see the San Diego Bay, only six blocks away, because the Federal Building was surrounded by much taller edifices. He could however look up and see his penthouse condominium on the 45th floor of the Pacific Majesty. The dozen top floors of the tower were visible above the courthouse across the street.

He had a camera installed on the western balcony of his condo, aimed down at the government piers. He spun his chair around from the window and grabbed his computer mouse, and clicked a desktop icon on his computer. His screen instantly switched to a live view of the Eldorado, tied to the big government pier jutting 200 yards out on the bay. By using the arrows on his keyboard, he could move the camera to point almost straight down, or zoom out to the ocean beyond Point Loma. Seeing his eighty-foot "mobile emergency command and control platform" safely tied to the dock cheered him up. He knew that no matter what happened in the city or to the country at large, he was only a matter of minutes from cutting the Eldorado's dock lines and running for the horizon.

The 45 story Pacific Majesty condominium tower had gone broke before it had been finished, a victim of the California real estate crash. The federal government had then stepped in and salvaged the project, securing most of the apartments for the use of federal employees at deeply subsidized rates, hence its ubiquitous nickname, the Fed Tower. The convenience of living near work could not be underestimated. Carjackings, 'express kidnappings' and home invasions were all too common for those who commuted into the city, especially for those who had the misfortune of living on the lawless east side of I-5. Downtown San Diego around the courts and government buildings swarmed with police and security cameras, and was relatively safe.

Bullard's next scheduled appointment was with Jay Lattimore Teague, the head of the San Diego IRS. Teague was a pompous ass who was a stickler for regulations. From Bullard's point of view, this had its advantages and disadvantages. On the plus side, Teague was a terrier when it came to confiscating the illegal property of citizens who were found hoarding gold or other prohibited valuables. On the minus side, he accounted for every single New Dollar, Euro and Krugerrand. There was no possibility of going in with him on skimming operations.

Teague had first requested the meeting to discuss some matter of urgency, but in reality, the only reason Bullard approved the request was in order to meet his newest acquisition, an IRS SWAT team leader who had just transferred in from Albuquerque.

Gretchen Bosch was a GS-14 who had gotten into hot water in New Mexico, for assaulting her lesbian girlfriend's ex-husband with a baseball bat. In addition, Bosch had received several reprimands for overzealously searching citizen's homes and property. On several occasions, it was reported that she had left private homes looking like Swiss cheese, after her team had drilled hundreds of holes into their floors, walls and roofs searching for contraband assets. When Teague requested the meeting, Bullard suggested he bring along Agent Bosch. Of course, his suggestion was a command.

Bullard's Chief Staff Officer had standing orders to send up disciplinary reports on federal officers within the Southwest division. When Bullard read the personnel file on Gretchen Bosch, he knew immediately that her talent was being wasted in the backwater of Nuevo Mexico. Besides, the new Marxist state government was already doing a fine job of shaking down its citizens, and it was leaving only small pickings for the IRS.

After his secretary announced the arrival, Teague rapped the mandatory three times on the office door and Bullard replied, "Enter."

Jay Lattimore Teague was wearing one of his black pinstripe suits, and black wingtips. Bob Bullard had never seen him dressed any other way. He knew that it burned Teague's Ivy League butt to be the subordinate of Bob Bullard, who had received his Master's Degree in Criminology via an internet correspondence course.

(In truth, a brainy previous girlfriend had earned the degree for him. Once he had received his Masters, he'd dumped her—but in the end, it was his name on the degree, not hers. The mandatory Master's Degree had been the last check-off on his ever-ascending path up to the lofty ranks of the Senior Executive Service. Although few ordinary citizens had ever heard of them, SES's were the civilian "generals," the entrenched high-ranking bureaucrats who actually ran the federal government.)

Bullard remained seated behind his massive mahogany desk. "Nice to see you again Jay, what can I do for you? Did you bring the new CART Team leader?"

The question threw Teague off balance. "Uh, yes, Special Agent Bosch is waiting outside. I'm not really sure why you want to meet a GS-14 though, it seems…"

"Oh, you know me Jay—I'm a very hands-on kind of leader. I like to get to know my new troops. Welcome them aboard. So, what's on your mind?"

Teague sat opposite Bullard, and pushed a small white envelope across the desk to his superior. "Take a look at these: they're showing up all over Southern California."

Bullard opened the flap on the envelope, and a dozen small gold coins about the size of dimes spilled out. Bullard slipped on reading glasses, and then reached into a desk drawer for a large rectangular magnifying glass. "Okay, I'm seeing some one-tenth ounce gold coins. What about them?"

"Well, sir, they're flooding the local economy! They're going to wreck any chance we have to stabilize the New Dollar, and that's going to mean big problems for the Digital Dollar program, and eventually for the conversion from the dollar to the Amero."

Bullard reached across his desk and pulled over a small high-intensity reading lamp, and trained the bright light on the coins. "Nice workmanship, first class. Those Indians do a fine job of minting." He turned all of the coins over, examining them with his magnifying glass. "Geronimo, Sitting Bull, Osceola, Crazy Horse—nice artwork. Nice. So, what's the problem?"

"Well, it's illegal, that's the problem!"

"How is it illegal? These are only one-tenth of an ounce, and with all of the different Indian chiefs, clearly they qualify as numismatic coins, collectibles. So how are they illegal?"

"Director Bullard, can't you see that these coins are a deliberate attempt to circumvent the gold law?"

"Not my problem, Jay. The law says that gold coins under a half ounce are legal, up to a total of five ounces of gold per person. These are only one tenth of an ounce, and besides, they're collectibles. So unless the law is changed, I'm not sure what you're expecting me to do about it."

"But the Indians are melting down all kinds of gold to make these coins, so the intent to evade the law is clear. What's the difference between an illegal one ounce Krugerrand, and ten of these?"

"The difference is that one-tenth ounce collectible numismatic coins aren't illegal, that's what."

"But…"

"Jay, what the Indians do on their reservations is their own business. That's settled law, just like the casinos. We're certainly not going to conduct any raids on the reservations, that's just out of the question. Okay?"

"But…!"

"That's all, Jay. If you feel that the law needs to be changed, fire off a letter to your Congressman. Now, send in Ms. Bosch. Thanks for your time." Bullard spun around in his chair, looking out of his massive armored-glass window, curtly dismissing the preppy asshole.

Jay Lattimore Teague was an idiot, if he expected help in combating the growing proliferation of the "gold dimes." Bob Bullard knew all about the new coins, he'd been out to the Golden Arrow and the other Indian casinos at least a dozen times. He'd seen the antique German minting machine in operation at the Golden Arrow Casino, and he knew the process from start to finish. Everything from gold wedding bands to gold ingots was accepted as payment at the Indian casinos.

Out at the Golden Arrow, the raw metal was melted down, purified, and minted into one-tenth and one-quarter ounce "collectible" gold coins. The Indian coins were then traded for thick stacks of blue bucks. The Indian casinos had become flourishing black market currency exchanges. The legality of this situation was somewhat undefined, but Bob Bullard's stance was as clear as a cut diamond: he would not interfere with the gold business on the "sovereign" Indian reservations.

At least, not as long as the Golden Arrow Casino continued to deliver 250 of their gleaming new "gold dimes" to him every week. At the current rate, one thin gold dime was worth $725 New Dollars. Next week, it would probably top $750, but the price in paper dollars didn't matter—his deal with the Indians was set in gold and only gold.

Ms. Bosch rapped on the door. Reading between the lines of her personnel file, Bullard already knew that she was a testosterone and steroid-abusing butch lesbian, with resulting anger management problems, a penchant for extreme violence, and no regard whatsoever for the civil liberties of Americans.

In other words, she was the perfect candidate to lead an IRS CART team running asset seizure operations. After studying her file, he was certain that he'd be able to recruit her into his private stable of crooked federal officers. Her CART team would eventually become his personal tool, doing his bidding and acting on his behalf. Jay Lattimore Teague would be unable to prevent this from happening. Unlike the last supervisor of San Diego's CART unit (an incorruptible Mormon who was currently being reassigned to Fargo, North Dakota), Agent Bosch promised not to be overly fastidious on the accounting end, after the assets were seized. There would be more than enough to satisfy both Uncle Sam and Gretchen Bosch, with a little left over for Bob Bullard.

Gretchen Bosch looked to be every bit as tough as her file photos and her reputation. Bullard rose from behind his desk and shook her hand across it. She had a grip stronger than most men, and her eye contact was prolonged and fearless. They were the same height, but Agent Bosch had the shoulders and arms of a serious weight lifter. She was wearing a man's gray sport jacket over a white t-shirt, and loose-fitting khaki slacks. This was a bit informal, but not out of regulation, and besides, this was her moving week. She was not yet on duty. Moreover, it was no longer permissible to demand old-fashioned gender-normed standards of grooming and attire. If Gretchen Bosch wanted to dress like a man and wear her hair in a flattop, well that was her business. Anyway, to Bob Bullard's thinking, it was better to deal with a straight-ahead dyke, than with a limp-wristed fairy, who on any given day might decide to prance into work wearing lipstick and a skirt. Both forms of on-the-job cross-dressing were now 100% protected as a matter of law, but Bob Bullard knew which type he preferred.

"Welcome to San Diego, Agent Bosch."

"I'm glad to be here sir. I appreciate what you did for me back in Albuquerque, getting me out of that jam."

Her voice was low and gravely, the result of either hard drinking, too much screaming during SWAT training, smoking cigarettes, or taking steroids. In her case, he decided it was probably a combination of all four. He could see that she had probably once been an attractive woman—if one was attracted to members of communist East German swim teams. Although her blue eyes sparkled, her crew cut and complete lack of makeup or lipstick announced her sexual orientation loud and clear. This didn't bother Bob Bullard. In fact, he saw it as a big plus. Gretchen Bosch obviously didn't give a shit what anybody thought about her. Her natural aggression (undoubtedly boosted by steroids and male hormones) had been amply demonstrated when she attacked her girlfriend's ex-husband with a baseball bat. Now it was up to him to channel her ferocity toward more productive ends.

"No problem, agent Bosch, I was glad to help. We need agents out here with your assertiveness. Southern California is too damned laid back for its own good, and I'm sorry to say that beach-bum attitude even creeps into our operators. Our contraband team needs a hard-charger to put the fire back into them. I think you've got what they've been missing."

"Thank you sir. You won't be disappointed."

"We've got a long list of suspected contraband hoarders, but the last CART team leader was too damn legalistic. He just didn't see the big picture, and frankly, I'm afraid it's not much better with your boss, Mr. Teague. Washington's not paying us to come up with excuses—they're paying us for contraband asset recovery. Are we on the same page, Agent Bosch?"

"Loud and clear, Director. I've got no time for pencil-neck geeks and their lame-ass excuses."

"Good. And remember, the asset recovery incentive has been raised to twelve percent. If you do your job to the max, that could double your salary. Maybe even more than that, if you're…creative. Creative, and aggressive. So don't be shy about using the bullion purchase lists—we've got names and addresses going back for years. As far as I'm concerned, anybody with a name on those coin dealer lists is fair game. That list is probable cause in my book. Use the ground penetrating radar, and the new tomoscopes for the walls. They've been getting great results. Ninety percent of the time, it's buried in their backyard, or hidden in their walls. You'll find some guns that way too, and that's all gravy."

"Yes sir."

"Good. So, you're reporting for duty next week?"

"That's right sir, Monday. This is our moving week."

"Do you want to stay downtown, or are you looking for a house?"

"Well, we have a little boy, and we'd like a yard for him to play in. We're staying in the Fed Tower until we find a place."

"Uh huh, great. That's where I live. I love it there, but I can understand your wanting a house. Just stay on the west side of I-5—don't even think about the east side. It's too dangerous. There are a few nice neighborhoods over there, but overall it's not worth it. At least the San Diego PD keeps the west side swept clear of dirtbags."

"We were thinking about finding a house up around Mission Bay, or Pacific Beach."

"Oh, that's nice up there, very nice. Seaworld, the beaches, all that. Have you checked the forfeitures and foreclosures printout? The July listings should be out already."

"Yes sir, we're using it for our house hunting this week," she replied.

This was one of the bennies of serving in federal law enforcement while the economy was in the toilet: being able to pick up plum real estate deals, for a fraction of what they would cost a civilian. This was especially true when you factored in the FEMP, the Federal Employee Mortgage Plan, which held interest rates to half of prime, and required no down payment. "You'll be able to save a bundle on a repo, just make sure the neighborhood is safe." Bullard rose from his executive chair, putting out his hand to shake hers again, and dismissing her. "Welcome aboard, Agent Bosch. I hope you have a productive tour in San Diego. We'll talk again soon."

"Thank you sir, I'll look forward to that," she growled cheerfully.

29

Logan's planned arrival time was ten AM, and at five after the hour they heard the faint sound of an airplane engine to the south. Less than a minute later, a white Cessna streaked over them thirty feet above the road, rocking its wings. The turbocharged Centurion was a high-wing single engine plane like the Maule-7 Ranya had flown from Texas, but it was much sleeker, with retractable wheels and a swept-back tail. Parallel blue stripes along the white fuselage were the airplane's only embellishment.

The plane flew beyond them, climbed into a steeply banking racetrack turn, and lined up on the road coming back. It was obviously a good flying trick to make a downwind landing with no margin for error, and all at minimum altitude below radar. The Centurion came roaring back toward them, wheels now locked down, crabbing against the crosswind.

It touched the road a thousand feet beyond the brown pickup truck that marked the nominal end of the temporary landing strip. Braking hard, it stopped only fifty feet from where they stood by the road. The engine was switched off and the propeller spun down and stopped. The left side pilot's door opened and Logan jumped down, wearing khaki pants, a matching khaki short-sleeve shirt, and tan hiking boots. He might have been retired from government service, but he looked like a professional aviator today.

They had already discussed and planned the seating and loading arrangements, and knew exactly what to do to minimize the plane's time on the ground. The co-pilot's right-side seat was already folded forward to allow Ranya to climb into the back. The disassembled wing and fuselage of the borrowed Border Patrol UAV drone extended from the center of the baggage area in the rear, and forward between the headrests of the rear seats. The men quickly brought the bags to the airplane, and Ranya passed them over the rear seats, loading them into the baggage area, followed by the Dragunov rifle. Their backpacks went onto the floor and the empty fourth seat on the left side in the back.

Then the three of them scrambled around to the tail of the plane and put all of their weight on its horizontal stabilizer, lifting the nose wheel up from the pavement. Once the nose was free, they were able to walk the Cessna around 180 degrees in its own space on its two back wheels, until it was aligned on the road facing upwind.

This accomplished, they climbed into their seats and both doors were closed and latched. They fastened and tightly cinched their seatbelts, and the men slipped on headsets. Logan switched the hot engine back on, waited for a few seconds, and eased in the throttle while the turbocharger spooled up with a whine. Then he let off the toe brakes and in a moment they were accelerating down the ribbon of gray pavement. At 60 knots the plane lifted smoothly into the air, and the pilot brought the wheels up. Ahead of them to the north rose the mountains that were their destination, already dominating the horizon.

"You don't get airsick, do you?" Logan asked Ranya, almost shouting. He lifted his right earpiece to hear her answer.

"No, I think I'll be okay today."

"Good, because we're not exactly flying a standard flight profile."

That turned out to be a major understatement. The plane, instead of climbing into the sky, dove and twisted into a dry creek bed with boulders and trees streaking past their wings.

Ranya sat behind Alex on the right side. She had an excellent view in all directions, blocked only by the forward headrests. If the Maule she had flown from Texas was a Jeep, the Cessna 210 was a BMW: faster, quieter and smoother. The Centurion's interior was much more elegantly appointed than the Spartan Maule 7. The four bucket seats were upholstered in honey-brown leather, with headrests and seatbelts like a luxury automobile.

They were nearly always below the level of the surrounding ridgelines, often shockingly close to red rock walls as they zoomed past. Logan had already explained that they were following a "radar route," keeping the plane in radar "shadows" below terrain. At times this meant that they could climb to over a thousand feet above the ground level, because mountains were blocking the known radar illumination, but most of the time they were below five hundred feet above ground level, and often below one hundred as trees flashed past. They hugged sandstone cliff walls so closely that Ranya thought they would clip off a wing.

At the end of what looked to be a box canyon, when it seemed certain that they were going to plow into the sheer rock face ahead, the plane pulled up hard at the last moment, cleared the wall and nosed over, leaving her floating weightless against her seat belt. In an instant they burst out over what seemed to be a mini-Grand Canyon of red and orange cliffs and buttes. The pilot immediately dove again and found a new streambed to follow, banking into its turns. She found it frightening and exhilarating at the same time, but she was not flying the plane, and she had no control over her fate. She could only trust her life to the pilot, and hope that Alex's faith in his flying ability was deserved.

Alex and Logan both wore headsets with stalk microphones by their chins, so she was excluded from their communications. Alex was also monitoring the plane's radios for any official notice of their low-level flight. All New Mexico law enforcement frequencies were pre-registered on their scanner. The Customs and Border Patrol plane's radios were equipped with the current federal encryption technology. They would be alerted immediately if they had drawn the attention of law enforcement at any level. She could see the large full-color GPS map screen in the center of the console between the two men, and could follow their route, which was laid out ahead of them.

Their destination was a section of a disused mining road on the edge of the Vedado ranch, fourteen miles south of the runway and the conference center. As the crow flies, this was only eighty miles from where they had taken off from the reservation, but their winding route snaked through the valleys and canyons, making wide diversions to avoid radar and populated areas. Even so, in less than an hour Logan reduced the throttle and put down the flaps, slowing the plane, which was already flying only 200 feet above ground level. Ranya looked ahead for something which might have been a runway, and saw nothing.

They were descending into another nameless valley, seemingly the hundredth of the flight. Halfway down the side of the mountain that rose to their left, buildings and other structures appeared before them, unpainted and rusting. The pilot made one more turn, and ahead of them, she saw the road, with a straight section a few hundred yards long at its end. She felt the wheels go down, as the ground came up to meet them. Lining up for the approach was a relief for her. It was the longest the plane had flown in a straight line during the entire flight.

The right side of the road was barren and spoiled, where the earth had been scraped bare. On the left side the mountain rose up steeply, covered in spruce and aspen. Beyond the strip mine, a line of heavy timber extended across the road. They touched down gently then braked hard, but instead of stopping, the pilot continued to rapidly taxi forward until the trees closed in around them from both sides.

She remembered hearing Logan say that the Centurion had a 39-foot wingspan, now she knew why that had been an important number. There were only a few feet beyond their wingtips to the thick forest on either side. The tops of saplings brushed the bottoms of their wings. When they were a hundred yards into the trees, Logan shut down the engine.

Motionless at last, swallowed by the silence, they pulled off their headsets, unbuckled and climbed down onto the old asphalt road. Ranya was thankful to put her feet back on terra firma. For much of the past hour, she had wondered if she would survive the flight. The ground immediately around them was fairly level, a rarity after what she had seen from the air. They were in a leafy green tunnel, the sky visible only above the road where the gently swaying branches did not quite meet. The warm air actually smelled sweet, like a living potpourri of fragrant balsams. Insects trilled and buzzed—cicadas perhaps.

As they had planned, their first order of business was to turn the plane around, to ready it to fly out on a moment's notice. The three of them once again walked behind the plane to the tail, and put all of their weight down on the horizontal stabilizer's unmoving front edge to lift the nose, so that they could spin the plane in its own radius. While turning the plane Ranya asked Logan, "Have you landed here before? How did you find this place? I'd never have thought you could land anywhere like this."

"That's the whole idea," he answered her cheerfully. "Sure, I've been here before. The trick is you never try to fly into a place like this without driving it first. At least I wouldn't! Not unless I lost the engine, but that's a different story—then you put her down wherever you can, and hope for the best. Anyway, I spotted this place from the air a couple years ago, and then I checked it out with a car. If a car can drive it at seventy miles an hour, then you're good to go. That's all we need, sixty knots of ground speed, and some clear space in front.

"Remember, I used to play the smuggler in training exercises. My goal was to land, unload and take off before the helicopters could catch me. Sometimes I'd just land and hide, and wait for them to fly past. They'd have to be right on my tail to know where I stopped. With trees like this, they'd have to be literally right on top to see the plane. Any side angle at all, and we're invisible from above—all they see is trees. If I got just a few miles ahead of them and I knew where I was landing, I could beat them. Not all the time, but often enough." He smiled at her, as they finished turning the plane. "It got pretty exciting at times. Like today."

In order to slide the disassembled UAV out of the plane, the right side door had to be removed. The UAV's separate wing section and fuselage were stowed from the extreme end of the cargo area, up between the headrests of the rear seats. Logan used a small hammer and a drift punch to tap the pins up out of their hinges while Alex held to door steady. When the hinges were free, he set the door carefully on the ground. Logan tilted the right side seats all the way forward and down, and gently maneuvered the long UAV components out of the plane.

Both men immediately went to work assembling the UAV, while Ranya stood guard with her Dragunov. The bottoms of the drone parts were painted sky blue, their tops were coyote brown. The wing section fit into a notch across the top of the fuselage, forming a cross, and was bolted in place. A pair of wheels was attached in front, and then the propeller, rudder and elevator were quickly installed. In twenty minutes, the Pelican UAV was ready for flight, and the men were running systems checks. The UAV came with a pair of laptops, a remote control console, and a UHF radio and whip antenna for its telemetry and video links. When the electronics were powered up, they were able to pan and tilt the video camera protruding from the belly of the little plane, and swing the rudder and elevators from side to side and up and down.

As an assistant dean of admissions at the University of New Mexico, Inez Ibarra Trejo could have used the perfectly adequate gym right on campus. Nevertheless, the trim fifty year old made the two-mile drive downtown to the elite *Club De La Buena Salud* women's fitness center every weekday at lunchtime.

The reason that she rarely missed her workouts was because the private women's club was one of Albuquerque's most productive sources of useful high-level gossip. Besides being a dean at the university, Inez Trejo was also a clandestine member of Felix Magón's secret Revolutionary Council.

Today she fiddled with the Nautilus machines, pretending to work on her shoulders, while listening carefully to a conversation between two of her acquaintances. Family Court Judge Galatea Obregon was pedaling a stationary bicycle next to her unlikely friend Frederica Chupatintas, who was the second in charge of the FBI's local Field Office.

Inez Trejo knew that Chupatintas also had a perfectly fine gym to use in the Federal Building only two blocks away, but she frequently complained that the male-dominated venue presented a "hostile environment," and said that she felt more comfortable at the all-female and Latina-oriented *Club de la Buena Salud.* Comrade Inez assumed incorrectly that Chupatintas also belonged to the club in order to pick up useful human intelligence, but in fact, that rationale had never crossed the woman's blissfully naive mind.

Neither lady was putting much effort into cycling; instead, they were engrossed in office chitchat. Both women were wearing stylish pastel-colored warm-up suits, which could not conceal that Chupatintas had skinny stork-legs, or that Galatea Obregon had a *culo* like two sacks of cement, and thighs to match. Even though she was almost a decade older than these two women, Inez Trejo took satisfaction from knowing that she was still in better shape than either of them, despite a few extra lines on her face, and her graying hair.

Inez was half-following some story of FBI office politics, but when she heard one of the names being discussed, she choked out a gasp and let go of her lat bar, causing the small stack of chrome weights to come crashing down. The name she overheard was Alexandro Garabanda! She quickly moved over to the curling machine, just a few feet behind the stationary bicycles, where she could hear every word.

"Oh, he's not really such a bad guy," said Frederica Chupatintas. "Who knows, maybe this diversity workshop will do him some good. It might broaden his horizons."

"I don't know," replied the judge. "These gay-bashers only take the training because they have to. It's never from the heart. A week in Santa Fe doesn't change them—it just teaches them how to be better at pretending."

"Well, even if they're pretending, isn't that an improvement?"

"Maybe. We'll see in six months, when I review their case."

"His ex-wife moved to San Diego, you know."

"Of course I know—I approved it. She's marrying her girlfriend, the one who whacked him at the picnic."

Chupatintas said, "I'm not sorry that she's gone. Don't get me wrong, I'm pro-gay all the way, but that Gretchen Bosch was one scary chick."

"That's quite a value judgment, Frederica," the judge said in a mildly scolding tone. "At least their little boy will be raised without all of that heterosexist baggage. Say, did you know that he was adopted? I've seen the original documents—it's really *quite* the soap opera. Brian Garabanda's birth mother was a gringo traitor, an Arab terrorist! But all of the records are sealed, so Brian will never know he was adopted."

"His mother was an Arab terrorist? You're joking!"

"No, for real. Her name is Ranya Bardiwell, she's Lebanese."

"You're right, that does sound like a *telenovela*," tittered Chupatintas. "So, what do you think the odds are of Garabanda ever getting visitation rights again? Believe me Galatea, he's far from the worst of the male agents I've dealt with."

"Hmm...realistically? I'd say very slim. Slim to none. It won't help Brian's social development to shuttle back and forth between two stable lesbian parents, and a bitter, heterosexist male father figure. Besides, Alexandro Garabanda's not his biological father anyway. There's no blood connection, so Brian won't really be missing anything."

Their conversation continued, but Inez Trejo didn't hear it, couldn't follow it. Ranya Bardiwell and Alexandro Garabanda, mentioned in the same conversation! The last time Comrade Inez had seen Ranya Bardiwell, the Arab girl's mettle was being tested against a wall, by Comandante Guzman's staged firing squad. The only time that she had ever seen Alexandro Garabanda was in the surveillance photographs from the cemetery, the ones that she had passed on to Basilio Ramos. These photos had led to the Jewish traitor Luis Carvahal being burned at the stake after the Rally for Social Justice. In her wildest dreams, she would not have imagined a connection between Bardiwell and Garabanda. This would require closer scrutiny, much closer.

When they were satisfied with the UAV, the pilot looked straight up at the patch of blue between the trees, and then checked his watch. "Al, it's only 12:30. Do you want to wait awhile, or put her up now? We've got weather coming in this afternoon, what do you think? Fly now, or wait? It might be too early. We might miss some of the jets if they're not all here yet…but on the other hand, we don't want to get caught by bad weather."

"We can bring it back and refuel it, can't we?"

"Sure, I guess so, but the longer it's up, the greater the chance of being compromised, one way or the other. And if we wait too long, we might get stuck in here if the weather turns nasty."

"How high over the place is it going to fly?" asked Alex. "You're sure they won't see it, right?"

"Pelicans should be 8,000 feet higher than the people they're spying on. Any lower than 6,000 feet above ground level, and there's a chance it might be spotted. Remember, the ranch is already at 6,000, so we're really talking about flying 14,000 feet above sea level."

"So if it's at 8,000 over the ground, it won't be seen or heard?"

"Above ground level, yeah, that's right. They won't see it. But the downlink transmission…that's another story. They might catch it, depending on what they're using up there at Vedado. Most scanners won't pick it up, it's pretty damn tricky. It frequency hops and transmits in bursts, all of that good stuff. It was made for the military."

"But even so, they still might catch it?"

Logan stared at the drone, and then glanced up at Alex. "You have to assume so. There's always a chance. We don't know what kind of electronic warfare gear they're using up at Vedado."

"Then let's fly now. Let's just get it done. Let's go see who's there."

The Pelican's miniature rotary engine was chosen for its silky smooth running, and when the little plane went zipping down the road, it was surprisingly quiet. Alex and Logan walked behind the taxiing drone until it was clear of the trees, and set for its takeoff run. Logan made final checks of the plane, the radio transmitter and his controls, lined the drone up perfectly by hand, and then looked at Alex and said, "That's it. She's ready."

"Okay then, let's do it."

After tearing down the road at full power for no more than 75 yards, Logan used his remote control "stick" to lift the Pelican into the air, its powerful gas motor dragging it aloft at a steep angle. When it was clear of the immediate obstacles around the old mining camp, he switched from manual control to a programmed ascent.

The plane was quickly lost from sight, corkscrewing up into the sky to its predetermined operational altitude, before it set off on the 14-mile flight to its station above the Vedado Ranch Conference Center, Wayne Parker's mansion, and his mile-long jet runway. It needed no further input from the ground after Logan sent its flight plan. Until it was given new commands, it would fly at the ordered altitude and then orbit above the GPS coordinates that were already programmed into its microchip brain.

The two men walked back down the lane into the woods and climbed into the Cessna, where the laptops and the radio could be run off the airplane's power supply. Only the system's whip antenna remained outside, connected by a white coaxial cable. On one side of Logan's screen they could see the UAV's current position and flight data, overlaid on a color GPS map. On the other half of the screen, digital representations of an altimeter, compass, air speed indicator and other displays gave the appearance of a virtual cockpit instrument panel.

On the second laptop, they could see the Pelican's camera-eye view in live streaming color video. This screen also showed the key flight information, in text and numbers overlaying the camera view. Both laptops could toggle between any of the screens, as desired, so that both men could see the same images. In twenty minutes the Pelican arrived over its first target, the Vedado Ranch's six thousand foot jet-capable runway.

Ranya remained standing outside the Cessna with her Dragunov rifle, providing their security. Besides the ten rounds in her rifle, she had two extra loaded magazines in her leather fanny pack, which she wore toward the front. If trouble found them, the Dragunov was their most powerful weapon.

Mommy and Gretchen were in the other room, with the door closed. That meant they wanted "private time," and he should not bother them unless the house was on fire. That's what Gretchen had told him a long time ago: not unless the house was on fire. And she meant it too. Once when they were having private time, she had come out in her bath robe with a very scary red face, shouting at him to shut up and stop crying. So even though they weren't in a real house, Brian knew that he should not do anything that was loud while they were having private time.

Brian was watching Sponge Bob on the television in the living room, but boring commercials came on, and he got up from the carpet and walked over to his toy bag, the one that he packed back in Albakirky. He had already played with everything in the bag ten times. He looked out of the big sliding windows at Sandy Eggo. He liked that name, even though he had seen a lot of signs and he knew that it was spelled San Diego. He was a good speller, but he still thought Sandy Eggo was a better name.

The two glass doors were not locked, and he could go out on the little patio if he wanted to. He didn't, because the little patio scared him to death. Out there, it was very windy all the time. He could look through the railings straight down at the street, down to where the cars looked smaller than Hot Wheels, and people looked like little bugs.

Brian knew that Spiderman wouldn't be afraid. Spiderman could swing right down the side of this building, and across the street to the other tall buildings. But Spiderman could shoot sticky spider webs out of his hands, and Brian could not.

They were just staying in this place for a week or two, that's what mommy said. Then they were going to get a real house, but with green grass and not just pebbles like in Albakirky. Brian didn't like being so far up in the sky. It didn't scare him, except outside on the balcony. He just didn't like it. Yesterday they drove over a bridge across Sandy Eggo Bay that was even higher than this building. Through the big windows, he could see part of the Bay, and even over to the ocean, but not that high bridge.

Through the windows, he could see lots of other tall buildings, and between them, there were airplanes flying on their way down to the Sandy Eggo airport. They all went the same way, from the right side to the left side. They were flying so low, sometimes they were flying lower than the buildings. They flew right over a highway full of cars, and then they landed. The pilots had to be really good pilots, to always land on the runway, and miss all of those buildings. Airplane pilot was a good job, one of the best, almost as good as astronaut or FBI Agent.

Brian knew that his Daddy flew in airplanes a lot. Sometimes he flew in small airplanes, when he was doing FBI work, catching crooks. He flew in the big airplanes with lots of people on them when he traveled to cities that were far away, as far away as Sandy Eggo was from Albakirky. He flew on airplanes just like these airplanes that were landing all day long, one after the other. The airplanes were close enough to see clearly, but far enough away that he could hold out his pointer finger, and his finger was bigger than the airplane. He wondered if his Daddy was on one of those airplanes that were landing every minute.

He had not seen him since that day they went to the toy store, except for a minute on the playground by his old house. He wondered if his Daddy missed him, as much as he missed his Daddy. He wondered if his Daddy had already forgotten about him, and that made him hurt inside, that made him feel like crying. He wished that he knew his Daddy's phone number. Mommy left her pocketbook on the low table in the middle of the room, and her little silver phone was in it. Brian wished that he could remember his Daddy's phone number. But it was no good wishing. He didn't know how to use Mommy's silver phone, and he didn't know his Daddy's phone number.

He just hoped that his Daddy was in one of those airplanes that were landing every minute. He hoped his Daddy would come to Sandy Eggo and get him.

30

"I count fourteen," said Alex Garabanda. "What kind are they?" His laptop's screen showed a long line of corporate jets parked nose to tail on the taxiway, which ran parallel to the wider asphalt runway.

Logan, sitting in the pilot's seat with the other computer on his lap, operated the drone's camera with input commands. The picture zoomed in until only one jet at a time was visible on the screen. A white cursor in the shape of a cross appeared on the ground. He could move it with laptop's touch pad, and then command the camera to aim at the designated spot. The Pelican was not flying directly over the runway, but was filming slant-wise from an angle. "Hmm…the first one is Gulfstream G-100, that's a 9 seater. Last time I checked, they go for over two hundred million blue bucks. Nice clear tail number, can you read it?"

"I got it." The plane's "tail number" was actually painted on the side of the jet engines, which were located on either side of the fuselage, between the wings and the tail. Garabanda copied the plane's number onto a notepad, as a backup in case anything happened to the computers, which were saving all of the transmitted imagery.

"But how are you going to know who came on it? The number will just tell you the corporation that owns the jet, and most of them are probably just charters anyway."

"Don't worry, Logan, I'll find out who the VIPs are. That'll be easy."

"I hope so—otherwise this is all a waste of time. Okay, the next one is a Cessna Citation. Hard to believe the same company made this Centurion. You get the number?"

"Got it."

"There must be a couple billion blue bucks worth of private jets down there today," said the pilot.

"I guess it's not every day you have a dozen friends drop in for lunch…in their own jets."

"You'd be surprised. I've been places and seen thirty or forty private jets stacked up like this. Palm Springs, the Super Bowl, the Key Largo Club… Alex, the jet set have their own world. We just live in it, but we don't count, not really. We're so far beneath them, that we're too small to notice. We're like the ants under their feet."

"Except for today," observed Garabanda. "Today, they're below us for once."

Logan continued moving the ground image down the runway, past the hangars along the eastern end. "Look, four Blackhawks. That would be the security, I suppose." The four-bladed helicopters were lined up abreast, their tails toward the side of the main hangar. This was at the end of the runway closest to the mansion, which was built on higher ground two miles away.

"The Blackhawks belong to the state guard," noted Logan. "I'll switch the radio to the cockpit speaker. If they go on alert, we'll hear it on the scanner."

"Those guys must be the Falcon Battalion," said Alex. "Ranya was right." He looked outside of the Cessna to where she stood watch, the Dragunov held horizontally at waist level, its weight supported by the peculiar necktie sling around the back of her neck. She was taking her job seriously, walking around the plane, looking in all directions. Her back was presently turned toward him, and with some pleasure he noted her long legs, and the sweet swelling of her hips below the narrowness of her waist, and the roundness of her—

He stopped himself short. Why, you dirty old man! She's young enough to be your daughter. Still…

Logan said, "I'll zoom in all the way—let's check 'em out."

Alex's attention snapped back to his laptop's screen. "M-16s and brown berets. See the silver shining on their berets? That's the Falcons for sure."

"You think they're expecting trouble?" asked Logan.

"Ahh, I doubt it. I think they're mostly for show. They're probably Magón's way of showing he's in charge of the New Mexico Milicia, that he has his own military units that answer directly to him. All of the guests had to see the Falcons, after they landed. See how they're right next to the airport road?"

After studying the troops and their four helicopters, Logan continued moving the cross-shaped cursor from jet to jet, until he had captured clear digital video of each aircraft's tail number, and in several cases, the corporate logos painted on their fuselages. When he finished, he said, "Okay, let's recover the UAV, and get the hell out of here."

"Hold on," said Alex, "While it's up, let's go see what's happening at the conference center. Swing the camera over two klicks to the southeast."

"Okay—I've already got it pre-registered. Here we go." The screen blurred for a few seconds, and then it refocused with razor-sharp clarity. "Nice place, is that a manmade lake?" Logan pulled the camera lens back for a wider view. Between the runway and the ranch's main buildings there was a kidney-shaped mile-wide alpine lake, glimmering silver with reflected mid day sunlight. The lake was surrounded by meadows and then by pine forests, which ascended the slopes of the surrounding mountains.

"I'm not sure. It has a dam there on the south side, but I don't know how big it was before. It's pretty, isn't it?"

"Looks like a slice of heaven. So this is what a few billion dollars can buy you." The camera continued panning past the lake.

Garabanda studied the picture and said, "Nobody's at the conference center, unless they're all inside. But there're no vehicles outside. Let's check out the mansion."

The camera view zoomed away for a wide angle, centered on the Wayne Parker residence, and zoomed back in. Logan said, "Nice place! It looks like a damn castle."

"It was a damn castle," replied Alex. "Wayne Parker had it dismantled and brought over, stone by stone. It's from Italy. Sweet, huh?"

"Whew! All it takes is money..."

"A *lot* of money."

"Well, there they are," said Logan. "The party's on the front porch."

The "front porch" was a terrace balcony that was at least two hundred feet wide, overlooking the sparkling mile-wide lake, which lay downhill across verdant alpine meadows. Seen from a slight angle in wide view, the people were barely recognizable dots.

"Let's go in and see if we know anybody," suggested Alex. "Hey, is this all being saved?"

"Yep, all of it. Everything we see is saved to the hard drive." Both men switched their screens to show the current camera view of the ground, 8,000 feet below the Pelican.

"Okay, let's zoom on down and see what we can see. Hmm…check out all the waiters. Looks like they're not holding back on the catering." There appeared to be more servants than guests, many of them carrying silver trays that flashed in the sun. White uniformed bartenders behind a long table upended dark bottles, keeping the trays filled with fresh flutes of champagne.

"Hey, now look at that!" Logan exclaimed. He switched the cursor from a cross to a white box, and put it around one person. "See him? The fat guy with white hair."

"I see him," said Alex. "Is that the closest you can go?"

"Uh huh, the zoom is maxed out. The only way to get in tighter is to drop some altitude."

"No, forget it, this is close enough. Yeah, that's Senator Kelly. Man, he's gotten fat! What a whale! Don't get between him and the buffet table," Alex joked.

"Or the bar."

"No doubt."

The radio scanner locked on a strong signal.

"Vedado radio, this is Gulfstream november whiskey zulu, seven niner three, over."

"Whiskey zulu, this is Vedado radio, over."

"Vedado, I'm twenty miles east at eighteen thousand feet. Request clearance, over."

"Gulfstream whiskey zulu, you're cleared for approach."

Logan said, "Sounds like we've got a late arrival."

"Yeah, we can check him out in a minute." The camera view remained locked on the mansion's wide terrace.

"Look, is that Senator Montaine? It sure as hell is! Your informant was right on the money. Kelly and Montaine—now there's a matched pair of bipartisan traitors."

Alex smirked. "I wish this Pelican came with little Hellfire missiles. I'd throw down some term limits right now."

"Yeah, *'You're fired,'* right?" Both men laughed, and Logan said, "Hey, who's the old geezer in the wheelchair, with the funky glasses? Is that who I think it is?"

"I don't recognize him," Alex responded.

"Well I do. That's Peter Kosimos, I'm almost sure of it. I didn't know he was in a wheelchair though—I always thought he was in good shape for his age."

"What is he, pushing ninety? I guess his staff can keep a secret. Who's he talking to?"

"Oh my God, it's Orozco!" exclaimed the FBI agent. "Pascual Orozco is here." Orozco was identifiable by his signature long white chin whiskers.

"Wait a minute—I thought he was leading a peasant revolt in Mexico?"

"Well," Alex remarked sarcastically, "it doesn't look like he's hiding out in the Sierra Madre today. Looks like he's doing a little networking with the rich and famous instead."

"And washing the shrimp cocktail down with champagne," noted the pilot. "Oh man, he is *so* busted! This isn't going to help his image. Anytime I've ever seen a picture of Orozco, he's wearing blue jeans and a peasant shirt. Now here he is in a suit, looking like a capitalist pig. It just doesn't match his Ho Chi Minh beard."

Alex laughed, "Ho Chi Minh, or Colonel Sanders?"

"Who's Orozco talking to? Who's the couple?"

"I'm not sure, but the man with the wrap-around shades might be our own ambassador to Mexico. Joe Calavera—he's one of the President's old college buddies. Well, I guess it figures he'd be here."

Logan asked, "Didn't Calavera marry a Mexican heiress?"

"Yeah, he did. Right after he was appointed ambassador. That must be her in the red sequins. She's not much to look at, they call her 'horse-face,' but she's worth three hundred *billion* blue bucks. High society doesn't get any higher than that! Her family owns about a quarter of

Mexico. I think she's the second or third richest woman in the world, that's what I read. So I guess that makes Joe Calavera the world's richest ambassador."

"I wonder what their prenuptial contract looks like?" asked Logan. "Become the ambassador to Mexico, and marry a Mexican billionaire. Or is that billionairess? Is that even a word? Anyway, it's pretty friggin' unbelievable."

"Truth is stranger than fiction—you can't make up a story like that," said Alex.

"I'm *sure* that Ambassador Calavera only has America's best interests at heart. No conflict of interest there."

"Well Logan, I guess it all depends on your point of view. I mean, if you don't believe in 'obsolete concepts' like independent sovereign nations, what's the difference who's paying you? Joe Calavera's been a big backer of the North American Community from day one. I guess he's just collecting his reward with horse-face."

"Look, look, here comes Félix Magón! This keeps getting better and better! I guess he's gotten over his grief for Governor Deleon."

"Yeah, the official mourning period must be over," said Alex. "What's it been, four whole days?"

Even from the current high camera angle, Felix Magón was easily recognizable by his slick black pompadour, wide pineapple face, and stubby physique. Unlike at the Civic Plaza "Rally for Social Justice," today was apparently not a good day for wearing a traditional Hispanic guyaberra shirt. Like the rest of the VIP attendees, *el gobernador* was dressed in a dark suit and tie for the Vedado conference.

While they watched, an aide handed Peter Kosimos a cell phone. After a brief phone conversation, Kosimos spoke with the man, and they both left the terrace reception. Kosimos steered his motorized chair down a long ramp to the driveway in front of the castle, and then into the side of a waiting van. Once the white van's own ramp was retracted and its doors were closed, it departed from the Parker mansion with a pair of white SUVs in the front and in the rear.

Logan asked, "Should we follow Kosimos, or stay at the party? Or should we just pack it up and bring the Pelican back? I think we've got plenty, don't you? I mean, we've already got the tail numbers, and lots of famous faces."

Alex pondered this, looking out through the Cessna's windshield at the surrounding pine forest. "No, let's wait until the new Gulfstream lands, and see who's still coming." They had mentally tuned out the intermittent radio chatter from the inbound jet, while they were studying the outdoor luncheon at the Parker mansion.

Logan said, "He should almost be down, let's take another look at the runway."

The video image held steady on a medium wide angle, over the tire-marked touchdown point on the eastern end of the runway near the line of hangars. While they watched, a white corporate jet appeared, and slid across the screen. A hazy puff of gray smoke briefly appeared as the wheels contacted the tarmac. Logan clicked the cursor directly on top of the jet, and the camera locked on and followed it to the end of the runway.

A half-dozen SUVs and vans surrounded the jet when it came to a stop at the end of the strip. One black SUV pulled in near the right front side of the Gulfstream, just ahead of the wing. Alex and Logan watched the cabin hatch open outward and swing down, forming steps. The border patrol pilot zoomed in to see who the new guest was, who deserved all of the attention and security. After a pair of bodyguards or aides exited the jet, they saw the still-familiar face of Dave Whitman, the former President of the United States. Even from a downward-looking camera, at a slant-range of almost two miles, there was no mistaking the unruly shock of gray hair, the puffy face, and the bulbous nose. He walked between bodyguards to the black SUV, and disappeared inside of it.

Both of the men sitting in the cockpit of the Cessna 210, fourteen miles to the south, were momentarily stunned into silence. Finally Alex asked, "Is that who I think it is?"

"Ay-up," replied Logan. "It's old Weasel Dave himself."

"Maybe it's a stand-in, a double," Alex suggested. "Sometimes he uses a double, for security."

"Then the double is somewhere else today, being seen. You know Whitman can't miss a party like this. Now we *can't* leave—this is too important."

Alex considered. They already had a large amount of video evidence stored on the two computer hard drives. The Pelican could remain aloft for another hour, but the longer they were transmitting radio commands to it, the greater their chance of discovery. At last he decided, "Let's follow Whitman back to the castle, and see everybody kiss his fat ass. That'll be worth filming, big time. Then we'll go."

"All right, sounds like a plan. They'll be there in five minutes."

However, the black SUV in the center of the little convoy didn't drive directly to Wayne Parker's mansion, as they expected it to. Instead, it forked off onto another asphalt road, leading around the side of the oblong alpine lake between the runway and the mansion. While they watched, the other vehicles in the convoy slowed and stopped, and the black SUV pulled around them and went ahead by itself. The other vehicles then followed at a distance. On the far side of the lake, on a grassy strip between the blue water and the dark green fir trees, the black SUV pulled off to the side of the road, close behind a white full-sized van. The other vans, pickups and SUVs stayed several hundred yards back from these two vehicles.

The side doors of the white van opened, and a ramp extended outward. Peter Kosimos steered his motorized chair out of the van, as David Whitman strode up to him, bent over, and the men exchanged prolonged handshakes.

The former President appeared to speak to his nearest bodyguard, and this man seemed to speak into his wrist. The other bodyguards immediately began backing away from the two principal VIPs, leaving them alone by the lake, within an outlying ring of security.

"Can you believe it?" said Alex excitedly, "Dave Whitman and Peter Kosimos, together, in private! One on one! Oh, man, this is friggin' awesome—this is history!"

"I'd give my left nut to hear what they were saying. Whitman wouldn't fly in just to say 'howdy' to Peter Kosimos."

"You can't get any closer?" asked Alex.

"No, the camera's already at max zoom. It wouldn't make any difference anyway—we still wouldn't be able to hear them."

"Logan, if we could just get in a little closer, there might be a way to 'hear' them. We could have a lip reader analyze the video, and tell us what they're saying."

"Are you serious?"

"Sure, we use lip readers sometimes, its court approved. Sometimes all we have is video. Sometimes a wire doesn't work, or the audio tape is unclear. Could you bring the Pelican down low enough?"

"She's at 8,000 feet AGL now. We might be able to get enough resolution from a mile, but it'd be risky. Is it worth it?"

Alex Garabanda thought about this for a few seconds. "To find out what Dave Whitman and Peter Kosimos have to say to each other? Yeah, I think so. Definitely."

"Okay then, down we go." Logan made the appropriate guidance inputs on his laptop, hit enter, and a compressed transmission was sent up to the UAV in milliseconds. The image of the two men by the lake slowly rotated and grew larger as the Pelican descended in a slow spiral.

Former President Dave Whitman walked beside the electric wheelchair, on a cinder pathway that led along the perimeter of the lake. Peter Kosimos asked him, "Did you bring the Secret Service here, Mr. President? Was that wise? Can you trust them?"

"Oh, hell no. I left them back in California this morning. Wayne provided this bunch, along with the jet. I'll be back in LA in two hours. For the record, I'm watching a movie, a private screening at a director's house. You know him—Stephen's covering for me. Hey, even I can sneak off the radar once in a while."

"I understand," sighed Kosimos. "It's so difficult to have any private life at all."

"Tell me about it," laughed the former President, whose sexual peccadilloes were infamous, and had almost led to him being thrown out of office.

"I must say, Wayne has been absolutely fabulous in arranging this conference," said Kosimos. Even thirty years after becoming a United States citizen, the Romanian-born multi-billionaire retained his Eastern European accent, and stilted speech patterns. Although legally an American, he spent most of each year traveling between the dozen homes and offices his foundations maintained on every continent except Antarctica. The 87-year-old man's legs were withered, and his head hung crookedly, but his voice was as clear and strong as his mind. "Wayne is a prophet who is not appreciated in his own land. I only hope that one day, he'll be recognized as the world hero that he is."

Speaking confidentially with Kosimos, the former President dropped his usual folksy Southern accent. "I couldn't agree more. Did you know he's donating this entire ranch to the UN, as a World Conservancy Site? A million acres..." Whitman paused and looked far across the lake, and up at the timber-covered mountains which rose around them.

"Mr. President, Wayne's philanthropy is...beyond measure. His actions in the service of humanity are almost without parallel, but he is only ridiculed and mocked in his own country. Yet despite all of the attacks on his character, he's been helping to lay the foundation of global governance for decades now."

"One could say the same about you, Peter."

"Oh, you flatter me, Mr. President."

"Please, call me Dave."

"Thank you...*Dave*. I must say, I'm quite honored to be on a first-name-basis with the next Secretary General of the United Nations."

Whitman smiled broadly. "Now Peter, that's just a rumor—unless you know something I don't know. As an American, I can't even be nominated for Secretary General. Nobody from the Permanent Five of the Security Council can."

"I assure you Dave, that is *not* going to be an impediment. That rule is unwritten; it was only a gentleman's agreement among the P-5, from the UN's first days in San Francisco. Given the extraordinary financial crisis facing the world today, that unwritten rule will be set aside—and why not? The people of every nation see you not as an American, but as the leading citizen of the entire world! Mr. President, *Dave*—if there is one man the world needs at this moment in history, it's you!"

The former President bit his lower lip, attempting to keep a somber face while hiding his delight. Ever since he had stepped down from the Presidency after his eight years in the White House, it had been his ultimate goal to become the leader of the United Nations.

"So, you think it's possible for me to become the next Secretary General?"

"Not 'possible,' Mr. President, it's a certainty. The way has been prepared—you have only to agree to serve."

"Well, my only remaining ambition in life is to help the people, all of the world's people. So of course I would serve."

"Good, good. You don't know how happy that makes me, to hear that! I feel that such a burden has lifted, knowing that the torch will be passed on."

The former President horse-laughed, "I'll admit, it makes me kinda' happy too!"

"Excellent. Now, when you become Secretary General, and I think you will, you *must* use your powers of persuasion to achieve our next and *most* important goal."

"And…that is?"

"The only way we'll be able to end this global depression is if we harmonize the economies of all of the nations. That means moving toward one currency, and one central bank. The people of the world *must* understand that the global economy is so interconnected today, that it functions like one single engine. Mr. President, one engine cannot run with pistons of different sizes, all running at different speeds!"

Kosimos continued with his pitch. "Dave, I'm not proud of the fact that I accumulated billions of dollars by speculating on those currency differences. It's not a productive use of capital, to say the least. But at least since then, I've tried to use my fortune to advance social justice around the globe, the entire globe. And now, as one who understands these economic differences, these imbalances, I'm telling you, the time has finally come—we *must* harmonize the world's economies! And that means one currency, and one central bank. There's no other way out of this depression."

"Peter, I'm with you, but trust me on this: most Americans will never accept it. They'll never go along with a central world bank. Not in a million years. It's a complete non-starter."

"Ah, but Mr. President, we already have it! At least, we have the nucleus, and that is enough to begin."

"You mean the World Bank?"

"No, no—I mean the BIS, the Bank of International Settlements, in Geneva. It already exists—it just needs greater statutory authority."

The two men came to a white marble bench along the path, near the shimmering blue lake waters. The former President said, "Let's stop here. I could use a rest. You know, the old ticker's not what it used to be."

"Yes, of course." Kosimos steered his motorized cart into a turn and stopped beside the end of the stone bench.

Whitman sat down, breathing heavily. "Peter, you know I'd love to see a world bank, a UN world bank, world money, global taxes, all of that. I just don't think it'll fly in the states."

"Even now? Even with the American economy in a shambles? With twenty percent unemployment and hyperinflation? Dave, even Americans will see the need for a single world currency, if the idea is communicated effectively. And I think that you can sell the idea—in fact, I *know* that you can." Kosimos chuckled, his weak laugh turning into a wheeze. "You might say I'm *banking* on it. Pardon my poor attempt at humor."

"But how can I sell *any* new currency? The dollar's become a joke, so why would Americans accept a new global currency to replace it? They don't trust any paper money any more, not after the dollar collapse, and this blue buck fiasco. The federal government can pass all the laws it wants to, but they can't make people trust paper money! Not after what they've been through. And outlawing gold, well, that was a *huge* mistake. That just showed how out of touch with reality Washington is, and how powerless they are. That was stupid, and I said so before the gold ban was passed." Whitman leaned down and picked up a handful of pebbles, and began to toss them into the lake twenty feet away, sending out intersecting rings of ripples from each splash.

"I agree, that was a mistake, it was not well thought out. There could even be a place for a certain amount of gold backing for the new world currency. At least at first—as a selling point."

"Peter, we can talk about finance later, I need to change the subject. I can't stay, I can't even drop by Wayne's place—it's too high profile. I'm speaking at UCLA tonight, and I'm getting right back on that jet as soon as we're done here. Have you spoken with Orozco and Magón yet, about the Southwestern plan?"

"You mean the Pakistan Solution?"

"That's what they're calling it now?" the former President asked, raising an eyebrow.

"Informally, yes. The basic plan is as we've discussed. Voluntary population transfer, and an autonomous region status for the Southwest—but within the North American Community framework, of course. Yes, that seems to be the direction in which we're moving. As far as the new boundary, the main sticking points are Denver and Las Vegas, and where the line will be drawn across Texas."

Whitman adamantly stated, "We need to keep all of Colorado, Utah and Nevada, or it'll never fly in Congress—and the President will veto it for sure. I know her mind on this—the political cost would be too high."

"Orozco and Magón want Denver, Las Vegas and Houston," countered Peter Kosimos. "They say that's the price of peace in the rest of the United States."

"Houston's out of the question—the Texans will fight."

"Mr. President, where the line is drawn across Texas will be part of the final negotiated settlement. The Anglos in Texas will just have to accept—"

"Peter, you don't know the Texans! They won't accept any settlement that puts the line east of Houston—there's just no way. Houston and Dallas have to stay in the United States, and that's non-negotiable. Tell them to draw the line at San Antonio, and make it a border town. Split it down the middle, we can live with that."

"Take it easy, I'm only a messenger here, just an 'honest broker.' I'll raise your concerns this afternoon with Orozco and Magón."

"Do they really expect to get any of Colorado? If we hold out for the Utah and Colorado lines to be our new southern border—"

"They want to keep Denver," said Kosimos. "A 'Berlin solution' has been discussed, with the state of Colorado remaining in the USA, but with Denver having a special status, with a corridor running south."

"Houston, Denver and Las Vegas? They're asking for too much! It'll never fly."

"Nothing has been carved in stone Mr. President—those are only the opening bids. This is just an informal preliminary conference, to explore the options. In any event, nothing will be decided before the Constitutional Convention in September."

One hundred yards behind the former President and the billionaire currency speculator, a bodyguard holding a pair of powerful binoculars was scanning beyond them and across the lake, searching for even the slightest hint or sign of a concealed sniper. The chance of a sniper attack was minimal, because Kosimos and Whitman's conversation by the side of the lake was unplanned, the spot being spontaneously chosen by both men. No sniper could have known the location ahead of time, and gotten into position in advance of their arrival. Besides, the lake was over a mile wide, nearly 2,000 yards, and therefore it was beyond the extreme limit of even the most skillful sniper, with the most advanced rifle. Behind the two men on the landward side, the meadows and woods swarmed with dozens of security men.

The marsh across the lake would have been a perfect hiding place for a sniper, so even considering the great distance the bodyguard was diligent in his search. He was a professional. Even so, he became mildly distracted by a stilt-legged white egret, walking in some shallows half way across the lake, searching for a small fish to spear.

They were both searching, the bodyguard mused. He guessed that in the local food chain, these small egrets might also have to fear becoming the meal of yet another predator, perhaps a hawk or falcon. The bodyguard raised his binoculars, wondering if he might spot a highflying raptor. With his standard procedure adapted from searching for human enemies to searching for a predatory bird, he methodically quartered the empty blue sky above the lake, and was rewarded with a fleeting image of a passing …a passing what? What the heck was that? It was no bird, he knew that much! He tried to find his target again, scanning with his binoculars, while calling his own supervisor with his walkie-talkie, even though the man was sitting in an SUV only twenty yards away.

"Harry, have we got any air assets up?" There were several different security outfits represented here on the ranch today beside their own: Wayne Parker's, Peter Kosimos's, the New Mexico "Falcon" Milicia, some Blackhawk helicopters from the state guard…maybe whatever he saw up there belonged to one of the other outfits. Maybe he was just being paranoid, and had only glimpsed the passing of a small plane at very high altitude. But the airspace above the Vedado Ranch was supposed to be closed today, except for the arriving jets…

He thumbed the send button on his radio again. "Harry, I just saw an airplane or a drone up there, I'm pretty sure. Anybody here have a drone up, over?" It couldn't be ruled out. It might even be the Secret Service, miffed that their charge had slipped his leash for the afternoon. Maybe they had tracked him from LA, and were putting a protective "eye in the sky" above him.

31

The Cessna's radio scanner jumped onto the new transmission. An unknown voice speaking in English flatly said, *"...saw an airplane or a drone up there, I'm pretty sure. Anybody have a drone up, over?"*

"We're busted! They're onto us," said Alex.

"Oh crap. Sounds like they got it visual, not electronic."

Then a different American voice replied to the first man. *"I'll check, but I don't think it's ours. Let me make some calls. Let's not go off half-cocked, over."*

"Should we pull back our principals, over?"

"Let's make sure of what we've got first. Break, break—tacnet four two—anybody on tacnet see an airplane or a drone up there?"

Waiting outside the jet hangars, Comandante Ramos was beckoned to his commo truck by Lieutenant Almeria, and he hurried over to the silver-gray Toyota SUV.

"What is it?" he asked, absorbing Almeria's excitement.

"They're talking about a drone. One of Parker's security men may have spotted something above us. They don't know if it's friendly."

"We were never briefed on a drone, were we?" asked Ramos.

"Absolutely not."

"Then tell them that! I'll get the pilots ready. If there's a drone, then it has a controller. If it's not on a satellite link, then it has a ground control that can't be too far away. Try to find their transmitter, see if it's nearby."

"Sí Comandante! Immediately!"

"If you find the location, pass it to me on the primary Blackhawk frequency—Falcon Leader, aboard Puma 1. We're going up!" Ramos strode over to a narrow strip of shade along the side of the last hangar, where some of his NCOs were sitting on folding chairs, a hundred yards from the four Blackhawks.

"Get ready boys, there might be something happening. Sergeants, move your squads to the helicopters." Ramos had known that the Vedado Ranch meeting was of high importance to the state government, because his request that the helicopters be armed with machine guns had, to his surprise, been approved. On each side, between the pilots' cockpit doors and the large sliding troop doors, the Blackhawks also had a one-meter square gunner's port. Today, each open port was mounted with a belt fed M-60D 7.62mm machine gun, on a swinging pintle mount that hung just outside of the fuselage.

"Logan, let's pack it up. Once they radio-direction-find us, we're screwed. We're not going to have time to recover the Pelican, just ditch it—we've got to haul ass."

"Not yet," said the pilot, feverishly entering commands on his laptop, data-linked in real-time to the UAV.

"Let it go, Logan!" There was urgency in Alex's voice. "Set it to fly into the mountains, send it into a lake, it doesn't matter, but let's get the hell out of here! We've already got enough video."

"No, wait—just give me another minute, just one more minute!"

On his laptop's screen, Logan could see that Whitman and Kosimos were still sitting by the side of the lake, talking. He clicked his cursor's crosshair on the stone bench, entering it as a target point on the GPS. Next, he pulled back the zoom lens to a wide view, and then panned and tilted the camera from its sideways slant angle, to directly forward. This gave him a conventional pilot's perspective. Once that was done, he pushed the tiny manual control stick forward, putting the Pelican into a steep dive. From 5,000 feet above ground level, the UAV picked up speed until it was traveling at over 120 miles an hour, on a westward heading that took it away from the stone bench by the lake.

Thirty seconds later, he rolled the UAV onto its back and then pulled it into a downward loop, reversing its course and bringing it back toward the lake. He continued descending, watching the lake approaching ahead of the drone, until it was skimming above the water. Then he switched the Pelican back onto autopilot, and commanded it to "Go To" its last designnated GPS target point. The UAV's microprocessor brain flew the craft at its maximum level flight velocity of 95 miles per hour, directly toward the stone bench.

Logan tapped his keyboard and his laptop's screen split into several images. The top half showed his real-time pilot's-eye view, forward from the nose of the UAV. The bottom of the screen showed an overhead GPS map, and the drone's "virtual instrument panel." On the GPS map, a tiny blinking triangle represented the Pelican's current position, and a square icon showed the stone bench target at less than 4,000 feet away and closing. With the drone flying straight and level, at 2,000 feet out Logan switched back to manual control, looking "ahead" of the Pelican using the laptop's video screen as his virtual window, until he visually picked up the two men sitting by the edge of the lake.

His temporary lead bodyguard jogged up and insisted, "Mr. President, we need to move out right now, sir!"

"What's the problem?" drawled Dave Whitman.

"We're not certain. An aircraft, a drone—something's up there." The bodyguard pointed skyward.

Whitman shielded his eyes with his hand, and looked up as well. "Well I don't see anything. Are you sure?"

"They fly too high; you won't see it."

"Are you sure it's not one of ours? I mean, who'd be spying on me?" The former President smiled, and said, "Oh, I'll bet it's only the Secret Service. It just burns those boys up when I ditch 'em like I did today."

"Maybe we should just go, Mr. President," said Peter Kosimos. He pulled on his electric wheelchair's toggle control and it began to roll backward toward the service road. His white van was already driving toward them.

At that moment, they both saw and heard a tiny buzzing black dot in the distance across the lake. Before the thought could fully register, the dot grew in size until they could just make out wings on either side of it.

For long seconds they simply stared in fascination, unable to avert their gaze. At first, it seemed totally unconnected to them, an accident, or just a coincidence. It seemed so ridiculous, perhaps someone was playing a practical joke, preparing to fly over them and give them a fright. The plane's distance was hard to estimate, it seemed so tiny, and therefore, still quite far away. Only gradually did its actual diminutive size become evident.

Whitman's uncertainty about the plane's size compounded his confusion over its distance, and its inbound speed. Was it a real airplane still some distance away, or just a model? Before he could decide whether to fall to the ground or run away, the plane had grown to a formidable size, and seemed to increase its speed exponentially as it closed the distance.

For another few moments, the former President considered running to the Suburban that had picked him up at the jet. Or maybe the big SUV would drive into the path of the little plane, blocking it? That, or the plane was only a toy, and it was going to fly harmlessly over him.

These ideas simultaneously jammed his mind, and he froze in place. The little plane swiftly grew to an enormous size, racing directly at him, until there was no time left. Now there was barely enough time to duck behind the only substantial protective cover available to him.

On Logan's laptop, the lake's shoreline abruptly expanded to fill most of the screen's video display. Fir trees upslope behind the two men enlarged and appeared to spread apart. Logan could see a pair of men still huddled by the stone bench, motionless. Dave Whitman was crouched directly behind Peter Kosimos, who was in his motorized wheelchair. Both men's eyes were wide, their mouths hanging open, staring directly into the Pelican's unblinking camera lens. Their well-known faces grew huge, filling the entire screen, and then disappeared. The video image flashed and went white for an instant, and then turned solid blue.

Until the discovery of the drone, Comandante Ramos had frankly been more concerned with the appearance of his men, than with the remote possibility that they would be required to engage in combat today. They had been wearing their brown berets instead of Kevlar helmets, with their camouflage uniforms starched and pressed. Their black paratrooper boots and their silver falcon insignias had gleamed in the sun. He had positioned them near the airport road running past the hangars, so that all of the arriving VIPs would get a good look at his elite Falcons, as they were driven from the runway to the Parker mansion.

The "fashion show" was over, Ramos grimly noted. The Falcons of Beta and Gamma platoons were divided into four squads of ten men each. Now each man was sitting on one of the metal pipe-frame seats in one of the four Blackhawks. Their turbine engines spooled up and their four blades began to turn until they were invisible rushing halos, shaking the helicopters like enormous washing machines. Their helmets were all securely chin-strapped; their M-16 rifles were pointed downward at the decks between their feet. Ramos was handed an extra flight crew aviation helmet to put on, connected by a wire to the aircraft's radios and intercom. He slid the clear plastic face shield up out of the way, put on the helmet, and adjusted the chin microphone. He was crouched between the crew chief and the gunner, behind the pilots aboard Puma 1, when the message came from Lieutenant Almeria. His communications officer was calling on the state guard's encrypted radio channel.

"Falcon Leader, do you hear me, over?"

"Yes, loud and clear."

"The drone is hostile, repeat hostile, and it has crashed, repeat, crashed, over."

"Crashed? What does that mean? Over."

"It's down, I don't know the reason. I did isolate its control channel before it went down. It was directed by a ground radio, not by satellite. It was using data compression and frequency hopping, but I found it, over."

"Were you able to fix a location for the ground radio? Where are they?"

"I don't have a precise location. It was line-of-site from the drone to its ground control, and there are mountains in between. I estimate fifteen to twenty kilometers southwest, over."

"That's the best you can do for a location, over?"

"Sí, Comandante. The drone's radio is no longer transmitting, but it was sending from the azimuth 220 degrees from here, over."

Ramos redirected his words via intercom to the pilot in front of him. "Puma 1, did you copy that location?"

"Yes sir," responded the helicopter pilot, nodding his helmeted head a yard in front of the Comandante. "Range is fifteen to twenty kilometers, along the bearing two-two-zero degrees."

"That's right, now let's go! Puma 1 and 2, we will begin to search for the transmitter. Puma 3 and 4, you will orbit above the ranch center, above the meeting places. But be alert: this drone might have been a diversion, to pull us away."

The two Blackhawks on the right side of the apron pulled pitch on their already spinning rotors, their tails rose, they began to roll forward and in moments, they were lifting skyward and banking to the Southwest. Ahead of them, mountain ridges rose thousands of feet above their ground level, to a maximum height of over eleven thousand feet. Their quarry was only a matter of minutes away, if they could locate them in the search area Teniente Almeria had provided, before they escaped.

The helicopters passed in front of Wayne Parker's stone mansion at an altitude of four hundred feet above ground level. Ramos briefly observed the Very Important Persons, gathered on the wide reception gallery overlooking the pastoral valley and its alpine lake. On the radio, he heard (in English) that the drone had crashed, "resulting in one fatality." Although the Falcons were serving as the Quick Reaction Force, the actual security around the VIPs was being provided by gringos, private "contractors" paid by Wayne Parker. How the crash of an unmanned drone could result in a fatality was a complete mystery to the Comandante. A long line of SUVs and vans were pulling into the driveway in front of the mansion, while men in dark suits and a few women in shimmering dresses scurried for vehicles, crouching among their bodyguards. Whatever had happened with the drone had evidently been enough to spoil the party.

The pair of Blackhawks continued to climb for altitude, and in a few minutes they crested a treeless ridgeline, and dipped into the first of a series of valleys. The two helicopters flew abreast, spread apart by one kilometer, to be able to search a wider corridor on their first pass. It would be a miracle if they could find the transmitter team in this rugged terrain, now that their radio had gone silent. As long as they flew along the bearing of 220 degrees, they might find something, perhaps a vehicle, or a squad of men hiking out. Of course, if their adversaries committed an error and made another radio transmission, they would be located almost instantly. This was Comandante Ramos's greatest hope.

Behind him, the ten Falcons from Beta Platoon's 1st Squad sat strapped to the aluminum and canvas seats, armed and eager for action, the troop doors all the way back to permit a rapid egress upon landing. Puma 1's crew chief and gunner sat on each side of the Comandante facing outboard, wearing green aviation helmets with their visors down, and also connected on the intercom. Their gloved hands clutched the twin vertical grips of their external pintle-mounted M-60D machine guns, as they leaned out through their square gunners' ports, searching for targets. A green steel box full of linked ammunition was racked up on the mount beside each machine gun, ready to fire.

Aboard the Cessna Centurion, the encrypted radio transmissions between the Falcon officers and the Blackhawk pilots had been heard as squeals and static. Logan attempted to decrypt the noise into intelligible speech, but he was unsuccessful. The frequency being used and the length of the comms told them that the state guard Blackhawks were on the alert, and might even now be on the hunt—for them. The Pelican's laptops and radio were hurriedly disconnected, and the men slid them into soft cases, and passed them over to the rear of the aircraft.

While the UAV had been aloft, they had seen the Blackhawks parked in a line outside of the main jet hangar, and had seen the troops waiting around them. If the helicopters were now searching from the air, their pilots would not know precisely what they were looking for, but a white airplane parked on a straight road would certainly draw their interest.

With recovering the destroyed Pelican UAV no longer a concern, the men rushed to reinstall the right side door while Ranya stood guard, with the Dragunov across her chest at port arms. Just before they could all climb back into the Cessna, they heard the distant rumble of rotors beating the air, and the whine of turbines. The Blackhawks! The three conspirators froze in place by the plane, as the sound of the helicopters grew louder and closer, and then actually passed over them, crossing their hidden road at an angle, one on each side of them. Parked beneath the thick cover of the concealing spruce and maples, they never saw the helicopters in that narrow slice of blue sky between the pine branches directly above them, but there was no mistaking their hostile intent.

"Falcon Leader, this is Puma 2. We're at twenty kilometers from base now. What are your instructions, over?"

Ramos considered his next move. He had great faith in Lieutenant Almeria's expertise at radio direction finding. Someone had been transmitting from this area. Perhaps because of the intervening mountains, Almeria was slightly off in either his range or bearing, or both. "Puma 1 and 2, return along the same azimuth, but let's open our separation distance to two kilometers, over."

"Roger, Falcon leader."

Both helicopters banked and circled outward, until they were again running on parallel tracks, but now back toward Wayne Parker's runway and hangars.

They waited for the sound of the helicopters to fade. They were unsure if they should prepare to take off in the plane, or get ready to run into the forest, to try to escape and evade on foot. The men were climbing into the airplane when the whining turbines and thumping rotor noises once again began to build. Even through the trees, the sound of the Doppler shift of the Blackhawk engines made it clear that the helicopters were coming back for another pass.

None of them spoke or moved. They were three rabbits cowering under the shadows of eagles, in mortal fear of being seen or heard. Once again, the rumble of the rotors and the scream of the turbines passed down either side of them. Once again, by pure good fortune, they were spared the straight-down view that would have immediately betrayed the gleaming white wings and fuselage of the Cessna. Once again they waited, almost afraid to breathe, as the helicopters passed them by and continued toward the north.

"Puma 1, this is Puma 2. What's that between us, over?"

The pilot of Ramos's helicopter replied, "Puma 2, that's an old copper mine. Do you see something there?" He had a folded air map in a clear plastic envelope, Velcroed to his thigh.

"Uh, negative 1, but there are some buildings and sheds down below. They could be hiding our targets. Falcon Leader, request permission to land and search them, over."

Ramos squeezed the intercom switch on his wire lead, and replied, "Roger Puma 2, go ahead if you have enough space to land. Don't take any chances if it looks too tight. I see some poles and wires, use caution. We'll orbit in case you flush anyone into the open, over."

Puma 2 hovered above the rutted dirt and weed-filled clearing between corrugated metal sheds and abandoned machinery. Rusty cranes, derricks, pipes, pumps and gantries cluttered the level area along the flank of the mountainside. An old asphalt road curved downward from the edge of the mountain past the abandoned mine pits, then ran straight for a few hundred meters, and disappeared into the thick pine forest that covered most of the mountain. At an altitude of 100 meters above the ground, the pilot rotated his craft through 360 degrees above the clearing. The pilots and the crew were scanning for obstacles that might impede the landing. When they were satisfied with the landing zone, the pilot began to settle the bird down. Meanwhile Puma 1 circled overhead in a tight racetrack, banking tightly over their comrades with a clatter of rotor noise.

"Oh shit, they're back! Now we're screwed!" Logan stood by the open left-side door of the Cessna, gasping. "They can't miss us now—they must know we're here, they must have seen us!"

Their airplane was concealed in a leafy tunnel, facing back out the way they had taxied in, a hundred yards from the edge of the woods. The sound and vibration of nearby helicopter blades instilled terror into them.

Alex Garabanda stood behind the open right door. "Maybe, and maybe not. If they saw us, they'd be right on top of us. They're not on top of us, so maybe they're just fishing."

The noise of one helicopter was steady, directly in front of them, and then they saw it, turning slowly and descending, directly in line with the road that was their runway exit out of the woods.

"Oh my God!" Logan blurted out, "They *must* see us! That's probably as close as they can land—"

"Maybe, but where's the other one?" asked Alex, stepping out from beneath the wing and scanning above them through the treetops.

From behind them Ranya shouted, "Alex, shut your door and get out of the way!"

He turned around to her, saying, "What?" She was kneeling behind the Cessna's tail. Her rifle's long barrel was lying across the horizontal stabilizer, aimed along the side of the plane, directly at him.

"Shut the door Alex! Shut the door and get out of the way!"

He slammed it shut and jumped away from the plane.

She had been watching the sky-blue open space above them, and down the green corridor toward the opening at the end of the trees. She had seen the Blackhawk dropping through the leafy slot at the end of their tree cover. She instinctively knew that it was going to land in the open space of the former strip mine, alongside their runway road. As soon as the helicopter touched down, it would disgorge a dozen troops.

Outrunning the Falcons in these woods would be impossible, especially when they had helicopters scouting above them and directing their pursuit. Other helicopters would drop off more troops ahead of their escape route. They would soon be cornered, and then killed or captured. To Ranya it was not an option to go down without fighting. She crouched low behind the plane's tail, with her right knee on the ground and her left foot forward. The plane's horizontal stabilizer made a perfect bench rest, her left hand supporting the bottom of the Dragunov's wooden forestock.

While the helicopter was still above the Cessna's high wing as seen from her perspective, there were too many tree branches in the way to risk a shot. She was also aware that the rifle's scope lay above its barrel, and a clear view through the scope might send a bullet into the Cessna's wing, straight into its gas tank. Most importantly of all, she knew that her first shots had to be perfect. Once warned of their presence by ineffective fire, all four Blackhawks would swarm down upon them, eventually bringing the entire Falcon Battalion. Finally, she silently said a prayer that the

South African had kept his rifle accurately sighted in, perfectly matched with his Russian sniper grade ammunition. If the scope was not sighted in, her shots would mean nothing.

The helicopter continued its descent, after slowly turning until it was facing her. Then the descending Blackhawk disappeared momentarily from her view, blocked by the Cessna's wing.

She pressed her right eye against the soft rubber cup at the back of the Dragunov's scope. Its unusual range-finder was useless to her; she had no experience with it. She guesstimated that it was one hundred yards to the tree line, and another two hundred to the clearing where the helicopter was landing. Three hundred yards. The scope was only four power, but that was plenty of magnification for the relatively short distance. If the helicopter landed safely, it would unload a dozen troops. She knew that the Falcons were by no means cowards, that they could run far and run fast, and that they could shoot their new M-16s very, very well. So it must not be allowed to land...

The Blackhawk appeared beneath the Cessna's high wing, facing directly toward her, bug-like. The apparent distance was only two hundred feet through the scope, an easy shot. Dust and debris swirled up and around the helicopter, whipping the tree branches. The Dragunov was operated like a stretched-out AK-47. Its first round was already chambered and she pushed the safety lever down, keeping the scope sighted on the Blackhawk. The pad of her right index finger slowly took up trigger pressure, holding low, and waiting for the helicopter to descend onto her aiming point. Instead of a crosshair, the scope showed four upside-down V chevrons, one above the other. She guessed that the tip of the second chevron from the top would keep her on target at this range.

She saw the Blackhawk's two fat wheels and its underbelly, and the three-part Plexiglas windshield. Through the window glare, she could even make out the helmeted pilot's outline. She put the tip of the scope's second black chevron just under the helmet, squeezed the trigger, and let off a shot that erupted with a resounding blast. She immediately moved her shoulder and swung the chevron aiming point to the opposite windshield and fired again, reacquired and made another shot at the same spot. The recoil and the muzzle blast were now unnoticed and unheard; she was in the zone, in the bubble, her entire universe encompassed within the Dragunov's scope. She swung the chevron sight back across to where she had made her first shot, but before she could fire again, the helicopter rolled on its side and dropped from her scope's view behind the curtain of trees, too quickly for her to follow.

32

Orbiting above the old strip mine, Comandante Ramos watched as Puma 2 descended into the clearing between the rusty metal buildings and mining equipment, churning up dirt and leaves with its rotor wash. When it was about twenty meters above the ground Puma 2 suddenly lurched and rolled to the left, then dropped like a stone while he stared in horror. The spinning rotors struck first and exploded, flying off in all directions like broken missiles. The helicopter impacted the ground at an angle on its nose, crumpled and finally came to rest lying on its left side, in a sickening but possibly survivable crash landing. What in the hell? Had Puma 2's rotors hit a wire or a pole on its way down? It must have! It was a cluttered landing zone, too full of potential obstacles. He should have known better than to permit their landing attempt, which had ended in complete disaster.

"Get down there!" he yelled to his pilot over the intercom, "Can you get down near them—is there enough room anywhere else?"

"I don't know…no, no, I don't think so!"

"Well try, try dammit!—Puma 2, Puma 2, do you read me over?" Ramos paused, and repeated his message—there was no answer but static. "Puma 3 and Puma 4—*atención, atención*—Puma 2 is down, I repeat, Puma 2 has gone down! Come on, get moving, get out here now!"

While his pilot maneuvered toward the clearing, he saw that the Blackhawk had crashed partly on a road running through the jumbled-up mining operation, a stretch of road he had not noticed before. The paved road led in a straight line, directly into a thick stand of pines, directly into the trees, and he thought he saw something white in there, something…then he looked back down at the wreckage of Puma 2 below him.

"Oh dammit, *now* look!" yelled Alex, "It's right across the road!" The broken helicopter lay on its side, straight ahead of the Cessna. The men were still standing on either side of the plane. "Logan, can you do it, can we make it out?"

The pilot stared straight ahead of the airplane, estimating distances and heights, and then he answered, "No, we can't make it. It's too close, too high—it can't be done!"

"Then what?" implored Alex.

Logan didn't hesitate. "Turn her! Turn her around again! Come on!" He jumped back to the Cessna's horizontal stabilizer, where it joined the narrow taper of the fuselage beneath the swept back tail. "Come on, push it down!"

Ranya slipped the Dragunov over her back, held by its necktie sling. The three of them leaned over the stabilizer, pushing down on the back of the airplane until the nose wheel lifted from the roadway, and Logan led them in walking the plane in another tight circle, until they had again turned 180 degrees and were facing deeper into the woods. He didn't wait but ran for the left door and climbed in, standing on the toe-brakes as he switched on the engine, the propeller an immediate roaring blur in front of them. Ranya had to climb into the back seat through the right side door, and it was a small opening. The copilot's seat was in the way and she couldn't find the catch to tilt it forward. Logan was screaming at her to get in, and Alex was pushing her from behind, but her four-foot long Dragunov rifle was catching against the wing and the fuselage as she tried to climb inside!

Logan reached across the cockpit with something bright orange in his right hand, some kind of emergency rescue tool. He swiped it across her chest and the long rifle fell free. Then he flipped the copilot's seat forward and Alex shoved her into the back onto her face, and as soon as he had put one foot inside of the Cessna, Logan let off the brakes and they began to roll forward.

Ranya squirmed into an upright position looking forward, and could see only trees. She looked behind, through the Cessna's sloping rear window back at the way they had come, and she saw a second Blackhawk hovering above the wreckage that she had created.

They were thirty meters above the smashed helicopter. There had scarcely been enough room in the landing zone for one Blackhawk, or as it had turned out, not even enough room for one. Ramos leaned out the open troop door behind the Blackhawk's crew chief. He could see a pair of camouflage-clad figures below him, trying to climb up and out of the crashed fuselage. Think! To rescue his men, they would need to rig for fast-roping. He hoped that the fast-ropes had been packed, as his squads had been briefed to do. Did his men all bring their thick leather fast-roping gloves? Or could the pilot bring the Blackhawk down close enough to the wreck for his medic to jump directly onto its hulk? Could they descend low enough to jump, without the rotors striking one of the rusty metal obstacles that had brought down Puma 2? Alternatively, they could look for another nearby landing zone, but then his troops would need to make their way back to the wreck on foot, which would take more time. Think! Think!

He tried to remember where the closest possible landing zone might be, based on his memory of their recent over-flights. Little of this area was flat enough to land on, and most of it was covered in trees. Beyond the woods ahead of them, it became clear but very steep, descending sharply toward sheer cliffs and down into a wide valley with an intricate system of side canyons. He was about to ask his pilot over the intercom where they could land, while he leaned out the open side door. Down the road toward the woods, he saw movement, a flash of white, something that did not belong. What was that? What? A truck? A car? No. What? A plane?

"There! There, do you see that?" Ramos screamed to his pilot over the intercom. "In the trees, do you see it?"

"Uh, roger, I see...something. What are your instructions?"

Ramos hesitated. Should he leave his injured or even dead Falcons, to pursue what might be an optical illusion, a mirage?

The Centurion taxied forward, bumping over cracks and ruts. The road curved ahead of them as the trees thinned out and became sparse. They were skidding down slope now, then the road turned hard to the left, and there before them was an almost straight run of road, but it was very short, less than a hundred yards and beyond it there was only sky as the mountain fell away. Logan measured the distance, guess-timated the slope, computed his current and required speed and made his decision. He had already set 20 degrees of flap in readiness, now with his right hand he pushed the throttle knob in all the way, committing them to flight. The hot engine immediately revved up to full emergency power, all 320 turbocharged horsepower screaming, causing the plane to vibrate madly as it leaped forward down the rutted trail.

"Falcon leader, this is Puma 3. We're on our way—we have you in sight. ETA one minute, over."

Ramos sighed, grateful that the other pilots had been alert and anticipated his emergency call. "Roger Puma 3."

A new voice broke into the net. "Falcon, this is Condor. We have a truck patrol in your area. They should be arriving in about ten minutes, over."

Ramos cursed silently. "Condor" was Carlos Guzman, Comandante of the 5th Battalion. His troops were serving as perimeter guards, patrolling the roads on and around the Vedado Ranch. Ramos knew that it was imperative that he get down to Puma 2 before that power-hungry Peruvian bastard arrived on the scene and usurped his authority. On the other hand, he knew that in order to salvage the fiasco that had unfolded below him, he would have to quickly pursue and either capture or destroy the aircraft that he thought he had seen hidden under the trees.

He made his decision. Ramos switched to "intercom only," and gave his pilots their orders. "Let's find the airplane. Follow the road through the trees. Machine gunners: open fire as soon as you have a shot."

The Blackhawk dipped its nose, gaining speed racing toward the tree line, leaving the survivors trapped within Puma 2 to await rescue from the other helicopters. In seconds they were over the trees, tracing the ribbon of asphalt that was now clearly visible beneath them. Ramos crouched behind the pilots in the middle, in order to see out of the front windshields as they accelerated across the treetops above the mining road. The trees thinned out, and the mountain ended ahead of them, the land abruptly dropping away. And there it was, just below and ahead of them, a white airplane on the ground, going straight for the edge of the precipice!

The Centurion, already rolling downhill, swiftly picked up speed. In seconds, the indicated airspeed was fifty knots as the road made another sharp leftward turn directly ahead of them. They couldn't possibly follow the turn at this speed, so Logan pulled back on the yoke, and the Centurion staggered drunkenly into the air, its wheels clearing a rusty guardrail by inches. The stall warning horn began blowing even as he pushed the yoke back in, nosing over into the yawning vastness of the red and brown space that opened up below them. He immediately brought the wheels up, and the Cessna began piling on air speed, as it hurtled down toward the earth a thousand feet below.

The plane unexpectedly disappeared from Ramos's view, dropping too low to be seen from his position at the rear of the helicopter's cockpit. The pilot pushed his cyclic control forward, diving after the white high-winged plane, but Ramos stopped him. "No, no, stay over him, just stay on top of him! On top and behind." He didn't know the maximum speed of the small single-engine airplane, but he was almost certain that it was slower than the 200-knot maximum of the Blackhawk. The small planes he had flown in as a boy, before his mother lost her TV job and the money ran out, had cruised at 160 or 170 knots, maximum. The little high-wing Piper Supercub, which the Falcons sometimes used for reconnaissance and over-watch, was capable of only 150. If they stayed above the white plane, they would quickly force it down, or get into a position to shoot it down. The prop wash from the Blackhawk's rotors alone would be enough to drive the plane into the ground if they flew directly above it. There was no possibility that the airplane could escape.

They were a few hundred meters above and behind the plane when the right-side machine gunner beside him began to fire. He was leaning out of his gunner's port, the M-60's barrel aimed forward and down, aiming carefully and then letting go with short bursts, sending golden brass cascading away in the slipstream. The pilot "crabbed" the Blackhawk, flying forward at a leftward-skewed angle, to give his right side gunner a clear field of fire ahead of the craft. Ramos stood behind the gunner, just in front of the open right-side troop door, leaned against the inside of the fuselage for support and put his head outside, blinking against the hurricane until he pulled his clear visor down. Red tracers streaked away from the Blackhawk and all around the fleeing high-winged airplane, yet somehow, it seemed to be actually pulling ahead of them, opening up the distance as it continued to dive!

He turned back to the cockpit, grasping the high back of the copilot's seat for balance, and yelled into his intercom, "Pilot, can't this machine go any faster? They're getting away! After them! Catch them, catch them!"

The Cessna dived, twisted and banked so violently that at several points it nearly rolled its wings beyond vertical. Ranya was looking out of the plane's rear window, and saw the Blackhawk, a monstrous prehistoric predator looming behind and locked in pursuit, impossibly close. She recognized the red tracers streaking past them, she knew what they meant—she'd seen them before, from the dying end. There was a metallic "twang" that she heard above the engine noise, and a few seconds later, there was another. Logan continued his plunge for the valley floor, building speed while also weaving and jinking, throwing her from side to side against her seat belt.

The sight of the giant black chopper following behind them filled her with terror. It was coming after her personally, as if madly seeking revenge for its dead brother! She looked forward again, and saw red earth filling the entire front windshield, coming up to meet them, no sky to be seen. At last Logan pulled back on the yoke, mashing her against her seat with the g-forces until they leveled out and skimmed through a dry river wash. She looked behind again, the insect-like helicopter was a little further back, and much higher.

The men both had on their headsets; it was no use trying to communicate with them. All she could do was try to control her fear, pray, and hope for the best. Once again, her life was out of her hands, once again she was merely cargo, along for the ride, possibly the last ride of her life. She looked forward, and wished she hadn't. Directly ahead a curtain of cumulous clouds soared tens of thousand of feet above them, an opaque gray-black wall.

While she stared at it in wonder, the wall was lit from within by a flash. A lightning bolt shot across the short distance from the bottom of the cloud bar to the ground ahead of them, and a second later the Cessna was struck by an explosive thunder bang. What she saw terrified her, but she could not close her eyes. Sunlight shone through a cleft in the squall line, turning the bottom edges of the clouds to brilliant silver and gold. She glanced between the front seats and could see on the panel in front of Logan that the Cessna was indicating an airspeed of 217 knots.

The wall of clouds was drawing closer, when she heard the ping, followed by another a second or two later. She looked back—the helicopter was hundreds of yards behind them and above. She looked out the right door window, and saw the jagged tear a few inches back from the front edge of the wing, a yard from the fuselage. The thin aluminum was puckered outward, as if it had been stabbed through by a giant ice pick. A fine mist streamed straight back from the hole. She wondered what would happen if a burning red-phosphorous tracer bullet hit one of the Cessna's gasoline-filled wing tanks. There was another hole through the flap on the trailing edge of the wing. She shook Alex on his shoulder, and pointed up to the damage. He looked at it briefly, nodded calmly, and then they plunged headlong into the clouds.

"Why are you slowing down?" screamed Comandante Ramos. "They're getting away!"

"What? Are you blind? Look ahead! *¡Chubascos y Tormentas!* Thunder clouds!"

"But they are going under! Follow them down, follow them!"

"Are you crazy, follow them into thunder and lightning? There's no space below the clouds! It's suicide!"

"If they can make it, so can we! Catch them!"

"You're crazy! You may be a Milicia 'Comandante,' but I'm a Major, a *real* Major, and I'm the captain of this aircraft! I refuse to put our lives in danger for you! It's madness, and it's a violation of every safety regulation that—"

Ramos screamed back, "*Hijo de puta*, don't tell me about regulations, you *maldito* coward!" He snatched the new Glock from his holster, and held it to the pilot's helmet, his left hand grasping the back of his cockpit seat. "You follow that plane, or I'll shoot you now, for cowardice in the face of the enemy!"

"Then shoot, you lunatic! The enemy is not only in that airplane, it's ahead of us! Look!"

The white plane disappeared into an opening in the bottom of the wall of clouds, through a notch like an inverted V. The bottom of the clouds now extended to the ground ahead of them, from north to south and obscuring the mountains as far as they could see.

When they were a half mile from the solid wall of cumulous, the sky suddenly turned dark, and the air temperature plummeted. The helicopter began to be buffeted, shaking and lurching sideways, up, down. There was no way forward, except through the black wall. They were flying at 7,000 feet above sea level, in an area jammed with 11,000-foot mountain peaks. Ramos felt the frigid air blast through the open troop doors, followed by a pelting of freezing cold raindrops, and then hail.

He looked into the cabin behind him. The Blackhawk's helmeted crew chief pushed up his visor and stared at him with murder in his eyes. His Falcons were looking away, out of the craft, as stolid and unflinching as if they were taking a daily cross-town bus to work. Some of them were actually grinning, enjoying the moment. Live or die, his beloved Falcons were addicted to danger and excitement, and they were getting plenty of both today. He calmed himself, acceded to reality, and holstered his pistol. "Okay. That's enough. Let's go back to Puma 2."

The Blackhawk immediately banked and reversed its direction in a tight half circle, its rotor blades popping. The men on the low side leaned outward against their chest straps, and they raced away from the menacing wall of clouds.

33

The Cessna punched through the western edge of the cumulous and out into brilliant sunshine, after being tossed up to 14,000 feet by the updrafts. Logan considered them lucky to be alive, lucky to still be flying, but he kept these thoughts to himself. There was no reason to tell them how insanely dangerous it had been to fly into that winking "sucker hole" of blue sky at the base of the thunderheads. Flying into thick cumulous could result in being thrown into a spin or slammed into the ground. Flying into sucker holes in a mountainous region was even stupider. Once flung out of controlled flight by the hurricane-force up and down drafts within the thunderheads, you risked plowing straight into unseen "cumulo-granite."

As it was, they'd been pelted with rain and beaten with hail, and had seen a glazing of ice form on their wing's leading edges. Once through the clouds and bursting back out into brilliant blue, Logan dived again for the cover of the ground, but they quickly determined that they were no longer being pursued. Flying into an ugly squall line that was spitting out thunder and lightning had been a desperation move. It now seemed that the Blackhawk had not been as desperate to pursue them, as they had been to escape.

They all knew they had been hit. They'd seen the red tracer bullets flashing past; they had heard the pings and snaps. Two exit holes were visible near the wing root on the right side, and they'd lost the right tank's fuel. Now it seemed like they were losing fuel from the left tank faster than they were burning it.

Logan had to decide where to go, which meant, where to land. The northern and the central parts of New Mexico were solidly in the grip of the radical state government. He thought that the Navajos in the Four Corners region were neutral, but he had no connections there, nowhere he could get the plane patched up and refueled. Some of the western counties he knew were hotbeds of resistance, he'd heard this from friends who had left the federal agencies, or had been forced out of New Mexico law enforcement. From the rumors he'd heard, no place in New Mexico was more defiant than Cantrell County, south of Gallup along the Arizona border. He guessed the one wing tank of fuel remaining would be plenty to make the distance they'd need to land there, in what he hoped would be friendly territory.

They had gotten some breaks, he had to admit. They had beaten the pursuit by the Blackhawk, and they had survived penetrating the squall line. The radio scanner was quiet, there was no all points bulletin out statewide to be on the lookout for a white Cessna. They were well north of the line of heliostat radar balloons along the border, which were oriented southward, looking deep into Mexico. In any event, these radar balloons were not very reliable, and they were out of commission more often than not. The right wing tank was empty, but at least the ugly puckering exit hole had not spread or grown. The plane's controls and instruments were all performing normally.

"How far can we go on one tank?" asked Alex. They were communicating through their headsets and the attached chin mikes.

The pilot looked again at the gauge. "We're showing three quarters in the left tank, maybe thirty gallons, but I think we're using it too fast. The left tank might be damaged, I can't tell yet. California's out, that's for sure."

The ground fell away to their right in brown folds extending to the western horizon. Just to their left and above them was a vertical red and tan escarpment, looking almost like one side of the Grand Canyon, which had somehow lost its opposite twin.

"How much time have we got? How far?" Alex had an air map partially unfolded on his lap. The GPS display in the center of the instrument panel showed a tiny airplane icon flying south-southwest down the western side of New Mexico.

"Ripley's got a decent municipal airport, we can probably get repaired and refilled there. Punch in FBO Ripley as our destination."

Alex found the Ripley airport on his air map, and then worked on the GPS, pushing buttons that expanded the scale of the presentation. He marked the airfield on the GPS and, then hit the "Go To" button. All of the information about the airfield was stored in the GPS's memory, and was now displayed on the screen. "Okay, here we go. FBO Ripley: 4,800 feet of asphalt runway, at 6,300 feet above sea level. Right now it's 138 miles away, on course 205 degrees. Can we make it on what we've got?"

"Oh sure," relied Logan, "We should make it easy, as long as the left tank is reading true. Let me switch to autopilot, and I'll do a little fuel consumption arithmetic."

The plane began to diverge away from the two thousand foot high line of cliffs that had recently been their cover and protection, concealing them from easy observation against the blue sky. A red stone monument soaring as high above the plain as the massive escarpment stood by itself several miles off to the west. The Cessna flew through the open space between the red wall and the towering rock island. They had already flown past a dozen of the imposing rock formations, all different, all magnificent.

"John Wayne country," said Alex, briefly turning to face Ranya in the back seat. "I love flying over this part of New Mexico. I always expect to see wagon trains and stage coaches down there."

Dirt roads scraped from the barren landscape led to small homesteads, mostly trailers or shacks. Logan believed that the Indians and other hardy souls who eked out livings in the dry and dusty territory below them might have been dirt poor in worldly possessions, but they lived in the midst of some of nature's supreme beauty. Anywhere else, each of these staggering pinnacles, with sheer sides soaring thousands of feet high, would have been a famous tourist destination in its own right. Only here in this part of the Southwest where there were so many, did these monumental geological formations each exist in relative obscurity.

The aircrew of Puma 1 was silent and stone faced on the return flight, pointedly ignoring their passengers. As soon as they arrived over the old copper mine, Ramos and the Falcons of Beta Platoon's 1st Squad rigged for fast-roping, and quickly slid down to the ground alongside the broken hulk of Puma 2. The most critically injured survivors of 2nd Squad had already been hoisted aboard Puma 4 in medevac litters, and the helicopter had just departed for Santa Fe.

The leading elements of the 5th Battalion arrived shortly after. Their truck convoy drove into the crash site from the same road where Ramos had first seen the white airplane. Comandante Guzman arrived at the scene of the wreck to help coordinate the medevac of the less seriously injured. Ramos and Guzman stared at the crumpled fuselage in silence. A short distance away, six pairs of boots stuck out from a covering shroud of green ponchos.

It could have been worse. Even though the crash site stank of kerosene, at least Puma 2 had not exploded or burned on impact, so they were able to walk around its smashed fuselage and carefully examine it. The Blackhawk had fallen from the sky while hovering over its intended landing zone. It was now clear that it had not struck a tower, a wire, or a tree. The open space into which the helicopter had fallen was not large, but it was sufficient, with no obstacles near the radius of its spinning rotors.

The reason for its crash was not long a mystery. Even with Puma 2 lying on its side, even with its three segmented forward windshields buckled, cracked and partly hanging loose, the reason for its plummet was now plainly evident before the two Comandantes. There were two bullet holes in what had been the right side windscreen, and one in the left. Controlled by a dead hand, the Blackhawk had rolled over and then dropped thirty meters to the ground, impacting on its left side and pancaking.

After seeing the dead pilot's head wound, they surmised that he had been killed almost instantly by a rifle bullet. As experienced soldiers, they knew that head shots often resulted in spasmodic reflexive jerking of the limbs. Puma 2's pilot, shot through the top of his skull, had probably jerked his cyclic control stick and his foot pedals hard to the left, tumbling the craft to the ground. The copilot in the left seat had apparently not been shot, and had survived the crash, but instead had bled to death while he was trapped and pinned inside of the twisted wreckage. As always, the pilots were the weak spot of a helicopter, especially when hovering near the ground. Instead of installing thick (and very heavy) bullet-resistant windscreens, the Blackhawks depended on the "spare" pilot for their safety from small arms fire. Too close to the ground, with a steady hover presenting an inviting target, this insurance policy sometimes failed.

The two glum Comandantes did not chat or pass the time of day. Standing together in the space between the wreck and the trucks of the 5th Battalion, they took reports from junior officers and sergeants, and gave terse instructions. The mangled green-black fuselage almost looked at home amidst the derelict mining equipment on the scraped hillside.

A 5th Battalion sergeant approached them both, his M-16 rifle slung over his back, carrying another very different rifle in front. Today the 5th Battalion troops were wearing the same surplus woodland pattern camouflage BDU uniforms as the Falcons, but without ballistic body armor vests. Unlike the Falcons, who were still wearing their kevlar helmets, these troops were wearing plain brown berets, without insignias. The Sergeant saluted, and then held the strange rifle at port arms as he stood at attention before them. He addressed Guzman. "Comandante, we found this rifle in the forest, on the side of the road."

Ramos quickly stepped toward the man, and took the rifle from him. It was the Dragunov. *His* Dragunov. "Thank you, sergeant. We'll need this for the investigation."

Guzman grunted and turned toward Ramos and the rifle, fingering a blue necktie that was improbably hanging from its barrel. He ran his hand down the silk, to where it appeared to have been neatly cut. A second, more colorful silk tie was tied to the butt. The sergeant had wrapped it around the rifle's laminated wood stock, to keep it from dragging on the ground.

Guzman said, "Well Comandante Ramos, *that's* not something you see every day. A Russian Dragunov, with a pair of neckties for a sling—and cut in the middle. Do you think this belonged to the sniper, the sniper who shot down your helicopter?"

Basilio Ramos's mind was spinning, trying to factor the angles presented by this unbelievable discovery. "I don't know. Perhaps. Perhaps it did." He was flushed, almost panicky, wanting desperately to leave with the rifle, to make it disappear, but there were too many eyes watching their little drama.

With one hand Guzman put a strong grip on the rifle's scope, and with the other, he reached under and extracted the box magazine. Then he stripped out the remaining rounds, counting them while they dropped to the ground. "Six unfired *cartuchos*. One still in the chamber makes seven. Plus three bullet holes in the windshields, two dead *pilotos*, and one crashed Blackhawk. How do my numbers add up, Comandante Ramos?"

He was speechless. His Falcons all knew that they had recovered a Dragunov rifle last week, from the South African who had ambushed them on the way back from the rifle range. Jan Pieter…something? That was the man. Of course he recognized his own neckties, and he wondered if anyone else did. He had rarely worn them, he could not even remember the last occasion.

Nevertheless, he knew exactly what this discovery meant. His fingerprints would be all over the rifle, which did not concern him so much, since he had a good reason to be touching it now. What concerned him were the other fingerprints that might be found on the rifle. Worse, his men were sure to make a connection between last week's Dragunov recovered from the South African, and this rifle. It was too much of a coincidence for anyone simply to disregard.

Ramos knew exactly where this rifle had spent the last week, and he knew just who had cleaned out his safe and stolen it. The fates were conspiring against him, there was no other explanation. He responded weakly, "Yes, of course, this might be the rifle that killed the pilot. We'll take it for the inquest."

Guzman handed him back the empty magazine, leaving the golden-colored cartridges on the ground. "What are the odds, Comandante Ramos, of finding a Dragunov here? That's a rather uncommon rifle, isn't it?" His coal-black eyes had a burning intensity.

Ramos attempted a nonchalant tone. "Oh, you know the Americans—they're crazy about their guns. Until a few years ago, they were allowed to own almost any weapon they could pay for."

"Yes, perhaps so…I've often heard that. A strange national custom indeed—and very dangerous. Well, anyway, I'm sorry for the loss of your men, and the aircrew. My battalion will do anything that it can to help. Our humble trucks may not be as swift as your Blackhawks, but they are at your service." His comment dripped with sarcasm, with the two officers standing in front of the crumpled hulk of Puma 2.

"Thank you, Comandante Guzman. The 5th Battalion's support is always appreciated."

"Just doing my duty, Comandante Ramos, as always. We must all do our duty, must we not?"

"Yes, of course." Ramos turned to leave, but there was really no-where to go. He was now in the humiliating position of being forced to depend on the Peruvian's pickup trucks, to take his men back to their own vehicles at the Vedado Ranch airstrip. After the chain of disasters that had transpired in the last two hours, he was not about to call the Blackhawks, and request that they return to lift out the rest of Beta platoon.

The Cessna Centurion's low fuel alarm began flashing ten miles north of the Ripley airfield. They were five miles from a routine landing when without warning the engine RPMs spun up, and the engine coughed, sputtered, choked and died. After two hours of hearing the steady roar of the turbocharged motor, they were overcome by the silence that meant they were suddenly flying in a glider. A new whistling noise could also be heard, the air rushing over and through the plane's new collection of bullet holes, some seen, some unseen.

They had known that they were edging toward fuel starvation, and as a precaution Logan had been flying 800 feet above State Road 14. The road was 6,200 feet above sea level, a low elevation for Cantrell County, near the Arizona border. The county was larger than the state of Connecticut, with a population of less than five thousand, half of whom lived in or near the town of Ripley. The two-lane paved road ran southwest down the center of a broad valley, between mountains that rose to above ten thousand feet on either side. The road was clear of traffic, the engineless Cessna 210 was a passable glider, and Logan had no trouble putting down the gear and making a smooth landing.

He said, "This is one more reason why I like a high-wing plane," as he nodded to the low barbed wire cattle fence about twenty feet to the right side of the road, and slightly down slope. In fact, the fence was far enough from the plane's wingtip not to matter, but the point was made. He taxied a short distance to a dirt turnout area, obviously used for many years by trucks and other large vehicles to stop and turn around on the narrow road. The men opened their doors and climbed down, followed by Ranya, all of them eager to stretch their legs. They walked around the plane, counting the bullet strikes. There were three in the wings, and one in the fuselage above the luggage compartment. The most serious was the one that had torn through the front of the right wing tank from above.

"So, who's going for gas?" asked Ranya.

Alex replied to her query with a smile, "I'd hitchhike into town, but I think you'll have better luck getting somebody to stop." They were all feeling rather chipper, having cheated death several times today.

"Yeah, well, I'd be happy to flag down a car with my Dragunov, but Logan cut it loose back at Vedado, and then *somebody* forgot to grab it."

"Hey, it seemed like a good idea at the time," said the pilot. "You were having a little trouble getting in the airplane with that rifle strapped to your back."

"Kind of like the Three Stooges," added Alex, stretching out his arms and flexing, while bouncing on his toes.

Logan walked down the dusty slope to where tall weeds grew against the wire stock fence, and answered the call of nature with his back to them.

She asked Alex, "Are you sure there's no Milicia around here?"

"Pretty sure. This is cowboy country. I think we're safe."

"So who's walking, you or Logan?"

"You mean to get gas?"

"That's the plan, isn't it?"

Logan returned and the three of them stood in the shade beneath the high wing, discussing what they knew about Ripley, which wasn't much. The airfield was two miles south of town, on the other side. While they were talking, a car appeared over a low rise, approaching from the direction of town, but it stopped in the middle of the road a half mile away. While the three of them watched in silence, it paused for a long minute on the crest of the hill, and then it backed up, and disappeared.

Alex said, "It shouldn't be long now."

"What shouldn't be long?" asked Ranya.

"The welcome wagon."

Ten minutes later, a Jeep and two pickup trucks climbed into sight where the earlier car had paused. They stopped along the side of the road, and about a dozen men climbed out, all of them carrying long arms. The men broke into three groups, one squad on each side of the road, and one remaining behind the Jeep. The flankers spread out in the brush on either side of the road in lines abreast, skirmish lines to allow them to direct all of their weapons toward the unknown threat to their front. These two groups moved forward in alternating bounds, until they were both only two hundred yards from the plane on each side of the road, then they sank down behind brush. After these men disappeared from view, the Jeep began to edge forward down the road at a walking pace, shielding the third group of men. No driver was visible in the Jeep.

"Well, I'm impressed," said Alex.

"Yeah, it sure looks like they've done this before," noted Ranya. "Now what?"

"Just stay cool, and go with the flow."

When the Jeep was also 200 yards away, it stopped and a man with a bullhorn hollered in English, "Who are you, and why are you here?"

Logan said quietly, "Well, at least they're speaking English. That's a good sign."

Alex quipped, "I don't suppose I should say we're federal agents?" Finally, he yelled down the road, "We're refugees! We ran out of gas!"

"Refugees?" whispered Ranya, rolling her eyes. "Refugees?"

"You have a better idea?" he whispered back.

The spokesman for the squad walking behind the jeep called back, "We're coming down to you. Step out into the sunshine, and keep your hands visible."

Whoever was driving the Jeep was crouching too low to be seen. The Jeep stopped a hundred feet from the plane, in the middle of the road. The four men went past it and continued walking forward, also in a skirmish line spread across the road. Their rifles were shouldered, but pointed down toward the asphalt at an angle. They were all dressed somewhat differently, but all of them wore various types of body armor and combat vests. All of them had on identical tan ball caps, which said DEPUTY in black letters across the front.

They finally stopped when they were only twenty feet away. Alex, Ranya and Logan stood perfectly still, facing the four riflemen. Two of the men carried either military M-16s or civilian AR-15s, it was impossible to determine which. One carried a black FN-FAL, a Belgian-designed 7.62mm battle rifle

The leader of the four was a hearty-looking late-middle-aged man with a closely trimmed gray beard. He was carrying an M-1 Garand, a World War Two era battle rifle recognizable by its lack of an external box magazine. It had been his voice on the loudspeaker. "You just said you were 'refugees.' You mind explaining that?" The four men appeared to be Anglos, but with all of them wearing caps and sunglasses, this could not be known with any certainty.

Alex glanced at Logan and Ranya, and then answered for them. "Can I show you some ID? This is going to take a little while to explain."

The man spat tobacco juice on the ground between them. "Explain away. You're not going anywhere today, I expect." He pointed up at the damaged leading edge of the right wing.

"You're all deputies?" asked Alex.

"That's right. Cantrell County Sheriff's Office. Now, where's that ID? And how'd your airplane get shot up?"

Alex removed his leather credential holder from a breast pocket on his vest, and flipped it open, showing his identification card and his gold shield.

"What's that, FBI?" asked the leader, moving closer and squinting.

"That's right."

"You're all FBI?"

"Nope, just me."

The man paused, and then asked, "So, who put the holes in your airplane?" It was clear that the Cessna had been fired upon from above and behind, by the outward-curling metal slivers.

"The Milicia, in a Blackhawk helicopter. Up in Torcido County."

The leader's walkie-talkie squawked, and he excused himself and walked back down the road, his back to the "refugees," while his other men kept them covered. After a minute he returned. The two pickup trucks that had remained behind were driven down the road and stopped behind the Jeep. "Okay, load up. You can tell us all about it in town. Get in the trucks—one of you in each." The flanking squads emerged from the brush and rejoined them.

Ranya turned to climb back into the plane, but she was stopped by a rifle barrel laid across her chest. Their bearded leader said, "Don't worry about your stuff. We're a lot of things, but we're not thieves. We'll leave a guard by the plane. Just climb into the back of that blue Chevy, thank you very much."

Alex asked, "Let me get something—a laptop. What's on that computer can explain the situation better than anything I could ever say."

The leader of the deputies hesitated, and then replied, "Okay. Get it."

Frederica Chupatintas was working in her office with the door closed. She was slogging through the backlog of work left for her to handle as the acting Special Agent in Charge. The SAC was still back East at FBI Headquarters, and he had left a mountain of undone and overdue work for her to deal with in his absence. Typical male. Bastard.

To make her life more difficult, the internet had been out most of the afternoon, and when it finally came back on she had over forty new emails to answer. Most of them she could quickly scan or delete, and some she left marked as unread, to handle later. One email contained routine BOLO information, "be on the lookout" notices concerning fugitives of particular regional interest. She quickly scrolled down the list, and a female name jumped right off the screen: Ranya Bardiwell!

Well, wasn't this a most amazing case of visual déjà vu! She had first heard that name only hours earlier at the downtown women's health club, when her friend Galatea Obregon had mentioned it. What had Galatea said? Bardiwell was an Arab terrorist, who was the birth mother of Alexandro Garabanda's adopted son. Five-year-old Brian Garabanda was now in San Diego, with Alex's ex-wife.

She clicked the link and scanned the brief informational paragraph, and the pair of attached prison photos. Bardiwell was 5'9" according to the height lines behind her. Her head was shaved to dark stubble, and she had a hard, defiant look in her eyes. Bardiwell was considered armed and extremely dangerous. She was the only suspect in the murder of a federal officer, which occurred while she was escaping from the federal transit center in Oklahoma City almost two weeks earlier. It was amazing to see the name Ranya Bardiwell in print, after hearing it for the first time earlier in the same day. Frederica Chupatintas read the paragraph several times.

The adoption records were sealed, that's what Galatea had said, and so there was no particular concern. Still, perhaps it would be better to err on the side of caution, and shoot an email out to Garabanda's ex-wife. Wasn't she marrying the female IRS agent who had struck Alex Garabanda with a baseball bat?

Gretchen Bosch—that was the woman. A nasty piece of work, yet still, she was a fellow federal law enforcement officer. Bosch had a standard federal government email address: first initial, last name, at cid.irs.gov. This fugitive Ranya Bardiwell could somehow have stumbled onto the adoption record—anything was possible. She might conceivably even be searching for her child. It couldn't hurt to warn them of the possible danger. A quick note and a link to the BOLO notice was all that it would take. There. Done, sent, and on to the next email in her in-box.

34

The laptop computer was set up in the middle of a varnished pinewood table. The three stranded aviators and the deputies were in the back room of Charlie's Steakhouse on Main Street in Ripley. There was only one long table in this rectangular room, which was evidently used to accommodate private parties. The three self-described refugees and the Sheriff sat at the table in front of the computer's screen. Most of the dozen deputies from the road dragged over more of the room's oak and leather chairs, and clustered closely behind them.

Ranya sat next to Logan on the right side of the computer, sipping a cold Coca Cola from the can, savoring the crisp, sweet flavor. Once again she was the only woman in a room full of men, only this time they were gringos, speaking English with a peculiar accent she couldn't quite place. She decided that these Southwestern cowboys had created their own unique twang.

The Sheriff of Cantrell County had met the deputies at the restaurant, and arranged for the private meeting. The room was paneled in honey-colored knotty pine. A brass ceiling fan circled quietly above them. The walls were decorated with antique rifles, and some very impressive racks of elk antlers. A massive stone fireplace dominated the end of the room opposite the entrance door. The rest of the wall space not holding up historical Old West firearms or antlers was filled by framed photographs. The pictures showed camouflage-wearing hunters cradling rifles, crouching over or kneeling by freshly shot elk, enormous beasts with wickedly tined antlers to shame any deer or moose. Ranya thought it was almost inconceivable that there could have ever been so many elk in the entire state of New Mexico, and these were just the ones that had been shot, photographed, and hung on the walls in one room of Charlie's Steakhouse!

The deputies' rifles were left leaning against the wall by the door. There was an assortment of FALs, M1 Garands, AR-15s, AR-10s, and bolt-action hunting rifles topped with scopes. Ranya noted that this could not have been an unusual occurrence, because there was a slotted rifle rack screwed to the wall to hold their barrels. The men had stripped off their bulky body armor, and were mostly dressed in jeans, hiking boots, and a variety of shirts. Some of them were wearing mix-and-match camouflage shirts or pants from the last half dozen of America's wars, but none in complete sets. Judging by their work clothes and coveralls, there was a welder and a mechanic among the deputies who had come to investigate the downed airplane.

Unlike his deputies, the Sheriff wasn't wearing civvies or cammies, but instead a tan police uniform complete with shoulder patches and a silver badge. He was an average-looking man in his forties, with short brown hair, and a cop's trimmed mustache. A laminated nametag above his right pocket identified him as Sheriff Leander McNally. A five-pointed star adorned his chest above the opposite pocket. He sat front and center between Logan and Alex, watching the view of the jet runway as the film began.

"So this is Vedado Ranch, Wayne Parker's place?"

"That's right, up in Torcido County, near the Colorado line," Logan answered.

"I've heard of it. Biggest private ranch in the state. And you just made this movie a few hours ago? That time stamp is correct?"

"Yep, that's the right date and time. 07-02, that's today." The screen showed the first shots around the Vedado Ranch airstrip, with the color picture zooming in to capture images of the tail numbers of the assembled private and corporate jets.

"You shot this from your Cessna, and they never saw you?"

"Oh no, we took it from a UAV," replied Logan. "A drone."

"A drone?" The Sheriff was visibly impressed. "So, where's the drone? How'd that work out?"

"Just watch," said Logan. "See these four Blackhawks parked by the hangar? We shot one down, and another one shot up our airplane. They were carrying Milicia troops from the Falcon Battalion."

"You shot down a Blackhawk?" asked Sheriff McNally. "No kidding? How'd you manage that?"

"That was later," said Alex, who was sitting on the left side of the Sheriff. "Actually, she shot it down, with a Russian Dragunov rifle." Alex gestured to Ranya, who was sitting on the other side of the Sheriff and Logan. The rest of the 'welcoming committee' had pulled their chairs up close behind them, or were standing and leaning over the chair backs to see the show.

Logan stopped the video, freezing it on a frame showing the four Blackhawks parked on the tarmac, with their tails toward the largest hangar. "We were controlling the drone from fifteen miles away. Our Cessna was hidden under some trees. They spotted the drone, and the helicopters came searching for us. I guess they RDF'd us. You know, radio direction finding. Maybe they found our signal—I thought it was secure. Anyway, one of these Blackhawks was landing in an LZ a couple of hundred yards from us, and she hit it with a rifle. Nailed the pilot, I guess. Down it went." Logan used his left hand, held out flat, to indicate how the helicopter had been descending when it suddenly rolled over and dropped to the ground. He struck the edge of his hand on the table like a karate chop.

The deputies who were sitting and standing behind them nodded to one another, murmuring. Alex said, "Let's watch the whole video, and take it all in sequence, okay? It'll make more sense that way."

"Okay, sounds reasonable," replied the Sheriff.

Alex narrated, with some comments added by Logan, but the video itself made their case. When they saw the VIP reception on the giant terrace in front of Wayne Parker's imported Italian castle, the deputies began to recognize faces, and they became agitated and then angry. Besides Parker, the two Senators, the next president of Mexico, the American ambassador to Mexico and Peter Kosimos, they identified several other notable billionaires and politicians.

There was even a famous blow-dried "conservative" media figure, who had once been a Presidential spokesman. His incongruent appearance was greeted by the deputies with curses and swearing. One older deputy offered the unconfirmed but adamant opinion that all of the American participants at the Vedado conference were senior members of the Council on Foreign Relations. This charge sparked a heated discussion about that private group's inordinate influence on United States foreign policy, particularly concerning their relentless drive to merge Canada, America and Mexico into the North American Community, with no internal borders.

Then they watched the wheelchair-bound Peter Kosimos leave the luncheon in his white van, and they saw the Gulfstream jet land on the runway, and the deputies grew silent again. In astonishment, they saw Dave Whitman step down onto the tarmac, and ride in a black SUV to his impromptu lakeside rendezvous with Kosimos. The deputies were muttering to one another and bitterly cursing, watching the ex-President and the billionaire currency speculator conferring in private by the lake.

Alex said, "We brought the UAV down 2,000 feet to get a good look at these two, so the resolution and the angle are pretty good. We might be able to use lip readers to catch some of what they're saying. Anyway, I don't think they just met to discuss the weather. Okay, this is when they spotted the drone. We started to pick up radio chatter from their security men. See the bodyguard coming over?"

"So this is the end of the video?" asked the sheriff.

"Not quite. Logan did some fancy remote-control flying here." The camera view tilted up and zoomed out to show a wide-angle picture of a mountain range. Then the brief view of the sky and the horizon disappeared and the screen again showed only forests, meadows and lakes, turning and spinning. The view swirled and blurred, and finally steadied again, rushing across treetops and a meadow, and then across a sparkling blue lake. Pine trees beyond the lake began to come into focus, as the distant shore rushed closer. Two shapes at the lake's edge became men, two faces expanded to fill the entire screen, and then the image flashed and went white.

The sheriff spoke for them all. "What in the HELL was that? Who? Uhh, can you back that up, and play it again, but slower?"

This was also the first time that Ranya had seen the UAV's film, and she was also studying it intently.

"No problem," said Logan, jabbing commands on the laptop's keyboard. The images began moving again, the drone's camera eye rushing across the lake waters. He slowed the forward progress until the video was moving frame by frame, and when the men's faces were clearly visible, he froze the picture.

The sheriff exclaimed, "Hell yeah, that's Weasel Dave Whitman and Peter Kosimos! Ho—ly crap! Did you kill 'em?"

"We don't know," responded Alex. "Maybe. We heard them mention a fatality on the radio, but not who."

The Sheriff was quiet, his brow furrowed, stroking his chin. "Hmmm. Now don't this just beat all? Don't this just beat all..."

"Sheriff," asked Ranya, "Are you going to turn us in? Arrest us?" She was an escaped federal fugitive, and here she was in a closed room, surrounded by local law enforcement officers—although they were like no other cops that she had ever seen before. Except for the Sheriff, they were wearing no police uniforms, beyond their tan DEPUTY ball caps. She hadn't even been frisked back on the road, and she was still carrying her barely concealed pistol—as were all of the deputies as well.

"Huh? What?" responded the Sheriff, confused. "You? Turn you in? To who? The Milicia? The communists up in Santa Fe? Naw, don't worry about that, we don't deal with them—we don't deal with them at all. Hell, it seems to me the only thing ya'll are guilty of is crashing a leadership party of the New World Order. If you ask me, you should get a medal for that! Naw, I'm not worried about it—Vedado Ranch sure ain't in my jurisdiction. But just to be safe, I guess we ought to get your airplane off the road. Can it fly a few miles, if we put some gas in it?"

"Sure, it'll fly," said Logan. "No problem."

The Sheriff turned around in his chair to address his deputies, who were huddled close around him. "Gentlemen, can we join you at the bar in a little while?" This was apparently his polite way of asking them to depart, and they rose to file out. "Not you, Halsey." This was his Chief Deputy, the bearded squad leader from the road. He returned to the opposite side of the table, and took an open seat. He was wearing an old-style desert camouflage BDU blouse.

When the room was cleared out and the door was closed again, Sheriff McNally asked Alex, "So, where were you planning on flying from here?"

"California. San Diego," he replied.

"What the hell for?" responded the Sheriff, surprised. "Cali's even worse than Santa Fe! You ought to be heading north, to the free states."

"We would be," said Alex, "but we've got a personal situation to take care of out there. After that, we probably will."

Logan said, "Alex…I've got a problem. I've got until tomorrow to get the Cessna back to Tucson. After that, it's going to be radioactive. But I can't return it all shot up, so that's out the window now. And since I can't turn it in all shot up, well…I've got a real big problem. Alex…we need to talk about California."

"What do you mean?"

Logan was distraught, obviously pained to be backing out. "I mean, we can't fly the Cessna tonight, not to California anyway, not with the fuel tank the way it is. Plus, the Pelican crashed up there at Vedado, and it won't take 'em long to put the pieces together, and find out where it came from. Maybe they already have. So I can't just go back to Albuquerque now, and pretend like nothing happened. And I can't leave Trudy back there either. I just can't."

"Okay…so what're you thinking?"

"Well, I've got until tomorrow before that plane's red hot. I'd like to get the plane patched up tonight, and fly back to Albuquerque. I'll pick up Trudy on a road, just like I picked you guys up, and we'll head north to the free states. I can just swing that, if I get it done tomorrow before the Cessna's posted as missing overdue. Ranya, I'll give you back what you paid me. I'm sorry, but I can't take you guys to California."

Alex thought about this. "Okay, we understand. Your wife comes first. But she needs dialysis, doesn't she?"

"Right, she does…but Alex, I burned all my bridges in New Mexico today. They're going to put the pieces of that Pelican back together, and then…"

"Yeah, I get the picture. You have to look after Trudy. You have to get her out of there."

"Thanks…"

"Don't worry about the refund," offered Ranya.

The sheriff cut in. "So, you two are needing a ride to San Diego? Is that all?"

"Well...yes," said Alex. "You can do that?"

"No, not me, not personally, but I can find you a plane and pilot. You might say that general aviation is one of our fortes around here—it's almost up there with horses and hunting. It's damn sure safer than driving any distance these days! How soon do you want to leave?"

"How soon can we leave?" asked Ranya.

Sheriff McNally told his Chief Deputy, "Go get Flint." The bearded man left the room and returned a minute later with another one of the "reception committee" from the road.

"Hey Flint," the Sheriff said, smiling, "How soon can you be ready to fly a pair of desperados to San Diego?"

The skinny pilot was holding a fresh bottle of Dos Equis beer. His face and neck were ruined by livid red pockmarks, but he carried himself with cocky assuredness. He sported a dirty-blonde mullet haircut: short in front and long in the back. He appeared to be in his mid-thirties, and was wearing his deputy's ball cap on backwards, pushed far back on his head. He was wearing faded blue jeans, and a USMC digital desert camouflage shirt. Ranya could see the subtle swell on his hip where he carried his pistol beneath the untucked shirt. Most of the other deputies had been open-carrying holstered pistols in plain sight. He sat down next to the Chief Deputy, across from the Sheriff and the three strangers.

"San Diego? We can go right now, almost. But it'll cost—aviation gas ain't cheap, or easy to come by." He asked, "Can you pay for the gas?" and Alex nodded assent. "I'll need to fill up at both ends, so call it 120 gallons, at seventy-five blue bucks a gallon, or whatever I have to pay for it. And I don't think you'll want to land anywhere they're going to give you the old biometric rectal exam, am I right?" He pulled off his ball cap, set it on the table, and ran his fingers back through his hair, glancing at each of them, but lingering on Ranya.

By his Southern accent, she thought that Flint was a transplant to New Mexico, maybe from Georgia or the Carolinas. She pegged him for Appalachian hillbilly stock. Scots-Irish, maybe. Skinny and as hard as flint, like his forebears. The thought crossed her mind that perhaps he'd survived the "monkey pox" she'd heard of since her escape. So that's what it looks like…the scars were indeed dreadful.

"Yeah, you're right about that," answered Alex. "We had somewhere a little more discreet in mind."

"Then I know just the place, but it'll cost extra. It's an Indian casino in eastern San Diego County. I've flown in there a couple of times. If you can pay, you can get anything you need there, and I mean *anything*. No questions asked, and *no cops*." Flint said this with his official sheriff's deputy ball cap resting on the table in front of him, yet with no evident sense of irony. If Sheriff McNally had noted the paradox, he didn't let on either.

"Great, that sounds perfect," responded Alex.

"All right then, call it…" He paused, considering. "Call it a hundred thousand blue bucks, all up. That's for the gas, the plane and my risk—and you've got yourself an air charter. Half now, and half in San Diego." His eyes flitted between them, as if he expected his price to be challenged, and he was prepared to negotiate.

Ranya coolly asked him, "Would you prefer that in paper dollars, or gold coins?"

Their new pilot's blue eyes lit up. "Do you really have to ask?"

"Just being polite. I'll pay you fifteen Krugerrands. One-ouncers." Ranya reckoned Flint thought he was getting the best of her…well, let him. He'd be a motivated flier.

"Okay then, you've got yourself a charter." He reached across the table to Ranya, and she shook his hand, while trying to look him in his eyes without cringing at his pitted face. After letting go and sitting back, Flint took a drink from his beer and said, "But first, we'll pour a little go-juice into your Cessna, and then I can fly it off the road for you. I've—"

"Oh, I think I can handle it," Logan quickly responded, chuckling.

"You should have seen the last road he took off from," said Ranya, sticking up for him. "A hundred yards, and off a cliff." She made a steep diving motion with her hand.

"With people shooting machine guns at us," added Alex, grinning.

They were all laughing now, and Ranya continued the banter. "That Blackhawk would have caught us too, if Logan hadn't of flown straight into that hailstorm."

Flint looked at the old Border Patrol pilot with new respect, leaned across the table again and shook his hand. "Well Logan, sounds like you're my kind of aviator. You fly in Afghanistan? Iraq? Iran?"

"Nope, just the border wars. I did my flying time in the Border Patrol."

Ranya thought Logan was used to being underestimated. He was a man you would not glance at twice in a checkout line, or passing on the street. He was just an average fifty-something white guy with middle age spread, black hair streaked with gray and mopy hound dog eyes. Ranya had to admit to herself that she'd misjudged him when they'd first been introduced at Alex's house Sunday night. She'd inwardly questioned Alex's judgment, in bringing such an apparent milquetoast into their conspiracy, but Logan had proven to be a tiger when it counted: in the air.

Flint said, "Pleased to meet you, sir. If you want a new paint job after we patch up your bullet holes, I know just who to talk to at FBO Ripley. We'll get your Cessna into a hangar, and spray the whole thing tan or beige—whatever we've got that suits you. No stripes and a brand new tail number. How's that sound?"

"Are you kidding? That'd be fantastic," Logan replied. "Al, like I said, I've burned all my bridges on this one. I'll lose my pension and my medical, I'll—"

"Don't worry about it Logan, we're all square," responded Alex. "It's not like it's my airplane—do what you need to do."

The Sheriff asked, "Aren't you folks hungry? They make a mean elk burger here, and they serve a steak like you've never seen before."

"I'm starving—bring it on," said Logan, and the others agreed.

The Sheriff told Flint, "Go fetch Carmen on your way out, and have her bring three menus and a round of *cervezas*."

The deputy nodded, picked up his hat and his beer, and left the room.

Ranya asked, "Sheriff, aren't you all putting yourselves at risk, helping us like this? What if the Cessna was tracked here on radar?"

"Then I'd have heard about it on the radio, or seen something on the computer. But there's been nothing, not a peep."

"But that doesn't mean that word won't get back to the Milicia," she said. "Somebody sees the airplane on the road, makes some phone calls.... what if they come down here in their Blackhawks?"

"Honey, I appreciate your concern, but I think we can take care of ourselves. You know, we have nine paid deputies, 140 reserve deputies, and more than 300 auxiliary deputies in this county. Most of them are ex-military, and they're all hunters—real shooters. We've got Rangers, Special Forces, you name it. Believe me: the Milicia doesn't want to tangle with us. They steer clear of Cantrell County."

Ranya said, "But what if they come down here in their helicopters and stay out of rifle range, and just use their machine guns, or maybe even rockets? What if they just stand off and hammer you from the air?"

"Well, I guess it could come to that. I mean, yeah, I know it could. But if it did, then they'd have a lot more to deal with than just cell phone towers getting shot up. Did you ever hear of the Former Lawman's Association?"

"I know that the state fired all the cops who couldn't pass the Spanish test," she said.

"Yeah, that's right, at least in the cities they did. And you know what? There might just be a few of them FLA boys right here in Cantrell County nowadays. And guess what—they've still got plenty of friends on the inside. Friends in Santa Fe, Albuquerque, Las Cruces, everywhere. Trust me on this—not everybody who speaks Spanish and draws a government paycheck supports those communist sons of bitches up in Santa Fe! Not by a long shot! If they were planning some kind of attack, we'd hear all about it ten minutes after they dreamed it up."

"Not the Milicia, Sheriff," said Ranya politely. "They've got good security—I know that for a fact. And a lot of them are hard core, with serious military training. At least the Falcon Battalion."

The Sheriff chuckled dismissively. "We're not too worried about the Milicia, not from what we've seen. You know, up there in Santa Fe, they talk a good game, and they put on a fair show. Maybe they're not half bad at burning ranches on their territory—but they'd be way out of their league in Cantrell County. They mess with us, and they've got a couple hundred pissed off lawmen, soldiers, and hunters to deal with. And not just from New Mexico either: we've got plenty of new folks from Phoenix and Tucson, and let me tell you: the Zonies are done with getting pushed off their land."

"What's the matter with Arizona?" asked Ranya.

"Oh, not too much, just power outages, water shortages, and gang warfare. I mean, just try living in Phoenix when it's 115 degrees in the shade, without electric power. Drinking swimming pool water gets pretty old, when it's green and nasty."

"Gross! What's the matter with their electricity?"

"Everything. The grid's real shaky over there. The lakes are too low to get much hydropower, and they're having trouble buying enough gas and coal, so their power plants aren't exactly running full tilt. They've only got one nuke and that's not enough. And then there's the folks who just can't stand seeing one part of town with electric power, if they don't have it. They shoot at transformers and power line insulators just for the hell of it, just to screw over the areas that have their act together."

Halsey, the bearded Chief Deputy, added, "What it is, is the rich neighborhoods are a lot easier to rob when the lights all go out. Them Mexican gangs are unbelievable over there now. I mean, calling 'em gangs don't hardly even cover it. They call 'em *pandillas*. They're more like Mad Max armies, and what police stuck around are terrified of 'em. They'll knock out the power to a neighborhood, just before they go in with ten or fifteen carloads of gang bangers. Then they go house to house like Comancheros—and it ain't pretty. Especially if you got women or daughters around."

Ranya paused, digesting this, thinking of the terror brought to ordinary suburban families by the lightning arrival of thirty or more armed robbers, rapists and killers. "Damn…I had no idea Arizona was like that," she said. "Are they Mexicans in these gangs, or Mexican-Americans?"

Halsey snorted. "What's the difference any more? It's not like we've got any kind of a border. Those gangs convoy up and just drive back and forth into Mexico. Pancho Villa rides again, only now he's riding in trucks and SUVs."

"But what about the Border Patrol?" she asked.

"Border Patrol?" Halsey spat in his cup. "The Border Patrol's scared to death of the *pandillas*—they just hide. You got a dozen trucks full of *pistoleros* with AK-47s coming, you think the Border Patrol's gonna jump out and get in their way? Hell no—they run and they hide. Sorry Logan, but that's a fact. They know the federal government won't back 'em up—Washington doesn't want an 'incident.' Hey, you know something? As bad as it is in Albuquerque and Santa Fe, at least the Milicia keeps some kind of order. Southern Arizona's just completely out of control."

"Yep, it's bad over there," agreed the Sheriff. "It just plain sucks to live in Phoenix or Tucson, and a lot of folks have given up and left. Most of 'em head north, but we get some of them. We have plenty of room in Cantrell County for folks who bring something to the table. Sometimes, it's just military experience, and that's fine. It's all been by word of mouth, and they just started coming. That's how we got folks like Flint, just friends of friends, lots of ex-military buddies. We've picked up almost a hundred new families in the last year alone, and almost every one of them joined the Deputies. I won't lie to you, it's not easy living here, it's damned tough—but at least you don't have to worry about your kids getting their throats slit for their sneakers. Compared to southern Arizona, life here is *tranquilo*. But if the Milicia came down here and attacked our homes, well then, the proverbial *mierda* would hit the fan—big time. We'd have no reason not to go on the warpath and start taking scalps. Folks around here all say the same thing: they won't be chased off their land. This is it, do or die. This is where they'll make their stand. Just let the Milicia come down here. Just let them try."

Halsey spat into his cup again and expanded on the Sheriff's theme. "There's at least five hundred folks in this county that can shoot a horsefly off a cow pie a mile away, and that's on a windy day, and they're all windy. Around here, kids get a rifle before they get a bike. Folks like that, you just leave 'em the hell alone, if you got a lick of common sense."

The Sheriff said, "Just between us, that's mostly what the 'cell phone tower jihad' is about. It's just a friendly warning to Santa Fe: don't push your luck, amigos—you're in our range. So it's sort of 'live and let live' between us and the reconquistas, at least for now. I mean, this is one mighty big state! Did you know that New Mexico is number five, right after Montana? Well, that means we're big enough for the communists to just stay the hell out of these parts. Plus, there's no Spanish Land Grants down here to give 'em an excuse. Believe me, Santa Fe don't want to kick over a nice quiet little hornet's nest called Cantrell County. No ma'am, they most surely do not want to start a blood feud with us."

"And we're not the only county that feels this way, not hardly," said the Chief Deputy. "If you've been hanging out in Albuquerque and Santa Fe lately, you might have the impression that the communists are running this state. Well, that'd be a very wrong impression. You seen any signs written in Spanish around here? Hell no, and you won't. Santa Fe hasn't sent a state car into this county since the election: they know better. Now we just run our own affairs as we see fit."

Ranya said, "I passed through Mountainview last week, that's a little town southeast of Albuquerque."

"We know where it is," replied the Chief Deputy.

"There were no signs up in Spanish there either," she said. "None that I saw, anyway."

"I suppose," said the Sheriff, "that you can tell there's no love lost between us and the communists up in Santa Fe, and there ain't. But this fight's not about Spanish or English! We got no problem with the Old New Mexicans, none. They're family, kin you might say. A bunch of my best deputies are Spanish. Hell, aside from the Indians, they were here first, right? And besides, we're all married in together, we always have been. We've all got Spanish cousins and in-laws, so it ain't that. No, it was those damned illegal aliens—New Mexico just plain got over run! It should have never come to this—and it all goes back to the federal government in Washington. If those traitorous Quisling bastards had done their lousy jobs and stopped the invasion years ago, we wouldn't be in this mess today! And now it looks like those traitors in Washington are getting ready to sell off what's left of America, at that bogus Constitutional Convention in Philadelphia."

Halsey added, "Yeah, that's going to be the mother of all traitor conventions. That's where the communists are going to stick in the knife, and break off the handle. You can just feel it coming."

The Sheriff said, "So anyway, we can appreciate what you folks did up in Torcido County today." He looked directly at Alex, and then at Logan. "You remember that oath we lawmen all took way back on Day One, when they swore us in?" The Sheriff held up his right hand, and looked across the table at his Chief Deputy. "I do solemnly swear to support and defend the *Constitution* of the United States, against all enemies, foreign *and domestic*, so help me God." Well, as far as I can tell from your computer movie, that little get-together up at Wayne Parker's ranch today, that was nothing but a traitor convention—all domestic enemies, every last one. If you'd a dropped a Daisy Cutter right on Wayne Parker's mansion and cratered the whole place, down here in Cantrell County, we'd have stood up and cheered! So if you nailed Whitman and Kosimos with that UAV drone, well, I'd say that the taxpayers never got a better return on their money, ever."

Halsey said, "Yeah, if that wasn't the head of the snake, it was damn close to it."

"Yes sir, it was," the Sheriff agreed, nodding. "So I just want you to know, we'll do whatever we can for you here in Cantrell County. If things don't work out for you in California, if you need somewhere to keep a low profile for a while, this is the place. We've got two square miles for every man, woman and child, and we'd love to have a few more patriots move in. Logan, I'm sorry we can't help your wife out, we don't have a dialysis machine, but it sounds like you've got a good plan going, to fly her up north. And a crackerjack pilot like you ought to make a decent living, what with his own Cessna 210, am I right? Once it's repainted, I mean."

Logan gave him a look of surprise at this candor.

"Yeah, yeah, I know, a Sheriff ought not to talk like that. But things are different today. Everything's different today, everything! Right and wrong? Legal and illegal? Those are important, sure—but right now, they're not the *most* important thing. Right now, everything just comes down to patriot—or traitor. Everybody has to pick a side, and I know which side I'm on. The same side as you folks—and proud to be. Right to the bitter end, even if it's a lost cause."

35

James Holcomb almost never left the San Diego Federal Building before Bob Bullard. If Bullard stayed late, so did his Chief Staff Officer. By six o'clock in the evening, he'd usually be found hovering nearby in the DHS director's offices, hoping to hear Bullard say, "Jim, why don't you knock off for the night?" Holcomb rarely if ever heard those words.

Tonight Holcomb came into the inner office and placed a printout on Bullard's desk, while his boss finished a phone conversation. After he hung up the phone, Bullard picked up the paper, and slipped on his reading glasses.

"What's this?"

"Boss, you asked me to let you know if anything popped up on Ranya Bardiwell."

"Who?"

"Ranya Bardiwell, the Arab. She escaped from federal detention in Oklahoma two weeks ago. You know, the Malvone affair, back in Virginia?"

"Gotcha, I'm tracking. Let me read it."

From: Frederica Chupatintas, FBI ASAC Albuquerque Field Office
To: Gretchen Bosch, IRS Criminal Investigations Division San Diego
Subj: BOLO Escaped Federal Fugitive Ranya Bardiwell

Hi Ms. Bosch,
You may remember me from the Albuquerque FBI Field Office. Anyway, I just came across a BOLO notice that may be of personal concern to yourself and Karin Bergen. To make a long story short, I have learned that the federal fugitive Ranya Bardiwell (see attached link) is thought to be the birth mother of Ms. Bergen's son Brian. The adoption records are sealed, and there is no reason to believe that Ms. Bardiwell is aware of Brian's current name or location, but I thought I should give you a head's-up.
Frederica Chupatintas

After scanning the printed email, Bullard said, "Interesting. Small world, huh? I had Gretchen Bosch in here just this morning. Well, I think she can take care of herself. Nice catch Jim, but I don't think it's a problem. Keep checking though, you never know."

"Will do boss."

Bullard reread the letter, while Holcomb stood in front of his desk. Sometimes strange coincidences happened in life, that was a given. Still, his antennas were twitching. Unseen wave patterns were welling to the surface, he could feel it.

"And Jim…go ahead and put taps on their phones and emails for the next week. Check the transcripts, and let me know if anything funny pops out."

"Taps on who?"

"Gretchen Bosch and her girlfriend. Umm…and her ex-husband."

"Her ex-husband?" asked Holcomb, looking surprised. "Gretchen Bosch was married to a man? But I thought she was a les…"

"No, not Gretchen Bosch—her girlfriend's ex-husband. I forget her name, look it up. Her ex-husband's an FBI agent in Albuquerque. If Bardiwell tries to make contact, it might show up on the tapes."

Flint wore night vision goggles, and didn't say much during the three-hour flight from Ripley, across Arizona and the bottom of California. The cabin interior was completely dark, with only the faintest glow from the instrument panel. Once again, Alex sat up front in the co-pilot's seat on the right side. Ranya didn't begrudge him this. Although he wasn't a licensed pilot, he knew far more about flying than she did, and he knew the esoteric radio procedures. If their hired pilot tried any kind of a double cross, well, she was sitting behind him with a pistol, and there was a second set of controls in front of Alex. (She now had five extra pistol magazines and four boxes of Cor-Bon ammunition for her .45 caliber pistol, all of it purchased at the "Gun and Pawn" on Main Street in Ripley.)

They lifted off from the town's nondescript towerless airport just after dusk. The plane was a four-seater Piper Cherokee, with low wings that swept up from the bottom of the fuselage. They had to walk across the wing root to climb into the cabin, a new experience for Ranya. After her recent flights in high wing planes, the Piper seemed to offer the entire sky to her. The tradeoff was losing a swath of terrestrial landscape on each side of the plane, not much of a loss on a night flight. She decided that on balance she preferred high wing planes. The Piper's three wheels didn't retract, and the plane cruised at only 160 knots of airspeed, which she now realized was not fast enough to outrun a Blackhawk helicopter if they were jumped en route.

They flew low-level through the mountain passes from Ripley the short distance to the state line, and then the pilot called in a bogus flight plan from Springerville Arizona, to Palm Springs California.

Their flight path took them across Arizona just north of Phoenix. Ranya was sitting on the left side behind the pilot, so from their cruising altitude she was able to see the lights of the vast city spreading to the southern horizon beneath her. While she watched, an entire rectangular section pulsed off and then back on, and then went black. A few moments later, an adjoining square went dark, and then another. In just a minute, half of the lights of Phoenix were extinguished, leaving enormous black spaces, crossed by highway lights that must have been on different power circuits. In a few more minutes Phoenix was behind them, and once again they flew over a completely black world. For a while Interstate 10 provided some frame of reference, and she could see occasional headlights inching along it, but the highway gradually diverged off to the north of their air route. Sitting in the darkness, she wondered how they would find Brian in a city of more than a million people. She worried about whether she could truly trust Alex, or if he was planning to ditch her once they found the boy. Eventually she nodded off into dreamless sleep.

Three hours into the flight, the pilot cancelled his declared flight plan, and called in a new flight plan to a private airstrip in eastern San Diego County. Their new destination's runway was clearly lit, and the pilot pulled off his night vision goggles before he brought them down smoothly and taxied to a stop near a row of hangars. They were met at the plane by an SUV. After more than three hours of flying through pitch darkness, they were glad to be on the ground again, and with enough ambient electric light around them to see clearly.

Flint went off to arrange for refueling and a tie-down for the night. Ranya had paid him four more one-ounce gold Krugerrand coins to lay over for four days at the casino's hotel. He was to wait for their phone call or even for their sudden unannounced arrival, and he was to be ready for an immediate departure at all times. Alex gave him a new prepaid cell phone, and instructed him never to use it, but only to leave it turned on, and await either their call, or their arrival. The pilot knew that he might even be asked to land on a road for the pickup, for which he happily agreed to be paid extra.

Unloading the plane was a cumbersome process for the stiff and tired passengers. The driver of the SUV was wearing a tan casino uniform with shoulder epaulets. He spoke to them in unaccented English. He was accompanied by a security guard, also in uniform, carrying a compact M-16 carbine. Ranya thought that both of them could quite possibly have had some Native American blood flowing in their veins, but perhaps there was somewhat more of the Italian vintage.

"You're John and Mary, from New Mexico?" asked the casino rep.

"That's us," replied Alex.

"We've been expecting you. Are you hungry? Thirsty?"

"Thirsty," answered Ranya. "Very." She had drunk nothing before the flight, since there were no bathrooms aboard single engine prop planes. You sat down, you strapped in, and that was that until the flight ended.

“Are these all of your things?” the driver asked, looking at their mound of baggage.

“This is it,” said Alex.

“Well, let’s go then. Whatever you need, we have it. Whatever you want, just ask me. I take it you want to avoid the main registration area?”

“That’s right,” replied Alex. “We’re tired; we’d like to skip the formalities.”

“No problem, I understand.”

They loaded their luggage into the back of the SUV, climbed into the middle seats, and drove away from the runway past a connected line of hangars. Two winding uphill miles later, they came around a final switchback and saw the brilliantly lit, neon encrusted Golden Arrow Casino Resort and Hotel. They were in San Diego County, sixty miles east of the city.

36

Thursday July 3

Ranya's new wig fit well enough, even though it pulled and itched just a bit. She shook her head vigorously, and was satisfied that it wouldn't slip. She studied herself in the hotel room's wall mirror, admiring the transformation. The medium-blond hair felt and looked incredibly natural, flowing onto her shoulders. It was full enough around the sides to help conceal her face from cameras, especially when combined with stylish oversized sunglasses. No one looking for Ranya Bardiwell with short brunette hair was going to see her today.

Satisfied with her appearance, she went back to the task of packing her new luggage. The black bag was open, lying across her bed in the casino's hotel. The heavy-duty nylon rolling case was more suitable for carrying the heavy load of gold, without showing any outward strain. Most of the clothes going into the case had just been purchased in the casino's fashion boutique, including the turquoise-colored tank top she was wearing. She also bought some souvenirs, including a white sweatshirt with San Diego and a sailboat design on the front.

Because she was wearing her black designer jeans and a form-fitting top, her .45 went back into her leather fanny pack. Even in the relative safety of her private room, she kept the pistol on her right hip at all times. The do-not-disturb sign was hanging on the doorknob outside, and if she heard as much as a brush against the door, she was prepared to draw. The room provided shelter but no safety. It was a cave with no rear exit, a trap, and she was anxious to leave it. She had thought that she would be able to spend Thursday morning relaxing, but found that she only wanted to get moving. The city of San Diego was drawing her as if by its own gravitational pull.

The television was set on a cable news channel with the sound turned low. She half noticed a story showing a team of brightly dressed emergency rescuers being roped down a cliff to some kind of a crash site, at night in the rain. The caption beneath the picture captured her full attention: "Billionaire Philanthropist Peter Kosimos Dead in Colorado Car Crash."

Ranya snatched the remote control and pushed the volume up, while calling through the suite's partly open interior door. "Quick! Put on TOP News!"

Over the rescue footage, a female reporter's voice said, "—last night Kosimos was returning from his foundation's North American headquarters in Aspen, when his Mercedes skidded off of this canyon road in a rainstorm. The driver was thrown from the wreck and survived the plunge into this ravine, but he was unable to call for help, and walked for several miles before being found." A helicopter camera shot showed the rescue team in red and yellow jumpsuits rappelling down a rocky slope in the darkness. Reflective tape on their jackets glowed eerily under searchlights. Kosimos's black Mercedes limousine was a barely recognizable pile of scrap metal, wheels-up, at the bottom of the canyon.

Alex rapped softly on the inner door of the suite, between their rooms. "Are you dressed?"

"Yes. Come on in."

"Wow—nice hair! Who's the blondie?" He entered her room in his new tourist garb: a gray and brown Hawaiian shirt, and Levis blue jeans. "I saw it already on CNN. Kosimos is dead, so I guess the drone nailed him. Well, good riddance. I was wondering how they were going to release the news. You know we're onto something big, if they had to fake his death outside of New Mexico. Any mention of Whitman?"

"No, none," she answered. "Weasel Dave must have lucked out again. If he was dead, I think they'd have said something by now."

"Anything on the Blackhawk crash?"

"Not a word. I guess it never happened."

"No, I guess not," he agreed sarcastically. "Oh, that reminds me—the next helicopter for La Jolla leaves at 11. Are you going to be ready?"

"I'm almost ready now."

"Hey, were you okay with paying thirty ounces for the car? I know that's a big chunk of change."

"You gotta do what you gotta do," she replied evenly. "If we return it in one piece, I'll get 25 ounces back anyway. It'll be worth it if everything works out—I just hope it's not a rip off. I mean, how do we know they'll have a car waiting for us at all? How do we know we're not being scammed?"

"Flint seemed pretty sure about this place. I guess the Golden Arrow has to protect its reputation. Ripping off high rollers would be bad for business. Word would get around, and then who would come way out here?"

"Do you think we picked the right car?"

He said, "Yeah, an Explorer should be fine for what we need. It's big enough, but not too big. We don't want something we can't park downtown. The main thing is super dark tinted windows."

"We're really on our way now, aren't we?"

"Oh yeah, we sure are."

"So far, so good."

"So far, so good." Alex thumped his chest with the palm of his hand. "Hey listen, I've only got one vest, do you want to wear it? I feel bad, wearing Kevlar when you don't have any."

She held out her arms, showing how her tight aqua tank shirt clung to her narrow waist, and how her bust line was nicely prominent. A slim line of skin was visible between her leather belt and the bottom of the thin cotton shirt. "You really think it'll fit under this, without showing?"

"I guess not," he laughed.

"Don't worry Alex, if there's any shooting, I'll just get behind you, and use you for cover."

"Deal." He put out his hand, and she shook it.

"Thanks for inviting me up, Director Bullard."

Ramón Devlin, the San Diego Chief of Police, was grinning like an idiot. He was clearly overjoyed to be in the private office of the Regional Director of Homeland Security. Devlin looked like a shorter version of former Mexican President Vicente Fox. Like Fox, he was of Castillian Spanish and Irish ancestry, without any hint of *mestizo* blood in him.

Devlin probably thought he had been summoned to Bullard's office to be offered a federal position. He was clearly in brown-nose mode, wearing his full dress uniform. Everybody knew that being police chief of San Diego was a no-win job, a job you just tried to survive until a better offer came along. The previous police chief had been assassinated after only five months in the position, and the job had then gone unfilled for another three months, until someone brave enough—or stupid enough—had been found to take it. Ramón "Ray" Devlin was that man. It was understood and accepted that anyone who planned to do the job—and live to see his next birthday—would be someone willing to accommodate the Mexican gangs and cartels that now virtually ran most of San Diego.

Bullard stayed seated in his executive chair, behind his massive mahogany desk. "Great to have you Ray, take a load off." Devlin sat across from him, his hat on his lap. "Look, I want to get to the point. I drove up to Mission Bay to film a new public service announcement this morning, and I saw some things that bothered me. My CSO took some pictures, and put together this little presentation."

Jim Holcomb was sitting across the office on a black leather couch, and he pointed a remote control at the opposite wall. A six-foot plasma TV burst into light. The first picture showed a green overpass sign, covered with angular slashing gang graffiti. Every five seconds, another picture appeared. There was red and black graffiti on the cement sides of a graceful bridge over a sparkling blue harbor, there was graffiti on the side of an upscale Italian restaurant, there was graffiti on the wall in front of a public elementary school.

"Ramón, we've got a problem."

"Oh, I hate graffiti Director Bullard—it's a scourge. But those little pricks are—"

"Ramón, do you recognize where these pictures were taken? We're not talking about Chula Vista or Ciudad Nacional—this was in Mission Beach! Come on! I mean, I don't give a rat's ass what they do in Montclaire or City Heights or any other shit holes over there—if those people want to live like they're still back in Tijuana or Baghdad, that's their problem. But this was in Mission Bay, for crying out loud! I mean, we're talking about Seaworld! Foreign tourism is just about all we've got left—what do you think our guests from Japan and China think when they see gang graffiti like that? Ray, I don't ask for much from you, but can you at least hold the line at I-5?"

Chief Devlin was taken aback, his thick neck and face a bright red above his tight collar. "But there's fifty rat-holes where they can slip through, and even with all of the cameras our response time—"

"Don't give me response time Ray, give me results! Break some heads! You find those tattooed *maleantes* west of I-5, put the hurt on 'em! If your cops find a spray can in a car west of the 5 and the guy's not a professional painter, then slam his hand in a car door. Come on Ray, I let you run your own show on the other side. We both know you've got your own arrangements over there, and I'm not sticking my nose into your business. I understand it's tough just trying to keep the peace over there, much less enforce the law. I get that. All I ask, is just keep that gang shit east of I-5!"

Bullard knew that Devlin was in an impossible position, trying to maintain law and order on the wild mesas east of the coastal interstate highway. Dozens of the densely populated hilltop neighborhoods were cut off by canyons or freeways, and only had one or two access roads. Single police units never went into these no-go zones on routine patrol; it was far too dangerous for them. The risk of being cut off from backup and subsequently killed or kidnapped was too great. Derelict vehicles, steel cables and trash dumpsters would be dragged across the chokepoints, leaving any police units trapped inside. As a result, the police never went into many areas except on blitz raids, with a dozen or more patrol cars, SWAT units, and helicopters overhead. The rest of the time, these no-go zones were gang territory, controlled by the most vicious thugs imaginable.

The positive side of this grim reality was that more of his police patrols could be concentrated where they could actually do some good, on the civilized coastal side of I-5.

"But the ACLU will…"

"Oh, don't get cute with me Ray. Screw the ACLU—I got dossiers a mile long on all of those goddamn communists, and most of 'em are perverts too. Don't worry about that end—I'll take care of it. I just want you to put the fear of God back in the gang bangers. Teach them a little respect. Look, they already own eighty percent of the city. Just send them a message: stay the hell out of our side of San Diego! Understood?"

Chief Devlin choked, swallowed, and stammered, "Understood."

"Now, I've been hearing some new rumors about a group called *Los Cazadores*, the Hunters. The word is, they're-off duty San Diego cops. Tell me what you know."

"Uh, well, really nothing! I mean, it's just rumors, nothing's been proven…"

"Yeah, yeah, nothing's been proven—but somehow gang bangers keep winding up behind dumpsters, with two slugs in the heart, and a bullet hole in the forehead." Bullard put two fingers of one hand on his chest, and another just above his eyes. "And nobody ever hears a shot. Almost like *somebody* was using suppressors…"

"But Director Bullard, there's never been any direct connection—"

"You're completely missing my point, Ramón. Personally, I think the Hunters are the best thing your department's got going. Aside from the obvious social benefit, it saves the taxpayers a fortune in court costs and jailing. Especially if your cops catch any of those little tattooed shits west of I-5. Understood?"

Chief Devlin was shaking, but appeared relieved at the same time. "I…think so."

"So if you've got any Internal Affairs investigations looking into the Hunters, drop them. Forget it. And if your cops do nothing else, tell them to keep the bad boys out of coastal San Diego! If I see any of those tattoo-faced *cholos* with the shaved heads west of I-5, I want to see them shaking with fear, or pushing a lawn mower, got it?"

"I've got it."

"Great. Thanks for your time, Ray."

After Police Chief Ramón Devlin's hasty departure from the director's office, Bullard leaned back in his chair and cracked his knuckles. "I think I got his attention," he told his CSO. "I think we'll be on the same sheet of music from here on out. Thanks for putting together the slide show."

"No problem boss."

"Hey, anything else come up on that fugitive, what's-her-name, Bardiwell?"

"Ahh, no—but I've seen some other really weird stuff coming out of New Mexico. You know that Peter Kosimos was killed last night?"

"Yeah, a car accident in Colorado."

"Well, it might not have been in Colorado, and it might not have been an accident. I've been reading some very interesting emails between

Wayne Parker's people, the Kosimos Foundation, and the governor of New Mexico."

"Go on..."

"Well, for starters, Kosimos was at some kind of a party that Wayne Parker threw yesterday. That's confirmed. Parker has a million acre ranch in New Mexico, up near Colorado. I've put together a partial guest list, and almost everybody on it used some kind of a cover story to attend. All different reasons, I mean. Or they just never went, officially, but they were reported as being there by some of the other guests. It's all very strange."

"And you think Kosimos was killed there, and the accident was staged some where else?"

"Sure seems that way."

"Why?"

"Take a look at this guest list." Holcomb slid a single-page printout across Bullard's desk.

"Hmm...Senator Kelly, Senator Montaine, Ambassador Calavera, Kosimos, Governor Magón—holy shit—Pascual Orozco? Hmmm...now isn't that interesting. Now, why would...?"

"Some of them have been emailing back and forth, using encryption." Bullard's CSO chuckled. "At least, they *think* they're using encryption, but we're reading every email. I just love how that works...thank God for the NSA. But even after we break their emails into clear text, some of the names and places are in a word code. Anyway, it's looking like Kosimos was killed on Wayne Parker's ranch, and his body was moved to Colorado. Somebody went to a lot of trouble to disconnect him from whatever happened at Parker's ranch."

"Interesting. Let me know if it turns into anything."

When Brian woke up, Gretchen was already gone, thank goodness. Mommy made him Fruit Loops and orange juice for breakfast, even though he was still in his PJ's. She let him eat it at the low table in the living room, while she took a shower. Way out through the glass doors, he could see the airplanes landing at the airport. He watched cartoons until Mommy came out wearing her bathrobe, with her hair wrapped up in a big green towel. When she came out, she took the remote control away, and that was the end of the cartoons.

She switched channels a lot, mostly boring grown ups talking to each other. Some of them were very serious, and some of them laughed and joked a lot, but either way, Brian didn't understand what they were talking about.

Then a commercial came on, showing another boring old grown up, standing up and talking with the ocean behind him. He said, "Hi, I'm Bob Buller," and for some reason, that made Mommy get very excited.

"Oh my God! Bri-Bri, that's Gretchen's new boss! I mean, her *really* big boss! Did you know that Gretchen met him yesterday? She did! Oh my God!"

Mommy grabbed her leather purse off the low table, and dug into it. This was a moment Brian had been waiting for and planning for since yesterday. He got up from the carpet, and snuggled next to her on the sofa, hugging up against her while she opened her silver phone. She pushed a button on top that said ON, and the little screen lit up, like a tiny television. She pushed another button that said "CONTACTS," and the little screen showed a list of names.

The first name on the list, right on the top, said ALEX. Brian knew that ALEX stood for Alexandro Garabanda, his Daddy. But Mommy pushed another button with an arrow pointing down, and each time she pushed it, another name turned colors, down the list, until the name that was a different color said GRETCHEN. Then Mommy pushed a green button that said SEND, and held the phone up to her ear. In a few seconds, she was talking.

"Gretch! Hey girlfriend, guess who I just saw on TV? Bob Bullard! Yes! Uh-huh, only the 'Southwest Regional Director of the Department of Homeland Security,' that's who! And *you* were in his office, for a one-on-one! Oh…my…God! Oh yeah, that is *so* big time—you are *so* awesome!"

Mommy kept talking to Gretchen, but Brian didn't pay attention to what she said. It didn't matter. He had found out the grown up secret to using Mommy's phone. The secret of the phone was ON—CONTACTS—ALEX—SEND.

Brian wouldn't forget the secret!

At 9:30 AM, Basilio Ramos and Comrade Inez met for the second time by the duck pond, in the heart of the university campus. The pumps and fountains were still not working. Brown and green algae covered half of the pond, and no ducks were in the water or on the shore. Once again, they sat in the obscuring shade beneath the overhanging willows. It was almost exactly one week since their last meeting. Basilio Ramos had rushed back to Albuquerque, and he had not had a chance to shave. He had changed from his camouflage uniform in a university lavatory. His jeans were not pressed, and his green Polo shirt was wrinkled and unwashed.

Inez was wearing another pants suit today, her brown one this time. She wore an oversized khaki ball cap with her gray ponytail pulled through the back, and her dark sunglasses.

"Basilio, I'm so sorry to hear about yesterday…"

He felt as if he had not slept in days, and knew that he looked terrible. "It was a disaster. A complete disaster."

"Have you been home yet?"

"No, we just drove down from Torcido County. I got your page on the way."

"Don't go home then, or to the Falcon Academy."

He looked at her quizzically. "Why not?"

"Basilio, we had a meeting of the council this morning…"

"Without me? But I'm—"

She raised her hand, cutting him off. "Magón had instructions for us: there was no discussion. Basilio, you're to be replaced as the leader of the Falcons. The Falcons will become the Reconnaissance Company of the 5th Battalion. Carlos Guzman…"

Ramos began to stand up. "*¡Ese hijo de…!*" he nearly shouted.

She patted him on the knee, urging him back down. "Basilio, calm yourself. The order came from the governor himself."

"And me?" he asked bitterly. "What is to be *my* new position?" He dropped back onto the bench.

"That…hasn't been determined yet. You'll be notified, after the inquest. You're officially on leave. There are many questions about the crash, and even about the rifle used to shoot the helicopter. Do you have the rifle?"

"Yes, I have it."

"Basilio, there are many rumors; even I don't understand them all. Many rumors, and many questions. Is it true that you drew your pistol on a Blackhawk, and aimed it at the pilot, and threatened to shoot him?"

"Yes, that coward was—"

"So it's true?"

"It is, but I can explain it. When will this inquest be held?"

"Next week, maybe. It hasn't been scheduled. But Basilio, I must tell you, perhaps there will not be any inquest at all."

"I don't understand. No inquest?"

"The situation…it may be resolved by *other means*. I'll do what I can for you, but it's out of my hands. You have very few friends left in Santa Fe, after what happened yesterday."

"Am I in…personal danger?" Ramos understood all-too-well that he was part of the small circle of conspirators involved in the assassination of former governor Agustín Deleon. It had occurred to him that this fact represented an ongoing risk to the new governor, Félix Magón, who had personally given him the orders for Deleon's permanent removal from power.

"Danger? I don't know. Possibly. Possibly. You might even want to consider… relocating. As soon as possible."

He kicked at the dirt with his black shoe, looking down. "I appreciate the warning."

"Basilio, you know I've always had a soft spot for you. I know that's not very professional of me. A revolutionary should not have such weaknesses, but I don't want to see you come to harm. But that's not the only reason I asked you to meet me here, just to warn you. I have something else." There was a canvas bag like an oversized purse or book bag on the bench beside Comrade Inez. She withdrew a large manila envelope, and slid out a stack of color photographs. "Look at these, and tell me if you recognize anyone. They were taken Sunday morning, but I only learned of them yesterday."

Ramos flipped through them; they were snapshot-sized copies of surveillance photos. Inez had a direct connection into the Special Surveillance Group. He knew that she was doing him a favor, and perhaps even putting herself at risk, by sharing classified SSG material with someone under such a darkening cloud of suspicion.

The photos showed a small playground in what appeared to be an ordinary Albuquerque neighborhood, identifiable by the Sandia Mountains visible in the background. There was a man on a cement bench, and then he was standing, and was joined by a blond woman. They appeared to be talking, but at a distance of a few meters apart. There was also a small child in a pink jumpsuit. Ramos said, "The man seems familiar. I'm not sure, am I supposed to know these people?"

"There are more, keep looking."

In the following photos there was a muscular man with a crew cut, holding a video camera while standing by a black pickup truck. There was a line of parked cars in the foreground of a long shot, with the playground in the background. From the perspective and foreshortening, he could tell that the SSG photographer had been a long way off with a telephoto lens. The car in line closest to a stop sign, parked at right angles to the playground, was a very small boxy wagon, white on the sides and black on top. It was one of those two-seater electric cars, with the roof made of solar panels, and the entire back area given over to batteries beneath its cargo deck.

The hair on his neck began to tingle. There was someone sitting in the driver's seat of the electric car, but it was hard to make out. He flipped through more photos. The driver was wearing a ball cap. In one photo, the person sitting in the car could be seen holding a small pair of binoculars. He turned to the next picture, and the driver's face was partially visible in profile.

Ranya Bardiwell. He took a deep breath, and closed his eyes.

"Basilio, this is the woman who was with you at the reception."

Inez did not ask him, she stated this as a fact. He glumly nodded yes.

"She is the Arab girl, your rifle expert. Have you seen her since Saturday night?"

He slowly shook his head. "No." He continued to flip through the photographs, not really looking, his mind spinning.

"Well," Inez offered, "I've learned quite a bit more about this young woman in the last 24 hours. You knew that she was in prison for five years, and that she escaped?"

"Yes."

"Did you know that she had a baby, while she was in prison? The child in these pictures is her son. His name is now Brian Garabanda. When he was born, he was given to an FBI agent for adoption."

Ramos was stunned by these continuing revelations, one after another. "Her *son*? Given to an FBI agent?"

"Yes. The child was given to Supervisory Special Agent Alexandro Garabanda. Garabanda was Luis Carvahal's agent handler, before last Saturday. That blond woman in these pictures is his ex-wife, Karin Bergen."

Ramos absorbed this information, and then said quietly, "That's what they did in Argentina, during the Dirty War. In the 1980s."

"Excuse me?"

"That's what they did with the babies of the *desaparacidas*, the disappeared ones, the women who became pregnant in the detention centers. The clandestine torture centers. They gave the babies to the secret police in Chile, to raise as their own. They gave them to the Chilean DINA, to any DINA agents who wanted a child."

"Yes, so I've read. And it happened in Venezuela, and Peru and many other places. I suppose it always does, in a dirty war."

"Inez, you said, 'his ex-wife'?"

"Karin Bergen-Garabanda. She dropped her husband's name. She left Nuevo Mexico for San Diego with the child last Sunday, after this meeting on the playground. I didn't put all of this together until yesterday, when I found out that Ranya Bardiwell was the child's birth mother. I put in an intelligence request for all available information on Garabanda, and that's when I learned of these SSG photos. Garabanda was the subject of the playground surveillance, not Bardiwell. The SSG doesn't know who she is in these photos; she's marked as an "unknown subject." And I received some other reports on Garabanda: listen to this, this is interesting. He's supposed to be in Santa Fe all this week, at a conference. The SSG went into his hotel room, and they found only a cell phone, set up as a relay. Garabanda wants people to think he's somewhere he's not. The question is, why? Where would he be going? I can only make one guess."

"So can I," said Ramos, slowly pounding his knees with his fists.

"San Diego."

"Yes, San Diego," he agreed. "And I have something for you, Inez. I know Bardiwell was at the Vedado Ranch yesterday. In fact, I'm positive."

"How do you know this?"

He was silent, staring at Ranya's best surveillance photograph, her face captured in profile, wearing a dark baseball cap.

"The rifle? The Dragunov?" she asked.

"You know about that?"

"Of course I know about the rifle. For one thing, I've read Guzman's debrief. *El Condor* is not exactly your biggest fan."

"I know," he said bleakly.

"In his report he wrote about a pair of men's neckties attached to the rifle, and cut in the middle. He didn't know what it meant, but now I have a guess."

"Enough—you know everything. She ran away from my house Saturday night after the reception, and she took the rifle with her." Ramos hoped that she would not connect the electric car in the pictures to Professor Johnson, and Professor Johnson to himself. He hoped that disgusting aspect of this case could be kept from discovery. He hoped that they would eventually blame Bardiwell for the professor's disappearance—anything but what had actually happened in his bedroom on that night.

"Yes, that's what I guessed, that she took the rifle from your house. But nobody else knows of this, no one! Not the SSG, not Comandante Guzman—only you and I. At least for now."

Ramos laid his forehead on the palms of his hands, his elbows propped on his knees. "Inez, what should I do? How much time do I have?"

"I don't know, but Basilio, there's something else we need to discuss. Things must look entirely black to you now, but there is one aspect of this affair that might present you with an opportunity—an opportunity to recover. The people on the small airplane you were chasing yesterday, the ones who shot down Puma 2, they were controlling a pilotless drone aircraft. What the *Yanquis* call a 'U-A-V.' They were watching the Vedado conference, from above."

"I heard a drone mentioned on the Vedado Ranch radio net."

"Then you know that the drone was used to attack President Whitman and Peter Kosimos? Did you know that?"

"I only heard that the drone crashed, and there was a fatality on the ground."

"Did you know that it killed Peter Kosimos?"

"I saw the news this morning. I heard that Kosimos was killed in a car accident in Colorado. He was killed by the drone?"

"It took his head off. Dave Whitman didn't receive a scratch, other than being soaked with Kosimos's blood. Now, here's your opportunity. The drone was sending down video imagery from the Vedado Ranch conference. Certain of the attendees don't want to see that film on television, if it exists. I'm informed that the drone was a type that would be recording directly onto a computer, some kind of portable computer. We know that the drone was taken from a Border Patrol base near El Paso, by a retired Border Patrol pilot who also 'borrowed' a white Cessna 210 airplane."

"It was a white Cessna we were chasing yesterday."

"The pilot's name is Logan Crawford. According to government flight logs we've been able to check, he's flown with Garabanda before."

"So where is this Crawford? Where is the Cessna?"

"We don't know. He hasn't been seen since he signed out the airplane on Tuesday. He has a wife in Albuquerque, but she's gone too. The SSG went by their house this morning. There was breakfast on the table, and signs that someone packed in a hurry. Both of their cars are gone. It looks like she fled."

"That figures," mumbled Ramos.

"The Dragunov rifle was found where we think they were controlling the drone, so that puts Bardiwell and Garabanda together yesterday. Now, not even the Special Surveillance Group knows about the connection between Bardiwell and Garabanda, because they don't know what the rifle means, at least not yet. And from what we can tell from our Federal sources, the FBI doesn't even know that Bardiwell has been in New Mexico, or that Garabanda is only pretending to be in Santa Fe. So we have an edge Basilio, an advantage we can exploit! Only we know who was controlling the drone, and where they're probably going next. Now, here's your opportunity: if you found Bardiwell and the FBI agent, and if you recovered the computer with the video record of the conference, if you permanently removed the risk that this Vedado meeting would ever be seen on television...well, certain very influential parties would be extremely grateful. Grateful enough to cause Félix Magón to be in a forgiving mood. Maybe even more than forgiving."

"I see." Ramos looked up, a glimmer of hope lifting him from the pit of despair.

"Basilio, I would grasp this opportunity."

"And you think they're going to San Diego, after the child?"

"Probably. Where else?"

"So if I find the child first..."

"Yes! And I know where the child is—I've been busy, Basilio! The child is staying with his mother, in a condominium tower in downtown San Diego. It's called the Pacific Majesty, it's very new. This building is leased by the United States government; they use it to house federal employees. The child and his mother are staying in apartment 4124, with another federal agent. You see, they're *lesbianas*, this agent and the child's mother. Gretchen Bosch is her name—she works for the IRS. So that's where you'll find Bardiwell and the FBI agent: I think they're together, trying to find the child. But you'll have the advantage—they won't know they're being pursued. Now here is your mission: If it's possible, if you can, bring Garabanda and Bardiwell back to New Mexico—preferably alive. Alive, to be thoroughly interrogated. We must know everything that they know, and if they've given copies of their film to anyone."

"What if it's not possible, what if I can't find them, or bring them back?"

"If you can't bring them back, then eliminate them—but try to bring back the computers. If you have to kill them, kill them. Do what you must, but try to get the computers. Time is of the essence—every day that this mission is not accomplished means a greater chance of the film being released. We need to know what's on the film, and who has been given copies."

"For damage control."

"Yes, quite right, for damage control. And to make sure that any film of the Vedado Ranch conference isn't released."

"It may already be too late! They may already have released it."

"Perhaps, so I wouldn't waste any time finding them. In any event, I don't think it would be played on television. I think the federal government would use the Patriot Act to stop it, I don't think the networks would run it. But even if it was shown, if Bardiwell, Garabanda and the Border Patrol pilot are eliminated, then the tape's authenticity can be challenged and destroyed. You understand how this works: 'experts' will call the film a fake, a computer-made forgery, and nobody will be alive to dispute that claim."

"All right Inez, I'll do it," said Ramos, his mood lifting. "I'll take some of my best men. But I'll need some logistical and communication support..."

"Of course. I'll serve as your point of contact at this end. I'll have a phone number and an email address monitored around the clock for your support requests. I'll do everything I can for you from here. On a deniable basis, of course. But you must succeed at this mission Basilio—otherwise, I would not return to Nuevo Mexico."

37

Ranya was surprised by how quiet the interior of the helicopter shuttle was. There were seats for seven passengers, but only five were on the flight this morning. Their destination was the seaside town of La Jolla, "the jewel," located ten miles north of downtown San Diego. She had completed her transformation to a lady of means; she was glamorous from her blond wig to her gleaming new $1,500 white Nike running shoes. After a room service breakfast, she had gone shopping in the casino's boutiques, putting everything that she needed onto her room tab.

Their bill was paid in the manager's office, in gold. Their total for the two-room suite, their room service meals, the boutique, the men's clothing store, the new luggage and their helicopter shuttle flight to La Jolla was converted from $33,840 New Dollars to 4.75 ounces of gold. The one-week rental of a Ford Explorer SUV cost five more ounces, along with a hefty 25-ounce "security deposit." In effect, they had bought the vehicle, which would be delivered to them in the safety of La Jolla.

She paid the 34.75-ounce bill with 35 Krugerrands, and received three tiny gold coins in change. Two were slightly smaller than a dime, and the other was even smaller, only about the diameter of a .45 caliber shell casing. Close examination revealed that each was struck with an arrowhead on one side, and the profile of a famous Indian chief on the other. The manager suggested that she exchange more of her one-ounce gold coins for the more "useable" 1/10th and 1/20th ounce coins. He assured her that the gold coins were accepted readily across Southern California, despite anything to the contrary that she might have heard from the government. Ranya accepted his offer, trading ten of her one-ounce coins for one hundred "gold dimes," as the manager off-handedly referred to them. He also quoted her the current exchange rate of gold to paper dollars, so that they would not be taken advantage of in San Diego. Today, one ounce of gold was worth $7,125. She didn't ask who set the price, it didn't seem to matter.

Dressed in their new clothes, they rolled their own luggage from a hotel side entrance along a paved golf cart path, to the helipad where a sleek cobalt blue Eurocopter was waiting for its 11 AM departure.

She sat in the back of the luxury helicopter next to Alex, with their bags on the empty seat and at their feet, eschewing the separate luggage compartment located behind them. The seats were soft cream-colored leather, almost as comfortable as the seats in Basilio Ramos's Jaguar. An executive wearing a charcoal suit took the empty cockpit seat next to the pilot—the civilian chopper only had one set of controls, on the right side.

Two women, trim and attractive thirty-somethings, sat in two of the middle seats. Both were wearing designer everything, from top to bottom. Ranya guessed that their visible jewelry was worth enough to feed a small African nation for a year. She wondered if their obviously rich husbands were getting their money's worth.

The helicopter's turbine moaned, its blades began to spin, and a few moments later they lifted off. The reason for the casino's profligate use of night time electricity was immediately visible: a nearby barren mountain ridge sprouted a row of a dozen enormous white towers, each topped with a slow-turning three-bladed propeller. Evidently, the casino Indians were plowing their profits back into building their own independent infrastructure.

She thought that the land beneath them could have been New Mexico between Albuquerque and Santa Fe, but more gray than red. There were the same boulders, dry hills carved by ravines, and the occasional green valley following a meager watercourse.

Ranya listened carefully to the rich women in front of her, trying to pick up their accents and the current slang, in order to better her own ability to pass herself off as one of them.

"I always sit next to the dealer, always. I just wait for a seat to come open, or I won't play. I'm sick of stupid amateurs who don't know how to play blackjack—they just screw up the cards I should get."

"How much were you up last night?"

"Ninety five thou. I should have quit, but I couldn't! Still, I had a good night. Paid for my room, the flight, everything."

"Don't you love getting paid to gamble?"

"Oh, you know it!"

Both ladies giggled.

"Too bad we can't claim these trips as a deduction. 'Reason for visit: to exchange paper for gold.' I mean, have you tried to pay for *anything* with blue bucks lately? Even my pool boy wants gold!"

"Are you still using Roberto? He's a cutie."

"Oh, *God* no. I caught him stealing, and I canned him. And that's not all—I made sure the little creep lost his crossing permit. It'll be a cold day in hell before *he* works in La Jolla again. Good riddance!"

"You fired him? What did he steal?"

"Not much. Towels, mostly, and some liquor from our pool bar. But it's the principle of it. I just can't stand a thief."

"I know what you mean."

"So, what are you doing this afternoon?"

"Oh, I thought I'd go up to Rancho Santa Fe, and play tennis with Talia and Stephanie at their club. Maybe swim some laps."

"You're not driving, are you? Remember what happened to Monica. Her husband paid two million, and they *still* cut off her ear."

"Oh hell no, I'm done with driving. I'm flying. I'm not taking any chances."

"That was so *awful* what they did to Monica! They could have just sent her ear rings for proof, but no, the sick bastards had to mail Ronnie her ear too!"

"Yeah, well, I guess it worked. He paid up fast after that."

"Hey, how much kidnap insurance do you guys have?"

"Ten mill."

"Same here. But I'm still never driving east of I-5 again."

"Are you joking? I won't even drive *on* I-5."

"Who needs to go east of I-5 anyway? Just send a servant, if you need to get something over there."

"A-men!"

Bob Bullard was sitting behind his desk, idly clicking between surveillance camera views of San Diego. He was waiting for his next scheduled visitor to be announced, before helicoptering up to LA for a quick afternoon visit. Jim Holcomb knocked and entered.

"Boss, the fireworks are all set. For our end of it, we're putting all of the federal tactical teams on standby."

"Uh-huh, good. We don't want any problems. Washington wants to see that San Diego is still an All-American city—these Navy bases mean a hell of a lot to them. They call San Diego the 'western anchor,' and they don't want to see it end up like Los Angeles. So, they finally got the fireworks problem straightened out?"

"Yes, but what a nightmare that was! Just try to find one COSCO shipping container in the whole Port of Long Beach, when they have a three-week backlog! But we lit some fire under their asses, and they found it. The container was trucked down last night with a police escort. Those Italian brothers are going to run the show out on the bay, same deal as every year. They're already loading the barge."

"So how big is this show going to be? We want a good one," said Bullard.

"They say they have enough rockets for a solid half hour of the big stuff, plus a gigantic grand finale—heavy on the red white and blue. We're still working out the city government logistics, but it's going to happen—the mayor's office has agreed to cooperate. Mayor Valdepeñas was dragging his feet, but we finally got him on board."

"What was his problem?"

"Oh, he just doesn't want to look like a gringo-lover," explained Holcomb. "I don't think he really cares about the 4th of July one way or the other, himself. He just wants to show his political base that he's not a Yankee lap dog. Word is he's getting ready to run for governor. You know how they are—*Aztlan Aztlan, Über Alles…*"

"What's that, German?" asked Bullard.

"*Aztlan über alles*? Well, yeah, I mean, it's all about race for those guys. 'For *la raza*, everything. Outside of *la raza*, nothing.' That's their official motto, you know."

"Well Jim, it's not like the *reconquista* boys kept it a big secret, what they planned to do after they took power."

"You've got that right," Holcomb agreed. "What did anybody expect, after they elected one of the founders of FEChA as the mayor of Los Angeles? I mean, those FEChA guys wrote the Plan of Aztlan in the first place."

"FEChA, smecha," scoffed Bullard. "This is all just power politics. In the end, it just came down to numbers. Racial politics, and raw numbers. Out with the old, in with the new. The Anglos wouldn't fight for California when they had the chance, and now their time is over."

"Well actually, they did fight, or at least they tried. They passed Prop 187, remember? But the judges threw it out."

"Oh, come on, that wasn't much of a fight. Face it, the Anglos rolled over. The *la raza* crowd called 'em racists every time they made a peep about illegal aliens, and the gringos crawled into a corner and hid. The liberals out here thought they could hold hands and sing Kumbaya with the *reconquistas*, and everything would be mellow... Obviously, they thought wrong. The conservatives, they were a lot smarter. They voted with their feet, they just took off. And every Anglo that left was replaced by three or four more illegals…"

"And their anchor babies," added Holcomb.

"Yeah, and their anchor babies—millions and millions of *reconquista* anchor babies. Instant citizens, instant welfare cases. And then came the big amnesty…and that was all she wrote." Bullard pushed away from his desk, leaned back in his black leather executive chair, and sighed. "You know, I wonder if this'll be the last big 4th of July in San Diego?"

"Why would it be?" asked Holcomb.

"Oh, I'm hearing rumors, that's all. After the Constitutional Convention, who knows what's going to happen? Everything might be changing around here, everything. The California delegation to the Con-Con are all Aztlaners, and they won't sign off on any amendments unless they get autonomy for the Southwest. Nothing is going to pass out of the Philly Con-Con unless the Aztlaners get what they want, right off the top."

Chino finally arrived, riding the green Kawasaki KLR-650 on-and-off road bike from Ramos's villa in Sandia Heights. He was wearing jeans, a dark windbreaker, and a black full-face shield helmet. The Comandante of the Falcons and his specially picked team of Zetas were waiting at Coronado Airport, a small general aviation airfield in northeast Albuquerque, not far from his villa and the Falcon Academy base.

The bottom of the Twin Otter's open side cargo door was four feet above the tarmac, and the Zetas wasted ten minutes searching around the hangars until they found a twelve-foot scaffolding plank sturdy enough to use as a ramp. Corky Gutierrez, the plane's pilot, arrived in his little white pickup while they were pushing the bike up the wooden board. He was the former owner and operator of Coronado Air Sports, a parachuting and sightseeing company.

He braked hard, got out, and marched up to the Comandante. "I was just at flight ops—what's this about you selling my airplane, Ramos?" he demanded.

"Can you wait until we get this damn bike in the door?" Ramos turned his back on the pilot. The Kawasaki weighed several hundred pounds, and it was no easy task to roll it up the steep ramp. Two men were on each side of the bike, steadying it and pushing it. Once its front wheel was inside of the fuselage, Chino climbed aboard, and walked it across to the right side of the plane, to lash it to the cargo tie-down bars.

"Ramos, you're not selling my Otter! No fucking way, Jose!"

Corky Gutierrez was a sorry excuse for a Latino man. He was half gringo anyway, on his mother's side, and with his wild brown hair, bristly walrus-like mustache and green eyes, he looked more like a hippie than a warrior for Aztlan—which he was not, and never could be. Today he was wearing typical dress: a faded ball cap, a red Hussong's Cantina t-shirt, khaki cargo-pocket shorts, and ratty sneakers. Beyond his Albuquerque house, his girlfriend, his hangar and his airplanes, his loyalty was an open question. Today his questionable loyalty was a minor consideration. With Ramos and five armed Falcons on board, Corky's allegiance would be 100% guaranteed.

Corky Gutierrez was the Otter's pilot and former owner, before the plane had been confiscated by the state for the use of the Falcon Battalion. He continued to fly for the Falcons on a contract basis, paid mainly with promissory notes and some occasional blue bucks. Ramos understood that Gutierrez hoped to regain outright ownership of his planes, and he played up to that hope.

This was a standard tactic during liberation struggles, to enlist property owners in effect to work for the state, while vainly attempting to retain control over their former property. Sometimes this was done with ranch owners, who gave up legal title to their land while staying on as a "consultant" or a "manager," in the futile hope of regaining ownership after a future regime change. In this way, ranch operations could continue without disruption, or in this case, the Twin Otter airplane could be kept flight worthy, and available for the use of the Falcons as needed.

"Corky, we're not selling the airplane. We just had to put something down on the flight plan. We couldn't say, 'reason for flight: kidnapping two *gabacho* traitors in California,' now could we? Look, we'll just fly to San Diego, stay a few days, and fly back. We'll say the buyer didn't like the plane, whatever. It doesn't matter—it's just a cover story."

"You're not lying to me, are you?" Corky was calming down.

Ramos held up his right hand. "I swear to God."

"And you're paying for the gas?" the pilot asked.

"I wouldn't say 'paying' exactly," explained Ramos. "But that goddamned *maldito* fuel truck better be here in five minutes, or somebody over at flight services is going to die! They'll take my paperwork if they know what's good for them—they can send an invoice to the state. Hey Corky, you know those *rulacho* assholes, why don't you run over there and get that fuel truck moving? Tell them what I said: five minutes, or somebody's going to die!"

The Comandante knew that even out of uniform, his Zetas were a terrifying group. Maybe even more terrifying, without the discipline implied by their uniforms. Corky Gutierrez jumped into his Japanese minipickup and tore across the tarmac back toward flight services.

With the motorcycle aboard and secure, the wooden plank was shoved inside. It was replaced by the Otter's own hinged aluminum ladder, which hooked to the sill of the cargo door. The airplane's actual cargo door rolled up inside and out of the way, for opening in flight to conduct parachute operations. Gear bags and equipment boxes were carried from Falcon Battalion pickup trucks, and loaded aboard.

Depending on the mission, the plane could be left entirely open for cargo, or it could carry twenty persons in seats, or up to thirty parachutists sitting on the bare cargo deck. For this trip, they had installed one row of six seats down the left side of the plane, between the cargo door and the cockpit bulkhead. This kept the right side and rear of the cargo area open for their baggage, weapons, equipment and the motorcycle.

Ramos carried a bundle from his own jeep, a black nylon zipper case. The dead South African's Dragunov rifle was going with him to California. Perhaps he would be able to use it on this mission, if a long shot was his best option. But no matter what, the incriminating rifle was not coming back to Nuevo Mexico, even if he had to throw it out of the airplane in flight. He stood at the open hatch; the cargo deck of the Otter was at the level of his ribs. He leaned inside of the plane, and slid the rifle case forward just along the inside of the fuselage. It fit beneath the aluminum legs of the removable seats, stowed all the way on the left.

One more rifle case attracted no particular attention. His Zetas were also bringing scoped M-16s, M-4 carbines, and several bolt-action scoped hunting rifles. In fact, these were the very rifles that Ranya Bardiwell had sighted-in. It would be pleasantly ironic to use one of these rifles to nail the bitch, if she couldn't be captured alive.

Although they had the long guns in order to cover every contingency, it was more probable that they would need to use firearms that were more concealable in the city. For close range work, they brought a selection of .45 caliber Ingram MAC-10 machine pistols, extra magazines, ammo and suppressors, as well as their own personal sidearms. No matter what situation they confronted in San Diego, Comandante Ramos was confident that his team would be able to adapt, overcome any problems, and accomplish their mission.

Even though rumors of his being relieved of command of the Falcon Battalion were beginning to circulate, the Zetas did not question his orders to prepare for a one-week special covert operation in San Diego California. Even Lieutenant Almeria responded without question, bringing his portable communications and surveillance equipment, which were packed in a variety of metal and fiberglass cases. The pudgy glasses-wearing Almeria seemed excited by the prospect of an undercover mission in California, eager to join the elite Zetas on a special operation wearing civilian clothes. Ramos knew that tech support troops usually were thrilled to come along on these ops with the shooters. It made them feel like James Bond, for once in their lives.

The four Zetas he had specially selected for the mission were more blasé. In or out of uniform, it was all the same to them. Chino and Salazar had both spent years in San Diego and Southern California, and were looking forward to visiting old friends. Carlos Mendoza he picked because he was easy-going and made few demands, while being extremely loyal and dedicated to his Comandante. Genizaro he picked, well, because he was Genizaro. He could be depended on to follow orders without question, and pull the trigger, no matter what.

While it was true that Comrade Inez had given him this mission, Ramos had no way of knowing at what level of the state government it had been cleared and approved, or if it had been at all. If he could bring back Ranya Bardiwell and Alexandro Garabanda, and the recording equipment that had filmed the Vedado meeting from the drone, he might yet salvage his command. If not…well, he'd lose his villa at the very least. Of course, considering what Ranya Bardiwell was likely to reveal under interrogation about the circumstances of her last night at his villa, Basilio Ramos considered it highly unlikely that she would make it back to Nuevo Mexico alive…

It briefly crossed his mind that he was in a similar position to Corky Gutierrez. Corky worked for the state because he wanted to keep control of the Otter, his other smaller airplanes, and his house. Now Ramos was doing the same, because he wanted to keep his command of the Falcons, and "ownership" of his villa in Sandia Heights.

While his men finished loading the plane, Corky returned in his battered Nissan *camioneta*, followed by the fuel truck. The fuel truck driver avoided even eye contact with Ramos. The driver swiftly pulled out the black hose, climbed his ladder and gassed the plane. He departed in his truck just as quickly, without as much as a hint of the usual invoice-bearing clipboard, providing Comandante Ramos with his first smile of the day.

For the flight, Corky took the left side pilot's seat, and Ramos sat in the copilot's position. As the mission commander, he wanted to get a good look at San Diego from the air, before they landed. The Otter was a proper airplane, with a real cockpit that was separated from the cargo area by a bulkhead with a narrow doorway, but no door.

Corky obtained ground clearance, and taxied to the takeoff point at the end of the runway. The pilot reached up pushed the unusual overhead throttles forward, and the Otter began to roll down the runway with a roar, vibrating madly. At sixty knots of airspeed, Corky pulled back on his yoke, and the plane lifted its nose skyward and some of the vibration disappeared. The Twin Otter wasn't a fast airplane by any means, but at short takeoffs and rapid climbing, it was a champion, and Basilio enjoyed the sensation of being pressed back into the seat. He was breaking free from Nuevo Mexico. His problems always seemed to diminish when he was strapped into a metal beast that was lifting away from the earth. Flight always meant freedom to Basilio Ramos, at least temporarily.

While Basilio Ramos and his handpicked team were taking off from Albuquerque, the executive helicopter flying from the Golden Arrow Casino was preparing to land in La Jolla, by the Pacific Ocean ten miles north of downtown San Diego. They could have taken another flight directly to the downtown San Diego International Airport, but Alex was concerned that the security check might be more thorough there. They were carrying concealed firearms, not to mention Ranya's gold, which was far more than the legal maximum of five ounces. The manager at the casino had told them that they would not be wanded or checked when landing in La Jolla, but the unexpected was always a risk. The jet helicopter flight across San Diego County took half an hour.

They crossed the north-south running I-5 freeway, and the helicopter descended toward a prominent hilltop, which rose steeply above the highway that ran along its eastern base. Most of the crowded residential neighborhoods of San Diego they had flown above seemed to be concentrated atop sprawling mesas, divided by steep canyon green spaces. Many of the highways used the bottoms of these canyons as their pathway through the hills, and Interstate 5 was the last highway before the coastal foothills and the blue Pacific.

Several acres on the top of the hill they were descending toward were scraped flat and paved over. Only wind-bent scrub brush and tall grass surrounded the asphalt square, which was larger than a soccer field. There were five yellow landing circles, one in each corner and one in the center, marked H-1 through H-5. Two spots were already occupied by choppers dropping off and picking up passengers. Their pilot set down on H-3, asking them to wait for the blades to stop turning before disembarking. He climbed out first and assisted the ladies in stepping down onto the tarmac, and then he helped them to unload their luggage.

Alex had purchased two identical black rolling travel bags at the Golden Arrow Casino shops. They were each four feet long, and big enough to consolidate their smaller gear bags. Between the two of them, they could carry everything in one trip, a critical consideration. Considering what Ranya and Alex were hauling, their bags could not be left outside unattended, ever.

The road leading up to the heliport ended in a traffic circle, where yellow and orange taxis were waiting. Alex intentionally dawdled, pretending to look for something in his bag, while the two women who had accompanied them from the casino took the first taxi, and the executive who had been sitting in the front of the helicopter took the second. Only then did he begin to move toward the taxi line, pulling his rolling bag with Ranya behind him. He was wearing the gray and brown Hawaiian shirt he had just purchased at the casino shop, and new blue jeans. The flowered shirt pronounced him a harmless tourist, and the untucked bottom easily concealed his .40 caliber Sig pistol. The shirt's broken-up design also prevented his thin lightweight body armor from printing through at the top or bottom.

In his capacity as an FBI Special Agent in Albuquerque, he had been comfortable wearing his "outdoorsman's vest" and BDU-style tactical pants, but here in San Diego California, they would set him apart, and to the knowing eye, proclaim him to be either an "operator," or a wannabee. Here in San Diego, he wanted to be an ordinary wealthy tourist, nobody of particular note.

They were running on blind faith and sheer momentum. They both knew that they could have been informed upon at any point along the line. Flint might have dropped a dime, or one of the staff at the Casino might have made a call. It was impossible not to be videotaped in a casino, and there was no way to know where the digital videos were being fed. If they had been set up for arrest, it might logically come right now, on this barren hilltop where they were virtually trapped.

The third taxi in line was a beat up yellow mini-van. The driver appeared to be in his late sixties at least, well beyond cop-age, so Alex judged that it was not an undercover vehicle. They approached on the sidewalk that ran downhill from the landing pad, and the driver got out and lifted up the rear hatch.

"Where to folks?" he asked, with an American accent. He had long flowing snow-white hair, combed straight back and hanging over his collar. Despite his years, he was wearing stylish wrap around sunglasses, and looked almost like an elderly Hollywood movie star. He was also wearing a Hawaiian shirt, showing old-fashioned "woody" station wagons, with surfboards on top.

"Just down to La Jolla. Prospect Street." Alex lifted their bags into the rear luggage compartment, not wanting the driver to feel their unusually heavy weight. Then he sat in the front passenger seat. Ranya opened the sliding right side door and sat behind him.

A printed document taped to the dashboard announced the fares by zones; there was no meter. The minimum charge was $90. Alex mentally calculated that this would have been $900 dollars in the old pre-conversion greenbacks—quite a steep price for a short taxi ride.

A serpentine two-lane road took them steeply downhill, past stunning villas with breathtaking ocean views. Each switchback presented them with another panorama, a constantly changing visual feast. To the north, para-gliders slipped along rugged cliffs above the surf, where the sea breezes were turned upward. Small sandy beaches were punctuated by rocky points, the blue ocean rolling across them in long white streaks.

"Beautiful, isn't it?" asked their driver, sweeping the vista ahead of him with a gnarled hand. "One of the things I never get tired of. You know that old Beach Boys song 'Surfin' USA?' Well, that was me, fifty years ago. '*All over La Jolla*,' that's what they said in the song, and we did, oh man, we did! I switched to long boards after I hit forty, and I surfed until I was sixty. Windansea is right down there, it's one of the most famous surfing spots in California. Oh man, we've got so much great California history here, you just don't even know where to start."

Above the driver, taped to the sun visor next to his license, there was a color picture postcard showing a white cross on a hilltop. Judging by the size of the people standing all around it, the cross was at least thirty feet tall.

Alex said, "I haven't been to San Diego in five or six years. Wasn't that cross in the news? Wasn't there a court case?"

"A court case? There sure was. It was a real donnybrook." The old driver ran his fingertips across the faded photograph. "That was the Mount

Soledad Cross. They had a cross up there ever since 1913, and they made a war memorial with that big white cross right after Korea, back when I was just a kid. It was a real landmark; you could see it up there against the sky from miles and miles around. The ACLU tried to make them take it down for years, since it was on public property. The county sold the land to private owners, but the judges said it didn't matter, that it was a sham sale just to keep the cross up. So then the county took the land back, and tried to give it to the federal government as a federal war memorial park. No dice. The judge wouldn't allow it.

"It was a real fight, it went on for years. Veterans chained themselves to the iron fence around the cross, old ladies were getting dragged away by cops in riot gear—man, it got ugly. There were candlelight vigils and pray-ins, but in the end, it just didn't matter. Everybody thought the cross would at least stay up while the final appeal went to the Supreme Court, but it didn't work that way. A few months after the protests died down, while everybody was waiting on the Supreme Court, the county came in at night with a crane and a flatbed truck. They cut it loose with jackhammers, and they hauled it away. In the morning, it was gone. All that was left was rebar and rubble. It's a real shame—you used to be able to see that cross for miles and miles."

"So what happened to the property?" asked Alex. "Is it still a war memorial?"

"Oh no, a year after the cross got knocked down, the county sold the property to another private developer. It didn't really matter any more, once the cross was gone. The county decided to make some money off of the land, I guess."

"What is it now? Houses?"

"The place where the cross was?"

"Right, what did they do with that place?"

"Are you kidding?" The driver turned briefly to Alex with a quizzical look. "You just landed on it—the Mount Soledad Heliport. I guess I shouldn't complain though, almost everybody who lands there catches a taxi. Most of the folks who live on this side of I-5 don't like to drive on the other side, so they take a lot of helicopter rides. It's gotten to be a huge business, helicopters, because of all the kidnappings and carjackings. Still, it's a real shame about that cross. That was a nice piece of California history that we lost."

38

It was the best merry-go-round ever. Gretchen stood outside and made a movie with her video camera, while Mommy rode on a black horse that went up and down next to him. The music was really loud and it was fun, but it went very fast and made him get dizzy. They were in Seaport Village, which was a lot of little stores and eating places, right by Sandy Eggo Bay. It was close, so they walked there from the condo, between lots of tall buildings down to the water.

At Seaport Village, Brian's Mommy and Gretchen were shopping a lot. His Mommy bought him a kite that looked like a shark in the kite store, but he didn't get to play with it. Maybe tomorrow, they said. It's a big kite, so it needs a big field, that's what Gretchen said. But they did get to stop to buy ice cream, and Brian got to ride on the merry-go-round.

Gretchen was wearing her blue farmer pants, with the square flap that covered her front, but let everybody see her big arms and scary tattoos. Farmers named John wore overalls like that when they drove tractors in Brian's picture books. Gretchen lifted dumbbells all the time to make her arm muscles get bigger and bigger. She wore sunglasses like two mirrors, so you never knew if she was looking right at you or not. Brian was wearing the same kind of overalls, but with a red t-shirt underneath.

Brian thought that his Mommy looked pretty, wearing her shiny green dress that hugged her skin. The wind was making her hair blow around, but that's how Gretchen liked it. Gretchen never had to worry about the wind blowing her hair around, because she hardly had any!

They were sitting at a table outside in the sunshine, with lots of happy people walking by on a wide sidewalk, right next to the water. Some people rode by on bikes, and there were even little wagons, where people sat in the back, and another man pedaled half of a bike in the front. Brian could see the top of their condo building from there, and lots of other tall buildings too. A big Navy ship, the kind that airplanes landed on, was parked way across the Sandy Eggo Bay. In between there were sailboats and motorboats, and the big blue bridge they drove across.

Gretchen Bosch said, "The CART team's going to be on standby tomorrow. Just in case. All of the federal tactical units will be on alert. It's the old multi-agency cluster foxtrot."

"Just in case of what?" asked Karin. "It's only the 4th of July, what's the big deal?"

"Just in case somebody tries to mess it up," replied Gretchen. "Terrorism, the Mexicans, whatever."

"Are you going to be on call?"

"Me? Hell no. I'm not officially reporting until Monday, same as you."

"Are they having fireworks tomorrow?" asked Karin.

"Oh yeah, big time," Gretchen growled. "Over the bay, right out there."

A group of college-age Asian girls flashed by on roller blades, zooming down the bayside promenade, grinning and laughing. Each slim young woman was dressed in a spandex outfit, 100% color-coordinated from their skates to their helmets, including their elbow and knee protection. Every single item sparkled with newness.

After they were past, Gretchen barked, "Damn! When did we get invaded by the Chinks? You notice there was almost nobody shopping in Seaport Village but Chinks? Mexicans I expected, but when did we get invaded by the goddamn Chinese?"

Karin wiped some vanilla ice cream from her son's chin with a paper napkin, while a pair of San Diego cops in shorts zipped by on police department mountain bikes. "Brian, do you want to see fireworks tomorrow, for the 4th of July?"

"Uh-huh," he answered. "I like fireworks."

Gretchen said, "We can go out on the government dock to watch the fireworks. Federal employees and dependents only. We'll be right out there, real close to the show. We won't even have to drive—we can just walk down Broadway and out on the pier. That's the same pier where Bob Bullard keeps his Homeland Security boat."

"Hi, I'm Bob Buller," said Brian, mimicking the frequently aired DHS public service announcement. After they had seen him on television, Gretchen had pointed out his eighty-foot yacht, which was visible from the balcony of their condominium.

"Hey, that's pretty good, kiddo," said the mannish IRS Special Agent. "That's right, 'Bob Buller' keeps his big boat there. You want to go out there tomorrow and see the fireworks, and get a look at his boat?"

"Okay," replied Brian, a little hesitantly.

Gretchen Bosch finished her ice cream first, and stood up and stretched and flexed. "You know, Director Bullard made me an interesting offer yesterday, he said it could almost double my salary."

"How?" asked Karin.

"The 12% RIP—that's the new Recovery Incentive Program. It sounds like he's pretty liberal-minded on the forfeitures. I'll get to keep 12% of the auction value of any property we recover, but for gold, that's just chump change. They figure the price of gold in dollars at the official rate, which is a joke. I'll just keep as much gold as I can find. That's what everybody does already. I mean, gold is the best money there is, only an idiot would turn it in for paper blue bucks."

"But Gretchen, gold is illegal, isn't it?"

The IRS Agent laughed dismissively, while swinging on her daypack. "Karin, you are one silly little airhead, you know it?"

Another pedicab approached them along the promenade, pedaled by a panting middle-aged American man wearing a Padres ball cap, a t-shirt, frayed cut-offs and flip-flops. On the sides and back of the cab were photographic advertisements for gold and diamond jewelry, but the vertical writing on each side of the pictures was entirely in Japanese and Chinese characters.

In the back of the cab sat a young Asian couple. Behind them were stacked shopping bags and boxes, all with designer logos or the names of upscale stores. They could have been honeymooners, the groom about thirty, and his slender bride a few years younger. Each was dressed immaculately, the husband in a new cream-colored suit and tie with a matching Panama hat, his young wife in a flowery red sundress with a matching chapeau. The man said something to their pedicab driver, and he stopped the cab even with Brian, who was standing near the table watching all the people go by.

The attractive young Asian woman was sitting on the pedicab's seat closest to Brian. She held up a camera and politely asked, "Picture? Prease to take picture of brond baby boy, with brue eyes?"

Gretchen Bosch indignantly stood to her full height and stepped forward, in front of Brian. "Not only no—*Hell* no! *No*, you may not take a picture of our '*brond'* boy! Number one: He's not *brond*, he has light brown hair. And number two: Why don't you all just go back to China, before we drop another big one on you!"

The Asian man's eyes narrowed, his wife was left open-mouthed, gasping and speechless. The exhausted pedicab driver stared straight ahead, a dumb beast of burden, awaiting his next command. The two San Diego police on their mountain bikes, sniffing trouble, reappeared and paused across the promenade, watching from behind identical dark sunglasses.

The Asian man hissed at Gretchen, "Number one: We Japanese, not Chinese. Number two: America not drop *big one* on China—America only drop *big one* on Japan, long time ago. Now China already have many *big ones* here in United States, maybe in San Diego. If American President drop *big one* on China, Chinese President push one button, and United States finish! Understand? *Finish!* So nobody drop *big one* on China. And number three: You feed *blond* boy very good—when I come again to San Diego, next time *he* pedal rickshaw!" Then the smartly-dressed

Japanese man turned forward to his pedicab driver and ordered, "Go now Big Johnny! You pedal fast, I give you big tip, hundred blue buck!"

The pedicab rolled away, while Gretchen Bosch clenched and unclenched her fists, her face scarlet with rage. She would have happily strangled that goddamn Jap, snapped his pencil neck and thrown his scrawny oriental body over the low wall into the bay. However, with the two San Diego police officers watching the entire confrontation, she was powerless to react. The IRS Special Agent knew that nothing, absolutely nothing, would torpedo her career as thoroughly as an "incident" involving a couple of San Diego's treasured Asian tourists, the California economy's very last golden goose.

The manager at the Golden Arrow Casino had instructed them to wait in the Jury Room Bar and Grill in La Jolla for their SUV to be delivered. They had not wanted their taxi driver to know their true destination, and they let him drive several blocks past the restaurant on Prospect Street before getting out. Alex paid him $300 in blue bucks to cover the $240 fare. They waited for his yellow mini-van to disappear, and rolled their luggage up a side street jammed with boutiques and galleries to a paved alley, and walked down it into the back entrance of the Jury Room. They performed what surveillance detection procedures they could, stopping to look into windows, using them as mirrors to watch behind them, while understanding that such methods were largely futile in an era when surveillance cameras bracketed every city block. They walked without any conversation, hyper-alert.

Inside the upscale bar and grill, they chose a corner dinette with a view across Prospect Street through a plate glass window. There was enough room under the large table for their bags. Slices of the Pacific Ocean could be seen between the small hotels, posh restaurants and financial services firms on the other side of La Jolla's "Rodeo Drive." They could also watch a television above them on a ceiling mount.

"I could use a drink," whispered Ranya, as they settled into their seats. "I'm ready to pull out you-know-what every time anybody even looks my way." Her brown leather fanny pack rode on her right front hip. She had tied a small leather strap to the zipper pull, and she could yank it open with her left hand and draw her .45 pistol with her right almost as fast as if it had been in a proper concealment holster. The more anxious she was, the further to the left the zipper was kept open. It was half way open on the walk from the taxi.

Alex sat across from her. "I'm nervous too, it can't be helped. We just have to be as careful as we can, and push ahead. It's all we can do."

A short Latina waitress came and took their orders, struggling with basic English. Iced tea and club sandwiches for two cost $379, with tax.

The entire menu was printed on a single sheet of cheap paper, obviously to facilitate frequent price revision. Ranya remembered the menu at the Ancient Pueblos diner in Mountainview New Mexico, with its grease pencil prices written over the old printed ones. She remembered meeting the doomed Michigan college students there, on their way to join the revolution. The college students at the Ancient Pueblos had been unable to scrape up enough money for coffee and pancakes, as well as gas for their van. A few hours later, they were all dead, except for Kalil, who lasted another day…

The lunch crowd began filtering into the Jury Room, mostly well-dressed Asians, uniformly dripping with gold watches, bracelets, and chains. Half of the shops on Prospect Street were jewelry stores, and they were clearly not lacking customers. Honeymoon couples, executives and groups of fashionably dressed young women strolled the sidewalks, clutching shopping bags. During their brief time in La Jolla, Ranya had noticed that the signs in the windows of the art galleries, jewelry stores and boutiques were written in Chinese, Japanese, Spanish and English. Stationed outside of many shops were black-uniformed private security guards, carrying riot shotguns on slings. A young woman in a traditional black and white maid's uniform passed their restaurant window, pushing an enormous baby carriage. She was trailed by a pair of obvious bodyguards, their eyes hidden behind sunglasses, their heads on swivels, and their suits bulging around their poorly concealed firearms and ill-fitting body armor.

Pretty Anglo and Latina girls, many of them only teenaged, cruised the sidewalks in skimpy mini skirts and halter tops, waving to men in slowly passing Jaguars and BMWs. Laughing Asian men riding in the backs of human-powered pedicabs bantered with the young streetwalkers along the curb. A pair of La Jolla police officers whizzed by on gyro-balancing Segway electric scooters, ignoring the teen prostitutes climbing into luxury cars. Nothing that Ranya had seen since her escape had prepared her for the opulent decadence of Prospect Street.

"Alex, have you ever been to South America?"

"No, why?"

"I spent six months in Colombia once. La Jolla reminds me of part of Cartagena, that's all."

"You mean the ocean, and the cliffs?"

"Kind of. But I was thinking more of the private guards with the shotguns, and the teenage hookers."

Alex smiled wistfully. "Welcome to the new California."

"I guess."

He said, "Did you notice that all of their shotguns have licenses taped on the stocks? Private security is big business out here, but it's all regulated. California's still not a concealed carry state, it never was. Only licensed security guards can carry. No guns for the peons…at least no legal guns."

Ranya leaned across the table and whispered mock-seriously, "So, does that mean we're…breaking the law?"

He smiled. "Probably about a hundred."

"In for a penny, in for a pound," she said. "I'm going all the way, no matter what it takes."

"So am I. All the way." Alex reached across the table to her, an invitation to shake hands, while looking her full in the face.

She accepted his hand, and shook it firmly, returning his eye contact. It was only the second time they had touched, other than casually brushing one another by accident, since she had cut him loose from his easy chair last Sunday night.

Televisions were set up in the high corners of the Jury Room lounge, tuned to CNN. The death of Peter Kosimos in the automobile crash outside of Aspen was still in the news rotation, but there were no new details, only brief retrospectives on his life "dedicated to working for social justice and human rights." Former President Dave Whitman was shown speaking before a crowd in a vast auditorium at UCLA. The news reader mentioned that the subject of his speech was accelerating United States integration within the North American Community, and the benefits the new Amero currency would bring to all of the citizens of the continent. The UCLA video had apparently been taped last night, after Kosimos had been killed by the drone. Weasel Dave Whitman appeared to be in perfect health and high spirits, still living his charmed life.

There was still no mention of a Blackhawk helicopter crashing in New Mexico.

The news broke for commercials. Alex considered these more significant, and certainly more honest, than most of the so-called news reports he had seen. The "bold new Nissan Conquistador" SUVs proudly featured armored windows and doors, fully protected engine compartments, self-sealing gas tanks, automatic fire suppression systems, and "run-flat tires" as standard equipment.

Next, there was some kind of a public service announcement. It began with an elderly white man in a black tuxedo, sitting on the ground inside of what looked like a bank vault. The entire floor of the vault was covered in gold coins and bullion bars. The old man was raking his fingers through the gold with an ecstatic look on his face, lifting the coins up above his head and letting them spill through his fingers, giggling with delight like a spoiled child in a billion-dollar sandbox.

The opening scene faded, and was replaced by a distant aerial view of a massive strip mine. Barren earth was carved away in dozens of terraces, one above the other, extending in every direction. The camera slowly zoomed in, until barefoot brown-skinned children wearing filthy rags could be seen attacking the soil with picks and shovels. A boy passed by the camera, straining to carry two enormous metal canisters, hanging from a wooden yoke across his shoulders. The dripping galvanized tanks had the word "cyanide" stenciled on them. A silky female voiceover said, "Illegal gold hoarding only leads to exploitive labor practices, and environmental calamity. One single gold coin means that 500 tons of toxic waste are produced, toxic waste that poisons rivers and destroys ecosystems."

The camera slowly panned across the open pit mine, revealing hundreds of pathetic wretches clawing at the earth, and blasting torrents of mud loose with high-pressure water hoses. The soft female voice continued. "During today's difficult economic times, the only responsible place for America's gold is in Fort Knox. Gold hoarders and speculators are criminals, who only serve to destabilize the global economy. Gold hoarding leads to exploitive labor practices, and environmental ruin. And if those aren't enough reasons to obey the law, here's another: ten years in prison for illegal gold hoarding."

The scene abruptly switched from toiling third-world child miners, to a gleaming wall of bullion bricks. Golden jail cell doors slammed together in front of the golden wall with a loud metallic crash. A stern male baritone voice then announced, "Gold: it's just not worth it!" The public service announcement concluded with that phrase printed across the screen, along with an admonition to call 1-855-USA-GOLD to report illegal gold hoarding. Smaller print under the toll-free number reminded viewers that large cash rewards were offered, for those who reported illegal gold hoarding to the proper authorities.

Alex and Ranya watched the announcement with straight faces, both of them attempting to suppress any hint of a smile. When it finished, Alex looked across at Ranya and winked, while attempting to keep an expressionless poker face. At the same time, he pushed a gold-laden bag beneath the table with his foot, into Ranya's legs. Ranya cracked first, just a small snicker, and Alex followed, hiding his grin behind two folded hands, and then they both totally lost it, shedding tears of laughter while staring at one another.

They were still occasionally chuckling at their new inside joke, whispering "Got gold?" or "It's just not worth it!" to each other, when their SUV was delivered. A young American Indian-looking man in jeans and a red polo shirt entered the dining area from the back. He was wearing the agreed-upon Miami Dolphins baseball cap as a recognition sign, and he approached close enough to their booth to be seen. They followed him past the bar and out the rear exit with their luggage. Standing in the alley, he handed Alex the car keys and an envelope full of papers.

Alex took a look at the black mid-sized SUV and said, "What is this? It's not an Explorer, it's a Dodge Durango! That's not what we agreed on."

"I know, I'm sorry. We had a problem at the last minute. Believe me, this one is better than the Explorer—it's loaded. More horsepower, better paint, everything. All right?"

Ranya shrugged, and Alex said, "Sure, I guess."

"Okay, good. It's got a full tank of gas. When you're finished, leave it somewhere safe, and call this number. When we pick it up, you can get your security deposit back. Any questions?"

Alex asked, "What about driving downtown? Any problems we should know about?"

"No problem if you stay on this side of I-5. It has a GPS map; it'll tell you the best way to go. You can use I-5, but I'd just take Ingraham south past Seaworld, follow Harbor Drive by the airport, and you're there. If you have to go east of I-5 and you want to get back over, don't worry—it has a La Jolla residency sticker in the window. But if some cop is being a real asshole, just use your judgment—there's not many legal problems a gold dime can't solve around here. Even so, I'd just recommend you don't go east of Interstate 5 *at all*. Okay?"

"Okay, but what if we want to drop it off back at the Golden Arrow? Can we do that?" Alex's idea was to drive straight to the casino and their waiting airplane, as soon as they were able to find Brian.

The car delivery man looked at them both carefully, and asked, "Have you been driving in California lately? The last few years?"

"No," responded Alex.

"Where are you from?"

"New Mexico."

"Well, driving is different here. Like, let's say somebody pushes a baby stroller right in front of your car, what do you do?"

"Stop," he replied.

"Wrong answer! Keep going! It's a trap, it's a carjacking trick. Don't worry, there's no baby, and they'll jump out of the way. They want you to swerve off the road—and then they've got you. Same thing if you see an accident, and it looks like somebody's hurt and needs help. Just keep going, don't even look back! Somebody jumps right in front of your car, waving his arms? Speed up, aim right for that sucker, he'll jump out of the way. Stop for him, and he'll know you're an easy target, and his friends will rush you from the sides. They'll put a hammer through your side window and a gun to your head, or a knife to her throat. So keep your windows all the way up, and don't stop, no matter what. Even if you get flat tires—keep going. They'll put bent nails on the road, to make you stop. Don't! Keep going, always keep going, drive on the rims if you have to, but don't stop where they want you to stop, get the hell out of there. And whatever you do, don't drive at night on the other side of I-5. If it's bad in the daytime, it's ten times worse at night. The highways are so-so, but the *barrios*? Forget it—don't even think about it. Cops don't ever go in the barrios at night, unless it's at least ten cop cars with a helicopter overhead. Two of you guys in one car? Forget it."

"But what if we do decide to take it back to the Golden Arrow to drop it off?"

"Then daytime only. Early morning would be best. Take Interstate 8 east all the way, and keep your speed over 100. Don't stop for anything."

"What about the cops?"

"What cops?" he scoffed. "Over there, there's no cops. That's why you're better off just leaving the car here in La Jolla, and phoning it in. Be smart: take the helicopter back to the Golden Arrow, and pick up your deposit. Okay?"

"Okay," agreed Alex.

"That's it then, enjoy your stay in San Diego, but above all, be safe, all right? There's nothing east of I-5 you want to see anyway. There's places over there you wouldn't last five minutes, day or night."

They loaded their luggage into the back of the SUV, and left the delivery man standing behind the restaurant. The tags and window stickers were current, and would permit the vehicle to cross freely into downtown, by showing that the owner was a resident of coastal La Jolla. The Durango came equipped with a color GPS map display built into the center of the instrument display for navigation. It had heavily tinted side and rear windows, as specified by Alex.

Alex drove on a winding tour of La Jolla, doing a surveillance detection run. Then he parked the Durango in an empty garage behind an upscale apartment complex, removed a device like an electrician's Ohmmeter from his luggage, and thoroughly examined the car for bugs or tracking devices. It was clean. There was no built-in cell phone, and the Durango's GPS was strictly a receiver, with no transmit capability. Finally satisfied, he headed out of La Jolla, southbound along the coast.

"You know, I never saw the Pacific before today," said Ranya, sitting in the Durango's front passenger seat, staring out the window to her right. They were passing through Pacific Beach on Mission Boulevard, just a block away from the cliffs overlooking the ocean. "It's totally different than the Atlantic, at least around Virginia. It's all flat back there, just straight flat beaches. Not like this. This is much prettier."

"It's not all like this," observed Alex. "Some parts have flat sandy beaches like back east."

They drove in silence, stopping for frequent lights. Surfers in black wetsuits carried their boards toward the beach, adults on long skateboards rolled right down the street alongside of cars. There seemed to be a tattoo parlor, a taco stand, a bar and a surf shop on every block.

"You know," said Ranya quietly, "I don't feel too good about yesterday. I didn't know I'd feel this way."

"What way?"

"The Blackhawk. I killed people yesterday, I know I did. I aimed right at the pilots, I could see their helmets, I could almost see their faces. There's no way a helicopter goes down like that and people don't die."

She sighed, and continued. "You might not understand this, but the Falcons weren't all bad people, not really. I didn't hate them. Basilio Ramos, I hated him, sure, but not all of his troops. Most of them were just soldiers, soldiers fighting for what they thought was their land. I mean, they really believe it, they really do."

"I don't hate them either," said Alex. "How can you blame them for wanting to take New Mexico, for wanting some free land to call their own? I blame our politicians—they held the door open for the invasion. If they couldn't see what it would lead to, they should have. Protecting the country from invasion is right in the Constitution, in black and white. That's one of their most basic responsibilities, and they blew it."

Ranya recalled the 'ten blind men,' the worst shots of the Falcon Battalion, and their punishment run up the mountain trail behind the Comandante's villa. It now seemed like ages ago. She remembered these Falcons with some fondness, how they had welcomed her on the run and treated her with respect, and she wondered if any of them were on the helicopter she had shot down. Then there was the Blackhawk's aircrew, and the pilots. Flying the helicopter was just their job, and now wives and children were probably grieving for fathers they would never see again. She had taken careful aim at them, pulled the trigger, and sent their helicopter crashing into the ground.

"Can we stop for a few minutes?" she asked. "I want to see the beach." Mission Boulevard was high above the ocean here, and they could only catch glimpses of the distant horizon between the low buildings.

"Okay, sure." Alex made a right turn between a bicycle shop and an Irish pub. The road dead-ended in a turnaround circle, between two small hotels. Ranya stepped out, and walked across the cement boardwalk to the edge of a bluff. The white sand beach was fifty feet below her. The waves rolling in a hundred yards away made the same surf sound she had grown up with in Virginia. She stood with her arms folded, the steady sea breeze lifting strands of blond hair around her face, the smell of the salt air bringing back a flood of memories.

Alex locked up the Durango at the end of the cul-de-sac and joined her after a minute, standing quietly off to her side.

"Did you ever kill anybody?" she asked, without turning to face him.

"No."

"Well it's not a good feeling." She didn't mention the people she had killed before, six years ago. That had been different, that was war. Maybe only a dirty war, but war. They had it coming, after what they did to her father. Yesterday was different, somehow. The Falcons were not all her enemies. Yes, the Falcons were fighting a war…but it was not *her* war.

"They were soldiers, with rifles," said Alex. "They would have killed us or captured us, if you hadn't of done what you did. It was us or them. Kill or be killed. You're the reason we got away."

She sighed. Kill or be killed? She had heard that line before. Heard it, said it, seen it, done it. There was Kalil, at the wall: *kill, or be killed.* She heard El Condor's words: *so far, I have not been killed.* She thought of Warden Linssen, back in D-Camp. The assistant warden's death had been the price of Ranya's freedom. There were no easy answers, no formulas to apply in every case. After several minutes of staring down the coast toward downtown, she asked, "Do you recognize that fishing pier?"

"No," he answered. The wooden structure was a half mile to the south, extending a few hundred yards out over the ocean, the surf tumbling through its hundred spindly legs.

"It's the one in the Homeland Security commercial. 'Hi, I'm Bob Bullard.' That one. They filmed it from the other side, from the south, but it's the same pier."

"I recognize it now."

She said, "We're close, aren't we? Close to Brian."

"Very close."

"He's just a few miles away…"

"Yeah, he is. Come on, let's go find him." Alex turned away from the ocean, and a few seconds later Ranya followed.

39

The last time that Basilio Ramos had flown low over San Diego in a prop plane had been two decades ago, during the golden years of his youth. That had been in a much smaller twin engine Piper Navajo, and he'd never forgotten the experience. A television producer, a 'friend' of his mother, had flown them from San Diego to Cabo San Lucas in his private plane.

From 5,000 feet the city looked the same as he had remembered it: not quite as dry as Albuquerque, a series of small mountains and foothills descending to the ocean. Most of the houses were crammed onto flat-topped mesas, with wide canyons and deep ravines splitting them into distinct areas. Highways furrowed the canyons, exit ramps led to roads that followed smaller side canyons up to the mesa tops.

Some things were clearly different this time. For one thing, there appeared to be many more houses than he had recalled seeing before. Seemingly, every acre of every mesa that was less than vertical was jammed with a half dozen or more tract homes. The flat bottoms of the empty canyons were now covered with blue tarps and tents, cardboard and plywood shacks. These were familiar to him from Central and South America: squatter camps. Another difference struck him as well: mile after mile of the highways crisscrossing San Diego had high cement barrier walls on each side, giving them the appearance of industrial chutes carrying ore to a smelter.

"Can you put us into a pattern for a go-around?" he asked his pilot on the intercom. "I want to get a good look at the city."

"I'm already assigned. We're going out to the ocean and back for our approach. We can't go south, it's restricted air space around San Diego International."

They were taking the Otter into a general aviation airport ten miles northeast of downtown. *Aeropuerto Chavez* occupied its own mile-square mesa, surrounded by steep slopes and ravines. On the instrument panel GPS display, they could select English or Spanish, and Ramos had been amused to see that in the English version the airport was still called Montgomery Field. He could only guess if *Aeropuerto Chavez* was named after Cesar or Hugo, or someone else altogether.

They flew parallel to and beyond the east-west main runway, while descending through four thousand feet of elevation toward the ocean five miles beyond. One more highway divided inland San Diego from the two-mile-wide coastal strip: Interstate 5. Ramos remembered it well. It ran from Seattle to San Diego, and terminated at the border with Mexico at San

Ysidro, twenty miles south. The crossing there into Tijuana was said to be the busiest in the world.

Over the ocean, Corky put the Otter into a left bank and turned south, presenting Ramos with a direct view south toward San Diego Bay, the Coronado Bridge, and the dozen skyscrapers dominating downtown. One of those high rises contained the five-year-old Brian Garabanda, the key to finding Ranya Bardiwell and the FBI agent.

The thought warmed him that he was on her trail, and she had no idea. She had ruined his life, blackmailed him, wrecked his reputation as a leader of elite troops, but soon he would have her in his grasp. She would not enjoy his grasp, oh no, she would not! He thought of the final minutes of the Zionist traitor Luis Carvahal, chained to the tree by his neck, screaming as he burned. He remembered the cocky attitude of the radio talk show host Rick Haywood, before he had been dragged behind a truck and skinned alive. Then he thought again of Ranya Bardiwell, and how much more he hated her.

After less than a minute, Corky made another banking left turn, heading east again over the mesas toward the foothills. They flew beyond Chavez field, made the final turns to pick up the approach, and lined up on the runway once again heading westward. They were flying at just over a thousand feet above the ground when the airport's mesa loomed in front of them, and suddenly they were over the runway. The Twin Otter touched down with a slight jolt and bounce, and the Zetas were in San Diego.

A room on the fifth floor of the downtown Holiday Inn became Alex and Ranya's command post. It cost Alex one gold dime above the advertised $799 a night price to obtain a room with a view of the Pacific Majesty. Their room's grimy window looked south down Harbor Drive, across three blocks of cruise ship terminal parking lots toward the Fed Tower. Alex was comfortable in Holiday Inns. They had served as operational bases throughout his FBI career. They were low profile, but had the high-speed internet connection he needed to set up his surveillance gear. His own laptop, once hooked up, became the nerve center of their effort.

Ranya watched him quietly, while he methodically plugged accessories into his computer on the room's desk. Her blond wig was thrown on her bed, her own short brunette hair was pressed flat to her head.

"Okay, I've got Karin's cell phone number locked in. Any calls to or from her phone, and we'll be silent third parties. We'll hear everything, and it's all recorded."

"Will they be able to tell you're doing this?"

"They who? Karin? No, nobody can tell. If you have the right equipment and the right accounts, you're good to go. I'm not even using my own account, I have a couple of dummies. They've been dormant, but they'll work, and they can't be traced to me. Trust me—this is all basic stuff. This is what I do. At least, it's what I used to do."

"So we'll hear every call that Karin makes?"

"And the Beast. Gretchen Bosch. In or out. And anybody they talk to, we can capture those numbers too."

"Don't you need a warrant or a judge to do this? You know, a court order?" Ranya was smiling coyly when she asked this.

"Oh yeah, I must have forgotten," Alex said, slapping his forehead. "It was on my to-do list. I guess it slipped my mind."

"Just add it to the other hundred laws we've broken."

"Why not?"

She said, "In for a penny…"

"…In for a pound," he finished for her. "They can only hang you once, right?"

"That's right, they can only hang you once." There was no humor in her voice when she said this.

"Now when they use their cell phones to make plans, we'll know. If we get lucky, we'll hear them talk about where they're going, and we'll get there first."

"You can do this for anybody's phone?" she asked. "Anytime?"

"Pretty much, but cell phones are the easiest. Of course, normally I'd need a warrant. But there's no physical reason why you can't. You just need this equipment. That's what we used the dummy accounts for: fishing expeditions. Once we made our case, you know, sort of 'unofficially,' we'd scrounge up some probable cause to get a court order. Then we'd use our regular accounts and start recording all the calls. You know, legally."

"Man, that sucks so bad."

"It's been this way for years," Alex said. "It's not exactly a secret. And it's not just for listening to calls. Cell phones have GPS built in now, so I can tell where Karin is to within ten feet. At least, I can tell where her phone is. Look, I'll show you how easy it is."

Ranya shook her head. "I wouldn't use a cell phone then. No way."

"Then you're one in a hundred. Most people start hyperventilating if you move their cell phones ten feet out of their reach. Okay, that's done—we're good to go on their phones. Now let me see about getting into the homeland security camera net." Alex typed on his laptop, going through a series of new web pages and logins. "This might take a little time, I haven't done this is California. Oh—that was easy, here we go, I'm getting it. That's it! I'm in. Check this out, let's see where we are."

A color street map of San Diego appeared on the laptop's computer screen. Alex zoomed down the scale until the screen was just showing the city blocks immediately around the Fed Tower. Dozens of tiny camera icons appeared. He clicked on one, and a few seconds later they were rewarded with a live view of Broadway, taken from a high angle down towards the County Courthouse. The camera view took up a quarter of the screen, leaving the rest for the map.

He clicked another camera icon, closer to the Fed Tower, and saw a view from across the street down toward the main entrance foyer, and the fountain in the center of its own small plaza. There were a pair of revolving entrance doors in the center of the building, and anti-vehicle obstacles disguised as massive flower planters evenly spaced along the curb on Broadway, fifty feet away. The first three stories of the tower were concrete, with no windows. The place was built to be a hard target.

"Okay, we'll save that one. Let's keep looking…"

"Can you do this anywhere, in any city?"

"Not everywhere, but in cities—especially downtown—well, there's almost nowhere that's not covered by cameras. I can't tilt, pan or zoom though—we're just getting the raw feed. Whatever the camera sees, we see. Okay now, that's a good one."

The camera showed the side of the Fed Tower, overlooking the entrance to its parking garage.

"That's another keeper—I'll save that one too. Now, if we keep an eye on the front doors and the garage entrance, we'll either see them walking out, or driving out. Let me split the screen up so those two views stay on top, and then you can play with it. You should get used to navigating around the city. It's just like a video game. Once you get the hang of it, it's sort of like swinging from building to building. You can go around the block, follow somebody, whatever you want."

"What happened to just sitting in undercover cars on a stakeout, eating fast food and telling corny cop jokes?"

"Oh, that's old school. We still do it when we have to, but in a city like this, why bother? And why take the risk? If we hang around down on the street, we're more likely to compromise ourselves than anything else. I don't want to even go near the Fed Tower, not until it's time to get Brian. That building is watched like a hawk—count on it. All of these surveillance cameras we're looking at? They have people paid to watch them, 24-7. Walk past the Pacific Majesty a few times, it'll be noticed, and it's all recorded. No, it's better to just stay away from there, and use their own cameras against them. If we see Karin's 4-Runner coming out, we'll be able to follow it by her cell phone's GPS position. If we already know where she's going from her cell phone calls, we can get there first. Once I find her car parked outside on a street, I'll stick a tracker under her luggage carrier. That big black box on her roof rack is perfect; I can hide a tracker under it easy. That way, even if she turns her cell phone off or leaves it home, we'll be able to follow her car. Plus, the luggage box makes it easy to follow her car in traffic. We won't have to be too close behind her. We can stay a few cars back, just eyeballing that luggage box. That's important, since we only have one car. We can't afford to spook her."

"Once we find her, then what?" asked Ranya.

"If it's just Karin and Brian, I've got some non-lethal happy gas. Karin doesn't know you from Adam, so you can walk right up to her, and give her a little spritz in the face. She'll be disoriented, sort of tripping out. I'll get Brian, and that's it. We'll drive straight out to the Golden Arrow and get on the airplane."

"What happens to Karin?"

"After you give her the happy gas? She staggers around like a drunk for a few hours, or she falls asleep. Not exactly a reliable witness, either way. Cops won't listen to a word she says. They'll assume she's either on drugs, or she's a lunatic. She won't make any sense."

"You think it'll work like that? That easy?"

"Why not? They have no idea we're in town, so they won't have their guard up."

"What if 'the Beast' is with them?"

"Gretchen Bosch? We'll just have to improvise. If the happy gas doesn't work, I've also got a Taser, and if it comes down to it, then there's always bullets—they work pretty good too. We'll see. You want to play with the cameras now?"

"Sure."

Chino and Salazar took off on the Kawasaki as soon as it was unloaded from the Otter. Chino sat in front, Salazar was behind him with a compact MAC-10 submachine gun tucked against his chest, concealed beneath a black wind breaker. Both men wore black helmets with dark face shields. The two former San Diego gang members had the mission of making contact with their old *compadres*, in order to arrange for ground transportation and a place for the team to stay. Guarded cell phone calls had been made, and their arrival was expected, but the actual arrangements had to be made face-to-face.

Comandante Ramos didn't worry about their physical safety driving through San Diego. There was almost nothing as dangerous in a city as two men on a motorcycle. A *moto* could outmaneuver any car, and the man in back with the weapon could defend them, or attack a target with concentrated full-auto firepower. The bike could then escape through heavy traffic or squeeze through tight spaces, or even go off road to evade pursuit. There was a very good reason why two men on a *moto* struck mortal fear into executives from Tijuana to Tierra del Fuego: it was frequently the last thing that they saw, before being riddled with bullets.

It was after seven PM when they returned to the airfield. The motorcycle was leading a jacked-up four-wheel-drive Dodge crew cab pickup, with custom bumpers and oversized tires. The truck had a low camper shell over the back, which matched the truck's dark blue color. The narrow side windows of the camper shell had been removed, and Ramos knew that this was to allow *pistoleros* with AK-47s or other serious weapons to fire from inside. It was a war-wagon, and its message was clear: attacking it would only be undertaken at great risk to the attacker.

The truck pulled up close to the Otter, and they loaded their baggage, weapons bags, and surveillance equipment into the back. Ramos noted the thick steel plates welded inside the cargo bed as armor. The rear bumper was made of parallel steel pipes. Foot-long horizontal steel rods were welded to the bumper and tailgate, pointing rearward as anti-ramming protection. Any vehicle crashing into the truck from behind would have its radiator and engine impaled.

The *mestizo* driver of the truck had some of the same neck tattoos as Salazar, including 13-13 in Germanic script. Like Chino, he also had seveal red and blue teardrops tattooed beneath the corners of his eyes, representing friends lost, and enemies killed.

Chino and Salazar again rode the motorcycle ahead of the truck as they left the airport. Corky Gutierrez stayed with the plane. He was useless to them beyond his skills as a pilot, and he could best serve their needs by keeping the Otter ready to fly. Mendoza stayed at the airport with Corky, to "assist" him. They all understood his true function: to eliminate the possibility of Corky flying away, and leaving them stranded.

Ramos sat behind the driver in the four-door crew cab truck, next to Lieutenant Almeria, his communications officer. Almeria seemed out of place among the tough *vatos*. This soft fellow with his gold-rimmed eyeglasses looked completely non-combative, but his special skills were essential to the success of the mission. Genizaro sat in the front passenger seat, a .45 caliber MAC-10 machine pistol on his lap. It was loaded with a thirty round magazine extending from its grip, and a long thick suppressor fixed to its stubby barrel.

This was Chino and Salazar's city, their home turf, and Ramos worried about them keeping their edge and staying focused on the mission. They had been disciplined troops in Nuevo Mexico, but there would be many old temptations to revisit in San Diego. The sooner this job was completed, the better. Ramos knew that every day the team remained in California, they would tend to drift away from his control.

He hoped the mission could be completed in two or three days, maximum. The boy Brian Garabanda was the focus point, the bait. All the Zetas had to do was find him and watch him, and then they would find Bardiwell and the FBI agent. The two traitors would be like a pair of tigers stealthily approaching a staked goat, unaware of the hunter waiting in his concealed blind. They had the cell phone number of the boy's mother, and

Almeria would be able to listen to her calls, and track her location. It was a reasonable assumption that the FBI agent would have a similar capacity. The trick was in anticipating Garabanda's moves, and outmaneuvering him. Their great advantage was that the FBI agent didn't know that while stalking, he was also being stalked.

The entire airport occupied its own mesa, surrounded by miles of chain link fence topped with razor wire. The Kawasaki led them to a highway that ran directly past the end of the airfield. They exited through an automatic gate operated by armed guards, and quickly merged onto the 805 freeway, heading south to where they would stay for the night in a house provided by Chino's old *carnals*, his gang brothers. Both sides of the freeway were walled in by twenty-foot tall concrete noise barriers, which Ramos couldn't help but think were more truthfully people barriers, dividing the city into more "manageable" segments. The concrete walls were covered in murals and graffiti for miles, with shifting gang symbols denoting who controlled which territory.

The freeway soared over some valleys on high bridges, and then ran up other canyons and across the mesa tops. Compared to Albuquerque, some of the green hillsides reminded Ramos almost of Hawaii, or at least of Mazatlan or Puerto Vallarta. There were many types of palm trees, and a wide variety of unusual tropical species never seen in arid New Mexico. Luxury homes partly supported on stilts were built one above another on some of the slopes.

They followed as the motorcycle took an exit into a middle class neighborhood of small homes, and a few minutes later the bike made a series of quick turns and drove beneath the highway they had just been on. One shoulder of the mesa was cut off by the highway, leaving a neighborhood stranded by itself. The only way into this small section was through the underpass tunnel they had just penetrated.

They followed the motorcycle through more turns and finally to the end of a cul-de-sac, with pleasant upper-middle class homes on either side. At the end of the traffic circle was a massively high and thick hedge. An archway had been carved into this wall of vegetation, just large enough for one vehicle. A chain-link gate rolled open behind the hedge at their approach. On the other side of the green wall, they entered a new realm, a small estate of a few acres.

This secluded property occupied the tip of one finger of the mesa. In the center of the neatly trimmed lawn, there was an ultra-modern three-story white custom home composed of plate glass, angles, terraces and balconies. The area around the house was landscaped with luxuriant tropical plants, rock gardens and decorative pools with small fountains and waterfalls. There was a line of tall palm trees along the property's cliffside border in the back. Beyond the palms, steep canyon slopes fell away, and another mesa rose a mile beyond.

No other nearby houses were visible, the property was enclosed entirely within the wall of hedges on the landward side. Ramos thought that the home was not quite as large or majestic as his villa back in Albuquerque, but it was certainly in the same league, and its geography made it a nearly impregnable fortress. Dusk was falling, and the lights of the homes on the hillside across the canyon were flickering on. It wasn't as dramatic as his view of Albuquerque and the Rio Grand Valley, but it was very charming, with the row of palm trees behind the mansion silhouetted against the orange and pink sky.

Two men in jeans and t-shirts were playing ping-pong on a table near the opening in the hedge. Another man played Frisbee with a trio of enormous Rottweilers, who leaped and rolled on the lawn, battling each other for the chewed-up yellow disc.

This was the home of Chino's San Diego *padrino* or godfather, within "*La Eme*," the Mexican Mafia. Here, Comandante Basilio Ramos's standing within the Milicia de Nuevo Mexico would count for almost nothing, and he would have to depend on Chino and Salazar to procure what they needed to complete their mission. Primarily they required a clean vehicle, which could transport them back and forth into the high security zone of downtown San Diego.

Here, Basilio Ramos could no longer simply give orders. Here, there were no camouflage uniforms, no brown berets with Falcon insignias, and no web belts with holstered pistols to denote authority. Here, they were all just *carnals, cholos,* wearing jeans and casual shirts. Here, he could only rely on the loyalty that he had instilled in his men over the past months. If Chino and Salazar decided to desert him now, he couldn't prevent it. To finance the entire operation, he had only the fifty remaining ounces of gold that Ranya had not found and stolen. It was a narrow margin.

The war wagon pulled up the drive, and parked in front of the house. Now it was time to meet the San Diego *jefe* of the Mexican Mafia, and see if Chino and Salazar's frequently mentioned relationship would result in assistance, or rejection. Ramos stepped down from the big pickup truck feeling like an unacknowledged country cousin, meeting a rich uncle for the first time. He squared his shoulders, took a deep breath, and walked up the flagstone steps leading to the front of the imposing house. The fragrance of honeysuckle and frangipani sweetened the calm twilight air.

40

Alex looked over and said, "Brian's bedtime was hours ago, you don't have to stay up. Nothing's going to happen tonight." He was lying on the bed closest to the door.

"Is the television bothering you?" It was nearly midnight. She was sitting up on her bed, leaning back on pillows propped against the headboard.

"No, no problem."

She was physically tired, but too mentally wound up to sleep. Brian, her son, was sleeping three blocks away. Tomorrow they might have their chance to find him, and rescue him. Rescue? Was that the right word? Recover. They'd be able to find him, and recover him. No, be honest—the correct word was *take*. They were going to find Brian, and *take* him. And so what? Hadn't Brian been taken from her, his own mother?

Tomorrow was the 4th of July. Karin was certain to leave the Fed Tower with Brian, and then they would take him away. Finally, she'd be able to see her son, to hold him, and then…what? She didn't know. Could she ever become the mother to a child she had never known for the entire five years of his life? She didn't have an answer.

And what about Alex? Once they had Brian in the Piper Cherokee, once they lifted off from the Golden Arrow Casino's runway, where were they going? After five days together, they still hadn't discussed the future beyond finding Brian, except in the most general terms. She still had more than three hundred ounces of gold left in her "operational fund," even after financing the airplanes, the casino hotel and shopping spree, the helicopter shuttle, the Dodge Durango, and the Holiday Inn. This much gold could be enough to start a new life, when they arrived wherever they were going.

But would Brian ever accept her? Ranya realized that she'd have to keep Alex in the picture, there was no other way that Brian could grow to accept her presence.

Alex, lying on his back on the other bed, only ten feet away. He'd never made one pass at her, and she didn't know what to think about that. She was grateful, she supposed. He was, after all, twenty years older than she was. Not that she was worried, not even in a single hotel room over night—not with the .45 under her pillow. But even without the pistol, she wouldn't be worried. No, sexual assault wasn't her fear, not after spending five days with him. So what was the remaining fear? Aside from the obvious, aside from the ever-present dread that the door might be smashed down at any moment, by a federal assault team dressed in black…

Her other remaining fear was being ditched. She'd basically brought Alex this far, paying for the airplanes, the hotels and the Durango. Now it was all his show, using his telephone and video camera monitoring systems. What did he need her for anymore? If he had the chance, would he grab Brian, and abandon her? It was hard not to consider the possibility. Experience had taught her that there was no percentage in trusting people, in caring deeply for people. You could make the commitment, and it was still damned easy to wind up alone, inside a small cement room with a locked steel door. Alex could even be setting her up to be arrested. Could he be stringing her along, waiting for the right moment to drop the trap? Didn't FBI agents routinely do that, build false trust and play on emotions, in order to entrap their targets? Could he be using her, the same way that she had strung Basilio Ramos along, and used him?

She wondered how Basilio was doing. With Peter Kosimos dead and one of his Blackhawks down, his security gig at the Vedado Ranch conference must have been a complete disaster for him. Basilio might even have been aboard the crashed helicopter. Perhaps even now he was dead in the wreckage. But dead or alive, Basilio Ramos was a thousand miles and two states away. If nothing else, at least she'd slipped free of him.

The weak air conditioning in their room at the Holiday Inn room was apparently turned off for the night, and the windows didn't open. Only a feeble stream of stale air came out of the vents, no matter how Alex adjusted the thermostat. After giving up on climate control, he turned down the bedspread and the top sheet, and lay on his back wearing a gray t-shirt and his blue running shorts. Ranya sat against the headboard of her own bed a few yards away, channel surfing with the volume turned down low. The flickering television was the only light on in the room.

She was wearing a black t-shirt and matching black running shorts. He couldn't help but observe that Miss Bardiwell looked awfully hot, with her long sleek legs crossed at the ankles, and her curvaceous figure clearly outlined, and he had to remind himself of their age difference. They'd seen all of the cable news shows through several repeats of the headline stories; they'd even seen Bob Bullard with the Pacific Beach pier behind him. They'd seen the child miners, and again they laughed together at the blunt warning: "Gold: It's Just Not Worth It!"

The digital clock on the small lamp table between their beds blinked over to 12:00. It was Friday the 4th of July, a government holiday. This might be *The Day*. Karin and Gretchen were certain to go out somewhere with Brian—to the beach, or to a picnic, but somewhere. When Brian was taken outside, they would be following right behind, on foot or in the black

Durango. Separating Brian from Karin (and possibly from both Karin and Gretchen) was going to be tricky, but with the element of surprise, it was very doable. Once they had Brian, a fast one hour drive out Interstate 8 would bring them to the Golden Arrow Casino, where Flint was waiting with his airplane.

But then what? Where would they go? Where would they tell their pilot to fly? Cantrell County was an option, but Alex knew that Cantrell County was on borrowed time. Eventually, the *reconquista* civil war was going to sweep across that county, despite the bravado and marksmanship of its citizen-deputies. Anyway, he'd had more than enough of New Mexico. New Mexico was his last assigned duty state, and no place for a renegade FBI supervisor. No, if they were going to bolt, they'd have to go north, somewhere. Idaho, Montana, Wyoming…somewhere. These were the "free states," according to many.

But what did Ranya want? What were her expectations? She believes that I stole Brian from her. She as much as blamed me for the five years she spent in non-judicial detention. Would she ever completely forgive me for those five lost years? Would she take Brian and run away with him, the first chance that came along? Could she make room for me in her life? How would they share Brian, after they had him back?

When would they even be able to talk about these things?

First things first. And the very first thing was: *get Brian.*

What was the use of even thinking about the rest of it, until then?

41

Friday the 4th of July

Early morning. Their bags were packed, Alex and Ranya were prepared to leave their room in the Holiday Inn on a moment's notice. Only the laptop and its accessories remained on the desk, ready to be unhooked and shoved into waiting cases. They took turns watching the computer screen, monitoring four current video camera images around the Pacific Majesty. Two of these cameras were in stationary positions, but two were under operator control. These cameras occasionally panned, tilted, and zoomed independently.

One of the primary cameras they were monitoring showed a long view down Broadway toward the bay, a half dozen blocks west. It covered the entire width of the avenue, including the main front entrance of the Pacific Majesty, seen at a downward slanting angle. "Broadway 7" was a live camera. Somewhere, someone was sitting in a security control room, intermittently manipulating it. When it was set on its usual wide angle, people walking in and out of the Fed Tower's main entrance were only discernable in their general details: man or woman, suit or dress, hat or long hair. This was okay, Alex was confident that if Brian walked outside with Karin, he'd be recognizable. There just weren't that many kids going in or out of the Fed Tower.

While Alex watched, Broadway 7 began to move, and he selected full screen to enlarge it on his computer. The camera tilted down slightly as it zoomed in, until its frame bracketed a man standing on a cement traffic divider, next to a left turn lane at Broadway and India. The man appeared to be walking along a row of cars. The color video image was surprisingly crisp and steady.

"Ranya, check this out."

She sat on one of the upholstered room chairs, beside Alex. "Is he holding a sign? What's it say?"

"He keeps turning. Wait, there it is. Um, it says, IRAQ WAR VET. Ah, shit…the poor guy's only got one arm. Look, the sign is pinned to his shirt."

The man was wearing an old desert uniform, three pale shades of tan. He was holding what looked like a matching desert uniform cap upside down in his left hand. He limped toward the direction of the camera, past two luxury sedans and an SUV stuck waiting in the turning lane. Long brown hair and a short beard covered his collar and obscured his face. His right sleeve was folded up and pinned beneath his shoulder.

When the left-turn arrow switched to green and the cars pulled away, the man walked back to the utility pole near the end of the narrow traffic island. He crouched down and pulled a plastic water bottle out of a back-pack resting on the ground against the pole, and took a drink. A brown sleeping bag was strapped beneath the pack.

While his back was turned to the camera, another car rolled up behind him, it was immediately identifiable from above as a San Diego Police Department black and white cruiser. It was followed by another, and when both units were stopped in the turning lane, two police officers stepped out, and strode up to the Iraq veteran, who stood to meet them. It was obvious by the body language of all three men that harsh words were being exchanged.

The veteran slapped his cap on his head and put up his one hand in a fist, turning and taking a fighting stance, causing the police to step back and pull out their batons. A standoff ensued while one of the officers spoke into the radio mike clipped to the epaulet of his uniform. After a minute, some kind of a deal seemed to have been reached with the veteran, who relaxed and allowed the officers to approach. When they were close, the two police suddenly seized the veteran by his shoulders, roughly guided him to the back of the first cruiser, and pushed him down inside by his head. The police cars then departed as rapidly as they had arrived.

Alex and Ranya made eye contact and shook their heads in silent agreement. Whatever it was they had just witnessed, it wasn't right. Alex switched back to the four-camera display, and they continued their surveillance of the Fed Tower.

Bob Bullard had computers in most of the rooms of his penthouse atop the Pacific Majesty. On weekends and holidays, he liked to give the city a quick inspection over breakfast, with his personally chosen sequence of downtown security cameras. Between toasted bagels, fresh fruit, orange juice and coffee, he had noticed a beggar, bold as brass, standing on a traffic island right in the middle of Broadway. He had Police Chief Ramón Devlin's personal cell phone number on speed dial, and he immediately reported the vagrant. Five minutes later, Bullard had a reason to call him again.

"Nice work Ray. I appreciate how quickly you handled that situation. I know it's not easy, but we have to draw the line. No panhandling means no panhandling, even if it's a tearjerker like that one-armed G.I. Joe. Uh huh, right. East of I-5, I could care less, but you can't let it start up again downtown. You let one bum get away with begging in traffic, and you'll have ten bums on every corner by tomorrow. That's exactly right, and then we'd be right back where we were last year. Nah, no charges. Right, tell them to drop him off at the vet center on East El Cajon. If he wants to come back downtown, he'll have a hell of a walk. Thanks Ray. Later."

The veterans center would be perfect for the vagrant, Bullard mused. The vet would feel right at home sleeping on a cot in one of the twenty-man tents. Standing in a chow line for a ration of free slop would be nothing new for the old soldier. Times were hard, and expectations were low.

Beggars could not be choosers.

Basilio Ramos had visited the city twenty years before, with his mother. They had gone to the famous San Diego Zoo and to Seaworld, and stayed for a long weekend with friends in the Santa Ana section. It had been a pleasant middle class area of San Diego then, with detached homes on shady streets. This morning Ramos and his small team of Zetas had to drive over to Santa Ana in the big crew cab truck, to pick up their van and the local driver who would take them downtown. Once again, Chino and Salazar rode ahead of them on the Kawasaki as armed scouts.

Last evening they had spent only an hour at the *padrino's* cliffside estate, before being driven to an empty house in the same mesa-top enclave. This fully furnished Mexican Mafia safe house was where the team spent the night going over maps, discussing possible snatch scenarios, drinking beer and watching television.

During his brief audience with the local godfather, Ramos was surprised to hear that the man was very interested in acquiring property in Nuevo Mexico, perhaps one of the confiscated ranches. Ramos concluded from this conversation and the high level of respect he had been afforded, that rumors of his personal and professional problems had not been signaled ahead to San Diego. Chino and Salazar even lauded him to the gang boss as "*El Che Guevara de Nuevo Mexico*."

Driving through Santa Ana on this Friday morning, the Comandante couldn't believe what a different world he was in now, compared to his youthful memories of suburban San Diego. Every foot of curb space was occupied by parked cars, and more cars were parked on sidewalks, driveways and yards. Many were stripped or burnt hulks. The green lawns and manicured shrubs he remembered were gone, along with the trees and their shade. Chickens scratched in the dust, goats ripped at the remaining greenery where they could find it.

Some houses may have been occupied by only one family, but it was clear that most had been converted into multi-family boarding homes or mini-apartments by the amount of cars parked on the front yards. The actual apartment buildings were now decaying slums. A vast number of shabby RVs and trailers parked in driveways had obviously been turned into fulltime stationary housing. Many homes, RVs and trailers had been enlarged or even connected together with the addition of shack-like extensions. "Informal" electrical wires crisscrossed between poles, buildings, homes, shacks and RVs, a pervasive overhead spider web of bootlegged electricity being tapped from every power pole.

The sheer number of people on the sidewalks, streets and yards was just staggering. It seemed as if most of the population of Mexico had been picked up and dropped into the San Diego suburbs. It was the 4th of July, a Yanqui national holiday, but there was not even one United States flag to be seen. There were only the tricolor flags of Mexico, proudly proclaiming the de-facto reality of *reconquista* in red, white and green.

In the 'better' areas, every house had stout burglar bars over their windows and doors. Many homes had enclosed front porches resembling cages, or holding cells. Most of the small yards were fenced with chain link, or were enclosed within high cinder block walls, topped with vertical shards of broken glass set into mortar. More than anything, it reminded Ramos of the barrios around Caracas, Rio, Mexico City or a hundred other Latin American cities.

The house in Santa Ana where they picked up their van and driver was protected by a ten-foot high fence made of rusty iron rebar. The metal bars were spaced six inches apart, and the top of each rod was machine-cut at a wickedly sharp angle, to form an effective spear point. The vertical bars were haphazardly welded together with random pieces of scrap angle iron. Ramos reflected that the level of crime must have been enormous, to drive people to take such extreme—and extremely ugly—measures to defend their property. This made him wonder about local police protection, and he kept an eye out for patrol cars, but he saw none at all.

Their cargo van was sparkling white, with high quality black vinyl graphics on both sides announcing that it was owned by the Magic Chef catering company, *El Cocinero Mágico*, complete with telephone numbers, and a cartoon portrait of a winking chef. The lettering and the art were being applied to the sides of the van as they arrived. The extended-length van and the driver who would take them safely into downtown San Diego had been arranged through Chino's local Mexican Mafia contacts. The cost to Basilio Ramos was 1.2 ounces of gold per day—after a "*depósito de seguridad*" of fifteen more ounces.

Their *coyote* driver charged an additional half ounce of gold for taking them past the security controls into downtown. The motorcycle, the weapons bags, Almeria's communications gear and the four members of his team went into the back of the van, sitting on the deck. Ramos sat in the front passenger seat. The driver had no visible tattoos, no facial piercings and a normal medium-length haircut. He was dressed in a white caterer's uniform to play his role.

The house where they picked up the van had a detached two-car garage, which had been converted into a paint-spraying booth. A dusting of over-spray covered the yard. More cars that were being taped and papered in preparation for spraying were parked on every square meter of the small property.

This residential automobile painting operation was not unusual for the area. On many blocks, every other house had been converted into a business: a beauty parlor, an automobile repair shop, or a mortician. These homes-turned-businesses were painted in garish yellow, red, purple, and green.

Every block had at least one combination moneychanger, pawn shop and loan shark, with the walls of a former house announcing that they traded dollars, pesos, gold and silver at the very best rates in town. The universal symbol of these businesses was a large depiction of a balance scale, painted on prominent walls. The symbol C/S (for "con safos") was painted by these scales, meaning that these businesses were under gang protection, and hence they were "untouchable." In the new San Diego, balance scales stood for anything but justice.

Every intersection supported a contingent of men, women and children walking into the stopped traffic to sell flowers, chewing gum, or small bags of nuts or fruit. It seemed like every open piece of sidewalk had a hot dog or ice cream vendor selling from a pushcart. Prime street corner locations were occupied by groups of young men all wearing the matching jerseys of various sports teams, such as the Chargers or Raiders. What they were selling was not in much doubt.

Alleyways and walls were covered with graffiti, murals or gigantic painted-on Mexican flags. ¡FUERA GRINGOS! (Gringos Out!) and ¡AZTLAN SÍ, YANQUIS NO! were commonly painted sentiments, but it was obvious to Basilio Ramos that the last gringos had departed years ago. From street to street, the horns and violins of *ranchera* music blasting from cars competed with the thumping base and angry verse of Latino hip-hop.

On every block, there was clear evidence that basic city services had collapsed. Trash was piled up in car-high mounds, and some of these were being burned, sending clouds of acrid smoke wafting across the neighborhoods. Sewage backed up from drains, running down the gutters and forming stinking black puddles, not surprising with several families living in every house. Old refrigerators, gutted washing machines, discarded furniture and mildewed mattresses occupied much of the space between the curbs and the security fences marking the property lines.

Basilio Ramos couldn't understand Chino and Salazar's fondness for the place. It must have been their youth—they had no memory of how nice the Santa Ana section of San Diego had been twenty years ago.

At nine o'clock, the van was creeping along in heavy traffic on El Cajon Boulevard. The Comandante calculated that at this rate, it would be more than an hour before they made it downtown to begin their surveillance. The traffic light above the next intersection wasn't working, it wasn't even flashing. It was just out, swaying but dead. As a result, traffic in both directions had to just bull through the gridlock, relying on their horns and sheer intimidation. The lines of cars would move ahead twenty feet, and then stop, providing a captive audience for the armies of street vendors. The slow traffic speed seemed to suit the condition of the asphalt streets, which if anything, were in an even worst state of disrepair than back in *Búrque*, with potholes that could be more accurately described as craters. Many of the holes were connected in long rutted chains, forming small canyons, and the driver had to maneuver to keep two wheels on either side.

On the sidewalk near the intersection, Ramos noticed a flurry of commotion. A group of young men wearing Raiders jerseys, black knee-length shorts, white knee socks and black boots were circling around someone, but it was no friendly football huddle. The men in the group all had shaved heads, goatees, and were all wearing sunglasses. A single taller man in the center of the group had long chestnut hair, and a short beard. Between the *cholos*, Ramos could see that the tall white man was wearing, improbably, an old-style desert camouflage uniform. He was spinning and turning, holding up a fist, but the gang was getting the best of him. Ramos saw that the *vatos* were tossing a hat between them, a uniform cap that matched the man's shirt and pants. While the gringo turned one way, another punk slapped or punched him from behind. This was the old 'game' of bear baiting, which would inevitably result in the man going down to the ground exhausted, to be kicked and stomped senseless or dead beneath their boots.

The van inched forward, and he could see that the man who was being so cruelly taunted had only one arm, and a small paper sign pinned to his chest.

The sign read: "Iraq War Vet."

"Stop the van!" barked Ramos, slamming his hand on the dashboard.

"What?" asked his driver, puzzled, since they were finally rolling up toward the intersection.

"You heard me—stop this van, now!"

Before they came to a complete halt, Ramos threw open his door and leaped out, lifting the bottom of his checked shirt with his left hand and drawing his Glock with his right. To the amazement of the preoccupied gang members, street vendors, passers-by, and other drivers and passengers stuck in traffic, Basilio Ramos seized one of the unaware street punks from behind by a handful of gold chains, jerked him back off balance on his heels, and then snapped him upright. He jammed his Glock's muzzle hard into the vato's right ear, and used him as a human shield.

"*Hijos de putamadre*, give him his hat, or I'll blow this *pendejo's* shitty brains back to hell! *¡Hazlo!* Do it now!" Ramos violently shook his hostage for emphasis.

The one-armed Anglo veteran straightened up, his chest heaving, breathing deeply through flaring nostrils. One of the gang members picked his uniform cap off the ground and handed it to him, while nervously eying the screaming *pistolero loco*. Ramos was so intently focused on the drama in front of him, that he didn't notice that Chino, Salazar and Genizaro were now backing him up on either side, their leveled Ingram MAC-10s gaining him vastly greater respect.

Ramos hissed, "Now, get the hell out of here! Move it!" as he shoved his captive forward almost onto his face. The cholo staggered and caught his balance, just in time to take off running after his friends. They were out of sight in seconds.

The Comandante was shaking, and he calmed himself down with effort. He and the one-armed man were the same height, taller by half a head than the common mestizo street punks he had chased off. The crippled man was gaunt and hollow-eyed. There was a small American flag patch sewn onto his left shoulder, above his good arm. There wasn't even an amputation stump on the right side, nothing for a prosthetic.

A sewn-on tag above one uniform pocket said U.S. ARMY, above the other, it said FREMONT. The man's thick chestnut hair and trimmed beard partially hid his burn-scarred right cheek and missing ear. The rest of his weathered face was prematurely aged by war and hunger, two conditions that Basilio Ramos recognized first hand. He was probably around thirty years old, but looked almost fifty. In English, he asked the one-armed man, "Where are you going today, soldier?"

"Downtown. *Back* downtown. The police kicked me out this morning, but my pack is still there. I'm going back to get it, if it's still there—police or no police."

Ramos stared into the crippled veteran's steel-gray eyes, thinking. It was at least seven or eight miles to downtown San Diego. Then he quietly said, "We're going that way, we'll give you a ride. Get in, if you want." The veteran shrugged, and glanced around the street as if considering his lack of better options. He walked over and climbed into the open passenger door of the van, and crouched in the space between the two front seats. The three Zetas returned to the back and slammed the side door shut behind them with a bang. A blue canvas curtain divided the front of the van from the cargo area, concealing their presence. Given the recent display of automatic weapons, the traffic had magically melted away from the *Cocinero Mágico* van. They were soon through the intersection and making good progress westbound on El Cajon Boulevard. Ramos offered the veteran water from a plastic bottle, and he gratefully drank it all.

"Why did the police kick you out of downtown?" asked Ramos.

The veteran sighed, and whispered, "For…begging." He stared straight ahead, just over the dashboard, which he held with his one hand to steady himself. "They said I can't ask for money. I didn't know that was the law here. I just hitchhiked here from Arizona. It took me a week—a hard week."

"You lost your arm in Iraq?"

"Yeah. Yes. Iraq."

"A bomb?"

"Yes."

"Don't you get a pension from your government?"

The veteran huffed a bitter laugh. "A pension? No, I don't get a pension. I was only in for eighteen months before...this. I get a disability check, but it's a joke. They never changed the amount after the money changed to blue bucks. Once a month, I can buy a few nice meals with the nine hundred dollars I get, or I can eat rice and beans for a couple weeks. But after that, I get nothing. Not unless I want to stay in a 'veteran's center,' and live worse than a goddamn prisoner of war. And I just got here, so I can't pick up my check until Monday, because of the holiday. Maybe not even then. The VA always screws up the paperwork, when you don't have a permanent address."

The van left El Cajon Boulevard and merged onto a highway, driving south in light traffic. Once again they were in a chute between high concrete walls, which were covered from top to bottom in graffiti, gang slogans and informal business advertisements. After a few miles their driver exited, heading west on surface streets toward downtown near the base of the Coronado Bridge, which vaulted skyward before them.

The Comandante said, "Listen, I'm sorry, but we can't take you all the way in."

"I understand. It's okay. I can walk the rest of the way."

Their driver pulled over to the curb.

Ramos stepped out of the van to allow the veteran to climb past his seat. They had stopped in an area of warehouses and industrial businesses, surrounded by high chain link and barbed wire. None of the businesses seemed to be open, either because of the holiday, or because of the economy. Trash blew down the sidewalk, and dusty weeds grew from every crack in the cement. There was no one else on the street.

"Good luck, Fremont," said Basilio Ramos, as they locked eyes for a few seconds.

"Thanks for the ride. And thanks for what you did back there."

"No problem. *Vaya con Dios*, soldier." Neither man put out a hand to shake.

The one-armed veteran turned and limped away down the sidewalk. Ramos climbed back into the front of the van, and their driver made a U-turn on the empty street.

When they pulled ahead, Genizaro reached forward and yanked the curtain aside and demanded, "Comandante, we have a mission, this is serious business! Why did you stop to help that fucking *pinche* gringo?"

"Why? Because he was a soldier, like us. A veterano."

"No Comandante, no, he was not like us! You heard him—that Yanqui lost his arm fighting an imperialist war of aggression, not a war of liberation!"

"It doesn't matter. He was still a soldier. You could end up like him. Any of us could."

"But Comandante, gringos like him shot down our helicopter, and killed six of our comrades! Gringos like him killed our brothers from Alpha Platoon last week in Búrque! Have you already forgotten them?"

"No, I haven't forgotten! But he didn't shoot them—his war is over, long over." Ramos didn't say any more after that, and Genizaro didn't push the issue, but the belligerent Zeta grumbled loudly as he sat back down on the cargo deck.

Comandante Ramos couldn't explain his complex feelings to these men. Perhaps he could discuss it with his communications officer, the more cultured Teniente Almeria, but never with these hot-blooded but simple mestizo fighters. Yes, Basilio Ramos recognized that on some level, he did sympathize with the plight of the wounded gringo soldier, crippled and disfigured in war—any war. The Yanqui soldier was only a pawn in any case.

But on another level, he understood what the veterano vagabundo truly represented: he was a walking, breathing symbol of Yanqui defeat. Powerless, impotent, beaten; an object of pity, not anger. In Cali—and soon in all of Aztlan—the old gringo fighters were mere shadows, hollow men, yesterday's warriors. As a force, they were finished, reduced to begging for alms in their former stronghold. Ramos almost wished that he had given the beggar-soldier Fremont one of the small gold Indian coins, a magnanimous token to cement their relationship of victor to vanquished.

Their driver approached the crossing point, and Ramos tightly closed the fabric curtains separating the two front seats from the back of the van. The crossing point was a highway underpass near the eastern base of the Coronado Bridge. The road passed through a square opening in the cement, the barrier wall on the side of Interstate 5 rising far above them. A single black and white San Diego police cruiser was parked in the bright sunlight a hundred feet away on the other side of the box-like tunnel. Two policemen stood near the patrol car, carrying MP-5 submachine guns on slings, scanning the occasional traffic that rolled through. Both officers were wearing black ball caps; both had cop mustaches and wore black sunglasses. The van slid through the darkness, and Ramos relaxed slightly when he recognized them as *carnals*, Hispanic brothers. One casually held up his hand, and blocked the vehicle's path.

The van's driver was prepared; his window was already down. As one of the cops approached, the driver held up his California driver's license, his national ID card, his downtown entry permit and his business license for inspection. Ramos glanced over, and could see two small gold coins fastened to the back of the driver's license with a paper clip. The policeman examined only the driver's license, turning away for a moment, and then he handed it back and waved them forward. The small gold coins were gone. They were inside of I-5, two miles southeast of downtown, the city's skyscrapers rising before them.

Their taciturn chef-coyote was suddenly light-hearted, almost carefree, after successfully penetrating the forbidden zone once again. "You don't have to worry about *policias* leaving downtown," the driver advised. "The only extra security is on the way into *el centro*, and now you're past it. Just keep your men with the gang tattoos in the back as much as you can—there are secret police who will kill them on sight, you understand that?"

"Yes, I understand. And so do they."

"Okay, good. When your mission is finished, you can leave downtown from anywhere—the police don't care about that. You know the way back to where we started?"

"No problem. *El Chino* will be driving. He's from San Diego."

"All right then. I'll jump out up here—I have friends around the corner on the next block. *Buena suerte*—good luck."

Brian saw that Gretchen was wearing her running clothes, a loose green t-shirt and the same stretchy black pants she wore when she went for rides on her bike. She had a special pair of sneakers that she only wore when she went running. She told Mommy that she was going to run by the bay. She was going to run ten K. Brian knew that ten K was very far. It meant that Gretchen wouldn't be back for a long time. After she left, Brian's Mommy let him have the remote control, and she went into the bedroom and closed the door, but not all the way. In a few minutes, Brian heard the shower running. He quietly walked to Mommy and Gretchen's bedroom, and peeked inside. Mommy's clothes were lying across the bed, and her bathroom door was closed tight.

This was his chance—he had enough time right now, if he hurried! He ran back to the living room. Mommy's leather pocketbook was on the little table by the end of the sofa. She kept her cell phone in a little black pouch inside of her pocketbook. He pulled it out, and sat on the sofa, took a deep breath and opened it up.

He remembered what to do. He pushed the ON button, and the little television lit up. He pushed CONTACTS, and the list of names appeared. The first name said ALEX. It was already a different color than the other names, so he pushed the green SEND button, and held the phone up to his ear. He could hear it buzzing on and off.

After seven buzzes, he heard clicks, and then his Daddy's voice! Brian said, "Hi Daddy!" but his father only said, "You've reached the voicemail for 505-555-4522. Leave a message after the tone." It wasn't really his Daddy; Brian understood with a sinking heart, it was only a tape machine. But it was his Daddy's voice, and he suddenly realized it was a way to leave a message for him! His Daddy would hear his message, and find a way to come and get him!

42

Ranya was taking her turn monitoring the computer, while Alex watched cable news with the sound muted. About once a minute, someone went in or out of the Fed Tower's revolving glass doors on Broadway.

"Look, is that Gretchen?" she asked.

Alex twisted the upholstered easy chair toward the desk and the laptop, reached over and tapped a command on the keyboard. The one-quarter size view of the building's entrance went full screen. "That's her—the Beast."

Gretchen Bosch was wearing a green t-shirt and black bicycling shorts, stretched over the powerful thighs of a serious body builder. She had a white sweatband around her head, and with her crew cut, it was almost impossible to tell that she was a woman. While they watched, Gretchen went through an elaborate process of stretching out, and then she disappeared running down the sidewalk on Broadway, toward the harbor four long city blocks away.

While they were both watching the screen, the laptop's speakers began to sound the tones of a phone number being dialed automatically, followed by ringing.

"Excuse me—let me sit there, okay?" Ranya vacated the hardback chair in front of the computer, and Alex settled into it, typing rapidly, causing the screen to shift to another window. "That's Karin's phone, she's making a call. There's her number, and that's the number she's calling, see? It's ringing."

Alex stared at the number Karin had dialed.

Ranya said, "505, isn't that the Albuquerque area code?"

"That's...*my* phone number! Karin is calling me! Oh jeez—now what?"

They both heard Alex's recorded announcement: "*You've reached the voicemail for 505-555-4522. Leave a message after the tone.*"

But it wasn't Karin's voice they heard next.

"Hi Daddy. This is Brian. I'm in San Diego. I hope you can hear this sometime. I really miss you a whole lot. San Diego is okay, but I wish I was with you. We didn't go to Seaworld yet, but we went to a beach.

Next week we're going to move to a house, but right now we're in a tall building. There are red trolley trains that go by our building, but Mommy doesn't want to ride on the trolley. Maybe if you come to San Diego, maybe you can take me for a ride on the red trolley train?"

There was a long silence, and then the child began speaking again, with pauses between each sentence.

"Daddy, did you know today is the 4th of July? Tonight we're going to see fireworks. When it gets dark, we're going to walk over the trolley tracks, down to where Bob Buller keeps his big boat. Bob Buller is Gretchen's boss. I can see his boat from our balcony. The fireworks are going to shoot up over the water.

So Daddy, if you can hear me, I miss you a lot, a whole lot. I hope you miss me too, because it's pretty terrible not being able to see you...

Uh-oh, Mommy's shower just turned off. I love you Daddy. Bye-bye."

They both stared at the computer screen, at the two phone numbers, Alex sitting in the chair, Ranya holding the back of the chair and leaning over his shoulder.

Ranya spoke first, choking with emotion. "Was that saved? Can we hear it again?" She had never heard her son's voice before, and a tear spilled onto Alex's neck.

"Sure, it's all saved."

"He's a great talker!"

"Oh yeah, Brian's as sharp as a tack. He was talking at fourteen months."

"Did you hear what he said at the end, about 'Mommy's shower'? It sounds like he was sneaking the call."

"Right, I think so too," Alex agreed. "He was sneaking it."

"But he's only five—and he knows how to use a telephone?"

"I'm telling you, he's smart, *really* smart. He figures things out."

"Will she know he used the phone? Will it show, will she check?"

"I don't think so, not if he puts it back the same way he found it. There's no reason for her to check."

"He must be a clever little guy." She wiped her tears with the back of her hand.

"Oh, he is. He takes after his mother. His *real* mother."

"And he's brave—like his father," said Ranya. "Like both of his fathers."

"He knows about Bob Bullard, can you imagine that? He said that 'Bob Buller' is Gretchen's boss, that's Bob Bullard, but how would he know that?"

Ranya hesitated, and guessed, "The television. '*Hi, I'm Bob Bullard.*' They must have seen the homeland security commercial. Karin must have told him 'Bob Buller' was Gretchen's boss."

"That makes sense," Alex agreed. "He was telling me where he's going to be tonight—*on the dock where Bob Buller keeps his big boat.* A dock he can see from his balcony."

"And he told us when: when it gets dark. And he told us they're walking, that it's only a few blocks. He told us everything! What do you think? Is it doable?"

"It's doable," said Alex, "If we don't get a better chance before that."

"If we grab the boy, we could hold him for ransom," suggested Chino, who was in the front passenger seat. Basilio Ramos was now driving the white catering van. Chino was wearing a brown turtleneck long-sleeve jersey, to conceal the gang tattoos on his neck and arms. The small teardrops tattooed beneath the corners of his eyes were not so noticeable when they were obscured by his sunglasses. "If we take the boy, we could force Bardiwell and Garabanda to come to us."

Lieutenant Almeria was in the back, sitting on the floor with his laptop computer, wearing headphones. Genizaro and Salazar sat across from each other in the far back, playing cards between them. All of them were wearing long jeans, and except for Chino, they were wearing checked shirts in different patterns, loose and untucked to conceal their weapons, and their Kevlar vests. The green Kawasaki was tied against the left side of the cargo van, across from the sliding door. They were driving slowly down Harbor Drive, spending 15 or 20 minutes in various parking spaces, and then moving, always remaining within sight of the Pacific Majesty.

"That won't work. We just need to be patient, very patient. The child is in that building, in apartment 4124. Bardiwell and Garabanda will come around; you know they will. They'll be like tigers sniffing around the tethered goat, unaware that the hunter is also waiting and watching."

"Tigers are dangerous, even to hunters," observed Chino.

"But they don't know they're being hunted. We have the advantage."

Behind them, Almeria said, "Quiet! A call!" and they fell silent. The blue curtains were open in the middle. Almeria was situated at the front of the cargo deck behind the passenger seat, with his electronics mounted in a plywood box. After a minute, he pulled off his headphones, and said, "Comandante, you're not going to believe this—the child has telephoned his father in Santa Fe. His English is hard for me to understand, let me play the call for you."

Almeria pulled the headphone jack out of the computer, and they listened to the playback of Brian Garabanda's phone call several times, while Ramos translated his words for them all.

"Do you think Garabanda will check his voicemail for messages soon?" asked Salazar.

Almeria scoffed. "Voicemail? I would assume he's already heard the call, at exactly the same time that we did. The man is an FBI agent, so I'm sure that he has the same capability that we have to listen to cell phones."

"Then why didn't he answer, when his son called him?" asked Salazar.

Genizaro said, "The boy only called the phone left in the empty hotel room in Santa Fe, did you forget this fact already?"

"I'm not stupid, I know that! But calls can be relayed, can't they? Garabanda could answer from another phone, from anywhere."

"Perhaps," said Ramos, "But then Garabanda would be giving away his location. This tiger is no fool, he won't make a basic mistake like that. He won't rush into the open, to seize the staked goat."

Chino said, "But Garabanda will be watching for his son on Broadway, as the darkness comes."

"Yes, he will," agreed Comandante Ramos. "If they have no better opportunity today, that's when Garabanda and Bardiwell will strike—and we'll be waiting for them."

Alex carefully glued a gray mustache onto his upper lip, while leaning across the bathroom sink and looking into the mirror. His very basic disguise kit was unfolded and laying across the top of the toilet tank. A silicone nose extension went on next, the flesh-toned rubber matched to his skin color with makeup. Then he put on a scraggly gray-haired wig, and a crumpled brown fedora. Boxy black-framed glasses altered the look of his eyes. He slipped on a loose-fitting dark gray suit jacket, and he was ready.

He expected Ranya to laugh at him when he came out of the bathroom, but instead she maintained an impassive poker face, so he asked, "Well, how do I look?"

She glanced up from monitoring the computer screen, and gave a blasé shrug. "What, have you done something? You look about the same to me."

"Gee, thanks. Just what I wanted to hear."

She broke into a grin. "No, seriously, you did a good job Alex. You look at least 75. Why, that's a good ten or fifteen years older than usual."

He pulled off his brown hat and flung it at her, saying, "No respect, that's the trouble with kids today, no respect!"

"No, you look fine," she said, finally laughing after ducking the hat. "You really do look 75. At least."

"That's the idea. This is one of my best disguises. Nobody pays attention to us old farts, we're practically invisible. The trick is to look too broke to be worth mugging, without quite looking homeless. And all of this garbage I've got on my face keeps the digital cameras from getting a match, just in case."

"Nobody knows we're in San Diego anyway."

"You hope. But hard drives are forever. Once you're recorded by the cameras, they can go back and check anytime, even weeks or months later."

She replied, "Weeks later? I hope we're long gone by then."

"We will be, but you never know. Don't make it easy for them, ever. Never make assumptions about security." While he looked himself over in the room's wall mirror, he briefly thought about his meeting with Luis Carvahal in the Mount Calvary cemetery, when he had believed he was not under surveillance—a fatal error.

Alex left the Holiday Inn through a secondary exit at the end of the first floor hallway. The ten story Holiday Inn was located across Harbor Drive from the San Diego Bay. He walked across to the sidewalk that ran in front of the seafood restaurants and excursion boats on the bay side. A clipper ship longer than a football field was tied alongside the quay wall, its massive bowsprit pointing south toward Broadway. Its advertising signs declared it to be the Star of India, built in 1863, allegedly the oldest sailing ship still in operation, and now a floating museum.

Five minutes later he was in front of the enormous government pier which extended for at least two hundred yards beyond the end of Broadway at Harbor Drive. From the shore, the massive pier seemed like a rectangular extension of Broadway, it was at least a hundred feet wide at its base. To the south, another giant pier was home to the aircraft carrier USS Midway, now a museum. To the north, back toward the Holiday Inn, another long pier was occupied by moderate-sized harbor tour and excursion boats from fifty to over a hundred feet long.

The government pier in the middle was the exclusive territory of the security services, with small vessels from Homeland Security, Customs and Border Enforcement, the Marine Patrol, the Navy and the Coast Guard tied up to floating docks, which were attached to the higher permanent pier. Near the end of the pier, with its square transom facing the shore, was one larger vessel. It appeared to be a motor yacht, about eighty or ninety feet long. Alex stopped before he reached the government pier and took a few innocent tourist pictures with his digital camera.

A black iron fence ran across the base of the pier, but in the center, a wide vehicle gate was open. Alex shuffled along the sidewalk, his head down, until he was in the middle of the opening, and then he steered a right turn, nonchalantly shambling out onto the pier. A uniformed guard immediately stepped out of a cement and glass security post, his arms upraised.

"Hello, can I help you?" the guard asked in an overly loud voice, as he intercepted Alex's path.

"No thanks sonny, I don't need any help. I just want to walk out there and take a picture of the Midway."

"Well I'm sorry old timer, but this pier is only for federal employees on official business."

"I can't just walk right over there, and take a picture of the Midway?"

"Nope, sorry. Federal property. You have to stay out there and take it."

"All right, I guess." Alex put his head back down, and shuffled to the pedestrian crossing at the traffic light on Harbor Drive. This was a massive intersection, where the six lanes of Broadway ended at the six lanes of Harbor Drive. He pushed the button and waited. When the light turned green, he took care to walk as slowly as an old man with bad hips might, and no faster.

Across Harbor Drive, there were parking lots on the north side of Broadway and government buildings to the south. A long block up Broadway there were multiple railroad tracks that carried everything from heavy freight to the local light rail commuters. Alex was amused to note that the train stop there was called the Santa Fe Station, constructed in Spanish Mission style. The station building was only missing a cross on top to be mistaken for a small Spanish colonial cathedral, an architectural throwback amidst the ultramodern glass and marble high rises of downtown San Diego.

Alex stood on the sidewalk near the tracks—this must be where Brian watched the trains passing by. While he was looking around, a red electric-powered commuter train pulled into the Santa Fe Station from the north, paused while taking on and letting off passengers, and then crossed Broadway and continued toward the south. The placard sign above the conductor said "San Ysidro," the final stop at the Mexican border a dozen miles away. Alex looked upward and saw the top floors of the Pacific Majesty, two blocks further up Broadway. Even now, Brian might be looking down at the "red trolley train" that he wanted to ride.

Alex tried to take in everything from the point of view of a pedestrian with a small child. Where was Karin most likely to walk? At the same time, he scanned for hidden vantage points where his Durango might be parked to lay in wait. He tried to imagine how the approach could be made, where Brian's pickup would attract the least attention, and how they could exit the area the most smoothly. If they drove straight north on Harbor Drive, they would be able to pick up Interstate 8 where it ended in a nice section of Point Loma, on the safe western side of I-5. From there, it would be a fast dash east on I-8 all the way to the Golden Arrow Casino, where Flint would be waiting for an immediate takeoff. It could work. It would work. It had to work.

Behind the Santa Fe Station on the north side of Broadway, Alex seized a chance opportunity. A San Diego Gas and Electric emergency services truck was parked along the curb of a small access road. The back of the big white utility truck was twenty feet from Broadway. Three orange traffic cones were spread a few feet behind the truck, but no workers were in sight. The truck was clearly parked for the long holiday weekend. Alex casually picked up the two cones nearest the curb, one dangling from each hand, and dropped them in new positions a few yards closer to Broadway, effectively holding a parking space for the Durango.

Even the regional director of DHS could take off occasionally, mused Bob Bullard. Late morning on the 4th of July and he was still in his royal blue bathrobe, lounging on the western terrace of his penthouse, on the 45th floor of the Pacific Majesty. It was a hazy day, and Point Loma was lost in the low fog. A mile across the bay, the aircraft carrier Ronald Reagan lay alongside its Coronado berth at the North Island Naval Air Station. Below him was another carrier, the retired Midway, now a museum. At the next pier over from the Midway was his own eighty-foot Eldorado, looking like a toy in comparison. He always felt like a king surveying his realm up here, but he realized that it could all end quickly. The barbarians were literally at the gate, just across Interstate 5 and pressing hard. It comforted him to know that the Eldorado was always fueled up and ready to sprint for the open sea. His yacht was the ultimate golden parachute.

Bullard's cell phone buzzed in the pocket of his silk robe. Only a very short list of people had this number.

"Hello."

"Boss?"

"What's up Jim?"

"Ahh, something kind of weird. It's the Garabanda-Bardiwell thing. We've got taps on the FBI guy's ex-wife, right? In case Ranya Bardiwell tried to contact her."

"Um, yeah."

"I just emailed you a transcript of a call—you'll want to check it out."

"What's it about?"

"Well, the boy called his father in Albuquerque. Ranya Bardiwell's boy, remember?"

"I remember," said Bullard.

"Garabanda's an FBI Supervisor, the one that Gretchen Bosch smacked with a baseball bat."

"Got it, I'm with you."

"Okay. The boy left a voicemail for his father. He used his mother's cell phone. Not his real mother, his adoptive mother. Karin Bergen."

"So?"

"Well, it's the 4th of July, a government holiday, right? Why didn't Garabanda pick up for his own son? It seems kind of strange, that's all."

"Hmm…interesting. What do you think?"

"I think maybe he's not in New Mexico at all, that's what I think. Maybe he's a lot closer than that."

"Could be, could be. Tell you what…check it out. Send a local Albuquerque team, but not FBI. Have them check on Garabanda, tell them to put their eyes on him. I want sure and certain confirmation of this guy's location. Let me know if he's really in New Mexico or not. Keep it quiet though—we don't want to spook him. And they shouldn't let the FBI Field Office know we're looking, or the word will get back to him."

"Got it boss—be discreet. Just find out if he's there."

"That's it. Today's a holiday, so put a flash on the message, and make sure they do it ASAP. I don't want it slipping through the cracks because nobody's on duty there in New Mexico. And let me know what you find out."

"Will do, boss."

"Yeah." Bullard snapped his phone shut, and dropped it into his bathrobe pocket. He strolled back through the open glass door inside of his penthouse apartment. His computer was already on. He clicked on the email from Jim Holcomb, and his eyes locked on the pertinent section.

Daddy, did you know that today is the 4th of July? Tonight we're going to see fireworks. When it gets dark, we're going to walk over the trolley tracks, down to where Bob [Buller] keeps his big boat. Bob [Buller] is Gretchen's boss. I can see his boat from our balcony. The fireworks are going to shoot up over the water.

He smiled at the transcribed misspelling of his name, and wondered what Gretchen Bosch had told the boy. If Garabanda checked his voice-mail, he'd know where his son was going to be at twilight. If he returned his son's call, and he was calling from New Mexico, that fact would soon be known from the telephone intercepts. However, if he didn't return his son's call, the question then would be, why not?

Bob Bullard had been married and divorced three times, and he knew better than most men how bitterly acrimonious these custodial battles could be. Even so, he thought that an estranged, divorced FBI agent would have the *cojones* to call his ex-wife and ask to speak to his son on a holiday. But what if he didn't call his son? What would that mean? He vaguely remembered an old black and white Sherlock Holmes movie. In the story, there was something important about a dog that *didn't* bark.

43

Downtown San Diego, twilight

"Okay, it's them. They're coming," said Alex. "They're crossing Broadway at the light, so they'll be walking down our side. We'll go with 'plan A'."

"You're sure?"

"I'm sure." Alex was sitting behind the Durango's empty driver's seat. Ranya sat next to him on the other middle seat.

He was holding a small pair of binoculars, using them to watch the front entrance of the Fed Tower, two blocks up and across Broadway. Dusk was falling over the city, but with the binoculars, he was easily able to observe each person as they walked out of the building's revolving doors.

They had not checked out of the Holiday Inn, but the room was empty, everything was packed into the rear cargo area of the Durango. If they were successful with their plan, they would be driving directly to the Golden Arrow Casino—with Brian.

The Durango was parallel parked on the side street behind the Santa Fe train station, two blocks from the Fed Tower, and two blocks from the bay. The SDG&E truck and the traffic cones had not been moved, and Alex had been able to occupy his preferred surveillance location near the tracks.

The SUV's deeply tinted windows prevented anyone from seeing the two watchers in the vehicle from the sides or the rear. A nylon mesh curtain made them invisible from the front. The thin black gauze was similar to nylon stocking material. It was attached with tiny hooks to the ceiling liner of the Durango above the front seat headrests, and to the backs of the two front seats, forming a tautly stretched thin black curtain across the middle of the vehicle.

Anyone looking into the Durango through the lightly tinted windshield saw nothing behind the front seats but an empty black void, which appeared to extend all the way to the rear of the vehicle. The mesh was virtually invisible to passing pedestrians, yet Alex and Ranya could easily see through it and out of the front of the "empty" black SUV.

Ranya had been suitably impressed with this surveillance trick. Alex could not have guessed when he pulled the compressed material from its tiny storage pouch, that it would remind her of the black stockings she had used to bind Basilio Ramos to his bed, on the night of her escape from his mansion. She had never brought up the subject of her time under the Comandante's roof, and Alex had never asked.

When they were certain that Karin and Brian were coming down their side of Broadway, Ranya slipped out of the SUV's right side door, and disappeared down the sidewalk toward the bay. This was 'Plan A,' the better of their two options, to be used if their targets walked along the north side of Broadway with the flow of westbound traffic. Ranya was a blond again, wearing the white San Diego sweatshirt she had bought at the Golden Arrow Casino gift shop. Alex was wearing a plain black sweatshirt over his Kevlar vest. Both were wearing jeans, and running shoes.

A minute after Ranya's departure, Karin and Brian came walking down the sidewalk on Broadway. Alex sank down low in his seat, and was motionless as Karin and Brian passed in front of the black SUV, just a few yards away. Karin was wearing tight jeans and her matching silver-studded jean jacket, dressed for the chill night air to come. Her own blond hair was brushed back and held behind a hair band. Brian was wearing his denim overalls, with a green long-sleeved jersey underneath.

Karin was holding his hand as they walked past; she was on the curb side of the sidewalk. They didn't appear to be talking. It more than crossed Alex's mind that he might simply jump out of the SUV and run and grab Brian away from Karin…but he knew that was a foolish idea. They had a good plan, and he would stick to it.

After they passed, Alex pulled down the black nylon screen stretched across the middle of the SUV. When he could see that no one was following Karin and Brian, he quietly opened his door, stepped out, and slipped behind the wheel in front. When Karin and Brian were a hundred yards past his position, he turned on the engine.

It was going to happen. The snatch was going down.

Chino knelt by the Kawasaki, across Broadway from the main entrance of the Pacific Majesty condominium tower. He was holding a small wrench, pretending to make an adjustment to the engine as the cover for his surveillance. The bike fit unobtrusively between two parked cars, and he was not hassled during the hour that he pretended to work on it.

When he saw the blond *gringa* with the small boy walk out through the revolving glass doors, he put his hand into his black windbreaker's pocket, and pressed the transmit button of his radio three times. The mother and child crossed Broadway over to his side, and walked right past him while he crouched behind his motorcycle. He waited until they were a block further down the sidewalk before he put on his helmet, and slowly rode past them, scanning in all directions for any sign of the Zetas' real quarry: the two traitors, Bardiwell and Garabanda.

Two blocks further up Broadway away from the bay, the *Cocinero Mágico* catering van was waiting in a small self-pay parking lot, which was located in an empty nook between two mid-rise office buildings. When they heard the signal from Chino's radio, Basilio Ramos turned on the engine and slowly maneuvered out of their space, and made the right turn onto Broadway. Chino was their scout, their eyes. If Bardiwell and Garabanda grabbed the child as they expected, Chino would observe the action, and drop into position to follow them. The van would then stay in radio contact with him on the motorcycle, and follow to wherever the traitors took the boy. They would ambush them at an opportune moment and location. Taken by complete surprise, the two traitors would be no match for his Zetas. Kidnapping and street ambush were specialties of these men, and after their year spent in rural New Mexico, they were eager for action on the familiar streets of San Diego.

After Ranya stepped out of the Durango, she walked rapidly across the multiple train tracks and past the Santa Fe Station. The area where Broadway and its sidewalks crossed the rails was paved in red brick, built up to be even with the top of the steel tracks. The long city block between the tracks and Harbor Drive was occupied by a vast parking lot on her side, the north side. A chest-high chain link fence separated the lot from the sidewalk along Broadway. The chain link was an integral part of their plan: it would give Karin nowhere to hide, run or escape when the trap was sprung.

A minute later she was at Harbor and Broadway, just across the T intersection from the bay and the federal pier. After a pause, she turned around, and began to walk back the way she had come, but more slowly. Right away she saw a blond woman up by the tracks, leading a small child by the hand: Karin and Brian. She timed her pace to meet them in the middle of the long block.

To give her a reason to approach Karin, Ranya had an unfolded map of the city spread between her hands. She had chosen to wear her new white San Diego sweatshirt, to give herself the appearance of a harmless tourist. Her .45 was on her hip in her fanny pack, but she had no expectation of needing a weapon to accomplish her mission.

In the middle of the block she stopped and turned, staring in various directions as Karin and Brian drew near. Ranya stood between an electric utility pole and the chain link fence, to narrow the space in which Karin could pass.

And now Karin and Brian were only ten feet away, and closing. Ranya tried to appear cheerful but confused, even as her heart was pounding hard in her chest.

Wide-eyed and smiling, she asked, "Excuse me, do you know where Harbor Drive is?" She knew the question would sound disarmingly brainless. She held the open street map in front of Karin, forcing her to either respond or walk around, between the fence and the metal pole.

Karin began to say, "Look, I—"

Concealed behind the map in her right hand, Ranya held an unmarked aerosol container the size of an aspirin bottle. She let go of the map with her right hand, held her breath, put out her arm and from a distance of six inches, she sprayed Karin in the face with Alex's FBI 'happy gas.' The open map fell across Brian's head, blocking his view of the aerosol attack, and preventing him from breathing the fumes. Ranya held down the top button for a count of two seconds, following Karin's moving face while she gasped and choked. Ranya then slipped the spray can into her partly open fanny pack, and withdrew a small red Spiderman action figure toy. She crouched down to Brian's level; the child was pushing the map aside and looking up in wonderment between the two blond women.

"Hi Brian! I have something of yours!" Ranya pressed the toy into his hand. Brian stared hard with wide eyes at the little red Spiderman, then he looked at his mother, and he looked at the new woman. A black SUV pulled up to the curb next to them, braking hard. Ranya stood and jerked opened the rear passenger side door, saying, "Brian, look, your Daddy's here! Go see your Daddy!"

The little boy held the Spiderman clutched in his grip, looking up at Ranya, at his mother Karin, and at the black vehicle. Alex switched on the interior light and excitedly called out through the open door, "Brian! Hey Brian! Come here tiger! Come on, Daddy's here!"

Brian stared up at his mother—Karin was blinking and coughing, rubbing her eyes. He seemed caught, unsure, looking up at his mother, at a strange blond woman, and a black car with…his Daddy!

"Get in Brian, go see your Daddy!" urged Ranya.

"Come on Brian, come on, jump in!" called Alex.

Karin rubbed her eyes and peered into the Durango. "Al? Is that you? What in the hell…?"

Ranya gripped Brian by the wrist, put a hand behind his back, and guided him up into the back seat.

"Daddy!" he shouted, "You heard my call! You came!"

A middle-aged couple walked down the sidewalk, unsure of what kind of family drama they were witnessing, but they politely continued toward Harbor Drive without staring.

Ranya climbed in after Brian, and began to shut the door behind her—but Karin was in the space between the open door and the frame! This wasn't part of the plan. She'd have to either shove Karin bodily out of the way or pull her inside, and more people were walking down the sidewalk, more potential witnesses…

Karin slid inside the Durango next to Ranya, staring at her ex-husband in shocked wonder. "Al? Al! What the hell are you doing here? Do you live in San Diego now?"

Alex was half turned in his seat, appearing stunned to see Karin sitting inside of the Durango behind him, next to Brian and Ranya.

Karin was out of it, totally fried, Ranya thought. The FBI's "less than lethal" happy gas had worked as advertised. But now an idiotically giddy Karin Bergen was inside the car with them, and the right door still hung open beside her. Ranya said, "Alex—drive, drive, go!"

He punched the gas pedal and the Durango shot forward. The door snapped shut from the car's sudden forward acceleration. Ranya was sitting in the middle, between an astonished Brian, and a blissfully befuddled Karin Bergen.

"Alexandro Garabanda! Long time no see, Al baby! Hey, what's up man? Are you going to watch the fireworks too? The fireworks are out there, on the dock. You know, it's just for us feds—no regular people allowed. Hey Al, did you know that everybody's looking for you? Uh-huh, oh yeah Al baby, *everybody* is looking for you and…what's your name sweetie-pie? Barty-well? Oh yes indeed, *everybody* is looking for you guys!"

Basilio Ramos was driving the catering van, following two blocks behind Karin Bergen and her adopted son Brian. He planned to drive past her, and park on Harbor Drive. There was still enough daylight to see, but the details were growing a bit indistinct as the streetlights began to blink on. The mother and child were walking on the sidewalk, alongside an enormous parking lot on the last block before Harbor Drive. Pedestrian traffic was moderate. Individuals and small groups clustered at the red lights, began walking together on the greens, and then spread out at their different paces.

Karin Bergen and her son were halfway along the parking lot; another woman was walking in the other direction, back up Broadway. A black SUV, moving too slowly, was creeping along in the curb lane not far behind Karin Bergen. Ramos's pulse quickened, as he saw the critical pattern emerge. He accelerated toward the Santa Fe train station, but a slow moving mini-sedan was in front of him, and he was boxed in on the left side by a silver Mercedes.

A bell began clanging, and right in front of the van, traffic gates with red flashing lights dropped across the road—*¡hijo de puta!* The red train, the light rail, was snaking its way out of the covered train station, heading south in front of him! He looked ahead, staring over the small car in front. He saw Karin Bergen draw even with another blonde woman on the sidewalk, and then the red commuter train pulled in front and blocked his view completely.

Karin's unexpected presence in the Durango was a complication, but Alex knew that they could dump her out quickly enough, once they were a few blocks north on Harbor Drive. The Durango was still in the right lane, fifty feet from making the turn off Broadway. He switched on his right turn blinker, meticulously observing every conceivable traffic regulation. The light was green for him on Broadway, to allow him to make the turn without stopping, when a huge blue truck shot through the intersection directly ahead of them, running the red light northbound on Harbor!

But instead of continuing north and out of their way, the Sparkling Alpine Water truck slammed on its brakes, stopping across Broadway, blocking their path. Before it came to a complete halt, the four rolling side doors of the bottled water delivery truck shot upward into the roof, and they were presented with the sight of a squad of agents, clad in black from their Kevlar helmets to their boots, with black submachine guns leveled at the windshield of their Durango!

At the same time that the Sparkling Alpine Water truck full of storm troopers seized their attention in the front, a blue van and a black Suburban screeched to a stop just to their left, and more black ninjas spilled out, submachine guns leveled. An agent took two steps toward their driver's side window, and snapped it with a glass breaker. The safety glass cascaded down in a million gleaming pebbles, while another agent did the same to the middle window behind him. Black-gloved hands snaked down with expert precision, reaching for the inside handles, and yanking open the doors while other MP-5 sub machinegun barrels were thrust at their faces point blank.

Less than ten seconds elapsed from the moment that the Sparkling Alpine Water truck ran the red light, until Alex and Ranya were dragged out and slammed face down on the asphalt. This was only enough time to decide if they wanted to die in a blaze of glory by reaching for their pistols, or if they wanted to live for a few more minutes at least, and see what would happen next. With Brian sitting in the Durango, both Ranya and Alex made the same decision: to avoid a hail of machine gun fire.

While hard plastic kneepads pinned them down at the neck and the legs, ninjas looped and tightened nylon flex-cuffs around their wrists with the speed of calf-roping rodeo champions. Once secured, they were patted down, and their pockets emptied and pistols taken as they were rolled from side to side. Their personal effects were tossed into a large green canvas kit bag, held open by one of the helmeted agents for that purpose. Then Alex and Ranya were jerked up onto their feet by rough gloved hands, and stood in the middle of a circle of grinning black-uniformed agents. The

Kevlar ninjas had not broken a sweat, even in their black BDU uniforms, body armor, tactical vests, helmets, boots and gloves. And there, right in front of Alex and grinning the most broadly, was Gretchen Bosch, the Beast: black helmet, body armor, submachine gun and all.

"Well howdy Al! Looks like you went and wandered off the reservation, eh boy? There goes the old pension, right? But hey, don't worry, we weren't going to take a chance on hurting Karin or the kid—check this out!" She leveled her MP-5 at his chest, and squeezed the trigger. A plastic bullet smacked him in the sternum, leaving an orange paint splotch in the center of his Navy blue sweatshirt. "Simunitions, Al. Just simunitions."

She turned to Ranya next, grabbed a handful of blond locks and yanked off her wig, revealing the short brunette hair beneath. She tossed the wig into the green kit bag like an animal pelt, laughing. Then Gretchen Bosch addressed the other agents—all males—who huddled around her: "Okay gang, thanks for playing tonight. Give us a lift out to the pier now, and I'll take it from there. Bring their black SUV too, and then you can all go home for the weekend. Get your beauty rest boys—your easy days are over. I'll see you all Monday at 0700 for a run and a PT that's gonna' leave scars!"

Alex and Ranya were bodily thrown through the open sliding side door of the blue van onto their faces. Four agents climbed in after them, and the door was slammed shut. The green bag containing Alex and Ranya's personal items was tossed onto the front passenger seat, and Gretchen Bosch climbed in behind the wheel, whistling merrily.

From Gretchen Bosch's point of view, the takedown had gone about as well as she could have hoped. As they had predicted, Alexandro Garabanda and Ranya Bardiwell had taken the bait. Once Bob Bullard had seen the transcript of the call from Brian to his father's voice mail, the wheels had been in motion. The discovery of Garabanda's cell phone hidden in the empty hotel room in Santa Fe confirmed their suspicions.

The IRS Contraband Assets Recovery Team was already on standby for the 4th of July, so gearing up for the quick-fuse mission had not even been a stretch. They had been eager to demonstrate their skills, and she had to admit, they'd performed above her expectations. Gretchen Bosch was actually quite impressed by some of the San Diego CART team's tactics and equipment. The sky-blue Sparkling Alpine Water delivery truck was one of their best tricks. It could stealthily infiltrate even the most affluent neighborhoods, right up to the front of a home or a business, and then launch as many as sixteen fully armed agents, four from each empty cargo bay. If pure vehicle speed was required, as it had been tonight, the bottled water truck was equipped with a high-performance

Cummins turbo diesel, the same type used in fire engines. The four rolling doors on each side were modified to retract upward in less than a second. Unsuspecting homeowners never had a chance to destroy evidence or hide contraband assets, not when sixteen CART team agents sprang from the ubiquitous bottled water truck innocently parked at their curb!

Even Director Bullard had to admit to Gretchen that the federal security agencies had come a long way indeed, since his old ATF assault team had approached Mount Carmel in Waco Texas, hidden in the back of a cattle trailer.

Tonight, the sheer size of the water truck had served to "cross the T" in front of Garabanda's Durango, cutting off their escape. Then the shock effect of seeing eight armed federal officers directly in front of their SUV kept them from trying anything stupid. The other CART Team vehicles pulling up on their left side had them trapped in a crossfire ambush, before they'd as much as suspected that Karin's walk down Broadway was a set up. Once again, surprise, firepower and speed of action won the victory.

Gretchen pulled her secondary radio out of one of the dozen Velcro pouches on her black combat raiding vest, and pushed the transmit button with her gloved thumb. "Okay boss, we've got 'em. Everything's contained. Prisoners are in custody, no problems."

"All right, good job, bring them out to the boat. Tell your team to stand down—they can go home. Thank them for me."

"Will do, boss. On our way." Gretchen Bosch, Special Agent of the IRS and the new leader of the San Diego CART team, didn't stop grinning all the way out to the end of the pier. It was going to be a great tour of duty in San Diego.

It took less than a minute for the light-rail train to clear the tracks in front of the catering van, and for the gates to go up. What he saw in front of him made Basilio Ramos's stomach churn. Down at the end of Broadway, at the T intersection with Harbor Drive, there appeared to have been some kind of a major traffic accident. A light blue truck was stopped perpendicular across the westbound lanes of Broadway, and in front of the truck there was a cluster of vans and SUVs, and among them, men in black, and at least a dozen of them appeared to be carrying firearms! As the white Magic Chef catering van drove across the train tracks at last, the blue truck headed north on Harbor Drive. Several of the dark vans and SUVs then drove across Harbor Drive, and continued straight out onto the long pier, as a gate rolled open to allow them to pass!

Chino wasn't supposed to talk on the radio, not even with Lieutenant Almeria's promise of secure encryption. He was only supposed to follow the blond *gringa* and her child, observe if the child was taken, and follow whoever took the boy away. What Comandante Ramos was witnessing was not going according to the plan in any respect, and in desperation he decided to break radio silence.

"Chino."

"Yes."

"Did you see what happened?"

"Ah…yes."

"Well?"

"Ah…the subjects were taken…by another group. All of them."

"I saw that! Where are they?"

"Ah…in a blue van."

Behind him, Lieutenant Almeria urgently said, "Comandante! I have them, quiet! I have it, I have it! Ha! Those idiot *federales* haven't changed their encryption in months! Listen now, I've recorded it—it's in English."

"Okay boss, we've got 'em. Everything's contained; prisoners are in custody, no problems."

"All right, good job, bring them out to the boat. Tell your team to stand down—they can go home. Thank them for me."

"Will do, boss."

While Comandante Ramos watched from the driver's seat of the catering van, the black SUV and a blue van disappeared out onto the pier, and the iron gate across the base of the pier closed behind them. He knew what had happened: he was too slow! The gringo *federales* had beaten him to the punch, and they had taken the prize! Now what? Think! It wasn't over yet, it was not yet time to admit defeat, there must be a way—but how?

The rolling iron gate that stretched across the pier looked formidable, and it was clearly well guarded. A smaller pedestrian gate was open on the right side of the pier, but as he made the slow turn onto Harbor Drive northbound, he could see that the ID cards of a group of pedestrians entering the area were being scrutinized by uniformed guards.

So what could he do now? What? Think, Basilio, think!

Ramos said, "Almeria, play back the tape, the new one."

"Okay boss, we've got 'em. Everything's contained; prisoners are in custody, no problems."

"All right, good job, bring them out to the boat. Tell your team to stand…"

"Stop it there," insisted Comandante Ramos. "Bring them out to the boat. What did the child say this morning? Play the part about the pier, and the boat."

Almeria had his headphones on, and nodded. He found the digital recording, and the child's voice came out of the speaker.

"When it gets dark, we're going to walk over the trolley tracks, down to the dock where Bob Buller keeps his big boat. Bob Buller is Gretchen's boss. I can see his boat from our balcony. The fireworks are going to shoot up over the water, so the dock will be a really good place to watch from."

"There's only one big boat on that dock, and that's where they are," said Comandante Ramos. He spoke into his hand radio. "Chino, come here." He pulled the van over onto an area of slant parking on the right side of Harbor Drive, and stopped. In moments the Kawasaki was alongside his window.

"Did you see where the blue van and the black SUV went?"

"On the pier, you mean?"

"Yes, where on the pier?"

"All the way to the end. They parked next to the white *yate*."

Ramos paused, thinking. "Okay. Chino, we need to get on that yacht, if that's where they are. Look for a boat, something we can use to get to it from the water. Go!"

Chino took off on the bike. Ramos had to rely now on his initiative, scouting solo on his own. The white catering van was too conspicuous; it couldn't continuously travel back and forth around their zone of interest near the government pier. But he had faith in Chino. Although the half-Asian was a little taller than most of his Falcons, he had not picked Chino or any of his Zetas for their size or for their muscles. In fact, they were no bigger or stronger on average than the other Falcons. Nor had he chosen them for their shooting skill. Although they were all dead shots, so were many other Falcons. No, he selected his Zetas for their intelligence, cunning and loyalty. Now the Comandante would see if he had chosen well.

44

After a low speed ride of less than a minute, the blue van came to a stop. Alex and Ranya were face down on the metal floor, but lying in opposite directions, with agents laughing and joking above them. The van's side door rolled open and Ranya was given the gruff command, "Get up, girly." The voice was deep, but unmistakably female. It was the agent who had shot Alex with the plastic bullet, and yanked off her blond wig. It was Gretchen Bosch, the Beast. She said, "You first, Bonnie—we'll come back for Clyde in a minute."

Ranya was rolled onto her side, and powerful hands gripped her arms and jerked her up and out of the van. It was almost fully dark outside. She was in a narrow space between the blue van and the edge of a massive pier. An aluminum ramp led down to another lower floating dock. She was hustled down the ramp, with black-uniformed agents on either side and behind her. The floating dock was only a few yards wide, running for perhaps a hundred feet between the pier and a gleaming white motor yacht. She was pushed up more steps, into the cockpit of the yacht, and forward through a narrow door and inside, where she was turned around and pushed down onto an upholstered sofa. Gretchen Bosch dropped the green canvas bag containing their pistols and their things onto a table, and left the boat with the other agents.

Ranya recognized the voice before she recognized the man. He walked up some steps from the front of the boat, into this section, which was furnished and laid out like a posh living room. She thought he had seemed bigger on television. It was "*Hi, I'm Bob Bullard*," in person.

"So, Ranya Bardiwell, we meet at last…or should I say, we meet again? But I don't think we were actually introduced the last time. No, I believe I was shooting at you, you were shooting at me…sure doesn't seem like six years ago, does it?"

She glared at him and demanded, "Where's Brian?"

"Brian? Oh, Brian's fine. He's in the forward stateroom with his mother. You know his mother, Karin Bergen. What did you drug her with, anyway?" Bullard sat behind a polished mahogany dinette table across the saloon from her, and began rummaging through the green canvas kit bag that Gretchen Bosch had carried onto the boat. He found her leather fanny pack, unzipped it, and began to pull out its contents and set them on the table. He first removed her Jardine's Custom .45, raising his eyebrows and nodding in appreciation.

He placed the pistol on the table and kept looking through her fanny pack, and pulled out the small spray bottle. "Oh, here it is—an aerosol. Is this the new happy gas? Well, that should wear off in a couple of hours. By then, Karin and Brian will both be sound asleep, and we'll be twenty miles out to sea. Yeah, that's right—we're all going for a little cruise."

He continued unloading the green bag, removing Alex's FBI-issue Sig Sauer pistol and placing it on the table next to her .45. "So Ranya, I guess we're in one of those 'good news, bad news' situations. The good news is, you won't be going back into a supermax cell. The bad news is, you're going to get to see how long you can tread water, when you're all wrapped up in chain. As soon as the fireworks are over and the Coast Guard gives the all-clear, we're going to cast off and go for a boat ride—only you and Garabanda won't be coming back. Nope, this time the bad penny is going all the way down."

The Comandante's radio crackled. The *Cocinero Mágico* van was still parked a half block north of Broadway, in the angled parking area on the Harbor Drive service road. It was Chino's voice.

"Boss..."

"Yes?"

"I found us a ride. Do you see the big *barco de velas*?"

"I see it." Chino had to be referring to the giant sailing ship tied along the sea wall, a few hundred meters farther north.

"I'm near its front. Look for the *moto*."

Ramos pulled back onto Harbor Drive. The sidewalk and the service road across on the bay side were full of pedestrians. Many of them were sitting on folding chairs or blankets, getting ready to enjoy the fireworks show. He pulled over onto the service road opposite the clipper ship and parked again. Inside of the van, they prepared themselves for action. Their compact .45 caliber Ingram MAC-10 machine pistols were concealed inside of dark, bulky windbreakers. Extra thirty round magazines were shoved beneath their belts, inside of their waistbands. They were already wearing light body armor beneath their shirts.

Almeria was left in the van to maintain his communications watch, and move the vehicle as needed. The three men walked separately across Harbor Drive, through the waiting fireworks spectators who paid them no attention whatsoever.

According to signs along the seawall, the century-old clipper ship "The Star of India" had been converted into a floating museum and tourist attraction, and even more spectators were lining its decks tonight. In front of its bow, almost beneath the end of its long bowsprit, a metal ramp ran straight out from the quayside to a perpendicular floating dock. The green Kawasaki was parked there on the quay, and the three men walked down the ramp past it. Tied to the floating dock was a smaller classic sailing vessel, a schooner from the 19th century that was now a harbor excursion boat. All the way at the end there was a dark-hulled racing motorboat. HOMELAND SECURITY was painted along its side in tall white letters.

Chino greeted them at the end of the floating dock. He was wearing a black uniform and a black ball cap with DHS on the front.

"Where's the crew?" asked Ramos, looking Chino up and down approvingly. His white sneakers at the bottom of the black pants were his only giveaway. Chino turned completely around, showing off the HOMELAND SECURITY written across his back in large white letters.

"There were only two of them. They're in the little cabin now—I handcuffed them with their own *esposas*. And I've got another uniform."

The Comandante was beaming. "How did you manage this trick, vato?"

"Oh, it was easy. I guess the idiots thought they were the only ones in downtown San Diego with guns. I just walked out the dock like a common drunken *borracho*, and I ignored them when they told me to stop in English. Finally I acted like I was going to stagger right off of the end of the dock, and they tried to stop me. Nice guys, huh? That's when I showed them my MAC—that's all it took. We went inside the boat, and they took off their uniforms. Very cooperative. They're cuffed and gagged now, but they're okay." Chino laughed, "I guess they weren't ready to die for their homeland's security. So, who wants the other uniform? It's big, it'll fit anybody."

Gretchen Bosch pushed Alex down the ramp and onto the Eldorado, prodding him in the back with her H&K USP .45 caliber pistol. Once in the main saloon, she shoved him down onto the settee next to Ranya, pulled off her black Kevlar helmet, and dropped it beside them. "Okay kids, snuggle up. Come on, don't be shy." When they were close enough, their shoulders touching, she reached into a side pouch on her assault vest and pulled out another flex cuff. "Did you guys ever run the 'three legged race'? Your right, her left. Come on, lift 'em up. We don't want you running off and getting into trouble." She looped the plastic noose over one of each of their feet, and pulled it snug so that their two ankles were tightly joined.

"Where's Brian?" asked Alex.

"Is that all you can think of?" replied Gretchen. "He's not your kid anymore Al, didn't you get the memo from the Judge Obregon?" Then, with her prisoners secured, she turned around and addressed her new boss. She was in an ebullient mood, still flying along after the thrill of her new team's success with the street takedown. "Hey Bob, *nice* boat. *Sweet.* So, where do you hide the brewskies?"

"Down forward, in the galley. The fridge is on the left." He was still examining their effects, laying them out on the dinette table in front of him. Ranya's blond wig looked almost like a small furry animal when he pulled it out of the green bag.

She returned with two Karl Strauss Amber Lagers, twisted the caps off of them, and handed one to Bob Bullard.

She took a long drink, and then turned to Alex and Ranya. "You two really are a pair of fuckups, you know it? Fun is fun, 'thanks for a wonderful evening' and all that, but I think we're going to have to call it a night. Even though you're a lot of laughs, you're both getting to be a royal pain in the ass. Ranya Bardiwell the Arab terrorist, and Al Garabanda, from the almighty FBI…whoop-de-doo, I'm *so* impressed—Not!" She took another long pull from her beer, set it on the dinette table, and began to rip off the Velcro straps and unfasten the plastic buckles holding on her assault vest and her body armor. She dropped them on the deck, and then sat on the high captain's chair in the middle of the saloon by the forward windows, swiveling it around from the yacht's controls to face her captives.

"So, did Bob tell you we're going for a little boat ride tonight? Yeah, a moonlight cruise, right after the fireworks. Hey boss, what time do they start?" she asked, glancing at her watch.

"Anytime now," replied Bullard.

"How long is the show?"

"I think a half hour. Real Chinese fireworks. The good stuff."

As if he had been clairvoyant, a shrill whistling sound split the air, followed by a burst of light, a resounding thunderclap boom, and several echoes. Through the high pilothouse windows, glowing blue streamers could be seen cascading out like the leaves of a palm tree. Before the last blue embers faded just before reaching the water, another rocket exploded high above them. The third rocket continued racing high above the first two before detonating with a ker-umph.

Brian Garabanda came up through the forward galley and he saw Gretchen first, sitting on the high captain's chair. He said, "Mommy is sleeping. Can I watch the fireworks up here?" His presence was a surprise to the adults, but he was even more surprised to see his father on the settee. "Daddy!" He ran to him, leaped on his lap, and hugged him around the neck.

Gretchen said, "All right kiddo, you can watch the fireworks. But after that you have to go to bed downstairs with Mommy. Is that a deal?"

"O-kay… But why is Daddy tied up?"

"Oh, um, we're playing a grown up game kiddo."

"An FBI game?" Brian looked doubtful and worried while he clung to his father.

"That's right," said Gretchen, "A grown up FBI game. It's their turn to be 'it'."

Basilio Ramos drove the blue Homeland Security boat. He just barely nudged the throttles to keep its speed down. The Comandante was wearing the other black Homeland Security uniform, with the similarly dressed Chino standing next to him. Salazar and Genizaro were hidden, crouched down inside the cramped forward cabin with the two gringo crewmembers. The captives were all the way forward, stripped to their underwear, bound, gagged and blindfolded.

The bay was full of security boats with red and blue flashing lights, there to keep the area around the fireworks barge clear of civilian boat traffic. By keeping his speed at just enough to steer, Ramos was able to slip unnoticed past the civilian piers, and around to the end of the main government pier. Sure enough, a black SUV was parked behind a white SUV, alongside the long white motor yacht. A smattering of people wearing civilian clothes stood and sat near the end of the hundred-foot-wide pier, looking out and up at the fireworks show. One rocket after another blasted into the sky, exploded, and launched sparkling starbursts out in colorful streamers.

The white motor yacht was facing the open harbor. Ramos steered his vessel close to its bow, to come alongside parallel to it, as close to its side as possible. Chino had already prepared dock lines, and stood in the back of the DHS boat closest to the white yacht, ready to step across with a rope. Chino's own MAC-10 was secured to his chest with a sling made of bungee cords.

The two low doors to the interior of the DHS boat were already open. Salazar and Genizaro, still in their jeans and windbreakers, were waiting for the Comandante's signal to spring out and go on the attack.

A crewmember on the big motor yacht walked out onto the side of the deck at their approach, hailing them and waving them off. He was dressed casually in jeans and a white dress shirt, open at the neck. "No, no, not here!" he called out in English. "Don't tie up here!" The man gestured and pointed to the open space on the floating dock behind the yacht, and kept yelling. Ramos pretended not to understand, and maneuvered alongside the big yacht's cockpit, the lowest part of its hull, where Chino would be able to step up and across with no difficulty. As they expected, their Homeland Security boat and DHS uniforms allowed them to approach with a minimum of resistance. When the cockpit of the DHS speedboat was almost even with the very back of the motor yacht, Ramos waved Chino across, to tie their own stern line onto the larger vessel, and halt their forward progress.

Cesar Escoria, the Eldorado's boat captain, was relaxing up on the flying bridge, half way through smoking a fat *grifa* of strong marijuana. There was no better way to enjoy a fireworks show than sitting up on top of the yacht, leaning back in the padded helmsman's seat, feet up on the instrument console, totally lit, buzzed—*prendido.*

Tonight's sampling of *sinsemilla* came from Sinaloa, courtesy of an amigo who worked for Customs. The weed and the fireworks were both primo, but tonight's boat parade on San Diego Bay was disappointing. He remembered the old days, when there would have been hundreds of private vessels out on the bay for a night of partying before, during and after the fireworks. But with the price of diesel fuel and gasoline as crazy as they were, practically the only boats on the water tonight were flashing the red and blue lights of the security services.

Fortunately, the price of fuel was never an issue for Captain Escoria. Tonight after the fireworks show they were going to make a quick run offshore, and the Eldorado would burn a hundred gallons of diesel, more or less. It didn't matter, because he had a government credit card to refuel the boat. One of his standing orders from Bob Bullard was to always keep the Eldorado's tanks topped off. Tonight the boss was involved in some dirty work, wet ops, a one-way trip offshore for some individuals who would not see the land again.

Well, that was the boss's business. Cesar Escoria didn't mind one way or the other—that was all up to Bob Bullard. Catch a buzz, watch the fireworks, feel that booming in your gut, see the reflections of the lights on the water…and then take the boat offshore, under the stars. The half moon was already sinking in the western sky above Point Loma. By midnight it would be gone, and the only light over the horizon beyond San Diego would be starlight.

Escoria noticed one of the DHS forty-footers coming around the end of the pier; it was the same type Bob Bullard liked to take out on the week ends. Probably somebody that knew him from their frequent weekend trips was coming by to say hello, and brown nose the regional director of Homeland Security. Whoever it was, he wasn't steering too well, and he seemed to be a rookie by the way he handled the throttles: pushing them and pulling them off, causing the boat to almost porpoise forward with little jumps.

Now the Fountain racing boat was coming down along the Eldorado's starboard side, very close. What was this idiot boat driver up to? The Eldorado's white hull had a $700,000 linear polyurethane Awlgrip paint job, and that was a lot of money, even in blue bucks, even if the government paid for it. Was this fool going to just come banging along-side, and with no fenders? Shit—amateurs! Cesar Escoria heaved himself up from his captain's chair, and shambled down to the side deck to see what these DHS clowns were up to. They were really killing his buzz, these assholes.

"No, no, not here!" yelled Captain Escoria. "Don't tie up here! There's no fenders—you'll scratch the hull! Down there, go down there!"

The vessels bumped, and Chino climbed up from the DHS boat's stern with his rope, immediately looping it over an empty cleat on the Eldorado's side deck. Ramos killed the engines and bounded across as Genizaro and Salazar burst from the small compartment, and followed him over into the big motor yacht's cockpit.

"You can't—" said the yacht's crewman, coming back along the side deck from the middle of the yacht. He was cut short by a burst from Chino's MAC-10 at a range of only six feet. Even with its suppressor, the noise was considerable. Red stains blossomed on the dead man's white oxford shirt as he twisted and fell forward, hit the teak handrail below his hips, and flipped overboard into the water. The booming and crackling of the fireworks show continued without a pause, a quarter mile out on the bay.

Gretchen Bosch was returning to the main saloon from the galley with two more ice cold beers, when she felt a bang on the Eldorado's hull, then heard some footsteps thumping on the deck above her, followed by a chattering metallic piston noise that she instantly recognized. She entered the saloon and looked through the pilothouse windows just in time to see Bullard's boat captain fall overboard. She placed both bottles on the dinette table in front of Bob Bullard and turned toward the back of the saloon, already drawing her big H&K USP .45 from the tactical holster where it was strapped around the right leg of her black BDU pants.

She moved through the saloon to the cockpit door in the back and sidestepped to her left, getting cover behind the aft bulkhead and taking a half-second quick peek outside. There was a man in a Homeland Security uniform coming across the cockpit toward the door. There was another man in dark civilian clothes, no more than ten feet behind the DHS agent. He was holding a small sub machinegun leveled at the DHS agent's back! A terrorist!

Her entire awareness of the situation in the cockpit was the result of her split second glance. She threw her H&K pistol up to eye level in a two handed combat grip, supported against the left side of the open door as she looked outside again. She instinctively banged off three rounds at the terrorist who was creeping up behind the Homeland Security agent, two to the heart and one to the head, dropping him instantly. The unknown DHS agent was out of immediate danger, Gretchen was still integrating the battle information, making sense of it all, scanning for new threats. She stepped out into the cockpit when she saw another terrorist to her left on the yacht's side deck, and she raised her pistol to fire again.

Basilio Ramos was the first into the cockpit, followed by Salazar and Genizaro. Chino had killed an unexpected crewman on the side of the *yate* with a quick burst from his MAC-10. Even using a suppressed weapon, and with the fireworks show as sonic cover, they had to consider their approach compromised. Now speed was everything: get inside the boat and take control, before they completely lost the element of surprise.

Half of a face appeared for a moment in the cockpit door, then a pistol and yellow flame fountained out—Bam-Bam-Bam! Salazar was down behind him, there was no time to check him, they had to keep assaulting through, had to keep the momentum. A black figure stepped out of the cockpit door, Salazar's shooter, but he turned away, apparently not even seeing him, and Ramos understood: it was his DHS uniform! He wasn't shooting, because of the uniform. The shooter turned left, toward Genizaro, and Ramos rapid-fired three shots of 9mm from his Glock, right into the center mass of the shooter as he turned. The shooter fell back against the cabin superstructure by the cockpit door and slid down, leaving a red smear on the gleaming white paint.

Piss-poor body armor, thought Gretchen Bosch. It shouldn't hurt like this when you get shot in the old Kevlar. She was feeling terribly cold and heard a roaring, and at the same time her chest burned. Red-hot claws were ripping into her lungs as she went down and collapsed onto her side, while red white and blue rockets exploded over the bay in front of her. Body armor should stop this shit easy… Her last conscious thought was the memory of taking off her body armor inside the boat. Damn! Never take the armor off. Never. Next time… The rocket's glowing cinders faded as they reached the water.

Ramos kicked the pistol away from the dead shooter's hand with his foot, as Chino and Genizaro joined him in a hasty stack by the cockpit door. When he burst in, they were right on their leader's tail, immediately criss crossing, going for the corners, finding cover, clearing the room as they had done a thousand times both in training and for real.

But there was no threat, no waiting team of enemy shooters. There was just one single gringo standing twenty feet across the room toward the front of the yacht, holding up a small child in front of his chest, and holding a pistol in his other hand. There was also another man and a woman sitting on a sofa on the right side of the room, their arms behind them—the prisoners—including Ranya.

The man holding up the boy said, "Look, I don't know who you are or what you want, but there's been some kind of a mistake. You should just leave right now and save yourselves. There are at least ten armed agents on the dock, and fifty more out on the water all around us. So just leave now, while you have a chance!" He held the boy with his left forearm across the child's chest, a pistol held in his right, aiming at Ramos in the center of the three attackers. Genizaro and Chino slowly advanced along the sides, increasing their angle of separation.

"What's the matter with you?" asked Ramos, in English. "Are you out of your mind? Put that boy down!" Ramos continued moving forward slowly, his own Glock pistol aimed slightly above the man's head.

Bullard rasped out, "If you've just shot a federal agent, do you have *any idea* of how much trouble you're in? That's a capital crime, under special circumstances!"

"Special what? Are you loco?" asked Ramos. "Put the boy down!"

"No way! You're crazy if you think I'll put him down! If I put him down, you'll shoot me!" The man was holding his pistol extended in front of the boy, aiming it at the Comandante, while cutting his eyes between the other two gunmen. "Tell them to back out of here, or you'll die! You!"

"Bullshit," responded the Comandante. "If you shoot, it'll be the last thing you ever do, and you know it. So put the boy down."

"No!"

Ramos continued his slow, measured advance. When he was less than ten feet away he said, "Look, if you don't put him down, I might shoot you anyway. I don't care about the boy, and I don't care about you either, dead or alive. I only care about them." He gestured with his head toward Ranya and Alex, sitting on the settee couch. "I've come to take them, not the boy."

"But if you've already killed federal agents, then you'll kill me too!" Bullard held the terrified child in front of him, his left arm clamped across Brian's chest, his pistol held out over the boy's shoulder.

"Just put him down, you idiot!"

"You'll kill me!" Bullard was starting to panic.

"I could kill you anyway, *pendejo*! Put him down if you want to live!"

"Listen—I'll make a deal, I'll make you a deal!"

"What deal? You have nothing to offer me that I can't take." Ramos was six feet away, his pistol aimed just above Brian's head at Bullard's face.

"Oh, but I do! Let me go, you'll see, I have a *lot* to offer!"

Ramos hesitated a few seconds, and said, "Okay, enough bullshit: tell me now, or you'll die in ten seconds."

"And then you'll let me go, with the boy?"

"No boy! Tell me what you have to trade for your life, *pendejo*! Five seconds!"

"Okay—all right. I know where there's gold. A *lot* of gold."

The mention of his favorite precious metal immediately won the Comandante's undivided attention. "How much?"

Bullard wailed out, "Hundreds of pounds!"

"You mean ounces."

"No! Pounds, hundreds of pounds of gold. Thousands of ounces!"

Ramos stopped, and raised his Glock a fraction above Bullard's forehead. "Okay, I'm listening: where is this gold?"

"Promise you'll let me go…"

"Where is the gold? No promises, until I know that you're not lying, gringo!"

"If I tell you where it is, you'll let me go?"

"If you show me where it is, if we get this gold…then I'll let you live."

"You're telling the truth?"

"Are you calling me a liar?"

"What guarantee do I have?"

"Guarantee? You have my word, as a man of honor. I promise your life in return for this gold. Now, take us to this gold, or die where you stand—that is your only choice. Choose now!" Ramos leveled his pistol at Bullard's forehead again.

Bullard's right arm wavered and then fell, and he let the .45 caliber pistol tumble onto the floor. "All right. I'll show you, but then you'll let me go, right?"

"Where is it, damn you!" Ramos stepped to within a yard of Bullard, with Chino and Salazar on either side of him, moving in to point blank range. "Enough games! Tell us now, or you'll die in five seconds. One…two…three…"

A pair of submachine guns and a pistol were now aimed at Bullard's head from less than a yard away, making his hostage irrelevant. He allowed Brian to slide down to the floor. As soon as Brian's feet touched the deck, he darted to his father, and clung to him, burying his small face in his chest.

Bullard slowly raised both hands. "It's on this boat. It's in the aft cabin, under the bed. It's there. Now, can I go? I've told you the truth, there's a fortune in gold! Many fortunes!"

"Who are you, anyway?" asked Comandante Ramos in English.

"I'm Robert Bullard. I'm the Director of Homeland Security for the Southwest."

"Hold on—are you on television?"

"I am."

"I thought I recognized you. This is really quite a nice boat you have, Robert. Not too bad for a government job. Now, show us the gold, and you can keep on being the director."

Bullard led them at gunpoint to the master stateroom, one level down and behind the main saloon. The room was paneled in light colored wood and rich blue fabric. They stood at the foot of a king-sized bed, which dominated the center of space with its head against the aft bulkhead of the compartment.

Bullard, subdued, said, "It's under here."

"Well, open it up," demanded the Comandante.

Bullard turned back the bedspread, then reached beneath the end of the mattress and lifted up a flat panel, hinged like the hood of a car. A metal rod on each side lifted with the panel to hold it up. Beneath the painted plywood panel was a horizontal steel vault door. Its four foot width fit easily beneath the foot of the bed, and extended back under it for two feet. Bullard entered a combination on an electronic keypad on the door, and then leaned over and strained to hoist it up by a handle on the edge closest to him. Metal legs on both sides followed the heavy door, and locked in place to hold it up at a 45-degree angle.

Inside of the safe were two neatly packed rows of dark green ammunition boxes, each a foot long by four inches wide, with a steel carrying handle folded flat on top. There were fourteen boxes in all. Ramos reached down to pull one out, and it barely moved. "Damn!" he exclaimed, "What's one of these *hijos de putas* weigh?"

Bullard answered, "About ninety pounds, depending on what's inside."

Ramos took a two handed grip on the handle, and extracted the ammo box with visible effort, and set it on the deck at the foot of the bed. As a professional soldier he recognized the dark green box, it was the type the American factories packed with linked 7.62mm machine gun ammunition, and he had opened many of them. He pulled up the locking lever that held the top of the box down, and swung the lid up and out of the way.

Rather than the usual machine gun ammunition, inside there was a mass of small gold coins. They were not packed in plastic tubes or cases, but instead they were loose, a gleaming jumble filled to within an inch of the top of the rectangular steel box. He reached in and pulled up a handful of the small coins, the size of American dimes.

"They're all like this?" he asked Bullard. "All one-tenth ounce coins?"

"No. Some have bullion bars, and some have one-ounce coins."

Ramos and Chino stared into the vault, comprehending the enormity of the wealth before them. Twelve troy ounces to a pound, ninety pounds in each ammunition box, fourteen boxes, all at $7,000 an ounce... What ever that came to, it was a huge number—he could do the math later. Director Bullard had not lied: it was indeed several fortunes.

"You said you'd let me go. Well, I kept my part of the deal…"

"We will Bob, we will. But not here. We have a plane to catch, and you're going to drive us. We're going to Chavez Airport—we'll let you go once we're there."

"Chavez Airport? Where the hell is that, Mexico?" asked Bullard.

"What? Oh, it used to be called Montgomery Field," Ramos clarified. "You're going to make sure we get there, if you want to live."

Chino and Genizaro could only carry one heavy ammo can full of gold up to Bob Bullard's Lincoln Navigator at a time, seven trips each, under the still-exploding fireworks. A quick search of the black Dodge Durango SUV that their two captives had been driving resulted in the discovery of two laptop computers in their luggage. These were also transferred to Bullard's Navigator.

When they were finished loading the white SUV, Genizaro and Chino returned to the yacht's main saloon. Comandante Ramos was making a brief radio call to Lieutenant Almeria, instructing him to drive ahead to the airfield and make sure the plane was ready to take off. Bob Bullard sat on the same settee as the other two prisoners, but apart from them. His spirit was destroyed and he stared forward, away from Ranya and Alex. Still bound with their hands behind their backs, their morale had only been marginally lifted upon seeing Bullard's defeat. They had only changed their captors and their destination; they had not been freed. Brian still clung to his father, who whispered encouragement that he did not feel or believe.

Genizaro was the only Falcon still wearing street clothes; Ramos and Chino were dressed in black DHS uniforms. Salazar's body was not in the cockpit; Chino reported seeing him go over the side into the water after he had been shot.

The Comandante said, "Okay, that's everything, we're ready."

"What about the boy?" asked Chino. "Leave him?"

Ramos hesitated, and then said, "No, we'll bring him along—for insurance."

"I don't want a kid running around loose, no way," muttered Genizaro. He saw the .45 caliber pistol that Bob Bullard had been holding. It was still lying on the floor where it had been dropped, and he scooped it up and jammed it into the front of his jeans.

The Comandante turned to Ranya and Alex and said, "This is the reality. If you want the boy to be safe, you'll obey us, every step. If you don't…." Ramos saw the empty green canvas kit bag lying beside the dinette table. He crouched down, opened it up on the floor and said, "Okay Brian, we're going to play a game, just like hide and seek. You're going to hide in here first. I want you to sit down inside of this big bag for a little while. Okay? You do that for me, and we'll all go back to Albuquerque together on an airplane, I promise. Can you do that for me?" Ramos held the bag open, smiled as genuinely as he could, and pointed inside of it. Brian reluctantly let go of his father, who gave him a last kiss. He stepped into the opening, and then sat down. "That's it, nice and cozy," said Ramos. "That's fine." Then he zipped the bag closed over Brian's head.

"Okay," he said to Alex and Ranya next, "We're all going up. Yell, scream, try to run away or give us any kind of a problem, and Brian won't be happy—that's all I'm going to say. Chino, cut their feet loose." Ramos stood back with his pistol, while the half-oriental Zeta used a folding knife to cut the flex-cuff that held them together at the ankles. One rip of his serrated blade against the plastic, and the ankle restraints were severed.

Ramos held his Glock in his right hand, and the bag containing Brian in his left. "All right, let's go—nice and slow." Alex went first, with Chino in his Department of Homeland Security uniform behind him with his MAC-10. They were followed by Bob Bullard, with Genizaro behind him. Comandante Ramos gave them a short head start, then pulled Ranya to her feet, and pushed her out of the yacht with the muzzle of his Glock in her back. They walked across the cockpit, off the boat and up the ramp to the white SUV.

He noted Ranya's silence with some satisfaction. The Arab bitch was not usually at a loss for words, but now she said nothing. This didn't surprise Basilio Ramos. He had led other bound prisoners to their executions, and unlike in movies or cheap novels, they were never talkative. The doomed kept their counsel until their final moments, when they sometimes begged, cried, or prayed. But the walks to the execution spots were always made in utter silence…like tonight.

Bullard climbed into the driver's seat, his hands at ten and two o'clock on the wheel. Genizaro opened the right rear door and pulled the middle seat forward, and Alex and Ranya were pushed into the rear bench seat, their hands still flex-cuffed securely behind their backs. Ramos placed the green bag containing Brian in the back cargo area, on top of the fourteen boxes of gold, and closed the rear doors. The Comandante slid into the front passenger seat, and Genizaro sat behind him.

Bob Bullard was going to drive, that was the plan. With the high-ranking director behind the wheel, accompanied by two apparent agents of the Department of Homeland Security, Ramos guessed that no one would challenge their passage. Chino sat behind Bullard. He leaned forward between the two front seats, and held a long carving knife in front of the director's face, rolling its silver blade inches in front of his wide eyes. In English Ramos said, "He took this knife from your kitchen, I hope you don't mind." Then in Spanish he said, "Go ahead, give him a little tickle." Chino took the knife and pushed it straight through the back of the driver's seat, down low at the kidney level.

"Can you feel that now, Robert?" asked the Comandante.

Bullard squirmed and flinched, and replied, "I can feel it."

Ramos looked across and told him, "If you do anything stupid, if the police pull us over, anything…no matter what happens, he's going to kick that knife right through your guts. No matter what, you'll die, whether it's by bullets or a knife in your back, do you understand?" Ramos held his Glock across his lap, covered by his DHS ball cap.

"You said you were going to let me go…"

"And I will. I'll keep my word—after we get to the airport. Now let's go. Just drive us out of here nice and easy. Remember: if anybody stops us, you're going to see that knife come out of your stomach."

The fireworks were still popping, shrieking, whistling and exploding over the bay, and nobody paid any attention to the white SUV that was leaving the government pier. Even the distracted gate guard's attention was aimed skyward, until he belatedly noticed the regional DHS director's Lincoln Navigator. He hurried into his post to push the button and open the automatic gate.

They crossed Harbor Drive, heading straight up Broadway past the Pacific Majesty and all of the other office and condominium towers and government buildings, and then past the next section of older and lower office buildings and second and third tier hotels. The grand finale of the fireworks display was exploding in a solid torrent of noise and light behind them when they made the left turn onto 10th Avenue. This street fed directly into the 163, a divided highway that began there and went straight past *Aeropuerto Chavez.* In the few blocks before the one-way avenue became a highway, the white SUV passed close by a solitary man trudging along in the darkness on the left side of the street. He was wearing a dark backpack over his light-colored clothing, and he had no right arm.

The last fireworks boomed and the echoes died as the final colored lights faded. They were less than ten minutes from the airfield, and the waiting Twin Otter.

45

Chino, sitting in the middle seat behind Bullard, said "Comandante, we have everything: the woman, the FBI agent, and the computers. I think this will be very good for you, when we return to *Búrque*. Perhaps you will be given command of the Falcons again, or perhaps a new command."

Ramos had suspected that his men understood the seriousness of his professional situation, after the disasters at the Vedado Ranch. Chino was doing him a favor by confirming it. Ramos supposed it was a tribute to him that they had accompanied him on this mission, knowing that his remaining authority hung by a thread.

He wondered what other things Chino and Genizaro were thinking about (and especially about the depth of their loyalty to the regime in Nuevo Mexico), now that the Falcon Battalion was being disbanded and reformed. Comandante Guzman of the 5th Battalion would never keep the Zetas intact. The Zetas were too closely identified with his rival, Comandante Basilio Ramos. The Zetas would probably be dispersed among the entire Milicia, and have their special status obliterated.

This would be a bitter pill for men used to being considered the elite of the elite. To be reassigned to an ordinary Milicia company, and ordered to stand checkpoint or guard duty in Nuevo Mexico was not something the Zetas would accept, especially not these men who had just successfully completed a sophisticated and difficult covert mission in San Diego. They had captured the two traitors and recovered the laptop computers, and this meant complete success as Comrade Inez had defined his mission. But prisoners and computers were not the only things of value in the back of the SUV…

The Comandante said, "I'm not sure what will happen, back in Albuquerque. I'm just not sure. *Politics* are involved." He pronounced politics as if the word was poison. Then he paused, measuring his words, before plunging ahead. "Actually, I've been thinking. I've been thinking perhaps of taking a small…vacation…" He hesitated, unable to see the faces of his men sitting behind him, imagining their thoughts, guessing their level of ideological commitment to *La Causa,* the cause of liberation. "You know, our mission was to catch those two traitors, and we have fulfilled that mission. But our mission said nothing about the…other things. About the fourteen strongboxes…"

He let that thought ride in silence for a minute as the Navigator hummed up the highway in light traffic. Then Genizaro replied softly, "You know, Comandante…I've been fighting for the cause for many years, with very few opportunities for vacations."

"I agree with my comrade," Chino immediately offered.

"Comandante, the range of the Twin Otter is almost a thousand miles..." The thought lingered in the quiet interior of the luxury SUV.

"Perhaps..." suggested Comandante Ramos, "Perhaps...we could first fly south, instead of east..."

After a moment Chino said, "I know a place, Comandante, where you can hear the sound of the waves, and where the señoritas are as soft and warm as the tropical breeze..."

"But what about these *pocho* traitors?" asked Genizaro. "What about our duty?"

"*¡Chingalo!* I've had it up to here with our *duty*," sneered Chino. "I've had nothing but *duty* for too many years! We all have. It's our turn now!"

"But what about the traitors?" Genizaro asked again.

Ramos said, "I know of a *casa de putas* in Juarez, where they would pay well for the pretty Arab whore. But even if they didn't pay, I would give her to them! They'll inject her with *heroína* and *cristal*, and then they'll teach her to be an obedient *puta* with their fists. She'll serve twenty men every night, on her knees and on her back. And she'll do it forever, until she's a toothless old *bruja* witch that even the poorest blind drunk *borrachos* won't want."

Basilio Ramos said this, and he meant it. But he didn't mention that he intended to have the first go at Ranya Bardiwell. He would begin with a large dose of Libidinol, and progress to more painful measures. One way or the other, he would find out what Ranya had done with her filthy and vile blackmail photographs. Only after that task was taken care of, only then would he hand her over to the professional whoremongers, who would turn every single day of the rest of her life into a living hell of pain and degradation.

Brian Garabanda lay curled up inside of the cloth bag. It was very hot and stuffy, and he knew it wasn't really a game, and he felt like crying, but he didn't except a little. He could tell he was in the back of a car or a truck, he had heard all of the doors opening and closing. Three men were talking. He couldn't understand what they were saying, but they didn't sound nice. His Daddy and the other lady were probably in the car too. He had been put in the bag when they were on the big boat, but one of the men that aimed their guns at Bob Buller said they were all going for an airplane ride, back to Albakirky. So now he had to stay in this bag, until they went for the airplane ride.

And then he heard his Daddy! In a loud voice, his Daddy said, "Look Ramos, why don't you just let her go? Her and the boy both. She was only looking for her son—you can't blame her for that. Let her go, and I'll tell everything that I know. I'll cooperate…"

One of the other men shouted at his Daddy in Spanish, and Brian didn't know what he said, but it didn't matter. He knew that his Daddy was sitting right in front of him!

Ramos snarled in Spanish, "Why don't you just shut your *pinche* mouth, FBI man! There's been a change in plans, or didn't you hear? Is your *pocho* Spanish that bad, *gabacho*? We're not going back to *Búrque*, and we don't really care what you have to say, either of you. So don't piss me off, or I'll send you to hell the same way I sent the Jew traitor Carvahal, and I don't think you'll like it any better than he did!"

Brian knew that Daddy had come to Sandy Eggo to find him. And he *did* find him, but something had gone very wrong. Now Daddy was in a lot of trouble. Big Trouble. When they were on the big boat, he saw that his Daddy's hands were tied behind his back. The new lady's hands were tied too. He didn't believe it was an FBI game like Gretchen said it was. The grown ups were too angry.

Now they were going to go on an airplane ride back to Albakirky, but Brian thought it was for a bad reason, not a good one. Something very bad was going to happen there. But what could he do to help Daddy? Brian had no FBI agent gun. In the front pocket of his overalls, he felt something, and he pulled it out. By feel, he could tell that it was his little Spiderman. The new lady from the boat gave it to him on the street, when she had blond hair. But where did she find it? There was too much to think about, it was all too hard to understand. The toy made him feel a little better, even though it was very small, because it reminded him that Spiderman would never give up, never! No matter how much trouble Spiderman got into, he never, ever gave up trying!

Brian turned onto his belly and wriggled his knees under him, and began to feel around inside of the hot smelly bag. When they put him in the bag, he had felt some things inside of it. Now he groped with his hands and fingers, looking for what he didn't know, but he felt something pokey and pointy and jingly. In his mind, he could picture grown-up keys, he knew what they felt like, and sounded like. Daddy kept a little teeny flashlight on his key chain. Maybe other grownups did too? He separated the stuff on the chain, feeling each key, until he came to a little thing that was not like the keys, it was smooth. With both thumbs and pointer fingers he squeezed it, and a bright blue light flashed! It was Daddy's key chain, because that was Daddy's blue squeeze light!

On Daddy's key chain, there was also a little knife. He had found Brian playing with it once, and he warned him that it was 'razor sharp,' and he sliced a piece of paper in half with it. It had a silver blade and a black handle just like a real knife, but it was only as long as Brian's finger, when it was folded up. Then like a flash, like a firework rocket exploding, it occurred to Brian that he could cut a hole in the cloth bag with the little knife, and give it to Daddy!

Alex Garabanda didn't know where they were, or how long they had to drive until they would arrive at their destination. He had heard the men mention a Twin Otter airplane, and flying south instead of east. No matter where they were going, it was out of his ability to control. He was unarmed, his hands were tightly bound with flex cuffs, and he knew it was impossible to break them. Ranya was in the same position beside him, staring into the darkness out of the right side of the big SUV. They were both in the same utterly hopeless situation.

He was in the custody of Comandante Basilio Ramos of the Falcon Battalion and two of his men. Men so ruthlessly efficient that they had boarded the regional director of homeland security's yacht, and swatted aside his protectors like flies. They had even dared to kidnap Director Bullard himself, driving him right off of federal property in his own vehicle. If they could do all of that, there was absolutely no chance of overcoming them, not with his hands securely tied behind his back with thick plastic cuffs. His hands were bound so tightly that he was losing feeling in his fingers. But what did this matter, against the plans Ramos had in store for them?

"Flying south" meant flying deep into Mexico, beyond any hope of American rescue, even if his superiors knew where he was—which they didn't. It was hopeless. Old photos of DEA agent Kiki Camarena's body flashed through his memory. Camarena had been kidnapped right off of the street in Guadalajara in 1985 by corrupt Mexican police, acting on the orders of high-level *narcotrafficantes*. He had been brutally tortured for days by both government officials and narcos, who were working side by side to learn what the DEA knew about their high-level collusion in the drug trade.

Kiki Camarena's infamous fate was used as a cautionary tale in federal law enforcement training: if you go south of the border you're on your own, and you can expect only treachery and betrayal from every side. In Mexico, today as in 1985, it was assumed that every single policeman, military officer and government official was corrupt and working for the *narcos*. The only honest cops in Mexico were the dead ones, who refused the silver, and took the lead. Once they landed in Mexico, there could be no hope for rescue or even mercy from any quarter.

Bob Bullard couldn't understand what these spic terrorists were saying, but he had very little confidence that they would keep their end of the bargain and let him go. What happened to the other prisoners in the back of his SUV didn't concern him in the least, since they had no apparent value to him as bargaining chips.

If he couldn't depend on his captors to release him, could he depend on local police, the Federal Protective Service or the FBI's Hostage Rescue Team to save him, without him being killed in the process? They were already outside of downtown, across I-5, beyond the relative safety of the coastal zone. They were heading up the 163 to Montgomery Field. That was where they would either release him, or kill him.

He knew there was always the option of pushing the panic button, actually a combination of two buttons to push at the same time on the instrument panel. If he held down the stereo's CD ejector and FM/AM buttons at the same time for five seconds, coded radio alarms would be sent, and an emergency response would be triggered.

But under the present circumstances, with the Mexican gangsters sitting behind him and beside him, could he do it, push the two buttons down for five seconds? These men were not fools. They had boarded the Eldorado dressed in Homeland Security uniforms, and had immediately killed Captain Escoria and the new female IRS agent. Now there was a pistol and two sub machineguns aimed at him, and the tip of a long carving knife pricking him in the small of his back. Could he do it? Could he push the panic buttons without them noticing? Even if he did, how long would it take to mount a hostage rescue? He'd be dead hours before they could save him.

For Ranya, to come so far and to fail was the most agonizing torture of all. Brian was only inches away behind her. She could hear him whimpering in the green bag where he'd been zipped shut on the yacht. He didn't even know her; he wouldn't recognize the sound of her voice, so she couldn't even offer him meaningful comfort. What would become of poor little Brian, lost in the world like a wood chip in a tempest at sea? Perhaps it would be hoping too much that he would be returned to Karin Bergen, the woman that he at least knew as his mother.

Basilio had horrible, disgusting, cruel plans for her. That was to be expected, after the way she had left him in his villa—drugged with Libidinol, screwing the gringo professor to death. If what he said was true, if he wasn't just playing with her mind, she was going to be delivered to a Mexican whorehouse, addicted to heroin and crystal meth, and forced to work as a prostitute. She would rather die fighting than be turned over to that fate. But how could she fight, with her hands tightly bound behind her back?

Starting on the day that she had landed in the United States after returning from Colombia, she had been handcuffed too many times to count. With some steel cuffs, there was a chance, given enough time and privacy, to pass her hands beneath her bottom and work them around to the front. Bound more closely wrist to wrist with a nylon flex cuff, there was no chance. Her only "hope" might be to rush one of her captors, to try to force him to use his gun in self-defense.

Some hope—suicide by a gangster's bullet.

And that would still leave Brian all alone, terrified inside of the green canvas bag, left to whatever cruel fate Basilio Ramos chose for him.

His hands were going numb. The zip tie had been yanked too aggressively when they had first been applied, while he was lying prone on the asphalt. Alex Garabanda had felt them tingle, then burn, and now they were going cold, losing sensation. The back of his right wrist and arm was jammed against his spine; the back of his left wrist was pressed tightly to the pulse spots of his right. He knew that the nylon flex cuff, like a jumbo-sized electrical cable tie, was rated at over 500 pounds breaking strength. It tightened with tiny internal ratchet teeth, and it would never be looser. Once pulled down like a plastic noose, the flexible handcuffs could only get tighter. That was reality.

He had worn flex cuffs in training many years ago, but never this tightly, and never for this long. A new sensation enveloped the fingers of his left hand, another type of pressure, almost like a squeezing or kneading. He had expected the numb feeling to gradually leave his fingers, and this new feeling came as a surprise.

But then the new sensation turned to a tugging, a timed rhythmic pulling, and for a few seconds he was confused, and he looked at Ranya, but she had not moved, she was still staring out of the right side window at the darkness. If not her, then…what?

And then he knew. In his mind, the tugging and pulling suddenly became a clear image of what it was: a small hand was pulling his own, and he tried to squeeze back, to wiggle his fingers at least. He knew that somehow, Brian's little hand was beyond the crack of the rear seat where the seatbelts passed through. Clever Brian knew about this split, he had tracked small toys from the back seat to the rear cargo area of Karin's 4-Runner. Now he was reaching through, looking for comfort from his father, and giving comfort, and Alex squeezed back, pulsing his grip as they had done so many times when holding hands. It wasn't much, but it was something, a silent, secret, shared hello. Brian must have managed to unzip his bag from inside.

Alex hunched down and pushed his hands far into the space between the seats, taking both of Brian's small hands in his two crisscrossed hands…and he felt something different, something other than Brian's tiny fingers and thumbs. Something else, being pressed into the palm of his left hand.

Brian knew how things came off key chains. They went round and round the silver circles. The problem was, he couldn't work the squeeze light, and take anything off from the silver ring, because it took both thumbs and both pointer fingers to make the blue light stay on. After a minute of trying he gave up, and decided to just open the little knife while it was still on the key chain, and that's what he did. The blade had very sharp point, and so he held it carefully by its handle while pushing it through the canvas bag, on the side where he thought he had heard his Daddy's voice. The knife went through, making a little hole, but that wasn't enough. He remembered that the little blade had bumps on it like a saw, so he decided that maybe sawing was the best way to cut a hole in the bag. Soon he found the best way to push and pull, and he was able to slide his entire arm through the cut that he had made.

With one hand, he felt outside of the bag until he touched the back of the seat, and he felt down it until he could touch the crack along the bottom of the seat, the place where seatbelts went, the place where toys could get lost and fall through. He pushed and pushed his hand, until it went through the seats, and he felt around and found only nothing, and moved his hand from side to side—and his hand bumped right into grown up fingers! In a little while, the big fingers were squeezing right back, and he knew for sure it was his Daddy! Next, it was time to give him the key chain.

Once the knife was open, Brian couldn't close it. It opened with a snap, and it stayed that way. It was not easy pushing his hand through the crack in the seat, not with a bunch of keys and a knife, and it took him a long time but he did it, he pressed the key chain into his Daddy's hand! Along the way, something sharp stung him, but he knew he was doing an important job and he didn't stop, and he didn't cry. When he finally had both hands back inside of the bag, his right pointer finger burned, and when he put his finger in his mouth in the black darkness, he tasted blood. He was bleeding, and it hurt, but he didn't cry out.

The flex cuffs bound his wrists in an X and kept the fingers of his two hands apart, so it was difficult to move anything between them. He could feel a bundle of keys, could see the tiny knife in his mind. The black plastic handle was two inches long, shorter than a car key. The open surgical stainless steel blade was a little shorter, and it was serrated except for the last half inch near the point. The knife had been thrown in as a free gift on a law enforcement catalog order, and it had cut nothing more important than the occasional string or package wrapping. He maneuvered its handle into his right fingers, which were angled down to the left.

His left wrist was on the outside of his right, against the seat behind him. The inside of his left wrist, the pulse point, was the only place where he could conceivably slide the blade between his skin and the tough nylon flex cuff. If he misjudged the angles he could easily slit his veins, but it was not a time to be squeamish. The alternative was to share the fate of Kiki Camarena or Luis Carvahal. He didn't know how far it was to the airport that they were traveling to, but in case they were close, he couldn't take the time to be careful. He could tell nothing about his surroundings, the highway was isolated in a channel between high graffiti-covered concrete walls, two lanes in each direction, with a Jersey barrier down the center.

With his hands already numb, Alex couldn't feel exactly where the blade was sliding sideways, but he could feel the resistance beneath the flex cuff, and he twisted the handle to turn the serrations outward, and only with difficulty he began to clumsily saw the blade back and forth in weak little half-inch strokes. He could feel slippery wetness on his fingers but he only pushed harder and sawed faster. The handle became slick, the nylon bumping against the blade's serrations—until it popped apart without warning. Painful heat surged into his hands, as a wave of relief flooded his entire being.

The plastic cuffs were off, and his hands were free! He rubbed his wrists and flexed his fingers and hands. The SUV passed through an exit between the walls that enclosed the highway, that had enclosed most of the highways he had seen in San Diego. The exits were the only breaks in the barriers for long stretches. There were countless miles of these twenty-foot cement highway barriers, and a crazy thought came into his head at that moment—that if only those miles and miles of twenty foot high cement walls had been built along the Mexican border decades ago, we might have stopped the invasion, and we might have saved our country!

He kept his hands behind his back, and moved sideways a few inches to touch Ranya with his knee, and then his hip. When their shoulders were touching, he slipped his right hand behind her back over to her tightly bound hands and he squeezed them tightly, his hand wet and slippery, and she turned to him as if she had been given an electric shock, her eyes asking: How?

He told her with his eyes to be ready, and with the key chain and knife now in his right hand he found her flex cuff, and probing with his index finger, he guided the blade flat-wise beneath the nylon. There was no perfect way, no protected way, the only way was to push it through, between skin and cuff, jam it through, and turn its sharp serrated edge outward. With his free hand, he was able to push and pull with longer one-inch sawing motions, while his captors were focused on their route, and on their directions.

The big SUV turned onto a straight road through some kind of an industrial park, where only a few streetlights were still working. Ramos and his men were on high alert now, their machine pistols on their laps, obviously fearing ambush and getting ready to counter attack, ignoring their prisoners in the back seat. The van slowed and made a left and approached a high security gate. Their kidnappers' weapons were openly displayed for the uniformed security guards to see, this appeared to be an accepted level of precaution in a luxury SUV after dark. The private guard only glanced at the stickers on Bullard's windshield and at the DHS uniforms on Ramos and his other stooge, and the ten foot high chain link gate rolled open with a rumble and whine. After few turns beyond the gate, they were driving between parallel rows of identical airplane hangars.

Straight ahead there was an automobile parking lot, nearly empty, and on the other side there was another chain link fence, and another gate was visible in their headlights. This unguarded gate was already rolled wide open, and the SUV passed through it without slowing. Alex continued sawing with the tiny knife, visualizing the blade working against the nylon flex cuff, glancing at Ranya, who was staring straight ahead, as expressionless as the Sphinx.

The SUV drove across an expanse of asphalt past a dozen single and light twin-engine prop planes. Beyond them was a larger twin-engine aircraft, a white transport plane with high straight wings like a giant Cessna. A white van was parked just behind the plane's tail, shining its headlights down the left side of the fuselage. The van's lights were illuminating the plane's open cargo door, which was a four foot by four foot square opening, just behind and below the wing.

Ramos said to Bullard, "Take it nice and slow. Now, turn around and back in. I want the back of this truck ten feet from the cargo door, no closer. Slowly…that's it, a little more. Okay, back up, slowly—that's it, fine. Put it in park and turn it off. Good. Keep your hands on the wheel until I tell you something different."

The bottom of the wing and the horizontal tail elevator were both around nine or ten feet above the ground, and Alex could see there was no risk of the roof of the SUV running into them. Only the stationary propellers of each engine descended low enough to be a concern, and they were at the front of each engine, four feet in front of the wings.

Bullard whined, practically begging, "You'll let me go now?"

"Patience. In a little while." Ramos aimed his Glock pistol at Bullard with his left hand, with his right he reached over and pulled out the car keys. "You'll get these back after we take off. I'll toss them out on the tarmac. Once we're gone, find the keys and go home. Okay?"

Bullard croaked out, "Okay."

Ramos turned in the seat to address his two henchmen. "Alright, go ahead and load the gold."

Chino and Genizaro got out of both sides of the Navigator, and lifted the SUV's rear cargo door. Genizaro asked, "What about the boy?"

"Put him on first—that way the traitors won't give us any problems. Keep him in the bag."

Corky Gutierrez came out of the plane through the side cargo door, behind the left wing. A hinged ladder swung down to form crude steps, it was four feet from the tarmac to the bottom of the hatch. The plane's actual hatch rolled up inside the fuselage like a garage door, to allow for opening in flight, in order to conduct parachute operations.

"What are you waiting for?" the Comandante yelled to the pilot. "Get the engines running! I want to be in the air in two minutes—come on, let's go, let's go!"

"Are you sure?" asked Corky. "You want me to start up while you're still loading?"

"You heard me, do it! Crank her up!"

The pilot disappeared back inside. The two Zetas carried the fourteen heavy steel ammunition cans across from the back of the Navigator to the cargo hatch one at a time, sliding them onto the cargo deck at their chest level. Carlos Mendoza, who had been the pilot's "babysitter" while the team was in San Diego, took each box from that point. He stowed them against the rear bulkhead on the cargo deck, weaving a thick rope through their carrying handles to keep them from shifting in flight. Each steel box weighed about forty kilos.

First the right and then the left engine was switched on, coughing and belching before catching, then roaring with fury. The propellers disappeared, but with their props set at flat pitch, they were taking the plane nowhere. The plane's running lights came on next, red and green on the wingtips, white behind. Flashing white strobes blinked off of the transparent circles created by the whirling props, creating frozen propeller images.

"Okay," said Comandante Ramos, "That's all of the gold, what about the computers?"

"They're aboard," answered Chino.

"Then get the prisoners—we're leaving." He walked to the driver's side of the Navigator, between the van and the SUV, to check that Bullard was still obediently holding the steering wheel. He was.

46

The right side rear door opened in front of Ranya, and the ugly Zeta called Genizaro unlatched the folding middle seat and pulled it forward. He had to yell to be heard over the airplane engines. "Okay, the boy is already on the *avión*," he said in Spanish. "If you want to see him again, don't make any problems. You first, *chica*." He reached inside and grabbed the neckline of Ranya's white sweatshirt with his left hand, while aiming his MAC-10 machine pistol at her with his right, and began to pull her out.

Ranya's hands were still crossed behind her back. She leaned forward at the waist—it was not a simple process to climb out of the vehicle from the far back seat, without using her hands for support. She saw Genizaro's finger outside the trigger guard of his MAC, and she saw that the .45 pistol he had swiped back on the yacht was still tucked into his belt, Mexican-carry. She recognized the pistol: it was her Jardine's Custom, which she had taken from Basilio's bedroom.

Genizaro had to steady her as she bent forward and put one foot outside of the SUV's middle door. Then she tripped, off balance, falling against him with all of her weight, turning into him with her left shoulder. He raised his MAC-10, shoving it sideways against her to hold her back, grunting "*¡Puta estupida!*"

Her unbound left forearm came up to block the machine pistol, while her right hand swept up in a flashing arc toward his face. She had been holding Alex's keys since he had cut off her flex-cuff, the tiny knife ready for this moment. Its razor-sharp serrated blade struck him below his left clavicle, ripped through his windpipe, and exited behind his right jaw. A shower of blood erupted from his throat, and both of his hands flew to his neck to try to do the impossible, to stop the Niagara of his own hot blood.

They continued to lean against each other for a few seconds—he was still standing but rapidly weakening while clutching his throat. She dropped the key chain and grabbed the .45 pistol from inside of his belt with her right hand. Chino, in his black DHS uniform, was standing only a few yards behind his teammate when this unexpected flurry of movement took place. He raised his MAC but Genizaro was directly in his line of fire and he didn't shoot. Ranya snapped down the .45's thumb safety and tried to take aim at Chino one-handed. As she put the green glowing front sight on him and squeezed the trigger, the dying Genizaro twisted and collapsed against her and the shot went high and wild.

Chino backpedaled furiously, trying to run past the Otter's left wheel and wing strut and around the nose of the plane to get cover. Ranya aimed again, two handed now that Genizaro had dropped out of the way, and while she was squeezing the trigger she watched Chino's head disappear from the nose up, his cranium and half of his face were instantly gone! The headlights of the van and the flashing strobes revealed the cause, they illuminated a blurring circle—Chino had backed straight into the spinning propeller! His body continued its backward movement until it was stopped by the ground.

Ranya didn't dwell on the two men who were down, because she had seen Basilio Ramos standing on the other side of the white SUV before she had been dragged out. She spun to her right with her pistol still outstretched in both hands, looking for him.

Basilio Ramos was standing behind the Lincoln Navigator while overseeing the final step, the loading of the prisoners, when Genizaro opened the right door to pull out Ranya. With her wrists bound behind her back, she seemed to stumble off balance, when her hand unexpectedly shot up toward Genizaro's throat. What! How? Chino ran backwards away from her, and as Ramos watched, most of his head was hacked off in an instant—he'd gone into the spinning prop! Ramos stared in momentary shock as Chino's body tumbled backwards.

In his peripheral vision he saw that Ranya was holding a pistol, aimed at Chino's corpse. She began to turn his way and he stepped back, around to the opposite side of the white SUV. To reach the airplane's side hatch, he would have to cross ten feet of open space, directly under her gun. Did she even know he was there? There was no indication she did.

Ramos made a snap decision to use that open ground between the back of the SUV and the airplane to his advantage. He sprinted around the back of the Magic Chef van, keeping the white SUV between himself and Ranya to avoid being seen. From behind the right side of the van, he had a clear field of fire down the length of the Otter's fuselage. The van's headlights would shine on her when she crossed the open space to the plane, and they would blind her to his location. When she went for the plane and tried to climb its ladder, he'd have an easy ten meter shot at her with his pistol. The Glock didn't have glowing night sights, but at ten meters its ordinary sights would be enough.

Alex was crouching in the Navigator's open door, ready to jump out behind Ranya, when he saw the half-Asian's instantaneous propeller decapitation. The pockmarked goon who had come for Ranya was already down in a spreading pool of blood beside the white SUV, his throat slashed with the tiny key chain knife. The dead man had dropped his MAC-10 machine pistol when he fell, and Alex snatched it up as he hopped out of the SUV and over the body.

The two former captives huddled behind the open door of the SUV, shouting to be heard over the airplane engines. Only one shot had been fired, and there was no evidence that anyone on the plane had noticed.

Alex asked her, “Where’s Ramos? He was outside—did he get on the plane?”

“I don’t know, I didn’t see him, maybe he did.”

“Brian’s on the plane, he’s in the green bag!”

“I know!” wailed Ranya.

He said, “We have to get aboard…” It was three or four yards from the back of the Navigator to the open hatch of the Otter, which was four feet above the pavement, up an aluminum boarding ladder. “We can’t wait, we have to go, Brian’s on the plane!”

Alex stepped from the back of the SUV, and a pair of shots cracked out from behind the white van’s headlights and he jumped back behind the cover of the SUV.

Another man appeared in the Otter’s open cargo door with a pistol in his hand. Ranya immediately took aim at him with her .45 pistol and fired a pair of shots into his chest, and thinking ‘Kevlar vest’ she fired another pair to his groin and hip as he turned, and he fell forward from the plane onto the tarmac.

A sudden gust of wind blasted them as the engine noise grew and changed in pitch. The aircraft jerked and slowly began to roll.

“Where’s Ramos?” she yelled.

“I think he’s behind the van,” Alex shouted back, “I think I saw his muzzle flash. But we have to go for the plane, Brian’s on it! I’ll keep him down with this,” he said, lifting the MAC-10. “Are you ready?”

“I’m ready!”

“When I go—GO!”

They ran together to the moving airplane, Ranya behind Alex as he fired a full auto burst at the van one-handed, the MAC-10 pouring out a wild salvo of .45 caliber slugs.

Ramos saw someone move from the SUV toward the plane and he instinctively fired two quick unaimed shots from his Glock, and the figure disappeared back behind the vehicle. It was a man, so it had to be the FBI agent. The catering van Ramos was using for cover was a few yards behind the airplane’s high left elevator. The van was angled slightly toward the airplane, bathing it in the light of its headlamps. He stood behind the van’s passenger door so that he could remain concealed and fire right handed, waiting for the FBI agent to try to run for the plane again.

Mendoza’s face briefly appeared in the open cargo hatch, crouching to look outside. More pistol shots boomed out, and Mendoza tumbled onto the asphalt. The plane lurched and began to move, and a moment later, the

FBI agent tried for the plane. Ramos fired three or four fast shots, and a torrent of bullets slammed into the catering van. He ducked behind it again for cover as glass window fragments peppered his face, and then something struck his right foot like an axe!

As if things weren't already bad enough for Bob Bullard, everything went completely, totally to shit when they came to get Ranya Bardiwell out of the back seat. Somehow, she'd gotten free of the plastic flex-cuffs, and somehow she'd killed the short ugly Mexican gangster and grabbed a gun, and while Bullard continued to watch in astonishment the half-oriental gangster wearing the DHS uniform managed to stumble into the left engine's spinning propeller, removing most of his head in a split second!

This was followed a few seconds later by even more shots, and Bullard had seen enough. He was safe from pistol fire behind two inches of bullet resistant Lexan glass and a door sandwiched with Kevlar and ceramic panels, but they had the keys—what if they came back for him? Once the killing began, it was inconceivable that he would be left alive as a witness. Any deal to let him go was off the second the shooting began.

Out of the blue, he remembered that there was a spare ignition key taped to the bottom of the ashtray. Usually he had a driver when he used the Navigator, so this extra key business wasn't really his responsibility, but thank God that he knew about it anyway! Alone and unguarded now, Bullard pulled out the ashtray and peeled off the hidden key. He fumbled it into the ignition, switched on the hot engine, and dropped the SUV into drive with his left foot on the brake. He hunched down in the seat, floored the accelerator and the big truck launched forward and out of the line of fire. He sideswiped the open chain link gate, hit a parked car, skidded through the next sharp turn and kept going.

Alex scrambled up the ladder after Ranya as the airplane turned. They landed in a heap on the Otter's cargo deck, and crawled inside.

"Cockpit!" he yelled, untangling himself from Ranya and the loose bags and boxes piled into most of the open space. "Let's take the cockpit!"

There wasn't standing headroom inside the Otter, so they had to run forward bent over, climbing over more deck cargo. It was about twenty feet from the rear door to the cockpit bulkhead. There was a row of seats installed down the left side of the interior; the right side was stacked with boxes and luggage strapped to the fuselage. The interior was dimly lit by a pair of overhead lights.

Alex went first, with the Ingram machine pistol. The cockpit was divided from the cargo area by a wall, with a narrow vertical opening but no door. A man was sitting in the front passenger seat, behind the left side of the cockpit bulkhead. He turned slowly, as if afraid to see who was boarding the plane after the shooting had stopped—his friends, or his enemies. He was a pudgy-faced man in his thirties wearing round gold-rimmed glasses, and he slowly raised both open hands when he recognized the outcome of the firefight. In Spanish and English he calmly stated, "Your prisoner, señor. *Teniente Almeria, a sus ordenes.* At your orders."

Alex left their unexpected captive to Ranya and he continued into the cockpit, leading with his MAC-10, holding the warm suppressor with his left hand. The pilot was in the left seat, the right seat was empty. Both of his hands were clamped on the yoke in front of him, headphones were fitted over his ears. The brushy-mustached pilot turned around in his seat, his eyes wide at the sight of the stranger with the sub machinegun, and then he shrugged as if to say, "*Okay, now what?*"

Almost reading his mind, Alex demanded, "What do you think, I'm here to arrest you? Get this crate in the air! Just fly this son of a bitch!"

Basilio Ramos sat on the ground next to the van's front tire, holding his right foot, which hurt as if a tank's tread had just crushed it. The leather of his black cross trainer was shredded across the top, just inches behind his toes, and it was bleeding like a butchered pig's neck. Ranya and the FBI agent had made it into the Otter. Bullard had somehow gotten the big white SUV started, and had taken off with his tires squealing. Genizaro, Chino and Mendoza lay dead on the tarmac, a triangle of fresh corpses. The van's headlights shone across their bodies, their blood glistening in black pools beneath each of them. Before him was a scene of utter defeat and ruin. From Wednesday at Vedado Ranch until right now at this airport, Bardiwell and Garabanda had brought him only death, disgrace, failure, pain, injury and humiliation.

The Twin Otter lurched, the propellers threw back a new blast of wind, and it began to roll forward. The massive tail rudder shifted from side to side above him, and then the plane started to pivot to the left, to taxi toward the runway. Basilio Ramos knew that the moment of truth had come: he could sit where he was, put a belt tourniquet around his right ankle, and wait to be arrested. Or…

He pulled himself up by the van's door handle, and he hopped, hobbled and jumped on his good left leg, putting as little weight as he could on his injured right foot. Just as the airplane finished its pivot and began to roll forward again, he made it to the ladder that hung from the side of the hatch. He pushed off with his left leg, and managed to get the arch of his bullet-shot right foot onto its lowest rung, but it could not support his weight and it slipped through and he fell, catching himself with his elbows and the crook of his right knee as the Otter accelerated, painfully dragging him across the asphalt.

Alex shouted at the pilot, "That's right, you have a new boss! Just get this thing in the air!" The plane lurched and Alex lost his balance, and he decided he had better be in the copilot's seat during the takeoff. He dropped into the empty right seat, the MAC held sideways, aimed at the pilot. Alex took a quick look around the cockpit, and then forward where the plane's landing lights illuminated the empty airfield ahead of them.

Then he became aware of a sharp pain in his side that didn't diminish, even as he got his breath back. This was a pain under his right ribs, a deep pain like a cramp or a hard punch, and sudden fear enveloped him: *he'd been shot*. He laid the MAC across his lap and pulled up the bottom of his black sweatshirt, and ran his left hand down his smooth white Kevlar vest to where it hurt the most. He felt the protruding base of the projectile, the slug trapped inside the layers of fabric, but not penetrating. The slug was only an inch from the bottom edge of the vest. He knew he'd have a hell of a bruise there tomorrow. He'd seen them before on the luckiest cops and agents, the type of livid welts for which you sincerely thanked God.

Ranya had to secure the prisoner before she could look for Brian. Across from the row of seats was a pile of bags and boxes, much of which had clearly just been thrown aboard the plane. While holding the .45 on him, she grabbed a dark rag from the pile; the rag turned out to be a brown Milicia t-shirt. She thrust it to Almeria with her left hand, the cocked .45 still aimed at his face.

"*Su cubierta*," she ordered. "Put on your mask." He did as he was instructed. Once the brown shirt was draped over his head down to his shoulders and he was blinded, Ranya breathed easier. The New Mexico "Zia" design with the red star was crookedly centered on his face, and she briefly smiled. On the side of the plane opposite the seats were long bars for tying down cargo; lengths of line were looped over the bars. She shoved the .45 back under her belt, took a six-foot length of stout nylon cord and quickly tied a slipknot in one end.

"*Sus manos*. Give me your hands, together." Again he did as he was ordered, extending both arms, crossed at the wrists. Ranya pulled the loop snug around both wrists, tightly wrapped them several more times with crisscrossed lashings, and then secured his bound hands to the left armrest with knots that would need a knife to undo. She repeated the process more quickly with his ankles and finally she was satisfied. The entire hurried process of securing the prisoner had taken no more than one minute.

The plane was still taxiing on the ground, and at last she was able to search for Brian. She found the green canvas bag on the deck in the space between the second and third seats, and she pulled it into the cluttered passageway. She crouched and unzipped it, and opened it wide. Brian was curled in the fetal position, his eyes tightly closed, shaking.

She touched his hair, put her hand on his back, and said, "Brian! Brian, are you okay?"

He turned his face and opened his eyes, his entire body quivering.

Ranya said, "It's all right Brian, you're all right!"

"Is…is my D…D…Daddy okay?" he asked.

"Yes, he's okay Brian! Your Daddy's fine!" She knelt on the deck, and reached her arms inside of the bag and around his back, helping him to sit up.

"We're on an airplane, aren't we?"

"Yes, we're on an airplane. Your father is up front—he's helping the pilot."

Brian blinked at her, and said, "My Daddy flies a lot. FBI agents can do anything."

"Yes, they can." Her eyes filled with tears, she slipped her hands under his arms, and pulled him up until he was standing and she hugged him hard, and then boosted him onto the open third seat. "We're going to take off in a minute, so we need to get you buckled up, okay Brian?"

"Did you cut yourself?" he asked, while she settled him onto the seat and cinched the belt across his lap.

She looked down and saw that the front of her white San Diego sweatshirt was covered with a spray of blood, and her right sleeve was soaking red. She pulled up her right cuff; she had a deep gash behind her thumb that was bleeding steadily. "Yes, I guess I did."

"I cut myself too," Brian said earnestly. "When I gave Daddy the knife. Look." He held up his right index finger, and Ranya clutched it in her grip and then kissed his wound. She slid her other arm around his neck and squeezed him tightly, with her eyes closed against everything but tears.

Corky Gutierrez didn't taxi the Otter all the way to the eastern end of the runway. Instead he took a shortcut, saving several minutes. He rolled directly across the apron to the middle of the runway, already halfway down its length, and turned the plane to face west down the abbreviated remainder of its length. Alex approved. Clearly, the pilot was getting the picture. Anyway, for short field planes like a Twin Otter, mile-long runways were just three-quarters of a mile of wasted concrete or asphalt.

The T-shaped throttles for the Twin Otter were located on the ceiling between the pilot and copilot's seats, hanging down. The flaps were already set, the pilot held the yoke with his left hand, with his right he pushed the twin levers forward, and the plane shook and vibrated while it accelerated. After only three hundred yards as the plane was passing sixty knots, he eased back on the yoke with both hands, and they smoothly lifted away from the ground.

"We're cleared for Albuquerque," the pilot yelled across to Alex, who nodded agreement back at him. The fixed-landing-gear Otter was slow, but it climbed like an elevator. The pilot banked to the north and they continued to ascend as they flew up the coastline into the night sky.

This wasn't how it was supposed to end, thought Basilio Ramos, perched on the bottom rung of the ladder as the Twin Otter climbed and turned. He had a phenomenal view, but not one he could enjoy tonight. He could tell that they were flying north and then northeast, he could see the half moon low in the western sky, sending a shimmering orange trail across the ocean.

It wasn't over, he grimly thought, the wind blasting him in the face, trying to tear him from the ladder. Not yet. They thought it was over, but it wasn't over. The icy slipstream hurricane buffeted him, but he could endure it. By sheer determination, and using every ounce of his upper body strength, he hoisted his chest to the top of the three horizontal ladder bars, and was finally able to force his right heel into the corner of the trailing lower rung, followed by his left foot beside it. This accomplished, he pushed himself up further, finally getting his shoulders inside of the plane, the wind forcing him against the back edge of the open hatch, and pinning him firmly in place. This was hard work and painful, but pain didn't matter. Only getting inside of the airplane mattered—nothing else.

Inch by agonizing inch he dragged himself forward, and then he was in—and that was all that mattered. He was in. They were up front, smug with the sweet taste of victory in their mouths—but he was in, and he was behind them. He'd lost his Glock somewhere between being shot behind the van and climbing into the airplane—but he was in. He knew that there were plenty of other weapons packed in the back of the Otter.

Even up in the cockpit, the noise was considerable. Alex found the co-pilot's intercom headset, slipped the earphones on, and adjusted the mike position. He was at least quite familiar with this part of flying. "Can you hear me? Am I on?"

"I hear you," said the pilot. "We're out of restricted airspace now. I'm on our declared flight plan, course zero-eight-zero for Albuquerque, at 7,000 feet, speed one-four-zero knots. So, what's your new course?" Corky Gutierrez looked across at Alex, and at the machine pistol on his lap. "You don't want to go to New Mexico, do you?"

"Not exactly. But zero-eight-zero is good for now—just get us out of California." The pilot seemed unperturbed by the unexpected change in "management." Alex had known other pilots like that. They didn't particularly care for whom they flew, or what the cargo was in the back, as long as they were flying. Alex guessed that this was especially true when a new "co-pilot" was pointing a hot machine pistol at them after a gunfight.

The pilot asked, “Hey, you think you can get that cargo hatch shut back there? It’ll help with the fuel burn, and it’ll cut the noise way down.” He spoke perfect, unaccented English.

“Roger that.” Alex wasn’t about to leave the pilot unattended, in case he decided to make a radio call for help, or alter their course. He could have a pistol hidden anywhere on him or in the cockpit. No, he needed to stay in the cockpit, and keep the MAC-10 aimed at him.

Alex turned inboard, twisting around to the left in his seat, and waved to get Ranya’s attention. This sent a new wave of pain radiating from the bullet’s point of impact beneath his ribs, but with the slug on the outside of the Kevlar, he didn’t much care.

Ranya was sitting in the second seat, behind their captive who now had a dark hood over his head. He noticed that their new prisoner’s hands were already bound to his seat’s left armrest. He knew from experience that Ranya was good at tying men to chairs, and he chuckled at the memory of their first meeting.

She unbuckled herself and came forward and stood in the cockpit door, leaning over in the narrow opening. She had pulled off her blood-soaked one-day-old white San Diego sweatshirt, and was just wearing the black t-shirt she had on underneath. He noticed her hands and arms were caked with dry blood—so were his. She had a blood-soaked rag tied around her right wrist and thumb.

“Did I cut you?” he asked, almost yelling to be heard.

“Hell yes you cut me—but it was worth it!” She pointed toward his own hand, the one holding the machine pistol across his lap. “It looks like you cut yourself too. Even Brian cut his finger.”

Alex beamed at her. “Oh, he’s something—he’s a real tiger.”

“Brian said he gave you the little knife. How?”

“He put my keychain right into my hands, through the bottom of the seat—the knife was already open. I guess the keys were still in the bag with him. I told you he was smart! How is he?”

“If you can believe it, he’s sleeping. Poor kid’s just knocked out. This has all been too much for him—but he’s fine. He’s buckled up in the seat behind mine. You know he asked me about you, first thing. He was real happy to hear that his daddy was on board.”

Alex struggled to control his voice and said, “Hey, one thing. Can you go back and close the cargo door? It rolls down.”

“Sure. Just a minute.” She turned and went back into the cargo area.

The Otter had obviously been reloaded in a rush, with no order or planning. Ramos had difficulty making out any weapons cases in the heap of bags and boxes piled and tied closest to him against the rear bulkhead, just behind the open cargo hatch. The plane’s interior had been configured for the flight with a single row of six removable seats along the left side, with most of the cargo on the opposite side. He could see the butt of the cased Dragunov where he had left it. It was still on the deck under the seats, on the left side against the fuselage. The four-foot long rifle was too unwieldy to use within the close confines of the aircraft, but it would do if he could find nothing else.

He remained in a low crouch, hidden behind the row of seats, the wind roaring past the open square hatch just a meter behind him. There was a green canvas kit bag beneath the last seat next to the rifle case. Their pistols and small submachine guns were often individually cased and then packed into these canvas kit bags, the same type that he had zipped the little boy inside, back on the motor yacht. So many types of gear were packed into these big military hold-alls that finding a weapon might be a matter of luck.

Ramos was hunched behind the seat unzipping the bag, when he saw movement forward. He watched Ranya get up and move toward the cockpit, and stand in the narrow open doorway. She had removed her white sweatshirt, and was silhouetted all in black, bending over in the cockpit opening. Even then, Basilio Ramos couldn't help but observe that she had an exquisite figure, with the hourglass waist and round *culo* that had originally helped to seduce him and blind his mind to her treachery.

He rushed to check the contents of the open kit bag. On top was a sport parachute. He lifted it up to check underneath, but there was just another parachute. These were only Corky's emergency chutes, not weapons! He crouched low behind the seat while she turned around, facing toward him. He tried to pull the Dragunov's case back from under the seats, but it wouldn't budge. *¡Maldito hijo de puta!* Ramos cursed bitterly, desperately trying to yank the rifle case out. He felt for the zipper pull, and opened the bottom of the case, grabbed the rifle's skeletal laminated wood stock, and tried to pull it out. The *maldito* Russian rifle slid back a few inches, and then it seemed to catch on something and it would move no further. *¡Maldito Diablo Ruso!*

She was coming—there was no more time! At a loss for anything better at hand, he pulled the top parachute from the open kit bag, to use as either a weapon or a shield. Peeking out by the right side of the seat, he could see a pistol tucked into her belt at her waist. She was no more than five meters away. First he thought that she was somehow aware of his hidden presence, but a moment later a more logical reason struck him. The reason for her approach was as obvious as the four-foot square opening immediately behind him.

Of course, she was coming to close the cargo hatch! But she was armed, and he was not… She would see him before she reached the hatch, but perhaps not before he could ambush her. If he could subdue her, kill her, or just throw her out of the open door, then he would have only one other enemy on the airplane to overcome. If he threw her out and closed the hatch himself, the FBI agent would believe that she had accomplished her task, and he would remain unaware of the new danger on board. Ramos knew that he would be able to attack the FBI agent in the cockpit with perfect stealth, but only if he dealt with Ranya first. He sank down low, between the seat back and the open hatch, and waited for her.

Ranya paused to look down at Brian, curled on his side in his seat, sleeping. She could still hardly believe that they'd made it, they had Brian, and they were on their way out of California! What a roller coaster the last hour had been, beginning with her spraying Karin in the face with happy gas and meeting Brian for the first time on the sidewalk, when she had felt her first brief wave of euphoria. Then from the terrifying moment that they had been pulled from their car and thrown down onto the asphalt and flex-cuffed, she had been flung into the darkest pit of gloom, beyond any glimmer hope. And yet, now they were free, they were in a long-range aircraft, and they could go anywhere!

Free! She had her son, her stolen son, and after five long years she was free!

She could not take her eyes off Brian, sleeping crunched over on the seat, his folded arm for a pillow, looking like an angel with his little lips slightly parted.

They could go anywhere. They could fly back to Caylen Barlow's ranch in the Texas Panhandle. They could fly to Cantrell County in New Mexico. There were good people and standing invitations in both places.

But no, she thought, she'd had more than enough of the Southwest. "Aztlan" was no place for Brian and her. She had had enough of the dirty war, enough of the civil war, enough of the *reconquista*. The Southwest was slowly but relentlessly being conquered, county by county, and she knew it. It was time to go somewhere else.

She turned away from her sleeping son and studied the flexible hatch, it rolled up overhead on two curving guide rails. It had to have a latch somewhere. The plane was flying smooth and level, she had to lean over to walk in the five-foot high main cabin. She could almost touch both sides at once, with her hands outstretched.

It was uncomfortably noisy and cold inside the fuselage; she hoped it would be quieter with the hatch rolled down. After she closed the hatch, she'd go back to the cockpit and ask for earplugs, they must use them on a plane this loud. Earplugs, and a blanket for Brian, if there were any.

Halfway back down the narrow walkway between the seats and the strapped cargo, she looked up for the mechanism to release the door, studied the two roller guide rails that ran down on either side of the open hatch, and then she noticed the aluminum stepladder. It was still hooked to the bottom lip of the hatch. She looked down to see if it hinged upward, or if she should just leave it where it was, blasted by the slipstream, adding to the wind's roar. The thought of leaning out of the hatch of the airplane in flight to pull back the ladder terrified her, but she would do it if she had to.

Basilio watched her approach, he would let her get as close to the hatch as possible before attacking her. If he could take her unawares, if he grabbed her close enough to the open hatch he wouldn't need a weapon. He could tackle her, choke her, and throw her out. Choke her long enough to whisper goodbye in her ear, to let her know who had killed her, as she plummeted to the earth. He crouched low behind the last seat…

Ranya paused before the last seat. The square opening of the side cargo hatch was a black wind-screaming void. Where is the catch to release the sliding door? She wanted to close it without getting too near to the opening. She had a natural fear of the open door, thousands of feet up in the night sky, but her fear suddenly increased ten fold. There was something behind the last seat, she looked down and saw the front of a black shoe, and around the shoe on the aluminum deck was a pool of dark liquid, rippling with the vibrations of the fuselage. She drew the .45 from her belt just as the shape behind the seat exploded up and forward! In an instant she had the pistol out, the thumb safety pressed off, the hammer was already back as always.

And unbelievably, there was Basilio Ramos a yard away from her face, holding something in front of him as he charged! She stepped back at his approach and raised the pistol's barrel, as he raised his shield.

It seemed impossible, but here he was, crashing into her, his eyes wide and his teeth bared like fangs as he screamed his rage! She tried to hold him off with her left forearm; the .45 pistol was held back by her right side while she roughly pointed the muzzle at his chest and pulled the trigger, the booming of the pistol lessened by the ambient noise.

Ramos was still standing in front of her, still coming—her bullet must not have penetrated the rectangular pack he was holding in front of him. She quickly lifted the barrel to snap off another shot, but he followed the barrel's movement and blocked that one too. Without pausing she dropped the muzzle to shoot him in the groin, she moved the pistol faster than he moved his shield and again she pulled the trigger—and nothing! A glance down showed the .45's slide was locked back after the last shot, empty!

She was out of ammo, she had never counted the bullets since taking it from Genizaro, and she'd lost count of the rounds she'd fired. She was out of ammunition, and Basilio was laughing, standing erect now and approaching casually; grinning, winking and nodding his head gleefully.

But suddenly he went quite still, his smile completely erased.

Alex heard a pistol shot in the cabin and his content reverie was exploded. A second later there was another boom and he unbuckled and launched himself from his copilot's seat, nearly falling as he twisted himself around and through the narrow cockpit door, and down the cluttered aisle between the seats and the cargo.

There seen in the dim emergency lighting in the cabin was Basilio Ramos, holding something up as a shield, moving toward Ranya. The slide of her .45 was locked back, empty. Well, his MAC-10's magazine wasn't empty—he'd checked it in the cockpit. He had six or seven bullets left, enough for a good burst, enough to shred Ramos from belly to head. But the machine pistol was loaded with copper-jacketed .45 caliber hardball ammo. Over penetrating rounds or misses could do serious damage to the aircraft. One bullet cutting a cable or wire behind Ramos could result in the loss of the rudder or elevator, and send them spinning into the earth. Plus, Ranya was still in front of him, in his line of fire. All of these calculations took place in under one second, with detailed, crystal clarity.

She couldn't understand why Basilio suddenly hesitated, stopped and even backed up, until she heard Alex's steady voice behind her.

"Ranya, get out of the way so I can shoot this piece of shit."

She immediately jumped between two empty seats to give Alex a clear field of fire, turning sideways and pressing her back against the fuselage, watching them both.

Alex yelled to be heard over the engine and wind noise. "Ramos—this is for my friend, Luis Carvahal." He raised the MAC-10 to eye level, holding it out like a normal pistol in a two handed grip, taking careful aim from ten feet away.

Then in a flash the Comandante dropped and disappeared. The .45 caliber MAC-10 was unwieldy with its heavy suppressor and Alex didn't fire. Basilio Ramos was already out of the cargo hatch into the black night wind. The both stared at the square opening, then Ranya threw her arms around Alex's neck and squeezed him hard, saying nothing.

He dropped the MAC to his right side, put his other arm around her back and held her tightly in return and said, "It's over Ranya. It's finally over."

For Basilio Ramos, it wasn't over, not yet. He'd been through other impossible situations before, and made it out alive. He was a survivor if nothing else. When a grenade landed in his jeep in Brazil, killing his bodyguard, he was the only one unhurt. When his helicopter crashed in the jungle in Colombia, only he walked away, uninjured and uncaptured.

He couldn't tell how much altitude he had left, but he had a parachute clutched to his chest. As he leaped away from the Otter, he thrust his left arm through a leg strap, hooking it firmly at his shoulder. He ignored the tumbling and turning, there was no time to achieve a stable freefall position, no realistic way to put the parachute onto his back. With his right hand he felt for the deployment drogue, the small parachute used to pull out the main chute. He found it, and tore it away and threw it into the slipstream where it was grabbed by the passing air. In a second the nylon main chute erupted out of the pack and up, while he grabbed his left arm with his right, and held on literally for dear life. The opening shock felt like it had torn his elbow and shoulder apart, but he still held on. He had a canopy above him, and the entire earth below to land upon.

He looked down past his feet and could see nothing. He looked up at his moonlit parachute and saw with horror that it had a serious partial malfunction! The right side of his rectangular canopy was collapsed and fluttering, he was swinging in a growing circle as the parachute spiraled him down, the low half-moon going around and around him in a blur. There was no way to steer the chute while hanging from one leg strap under a partial canopy, no way to find the wind direction and head into it to lessen the landing speed, no way to pull the toggles and flare just before impact to slow his rate of descent. It was impossible to tell how fast he was coming down, but at least he was under most of a parachute canopy…

The unseen earth struck him as if he had been fired from a cannon into a stone wall. He both felt and heard his bones cracking on impact. Waves of heaving nausea rolled through him—but he was alive, he was conscious, and at last, he was blessedly *still*. There was no further distance to go down, his night sky descent was finished, and he remained alive! He lay on his face and chest against the good earth, and felt dry sand between his fingers, in his eyes and in his mouth. He was in excruciating pain from his head to the ends of his limbs, but he was conscious, he was alive—and he would not die tonight! The stars never looked more lovely, the half moon, low in the western sky, never looked more sweet!

Basilio Ramos complimented himself in spite of his agonizing pain. He had cheated death again! He was still alive! The rest was a matter of iron will and a test of his unbreakable determination. Now he had two reasons to live. No matter how long it took, no matter what he had to do, he would pursue them both until his last breath. Fueled by limitless hate, he would never give up his quest for revenge, not even if it took the rest of his life.

"So, where are we going?" asked Ranya, whispering into Alex's ear. She was still squeezing him around the neck with both of her long bare arms, their faces pressed together. The cargo door remained open behind them, forgotten.

"We?"

"You heard me Alex. Where are we going? You, me, and our son."

Our son… "I don't know," he answered. "The free states? Idaho maybe? How about Wyoming, or Montana? What do you think? Do you know anybody up there?"

"I think you should just tell the pilot to fly northeast until we're almost out of gas. We can decide later."

He lowered himself onto the empty fourth seat, and she followed him down without resistance, her arms still draped around his neck. She sat sideways across his lap, their cheeks lightly touching, sharing breath and watching their son sleeping in the seat in front of them.

Epilogue

The park ranger had to scrounge for a ride out to the call, the report of a dead body found near a natural spring on the edge of the Borrego Desert. A father and son had been flying a remote control model airplane at their campground. The model plane went down, and when they went to find it, they found human remains as well. Soon after the ranger arrived, he found the witnesses in the campground. He knew perfectly well that they were living at the spring fulltime, against the park regulations, but so what? Why mention it? Especially when he had to bum a lift out to the springs with one of the offending campers.

Halfway through the month and his office's meager allotment of gasoline was already finished, and they wouldn't get another credit put on their government account until August. For now, he was in the ironic position of depending on the good graces of the very people he would have written up for citations in the old days. The fuel rationing meant that most of the time the park rangers just hung around at headquarters, shuffling paper and playing computer solitaire. "They pretend to pay us, and we pretend to work" was how most of the rangers put it.

At least this group of "non-permitted long-term campers" kept the area around the spring-fed lake and their campground under the palm trees clean and orderly. He'd seen worse, much worse—biker gangs, Mexican Mafia meth labs and bizarre quasi-religious cults. This group was just trying to get through the hard times with a minimum of pain, and a little joy where they could find it.

The man who found the body said that he was a former aerospace engineer, and he made a joke about how he was now fixing model airplanes for a living. This witness led the ranger on foot a half mile east from the springs. They stopped at the edge of a small berm, almost a cliff or escarpment, which ran from north to south for hundreds of yards. It was no more than ten feet from where they stood at the rim, down to the level of the sandy desert that continued beyond.

The body was halfway down the angled slope. It was a male, partially buried in the sand. He was lying on his side, wearing only black fatigue-style pants. Long brown hair blew across what was left of his face. One leg was visible above the sand; the cloth at that knee was completely ripped away. The fingers of his right hand were curled into desiccated hooks, the skin abraded away down to the bones. His bare skin was burned red and black, and showed clear evidence of wild animal predation.

The witness said, "He's got no ID on him at all. No wallet, nothing."

"If he doesn't have any ID on him, it'll be a DNA job," said the park ranger. "Looks like he doesn't have any fingerprints left, and that face sure won't help much—not after the coyotes found him. I'll take some pictures, but I'll be honest: I don't think anybody is going to care enough to come out and collect him. Nobody's been reported missing out this way."

"Do you think the coyotes got him after he was dead, or before?" asked the man who had radioed in the report.

"I don't know. It looks like he was struggling hard here. Maybe he was fighting the coyotes, or maybe he was just trying to get up the slope."

"How long do you think he's been here?"

"Hmm…hard to say. The desert can be funny, what it does to a man. Hey, look there: his leg is broken, see?"

"Yeah, I noticed that," said the witness. Visible bone shards protruded through the dead man's blackened skin, beneath his knee. A tourniquet made from a nylon belt was strapped around his ankle, and the end of his bare foot was badly mangled, and encrusted in sandy black scabs.

"Man oh man, that had to hurt like the devil!" exclaimed the ranger. He slipped off his sunglasses and lifted his binoculars to his eyes, and surveyed the rippling sand to their east.

"You think his truck broke down out there somewhere?" asked the witness. "Maybe he crashed into a ravine." Even without binoculars, the dead man's back trail through the crusty sand was clearly visible, drag marks leading out into the trackless waste where shimmering waves of heat mirage made everything blur and disappear.

The ranger continued scanning through his field glasses. "There's no car or truck out there I can see. If I had the gas, I'd take my jeep and follow his trail. Maybe he was in a plane crash, I don't know. There's nothing out that way for thirty miles but sand and rocks. Think about it: he might have crawled for miles on that busted leg! He would have seen your palm grove from way off. It might have taken him days just to get this far and after all that, he just couldn't get up this final slope. Look at all the scratch marks, look how hard he tried! But he just couldn't push himself to the top with that busted leg."

"Poor bastard, he was so close," said the witness. "Another half mile, and he would have made it to the springs, and we could have saved him. Even if he'd just have made it to the top, we might have seen him."

"Yeah," said the ranger, "He was damned close. Poor devil almost made it. I'll bet he went through hell on earth before he finally died."

Regular mail delivery in the Texas Panhandle had been temporarily suspended, and temporarily had long since dragged on into permanence. If you wanted your mail, either you went to the post office twenty miles away in Tascosa, or you didn't get it. Mark Fowler had permission to pick up the mail for everybody at Caylen Barlow's RV camp, and on the days when he drove to Tascosa he became the unofficial mailman, as well as carrying passengers and general cargo in the back of his truck. The mail rode up front in boxes, under his watchful eyes and the protection of the .45 caliber pistol that rarely left his hip. As usual, he saved his most important drop off for last, including a small package that almost seemed to glow with significance.

The little package was addressed to Mr. Caylen Barlow himself, post-marked from Cody, Wyoming on July 16, with three cancelled $25 dollar stamps for postage. It was a square carton the size of a CD or DVD, and the return address said only 'Ranya, Free State Wyoming.' This had sent Mark Fowler's curiosity into overdrive, so he rode all the way up the long drive to Caylen's ranch house to hand it to him in person. He'd never admit it to a living soul, but he'd had a deep and abiding crush on Ranya Bardiwell from the first moment he'd met her at his outdoor shooting range, the day she took all the prizes with his best competition .45.

His old friend was sitting in his wheelchair on the shady veranda of his ranch house, listening to AM talk radio. The radio was turned up loud enough to be heard across the yard. The talk show host was shouting about the upcoming Constitutional Convention. The leaders of the Poor People's Party were threatening to surround the convention site in Philadelphia with two million demonstrators, in order to pressure the delegates into passing the "Economic Democracy Amendment." The white-haired rancher turned off the radio as his friend stepped out of his truck in front of the house.

A ceiling fan was spinning above Barlow, and a silver pitcher of iced tea glistening with condensation was on a table in easy reach. Even with the temperature still over 100 degrees in the late afternoon, the elderly ranch owner was wearing long pants, and a yellow short-sleeved shirt with buttons and a collar.

"Hot enough for you Caylen?"

The old man replied, "You call this hot? Why, it's barely warm. I'll tell you about *hot* someday, youngster. Say, whatcha got there for me big Mark? Anything worth putting my glasses on for?"

Fowler walked up the front steps with Barlow's mail. "Yep, I'll say. This one is from Ranya Bardiwell. Actually, it just says Ranya, but how many Ranyas do you figure we know? Looks like she made it out of New Mexico after all," he said, pointing to her name in the corner, and then to the postmark as he handed it over. "Maybe it's pictures or something."

"Sure, maybe it is," agreed the old rancher, turning it over and studying it. "Seems kind of heavy for just a CD."

"Well, aren't you going to open it up?" Fowler stood directly in front of his wheelchair-bound friend, making it clear that he was going nowhere until his own personal interest was satisfied.

Caylen Barlow fumbled to put on the reading glasses that hung around his neck on a piece of string. He took a small penknife from his pocket and attacked the thick brown wrapping paper, which was both taped and glued in place. Under the paper there were several layers of heavy-duty aluminum foil, and beneath the foil, the CD case was sheathed in layer after layer of fiberglass reinforced strapping tape.

As Barlow peeled the tape back, a small gold coin was exposed. He pulled it from the sticky side of the tape, and examined it closely with the magnifying reading glasses perched on his nose. It was about the size of a regular dime, or maybe a hair smaller. It had an arrowhead design on one side and the portrait of a scowling Indian's face on the other. Beneath the portrait it said, GERONIMO, and above it, 1/10 OZ. FINE GOLD. He continued to unwind the tape, and he had peeled off dozens of the coins by the time he got to the actual CD jewel case. He handed the thin gold coins to his friend Mark Fowler as he freed each one.

"Looks like she did okay for herself," noted Fowler, hefting several ounces of jingly coins in the palm of his hand.

"Yep, looks like she did indeed," agreed Caylen Barlow. "So what's gold going for these days, anyway?"

"In blue bucks? Almost $8,000 an ounce, last I checked."

At last Caylen Barlow opened the case, his old fingers shaking as he found the seam and cracked apart the plastic shell. Inside, there was a single photo between two CDs, one disc on each side of the case.

Ranya Bardiwell was shown from the waist up astride a chestnut horse, her face lit with joy. A small boy with light brown hair and blue eyes was sitting in front of her, holding the horn of a western saddle. The boy was wearing a camouflage t-shirt, a toy six-shooter holstered on his hip. Jagged mountains lined the distant horizon behind them. "My son Brian" was hand-written on the top of the picture, across the blue sky.

"You reckon that's Wyoming?" asked Caylen Barlow.

"I guess it is. Ranya sure looks happy. What a smile she's got!"

"Her boy too—handsome little feller. Wonder who took the picture?"

Mark Fowler thought, *I don't have a single clue, but I sure do wish it was me*. Then he swallowed hard and said, "Hey Caylen, what's on those CDs?"

The disc on one side of the case had a note written on it in black marker. It said: "Professor Johnson's Last Class—NOT for children!"

The other disc was inscribed with: "Crashing Wayne Parker's Vedado Ranch Traitor Convention—feel free to make copies."

"Holy Moly!" exclaimed Caylen Barlow, looking between the two CDs. "Christmas in July! Which one are we going to watch first?"

"Hell, I don't care—go fire up your computer, and I'll grab the beer!"

Matthew Bracken was born in Baltimore, Maryland in 1957, and graduated from the University of Virginia and UDT/SEAL training in 1979. He lives in Florida with his wife and two children.

DOMESTIC ENEMIES